I0608717

NEW ROCK NEW RULES

# NEW ROCK
# NEW RULES

## BOOK THREE OF THE NEW ROCK SERIES

## RICHARD SPARKS

CAEZIK
SF & FANTASY
**ARC MANOR**
ROCKVILLE, MARYLAND

✻

SHAHID MAHMUD
PUBLISHER

www.CaezikSF.com

*New Rock New Rules* **copyright © 2025 by Richard Sparks.** All rights reserved. This book may not be copied or reproduced, in whole or in part, by any means (electronic, mechanical, or otherwise), without written permission, except for short excerpts in a review, critical analysis, or academic work.

This is a work of fiction.

Cover art by Christina P. Myrvold; artstation.com/christinapm

ISBN: 978-1-64710-187-9

First Edition. First Printing. November 2025
1 2 3 4 5 6 7 8 9 10

CAEZIK
SF & FANTASY

An imprint of Arc Manor LLC

www.CaezikSF.com

For Lezli

# CONTENTS

MAP OF NORMARK

THE WINTER SEA

MONDTHAL

GREAT ICE LAKE

ICE PITS

OGRETZK

ISVELLIR

THE ICE LANDS

WHITBURN

THE

THE STOCKADE

SNOWLINE

ALDFELL

OSTENBY

SONDEHAFN

CHILMOUTH

THE NORTHERN OCEAN

Map by Jenny Okun

*Who's Afraid of the Big, Bad Wolf?*

# Prologue

**Come** *at once. All of you, armed and armored. E.*

Esmeralda.

I scrambled out of bed and threw on my clothes, my head fuzzy from the night's celebrations. We'd survived our trials overseas against overwhelming odds, so it had been party time at last—and *oh* how we'd partied. Making our unsteady way back at dawn to *The Red Rose*, our ship, we'd all been looking forward to a nice, long lie-in and a day without dangers, relaxing among friends.

That, clearly, we were not going to get. Even Qrysta was not quite her usual cool, calm self. "The hell's this about, Daxx?" she asked, as we hurried down the gangplank. Grell looked even grumpier than usual, his eyes bloodshot, his expression ferocious. An Orc with a hangover is not a pretty sight.

It was Oller who filled us in as we hurried after the Queen's Messenger: Old King Wyllard had died during the night.

According to the Royal Physician's later, official, report the cause was a dropsy, brought on by gout—which, though tragic, was a blessed release after all those long years of His Majesty's suffering. According to the gossip that was flying around, based on the Royal Steward's unofficial, but eyewitness, account, it was a threesome that had ended

1

him—His Majesty being galloped naked, on all fours, around the Royal Bedchamber, by two plump, enthusiastically spanking, and also naked pastrycooks.

"It was the way His Majesty would have wanted to go," he maintained, when questioned by Wyllard's extended family of ambitious kin. "Whooping, and laughing fit to burst, he was, and so burst he did! Fine way to go, with a grin on his face ...." But—no, *no*, that was not the *actual* way he'd *actually* gone, he "suddenly remembered," when told he must never speak such lies again, on pain of losing his tongue. "No, no, of course not, my lords! Died peacefully in his sleep, he did, our pious, saintly king. I found him myself, at daybreak, when I went to wake him: arms crossed on his chest, a pale sunbeam stealing in through the window and illuminating a smile of such holiness on his face as made me fall to my knees in veneration and sorrow. I was distraught, my lords and ladies. We had lost our beacon, our—"

*Yes, yes,* the family responded. *That's enough, now get out of here, and never besmirch the name of our late king again.*

Palace intrigue swarmed and buzzed. Cousin schemed against cousin, brother against sister, uncle against aunt. Esmeralda was going to need all the help she could get.

All eyes turned to us as we entered the Throne Room. Everyone knew who we were: Heroes of the Realm, just back from a perilous quest overseas. Huge Orc Grell, his brutal maul in his hands; Qrysta, neat but deadly sword-dancer with her twin blades; Oller, scrawny little cutthroat thief, as much a mongrel as Little Guy, the dog trotting beside him; myself our crew's battlemage-healer. I held Shift, my staff of power, so that everyone could see the red and green lights of her tourmaline heartstone glowing ominously. The threat we presented was unmistakable.

*They get the message,* Shift thought at me.

*Yes,* I agreed. *None of them want to tangle with the likes of us.*

But all of them wanted Old King Wyllard's throne.

And the crown that rested on it.

Commandant Blunt, known to one and all as Commandant Bastard, stood behind it, flanked by the chiefs of all the Orc tribes, arms crossed, glowering. We took our places behind Esmeralda's throne and waited. The Royal Family stared up at us, avoiding each other's eyes. No one said a word. After a long, silent while, Esmeralda, wearing her

2

own crown, entered through her private door. She seated herself on her throne beside Wyllard's.

"Thank you so much for coming," she began. "There's something we need to sort out. You all know that my co-monarch agreed that I won my throne by right of conquest?"

She let the question hang.

No one spoke.

"Well, there's still his throne, isn't there?" she said. "So, who wants to sit on it, and"—she pointed at Wyllard's crown—"wear this?"

They all did, of course, but no one was going to admit it. Cousin glanced at cousin. Brother glanced at sister, uncle at aunt. They all knew that if they made a claim for it, everyone else there would object. So, nobody moved.

Esmeralda waited, a patient smile on her face, happy for any of them to take the crown and share her burden. "No one?"

They fidgeted. Said nothing. Esmeralda looked at them all in turn, inviting them to make the fateful move. When no one did, she said, "Oh, well, perhaps we should just keep it for whoever I marry …"

She let that sink in. *Marry*. What a prize *that* would be! Not only the realm but also her hand in marriage. *The loveliest life there ever was or ever would be*. Smiles appeared on previously stony faces.

"As to who that will be," she went on, "I suppose we'll just have to wait and see. I'm in no hurry, after all I'm only sixteen. Meanwhile, I'll just carry on alone and do my best. I expect it won't be easy." She sighed. "I'm going to try to be a good queen, but it would be such a relief if I could share the load."

Heads nodded. Voices murmured that indeed they would do anything they could to help.

"That's so encouraging, thank you," Esmeralda said. "I'll try not to give you all too much to do. It's so nice to know that we're all in this together. I'd hate to be a bad queen who went around chopping the heads off everyone she was worried might try to steal her throne."

Her audience went still.

"I mean, imagine that, right?" she said, and her smile lit up the room. "Seeing enemies everywhere. That would have to be horrible. I'm *so* glad we're all friends."

I felt Shift's chuckle as it came up through my arm.

*Oh, very nicely done.*

# I

## The Big Fight

**Eastbay** was buzzing at the prospect of the Big Fight. It was the talk of the marketplace, and of every tavern and guildhall, as well as at the dining tables of the gentry, and in the kitchens of their servants. Commandant Bastard, "two-handed, against the best bloody Orc he'd ever seen"? Now *that* was going to be worth watching!

Commandant Bastard knew an opponent when he saw one. He never gave anyone respect unless they had earned it the hard way. The entire realm had, by now, heard about his bout with Qrysta near Mayport, at dual-wield, some months earlier; and the tale had grown in the telling. No one had believed that such a thing was possible: Commandant Bastard, fought to a standstill? By a *girl?* Well, that had been a turn-up for the books!

And now here was his new challenger—Grell, Qrysta's fellow in arms. And him not just a Hero of the Realm but also victor of some desperate campaign overseas which he, and his companions, had just won, against long odds. He was taller than Blunt, and wider, and a lot nastier looking, which was saying something. Commandant Bastard could freeze your blood with a glare. But this Orc .... People had watched him training, tirelessly, for hours against the Queen's Guards and against Orcs as scary looking as he was. Even several of them at once. He'd pulverized the lot, time and time again.

Blunt, meanwhile, had never been near the training ground. He was in his quarters with his long-lost wife and the son he'd never known. Normally, no one would have given this Orc's opponent a chance, but this Orc's opponent was Jack Blunt. And, normally, no one would have given Jack Blunt's opponent a chance, but he was distracted. Otherwise occupied. His mind on other matters. And his opponent was *the best bloody Orc he'd ever seen*, who was training himself into prime fighting form.

Maybe things were different, this time around.

Maybe it would be stupid to think that.

There was no doubt about it. This was going to be good.

I was looking forward to it myself, as much as anyone I talked to—and I had no more idea than they did as to where I would put my money, if I had to. I'd back Grell against anyone, two-handed. But I was terrified of Commandant Bastard. Grell was my *friend*. I should back him, surely? But Commandant Bastard was my master. I'd never seen anyone get the better of him. My heart said Grell, but my head said, *Are you an idiot?* So, I kept my gold in my purse.

Nyrik and Horm were taking bets left and right, but not from me. They urged me, "Come on, Daxx, have a flutter! Might as well have some skin in the game, eh?"

The Orcs were piling in on Grell. The officers and rankers of Her Majesty's army were all for Commandant Bastard. The odds hardly budged from even money either way. Queen Esmeralda declared that her Royal Steward would be the official custodian of all wagers. She didn't want anyone bunking off with the large sums that were accumulating.

All staked coin was locked up in her strong room in her private wing in My Lady of Eastbay's Castle, with two guards standing sentry outside. Any stakeholder not presenting himself every evening, to deposit his tally with her steward, would find himself locked up in the castle dungeons and all his holdings forfeit. An old head on young shoulders, was Queen Esmeralda. She was wise beyond her years.

"Some friend you are," Nyrik teased. "Not backing the bloke you been through the wars alongside of!" We were sitting in the snug bar of The Ship Aground, which the innkeeper had reserved for us at my request. It was a tiny room in a secluded, but comfortable, back-alley inn, with benches set into dark, wood-paneled walls behind three small tables around a fireplace. A serving hatch in one wall connected it to the main parlor of the tavern, and a door across one corner to the street outside. Horm was at one end of our table, Nyrik at the other. I sat between them, opposite the fire, my back to the wall. Flames danced in the grate. Candles threw shadows onto the ceiling. Voices drifted in through the serving hatch—rumbles, laughter, conversation—but, in the snug, it was private, and quiet.

We were finishing off our suppers of a rich eel-and-shoreweed stew, and brown bread warm from the oven, and a huge bowl of the best pickled vegetables I'd ever eaten. *Make them myself, in-house,* the innkeeper had told us. *Secret recipe, handed down from my grandmother,* he'd said. *Famous in Eastbay, our pickles.*

Horm, it seemed, disapproved of pickles. "It'll soon be spring, thank the gods," he said, "with something fresh and green to eat, the way nature made it. Not this embalmed stuff." He ate plenty of them nonetheless, crunching carrots and onions and radishes and sharp peppers between mouthfuls of bread and stew. They'd both been digging in with a purpose; and only now, it seemed, after they'd put away more food that I'd have thought possible, were they showing signs of easing off.

"Yes, well," I said to Nyrik, "I want Grell to win, of course. But I can't see it. Even though I've seen him take down monsters. I can't forget Commandant Bastard flattening him our first day in training, after you'd sold me to my Lord of Brigstowe's army."

"Sold?!" Nyrik barked, outraged at the memory. "That thieving Corporal bloody Smott *stole* you, mate, and you know it! Twenty poxy gold for a prize specimen like you?? You was worth well north of a hundred! I meet that sod in a dark alley one night—he's not coming out of it again, I can tell you that!"

Horm grunted his agreement.

A number of thoughts struck me, one after the other, knocking into each other like dominoes. They knew why I'd asked to see them. Everyone knew what I was now. People crossed the street to avoid me. Mothers hurried their children away from me, telling them not to stare.

I looked Nyrik and Horm over. Their clothes were far from new, and not recently washed. Scuffed boots. Worn leather belts. Empty purses. They'd been hungry and thirsty indeed. As well as the pickles, we'd worked our way through two large tureens of stew, and several ales, and a great round loaf of bread and a mountain of butter, and they hadn't held back. They'd lost their livelihood, I realized. They'd been slavers, experts in their field, before His Lordship of Brigstowe, and later Queen Esmeralda, had outlawed it. And now, here they were in Eastbay, long leagues from their woodlands, trying to make a little coin by edging bets on the Big Fight.

And no, I wouldn't have put it past them to sneak off with the money while all eyes were on Grell and Commandant Bastard. Another reason, I thought, for them to have a grudge against Esmeralda. I couldn't have that. Ez was my friend. Nyrik and Horm were my friends, even though our relationship had started out somewhat rockily. I wouldn't be here, now, I thought, if I hadn't bumped into these two—and, later, in some roundabout way, through them into Esmeralda. I was rich now, partly thanks to them. They, in turn, were poor now, partly thanks to me. It was odd to realize that I owed a great deal to people who had captured me to sell me into slavery. But I did.

"A hundred?" I said, mockingly. "For a scrawny, useless thing like me?"

Nyrik glowered. "Easily. Nice-looking lad like you. Young, strong, handsome; plenty of years o' work in you. Intelligent, can read and write. *And* think around corners. Marnie says she's never known a head for puzzles like yours. You couldn't fight for piss, but, well, how was we to know all you needed was that staff?" He nodded at Shift, who was leaning against the wall beside my bench.

"One-fifty, on a good day," Horm said.

"Yur," Nyrik agreed, glumly. He took a long pull from his ale, sighed, and looked into the fire, and grumbled, "Which that blasted day in Brigstowe most certainly was not!"

"No indeed." Horm grunted, and added, "Corporal bleeding Smott ..."

I held out my hand to him. "Done."

Horm leaned back, and frowned.

Nyrik said, "Eh?"

"One hundred and fifty gold. You got twenty from Smott. I'll give you the other one-thirty."

Horm's mouth fell open.

Nyrik stared.

He muttered, warily, "Are you pulling my plonker, Daxx?"

"I am not. One-thirty, not all of which I have on me at the moment, and we have a deal. And I consider myself cheap at the price."

They were still staring, unable to believe what they were hearing.

I leaned forwards, and said, "Look, lads. I wouldn't be where I am today if it weren't for you. And where I am today is, among other things, rich." I took my purse from my belt, and opened it, while continuing. "And, among other things, is also *bloody confused*. And I need your help. You know what I'm talking about. So, I'll buy my freedom from you with pleasure, and I do believe you could use the coin. Fifteen each for now," I said, counting out the gold, "and the rest tomorrow. Come up to the castle in the morning for it. And, my friends: my thanks."

They managed, finally, to exhale, as they shook my hand, one after the other, and then took the heavy gold coins—which they kept staring at in disbelief.

"You're thanking *us*?" Nyrik breathed. "Boiling hells, Daxxie! We're the ones as should be thanking *you*."

"Not bloody half!" Horm said. "That's … this is …." He raised his dark eyes, and looked into mine. Horm, I knew, was proud, as well as humble. He didn't complain. He didn't begrudge others their good fortune. He played the hand that life dealt him and just got on with the job.

So I knew what he was doing, when he spoke again.

He was taking me into his confidence.

"We was sleeping on the streets, Daxx," he said.

It had taken a lot for him to admit that.

I felt, in a way, honored that he'd told me.

I nodded and patted him on the shoulder. "Well," I said, to lighten the mood, "if I was you I'd get a room while there are still some available. The town is filling up fast."

"Too true," Nyrik agreed. "Half the realm's heading this way for the tourney, from what we hear." He turned to the service hatch in the wall behind him and rapped on the counter between our snug and the parlor.

The innkeeper's bald head appeared, filling the little space. "Yes, gents?"

"Another pitcher of this fine ale, mine host, if you please," Nyrik said. "And would you have a room for the two of us, for the next month?"

He held up a gold coin.

The innkeeper gaped. "Yes, sir, certainly, sir," he said, wiping his hands on his apron, before daring to reach for the gold. "The best we have, just the one floor up, at the back, nice and quiet, view over the garden, proper feather-beds—not like the straw ones up top."

"Sounds perfect," Nyrik said. "We'll take it."

The innkeeper accepted the coin as delicately as if it were a flower—and froze when Horm walked over and held out another to him.

"Pop that on our account, mine host, would you?" he said. "We'll be eating and drinking here most days, and we don't want to have to keep digging in our purses for coppers."

"No, sir, yes, sir, of course not, ha ha!" The innkeeper was bobbing, and ducking, and itching to take Horm's gold.

"Just give us a bit o' notice when our balance is getting low, there's a good chap, and we'll top it up, all right?" Nyrik said, with a breezy smile.

"Yes, sir, gents, anything you want, anything at all, you just send for me."

"That we will, matey," Nyrik said.

The innkeeper bowed, and grinned, and disappeared.

Horm rejoined us and sat down.

Nyrik said, with a sigh of both satisfaction and relief, "Well, that's us all right for a bit, then. Much obliged to you, Daxxie. You're a gentleman, and no question, I've always said that."

"No question," Horm agreed.

"You've done for us, and handsomely," Nyrik continued. "So, what can we do for you?"

We all knew what was coming; but before we got to the point, there was something I needed to say. "Three things."

"Three, hey?" Nyrik's eyebrows rose in surprise.

"One ... and this is the most important one: I know what you mean, and I appreciate your thanks, but you're not 'obliged.' You are not in my debt in any way. You don't owe me a thing, all right?"

Nyrik chuckled. "If you say so," he said, shaking his head.

I smiled back at him. "*Crazy bloody foreigners,* right? Look, that's just the way it is, in my book. We're here, where we are, because this is how we got here—which we wouldn't have done without each other. Who knew, right? So? Agreed?"

Nyrik and Horm exchanged looks.

I could see them thinking, *No skin off our noses.*

"No problem," Nyrik said. "Slate's clean between us."

"Good," I said. "So. Two: You no longer have a grudge against Queen Esmeralda."

They bristled at that and glared at me.

"I know, I know," I said. "She's outlawed your trade. Get over it—get a new one."

"Easier said than done, Daxx!" Horm objected.

"No doubt," I agreed. "Many things in life are, Horm. Look, I can't have you and her in opposition. You're part of our team, all of you. I need you and her on our side."

They clearly didn't like that. They started fidgeting with their clothes, their tankards.

"Okay," I said, "just think about it. Talk yourselves round. I understand it might take time, but just … please. Okay? Yes, change is *hard*. I get that. But—if you can?"

Nyrik shrugged.

Horm emptied his tankard, slowly, avoiding my eyes. The landlord put another pitcher of ale on the counter in the hatchway, and Horm got up with a grunt to fetch it.

I thought, *Best leave it with them. Up to them to sort it out.*

"The third thing," I said, when Horm sat back down and began refilling our tankards, "is the reason I wanted to see you." I waited. "I believe you know what that is."

"Yur," Nyrik said. "Everyone does. Talk of the town, you are, Daxxie. We heard you scared your crew shitless, howling your bloody head off in your cabin, banging on the door night after night of the full moon …"

Horm grunted agreement. "We have enough trouble with them buggers out in the Wildwoods."

Neither of them said the word. They didn't need to. Normal though I looked at that moment, in that inn, as we sat by its cozy fireplace. we all knew what I now was.

Werewolf.

I could see them swapping glances. Nyrik reached for his ale as Horm shifted on his seat, avoiding my eyes. The subject clearly unsettled them.

Nyrik, seeing me struggling, said, gently, "Tell us what you can, Daxxie, and we'll do the same."

I gathered my thoughts and began. "We sailed through three Moon Nights, on our way here to Eastbay. I was locked in my cabin." I shook my head at the memory of what had taken me over. "It wasn't anything like choosing the Form, on other occasions, when I could slip between *were*-me and *me*-self without effort. *On the Moon Nights, the*

*Form chooses you,* the Packfather who Gifted me had told me. Well, over those three long days and nights I came to see what he meant."

I paused and looked at the two Woods Kin, who were watching me intently. "The confusion of what I was going through was bad enough. What was worse, though, was the agony of this."

I took off my "masterpiece," the greenfire necklet that I had created myself. "It wasn't hanging on this," I said, holding it up by its leather lace. "It was on a silver chain."

Horm's eyes grew round. "Bleeding hells," he muttered.

I nodded. "*Burning* hells was more like it, Horm. And the silver was niblun imbued, strong as stone." I pulled down the collar of my jerkin so that they could see the livid burn scars around my neck. Nyrik drew in his breath sharply at the sight. "Only the gods know how I got it off. I clawed at it, and tore at it, and wrenched and twisted, my paws burning. Every second it was on me was torture."

"I can imagine," he said.

"Finally the damn thing snapped and I threw it aside. The last thing I remember is standing there, my chest heaving, my neck aflame, thinking, *What in all hells do I do? How am I going to deal with this?*"

My throat was dry as I recalled my terror. I took a mouthful of ale and continued. "I came to on the second morning of the moon's waning, face down on the floor of my cabin. I was drained, exhausted. I could hardly move my eyes, let alone my head. This," I indicated my greenfire pendant, "was lying inches in front of my face. When enough strength returned to my arm I reached for it—with a shaking, human hand. Not, thank all the gods, a paw. I hesitated to touch its broken silver chain. Would it burn?

"It did not.

"I gave the chain away to one of our crew—Gelbert, our purser. I do *not* want silver anywhere near me when the next Moon Nights take me again."

"Too bloody right!" Nyrik agreed.

"Since then, lads, I've been banging my head against it, this so-called Gift. Where does it lead? Am I going to be fighting with myself for the rest of my life? Will there be a winner and a loser? All that I've learned, for a certainty, is that there had been nothing I could do about it, those three nights. Now I need to know what I can do about it at other times, and what, at heart, it all means."

Nyrik glanced at Horm, who grimaced. Neither of them liked the subject.

But they knew more about it than I did.

"Look, lads. You told me you'd come across *Weres*. You've traded with them, right, in a way? You'd leave a goose for them, or something, and hope they'd drop some shinies that they might have picked up in return?"

Nyrik nodded. He didn't answer.

"So," I said, "what would you do, if you were me?"

Horm looked up at me from under his dark eyebrows. "You need to make yourself scarce."

"And the sooner the better," Nyrik said. "You'd think you'd be safe here, you being a Royal Companion, under the protection of the queen." He shook his head. "That don't mean there aren't folks here who think you'd be better off dead."

Horm said, "The only good Were being a dead Were, as they see it."

They let that sink in. Nyrik saw my discomfort, and said, "Leave town, Daxx. While you still can. You're not safe here. No more than a lone human is out in the Wildwoods on the Moon Nights, when the Packs are running."

"Yur," Horm added. "All it takes is a dark alley and a silver knife, and that's the end of you."

"Thing is …" Nyrik said, "well, as far as I know—*we* know—or anyone knows, really, anyone who isn't of the Pack: It's either one thing or the other."

A chill crawled up my spine at his words.

"You mean … I have to give it up, or lose my magic?"

"Not just your magic, Daxx. Everything." He let that sink in. "Your*self*." He leaned forward and fixed me with his dark eyes. "Thing is, mate: We don't know if it's even possible to give it up. Don't know anyone, up our neck of the woods, who ever has. All we've heard is, this 'Gift' of yours, as those of the Pack call it, is stronger than you are."

I didn't like the sound of that at all.

"So," he continued, "it calls you. And you go out into the Deepwoods, towards the Moon Nights, and then …" he tailed off, and shrugged. "Well. Then it takes you. And, um, off you go."

He looked back at Horm, who grunted and reached for the jug of ale. He refilled our mugs as a silence fell between us. I gazed at the fire in the hearth. I couldn't think straight. A jumble of feelings was flooding through me. I got *run* and *smell* and *hunt* and *eat* and *listen*, and *wait and watch*, and other sensations crowding into me, all at once. I fought to rise above them, to get on top of it all; but, even as my mind cleared, I knew for a certainty that I couldn't let that richness go—the ecstasy of connecting so profoundly, so intensely to the world around me. I'd never before felt anything remotely like it. I was so little, and would be so much less, without it—this new, seductive Gift. I couldn't bear the thought of it. In the Form, I was my *Truth*. The rest of my existence, my human life, was a shadow.

Nyrik saw me struggling. He leaned over and patted me on the back of my hand, then smiled. "And there you have it, eh?"

I looked at him, confused.

"Is this a gift ... or problem?" he explained.

His words echoed around the quiet little dark-paneled room. The flames crackled in the hearth. I stared into them as I considered what he had said.

*Gift or problem.*

I shook my head to clear my thoughts. But my thoughts were losing the fight against the sureness of my feelings. I *knew*. In my heart of hearts, I knew. This was who I truly was now. No—this was who I had truly been, all along, but only now had found, now that I had broken free from my own confusions, my own bullshit, my own petty restrictions. How absurd they were, how fake—the rules, the conventions, the formalities.

Formalities, I thought, or Form. It was no contest. *Out there* was where I belonged. In my Truth. With my Pack. Wherever, whoever, and whatever they were.

I raised my head, and looked at them—first Nyrik, then Horm. "You haven't answered my question."

Horm's eyebrows rose. "What would I do in your place?" He glanced at Nyrik, who nodded, as if there was only one answer.

Which Horm gave me. "Find your Pack."

It was, I saw, what I already knew that I had to do; but, somehow, from the way he said it, I knew that he meant, *Go, and never return.*

I stared at him.

Horn must have seen something on my face. "Don't have a choice, Daxx. None as get the Gift ever come back."

"Gods ... I don't want to lose ..."

Horm shrugged. "Don't see as how what you 'want' comes into it no more, mate. It's what you are, now, *want* it or not."

"We've lost several over the years," Nyrik said, "of the Woods Kin. Gifted, and gone. We see 'em, now and then, on the Moon Nights. We can always tell, *Oh, that's cousin Sarey*, and she gives us a nod and a look as she passes. But none of us wants the curse—I mean, Gift—thank'ee very much. We keep well clear."

"Mostly we hunker down inside a big tree while the moon's at the full and the Packs are running," Horm said.

"We'll wait out if we've left something for them, and watch 'em tuck into the geese or whatever, see if they drop any shinies," Nyrik said. "You can hear the buggers coming from leagues off, howling away. Plenty of time to nip up a tree. They can leap," he added, "and snarl, but they can't climb."

Silence fell.

We drank, each lost in private thought.

"Who knows, though," Horm said, lowering his tankard, "maybe it's different for foreigners?"

"Yur," Nyrik said. He leaned over and jabbed me in the shoulder. "If anyone can do anything different, it's our Daxx, with his head for puzzles."

"Whoo," I said, exhaling. "Well. It seems I'm going to have to try."

"That is does," Nyrik agreed.

"So. Where do I go?"

"The Deepwoods," Horm said. Nyrik was about to say something, when Horm continued, "And, I do believe, you have just hired yourself the best guides in the business."

He looked at Nyrik, who took a moment to understand and then nodded.

"That you have," he agreed. "No one knows the lie o' the land out there better'n me and Horm." He leaned over and rapped on the counter. The innkeeper's head appeared in the hatchway. "Keep our room for us will you, matey? We'll be back in time for the Tourney."

"Yes, sir, certainly, sir. No charge the nights you're not here—plenty of other customers will want it, so I won't be out of pocket."

"Excellent. Right." Nyrik turned back to me. "That's me and Horm sorted, now let's see about you."

"Thank you, lads. I feel …" I trailed off.

"You feel what?" Nyrik enquired.

"I was going to say 'better already'." I said. "But …"

Horm chuckled. "I know what you mean, mate. Who knows, eh? Just one thing, though, if I might ask?"

"Of course," I said, "anything. What?"

"Promise you won't eat us."

"I'll do my best."

I left the others with much to do. They could have done with my help, but they understood. I had a problem to deal with. *Solve the problems.* That had always been our motto.

Oller would take charge of the loot that we'd brought back from the helldragon's hoard and from *The Rose Revived.* He would consult with the experts: Thieves Guild fences, who knew more about gemstones than anyone; the Conclave of the Guild of the Arcane Arts, who would divine the magic properties of every item; Marnie and her Guildsisters of Coven, who knew secrets that even the GAA didn't.

Grell, as well as training all hours of the day, was responsible for our ship, *The Red Rose.* It had been Grell's idea to appoint Gelbert as purser. It was a good choice. Gelbert was an Eastbay lad, who knew the town and its chandlers and tradesfolk. Grell gave him orders for a complete refit of the ship, as well as an overhaul of the crew. We'd be needing a new captain, we all knew, if we were to sail her again, not some landlubber like myself—but that appointment could wait, for the time being.

Qrysta would be up to her neck in admin for the Royal Tournament. She would be overseeing the Palace Guard and the Royal Company of Heralds, who both had interminable amounts of protocol, and due form, and precedent, and palaver, which sparked disagreement after argument after negotiation. Contestants were arriving from every corner of the realm, as were bards, and mountebanks, and mummers, and dancers and chancers and riffraff.

Esmeralda, via Oller, summoned the Receiver of the Eastbay TG to a council with the Town Reeve, and the Clerk of the Watch, and the Tidemaster of the port, as well as Qrysta, the Captain of her Guard. She said that she knew she could rely on all of them to make their town proud that it could carry off this great festival without a hitch—

and what did they all think of the idea of a tax holiday? No import or export duties, to stimulate trade, for six months—like in the free ports that her friends had told her existed in Mourvania? *We might as well make the most of this influx of people from all over, right? Business would go through the roof, wouldn't it? And all of Eastbay would benefit. Coin would flow like water.* They all got the message. They promised her that there would be no hint of trouble, at least not from the locals, and any outsiders making mischief wouldn't be free to make it for long.

I so wished that I could stay to make the most of the festivities with my friends. I was more than ready for some relaxation after our escapades overseas; but they all knew that I had to go. They told me to get back as soon as I could. We were, after all, to be guests of honor at the Royal Tournament, which was going to be an occasion of joy and merrymaking as well as a celebration of our return.

Before dawn the next morning, Nyrik and Horm and I saddled up in the castle stables and rode through the sleeping town, the hooves of our mounts clattering on the cobblestones of the empty streets. A yawning night guard opened the gates. We trotted out into a damp, misty, early spring morning, and turned west and north for the Deepwoods.

# 2

## The Deepwoods

We rode hard for three days, farmland to woodland to hill country, always climbing, the far side of each valley rearing higher than the slope we'd ridden down. The weather grew colder, the trees taller, the ridges ahead of us steeper and more rugged. On the third evening we mounted the last crest, where we reined in and looked down at the endless forest below.

The land ahead dropped away into a blanket of dark green and darker shadows. In that twilight it seemed like a lake spread before us, stretching to the horizon. Days away in that direction, I knew, the land rose again, towards the moorlands, and the uplands, and—eventually—the Western Mountains, where the giants lived.

We could not see that far. We could see nothing but darkness below the ribbons of red and orange cloud in the blackening sky, and the sun settling into the rim of the world. From our vantage point the Deepwoods looked peaceful, if not exactly welcoming. I didn't want to go down there. What I wanted meant nothing. This had to be done.

"Best camp up here for the night," Horm suggested.

Nyrik groomed and fed the horses, putting blankets on them and giving them nosebags full of oats, then hobbling them so they could roam free to graze. Horm gathered wood and made a pile of it, into which Shift blasted flames, until the damp logs were dried out and burning. We ate facing the fire, cross-legged on our blankets. Cold and wet soaked up from the ground under us; but much of it evaporated in the Orbs of Warmth that I cast around us.

The night would be as comfortable as I could make it, which was not saying much. Nyrik and Horm were used to sleeping rough, being creatures of the wild. They found it easier than I did. On our first night I'd asked why they didn't unlock a tree for us to sleep beneath. "Be nice, that, wouldn't it?" Nyrik had said. "Horm and me, we've been through here many a time, but we're not from around here. The trees here have seen us before, but they don't *know* us, Daxx. We're trespassers on their turf. One day, why, they might welcome us as guests, and allow us in. Then we'd be out o' the wind and the rain. Their realm, their rules."

Another damp, cold night in prospect, then, and, in the morning, the descent into the Deepwoods. From which I might never return.

Towards midnight the rain came. Shift and I did what we could to shelter us. We lay there, wrapped in our cloaks, snoring, waking, listening to the night sounds: the mournful hooting of owls; bats squeaking; foxes yipping; the churring of nightjars; the wind gusting in the bare branches of the trees. How long the night seemed, in the fitful intervals between waking and sleeping. The moon above us was shedding layer after layer, night after night, teasing me, disappearing in her own sweet time. I watched her as she drifted overhead, in and out of passing clouds. There would be less of her tomorrow, and less every night, until she was nothing. Then she would return, I knew, stronger than ever—and stronger, certainly, than me. I found her enthralling; but, no, I did not love her. I feared her. *As she pulls the tides of the seas, she owns me,* I thought. *I follow in her wake. I dance to her tune.*

We woke before daybreak, ate hard bread and harder cheese, and rode on, down from the ridgeline into the Deepwoods. After a couple of hours, as weak morning sunlight filtered through the trees that leaned in above us, Nyrik reined in.

"This it?" he said. Horm nodded and rode on ahead past him, leading us off to one side, away from the direction we'd been heading.

We hadn't even been on much of a path—merely, it seemed, picking our way down as best we could. Now there was no path at all that I could see. There was just Horm, threading through the trees, over fallen trunks, around ditches, and damp bushes and thickets. I knew better than to ask what he was doing, or where we were going. We'd done all the talking we could think of—which hadn't been much.

They hadn't told me what they were planning, because they didn't want me to be disappointed if that plan came to nothing. *The which,* Horm said, with his usual pessimism, *it probably will.* They knew little about what lay ahead of me. All they could do, they said, was take me as far as their knowledge led them and then hand me on.

We rode through wet mists under dripping trees, until we came, at about midday, to a hovel. It loomed out of the shadows before we knew it was there. The ground around it had not been cleared. There was no enclosure. It was a simple, small structure: two sides of a rough triangle of interwoven pine branches leaning against each other, banked beneath tall evergreens and covered with turf. A curl of smoke drifted up out of a hole in its roof.

Horm nodded, pleased that the owner was home. We dismounted, and followed him to the door. He rapped on it, calling out, "Urn? It's me, Horm—and Nyrik, and a mate."

His words drifted away on the wet wind.

There was no reply.

"You in?" Horm said, after a while.

If there was a reply it might have been the faint growl I heard, which sounded like a large dog groaning in its sleep. It seemed to confirm something to Horm, who nodded, and reached for the door—which was merely a hurdle made of branches.

It rustled as he pulled it open. Horm ducked inside, and we followed him in.

The hovel's interior was smaller than the snug bar of The Ship Aground, and a lot less snug. The smoke that we'd seen hadn't been coming from a welcoming fire but from a few dull embers in a pit. There was an earthen smell, and a sense of brooding. I knew there was a presence, but couldn't see it. And then the shadows at our feet stirred, and something rose from the ground. It, whatever it was, unfolded itself from under a heap of pelts, and kept growing, and rising, and occasionally grunting, until it was blinking down at us, its long arms hanging by its side, its cannonball of a head jammed awkwardly below its shoulders and back against the hovel's roof.

The thing was huge, and undoubtedly powerful—possibly even as powerful as the exhalations that it heaved down towards us as its breathing rasped through its throat. Being taller than Nyrik and Horm, I was a couple of feet nearer the source of that breath than they were. It was all I could do not to gag at the stench and turn tail and run.

"'Ullo, Urnzie," Horm said, his voice affectionate, "you're looking well. Things good?"

"*Hooormmm!*" a deep, but undoubtedly female, voice rumbled, sounding pleased. "Yur, all fine. How's yourself? Long time no see!"

"We're good, Urn, thanks," Horm replied, as the gigantic thing picked him up in a bear hug, which he returned, as best he could, his feet a yard in the air. "And yeah, it's been too long, no question. Lots of bloody changes in the world these days. Been run off our feet, we have, me and Nyrik."

"Nyrik!" the thing said, and gurgled a deep laugh of pleasure. "What'ch you two scoundrels doing up this neck of the Deepwoods, hey?" Her voice was thick, and heavy, and peculiar, but understandable.

She reached a lump of a fist down towards Nyrik, which he bumped with his own.

"Coming to see you, o' course, Urnz," Nyrik chuckled.

"Uh-oh," she echoed Nyrik's wry chuckle with a deep one of her own. "Want something, yur?"

"That we do, Urnzie," Horm agreed, also laughing.

I had no idea what amused them, but I was making sure to be as still, and polite, as possible. This ... *thing*, I knew, could rip my head off with a twitch of her wrists.

Nyrik added, "On account of our mate here."

All three turned to me.

The cannonball head lowered itself to inspect me, up close and personal. Fierce, yellow eyes burned down into mine, as nostrils below them sniffed at me.

"Daxx, his name is, and he is a true gent, and a true friend," Horm continued. "Been very good to us, he has, and we'd be much obliged if you'd be good to him on our account. Daxx: Allow me to introduce my cousin, Urngra. Well, technically: my dad's second cousin's daughter, but we just shorten that sort of thing to *cousin* 'round these parts."

I waited, looking up at that alarming head.

Urngra smiled. It was not a reassuring smile, and it was less than a foot from my face, leaning down and breathing ferocious breath. Her teeth, I saw in the hovel's gloom, were even larger than Grell's.

21

"*Hhhhhhhhhulloooo,* Daxx," she said, in a blast of halitosis that parted my hair. She extended a gigantic hand, which I took and allowed to shake mine, which it did, like a puppy mauling a shoe. "Nice to meet you!"

"Hello, Urngra," I said, smiling as best as I could. "The pleasure's mine. Horm has told me a lot about you." Well, not perhaps a lot. Just that she could stun an ox with a single blow, as she had demonstrated on her fifteenth birthday.

"Urnzie not only knows the Deepwoods better than most, she also speaks like we do, when she wants," Horm said. "She don't only talk Ogre. Which is not the easiest language to learn, by the way. She has a foot in both cultures, my clever cousin, you might say. The which saves me the trouble of having to interpret, and my Ogrish is a bit rusty, I might add."

"Better than mine," Nyrik interjected. "All I know is *uuurngkf* and *fgroot* and *gnarra-rarra-yarrrngnhrrff.*"

"She is also," Horm said, with a big smile, "my favorite cousin."

Urngra gurgled with pleasure. It was the sort of pleasure that said, *Ooh, that looks tasty, I'll have a nice big bite of that!*

"There's only a couple of years between us, so we played all the time, as kids—didn't we, eh, Urnz?" Horm added.

"That we did!" Urngra agreed.

"By the time she was three, she was twice my size, so not only was she my best mate, she was my own personal transport!" Horm said. "I spent half my childhood on them shoulders, I did, us charging around hither and yon, making up games, telling each other tall tales, and getting up to mischief. So, if there's anyone I know who'll look after you, Daxxie, it's Urngra, 'cos she looked after me, no matter what scrapes we got into."

Urngra was looking from him, to me, and chuckling.

I caught her eye, and she gave me an unnerving wink.

"You'll be safe with her," Horm added.

That I could believe. I couldn't imagine anyone—or anything—wanting to mess with Urngra.

Urngra rumbled, contentedly, and asked, "Safe during what?"

"Ah," Horm said. "Daxx here has a problem."

"Yur?" Urngra looked at me, smiling, as if my problem would be something she'd enjoy putting firmly in its place.

Horm cleared his throat. "He's been Gifted."

Urngra went still. Her smile faded. Her eyes dulled.

The hovel went quiet.

Urngra stared at me for many long seconds.

She turned her head to Horm, and stared at him for many more long seconds, and said, as if he should have known better, "Are you asking me to interfere?"

"No, no, Urnz—wouldn't dream of it!" Horm said quickly. "I know what's what. We're not asking anything, blimey—least of all anything like *that!* No, certainly not, not *interfere*, in a million years. We just come to see you, in case, you might have, you know, an idea? As to how our mate Daxx might proceed. You knowing what's what, around these parts, for those who've been Gifted. And, er, where's where, so to speak. Daxx isn't one of us, obviously. He's not even from here. He's a foreigner, from overseas. He don't know what's got into him. He don't know what he should do. Or what he should think. Or where he should go, or who he should see." Horm tailed off.

Urngra was studying me.

Being studied by her, in that cramped, dark space, was not comfortable.

She lowered her cannonball head towards mine and growled.

I didn't know what to do, so did nothing.

*"Hrmmmnnnggggnnnn,"* she said at last, rearing back, as far as the low roof of the hovel allowed her. Her yellow eyes never left mine. She stared down at me, inhaling heavily, exhaling noxiously.

At last, Horm said, "We thought, you, might, know what to do …"

Urngra turned to him.

"What's in it for me?!" she demanded.

Nyrik and Horm unfroze, and looked at each other, and me, and shrugged, and chuckled, and Horm said, "Er, well, tell us what you think would be reasonable, and our mate Daxx here will tell you if he can afford it. He's rich. Not that coin means anything to you, o' course, Urnz, but, er … if he can meet your terms …?"

Urngra turned her head to me again. "Nnnng," she growled; and then nodded, slowly, and said, "Pack."

I still didn't know what to say. But, after a long while, it became obvious that everyone else was waiting for me to say something, so I said, "Yes," and then, "please."

Time stood still.

Urngra considered, her chest inflating and deflating like an enormous bellows, inches from my face.

"Thing is," Horm continued, "Daxx here isn't just your ordinary foreigner. He's a mage."

Urngra stiffened, surprised.

"How many of *them* you ever hear of getting Gifted, eh?"

"None," Urngra said, frowning. "They'll want to hear about *that!*"

"What we thought exactly," Horm agreed.

My curiosity was piqued. "They? Who?"

She ignored me. "Stave," she said, holding out a paw.

I unhitched Shift from my back and felt her shock as she woke abruptly in my hand. *Whoa! Ogre? What's going on, Daxx—no! Stop!*

Her scrambled thoughts turned to a squeal as Urngra took her from me.

"Hmm," Urngra rumbled as she inspected my beautiful, precious staff. Who was, plainly, terrified—and I'd never known Shift to be scared before. Urngra turned her in her hands, studying the red-above-green tourmaline heartstone that was Shift's eye. She stroked her hands along the staff's lustrous rowan wood. "Pretty."

In my head Shift was screaming. *Daxx! Make her hand me back to you!!*

*Calm down, she's a friend, she's going to help, it'll be all right—*

It wasn't. Urngra opened her mouth and bit Shift's head off.

I launched myself at Urngra. "No! Give her back!"

Nyrik and Horm were quicker than I was. And, between them, stronger than I was. They caught me before I could reach her. "Now then, Daxxie, calm down," Horm was saying. "Urnzie knows what she's doing."

Urngra was smiling as she chewed thoughtfully, as if she was appreciating how my staff tasted. Shift, clearly, did not appreciate being tasted. She shrieked as Urngra's jaws worked on her hard rowan heartwood—and then, suddenly, Urngra's cheeks were lit up in a blaze of red and green light from within. Her eyes widened in sudden shock. The reds and greens faded away as Shift's wails ceased abruptly. Urngra swallowed. "Woof!" she said. "*Spicy!*" She wiped her eyes, which had filled with tears, and belched.

"What did you do that for?!" I shouted, struggling to break free. I was stunned, thinking, *My healing! My protection, my damages! My*

*Shift.* I stared in horror at the shattered stick that I was holding. I had never felt more vulnerable in my life.

Horm seemed delighted. It made no sense—he knew how powerful Shift was. *Had been.* I was nothing without her, unarmed and defenseless …

"You're on, then, Urnzie?" he said, already knowing the answer.

"Yur," Urngra replied. "Fool's errand, but, well, anything for my favorite cousin."

She took my wrist in her hand, said, "Come on, then, you," and dragged me out of the hovel.

Out in the open air, I staggered as Urngra dropped my arm. Nyrik and Horm emerged behind us.

"Looks like you're in luck, Daxxie!" Nyrik said, clapping me on the back, while I stood frozen on the spot, stunned. "We'll be off, then. See you back in Eastbay. Try and make it in time for the fight, eh?"

"Yur, you won't want to miss that!" Horm added.

"I'll still give you five-to-four against Grell," Nyrik continued, cheerily. "Your four wins my five, or forty my fifty?"

They seemed as unconcerned as if we'd just had tea and cakes with Esmeralda. They were chatting away blithely—and going to leave me with an Ogre who had just bitten the head off my only weapon, my *friend*, and I was still reeling from the shock …

"Wait—what?" I managed. "You can't leave!"

"Don't need us no more, mate," Nyrik said.

"You got Urnzie now," Horm said, proudly.

"She bit the head off Shift!" I protested.

"For your own good," Horm pointed out.

"What??!"

"Can't go where you're going carrying one o' *them*," Nyrik said. "Bad things could happen."

"Bad things could happen to me without it!" I yelped.

"Nah, they won't, mate. Not with Urngra looking out for you."

"But—but …"

"Look, you don't know the way things are hereabouts, do you?" Horm said. "We do, Urngra more than anyone. You don't go swanning into the village *armed*, Daxxie. You go in quiet, and peaceful, and humble. All right?"

I looked from him, to Nyrik, and back again. I could feel my mouth opening and closing like a fish. But I couldn't think of anything to say. I felt helpless without Shift.

Among my scattered thoughts, eventually, a word that Horm had said echoed in my head. "Village?" I said. "What village?"

"The one my lovely cousin is taking you to, out of the kindness of her heart," Horm said, "where you'll find your answers. And very probably your new life, 'cos most who go there, stay there. It being more where they feel they belong. You know: like with like."

"Birds of a feather," Nyrik added, swinging himself up into the saddle.

"Only not birds, o' course," Horm said. "In that partic'lar village."

"Nor feathers," Nyrik agreed, chuckling. "Plenty of hair, though." He looked down at me with a cheerful smile. "I'm not trying to hornswoggle you, Daxxie, mate," he continued, "with my five-to-four. No cash down necessary—your credit's good with me. I wouldn't want you to think, *Ooh, Nyrik knows I'm never coming back. He's pulling a fast one, offering big odds against Grell. The little sod just wants to get his hands on my coin 'cos he thinks I'm going to stay here in the Deepwoods forever, and he won't have to pay up if I win.*"

"Nah, we'd never do that to you, mate!" Horm said, reaching out, and shaking my hand before I knew what I was doing. "You treated us right, we'll always do likewise, my word on it."

"You turn back up in Eastbay," Nyrik said, "me and Horm will accommodate your wager at five-to-four minimum—or longer, if the odds have shifted against your boy."

"Least we could do, after all you done for us," Horm agreed. He turned to Urngra. "You're the best, cuz!"

Urngra picked him up in another bear hug, saying, "You too, Horm. Look after yourself, and don't be a stranger now!"

"I won't, I promise," Horm replied.

Urngra twirled, Horm tiny in her huge arms, and deposited him in his saddle. They slapped hands, chuckling, and Horm turned his horse's head away, back in the direction we'd come.

"See you, Daxxie," Nyrik said, following him, leading my horse behind him.

"We hope," Horm qualified, over his shoulder.

"Wait!" I squawked. "Don't—"

But they were already swallowed up by the mist and the trees.

I stared after them. I'd never felt so lost. Betrayed even, although I knew they meant the best.

A large finger prodded down into my collarbone.

I flinched, and looked up at Urngra.

She was staring down at me. "You'll owe me!" She rumbled.

"Yes," I said, nervously, "thank you. Whatever you want, if I can do it."

"Whatever I want," she echoed.

"Yes," I said. "Well, within reason."

She gurgled a small laugh. "Within reason," she said, nodding. "Sounds fair enough. Although where we're going, reason doesn't come into it."

I didn't like the sound of that. But what choice did I have? I could hardly tell her that I'd changed my mind and head back to Eastbay.

"Off we go, then," Urngra said, and strode off down the slope, deeper into the Deepwoods.

I readjusted my pack on my back and hurried after her.

"Urngra," I said, "wait!"

She stopped. "What?"

"Where are we going?"

She stared. Frowned. "You heard."

I said, "The village."

"Yur. So why ask?" She set off again.

I hurried after her again.

"What village?" I said, when I'd caught up with her.

She stopped. "*The* village," she said, as if to an idiot, "where you need to go."

She turned away and strode on. Fast.

I ran a few paces and was at her side again. "What can you tell me about it?"

Urngra stopped. She stared down at me. "If you keep asking all these questions we'll never get there."

I didn't understand. "What do you mean?"

Her eyes narrowed as she stared into mine. Eventually, she said, "What do you know about Ogres?"

"Not much," I admitted. "Very little."

"Here's an interesting fact about Ogres," Urngra said. "Most people know this, but you, apparently, do not. It will answer your question and explain what I mean."

I waited.

She said, eventually, "Ready?"

"Yes," I said.

"Ogres," she said, "cannot walk and talk at the same time."

She let that sink in.

I saw that a response was expected, so said, "Oh."

"Strange, I agree," she said. "We can do both, just not simultaneously. It is not as if we don't have the requisite physiology. Like mastodons can't jump. It has baffled our finest minds since time immemorial."

Once again, I said, "Oh," which seemed to be about the limit of my conversational prowess.

"Now," Urngra said, still staring down at me, "I know what you're thinking. I'm only a half Ogre. Therefore, possibly, the above does not apply? Or, perhaps, I could walk and talk half the time? Or half walk, while half talking?" That thought seemed to intrigue her. "Maybe. Who knows? I've never tried. I also do not quite know what to make of the concept of a *half walk*. What would that be? A shuffle? A slow march? And half talking? Would I only enunciate half of each word I was attempting to speak—while doing the above-mentioned, if not yet properly defined, 'half walking?' How would that manifest itself? *'Howou- tha- manif- thelf?'* Mm. Not a particularly fruitful mode of communication, in my view. What would be the point, I ask you to consider, of us proceeding at a snail's pace—that being basically what a 'half walk' would be—talking gibberish to each other? Well, maybe *you* could speak just fine, while we *half walked*, but if I couldn't we'd a) be going very slowly, or, b) you'd be hard-pressed to glean anything informative from my truncated utterings."

She let that sink in—which, I have to confess, it really didn't.

"Anyway, irrelevant: half Ogre or not, I'm all Ogre when it comes to the *can't-walk-and-talk-at-the-same-time* affliction. So, if you want to get anywhere, don't ask questions, or we'll just be standing around all day arguing and not making progress. The other half of me being Woods Kin, though," she smiled, brightening up, "it balances out, I am happy to say, and I am an *excellent* dancer."

She executed a neat shuffle and turn. She was surprisingly light on her feet—which were hairy, and bare, and blue. Each of her toes ended in a black, inch-long talon.

"So," she said, "shall we be getting on? In silence? To the village? Where your questions will be answered? By those that know what you need to know? And where, if by some delightful happenstance there is

28

a musical soiree, I will be pleased to take the floor with you? Or I can solo, if you're not up to it and just want to watch."

"No, I'd give it a go," I said. "I'm no expert, but I do enjoy it."

"Good!" Urngra grinned. "Let's hope then, eh? It's not beyond the bounds of possibility. Musical lot, the Pack, and it's not just howling."

She turned away and strode on down the slope into the Deepwoods.

# 3

## The Small Fight

Urngra didn't bother with such concepts as *the easy way*, or *around*. Her idea of navigation was limited to *straight ahead*. Straight ahead took her through thickets, and bushes, and across ponds and bogs and streams. Her giant strides were more than twice as long as mine, but I must have taken ten times as many steps as she did, on my various detours around obstacles that she simply ignored. By midafternoon I was exhausted, and cold, and wet, and scratched, and splattered with mud. She showed no sign of tiring. She plowed on, in a beeline, not saying a word—just occasionally grunting, or growling, or throwing her head back and emitting a sharp, startling bark.

I was wondering how much longer I could keep this up before I dropped when the solution occurred to me. I thought, *Duhh!*, amazed that I hadn't seen it before—after all, I'd been worrying about *Pack*, and *Form*, and *Moon*, and *Gift* all the time, wondering what lay ahead. Knackered I might be, in human form—but to *were*-me, this marathon would be a stroll in the park.

I Turned and trotted up alongside Urngra, feeling not only smug but much better. I could keep going like this all day. The feelings of *smug* and *much better* lasted only until Urngra glanced down and noticed me. She roared, and clouted me with the back of her hand, sending me

30

flying. I landed in a ditch, my wits scattered, and looked up just in time to see Urngra launching herself into the air and dropping down onto me, talons out, mouth open, bellowing.

I didn't have time to roll away. All I could do was hold my four paws up in front of me to cushion the impact. She landed on top of them, knocking the wind out of me, her arms flailing wildly for any part of me that she could scratch or punch. I kicked, and pushed, and snarled, and hit, and blocked, while above me Urngra did the same. She was enraged, attacking me with everything she had.

Within seconds I was fighting for my life. My claws were sharp, but her talons were sharper, and she had a big weight advantage. Human-me would have been disembowelled in seconds, but my tough werewolf hide kept me in one piece—for a while, as least. I knew that my teeth were my best weapon, but I also knew better than to use them on her. She was stronger than me, no doubt about that, but I was quicker.

I scrabbled at her with my hind legs and managed to push my hips out to one side, from beneath her. I kicked as hard as I could, digging my heels into her pelvis, throwing her off, while grabbing around her upper arms with my forelegs and pulling, turning her onto her back. She thumped into the mud beside me, and I had a second or two before she could get up onto her feet again. I scrambled backwards out of the ditch, ran like hell to put some distance between us, and re-Turned, and dropped to my knees.

I waited, cringing and unthreatening, and said, "Sorry ...!"

Urngra was towering above me by the time I got the word out, her fist raised above my head for the hammerblow that would finish me.

The fist stopped.

Urngra glared. Her chest was heaving, and her throat gargling with anger.

"I was tired," I explained.

She was, I could tell, longing to flatten me.

She inhaled, deeply; held it, as if for the next action; and then exhaled, slowly. I was glad that I was not in *were*-form, as I flinched away from her awful breath. My *were*-nose would not have enjoyed the smell of it.

I tried not to look at her fist but held her eyes, my expression meek.

"Fucking *Weres!*" She growled it in a way that said, *I should do the world a favor and finish you off.*

31

I waited.

The longer she took before hitting me, I thought, the better chance I stood of surviving.

"Do you have a problem," I said, "with werewolves?"

She frowned down at me. "Are you kidding me?" she challenged.

"No," I said. "You're taking me to, this, um, village of them, so, I thought you—"

"*Everyone*," she interrupted, leaning closer, "has a problem with werewolves. Even bloody werewolves!"

I couldn't begin to put that particular two and two together, so just said, "Oh."

"And if you don't let the fuckers know that they have an even bigger problem with *you*, the next thing you know is one of them's sunk his teeth into you, and you're one of them yourself. And I'm not having that!"

"I wasn't going to bite you, Urngra. It's—"

"How was I to know that?!"

I had no answer, so ignored the question, and continued. "It's just a lot easier to keep up with you on four legs."

"Yur!" she challenged, nodding down at me, "and we're going along, all nice and easy, for an hour, or three, and the next thing you know your nose is telling you, *Hmmm, wouldn't mind a mouthful of that*, and you take a chunk out of my leg! And while I'm hopping about going *aagh, aaah*, unable to stand properly, you're tasting blood, aren't you? Yur! And that works on you, and you lick your lips and think, *Ooohm, yes, lovely—very tasty! Think I might just help myself to another slice o' that*, and I can't stand, let alone run, or fight; and two mouthfuls ain't enough, you decide, and you go, *Ah, might as well finish her off.*"

"I wouldn't. I'd never—"

"Been Gifted one moon month, and you're a bloody expert?!" Urngra sneered, jabbing me in the shoulder with a hard forefinger. "You have no idea, mate. *'You wouldn't, you'd never.'* Pff. *'You'* don't bloody come into it, Daxx. I'm not bothered when *you* are around. It's when *you* have gone that's the problem! And *you* wake up the next morning with a nice clear head, and a nice full stomach, as well rested as your sweet old grandma after a nice long nap; and you yawn, and stretch, and sit up, and feel fabulous, and there's bits of me strewn everywhere and blood all over the place. And you have no recollection of anything."

She stared down at me.

"I … what …?"

She ignored me and continued, "And you go *Ahh*, as you contemplate my scattered remains. And then you go, *Oh, well. I feel fine.* And you look around, and you think, *What a nice, sunny morning. Birds in the trees, sun in the sky. Everything must be all right. Pity about Urngra; I rather liked her. Jovial company. A source of much information about which I'd known nothing until she imparted it to me. Most insightful, I enjoyed meeting her—and, judging by the evidence all around me—eating her. Oh, well, that's life, eh? Or, in her case, not.*"

She stopped and waited, watching me.

Eventually, I said, "Is that what it's like?"

"As I've heard," she acknowledged. "Secondhand, of course. I've never been Gifted myself, obviously, thank all the gods. A couple of the fuckers have tried, but … well." She shrugged. Then she smiled, a little apologetically. "I wouldn't be standing here now, would I? If they'd succeeded. It was me or them. But, you know: Word gets around."

I didn't like any of what I'd heard. "And … what does that word say?" I asked.

"Basically?" she said. "What I just told you: *me or you.*"

"That's it?"

"Seems to be," she said, "for them as have been Gifted."

I couldn't think what to say. "There's no … alternative?"

She shrugged. "How should I know?"

"What happened to them? The ones who tried to … Gift you?"

"Spiked 'em."

"You what?"

She stared at me, as if surprised that she had to explain.

"Spiked 'em," she repeated. "Just the heads. We throw the rest away. Silver spikes, mind, or the buggers Turn back, even when dead—and who wants some poor forester, or milkmaid, or nibler, or woody staring down at you, eh? You'd feel sorry for them in human form. Quite put you off your sproj."

I knew I'd heard the word before, but I echoed it anyway, as I was struggling to keep up.

"Sproj?"

"Ogre hooch. What we drink, when carousing. Which is what drinking is, in our establishments—none of your gloomy sipping alone in a corner, staring into the fire. Carouse or fuck off, is the way we look at it."

She seemed to be less likely to kill me now, so I said, "Sounds fun."

Her shoulders relaxed, and her glare softened into something almost like a smile. "It is," she said. "And we like to decorate our inns and such with trophies. Adds to the ambience. We all contribute."

I cringed. "Werewolf heads?"

"Among others. Gryphons. Minotaurs. Trolls. Anything hostile and horrible. You'd be mocked rotten if you turned up with a goat or something. There's a tavern up in the Northlands that has an elf-wall. You could swear their eyes follow you around the room."

We'd fought pit elves on our way back up from the Floor Of The World. Vicious little brutes. I didn't think I'd find an evening's "carousing" with their cruel eyes watching me particularly relaxing.

I said, "I've been at an Orc feast. With my friends." I told her about our night with the Stonefields clan. It turned out that she knew them—Klurra, Chief Elbrig, the rest.

She grinned and punched me in the shoulder—in a friendly, if painful, way. "You," she said, "are coming with me!"

I said, "I know. To the village."

"*After* that," she said, with a grin and a wink, "for a night on the sproj!" The grin faded, as she thought it over. "Well, if you make it out of the village, that is."

The confrontation seemed to be over. I reached out a hand to her, and she wiped hers on the back of her tunic before taking it and shaking it.

"I'm sorry I Turned," I said. "I didn't know how dangerous I could be. There's a lot I don't know."

"No worries," she said. "Just don't do it again."

I said, "Not even at night, so I can sleep nice and furry and warm?"

Her smile faded and her huge hand clamped tighter around mine.

"Not if you want to wake up in the morning," she said.

I felt my knuckles collapsing under her grip. "I won't," I said. "I promise!"

She held the squeeze just long enough for me to get the message. Any increase in her pressure and the bones in my hand would shatter. I was on tiptoe, in pain, holding my breath …

She let go, nodded, turned away, and strode on, straight ahead.

I urged my tired legs into action again and followed her. I was drained. I was frightened. I was lost and confused. I was plunging ever deeper into the Deepwoods, unarmed and unprotected, trailing after a monster who had just been trying to kill me. I had no other choice. It was too late to change my mind now.

Three days later we reached the village. I was a mess. I'd been scrambling along in Urngra's wake as best I could, while I had no means of healing myself, nor of warming myself during the long, cold days and nights of our trek. I'd carried the sad remains of Shift for a while, hoping that I might make some sort of contact with her. She had, after all, awoken in my hands before I'd fitted her with her tourmaline heart. Remembering her former glory, it felt almost insulting, waving her around and casting everything I could think of, all to no avail. I was holding nothing more than a dead stick of wood. It seemed wrong to discard her, so I buried her respectfully—much to Urngra's bemusement.

On we went, down, and damp, and up, and cold. Urngra never tired. I was run off my feet. Hauling myself over fallen trees, wading through mud, and mold, and undergrowth, and water, shoving through bushes. Always hurrying to catch up with Urngra, who only spoke when we stopped—and, when we stopped, I was too exhausted for conversation. I had no words that I wanted to say aloud. The words that I kept saying to myself, in my head, were confused, and no help at all, and usually began with *f*.

"There," she said at last, having stopped.

There had been clearings, in the Deepwoods, on our way, but this was different. It was as if the other trees had stepped back, out of respect, and left this place to the oaks. We emerged from a wall of forest and looked at the open ground before us. It was quiet, and calm, and bathed in weak, late-winter sunlight. A hundred yards away the oaks rose, one tall, ancient tree after another, all rearing their twisted arms to the sky, the thin breeze rustling through their bare branches.

*Brooding*, I thought.

*Watching.*

*Waiting.*

Urngra turned and looked down at me. "Ready?"

I nodded.

We walked on up. Birds flitted among the branches, silent. Everything was hushed, as if holding its breath. The ground rose beneath our feet, until we were among the trees, each more massive, and older, than the last. I don't know when I realized that Urngra was holding my hand.

At the crest of the knoll stood the largest, oldest oak of them all. Its trunk was wider than it was tall; a massive, gnarled lump, from which long limbs forked up and out into the slate-gray sky, bare but for clusters of mistletoe.

I froze as we neared the shadow that spread around its foot. Two intense, mossy green eyes had opened in its trunk and were peering down, inspecting me. A gust of wind moved among the oak's branches, making it seem as if the tree was breathing. Its trunk parted, slowly, and opened, revealing a tunnel—a tunnel that led not down, which would have been possible, but straight on through, and beyond, which was not. I'd slept inside trees with Nyrik and Horm. I'd descended into the heart of the Tree of Life at the Floor Of The World, so I knew that trees held their secrets. Never before, though, had I walked *through* one, as if into a hole in the wall of a cliff that wasn't there.

I know that it wasn't there because I checked, stepping to one side of the giant oak, and then to the other. Nothing led out from behind it: But, from the front, something led into it, and off, and away. The green eyes watched us as we walked in below them. The tree closed behind us and we were in darkness.

We waited, hand in hand, letting our eyes adjust, until we saw that the gloom in the tunnel was not total. Faint points of light glowed all around us, in the floor, the walls, the roof. I leaned over to inspect one. It was a luminescent fungus, the size of a fingernail. Pale, gleaming roots poked down from above. The ground was soft underfoot, and spongy—lichen, I thought, not grass. Not enough light was being thrown for us to see much more than shadow ahead, but hundreds of points of light showed us the tunnel's outline. It was, I thought, like walking into the night sky, but a sky that smelled of moss and mud and damp.

We went on, and, eventually, down. Urngra was having to stoop, to avoid banging her head against the tunnel's ceiling.

She halted and peered down at me. "It's not too long," she said. "Less than a mile."

"You've been here before?"

"Now and then." Her voice echoed in the enclosed space. "When someone brings me in. Can't come in on my own. No one can who isn't Pack. Tree won't open for them."

"So that means I'm Pack now?"

Urngra stopped. "Well, Pack, or, Pack-*ish*," she demurred. "I doubt if it's that easy. You just stroll in and it's all sorted? I wouldn't think so. But how should I know? They don't tell. You've probably noticed that yourself? People don't tell outsiders things."

"So, you don't know what …." I struggled to find the words. "I can expect?"

"No. Something, no doubt. Welcoming committee; initiation ritual; hazardous test of worthiness, perhaps? Ceremony. Rite of passage. Single combat to the death. Who knows how they do these things?"

She waited. I knew she wasn't going to move until the conversation was over.

"I suppose we'd better find out," I said.

Urngra grunted agreement.

We headed on down the long, dark, mushroom-lit tunnel.

After a while, and a few twists and turns, we saw daylight ahead. We emerged at the top of a slope. A path led down, into more trees, some cultivated, standing in neat orchards. Many had clumps of mistletoe in their bare branches. Bushes grew beneath them: hedgerows, banks of shrubs. Early flowers brightened the road's verges—snowdrops, crocuses, primroses. This was farmland, not wilderness. There were streams, and sluice gates, and still ponds.

The sun was warmer here, and the sky cloudless. I heard bells—cowbells, sheep bells, goat bells, clonking softly as animals grazed in their pastures. Lambs and calves and kid goats bleated for their mothers. It could hardly have been a more peaceful, more idyllic scene. Why in the world, I thought, would anyone want to live anywhere else?

I gazed around as we walked on down. The roofs of cottages emerged ahead of us. Our footsteps crunched on the stony path. We saw livestock in the fields, but no people. The world, down here, was dozing in the mild afternoon sun. This was not what I had been expecting. What had I been expecting? A challenge, a horror. A problem. This was a solution. I would lay down my burden, I thought. *I will lie down by the side of that lazy little river, and watch the dragonflies dancing above the water, and fall asleep, and dream. Here is my space.*

As we neared the village, a dog rose from its scrape under a hedgerow.

It padded up to us, tongue out—a black-and-white sheepdog, I saw. It reminded me of Ezzie, Marnie's pup, who'd be almost fully grown now. I held my hand out to it, for it to smell.

It sniffed, and looked up at me in recognition, its bright brown eyes shining, its tail wagging. *It knows what I am,* I thought

It fell in beside us as we walked on down towards the village. The hedges on either side of the path became more orderly and trimmed. We passed a small gate, and then another. Beyond them were glimpses of gardens, and orchards, and buildings—woodsheds, barns, cottages. Around a final curve the path widened, leading to one corner of a village green, complete with duckpond. It looked like the most ordinary, typical, serene rustic village—quaint, unremarkable, well-kept and tidy.

The only odd thing about it was that it was deserted.

I said, "Is it always like this?"

Urngra stopped and said, "It livens up at night. This way," she continued, when she saw that the conversation was over. She led me along one side of the village green and turned off up a lane into a field between an avenue of ash trees, their bare branches dotted with the early buds of spring and shadowed with balls of mistletoe. As we crested a small rise, a house emerged ahead of us. It was dark, and wide, its lower half stone, its upper half timber and plaster under a thatched roof.

The sheepdog looked up at me, wagged its tail, and turned to go back.

I watched it trot away towards the village.

"Who lives here?" I asked Urngra as we approached the door. Yet more mistletoe hung on it, above a brass wolf head that held a brass ring in its teeth.

"Byrneth," she said, and thumped the door knocker.

"And who's he?"

"Him you need to see."

# 4

## Byrneth

"Urngra," the man said, peering up at her around the heavy wooden door as he opened it. He sounded wary rather than pleased. "To what do I owe the pleasure?" he added, in a somewhat sarcastic tone. His voice was low, not much more than a rumble in his throat.

"Let us in and I'll tell you," Urngra said.

He stepped back and held the door open to us. I followed Urngra inside into a small lobby.

"Shoes," the man said.

"Don't use 'em," Urngra muttered. She wiped her huge, bare feet on the doormat and strode on ahead.

I took my boots off and went in after her, into a long hall that was lit by guttering candles. It seemed to be part library and part laboratory. Bookcases lined the walls. Workbenches stood among tables and chairs. There was no ceiling overhead, just roof beams stretching up into the thatch. A log fire burned in a central hearth, throwing a warm glow into the gloom. On the mantelpiece above it sat another ball of mistletoe.

"Got a problem," Urngra said, nodding at me. "Him, not me. He's been Gifted."

The man looked at me and his amber eyes held mine. "That's always a problem," he agreed.

"Thing is," Urngra said "he's not your regular sort. You know, peasant or whatever."

"We make no distinctions here," the man growled. "All are equal, in the Pack."

"Yur, I know that," Urngra continued, "but Daxx here's a foreigner, and a mage, and a scholar. How many mages in your Pack, eh, Byrneth? Oh: Daxx—Byrneth," she waved a big blue hand between us by way of introduction.

The information seemed to interest Byrneth. He was a man of middle years, and middle height, and fairly unremarkable looking apart from his very remarkable hair. On top of his head rose a luxuriant black mane, swept back; below it, thick whiskers bushed out, black streaked with gray, all around his chin and up to his eyes. Tufts sprouted through his eyebrows, below his hairy forehead, and feathered his ears, and pushed above the top of his jerkin at his neck, and out from below the sleeves on the backs of his hands. His fingernails were long and black. His feet were bare and thickly matted with hair, and his toes ended in claws. His teeth, I noticed, were larger than normal. I'd been expecting that I'd meet werewolves, either in the Form or as their human selves; but this Byrneth, I realized, was neither one thing nor the other. He was both.

"Mage, eh, are you, Daxx?" Byrneth said, intrigued. "As in, wizard, sorcerer, that sort of thing?"

"Yes," I said.

He studied me, and then frowned. "So, where's your staff?" he demanded.

"Urngra ate it," I said.

Byrneth looked at Urngra.

"I know the rules," she said. "Moon Magic only in the village."

"Yes, but a mage who's been Gifted?" Byrneth said. "How many of them do we get?! None, that's how many. Not one, ever. And what use to us is a mage with no staff, if I might ask?"

Urngra looked down at him and snarled.

"Look," she said, "I'm doing this as a favor for my favorite cousin. My favorite cousin tells me that this gent here, Daxx, is a man of worth, who has been very good to him, and that I should do anything I can for him. What I can do is what few can do, and I did it, which is bring him here to you. Most poor buggers who get Gifted just get drawn into the woods towards the next Moon Night, and then they're off and away and gone.

"So, what you have here is a mage who's been Gifted. I don't know what to do about that, and the only person I know who might be able to sort him out is you. The which is why I brought him here. I was just obeying your rules, out of respect, eating his staff. Your realm, your rules. I didn't want your Pack ripping him to shreds out there in the village, on account of seeing his staff, before you got to take a look at him."

Byrneth sighed. " 'Sort him out'?" he echoed.

Urngra grunted. "Help the poor sod."

Byrneth shook his head, slowly. "There's no help."

"Then help him understand that, all right?" Urngra said. "Settle him in, nice like. Make him feel at home. If he's going to have to spend the rest of his life here, let him know what's what, and why."

Byrneth grunted. "*Why*," he repeated. "If we knew that, we'd all be a lot the wiser."

They fell silent.

To break that silence, I said, "If you tell me the problem, I could try to think of a why."

Byrneth turned his amber eyes on me. "If none of us have ever been able to work it out," he challenged, "what makes you think that you can?"

"I've been told I'm good at solving problems."

Byrneth leaned back, still studying me. "When were you Gifted?"

"Last moon month."

He snorted. "So, you know next to nothing. And you think you can solve our problem? That we've had for thousands of years?"

I considered his words. "If you like, I can tell you some other problems I've solved recently."

"Such as?"

"Defeating Jurun. Bringing Queen Esmeralda back from the Floor Of The World."

His eyes widened. "That was you?" Byrneth was clearly impressed.

"That was me."

He nodded. "I'd like to hear about that, indeed. We've heard all sorts of tales."

"I'll be happy to tell you everything," I said, "but it will take a while. Perhaps you could fill me in on this problem first? *Our* problem? So that I can start thinking about it?"

Byrneth hesitated. "It's not the usual way."

"Then what is?"

"You drink the drink, and dream the dream, and learn the lore," he said. "Then, you're Pack." He spoke with an air of finality.

I understood the word that he had left unspoken: *Forever.*

"So, at a guess," I said, "that's the problem. That there's no going back and that the change controls us too much—takes over."

He nodded, slowly. "*Gifted, and gone,*" he said. I recognized the phrase that Nyrik had used. "Normal folks don't like us. They don't want the Gift. We're safe here, where they can't come, or they'd have wiped us out long ago."

He sighed. "Once bitten, can't be unbitten. There's only forwards. That's just the way it is, Daxx. Always has been. Always will be." He held my eyes and spread his arms wide.

I knew what he meant.

*Look at me. This is what lies ahead.*

*For us. For me. For you.*

*Finality.*

My heart sank. "Does everyone end up like that?"

"This isn't the end," he said. "Not by any means."

*I studied him. That?* I thought. *That's going to be me? And maybe more than that?*

He saw my concern. "It's not as bad as it looks. You get used to it. Trouble is, of course, other people. Normal people—like the folks we leave behind, and Urngra here. They don't hold with our kind. Which is why we all eventually settle here in the village, or somewhere like it. A safe place. A hidden place, where we fit among our own. Out there it's dangerous."

I remembered the hunters who had been pursuing Graycote.

I thought I might as well tell him my story. "I was Gifted by a Packfather named Graycote, in another land," I said.

"Hmh," he muttered. "Never heard of him."

He didn't seem to want to say anything else, so I continued. "I saved his life from hunters who had filled him with silver arrows. I didn't know who, or what, he was—I just saw a man in peril of his life. I healed him. I'm a healer, as well as a battlemage. Graycote Gifted me, I think, by way of thanking me."

Byrneth's eyes narrowed as he mulled over what I'd said. I sensed that he'd never heard a story like mine before.

"Healer," he said.

I nodded.

"There's no healing of this."

"That you know of."

I thought I saw something flicker deep in his amber eyes, but it swiftly disappeared. "That we know of," he agreed.

Byrneth was contemplating me and thinking.

"Healer," he repeated.

"Yes," I said, "so let me ask you something: If I could heal you, Byrneth, would you want it?"

I watched him as he considered the idea. Perhaps it had been so long, since he'd been Normal People, that he'd stopped thinking about the possibility of having a choice. There was no either/or, in his world. There was only both.

"Don't know as I can say," he said. "For myself. I'm … accustomed, now. But for some as are here … why, it might well be that they would. Hard though it would be, to give up the Gift." He considered, then held my eyes. "As you will see for yourself, soon enough."

"I already have some idea," I said, remembering the flood of feelings that had coursed through me when in the Form. The glory of it, the *rightness* …

Byrneth understood. "Yes," he said, nodding slowly "I expect you have."

And I did. Because I now knew what it was, this Gift: a lure. A trap. Also: an escape. Above all, but not for long, it was a confusion. It gave you much to think about, but much more to feel. This Gift would tear anyone apart—until, eventually, you were more feeling than thought. And what could be wrong with that? Sitting, on a rock, under the moon, the world flowing into you, through your nostrils, your ears, your tongue. Completion. Harmony. Compared with the distracted, busy muddle of our scrappy human lives, when we never seem to know where we are going, or what we are doing, or much about anything.

The thought struck me: I'm here, now, and have cleared tasks after quests after levels; and if I keep going, why, one day the others and I will be heading out into the universe, aboard Eydie—my *other* gift; my own, personal spaceship that had been my reward for defeating Jurun—but how much more fulfilling might it be to go the *other* way? Not up and out and away: but down and in. To live, forever, at the level of feeling; of sensing. Rather than with a head full of cluttering thoughts and confusing ideas, plodding forever through an endless to-do list.

My mind cleared, and the conclusion was obvious.

I wouldn't be piloting Eydie as a werewolf.

The thought made me smile.

And then think again.

My next thought was, *Well? Why not? Skywolf. That sounds pretty good . . .*

Who knew what was and what wasn't possible?

*Problems, problems.*

*Solve the problems.*

Urngra brought me down to earth abruptly, when she said, "Right, I'm off."

I was startled. "Wait, what? You're not going to . . . take me back . . . eventually?"

She stared down at me. "You think you're going back?" she challenged.

"I must!" I said. "I'll work out a solution. I have—well, things to do!"

"Urr," she grunted. "Maybe as you'll be doing them here. Cheers, then, Byrneth," she said, turning to him. "Good seeing you again. I won't stay for a jar of 'shine; I know you'll have things to do to-night." She gave Byrneth a ferocious smile, then turned to me. "The last time Byrn and me and his lot got stuck into their moonshine, I couldn't walk for two days! Good stuff, that. Brutal, but you can't help helping yourself to more. It was nice meeting you, Daxx. Most interesting conversationalist. You owe me, remember? Whatever I want. Within reason."

"I do," I agreed. "Anything I can."

"Hmm," she growled and smiled. "Mage. Yes. Could be just what I've been looking for. Talking of which," she said, suddenly remember-ing, and fishing inside her sleeveless jerkin, "this is yours. I expect you could use it."

She opened her gigantic blue fist.

It was holding Shift's tourmaline heartstone.

"Passed it a couple of days ago," she said. "Not the most comfort-able dump of my life, if I'm being honest. All them edges. It's all right," she added, as I stared up at her yellow eyes in shock. "I washed it. In a stream."

Well, that was a relief.

44

I reached for the tourmaline and took it. It felt warm in my hand. The familiar sight of it gave me a glimmer of hope. "Thank you," I said. "Thank you for everything, Urngra."

"No problem," she said. "Anything for Horm. We'll meet again."

"You think?"

She nodded. "I think. Right, then, I'll leave you to it." She turned and stalked off down the hall and was gone.

"Remarkable woman, that," Byrneth said, as I tucked the tourmaline into the inner pocket of my jerkin above my heart. "She has her own way of thinking, like all Ogres, but I've never known her be wrong. Incomprehensible, yes. Half the time you have no idea what she's on about; but when you do, it turns out she's always right. And she was right to bring you to me first."

I said, "First?"

"Before meeting the others, here in the village. You being a mage. They'd have been ... wary. *Especially* if you'd had your staff .... Interesting, that," he considered. "Very interesting. Most wizards, and mages and such, know better than to be out and about at the wrong time. Some say they can see 'round corners, or know where we of the Packs are, from leagues away." He looked up at me. "Is that possible?"

"Yes," I said, thinking of Reveal Hidden Life, and the new skill line of Light Magic that Avildor had taught me. "I can do it myself."

"Well then," Byrneth said, "it will be no surprise to learn that your sorcerers, and so on, steer well clear of us. Or, if they meet us, they shoot first and ask questions afterwards. They've killed a lot of us, mages have. So, one of them walking in here, staff and all, would meet a very unwelcoming committee." He sighed. "All of which means, of course, that we have no one in our community who has the first idea how to look into what you and I have been referring to as our 'problem.' Perhaps you, being a mage, might discover something? With your skills. Even without your staff."

I said, "I can craft another." I held up the tourmaline heartstone. "And fit this to it. All I need is the right wood." A new staff might not be Shift, whose loss I had been grieving for days, but with the right combination of *stick and stone* in my hands I'd be armed and dangerous again.

Byrneth said, "And what is the right wood?"

"Rowan."

45

"Mountain ash." He nodded. "Plentiful hereabouts. Farnz will set you right. Our master carpenter," he explained. I must have looked surprised, because he chuckled. "These houses don't build themselves, Daxx. Made all this furniture, Farnz did." I took a moment to look at the chairs nearby. They were, I saw, skilfully crafted. "He'll sort you out on the morrow. You won't be needing a staff tonight. Moon Magic only is the rule here; Urngra was right about that." He nodded and then seemed to think aloud. "Moon Magic, Mage Magic—the old ways, the new ways ....Yes. Problems, solutions, changes ... who knows what we might learn, that we've been wanting to learn for so long?"

I agreed. "Well, let's try to find out."

"Indeed," he said. "Things are shifting, it seems to me."

I smiled, a little wistfully. He noticed and said, frowning, "What's so funny?"

"My staff," I said. "The one I had before, that Urngra ate. Her name was Shift."

His face cleared. He liked the convergence. "Good name. So, let's get you going, shall we?" He loped off down the dusty hall and stopped at a workbench at the hall's far end. "It's probably too much to hope you'll come out with anything more than anyone else has," he continued, "but, then, none of us has ever been a mage. Sit."

He pointed at a low stool. I duly sat, watching him as he found a flask, and various vials and pots. He measured out powders, and sprinkled them one by one into a mug, then added drops from the vials. He picked up a handful of pale, glowing mushrooms, which he crushed, and dropped into the mug. He added liquid from the flask. He swirled and sniffed, and nodded. He handed the mug to me.

"Drink," he said.

Cautious, I said, "What is it?"

He smiled. "Moonmead."

I hesitated. "What's in it?"

"Moonwort, picture mushrooms, mandrake root, wolfsbane, burdock, valerian, all steeped in our own mead," he said. "The which we brew here in the village, and you'll taste none better."

He took a swig from the flask, swallowed, smacked his lips and sighed with pleasure. He stoppered the flask, put it back where he'd found it, and waited for me to drink his concoction.

I was still wary. "What are 'picture mushrooms'?"

"They will show you," he said, "what it would take me all night, and all the morrow, to tell you. And they will do it much better than I could. Pictures being more instructive than words."

I looked down at the oily liquid in the mug I was holding. It smelled … ominous. I wasn't sure I wanted to drink it.

I looked up at Byrneth.

His amber eyes burned into mine.

"What does it do?" I asked.

"Like I said: pictures. I could *tell* you," he said. "This will *show* you." He raised his chin and crossed his arms. "Drink. It'll put hairs on your chest. Among other places."

I raised the mug to my lips.

Well, I thought, here goes.

I drank.

*I don't know how long I'd been asleep. A minute, or thousands of years. The man was bearing down on me. I could barely stand. The body of my mother was still warm beside me. The man raised his spear. The little girl, behind him, cried out in protest. The man stopped. He gestured. The girl came forward and loomed over me. The man turned aside and began to skin my mother. The girl smiled and reached out for me. She lifted me up and held me in her arms. She stroked my head, my back, talking to me, reassuring, loving. She tickled my ears. I was shivering with fear.*

*My eyes had only opened that morning, and now my mother was dead. The man killed my brothers, my sisters. He flayed off their skins and looked down at me, in his daughter's arms. She was stroking me, her fingers kneading my thin body. I knew that I was dead but for her. She smiled up at him, her eyes wide, pleading.*

*In a language that I did not know, she said, "Can I keep her?" He looked at me with disdain, and then at her, with love. He tousled her hair. And so, I was brought into her pack. Her pack disapproved. I was the other. I was the enemy. As I grew, I grew used to kicks, and blows. She fed me on scraps. I slept in her arms, under my mother's pelt.*

*Months later, I was chasing smells in the forest, ignoring her calling me, her voice fainter and fainter behind me, suddenly turning to screams. I ran back. She was struggling with two boys of another tribe. They pushed her to the ground, laughing, taunting. I burst out of the trees and flew into them. I tore the throat out of the older boy, who was kneeling over her, pulling at her clothing. The younger ran, screeching. I brought him down, and dragged him back to her as she recovered. Together, we returned to her pack.*

*That evening, they killed the boy and threw me his body. I was not sure how to respond. He smelled like them. He was their enemy. I ate. They laughed. They patted me, roughly, gently. I gorged. They watched, enjoying, eating meat from their fire.*

*We read each other. My tail. Their smiles. We had changed. They felt safer. I felt closer. From then on, I was one of them. When I whelped, I was among them, in their cave. My cubs did as I did. We were Pack. No others of their kind could live as we lived, for they did not have us alongside them. We were the first to live with their kind, and I was the first of the first.*

*We hunted for them, killed for them, guarded them. They traded our offspring among themselves, brought us mates. A community was formed. A Pack and a pact. We guarded their flocks. We killed our wild cousins, who would prey on them. We slept, and ate, and traveled as one. We were true to each other, and loyal, hound to master, master to hound. We herded, we guarded, we loved. Big or small, fast or slow, we slept in fields, in barns, on laps, by hearths, on cushions in castles and straw in stables. We knew it would always be thus. We did not see ourselves as slaves, or pets, or inferior. We saw only friends, in concord, in our Pack. They needed us, we needed them. They scratched our backs and we guarded theirs.*

*And then, the day came. Or rather, the night: the night when one of our two-legged Pack was Gifted under the full moon. He left us. He was neither us nor them. He, in turn, formed his own Pack, from those he Gifted to be like him. He was not like them, and not like us, but other: something different; a blending. The two-legged of our Pack avoided those who had been Gifted, feared them.*

*My mind shifted, and I, Daxx, was one of the Weres now. I saw, through their wild eyes, those poor, tamed fools, with pity. Shadows of themselves. Shadows of what they should be, and what we were. We were true, they were false. We despised them. I watched them with disdain, trotting behind those who had tamed them. We killed their cattle, their dogs, their families. The two-legged tamers filled us with silver and took our skins.*

*There would never be peace.*

Then, as I understood that picture, everything altered. The world of the wolf dream turned around me. Time halted and reversed. A kaleidoscope of images poured through me. Sounds rushed past my ears. A forest at night as I ran through it. A tower, rising above a snowfield, ringed by mountains. A moon. Yellow eyes opening and boring into mine. We stared, searching, surprised that we had found each other. Our thoughts said, together, *Who are you?*

I tried to reply but could not.

A voice said, *the Moon Mage.*

I could not tell, from the way he said it, whether that was his name or who he thought I was. The yellow eyes were pulled away from me, holding my gaze as they faded back into the moon.

*"Find me,"* he said, his voice dimming, *"in the Valley of the Moon."*

I jerked awake.

Byrneth was beside me. He caught me, as I fell from my chair.

He helped me upright, to settle on my seat, as I gasped for air. He gave me water.

I drank, shaking.

"So now you see," he said.

I could not speak.

"There will never be peace," he said.

Eventually, I croaked, "What?"

"You heard. The final truth, the last thing that is revealed, in the wolf dream," he said. "*There will never be peace.* So, now you know; and now you are Pack."

I found my voice and said, "That wasn't the last thing."

He frowned at me. "It wasn't?"

"No. After that, there was The Moon Mage."

Byrneth stared at me, surprised. "The who?"

"The Moon Mage."

Byrneth said, "Never heard of him."

"He said I must find him, in the Valley of the Moon."

Byrneth drew back, as if what I had said was absurd. He grunted a laugh. "Well, good luck with that."

"Why? Do you know it, where it is?"

His eyebrows rose. "Of course," he said. He got up from his chair. "Come with me," he said, heading for the door, "and I'll show you."

Outside, night was falling, as was thin, cold rain. Beside the evening star, high overhead, against the last of the twilight, the crescent moon shone beyond the skeletal ash trees.

Byrneth pointed up at it. "There."

I said, stupidly, "Up there?"

Byrneth turned to me. "That is where we go when we die," he said. "The Valley of the Moon."

I stared up.

Rain dripped down.

"Jar of something?" he suggested, to drown out my disappointment.

"Good idea," I said, and we set off. Byrneth didn't bother to lock up behind him. "No need," he said, when I asked him. "We don't have thieves here. A thief wouldn't last long in a village full of werewolves."

# 5

## What Lies Beneath

It was like an Alcoholics Anonymous meeting, only in a pub. Not that I'd ever been to one. All I knew about them was from shows I'd seen, where some character with the problem goes in and sits down in the circle and begins the process.

I hadn't been much of a drinker, IRL. A beer or two would see me through a hard night's gaming. On this world, though, things were different. Inns and taverns were everywhere, in every city and town and village—and there were more than a few, like The Wheatsheaf, that were miles from anywhere, on the long roads that traversed the length and breadth of the realm.

They all took pride in brewing their own creations. In Brigstowe barracks we had lived for Matty the Brewer's ales, which were excellent, and varied—and, to My Lord of Brigstowe's recruits, free, though rationed. Any meal, in any tavern, was usually washed down with the house's own brewage—at breakfast, small beer: thin, sour stuff, which I had come to love. It would cut through any grease, and, being hardly 1 percent alcohol, didn't interfere with the day ahead. Most importantly, because it had been boiled in the brewing, ale was safe to drink—unlike the local water, which might give you all sorts of ailments, being half mud and half sewage.

Lunch, after a hard morning's marching, might merit a mug or two to recharge the batteries—which you'd sweat out in the afternoon's exertions. Supper: well, that depended on the occasion. Something to help you wind down after a long day, most usually; or, occasionally, something more, to celebrate a success, or to drown the sorrows of a failure. Out in the farmlands there were ciders, and meads, and fruit distillations.

Here, in the village tavern, there was 'shine.

And it was quality stuff; a fine sipping spirit indeed, to be savored, slowly.

"A mug of whatever you fancy, chased by a sip of moonshine," Byrneth recommended, as we found our seats.

The tavern didn't have a name. It didn't need one, being the only one in the village. The locals made me welcome, quietly, warily. I sat among them, and—quietly, warily—sampled what they suggested. The ciders were particularly delicious. They weren't just brewed from apples and pears, but from plums, and berries, and apricots—and, unexpectedly, rhubarb. Not too strong, not too sweet, not too fruity: They were beautifully balanced. Easy on the nose and the tongue. And, for a little kick, to accompany them: a shot of 'shine.

I remembered Urngra saying that she hadn't been able to walk for two days after her most recent night on the 'shine here. *Just the one,* I told myself. Excellent though it was, I thought: *If this stuff could render someone as large as Urngra comatose—well, a little will be enough for me.* After all, I wasn't there to party. I was there to learn what I could, and to meet those who might well be the companions of my old age. Retirement, I thought. Here in the village, away from the busy world. Among these folks. This might well be my future. The rest of my life, the end of my tale.

The villagers were hamlet and farm folk, or people of the forests and hills. They were rustic and down-to-earth: full of their own wisdom, but not exactly what you'd call sophisticated. Conversation was, well, limited. It was informative, if you wanted to learn about pestilence in crops, or techniques for castrating goats; but, basically, I didn't. I respected their expertise; but my mind kept itching to think on other things. I didn't want to be disrespectful, so I listened, and asked what questions I could think of.

*But.* The wide world was calling. *The Royal Tournament. Grell versus Commandant Bastard.* It was hard to concentrate as they spoke, slowly, one after the other. My thoughts kept flitting off and away as I tried to keep a polite smile on my face and look interested. And, at one point, those thoughts flitted off and away to Alcoholics Anonymous. People with problems, telling their tales, seeking guidance; others nodding, listening respectfully.

*My name is Hrrolf,* I thought, *and I'm a werewolf.*

*Hello, Hrrolf.*

The thought amused me. Briefly. And then made my heart sink.

*My name is Daxx, and I'm a werewolf.*

Gifted, and gone. Isolated. Would the others, I thought, come and visit me here? Grell, Qrysta, Oller? Marnie? Esmeralda, even? Nyrik and Horm might, I thought. But then, maybe not even them. They hadn't brought me here themselves. They'd handed me on to Urngra.

I missed Urngra already. She had seemed like my last connection to the real world. I shook my head, staring into my mug of cloudy rhubarb cider. I thought, *so Jarnland is the new IRL, is it? Then what does that make this place, this village?*

The answer came quickly, and I didn't like it.

A.A. We were unable to get rid of our addiction—our werewolf selves. So we adjusted to them. Our stronger selves. And went to support meetings.

It was a game within a game—only, as Ken had said, *this isn't a game, it just looks like one.*

IRL, I'd spent every hour I could gaming.

I was, I had to admit, addicted to it.

Alcoholics are good at drinking.

Addiction.

Affliction.

That is who they are.

This is what I am, now.

And, as far as anyone could tell me, this is what I would be forever. I would grow old, among these kindly, softly spoken folks. I studied them, as they were talking, nodding, listening; thinking in the long pauses between each other's remarks. Their voices rumbled in their chests. Their faces were haired or hairless, their hands fingered or taloned, their bodies upright and solid or hunched, long-limbed, long-backed. They were all, clearly, in some stage of *neither one thing nor the other.* Those who had the most to say were the ones who looked the most far gone, their eyes more yellow than amber, their faces more hair than skin. Byrneth was, as he had told me, some way toward the end stage. *And at that end stage,* I thought, *what happens then?*

I tried to pay attention. I really did. I couldn't. I didn't want to be there. I didn't want to be *that*. My eyes kept wandering around the quiet, dark, comfortable room. Benches; tables; people. A goat turning on a spit by the fire. The slowly roasting meat smelled delicious. I could hardly wait to get my teeth into it.

"I know," a voice beside me said.

I snapped out of my reverie and looked at the man who had sat down beside me. He was older than me, about fifty: tall, powerful looking, and, like everyone else there, dark.

He smiled. "It was the same my first night here," he said. "Same as anyone else's. Takes some getting your head around."

I could hardly disagree with that.

"Evening, Daxx," he said, extending a hand, which I shook. "Name's Farnz. Byrneth tells me you'll be needing a good stick of rowan."

He pronounced it to rhyme with *how* and *now* and *cow*.

"Yes," I said, brightening. "I will."

"I've all you could want in my stacks," he said. "Well-seasoned, prime cuts. You're welcome to take your pick."

"Thank you, Farnz," I said.

He nodded at me. "Maybe as we'll be thanking you, one of these days."

I said, "I'll … be doing everything I can."

His eyes glinted. "Which is more'n any o' the rest of us can do, I'm thinking. None of us being mages."

I didn't want to give him any false hope. Or myself. I knew nothing. I didn't know where to start.

I didn't need to tell him that.

I took a sip of rhubarb cider and looked again at the fire. Above it, another ball of mistletoe hung from a smoke-blackened roof beam.

I said, "What's with all the mistletoe everywhere?" I nodded at the cluster of leaves shrouding their little white berries.

"Turnaways, those. Protection, they are."

"From what?"

Farnz shrugged. "That which wouldn't be welcome."

"Anything specific?" I wondered.

"Not that I know of. They ward off what needs to be warded, it is said. We all keep a ball o' moonberries in our homes. Must work, I suppose. We don't get anything unwelcome here."

I said, "Moonberries?"

"Our name for them. They look like little moons, wouldn't you say?"

I contemplated them. They did, indeed: pale little pearls, glistening among dark green leaves, like moons peeking through clouds. It was hardly surprising, I thought, that these folks would name them such; the moon being, as they saw it, their mother. I wondered how anyone could believe that a cluster of berries could act as a ward. How could a bunch of vegetation protect anyone, and turn away unwelcome visitors?

Superstitions had always seemed irrational to me. Turning the thought over in my head, though, there in the village tavern, I realized that I'd never really considered the subject closely—the *why* of how superstitions had arisen. Was there sense behind them? Was there some reason, however deeply buried, however long forgotten, that could explain them? Or were they just … folklore? Old wives' tales? I should, I realized, ask Marnie when I got back to Eastbay. I had a feeling that she'd know more about old wives' tales than anyone, and would know the wisdom within them that most people, including myself, could not see.

*Marnie.*

I'd chosen the staff that became Shift the way she'd told me to: in the dark, in her woodshed.

That had worked out well.

I decided that I should choose my new staff the same way. Tonight, in the dark, not tomorrow when I could see.

I explained that to Farnz, who nodded. We drained our tankards, told Byrneth we'd be back for our suppers, and left the tavern.

Farnz walked me through the darkened village to his home. Above us, the moon hung over the bare branches of the surrounding ash trees.

I was curious. "Farnz, can I ask you something?"

"Fire away," he said.

"Are you happy here?"

He chuckled, stopped, and looked down at me. He was taller than I was. His eyes glinted amber in the moonlight. "I believe you know the answer to that, Daxx," he said.

I said, baffled, "How can I?"

"Ask it of yourself."

He waited.

I asked myself, *Am I happy here?*

And then, *Would I be happy here?*

I couldn't see an answer to either question—until I realized what I should really have been asking:

*Are you happy being what you are?*

He nodded, seeing that I understood. His eyebrows rose as he waited for my answer.

"Yes and no," I said.

"And there you have it!" he agreed. He clapped me on the shoulder and we walked on.

"*Yes and no.* And what is happiness, by the by? A fleeting moment. It comes, it goes. We chase it. We hunt it, as we hunt our prey on the Moon Nights. Do we know it, before we catch it? Mayhaps we have some idea of what it might be—but is it what we expected, once we have it in our hands?"

I saw what he meant.

Once you've achieved a goal, you move on.

Once you own something you've longed for, the longing fades.

Yes, our achievements comfort us. We surround ourselves with our trophies. We look back with gratitude, with satisfaction. We like the familiar, the sense of knowing. But there is so much more out there. I was nowhere near ready to retire, to settle for what I had. I had far more waiting for me, out there, yet to aim for.

On the other hand, could I let what I had go?

It hurt just to think of it. In the Form, I inhabited a life of a richness I could never conceive of as a mere human.

My thoughts cleared and I saw the problem. *I'm being pulled two ways at once.*

Right. Good. Now we know what we need to do.

Solve the problem.

*Yes and no.*

*This or that.*

Something was beginning to come into focus.

I decided to share those thoughts. "Sometimes, yes, it may be what we expected, Farnz—but not always. Sometimes, it is a disappointment."

"Indeed," he agreed. "We realize that we have been chasing a dream. A will-o'-the-wisp. Worth the try; but it turns out to be not as good as what we thought we were looking for. And even when it is, does happiness last, once we have it in our possession?" He shrugged. "It comes, it goes. Then off we go looking for it again."

We walked on along the dark lane behind the village. An owl hooted from the woodland ahead of us. A cold wind rustled in the bare branches. All was quiet, and peaceful, and yet I was tense, on alert. "You said you knew how I felt, and that you'd felt the same, your first night here, and that everyone does."

"I was setting your mind at ease, Daxx. It's alarming. We're alarming. There's much worth learning beyond the alarm."

"Would you go back," I said, "to your old life, as—presumably—a carpenter, in a town, or a village?"

He grunted, as if not sure. "In my head, why, yes, as a thought. But no. That would be like a dream from the which you wake up. This is what I am, who I am, now. Go back?" he sighed. "Well, that's not possible anyway, is it? Who can ever go back? I've family and friends, back where I came from. Most here do. I wouldn't want to inflict this on any one of them. And who has any 'back,' anyway? We have only forward. So, first we deny, and struggle, and cast about to escape. Then we accept. Then we embrace."

He stopped at a gate in the hedge that ran alongside the lane and opened it. I followed him in, towards his cottage. He led me around to the back of it where the shadow of a tall building loomed.

I stopped. Something was bothering me.

What was it that I'd thought earlier?

*Yes and no.*

*This or that.*

I tried to see the connection between the two.

"You all right?" Farnz asked.

I shook my head. The idea, whatever it was, had faded into mist and slipped away. "Yes. I'm fine."

"No light, you say, for your choosing," he said. I felt his hand gripping my wrist. "Come with me, then, Daxx. I know where they are, what you need."

I followed him into his wood store. Smells of timber and sawdust and sap filled the night air. The thought struck me that he could lead me anywhere in there, and leave me among any kind of wood, and I'd never have known. But I knew at once, when I laid a hand on the first stick on the pile where he'd led me, that I was holding rowan.

"Take your time," Farnz said, "and much luck to you, in your finding."

He left me there in the darkness.

The choosing was more difficult than it had been in Marnie's shed, where all the woods had been different. Here they were all of a kind. Each rowan staff jittered and teased her way up my arm, and down into my chest and stomach. None of them were unknown, or wrong. They were like a litter of eager puppies, standing up for my attention, wagging their tails, all excited to be alive and clamoring to be chosen. I held each in turn, again and again, one after another, feeling the surges of delight passing between us.

As I held on to each, and stroked them, I realized that I couldn't decide on any of them. They were all so fine, so full of life and promise. I loved them all, wanted them all, hated the idea of disappointing any of them. I went round and round in circles, not knowing how I could begin to do what had to be done. The more I thought about it, and fretted about it, the more it tugged at my heart, each move of my hand from invisible stick to invisible stick hurting more than the last.

Literally.

The ache in my heart growing.

Sharper. Warmer. And *warmer* …

Until I realized that the heat was coming from outside me rather than from within.

I reached inside my jerkin to the hidden, inner pocket that lay above my heart.

My hand closed around the tourmaline.

It was glowing as I brought it out, the green and red lights swirling around it blooming into the dark of the cavernous woodshed. *The calm of healing. The fire of power.* I held it out towards the rowan staves and watched its lights reach down into them, searching, testing. Curtains of lights spread from it and hovered over them, waiting, watching, seeking. Fingers of green and red reached into the pile and around each stick, listening, learning, strengthening as they homed in towards each other, pausing, tasting, moving on.

At last, the lit strands gathered in towards the staff that the tourmaline had chosen—chosen as if it had already, always, known.

*This one.*

*There you are. Here I am.*

I reached into the pile for the chosen staff and drew her out, her head wreathed in dancing fronds of red and green.

When I took her in my hand, the tourmaline pulled my other hand towards her.

The hood of the staff's head opened. As the tourmaline heartstone neared it, lights flowed from it into the rowan wood, greens and reds merging into her new staff's browns. Shift was completing herself, her two halves merging, marrying, stick to stone. She was back. She was home. In her new home. Bigger, brighter, stronger—but the same merry friend that I had known so well and mourned so deeply.

She quivered in my grasp. Alive. Joyous.

I closed my hand over her, my thumb settling between the forks above her heartstone. Her essence came loud and clear up my arm in that familiar, teasing laughter that I'd thought I would never hear again.

*Shift!*

*Yes indeed.*

*It's really you?*

*None other. It's good to be back, Daxxie.*

*You survived!* I was so happy I felt giddy.

*I was only asleep. Mind you, without a stick to make me whole I'd never have woken up again. And you found me this lovely new staff of rowan! Isn't she a beauty?*

*She is. You are.*

I gazed at my old friend, returned to me renewed—and somehow, I felt, improved. Better, stronger than ever. I got a surge of hope. With her back in my hands: Well, who knew what we couldn't achieve?

Shift, I could feel, from the joy flowing into my arm, felt the same as I did.

*So, how've you been, Daxx?*

*Gods above and below! Worried out of my mind. Lonely.*

*Awww. How sweet. Busy?*

*You have no idea.*

*So fill me in.*

Happier than I'd been in weeks, I did.

Farnz was waiting for me in a chair by the fire in the kitchen of his cottage. When he saw us, he smiled.

He held his hand out and said, "May I?"

I handed him my staff. As he studied her, turning her over in his hands, I noticed what was different about her. She was Shift, there was no doubt about that. Her voice, that only I could hear, was the same as it had always been; but her tourmaline heartstone was reversed, green now above red. I wondered why that was.

"Fine stick o' heartwood, this," Farnz said. "Purple as mulberry juice. That's rare, for my lady rowan."

"Does it signify?"

He chuckled. "How should I know? You're the mage. I'm just a carpenter."

I wasn't settling for that answer. "So what is purple rowan to a carpenter?" I probed.

"Special. You don't make a chair of this beauty. No. You bring out what is deep within her, waiting to be revealed."

He handed her back to me. When my hand closed around her, the question flowed between us. *So? What is waiting to be revealed? Why green above red, not the other way around, as it was before?*

*Are things as they were before, Daxx?*

We both knew that they were not.

*Perhaps,* her quiet voice came, *we are going to be needing Heals more than Damages, wherever we are going next?*

*Almost certainly,* I thought. That was, after all, what I had come to the village for. Healing. A cure.

I felt calm at that moment, for the first time since I'd set out from Eastbay into the Deepwoods with Nyrik and Horm. The anxiety that had been clouding my mind since those mad Moon Nights aboard *The Red Rose* was replaced, at last, by a sense of relief. Somehow, I felt, I was on the right track.

I heard a chuckle and looked up to see Farnz nodding at me.

"Go on, then," he said. "Show us."

My thought exactly. I wanted to know what my new, improved Shift could do. I raised her, and then realized: well, perhaps not a Thunderstorm, in this quiet little kitchen, or a Flamefield. I didn't want to burn his home down, or blast it to pieces. Something less destructive would be tactful. Neither Farnz nor I was wounded, so there was nothing for me to heal.

"I wonder," I said, "how many mice you have hereabouts."

Farnz frowned and said, "Eh?"

I cast Reveal Hidden Life.

I'd heard that in any building, anywhere, you are never more than ten feet from a rodent. So I wasn't surprised when small, scuttling red outlines glowed all around us—in the wainscoting, under the floor-boards, and in the roof overhead.

What did surprise me was the pale ball of light hanging beyond the walls of the cottage.

I stared at it, wondering where and what it was.

Two yellow eyes blinked open within it, stared at me, and then blinked shut and vanished.

"That's weird," I said.

Farnz said, "What is?"

"I have no idea," I said. "Better take a look."

We stood up and went outside.

Clouds were covering the moon. I led Farnz to the back of his cottage, where the thick woods behind it should have been completely dark. They weren't. I studied the source of the light that shone among the tree trunks, hovering at about head height. I'd cast Reveal Hidden Life, but this was not a life-form. It was perfectly round, rather than shaped like an animal, or human. It showed white, not red, as a living creature would have done.

Beside me, Farnz said, "What are you looking at?"

I said, "You can't see it?"

"Can't see anything in this dark," he grunted.

"Take a hold of my staff," I said.

He reached for Shift, gripped her, and exhaled sharply.

"Whoo!" he said, stiffening as he saw the orb for himself.

We stood there, in the darkness, watching the pale ball of light, not wanting to move.

Eventually, Farnz said, "What in all hells is that?"

I felt Shift's curiosity through my hand. She, too, knew that this was something we had to investigate. I said, "What's over there?"

"Nothing. Woods. Trees. Undergrowth."

Neither of us liked it any more than Shift did. It was unexpected, and therefore unsettling. But we all knew that we needed to see what it was. We walked towards it, treading carefully, trying to make no sound.

There, among the dark, crowding tree trunks, it floated, like a child's balloon—but its edges were not solid. Its outline was blurred, the soft light within it gently pulsing.

I reached towards it. No heat came from it.

I passed Shift around it, above it and below it. We learned nothing.

I could hear Farnz breathing beside me. Neither of us wanted to speak.

Slowly, I walked around the glowing, pale ball, Shift held towards it, my eyes fixed on it, staring into its depths, wondering what it could possibly be.

Which meant that I was not looking where I was treading.

The ground parted beneath my feet.

# 6

## The Pact

I dropped into a shaft in the earth. Its narrow sides buffeted me around inside it, stones rattling down alongside me. I gasped in shock. Dirt flew into my mouth and up my nose. My eyes filled with grit. I screwed them tight and clamped my mouth shut, and tried to hold my breath as I fell, the air rushing up past me.

I plummeted, faster and faster, stiffening as I was kicked and thrown from side to side of the tunnel, dreading the shock that I knew had to be coming. I clung to Shift, wrapping my arms around her. I could feel her alarm, but her thoughts were as startled and confused as my own. We were being too jolted around to be able to think about anything, let alone casting a protective Shield over me. My heels struck an angle in the shaft. A moment later my back thumped into it, the impact making me yelp; which meant an open mouth that was instantly filled with filth—and then I was off into a series of impacts. Front, sides, shoulders, lurching down a steep slope, the wind knocked out of me, in an avalanche of stones and dust and mud.

The slope curved and leveled out. Shift and I tumbled out through the end of the tunnel, end over end and side over side, until I skidded to a halt, coughing, my lungs gulping for breath.

The racket that I'd brought with me faded away into silence.

I lay there, in the total darkness, my chest heaving, not daring to move.

Everything around me felt bigger and emptier.

I could tell that I was no longer in a narrow shaft. I also knew that my entry into this space had been far from quiet. If there was anything down there—anything alive—it could not have failed to hear me coming. I tried to steady my breathing. I failed. I coughed again. The sound echoed back at me from walls far away, and a roof high above. Twisting, and turning, as quietly as I could in that darkness, I tried to collect my scrambled thoughts.

I listened.

I heard nothing.

So, where was I?

In a big chamber. It felt like a cavern. It smelled musty, earthy, cold and damp. There was a faint breeze as if currents of air were stirring. That was all I got.

A drift of air on my face.

A smell of dirt and mold.

As quietly as I could, I rolled to my knees, and waited, staring this way and that into the darkness.

No sight.

No sound.

I didn't know whether that was reassuring or not.

Had I just fallen into some random sinkhole?

A sinkhole that had, what, "just happened" to open below a ball of light hanging in the woods? A ball of light that my cast had "just happened" to reveal?

I didn't think so.

So, what to do about it?

I considered, letting my aching body rest a minute. Pop up a Glow, so that I could see where I was?

*Bad idea*, Shift let me know. *Light this place up, and anything down here can see us …*

She was right. That might not be such a good idea.

*Anything alive* down here might not be friendly.

My ears strained into the empty darkness. They heard nothing.

I felt along Shift's length. To my relief, she had not been snapped. *I'm fine*, she let me know.

I asked her, silently, *are you sensing anything?*

*Nothing.*

Both of us in the dark, then. In more ways than one.

And then ... was that something?

A rustle. Shift, too, noticed it. *We're not alone ...*

A slither.

Something was scraping its way towards us.

What could make those noises?

Feet? Claws?

*Scales?*

I held my breath. Shift was still, on high alert.

I listened. She probed the darkness around us.

The sounds stopped. And then came another sound, softer.

Closer.

The sound of breathing. Sniffing. Holding its breath. Inhaling again, and again.

It was coming from above me. And from very nearby.

I felt a warm exhalation on my face when whatever it was breathed out.

And started inhaling me again. And again.

*I was being smelled.*

By something very close, and very, *very* large.

Shift let me know what to do. Trying not to make a sound, I gripped her and cast Reveal Hidden Life.

A huge shadow, outlined in hazy, unstable red, bloomed into shape in front of me.

It took me several moments to get my head around what I could possibly be seeing. The long nose that had been inspecting me was inches from my own. The rest of it stretched high above me and curved away into the distance. I had no idea what it was. All I could tell was that it was more than twice the size of the helldragon we'd fought under Wester Isle—and, I instinctively felt, far more than twice as powerful. Shift, too, was overawed at the sight.

My throat was dry with fear. My heart was thumping in my rib cage. I had never felt so vulnerable. I had no doubt that it knew that I was there, just as I had no doubt that I was defenseless against it. I stared up, frozen in place, at where I thought its eyes must be, waiting for an attack.

I could see no eyes.

And no attack came.

65

What did come was more warm breath as it sniffed at me, followed by a rumble as deep as an earthquake.

I looked over what I could see of that flickering red outline.

It had legs, so was not some monstrous serpent.

Its chest was long and low. Its hindquarters seemed to rear above it as if it was crouching down towards me.

The long, shadowy snout moved closer, and something wet, and abrasive, scraped up my cheek, leaving a dripping, sticky trail.

Shift jumped in shock. I wiped my cheek with my sleeve, thinking, *I've just been licked,* as the creature let out a long, low *hhmmmmmm* … and the back of my hand touched my face, where I had been licked, and … my skin there was dry, after all?

What in all hells was going on?

I did not know what was more worrying: the darkness; my confusion about what the damn thing was, with its sniffing at me, and its licking that wasn't licking, but had certainly felt like it—or whether it would be even worse once I could see it, than what I was imagining.

There was no point in avoiding it anymore.

Shift agreed, *Might as well find out what we're dealing with …*

I raised Shift and cast up a Glow, unable to bear being in the dark any longer.

The Glow rose and hovered above me.

I was alone, in an empty cavern.

There was nothing there.

I looked around, hardly daring to move.

There was just me, in a vast chamber below the earth.

Alone, and in silence.

I allowed myself to exhale.

And, just a little, to relax.

Okay, I thought. That was weird. A light in the woods, hovering above a concealed hole in the ground; a wild slide down on my backside; and then—what must obviously have been some bizarre hallucination.

Well. That's a relief. Shift agreed with me. *We need to get out of here.*

So now—how to get out of here, and back up topside?

I stood up, and dusted myself down and I set off across the cavern.

I heard a gasp, like a dry throat clearing. Then, on the edge of sound, a hoarse voice whispered, "Wait …!"

I stopped.

66

I listened.

Silence.

Nothing but a drift of cold air and the sound of my own breathing.

Had I imagined hearing something? I shut my eyes, to concentrate on listening.

The moment my eyes were closed I could see the massive shadow looming over me again, outlined in dark slashes of fuzzy, unstable red.

I stepped backwards and opened my eyes.

And saw that I was, indeed, alone in the silent cavern.

I held my breath, waiting. I heard nothing. Felt nothing.

I let out a sigh of relief. I must have been imagining things. Seeing things that weren't there, hearing things—

The weak voice spoke again.

"You're *real* ..." it said, unbelieving, in a croak that sounded as if its vocal cords had not been used in a long while.

I thought, *How do I reply to that?*

What could possibly be surprising about "being real"?

On the other hand, how real was this invisible ... *thing*, that was, without question, both not actually there and talking to me?

And which sounded more confused than I was.

"So many have come," the Voice murmured. "So many who turned out to be no more than my imaginings, my dreams. So many disappointments. So much despair. While I sleep on."

Silence fell between us again.

I needed to know what, or who, I was talking with. "Are you ... real?"

"I am."

"Then why can't I see you?"

"I am not there," the Voice murmured, "where you are. I am here."

"And where is that?"

"I ... do not know. But you must find me."

"I must? Why?"

"I have what you need. You have what I need."

That gave me pause. I had, indeed, come to the village with a need. I had not found what I was looking for. Could this ... whatever the thing was ... help me find it? "How do you know what I need?"

"You fell, did you not? A ball of light bloomed among the trees. It did so in response to your cast—as I set it there to do. You went to examine it. The ground opened beneath your feet. *You are a mage.*"

I could see no point in denying it. "I am."

"At last!" the Voice said. "After all these years. A mage. In the village. What she feared has come to pass. That is why she made the rule, *Moon Magic only, in the village.* So, it has started."

Where before he had sounded weak, and hesitant, and lost, now his voice was stronger and growing in confidence.

I said, "What has started?"

"The rupture. The awakening. The beginning of the end."

I wasn't sure that I liked the sound of that. "The end of what?"

"We have no time for questions," the Voice said, suddenly urgent. "You must get away from there. Help me and I will help you."

I was suspicious. "Help me how?"

"You have been Gifted," he said, as if the answer was obvious. "You seek the cure."

That was true. A cure was what I had come for. But Byrneth had said there was no cure.

I said, "There is one?"

"There is. I will lead you to it. It will lead you to me."

I was still confused. I'd heard a lot, but learned little. Who was "she"? What was his need, and why was it mine?

"I will explain, later, when you are safe," the Voice interrupted my thoughts. "You must leave, before they find you. Go to the library. On the top shelf to the right of the hearth, at the back, hidden behind the other books, you will find a small volume bound in black leather. It has no title. To most eyes, its pages are blank and it has no contents. You will know how to read them. What you seek is on the last page. Note it exactly. Replace the book—do not be tempted to take it. That would let her know that you found it."

"Let who know?"

"*Later!* That must wait, like so much else," the Voice insisted. "We are in this together now, mage. Have patience, do as I say, and get to safety. Write down what you read there, word for word, and leave the village. Tell no one. Run hard and fast. Cover your tracks. Do not go directly back to where you came from. Take the long way around—if you came from the north, head south. Put as much distance between yourself and here as you can, before they come for you. Watch the skies. Always be ready to hide.

"If you live, if you manage to lose them, find one who is wise in herb lore to help you with the cure. When you have taken it, your mind will be open to me. You drank the drink and learned the lore. That was your dream. This is mine. I have slept many hundreds of years. I sleep now. Do as I say and our dreams will merge. I will find you in them, and you will learn everything. And then, you will find me."

Okay, but .... It had told me that it didn't know where it was. So how could I start to look for it? "How do I do that?" I asked.

"That is for you to discover!" the Voice urged. "That is your task! If you fail, we all fail. You, me, those you love. Without you, I am finished. Without me, you are finished, all of you. Your tale will end, as mine ended, long ages ago. Yet now it has begun again, and our tales have converged. That was my hope: that, one day, one such as you would open the door that I left concealed. You have done so. The task has fallen to you. You are my only hope, as I am yours. Now go! Every minute wasted brings the hunt closer."

I had no way of knowing if it was telling the truth or not—but what it said alarmed me. I did not like the thought of being hunted. I had questions but saw that they had to wait.

I looked around me. "So, how do I get out of here?"

"The same way you came in."

"By climbing back up that shaft?"

"Not by climbing. By falling. You fell in. You fall out."

I felt the air in the cavern swirling around me, The ground shuddered under my feet and disappeared.

"Learn. Run. Hide," the Voice commanded, growing fainter as the noise of the wind blowing through the cavern grew louder and louder. *"Find me, before they find you!"*

His last words were lost in the roaring that filled my ears. I felt myself lifted up, and carried off and out, as the cavern dissolved, earth becoming air that turned me around and around and took me with it, higher and higher …

… until it released me, and dropped me behind Farnz—in a night that was now fouler, and colder, and wetter, and wilder than it had been when I fell into the earth.

Farnz barked in alarm and whirled to face me.

I'd fallen down, below him, and had now fallen back down from above him.

I got to my feet and brushed myself off. The rain was now sheeting down and we hurried to get out of it, towards the shelter of his cottage. Farnz, naturally, had questions as we ran. I did not have time to answer them. I told him that I had to go.

"Tell everyone that I was never here," I said. "You'll be safer that way, all of you. If anyone asks."

Farnz looked across at me as we ran, his dark eyes glinting in his rain-streaked face.

He said, "You're saying that someone will?"

I grimaced. "It's likely."

"Who?"

"Someone looking for a mage. Remember the rule? *Moon Magic only in the village?*"

He nodded.

"So, say something like, *No, we've not seen any mage—but maybe a mage could find a magic way in, with none of us any the wiser. Cloaked in magic—invisible, like. So, no one here in the village would be able to notice him, or her.* Be vague. Play dumb. And don't mention my staff. For which I am grateful."

We reached his door, soaked to the skin, and stopped under the little porch outside it, while the rain drummed harder onto its roof and the wind blew colder.

Farnz said, considering me, then Shift, "And to which you are welcome."

"I have to run."

He knew what that meant. *Time to Turn again.*

"Sounds like trouble brewing," he said.

"Sounds that way," I agreed.

"How d'you know all this?"

I thought of telling him, *I met someone.* But I didn't want to put him in danger.

"Best if I don't say."

I heard his grunt of understanding. He held out his hand.

I shook it.

"Thank you for the warning, friend Daxx," he said. "We'll do you right. Anyone comes looking for you won't hear a peep from any of us. You're one of us now. We look after our own."

I nodded my thanks and ran into the driving rain.

§

Byrneth, I knew, never locked his doors. It was easy enough to find the little black leather-bound book, tucked away at the back of the top shelf to the right of the hearth, just where the Voice had said it would be. Whose voice? I believed that I'd find out soon enough— if I survived my run the long way around back to Eastbay.

The little book's pages were blank. I cast Reveal and words appeared. I turned to the last page. On it was written, *Turnaway, For the Moon Sickness*. I cast Absorb, and the few lines of the potion's recipe copied themselves into the Infinite Notebook that Marnie had given me, that I kept in the pocket inside my jerkin above my heart, where I could quickly reach it.

I was about to replace the book on its shelf when a thought struck me.

I wondered what else might be on its other pages, hidden from eyes that could not read the invisible writing.

Perhaps the knowledge that they held might be useful. I cast Absorb All, then put the little book back where I'd found it, knowing that everything in it was now leaching into my Infinite Notebook. Marnie and I would study it all later. I cast Cleanse on the book, and then on the library itself, hoping that it might erase any trail I might have left. The feeling of urgency grew by the minute, as did my sense of approaching danger. Something was coming, I knew. The Voice had told me, *Run, as far and fast as you can.* I hurried out into the night and the rain that was lashing down through the avenue of ash trees. I Turned, and began to run.

My mind clouded. It is never easy to think clearly when in the Form. You feel, you hear, you taste: Above all, you smell, inhaling and learning the world through your nose. I galloped up the long road from the village, under the waxing moon. The cold rain fell harder and heavier by the minute, drenching my fur. Above me, dark clouds rolled in from all directions.

Odd.

Which way was the wind blowing up there?

Towards me, from every point of the compass, it seemed—while, down here, it was driving into my face, stinging my eyes.

I ran through the tunnel, its dry dirt floor crunching beneath my paws. The trunk of the monarch tree opened ahead of me, and, as I emerged into the oak grove I heard the first rumblings of distant thunder. It grew louder as I ran, doubling back north into the Deepwoods—

away from Urngra's hovel and Eastbay to the south and east. *Go the long way around.* Lightning cracked in the dark sky above the trees.

The Voice's words echoed in my mind.

*Watch the skies.*

I did, my ears straining into the night around me. Thunder boomed, closer now—but, unlike any thunder that I'd ever heard before, it did not fade into silence between thunderclaps. The air overhead shuddered as other sounds merged with the rumbling of the thunder, and the snap of lightning, and the sheeting of the cold rain: sounds that I was sure I was imagining, at first, until I knew that I wasn't.

The sounding of horns, the howling of hounds, the drumming of hooves.

Running as fast as I could, I looked up.

A shadow rolled across the sky, beyond the dark clouds, turning them black, like a wave breaking overhead—a wave that stretched from horizon to horizon. A host passed above me, riding on the air, driven by the storm. I knew that I was their quarry. I knew that they would not find me in the village. I knew that they would not stop there. They would cast about in every direction until they found my trail.

My old, human trail led south, with Urngra's, the way we had come to the village. *Let them follow that.* I plunged into a stream, and ran up it and along it, to hide my scent, league after league after league, pursued—I knew not how far behind me—by all the hounds of hell.

I ran. The stream ran east. It joined a river, flowing north to south. Which way? I had come from the south. I should go north. I turned to my left and ran. I ran all night, and all the next day. That night, the river curved back to the east. I left it, and ran through bush, and bog, and underbrush, to the north. By the next evening I had reached the sea. I stood under the shadow of the trees that crowded to the edge of the cliff top and re-Turned to my *me*-form, so I that could think through what I should do next.

I looked down at the expanse of the North Sea as my mind cleared.

A path of silver led across it to the moon rising over the eastern horizon. In under another two weeks, I reckoned, she would be full. Time enough to get to Eastbay and find "one who was wise in herb lore."

*Marnie,* I thought.

I waited for her reply.

None came.

With her mastery of her Awareness skill she would have replied instantly if I had been within range. I would just have to try every day to get through to her—the sooner she knew what I had learned, the better.

I could see, in the moonlight, that the cliffs fell away to the east. With luck I would find a way down them that I could manage on four legs. I hoped that I wouldn't have to climb down some steep cliff face, in the dark, in human form. I Turned and ran through the thinning trees as darkness fell. Before long I was on open turf, under an open sky, cantering down an easy slope towards the sea. The wind picked up, cold and salty, carrying the sound of breaking waves to my ears. I crossed rocks, and pebbles, and sand, until I reached the water, where I altered my course to the south, at last, on the long way round back to Eastbay.

By the time the first light of dawn grew gray in the sky off to my left I was exhausted. Running through water is hard work, even in the Form—especially when the breaking waves are pushing you inshore, and the ebb flows drag you back out to sea with them, and your pelt is heavy with seawater. My legs were numb. Long before the eastern sky turned from blue to red I saw dark shapes in the cliffs to my right. Caves. I trotted out of the water and shook myself dry. The first cave I came to was sheltered, the air in it still and quiet, in contrast to the harsh wind outside. It bore no trace of animal or human smells. I explored it, all the way to the back, which wasn't far, my eyes and ears and nose on full alert.

It was empty and I was alone.

I would sleep in the Form. I'd be warmer, in my pelt of wolf fur, and my senses would be sharper and better attuned to any approaching danger. First, though, I needed to try to contact Marnie again. Again, I got no reply. I slept, until evening.

When it was dark enough I set out again. Again, I ran all that night, and the next, through the tidal water. As each dawn broke, I holed up in another cave and thought to Marnie.

When at last she replied I heard her sharp old voice in my head as clearly as if she'd been in the cave beside me.

"I've been wondering what you've been up to, lad!"

I told her everything that had happened since I'd ridden out with Nyrik and Horm into the Deepwoods.

She didn't say much; but from what she did say, and the tone of her grunts of surprise, I could tell that she didn't like what she was hearing.

"The Wild Hunt," she said, when I'd finished answering all her questions. "Conclave will need to hear about *that*, and soon!"

I said, "You know about it?"

"As much as anyone does, and that's little enough. The Wild Hunt don't ride out for no reason, and it hasn't been seen in the skies in my lifetime. Which is longer than most."

"What is it?" I said.

"Trouble," she said. "A legend. Like Jaren and Jurun. A tale out of its time. Seems its time has come again, as his did for Jurun."

The association was not comforting. "Why me?"

"That's for us to find out. I don't like the sound of any of this, I can tell you that for nothing. Something's brewing—and your little jaunt is just a part of it."

I thought, *little jaunt?*

If this is a little jaunt, what was the bigger issue that was worrying her?

"Part of what?" I asked.

"That's what we need to learn. Mayhaps you'll see the picture clearer than we do, with that clever head for puzzles o' yours."

"Who's 'we'?" I said.

"Those of us who've seen the straws in the wind, and have been watching which way it's blowing. And it's making us uneasy. So, get yourself here as quick as you can, young Mastercaster. There's work to be done."

# 7

## The Curse and the Cure

TWO days later the masts in Eastbay harbor came into sight on the southern horizon. I'd slept until noon in another cave, but knew that I'd have to travel the last leg of my journey in daylight, as the town gates would be closed at dusk. I grew more and more anxious all afternoon, scanning the skies, and the shore around me, and the sea to my west and the hills to my east. All seemed empty. But I could not be sure; and, in midafternoon, even though I hadn't seen a soul, I left the water and scrambled back, across rocks and pebbles, into the woods that lined the cliff tops, leaving no paw prints behind me.

I'd just have to hope that I'd hidden my trail from any hunters, above or below. The risk of anyone picking it up seemed less worrying than running alone in the open. Out there, a black dot against the breaking water, I had felt conspicuous and vulnerable. Under the cover of the trees I ran inland, eventually finding the little road that led from the farms and villages that lay to the north of Eastbay. Staying back in the woods, where no one traveling on the road would see me, I turned south alongside it, in the opposite direction to the one I'd ridden out on with Nyrik and Horm. Not much more than a week ago that had been, but it seemed far longer. When I saw the walls of the town I stopped and Turned back to my *me-self*.

I'd drilled that instruction into myself, as I ran: *Stay out of sight. Re-Turn. Think.*

I felt the strength of my mind grow as the wolf-strength of my body dwindled.

As far as I was concerned I was still being hunted, even though nothing had come riding across the sky after me. Well, nothing *yet*. I knew that, sooner or later, they would. I knew they were looking for me. I knew they weren't going to stop until they found me. I knew they would look everywhere. Whoever "they" were.

I needed to hole up, among friends, and try to work out what to do.

I sat on a fallen trunk and studied the puzzle. I could see only a few of its pieces, none of them connecting. So, I thought: Stay ahead of the game as long as you can. Give yourself time to get the information. Find more pieces, fit them together, understand the picture, work on a solution.

*Game.*

The word echoed in my head. And then, *hunt*.

Hunters hunt game. I was the quarry.

*Hide,* I thought.

*Get help. Turn the tables.*

Turn.

*My* turn …

My mind cleared and I saw what I needed to do.

Though I could Turn into my *were-form* and back easily enough, I could not actually become someone else. I could, though, deceive anyone who did not have the eyes to see the truth of what they were looking at. Or, indeed—and I smiled at the thought of Little Guy— the nose to smell it. It would be good to see him again. And my other friends. They, I knew, would help me in any way they could. I raised Shift and laid a Glamour on myself.

As twilight fell, an unremarkable old peasant in unremarkable old clothes, trudged down the north road and in through the gates of East-bay, bent under the load he was carrying. He was not a notable mage, no sir; certainly not a mage who was the talk of the town because he was also a werewolf, as well as the queen's honored companion, and a Hero of the Realm. Perhaps I flatter myself. My reappearance might have made me the talk of the town once people had exhausted all the latest gossip from the Royal Court, which was gracing Eastbay with its presence; not to mention the Royal Tournament, and the upcoming Big Fight between Commandant Bastard and the best bloody Orc he'd ever seen. Those were far more interesting subjects of conversation than some worrying werewolf of a mage who was best avoided. As it was, the guards barely glanced at the unremarkable, old peasant as I plodded past them. They were bored, and tired at the end of the day, and looking forward to locking up, and going home, or to the mess hall in their barracks, or to a tavern. No one stiffened, and looked twice, and stared when I came in through the gates and headed for the town square.

I was in and nobody yet knew it.

I thought to Marnie, and she told me where to meet her.

The market square was crowded and noisy. In the twilight, torches burned in sconces set by every stall while vendors hawked their wares. The town was even livelier than it had been when I had left for the Deepwoods. The excitement in the air was palpable. The Royal Tournament was only days away now. There was feasting, drinking, music, dancing. In one corner, mummers were acting out a coarse melodrama to a raucous crowd—a fat knight, prancing around in a skirt that was his horse, being thwacked by gnomes with wooden swords, while onlookers jeered and roared. In other spots, jugglers, and animal handlers, and fire-eaters, and hustlers went through their routines. Bards stroked lyres, and sang well-known, well-loved ballads.

Lovers held hands. Rivals held back. No one wanted to make trouble, to break the spell. All were enjoying the moment. The atmosphere was at once excited and relaxed, and noisy and calm. The smells of cooking and the sounds of instruments and happy voices filled the air. It was party time. One morning, soon, they would all be at the tourney and the games would begin. Reputations, perhaps even lives, would be on the line. Nobodies stood to win fortunes. Spectators would watch their choices fall, or succeed and move on to the next bout, while the odds on them shortened, and they could press their bets, or lay them off. It was going to be *something*. Something special. All knew that. Everything else was in abeyance, waiting.

The old routine of real life would return soon enough. The queen's court would be gone, back to the capital city, Mayport. The tournament would be over. We'd all know who had won, and who had lost. Of course there would be a morning after. There always is. But if you're going to suffer the backlash, get some of the frontlash first. Tomorrow is tomorrow's problem. So, deal with it tomorrow. Now, in this buzzy, busy town, no one was looking beyond the present. It was an exciting time to be alive, and everyone was reveling in it.

I made my weary way through the throng, head down, old and tired and not worth a second glance. The apothecary's house was easy enough to find, tucked away as it was in a quiet backstreet. Its widows were shuttered and dark. It seemed deserted. A heavy iron knocker, shaped like a pestle, hung below an iron grille in the door. I lifted it and looked both ways, to check that the coast was clear, before rapping four times, as Marnie had instructed me.

I waited. I heard footsteps approaching.

The panel behind the grille slid aside and a candle appeared in it.

Two dark eyes glinted behind it, studying me.

As Marnie had instructed me, I said, "I've come for my powders."

The panel closed and the door swung open inwards.

I stepped onto the threshold. A tall, thin, gray-haired woman, dressed entirely in black, looked me up and down, the doorknob in one hand, a candleholder in the other.

She nodded, and smiled. She was by no means young, but she radiated vitality.

"Good job!" she said, clearly approving of my Glamoured appearance. "Looks nothing like you. Not that I know what you *do* look like," she added, stepping aside to allow me into what I saw was her shop, "but I know it won't be like what I'm seeing. Nicely done, lad. Name's Velaryn."

She held out a long-fingered hand and I shook it. "And yours," she said, holding up her other hand to stop me replying, "we don't say when anyone as shouldn't hear it might be around." She ducked out, turning to look up and down the alley outside, both ways, then coming back in and closing the door behind her.

She locked the door and slid two large bolts home, one high on the door, one low.

She turned back to me, and smiled again, and held up the candle so she could study my face.

She grinned. "Welcome to my home, young Daxx, looking like some old farm laborer."

I Cleansed the Glamour off myself.

Velaryn's eyebrows rose. She smiled. "Mm," she said. "Much better. This way."

78

She turned and walked across the creaking floorboards of the dark little shop. I followed her past its counter. A blaze of candlelight shone out as she opened the door to the room beyond, which was part laboratory and part kitchen.

Marnie was waiting for us.

Seeing her, after all I'd been through, was a huge relief. I felt safe.

Until I saw the look on her face.

"Right," she said, by way of a greeting, "let's get started." She held her hand out for my Infinite Notebook.

I retrieved it from inside my jerkin and handed it to her.

She opened it and read the potion's recipe, frowning. "Hmh! I don't know as I'd trust anyone as told me to drink *this*." She passed it to Velaryn.

Marnie and Velaryn, I could see, had much in common. Both were dressed all in black. Both were gray-haired. Both had faces crisscrossed with the lines of long and arduous lives; but Velaryn was tall, and thin, and cheerful, where Marnie was short, and stout, and sour.

I got the sense that these two had known each other for a very long time.

"What d'you think, Vel?" Marnie said.

"I think this would kill anyone as drank it," Velaryn chuckled.

I thought, *Well it's all very well for you, to be so nonchalant about it! I've been running hard for over a week. I've been hunted through woods, and bogs, and storms, and tides. I've been beaten up by an Ogre. I've been confronted by an apparition in a vault, deep below the earth, under a hidden village full of werewolves. I've been offered a cure and I've brought it to you—and you think it'll kill me and that seems to amuse you?*

"He said he needs my help," I pointed out.

"You won't be a help to anyone if you're dead," Velaryn countered. "Henbane? Black hellebore? On top of them 'moonberries,' as you call these little beads o' blight?" She picked up a handful of mistletoe berries and let them slip back through her fingers into the bowl. "Do you have any idea what any one of them can do?"

"No. That's why I've come to you."

"Deadly, the lot of them. And in doses far smaller than what this says. You'll need more than we could do for you if you drink this little lot," she said. "You'll need a Revivalist—and I've never been one o' *them!*" She snorted.

"Nor me," Marnie said. " 'Bring you back,' they say they'll do; but no one's ever what they were before, however much they might look like it. I've never seen anyone Revived who was more than a husk, even if the fools who welcome them back can't see it. Have you, Vel?"

"Never."

Marnie was clearly unsettled by this recipe that had come from the hidden book in Byrneth's library. Where this was leading was making her jumpy. Marnie didn't like being jumpy. She liked certainty. She liked to know where she stood. What she was saying was making me nervous. Velaryn peered over her shoulder, rereading the recipe, as calm as Marnie was troubled.

I said, "Maybe that's true for normal people. But for *Weres* ... "

Marnie went still, and stared at me, as she considered that. She nodded. "Vel?"

"Weres are different," Velaryn allowed.

"We can run far longer and faster than normal folk," I said, "when we're in the Form. We can scent, and hear, and feel, in ways the rest of you can't; and our hides are tougher than human skin. So—"

"So, you can drink what would kill a dozen of us and it won't harm you?" Velaryn challenged.

I had, of course, no way of knowing that.

All I had to go on was my encounter with the Voice in the vault.

I said, "Why would he kill me? If I have what he needs—whatever that might be? He's been waiting ages for someone like me to turn up. And he told me about this cure, this recipe; *and* he urged me to get out of the village as fast as I could. If he'd wanted me dead he could have kept quiet and left me there at the mercy of the Wild Hunt."

"And that's another thing," Velaryn said, her smile vanishing.

I studied her. "What d'you know about it?"

Marnie said, "You'll learn tomorrow. Conclave's been summoned, and they want to talk to *you*, laddie, urgently! Stirred up as a hive of bees they are. First things first. Kill or cure, it seems to me." She turned to Velaryn. "You?"

Velaryn nodded.

"Seems to me," she agreed. "It's the lad's choice, though."

They both looked at me, and waited.

I couldn't think what to say. I didn't see that I had a choice. *Kill or cure.* Well: *cure,* surely? Yes, I'd miss the intensity of the Form, which had shown me so many wonders that I could never have experienced without it. But I didn't want to end up consumed by it. I didn't know what was worrying them. And that worried me, because they were the experts.

Marnie saw my uncertainty.

She said, "We think—not just Vel and me, but others, those of us with the eyes to see, and the ears to hear, and the wits to understand—that there's more to this than meets the eye."

"Or ear. Or wit," Vel added.

Marnie nodded in agreement. She took a deep breath, and sighed. "We don't like the smell of any of this, Daxx, I'll tell you that for nothing," she said. "Something's brewing."

"And from all we can sense," Velaryn added, "it'll be something bad."

"And you, and your problem, are no more than a small part of it," Marnie said.

They watched me and waited for my response.

I thought, *a small part? This is—everything. This is* kill or cure. How can this be a "small part"? A small part of what?

A small part, presumably, of something bigger.

Something I knew nothing about.

Yes, I thought. A puzzle. A big picture. Of which I can't yet see anything, really. Except my own small part in it. I looked to my mentor. "So, what are you thinking?"

Marnie studied me with her one good eye. Something seemed to change in her expression as she considered my question. Eventually, she said, "I'm thinking that trouble seems to follow you, young Mastercaster."

Velaryn nodded in agreement. Then a thought struck her, and she frowned. Her eyebrows rose as she stepped forwards. She crossed her arms and studied me.

She looked down at Marnie, beside her, and suggested, "Unless it's t'other way 'round?"

That made no sense to me; but Marnie seemed to understand what she meant.

"Mayhaps you're right, sister," she allowed.

I said, "You're saying that I follow trouble?"

Velaryn glanced at Marnie, who shook her head.

"No," Marnie said. "She's saying you run ahead of it. *Warn* of it. And seems to me she may be right. Remember what you did before, when those lads brought you to me, Nyrik and Horm: you all empty and lost, the day we first met? You were ahead of it, of all of us, though none of us knew it—least of all you. Ahead of the game ...." She held my eyes. "Well," she decided, "if there's a game afoot, the best place to be is ahead of it. Wouldn't you agree?"

Which was exactly the conclusion I had come to sitting on my fallen tree trunk in the woods beyond Eastbay's walls. "I would, Marnie, yes."

"Even though we don't know what it is yet," she said.

Once again her eye dropped to the page in the open notebook on the table between us.

Once again I reread the words that had leached themselves into it.

*Turnaway: For the Moon Sickness. Fill a small silver cup with moon-berries. Heat spirit until it bubbles. Pour the spirit into the cup. Add a dozen grains of henbane and a pinch of black hellebore. Crush the berries in the mixture. Stir and let stand until cool. Drink all of it, swallow berries and all. Have a basin ready for the vomit.*

That didn't sound too reassuring.

*"A basin ready for the vomit?"* Velaryn said, as if she'd read my thoughts—which, if she had Marnie's skill, she may well have done. "Basin? You'll need a bucket! And we'll need these for the cleaning," she added, heading over to the sink. "I don't want my nice kitchen awash with your puke." She brought back two mops and two large pails, which she set down by my feet. "If you ever want to pump some-one's stomach in a hurry, black hellebore will do it."

I said, "It only says a pinch."

"Two pinches, and you'd be sick for a week," Marnie snorted. "Both kinds of sick, each nastier than the other. Three, and you'd never eat again. 'Only a pinch' will pack a punch, as you're about to find out."

I was hardly looking forward to it—but what did I have to lose? Apart from my breakfast—a rabbit, which I'd chased down in the woods and crunched between my jaws as I ran.

Marnie folded her arms, looked up at me, and held my eyes. "Are you sure about this?"

I grimaced. "No."

"Mm," she agreed. "Nor me. Well?"

I said, "I think I have to."

She didn't reply. She nodded, and both women went to the work-bench and began to brew. Marnie poured clear liquor from a flask into a pot, which she set over a flame. As it warmed, the scent of its vapours filled the room. They were both alluring and alarming. Velaryn filled a small silver cup with mistletoe berries, of which she clearly disapproved. "Poison, these are," she said, "to a normal person. Which, now, as you've said, you're not. Although," she admitted, "the winter birds like them well enough."

When the liquor bubbled she emptied it over the mistletoe berries. She added the henbane and black hellebore, and crushed them all up together with a stone pestle.

"The seawolves smeared their bodies with henbane in the olden days, the tales say," she said, as she pounded and stirred, "to make them fearless. And fearsome. Long years ago. They raided the coastlands in their longships, burned and destroyed holdings; killed all who faced them, and carried off women and childer. Out of some land to the north they came, as we've heard tell; but they've not harried this realm in many generations."

She set the potion aside. Pungent steam rose from it.

"Henbane," Marnie said. "Wolves. Makes you wonder, does it not?"

It did.

*Henbane. Moonberries. Black hellebore.*

It all sounded … challenging.

When the cup was cool enough to handle Marnie picked it up and brought it over to me. Gently, she said, "Best be ready to lie down."

I folded my legs under me, and sat cross-legged on the floor.

Neither of us said anything further.

Marnie handed me the little silver cup. "Rather you than me," she said.

The cup felt warm in my hands, but not too hot to drink. I stared at the potion. It smelled harsh, and worrying.

I was glad that I was not in the Form. My *were*-nose would not have liked the bitter fumes that were rising from the little silver cup.

I raised it to my lips and drank, screwing up my eyes and swallowing as fast as I could, so that I did not have to taste the potion.

I shook the berries into my mouth, chewed them quickly, and gulped them down.

I opened my eyes, and looked up at Marnie, and then at Velaryn.

*Well*, I thought. *That wasn't so bad.* I exhaled a sigh of relief. Everything seemed to be fine.

I actually began to feel relaxed.

Comfortable.

That was hardly surprising: I'd just ingested a very large dose of whatever strong liquor they had used for the potion. It was, no doubt, having a soothing effect on me, the way good liquor can.

I smiled, as I felt the concoction warm my stomach and soften my brain.

Neither woman smiled back.

The warmth in my stomach grew.

And grew.

And ...

I'll spare you the more graphic details. It went from not so bad to *so bad*. Marnie held the buckets. Velaryn grasped the hair at the back of my head and pushed my face into them as I knelt there, hurling. Mouth agape, I did nothing but bellow the letter *R* for longer than I can recount, again and again, *ARRRRRR*, as globules of rabbit sprayed out of my mouth, followed by everything I'd eaten that week, wave after wave after wave of it. Velaryn struggled to keep my head pointing in the right direction as my stomach and shoulders convulsed and heaved, throwing me around as I threw everything out.

I came to flat out on the floor. Marnie was wiping my lips and helping me up onto my elbows.

"As I said," she repeated, as she swam into focus, "rather you than me."

I was choking. My throat felt like a furnace. *"Hchhhuh ..."* I tried, then swallowed, then tried again. "How long was I out?"

"No more'n two hours," she said. "Gave us time to study your notebook. There's much in there that's new to us. I've leached it all into mine. Come in useful, them recipes will, I've a feeling. Up you get, then, and let's see."

It took a while to haul myself to my feet. I stood there, swaying, looking from Marnie to Vel. They were both blurred out by the water in my eyes. I couldn't remember ever having felt so weak.

Vel said, "All gone?"

I hiccuped. "I damn well hope so."

"Right, then," Marnie said. "It should be out of you."

I knew what she meant.

*Here goes,* I thought. I reached out, and took her hand.

Vel took my other hand in both of hers. She patted it as I closed my eyes and Turned.

But didn't.

Normally, it was effortless. I could slip between my *me*-Form and *were*-Form without a second thought.

I tried again.

Nothing.

I was still me. And only me. My *were*-self was no longer available to me.

I opened my eyes and looked at them.

"No?" Marnie said.

"No," I agreed. "I can't."

She smiled her old, almost toothless smile, and nodded.

"Turnaway," she chuckled. "Took your Turn away, those moonberries did. Not that you needed it today, on a day you could choose the Form. Will it work when the Form chooses you? That's the question. The which you'll find answered come next Moon Night."

I felt the relief of what she said flooding through me. My quest to the village had been worth it.

The quiet, candle-it room was coming more clearly into focus as I recovered my equilibrium. I looked around and saw that it was spotless.

"Was it ... bad?" I asked.

"Worse for you than us, I'd think," Marnie said. "A little mopping was all as was needed. You hit the buckets more often than not."

I was glad to hear it. "So now what?"

"You stay ahead of them," Marnie said. "They'll be coming for you. We've no doubt of that. You need to keep your head down and stay out of sight. And if you do show it, make sure you show another head instead of your own. No one other than those we can trust must see you. Let them see someone else—someone who looks nothing like you. You can't go back to the castle, no matter what you look like. Folks there will see you, whoever you are, and folks gossip. *No, haven't seen Daxx, but there's this strange old scholar no one's ever seen around here before turned up that the queen gave a room to*—and the wrong ears will hear. And whoever comes looking for you will be sharp enough to put two and two together."

"So you'll be staying here," Vel said. "And it'll be nice to have the company."

"Thank you, Velaryn," I said.

"Wouldn't be nice for her to have your mud and fleas and lice for company too, though," Marnie said, "so get them clothes off you, laddie. You'll find them all clean for you when you wake, washed and ironed and folded. Meanwhile, you need a good scrubbing."

I stood there, staring from one to the other of them.

Eventually, Velaryn gave a snort of laughter. "I do believe the lad's shy!" She grinned.

"No need to spare our modesty, Daxx," Marnie said. "We've seen more than many a birthday suit in our time. Who d'you think brings the babes into this world?"

Vel chuckled. "And lays out the dead. Young, old, everything in between. And as for the living: You should see one of our Coven nights, young Daxx."

"He should not!" Marnie snapped.

"Us all dancing, hither and yon, wild as wild, as naked as the day we were born," Velaryn breezed on. "Well, except for our boots, if we're outdoors and the grass is damp. Wouldn't hardly believe his eyes!"

She giggled. She clearly enjoyed teasing Marnie.

"A sight that's blinded more'n one man who shouldn't have been peeping," Marnie countered.

"True," Vel admitted. "But he'd have his memories, eh? Once seen, never forgotten?"

"The sight o' you gallivanting about in the altogether would be a fine last picture to take into the darkness!" Marnie snorted.

"I don't know," Vel said. "In my day, I turned many a young man's head."

"That's a day that's long gone," Marnie shot back at her. "And him young enough to be your grandson." She turned her one good eye on me, while Vel shook her head in amusement. "Come on, laddie. What are you waiting for? You need a scrubbing."

I saw that there was nothing for it.

I stripped off and dropped my muddy, lice-ridden and flea-infested clothes onto the floor.

I don't know if you've ever been scrubbed by two elderly women energetically wielding bristle brushes, and bars of soap bigger than their arms, and buckets of cold water: But, if you have, you'll probably agree that you enjoyed it less than they did. The water ran off me into the drain in the middle of the kitchen floor—at first black with mud, then brown, then brimming with rafts of richly scented bubbles.

Made the soap herself, she did, Velaryn told me. Infused with witch hazel and rosemary, for the flea bites, and oil of orange peel to kill the lice, and lavender so I'd smell nice. By the time the water ran clear, I did indeed. They stopped drenching me from their buckets, and toweled me off vigorously. Then they started beating me with bunches of twigs. "For the circulation," Vel said.

When they had finished flailing at me, they stepped back, breathing hard from the exertion.

"So?" Vel said. "How are you feeling?"

My skin was smarting from the thrashing that they'd given me.

Warmth and comfort bloomed all over me, infusing every inch of my skin.

I returned her smile with a bigger one of my own, and said, truthfully, "Fabulous."

# 8

## A Change for the Worse

Wrapped in the blanket that she had given me, I followed Velaryn up the narrow stairs, each wooden step creaking under our feet. Her candle threw pools of light ahead and off the dark walls around us. I could hardly put one foot in front of the other. I was running on empty. "No food tonight, Daxx," she had said. "Give your stomach a good night's sleep to settle. It's had enough to deal with for one day. I'll fill you up in the morning, don't you worry about that. You'll have all the breakfast you can eat."

Her tiny spare bedroom was tucked away at the top of the house, so low under the thatched roof that we both had to crouch in order to enter it.

She placed the candleholder on the bedside table as I climbed into bed. Soft sheets. Warm blankets. It had been a long time since I had slept in such comfort.

"Drink this," she said, handing me a potion. "And sleep well."

I drank. I lay back.

Velaryn smiled down at me, and stroked my forehead. "Sweet dreams."

She blew out the candle and left, closing the door behind her.

I drifted off into a cloud of comfort, thinking, *how nice ...*

Hours later, the dream came.

I found myself swimming out of the depths of the most refreshing sleep I had ever known. I was calm, confident, energized. I surfaced to see two familiar, yellow eyes staring at me out of a moonlit sky, passing clouds.

*Ah*, I said, pleased to see them again. *There you are!*

The Voice that I had last heard in the vault answered, *Yes.*

So, I thought: Thank goodness that that is all over. Problem solved. Now I'll learn what this is all about.

First, though: I owed him my gratitude. I should tell him so.

*I did what you told me to*, I heard myself say. *I drank the Turnaway. Thank you! I will miss the Gift. I am lucky to have known it. The smells, the sounds, the tastes. The speed and the power. But, no doubt, I am better off without it. I have places to go, and things to do, which I could not do as … that.*

The yellow eyes narrowed, as if surprised. The Voice said, *I don't think you quite understand.*

*Understand what?*

*You only have one place to go, and only one thing to do.*

That I had not expected. *Which is?*

*Find me before she finds you.*

That felt a bit rich. Yes, he'd solved my problem, but—who was he to order me about? But I didn't want to appear ungrateful.

*I really appreciate what you've done for me. But I have other things on my plate at the moment, and—*

*No. You don't. I lied.*

That brought me up short. *What?*

*I needed your total commitment. I only showed you half the picture. I gave you half the truth. I will give you the other half when you find me.*

I felt backed into a corner, and I didn't like it. *Why should I do that? If you lied to me?*

*Because you will die if you don't. You drank the potion. Your friend was right. It would kill any normal person. You are now a normal person. It is killing you. Without the Gift, you cannot withstand it. Within three moon months you will be dead, if you do not get the antidote. I have it. Your friend doesn't. By all means ask her. She will never have heard that there is such a thing. No one else knows of it. I will give it to you. No one else can. Do you now see your problem?*

I was stunned. If he was telling the truth, I was in trouble. But he'd just told me that he'd lied to me before. *Why should I believe you?*

*Wrong question.*

*What is the right question?*

*The right question is, why have I done this?*

*Well? Why?!*

*Carrot and stick.*

*I'm sorry?*

*You sought a cure. I gave it to you. But only half of it. That was the carrot. You have seen that it works. You cannot Turn, can you?*

*No …*

*Without the other half of the cure, you will succumb. This was the only way I could be sure that you will do what I need you to do. That is the stick. The poison is working in your blood. It will consume you. Any mage would understand.*

I kept thinking, *He's lying; he's lying.*

Even though I had a bad feeling that he wasn't.

*Can you prove that?*

*I already have proved it. The first half is true. You cannot Turn, any-more, into the Form. So, the second half is also true.*

*I only have your word for that.*

*On which your own future hangs. Your choice is simple: Believe me or do nothing. You have ninety days, mage. My advice is, come and get it.*

I was still struggling. I didn't like thinking that I'd been out-smarted, outplayed.

*And if I don't?*

*Then you will never see the answer. You will never know the truth. You will be dead. It's your decision. I can wait. I have waited hundreds of years, in this sleep. Eventually, another Gifted mage will come, in time, to the village. Another will unlock the door, and learn where I am, and find me, and unbind me. By when you will be long gone—just another old dream that faded away and amounted to nothing.*

The way he said it was almost as if none of this mattered.

And that I was of no consequence.

Was he lying again? He'd admitted that he'd already lied once.

The only way to prove that he was lying would be to call his bluff and stay here, and do nothing.

But if he wasn't bluffing, I'd stay here, and do nothing—and die.

That was a scenario that was not in my best interest.

Nor his.

I had no choice. He knew that and I knew that. I had to find him, within ninety days.

I said, *What can you tell me?*

*Watch*, the Voice said. *Listen. Learn.*

I did not reply. There was no need to, just as there was no need for him to speak further.

What followed was shown to me, not told.

I was flying through the night sky, over hills and snow-covered forests that became mountains and glaciers, leading to a vast sea of ice. At the far end of it, surrounded by tall peaks, some snow-capped, some aflame, stood a white, circular tower topped with wide battlements. Below them pale light gleamed behind its single, wide window. Beneath the tower, tunnels led through caverns of glistening blue-white ice. There was something down there. Something that I must find. There was something up there. Something that I must face. Years were passing as I watched: lifetimes; centuries. The light in the high room never dimmed, by day or night. Down in the white-blue caverns, something watched, and waited. I strained to see what it might be, as the vision faded.

Two yellow eyes were staring at me again, against the moonlit sky and passing clouds.

I felt the Voice's presence, waiting for me to answer. I conjured up the vision from the wolf dream. *The Moon Mage.*

*Yes. That is who you are.*

*The Valley of the Moon.*

*Yes. That is where I am. That is where you will find me.*

*But how do I get there?*

*You are a mage. Only a mage can.*

*Only me? I must come alone?*

*Only a mage who has been Gifted can pass the barrier.*

*I have lost the Gift. I told you: I made your Turnaway potion. I drank it.*

*You have lost the ability to Turn at will. That is all. You will see, come the next Moon Nights. They will take you, as they have done before, as they always will, only deeper now, and harder. Find me and your Gift will be greater than before. Where now it is your curse, it will be your reward. It is your choice, mage. Stay where you are, and lose. Find me, and win.*

*Win what?*

*I will show you.*

I'd had flying dreams before. Mostly they are confused, and scrambled, and don't last long before I plummet—or flounder about, swooping a few feet off the ground, flapping frantically, before lurching back down and falling in a heap. What followed was in another league entirely. I owned the air. I could go as fast, and as high, as I wanted. There was no gravity. I ran up, and away, and around, exhilarated, confident, the world circling below me, stars above in the night sky. I was in my element. This was where I belonged.

It was over before I'd begun to explore it.

And then I saw the alternative.

I was in a dark room, sitting back on my haunches, staring at myself in a mirror, lit by candlelight. I couldn't comprehend what I was seeing. My mind was scrambled, by scents, and sounds, and the taste of blood. My thoughts were fading as my feelings grew. My reflection in the mirror evaporated into mist. In front of me, Daxx, on two legs, was looking back at me, his eyes wide as my mind receded and the last of me blinked out.

I was lost, forever.

*Now do you see?*

*Yes. Yes, I do.*

*If you choose not to try to find me, the Turn will turn you inside out. There are only two endings to this tale, mage: the clearest of minds, or the darkest.*

The yellow eyes stared into mine, behind them the moonlit sky, in front of them the drifting clouds.

*Find me. Free me. And I will free you.*

I now knew what he meant. I would have the freedom of the skies. The glory of a greater life, free to run among the stars at will ...

The yellow eyes faded as the dream ended. I understood what I had been shown. I was neither the one thing nor the other.

Do nothing and the *one thing* and the *other* would tear me apart.

I knew where I needed to go and what I needed to do. I would find my way to the Valley of the Moon and face the challenges that awaited me there. If I reached the end, I would either pass through and come out the other side, or—not. *Find him, free him, and receive my reward: the Gift at my command, no longer a curse but a blessing. Fail, and fade into the dark.*

My story would end, or it would continue.

It was as simple as that.

I had to admit that it was neatly done.

He had trapped me.

I had sought a cure, an answer to my problem.

And the answer was simple.

*Do or die.*

I drifted off back into sleep, feeling clueless, helpless, and not knowing where to start. All that I knew, as I sank deep down again, was that I *needed* to start.

Ninety days. Three moon months. How? Where? Well, I'd just have to work all that out. Succeed, or die trying.

Win—or lose.

Win that freedom, that power, that ownership of the air. Or lose. And I'd be the opposite of whatever a werewolf was.

I'd look like a man, but I wouldn't have the mind of one.

I'd be gone.

Marnie's word echoed in my mind, as I drifted off.

*Husk.*

It was nearly noon when I woke. My eyes opened, slowly. Daylight shone through a little round window low down in the wall below the thatched eaves. I was lying on my side. I did not know where I was. All I knew was that I was snug, and warm, and in no hurry to leave this soft cocoon in this quiet room. I took in a deep breath, ready to exhale a sigh of contentment—and my nostrils filled with the rich smell of baking bread.

I was wide awake in a moment.

*Gods* I was hungry!

My clothes were, as Velaryn had promised, beautifully laundered, and folded on a chair by my bedside. I dressed and hurried down the creaking stairs towards that wondrous smell.

"There you are, then!" Velaryn said, with a smile, as I joined her in her kitchen. "Sit yourself down, Daxx, and fill yourself up—you've a busy day ahead of you."

I sat.

Velaryn set a plate in front of me.

As she had promised, it was filled with all the breakfast I could eat—and I'd never eaten a better. I needed it, after all that I had been through. Shoreweed seemed to be a local delicacy in Eastbay, and Velaryn had built an omelet around it, and mushrooms, and onions, and sharp peppers, and green peas, and shards of carrots for a bit of crunch, all fluffed up as light as a feather. It was accompanied by sausages, and bacon, and potatoes, and the morning's bread hot from the oven, slathered with butter.

"It's good to have a young man with an appetite about the place again," she said as she sat down beside me.

From the way that she said it, I sensed that Velaryn had enjoyed her long life in this house.

She kept refilling my plate until I couldn't eat anymore. As I ate, she told me that she'd be telling the neighbors, and customers at her shop, that I was her cousin Hernbert, also an apothecary, visiting from Whitmouth: So, I'd best get used to being called that.

Between mouthfuls, I said, "Peculiar name."

Velaryn's eyebrows rose. "And Daxx isn't?"

"Well, now you mention it," I admitted.

"There's been Hernberts in our family going back generations. I apprenticed with one, my great-uncle. Finest apothecary in the land, as all knew."

I remembered something that Avildor had once said. "A lie is best hidden behind the truth," I said.

"It is indeed," Velaryn agreed. "So, if anyone wants a cure for his piles, or a love-philtre for the lad she's dotty for, and shyly asks you—well, you just tell them we'll see what we can do. Folks can be coy about what ails them. They might not want to come to me, 'cos I know their wives, or parents, or neighbors. But mayhaps they'll pluck up the courage to sidle up to you, a stranger who might put in a word and help out. So, be prepared to play the part, lad."

Perhaps it was the comfort of having a full stomach for the first time in more than a week. Perhaps it was the word *play*. Whatever, I liked what I heard.

"Got it," I said.

*Play the part*, I thought.

*Yes. The game is afoot.*

*So, let's get in it, get ahead of it, find out what it is.*

When we did find out, just a few days later, we didn't like what we saw at all.

We saw that we were out of our depth, and out of time, and completely unprepared for the challenge.

"Right, then," Velaryn said, when I finished eating. She rose to her feet, took off her apron, and hung it on a hook behind the door. "Let's be on our way."

I wiped my mouth with a napkin and got up, feeling better than I had in days.

"Where are we going?" I asked.

"Conclave. Although not at the guildhall. We don't want all those porters and servants seeing us going in and out, and gossiping in the taverns. We need to keep a lid on this as tight and as long as we can, Marnie's adamant about that. We'll all know what we all know soon enough—although whether that's much remains to be seen. I'm in the dark myself, I'll tell you that for nothing. Glamour yourself up, Daxx. We don't want anyone seeing that handsome face what everyone in town would recognize in a flash. Although I'm happy enough to look at it."

I raised Shift and Glamoured myself as an elderly scholar.

"Urhm," Velaryn grunted, her face falling. "Not what I'd call an improvement. Still, should serve."

She led me out of the kitchen and through the shop, where she waved a hand at the door to the alley outside. The large, iron bolts obediently eased themselves back from the bars into which they'd been pushed home. Velaryn unlocked the door and we stepped out into the spring sunshine. The alley was quiet, and empty, but I could hear faint sounds coming from the distant town square. It was still party time in Eastbay. Velaryn closed the door of her shop, and waved a hand at it. I heard the bolts behind it slamming shut.

She saw me notice the sound, and said, breezily, as we set off along the alley, "There's not the thief alive who can open *magic* locks."

I said, "Yes, there is."

She turned and frowned at me. "You're a mage—you should know better than that!"

"I'm a mage," I agreed, "and I know a thief who can."

"Pff," she snorted. "I'll believe *that* when I see it!"

"He'll be happy to show you," I said.

Velaryn chuckled. "And I'll be happy to watch him fail. Still, he's welcome to try," she said.

I walked alongside her, enjoying the thought of seeing her face when Oller opened her door with his silver key.

We kept to side streets, taking a detour around the town square, stopping at last in another back alley outside another unremarkable door.

Velaryn knocked. The door swung open inwards.

It appeared that no one had opened it.

*Magic again,* I thought.

Well, that was to be expected.

Still, it was impressive.

"Vullo, Helaryn," a gloomy voice by our knees muttered.

I looked down. A small, mournful creature was holding the door open for us, one long, thin hand stretching up towards its handle.

I'd seen one like it before, at Marnie's cottage.

*Hogboblin,* I thought, automatically mangling the word.

It turned its gaze to me, and studied me with its large, pale eyes. "Housin Kernbert," it said, with a nod. "Elcome, coo wum din."

"Thank you," I said, once I'd translated.

"Hello Tob," Velaryn said. "How's things?"

"Uddy blawful, if you ask me, Vel!" Tob muttered, crabbing backwards to open the door for us. "Nut bo-one ever duddy bluzz. Stit shorm's coming, no woo tays about it. You wark my merds. It's onna be gugly."

"What makes you say that, Tob?" Velaryn asked.

"Huh? It's ucking fobvious. Any mucking foron can kee it summing!"

The Hobgoblin turned away, and led us on crooked, cautious feet into the house.

"Worse and worse, if Tob is worried," Vel muttered to me.

"I'm not the wonly un," Tob said, over his shoulder. "Every hucking fogboblin's as kervous as a nitten. So, you wigbigs better get your kinking thaps on, before the fat hits the shin."

Tob held open the door to the back parlor, where the Conclave was waiting for our arrival, and closed it behind us.

"Conclave" had sounded big and important when Marnie had said it the night before. I'd been expecting a large gathering of everyone who was anyone in the Guild of the Arcane Arts, all the high and mighty—probably in some impressive chamber. Instead, just six people were seated at the round table that took up most of the small room that we'd entered.

I knew that I'd be seeing Marnie there. I hadn't expected to see Mabel sitting next to her.

"Hello, 'Cousin Hernbert,'" she said, her brown eyes shining and a cheerful grin on her homely, happy face.

"Hello, Mabel," I said, inclining my head to our queen disguised under her familiar *scullery maid Mabel* Glamour. "This is a nice surprise."

"There's other surprises, and not a one of them nice!" Marnie cut in. "The which young Mabel needs to know of, because there's decisions to be made. And she's Mabel today because if I didn't Mabelize her she'd be noticed, and the last thing we want is any o' this to be noticed. Same goes for you, laddie! Glamour yourself up good and hard before you go anywhere. We don't need word of you being back in town to get about. Now, first things first."

She addressed the others at the table. "You all know Vel," she said, to the others, who nodded to show that they did. "This gent with her is the one I told you about, and the reason we're all here. As Mabel named him, he's Velaryn's cousin Hernbert, though that's no more his name than Mabel is hers. He's the one as trouble follows, and we need to know what the trouble is that he's warning us of."

She introduced the others.

Eilwen, Dean Auditory of the Eastbay College of Lore and Learning, sat leaning back as if asleep. An odd title, I thought. I wondered what it meant. Eilwen was a fey-looking, silent lady, who could have been fifty years old or five hundred. Her eyelids slowly half opened for a moment, just long enough to let her see as much of me as she needed to, before flickering, and drooping, and closing again.

Marnie introduced the twins, Sharyth and her brother, Aulber, as Historians. They seemed to have nothing in common—unlike the identical twins at The Wheatsheaf, Mindy and Mandy. They inclined their heads and I returned the gesture, but they said nothing as they watched me with alert, pale eyes. He was tall and reserved. She was short and intense, her eyes locked onto mine. I found her stare disconcerting.

The sixth person at the table was the only one who had risen to greet us. Marnie named him as Archmage Faldruti, Guildmaster of the local chapter of the GAA. Faldruti was, to my surprise—though I took care not to show it—Black. Clearly, I realized, as I shook his hand, this realm was not as monochrome as I had thought. As, well—why should it be? I remembered the dark-skinned warrior women I had seen in the marketplace in Freehaven. This was, after all, an entire world. There had to be more nations to it than just the two northern realms that I'd explored so far.

It surprised me to sense that Faldruti seemed, as he smiled at me and shook my hand, to think that he knew me, somehow.

"Welcome to my home, Master Hernbert," he said. "And if you would spare me a moment, after Conclave, we have guild matters to discuss?"

I nodded, and said, "Of course, Archmage."

He sat.

Velaryn and I sat.

"But first," he said, "your story. Marnie has told us how you and she met, and what you did for this realm. But of what happened to you in another realm—your Gifting, and all that has followed: We know little. We need to hear it all."

# 9

## Conclave

So, I told them.

I told them everything: my encounter with Graycote, in the wilds of Mourvania; my journey with Urngra through the Deepwoods to the village; my conversation with the Voice in the vault; and my run back to Eastbay, the long way around. I ended with my dream the previous night and what the Voice had told me.

That, of course, was news to Marnie. It was news that alarmed her. She sat bolt upright on hearing it.

She looked at Archmage Faldruti, who held her eyes, his expression grim.

She nodded, as if agreeing with something he hadn't said.

"A Binding," she said; and she didn't like the word at all. She shot Velaryn a glance full of meaning. Velaryn looked similarly troubled.

Mabel said, "What's a Binding?"

"Bad," Marnie said.

"In what way?"

"In every way, girl."

"It is an art no mortal practices," Faldruti said. "No mortal with any sense, that is. Any that do keep well away from the rest of us. If they're found out, that's the end of them. They know they can expect no mercy."

"It can't be risked," Vel explained. "Any mortal who casts a Binding might release a terror into this world that it can't handle. It's not for us to meddle with such matters."

"Some fools try, though," Marnie said. "Just as some fools will try anything. Never mind them—if it's a Binding we're looking at, young Mastercaster, we're dealing with powers mightier than we are. *Divine* powers."

"How do you know that's what this is?" I asked.

Marnie snorted. "Don't you listen? He told you himself. *Find me, and unbind me.* What could be clearer than that?!"

I said, "I don't know how to do either."

"And I don't know as you should!" Marnie snapped. "We've told you—it's an art no mortal practices."

"But if I don't ..."

She leaned back and stared at me, challenging me to work it out for myself.

It wasn't hard.

If I didn't find him, I'd die.

"The question is," Archmage Faldruti said, "unbind him from *what*?"

I looked from him, to Marnie, to Velaryn.

Marnie nodded. "And there you have it. Who is bound to what? And who did the Binding? Well, that's not hard to scry out. You, Gifted; what your Reveals showed you, in the vault; what your Voice told you, and the rule you broke—*Moon Magic only in the village:* This is Moon Magic, without a doubt. And that's her business, not ours. As to what she's up to, it's not for us mortals to interfere."

My head swam. I'd been told where to go, if I could find it, and what to do, if I could do it—and they were saying I shouldn't? "So I do nothing?"

Faldruti said, "Unbind the one, you also unbind the other."

Silence fell in the little room.

He, or it, must, after all, have been bound for a reason.

I understood. I was just one life. One person. Who knew how many lives would be at risk, if that "other" were unbound?

"How do I find out more? Are there books? At the College, or at the GAA?"

Marnie said, "You're not listening, laddie. Any book on the subject is destroyed if found. It's not an art for mortals."

I said, "So what should I do?"

No one seemed to know.

Mabel broke the silence. "What else do we know about Binding?"

No one answered.

"Well, it seems to me we know hardly anything," Mabel continued. "If I were Daxx, I'd want to know what I was dealing with."

Marnie said, gently, "We've told you, child. It's—"

"—an art no mortal practices," Mabel interrupted. "So, no one can tell him about it. Except the one who wants to be unbound. In Daxx's place, I'd go and find him and see what's what. Rather than just give up."

That didn't sit well with her elders.

"With respect, Your Majesty—" Archmage Faldruti began, but Mabel ignored him, and turned to me.

"Whatever you decide," she said, "you'll have my support."

I said, "Thank you, Your Majesty."

That matter settled, she said, "Right, now what about this Wild Hunt?"

Marnie looked across at Sharyth and said, "Sister?"

Historian Sharyth was about a third of Marnie's age—but in Coven, I knew, all were sisters.

She glanced at her brother beside her, who nodded. "The connection seems clear to us, although we cannot yet see what it means. The Wild Hunt has been held to be a portent of disaster, or a harbinger of chaos—all of which may be true, in this case. Disaster may be impending. We may indeed be looking at imminent chaos. But my brother and I have been considering the other face of the coin. We look up, and see the hounds, and the mounts and their riders, flowing across the sky—and by 'we,' I mean us, down here. Us mortals. No one alive in this age has witnessed it. It is so long since the Wild Hunt has ridden the skies that folk now think it no more than a legend. But what do *they* see, when they look down at us? What do they seek? What is their quarry, their game? And why?"

"Why Daxx?" her brother spoke.

"Hernbert, if you please, Master Aulber," Marnie reminded him.

"I used his true name for a reason," Aulber replied. "I will explain why, and I will not say it again. That reason is this: We must not be distracted. We must not look between Form or Truth; or Man or Wolf; or Mage or Glamour. He is all of those. He is the quarry. He is the game. We know of no other such, in our lifetimes, or in those of our parents and grandparents."

"Indeed," his sister continued. "Why this person, and why now? After how many scores of years?" She waited.

Eventually Marnie lost patience and snapped. "Well? Why?"

Sharyth held her gaze, and said, calmly, "That is what we would like to know."

Marnie grunted. She didn't like that answer. "So, how do we find out?"

"We have researched every tale that we could find. None who have been quarry ever lived to tell."

"So, you're saying that we don't know what we're dealing with?" Archmage Faldruti asked.

"We know what," Aulber said. "We just don't know why."

Marnie said, her voice filled with impatience, "So, tell us what you *do* know."

"Hounds. Horns. Horses. Hooves," Aulber said.

"Some say other mounts," his sister added. "Great cats, and bears, and chimeras; manticores, and wyverns, roaring with the wind; claws and paws drumming in the thunder."

She fell silent.

A thought struck me. "Wolves?"

They both nodded, in unison, as twins will.

"Some have said it's the howling of wolves they hear, not the belling of hounds," Sharyth said. "Others say it's both."

Marnie said, "Always at night?"

"No—always in storm, day or night."

None of us knew what to think. Or to say.

Marnie sighed. She turned to me. "What did I tell you, young Mastercaster? Trouble follows you."

"Or I run ahead of it," I reminded her.

Silence fell again.

I broke it. "Which, it seems to me, I'd better keep doing," I said. "If what Sharyth says is right, that no quarry ever lived to tell the tale."

No one wanted to contradict her.

That was when Mabel spoke up. "No quarry ever had *us*," she said, firmly. "And we're not going to let you run off on your own to get hunted down and killed. I don't care who they are, or where they come from. Archmage?"

"Of course, Your Majesty. You will have all the resources of the guild at your command."

Marnie added, "And Coven, but she knows that, being Coven herself." She looked at Velaryn. "Apothecaries?"

"I'll make sure of it," Velaryn said.

"Good," Mabel said. "Riding across the sky sounds like magic to me, so we fight magic with magic. And if it comes to war on the ground, we've got the Royal Guards, and every garrison in the realm, and all the foot soldiers and horsemen of every lord or lady's retinue, and every knight and his squire and household—not to mention an army of battle-hardened Orcs, who love nothing better than a good scrap. And the nibluns will remember what Da—I mean, *Cousin Hernbert*—did for them, saving their city. The Woods Kin will help too, mayhaps, if we send Nyrik and Horm to them. Riding through the sky chasing a lone victim is one thing. Riding through a storm of arrows and Firebombs into a reception committee like *we* can muster is quite another!"

Not for the first time I thought what a remarkable woman our young queen was.

"I appreciate what you're saying, Mabel," I said, "but I won't be waiting for the Wild Hunt to turn up. Or for anyone else who comes looking for me. I intend to stay ahead of them. And that means leaving Eastbay as soon as I can."

I could see that Mabel didn't like that. "You'll be alone," she said. You never left *me* alone. I'm not leaving you alone."

"I won't be. I'll have Qrysta, with your permission, and Grell, and Oller. And you've seen that we can look after ourselves."

Mabel nodded. "You'll have anything and anyone you need."

I bowed my head. "Thank you."

"And you'll come back," she added; and the way she said it, it was a royal command.

"I will, Your Majesty."

"You make sure you do." She looked at the others. "I apologize," she said, with an unconvincing smile. "I wouldn't be here, now, or be what I am, now, without Cousin Hernbert." She recomposed herself, and said, "So: Back to the matter at hand. Archmage?"

Faldruti's fingers were steepled together under his nose. His lips were drawn downwards and he was frowning. "I wish I had more, Your Majesty. Our guild will exert every effort to learn further." He shrugged. "But, for the moment, I am as in the dark as all of you." He shook his head. "We will do what we can," he promised, "to our utmost." He did not sound hopeful.

Mabel said, "Velaryn?"

Velaryn replied simply, "As will ours."

The twins had told us all they knew.

Marnie shifted awkwardly on her chair.

"So, we have all the guilds, and all the forces, and all the resources," Mabel said, "all working together. That has to be something. Right?"

It sounded good, in theory. It sounded unconvincing when she said it. Nobody needed to say the obvious: We didn't know what we were dealing with. We didn't know how to solve the problem because we still didn't really know what the problem was.

We all felt more unsettled than we had when this Conclave had begun; more challenged and confused.

No one knew what to say.

Where to start?

And then, her eyes still closed, Dean Eilwen inhaled, slowly, through her nose, and raised her chin from her chest.

All eyes turned to her.

I glanced at Marnie as she leaned forward, her body still, her eyes fixed on Eilwen. I looked down at her old hands on the table in front of her, both crossing their fingers.

Eilwen spoke, her voice dry, and weak, her eyes still closed. "Run and hide," she whispered.

She was, as far as we could tell, asleep. Or, perhaps, in a trance. She was with us in person, but far away in spirit.

I knew that the others were thinking what I was thinking. *"Run and hide"? That fits the Wild Hunt.*

In the silence, Eilwen's chest rose and fell with her slow, deep breathing. My own, I could feel, was much shallower, and twice as fast. Her face was a mask. Eventually, her soft voice came again. "Hide and run," she echoed.

*Yes, I that's what I did indeed, I hid and ran. And if I hadn't, I wouldn't be here now. So—now what? What happens next?*

We waited, our eyes fixed on her.

Out of the corner of my eye, I noticed Marnie fidget. She was anxious for more. Clearly, she felt that this was important.

Perhaps, I realized, this was why Eilwen was here. I knew nothing about her, beyond her title: Dean Auditory of the College of Lore and Learning.

Eventually, Eilwen said, "Don't assume."

I thought, *don't assume what?* I had no idea.

Eilwen spoke again. "Dead reborn."

In the silence that followed, I wondered, *Is that good? Is that bad?* I didn't know how to make sense of what she was saying.

In her chair, Eilwen stirred, as if agitated, her mouth working, her eyes screwed tight. Eventually, the words came, in a rush.

"Wield the broom

Sweep the sky

Sound the horn

Hue and cry ..."

She broke off and coughed, agitated. Clearly, every word had been a struggle for her. Her tongue slipped through her lips to moisten them. Something else was coming, we felt—but it didn't. All we heard were soft grunts coming from deep in her chest, as if she was listening to someone.

She nodded, as if she had heard and understood. Slowly, she turned her old face towards me, her eyes still closed. Her hand reached out towards me. When she spoke again, her tone was different, as if she was giving me specific steps how to do what she was telling us needed to be done. "Unlock the rune."

I tried to make sense of that. *"Unlock the rune"? What does that mean? Runes are symbols; letters, written on parchment, or carved into stone. Who locks runes? Is that even possible? How do you lock a rune? How do you unlock one?*

"Observe the moon."

*Okay, yes, that I can do. But ... please—we need more ...*

It seemed that I wasn't going to get more, and that was all she was going to say. Her chin dropped to her chest again and her breathing settled and slowed.

Eventually, I sensed the others around the table stirring as if they felt that the episode was over.

It wasn't.

"Assume the form," Eilwen mumbled into her chest, as we strained to hear.

"Unleash the storm
In fire and flood
And turn the tide."

Again, we waited, and listened, in suspense. The only sound in the room was Eilwen's deep, steady breathing. Was that it?

We waited.

Slowly, Eilwen raised her head again.

"Divide the blood," she added, nodding.

"Devour the sun
Let darkness fall
And end it all."

Behind her closed eyes she seemed to be looking up for something above her—for further guidance, perhaps?

It didn't come. After *end it all*, it seemed, there was nothing more.

She swallowed. She sighed and her head fell against the back of her chair, her body slumping down as all the tension left it.

The first of us to come out of the spell was Marnie.

"Well, now!" she said.

She pushed her chair back and got up, hobbling around the table to Eilwen, who had fallen into a deep sleep.

Marnie lifted Eilwen's hands out of her lap, and held them in her own. "So what's that, then, dear?" she asked, gently—and I'd never heard Marnie sound so respectful.

Slowly, Eilwen's head lifted. Her eyes opened. She looked around, puzzled, as if not knowing where she was. Then she found Marnie, and frowned, as if she'd been expecting to see something, or someone, else.

At last she recognized her. "What is what?" Eilwen said.

"What you just said, sister."

Eilwen relaxed. She smiled a faraway smile, as if she'd just heard happy news. She replied, "I said something? Oh, how *nice!* What did I say?"

Marnie told her.

Eilwen nodded, considering. "Well, I never!" she said. "I wonder what *that* means."

She chuckled, content. She had delivered. Now it was out of her hands.

Marnie nodded. "We'll see," she said.

Eilwen drifted off again, back to sleep.

Marnie let go of her hands, settling them back in Eilwen's lap.

"Good!" she said, stumping back to her chair, "finally we've got something to go on!"

Mabel said, "Did that make sense?"

Marnie answered, firmly, "It will if we put our minds to it!"

I had no idea what had happened, but I was encouraged that Marnie was suddenly energized and purposeful. She eased her old frame back into her chair, pulling her notebook out of her pocket. "It'll be in yours too, laddie," she told me.

I reached inside my jerkin for the Infinite Notebook that she had made for me. I opened it at the last page that had writing on it. Sure enough, there it was.

Velaryn leaned over my shoulder to look at it while Marnie read aloud.

*Run and hide*
*Hide and run*
*Don't assume*
*Dead reborn*
*Wield the broom*
*Sweep the sky*
*Sound the horn*
*Hue and cry*

*Unlock the rune*
*Observe the moon*
*Assume the form*
*Unleash the storm*
*In fire and flood*
*And turn the tide*
*Divide the blood*
*Devour the sun*
*Let darkness fall*
*And end it all*

"Now we're getting somewhere!" Marnie said.

It made no sense to me, even though it … resonated. "Can you explain?"

"No, but it's all there, even if we can't yet see it."

I frowned. "What is? And how do you know?"

Marnie snorted. "You stick to your job, I'll stick to mine! An Auditor doesn't speak unless spoken to. And all at this table, excepting mayhaps you, young Mastercaster, know it's not a one of *us* she's been spoken to by. Someone, or something, who knows more than we do has Informed her—one who can see *through* and *across* time and place, where we can only see *along*. Past, future—who knows? A Higher Power. That's the privilege a Dean Auditory has, lad. That's Lore and Learning. The main thing is: *We've been told.*"

I tried not to appear impatient or frustrated. My life was at stake. "Told what?"

Marnie shook her head. "You've skills none of us are near, lad. You can cast and blast and heal like none I've ever seen. But you're ignorant as an earthworm. 'Told what?' Told *everything!*"

I was still nowhere near understanding why she was so pleased. "So, we know what we need to do?"

"We will once we've deciphered. The which might not take too long, if we're lucky."

*Not too long* would definitely be good. "Can I help?"

"Knock yourself out."

I looked at Eilwen's pronouncements again. Some of them seemed graspable, even familiar. I had no idea what others meant. I felt that they all sounded more ominous than hopeful. Bits seemed to make sense—those that seemed to be about what we were dealing with. But what it all added up to was as clear as mud.

Okay, I thought: What do we always do, with a problem?

Turn it around and peer up its backside until you see daylight.

So: If it doesn't make sense, or any sense that we can see yet, what else have we got?

Well, let's start at the beginning. We have lines. We have rhymes. Eighteen lines. Nine rhymes.

So far, so straightforward. But if the sense was all over the place, so was the form. The lines rhymed, but in haphazard way.

But they still rhymed.

If it was not without rhyme, maybe it was not without reason.

I waited, for an insight.

None came.

I frowned at the lines on the page in front of me. *What aren't you telling me? What don't I see?*

I scanned them up and down, thinking, *What am I looking at? In general? In particular? What is all this? Any of it?*

I looked up at Marnie when she challenged sharply, "Well?"

I hesitated. "I can see what it says … but what does it mean?"

Marnie snorted. "That's for us to scry out. We've been *told*, lad—and a Dean Auditory doesn't waste a Telling. It'll all be there. All we need is the eyes to see it and the wit to know what we're looking at. So put that clever head for puzzles of yours to work, as the rest of us will be doing."

Mabel said, "While you're all doing that, what can I do?"

"Go about your royal business, child," Marnie said. "Give your people a show to remember."

The Royal Tournament was that all right.

But not in a way that any of us could possibly have foreseen.

The Conclave broke up. Marnie seemed to know that the meeting was over; and if a meeting was over, Marnie saw no point in wasting time in small talk. She and Mabel would see Dean Eilwen safe back to her rooms at the College. The twins were heading to the GAA, to get on with their research. "Cousin Hernbert and I have matters to discuss," Faldruti told Tob, when he came back for me.

"Got can I wet you?" Tob said. "Sea? Tandwiches?"

Faldruti glanced at me, eyebrows raised—but I was still full of Velaryn's breakfast.

"Nothing for me, thank you," I said.

Tob grunted, and crabbed out, closing the door behind him.

Faldruti gestured for me to sit down, then turned to me with a smile—the smile of someone who believed that we had something in common.

"Marnie tells me," he said, "that you're not from these parts either."

"She's right."

He nodded, rocking back and forth in his chair, and his smile broadened. "Then, my friend, you will know the word."

I thought, *word?*

I could see no point in pretending. I knew that I needed this man on my side. "I don't know the word, Archmage."

His smile faded. His brow furrowed. "Yet you are of the road?"

Again, I was at a loss. I had no idea what he was talking about.

He continued, and it was more of a statement reminding me about myself than a question. "You have come here from another realm."

"Yes," I agreed. "I have."

He waited. Eventually, he shook his head.

"Perhaps, in your realm, they do not teach what is taught in mine. That, when a mage travels, he will encounter others of his kind, who are also of the road. And that they will know each other to be such, and will confirm it with the word."

"No," I said. "This is the first I've heard of it."

His eyebrows rose. "Really? Well, it seems that you have something to learn just as I do, Daxx. Marnie has told me of your skills. It sounds to me that some of them far surpass anything we know here. That is knowledge that we lack. The whole realm knows of what you achieved at the Floor Of The World. I doubt that anyone else could have done what you and your companions did."

I couldn't think what to say, but knew that an answer was needed. "We did what we could."

"Indeed." Archmage Faldruti paused.

I waited.

He was considering what to tell me. "I have traveled the length and breadth of this world," he began, "as those of us who are of the road must. We all follow it to its end, but the road's end is different for each of us. For me, it ended here, in Eastbay. A fine town. I knew that I would settle here the moment I landed, after more than twenty years of roving, and seeking, and learning, and serving. I will go no further. My sons have taken to the road in their turn. Far and wide they are now. South, they went, east and west." He smiled. "It is mild, here in Eastbay, but this is as far into the cold lands as I will go. My sons headed to the sun, as if their father's blood were calling them. They send pigeons, when they can. My wife was raised here—in this very house. This is where I belong. And you?"

It was a question I had been thinking about a lot since my appearance in Jarnland.

I had no answer to it.

"I don't know that I belong anywhere, Archmage," I said.

He nodded, as if my reply pleased him. "Then you are of the road and *on* the road. For you, as for all of us, it will end where and when it so decides. Not in idleness. My feet may be still, but my mind is active, and my tasks are many. The journey's end is but the beginning. We arrive at our destination for a purpose. The road leads us where it will."

"Do you know your purpose, Archmage?"

He considered the question. "I know that it lies here. I know that it involves my wife, and my sons, and my duties here at our guild. I have lived. I have traveled. I have studied, in many lands, learning many languages, and much lore. My apprenticeship has been served. Now I serve as a master. But, perhaps, that is not all of my purpose, at the end of my road. Perhaps that purpose also involves you."

A thought struck me. He had traveled the length and breadth of this world …. "I'd like to hear where you've been."

He looked at me, nodding, and smiled.

"My road began in the island where I was born," he began. "It is a large island, off the coast of a large continent, the largest of all that I have traveled in. Far to the south it lies, under the tropic sun. There I served my apprenticeship, of seven years; and, when I was fifteen, I took ship, for the great landmass that lay to the west of my island. I walked, and settled, and studied with adepts of our arcane arts in places that I could never have imagined. Jungles, deserts, villages, cities. High among mountains. Deep in the realms of the dead. I learned and moved on. Always I came west, and north. I crossed the last sea, which became ever blacker, and colder. I landed here, and knew that I had come home. From my old home to my new one. My road had ended."

From what he had told me it had been a long journey, over many years and through many realms. He had seen much, and learned more.

But he had not seen, nor learned of, the Valley of the Moon. I asked him directly. He had never heard of it.

Another dead end, I thought.

Sometimes I amaze myself with my own stupidity. Faldruti might not have known; but someone else did. Someone who was just about the last person I'd have thought of asking.

He pointed me in the right direction that same evening—which I could have done for myself, if I'd only, to quote Marnie, *had the wit* to put two and two together.

# IO

## Impartment

All sorts of unsavory characters find their way into Thieves Guild hide-aways. If you're not TG yourself you can't get in, even if you know where the hidden entrance is. On our way to the branch in Eastbay, Oller explained the protocol to Qrysta and me.

"Anyone who's not TG needs a sponsor who will vouch for them with the Receiver. Then they can do their business in the trading room—which is the only room that non–TG are permitted to enter, in any hide-away—and no questions asked as to who they are, or what they're trading. Call yourself a fence, and why would they want to challenge you? All they care about is whether you give them a good price for their stolen goods. If you do, they're happy, and you have a deal."

Oller was, now, royalty in the TG. He had the ear and trust of the young queen, which made the Eastbay Receiver both proud and nervous. *Us, TG, at the highest levels of the royal court?* No Receiver had ever heard of such a thing! TG wasn't *inside*, let alone inside at the highest levels. If a thief was inside, he was almost certainly trespassing, and looking to steal something. Thieves were outside. Always had been.

When he'd made his number with the Eastbay Receiver, Oller had been sure to stress that he had no intention of throwing his weight about. He was TG to the core; Brigstowe born and raised; and when he said Brigstowe, he meant the *streets* of Brigstowe. Born on them, raised on them, and would've died on them if it hadn't been for the TG, and old Fingers who'd taken him on as his 'prentice. He'd never rat on the TG any more than he'd let down his queen. Fugitives together, they'd been, him and Esmeralda; outlaws, running for their lives—and you don't break those kinds of bonds. She wouldn't, no more than he would. Looked out for each other, they did, on the run. And look out for each other they always will.

The Eastbay Receiver got the picture. You don't get to be a Receiver by being slow on the uptake. It was as if Oller had shown him a Royal Warrant that read: Eastbay Thieves Guild, By Appointment to Her Majesty, Queen Esmeralda. *Any problems, chum, you've got a friend at court. Any problems, she's got friends in TG.* As a result, neither Esmeralda, nor the Receiver, had had the slightest hint of a problem with each other, all the time that she'd been in Eastbay with her court—and that was just fine with both of them.

So when, the next morning, Oller brought in a shady-looking, foreign-looking merchant, along with the Captain of the Royal Guard, and made his number with the Receiver, the Receiver signed us all in with a grin and a flourish. Qrysta he knew, of course, if only by sight. I could tell he thought, *Anything the queen wants, that's fine by me. Happy to oblige, Your Majesty.*

The "foreign-looking merchant" was me. Oller approved of my disguise. I looked, he said, no worse than most who came through the hideaway to do their business—and a lot less unpleasant than many. You have to be a good judge of character to make it to the rank of Receiver—especially when most of the characters you have to judge are anything *but* good. I'd taken care to position my appearance nearer *shifty* than *trouble*. The Receiver barely glanced over at me. Clearly, I fitted right in. Besides, he had something more pressing that he needed to discuss with Oller, and the two of them conferred, heads together. Oller nodded, and led us to the trading room, which we'd have to ourselves for as long as we needed it. Anyone else who came along with another outsider to do their business, well, they'd just have to wait their turn.

"Out-of-towners have been dipping their hands in where they shouldn't," Oller told us, as he showed us into the trading room. "Non–TG scoundrels. Can't be having that! There's plenty of TG come from all over for the tournament, but they know to come in and make their number, and learn what's guild-approved and what isn't. Receiver's got 'em locked up, wants me to have a word with them—show them the error of their ways. Can't have anyone mucking up Her Maj's tournament. Won't be long." He ducked out and left Qrysta and me alone.

"So, how's things?" we both said, at the same time, and both answered, at the same time, "Don't ask!"

I said, "Yours can't be worse than mine."

"Hah!" Qrysta growled. *"Nothing* is worse than heralds!"

"Yeah?"

"Yeah! What a bunch of whiny, snotty, self-important, smarmy know-it-alls. I could happily strangle the lot of them. Can you imagine a committee in which every member thinks he's chairman of the committee, and they're all only interested in committee meetings?"

I actually couldn't.

*"Uurrhh!"* she shouted, exasperated. "Points of order! Procedures! Minutes, amendments, protocols! I can't *wait* for this tournament to be over!"

"Won't be long now."

"Still too damn long," she muttered. "I didn't sign up for this shit."

I couldn't help smiling.

"What are you laughing at?!" she challenged.

"You'll understand when you hear what I've been through."

She frowned. "What does that mean?"

"Just that other people's problems put your own into perspective, Qrys. And are also entertaining."

"Well, I'm happy I've given you a good laugh," she said, sounding anything but. "If what you've been through is as bad as ass-numbing meeting after ass-numbing meeting, where everyone is politely, and formally, and minutely going over and over again through every damn detail that makes you want to scream—only you can't, because that would be bad form—*gaaahh!!"* She growled and crossed her arms. "There's no way it can be," she challenged. "So, spill."

I told her what I'd been through. When I finished, she was staring at me wide-eyed, her mouth hanging open.

I said, "You want to swap that for a few committee meetings?"

Qrysta closed her mouth, and blinked, and swallowed, holding my gaze and nodding slowly. "You, lucky *bastard!"* She shook her head and chuckled. "*Any* damn day of the week, Daxxie!" she said. "I'd rather be running for my life than bored to death."

I laughed too. "It's good to see you again, Qrysta."

"Likewise," she replied.

"So," I said, "talking of bastard: Grell or the Commandant?"

Qrysta snorted. "No contest."

"Huh? That's not what everyone else seems to think."

"Everyone else doesn't know shit."

I realized that she hadn't answered the question. "So? No contest— how, exactly?"

She tapped the side of her head with a forefinger. "Up here."

"Go on."

"Look, Daxx, I love Grello. We all do. I'd back him against anyone else. I don't care who that might be. But Commandant Bastard? Forget it! He's in Grell's head. He trained Grell up from a raw recruit. He beat the crap out of him again and again, in the castle yard in Brigstowe, in front of his mates. You were there. I mean, am I right?"

"You are."

"Doesn't matter if Grell is the better fighter now. And he is ridic-ulously good, by the way. He's been training all day every day, against the best, and crushing them all. Could even be better than Blunt, two-handed, for all we know—but we never will. Why? Because he knows he can't beat Blunt. He's desperate to get as good as he can. Result? He's overtrained. I keep telling him to ease off. And he keeps telling me to fuck off. He can't see the bigger picture, Daxx. Commandant Blunt has already won, without lifting a finger. It's all over bar the flattening."

I could see that she was absolutely sure about what she was saying.

I said, "So, you've got all your money on Blunt?"

"Gods, no," she said. "I could never bet against my crew."

That surprised me. I said, "You've bet on Grell?"

She shook her head at me in amazement. "Weren't you listening?"

"You're sitting this one out."

"Damn right, I am. I have no intention of losing my money, thank you, and no intention of rooting against my friend."

"Gotcha."

"What about you?" she said.

"Same," I said. "But I hope you're wrong. My heart's with the big guy."

"Yeah. Mine too."

Neither of us felt all that hopeful.

Qrysta sighed. "And on top of that, there's Jess," she said.

"What's up with her?"

"She's doesn't know anyone here but me. I train with her, when I can—which is hardly often, I'm so busy, and she'd train all day if she could. She's always bugging me, but I'm swamped up to my ears in godsdamn heralds. Thank the gods Evall is here. Thick as thieves, those two are, running around, getting up to all sorts of mischief."

I raised an eyebrow. "Anything serious?"

"How should I know? But he's a bookish lad and loves the libraries, while she can barely read. He's trying to teach her, but …"

"She'll have to learn if she's going to be a cadet."

"Oh, I've told her. Which makes her not sure about this whole cadet thing. She's keen to learn dual-wield, loves to spar with me, but all the rest of it …. You can see that it worries her. She'll be just about the youngest. And the smallest. And a girl. And a foreigner. And she won't know anyone in Mayport. Evall's staying here, until he can find a ship home to Normark. So, she'll be alone, and out of her comfort zone, and what does she know about the royal court, and manners, and formalities? She's the daughter of fisherfolk. Most of the other cadets are the sons of lordlings and knights. 'Who's this little upstart nobody from nowhere?' I mean, you can see it all already, can't you? Not to mention she'll be seen as the queen's pet. How many targets on your back can you have?"

I thought of my own schooldays, and said, "One is enough."

The way I said it made Qrysta look at me sharply. "Happy memories?"

"Some," I said, thinking of the learning and studying part, which I'd enjoyed—and because of which, I'd become a teacher myself. Other parts—not so much.

Qrysta got the message. "I guess you know the feeling. I'll just have to hope the other kids aren't too hard on her. They'll all be living in barracks, and even if I'm in the castle I won't be there to have her back most of the time—which she wouldn't want anyway, the other cadets thinking she had to hide behind me. Dammit, she's been through enough, poor kid."

I saw her point.

"Mind you," she said, brightening, "she's a quick learner, when it's anything practical. I told Oller all this, and he's been teaching her sneaking. As a way to take her mind off it. He says she's taken to it like a duck to water. Although that's kind of backfired. She can get close to her marks now without being noticed, so she's itching to try cutting purses. I said, 'You want to end up in the stocks again?' I dunno, Daxxie. She's quiet, and polite, and respectful, and keen, and butter wouldn't melt in her mouth—and a right handful. Talk about an iron fist in a velvet glove."

"And nearly a teenager," I pointed out.

Qrysta sighed. "And there's that," she agreed.

The door opened. Oller bustled in with an armful of boxes.

"Sorry about that," he said, setting everything down on the table, "I explained some facts of Eastbay life to our out-of-town visitors. Namely: You think where you are now is uncomfortable, chum? Well, do any of that nonsense again and you'll find yourself in a dungeon deep below our Lady of Eastbay's Castle, stretched out on her question-master's table by sweaty gentlemen in hoods, and some nasty-looking implements heating up on the coals."

"And?" Qrysta asked.

"They got the picture. Receiver's giving them the rest of the night in our lockup to contemplate it. So," he said, opening the chest and setting out its contents on the table, "turns out we picked up some interesting stuff on Wester Isle."

First, he opened the chest-within-the-chest, the one filled with heartstones. Each began to glow with its own-colored light. They were even more beautiful than I remembered.

"Biggest diamond I've ever seen, and that's a fact!" Oller said, as I reached for it. It was, indeed, huge—the size of a pigeon's egg. "Flawless," he said. "Clear as clear." I studied the gleaming jewel. A gentle, white spark slumbered deep within it—a spark, I knew, that could burst into white-hot flame when needed.

It made me smile just to look at it. "I know where this belongs," I said.

"Where?"

"With Marnie. For her oak staff. She's been looking high and low for a diamond heartstone for it. It'll pack a punch with this beauty powering it."

"She's all yours," Oller said, and I tucked the jewel into the pocket inside my jerkin, above my heart, next to Marnie's Infinite Notebook.

Watching me, Oller shook his head. "Worth a fortune, that diamond—and I say, 'Go on, off you go with it, then,' like it's nothing?! Not, 'Hoy, not so fast, chum, where's my cut?' I dunno what's happened to me; I really don't. I blame you two."

"As to these other heartstones," I said, looking through them, "they'll be the answers to many a mage's prayer. I suggest we sell them through the Guild of the Arcane Arts. I've met the Eastbay guildmaster. We have something in common: We're both foreigners. He'll steer me right. And we'll build up our bankroll. These won't go for coppers."

"They'd better not!" Oller snorted. "You won't see the likes of these again all in one place."

I thought about what he said, as I contemplated them, drinking in their beauty, each shining with its own light. All shades glowed out at us from the casket, from the densest violet of an amethyst to the ethereal red of a huge spinel. One of them glowed in two colors: a deep, blood red and the rich green of a spring meadow. I remembered how I'd thought of the heartstone that was now Shift's eye, when I'd first seen her, in the Thieves Guild trading room in Rushtoun. *Like the path of a sunset leading up a grassy hillside.* I picked the tourmaline up, and studied it. I unslung Shift, and compared the two heartstones.

Shift perked up immediately. *Whoa! What have we here...?!*
*Could almost be your twin.*

Shift did not reply. All her attention was on the other tourmaline. The closer I held them together the more their lights sought each other's out, and merged, in gentle swirls, as if they were exploring each other. We watched, as the red and green lights gathered in strength, and danced between them, flowing first this way, and then that. Eventually, the movement stopped, and both heartstones shone out like lanterns, green above and red below.

"Not this one," I said. "I can't let her go."

A warm glow of approval came up my arm from my staff.

"Spare battery?" Qrysta said.

"Yeah, mayhaps Neva could make you an amulet with that, and imbue it," Oller suggested. "Two of them, working together? Double your firepower!"

That thought made me wonder what else we could do with the other heartstones. I said, "Maybe we should keep a few back."

"They're portable enough," Qrysta said. "Rarer than rare."

Oller shrugged. "No need to sell 'em all at once."

We'd keep six back, we decided. We picked out the others, which I'd keep along with the tourmaline: a ruby, a fire opal, an amethyst, a topaz, and an olivine.

"Our good luck charms," I said.

"Yeah, well." Oller chuckled. "No doubt we'll be needing as much of *that* as we can get. Over to you," he added, closing the lid of the casket and handing it to me. He turned to the other boxes. "Now, this is the interesting stuff."

The oddities that we'd collected were just as I remembered them—and they looked no more 'interesting' now than they had when we'd first come across them, in the little side pile in the helldragon's hoard. But we knew that they were special, because they'd all reacted to my casting.

Each item, however nondescript it might look, was magic.

I asked, "You've had them checked out?"

"Yep. And not just by jewelwrights. Remember Junie?"

I knew the name, but couldn't place it.

He jogged my memory. "Esmeralda's fairy fucking godmother?"

"Oh, yes, right ..."

"She was the one as hid your tourmaline heartstone where I found it, in My Lady of Rushtoun's kneeler, in her chapel. Specializes in heartstones, does Junie. Knows everything about them. She knew when she found yours that it was a treasure. And that diamond you kept, *whoo!* Rarer than hen's teeth, diamond heartstones, and she'd never seen a finer. What Junie don't know about Divination isn't worth knowing, Marnie says."

He nodded at the little pile of trinkets on the table in front of us. "Some of them she could tell just at a glance, gawds know how. Ring of Speed, Brooch of Striking—just the things for you, Qrysta, eh? Speed through your foes, and your strikes guaranteed to hit home and hit hard: What more could you want?"

Qrysta's eyebrows rose. She picked up the ring, and the brooch, neither of which looked like anything much. "Well now," she said, slipping the ring on a finger, and pinning the brooch to her chest. She held her hand out in front of her and smiled at the ring.

"Others took her a bit of time for her to scry out, as she named it," Oller continued. "One of them, though, she couldn't work out at all. Turning it over and over in her hands, again and again, puzzling at it, muttering spells, even *biting* it; still couldn't figure it. She knew it was special, just didn't know in what way. It was me that found it!"

"We all know you're good at finding," Qrysta said.

"Complete bloody accident and all." Oller chuckled. "But I didn't tell her that, oh no. 'Finding's what I do,' I said, all casual like. She didn't buy it for a second. Fixed me with a stare as cold as Marnie's, then lifted her stave and laid a Truth on me. Damn thing bit me in the arse as sharp as a bloody ferret! I must've leaped a foot. 'You'd best not lie to me again, boy!' she said. I didn't."

"Which one is it, then?" I said, looking at the pile.

"We'll leave that till last. See if either of you can spot it. So, first up"—he picked out a thin, tattered glove—"pop this on, then, Q."

"It's too small," Qrysta said.

I said, "Not if it's magic."

She looked at me, puzzled, then understood. The glove grew to fit her hand as she slid it over her fingers. Only magic items do that. She looked at it, wiggling her fingers, trying to work out what was so special about it.

Oller said, "Feel anything?"

"No."

"Here," he said, holding his hand out for the glove. He put it on and crouched beside me. He gripped a leg of my chair, one-handed—then stood up, lifting me over his head.

"Whoa!" I gasped.

"I know! Not bad, eh?" Oller's voice came from below me. "Hold onto the seat, Daxx."

I did.

"One, two—*three!*"

On *three* I felt myself soaring towards the ceiling, before dropping back down. Oller caught me in the chair, again one-handed, and lowered me to the ground.

"*Very* impressive," Qrysta said. I could only splutter as my insides tried to settle themselves back down.

"Glove of Strength," Oller said, taking it off and handing it to me. "Imagine what Grell could do, wearing this. Could lift a mastodon. I'll have to warn him that it wears off quick, though, and won't work again for a while. And how about this, eh?" he said, reaching for a what looked like a cheap, pewter ring. "This one's for me." He put it on, and looked up at us with a grin. "Right, close your eyes."

We did.

A few seconds later, Oller said, fainter, "You can open them now."

120

We opened our eyes, and looked around for him.

He was nowhere to be seen.

"Where are you?" I said.

"Haven't moved, Daxxie!" he said, removing the ring, and then re-placing it. We could see him as plain as day. "I put my hand over my mouth to fool you. Just turn around this time," he said.

We did, and once again, Oller wasn't there.

"Ring of Blending, Junie says," Oller continued. "I melt into the background. Take your eye off me for a second and I'm gone. Even though I'm right here. It's not a Ring of Invisibility. Junie says there are no such things, sadly, but it's the next best thing. Just the thing for a sneaky type like yours truly, eh?"

"Perfect," Qrysta agreed.

"It runs out of power too, though, like the Glove of Strength, so I only wear it when I need." He slipped it into one of his many secret pockets. "It's good for ten or fifteen minutes, though. And if I can't make myself scarce in that much time, I *deserve* to get nabbed."

He picked up a grooved, iron band, which he handed to me. "How's about this one?"

I recognized it. It had reacted to my cast, on Wester Isle, by glittering and fizzing, so I knew that it was magic. It looked plain, and ordinary—just a dull iron hoop, with a deep groove running around its center. So dark a gray that was almost black, it was something you'd never look at twice. And wouldn't that, I thought, be exactly the way you'd *want* your magic gear to appear? Like that scruffy little glove: Nothing flashy, that people would notice and think, *Hullo, I'll have that,* or, *Now I wonder what that shiny thing is …?*

No. You'd want to sneak it past people.

Just as Oller was trying to sneak it past me now.

I said, "This is it, isn't it?"

Oller grunted, and then chuckled. "Can't fool you, eh, Daxx? 'Leave it till last,' and do I—bollocks! Well spotted, matey. I should know better by now than to try and slip a puzzle by you. All right, then, Mr. Cleverclogs: Show us what you've got."

What I had wasn't much. I cast Reveals at the iron band, as I had on Wester Isle; and, again, it glittered and fizzed in response; but it revealed nothing as the cast faded.

Well, nothing more than that it was magic, which I knew already.

My Divination skills were poor, but I tried them anyway. Again, nothing, beyond a weak glitter and fizz that were gone almost as soon as they appeared.

I heard Oller chuckle. He was enjoying my confusion. I wasn't ready to give up quite yet.

I turned the band over in my hands. I couldn't see anything remarkable about it at all. I felt it, carefully, all the way round, inside and out. Its edges were curved. It was solid, but not heavy. A thought occurred to me. It was, clearly, old. Who knew how long it had been in the helldragon's hoard? Decades? Centuries? Possibly—but there was not a single fleck of rust on it.

Interesting.

I held it close to my eye. I could see no sign of any coating on it, to seal it against the air. Surely, I thought, iron would have rusted. So, was it, indeed, iron? If not, then what was this metal that reacted to magic by glittering and fizzing? I hesitated for a moment, wondering if it might be dangerous, then hoped for the best, and slipped it on over my left wrist. It shrank, gently, to become a comfortable fit.

Time to check out its reaction to magic, then, while wearing it.

I raised Shift, and cast Divination on the bracelet. I could tell that she, too, was curious about this plain iron band.

As before, when I had cast Divination on it in the helldragon's hoard, I learned nothing; but, as before, the bracelet sparked and fizzed briefly, throwing off little gold flashes and glints. I could feel them jumping into my wrist. I slipped the bracelet off. There was no damage to my skin.

I checked it over, again and again, then shook my head.

"What am I missing?" I said, handing it back to Oller.

He chuckled. "You won't believe it when you see it. I'd never have found it in a million years, and I'm good at finding; it was pure luck. Ready?"

He held out the bracelet on the palm of his hand and looked up at me.

I nodded. "Ready."

"I had it in my hand like this, and I thought there was something on it, a smudge, so I licked my finger," he said, licking his finger, "and wiped it, like this." He rubbed it with his forefinger. "And I could swear it moved. I thought, *Hullo.* So, I put my other hand on it, and …"

He covered the bracelet with his other hand, and twisted his palms together, in opposite directions, as if unscrewing a jar.

He opened his hands, and held them out.

A half-size bracelet rested on each palm.

"Whoa!" I said. I hadn't seen that coming.

"Take a look," Oller said, passing one slender hoop to me.

I examined it.

It was perfect—by which I mean that I could see no sign that it had ever been anything but the metal hoop I was holding. It looked as if it had been made that way. There was nothing to show that it had ever been joined to the other hoop. Both edges were smooth, and rounded—and identical in every way.

"That's … something," I said.

"Ain't it just?" Oller agreed, happily.

"The question is, though: what?"

"Pop it on and I'll show you." He handed the other band to Qrysta, and said, "Put this on, Qrys, and stand over there."

"Right," Oller said, when Qrysta and I were at opposite sides of the room. "Cast something at yours, Daxx."

I raised Shift, and cast a Sizzle at my bracelet.

It sparked and fizzed and glowed yellow—and at the same instant, so did Qrysta's. She jumped in surprise.

I said, "Are you all right?"

"Yes, fine. Didn't expect *that*, is all. Doesn't hurt. But I can tell what it is, there's no mistaking it. Shock magic."

"You could throw thunderbolts at it, all she'd feel is a crackle," Oller said. "Try cold, or heat."

I tried both.

Just as she'd felt the jabs of electricity, she felt the cold, or the heat, as her bracelet glowed first blue, and then red. I then cast a Full Heal at mine, and hers, too, gleamed green, and she laughed as she felt the warmth of it spreading up her arm.

She looked across at me, and smiled.

We both understood what we had.

Qrysta said, "Comms …!"

Oller said, puzzled, "Eh?"

"Communications," I explained. "I can send her messages. Cold means go north, hot means south, damp means come back now—or

123

whatever we decide on in advance. And in combination, say, *x-y-z* could mean one thing, and *a-f-d* another. We could get pretty specific …"

"Don't need it," Qrysta said.

I looked at her. "What? This is *gold*, Qrys!"

"Red is dot, because it rhymes with hot. Green is dash. Because, well, green is the opposite of red. Means go, not stop. Makes it easy to remember which is which. So now, all we have to do is learn Morse code."

I said, "Now why didn't I think of that?"

"What's that, when it's at home?" Oller said.

We explained. He got it soon enough. "Clever, that," he said. "Foreign stuff, eh?"

"Indeed," I said.

"Only problem is," Qrysta said, "Daxx can send to me, but I can't send back, I don't have a staff."

"Don't need one," Oller said. "Tap it with your Ring of Evasion."
She did.

Her bracelet, and mine, glowed with a blue that matched the stones set into her ring.

"So, if I try this …" she said, touching her band to her necklace of ancient amber squares.

Our bands glowed amber in response.

"Amber dot, blue dash?" Qrysta suggested.

"Fine with me," I agreed.

"Junie said she'd heard of these, but had never seen one," Oller said. "She didn't know if they actually existed, or were just tall tales. What we have here, she says, is a Link of Impartment. She said, think of it like a link in a chain, but a chain that doesn't need all the other links between one end and the other. Just this one. Or rather, these two. Of which, it is both."

I said they could go on ahead and I'd meet them for supper at the tavern, but Oller insisted on accompanying me to Faldruti's house, so Qrysta came along too. Oller didn't want me carrying a chest of priceless heartstones through a town that was crawling with thieves. "They're not going to try anything when they see you're with me," he said. "Some of 'em would, given half the chance, and there are some tasty operators in Eastbay at the moment, I can tell you. Best thieves in the realm have gathered here, same as the best knights, and archers, and other hopefuls. They know what's allowed and what's not, while the tournament's on, but when have rules ever bothered thieves, eh? Specially for a chance at what you're carrying—a once-in-a-lifetime score, that'd be."

Tob opened the door to us, and led us into Faldruti's study. The Archmage was speechless at the sight of the chest of heartstones. He told us that he would entrust them to the Guild's Master of Enchanters, who would sell them on our behalf. He offered us wine, and food, but we thanked him, and told him that we already had arrangements for the evening. Tob showed us out into the twilight, grumbling about all the tuddy blorists tuttering the clown up, and plurning the tace into a pear bit, before closing the door behind us. We made our way through the winding backstreets of Eastbay to The Ship Aground.

# II

## A Death in the Family

There was no possible way that the Royal Tournament could be completed in a single day. Competitors had flocked to Eastbay from all over the realm and beyond. There wasn't a room to be had in town for love nor money. The fields beyond the town walls were overflowing with tents, and pavilions, and stables, and smithies. Some categories had so many entrants that the victors were going to have to fight their way through ten bouts or more. There were rich prizes to be won, which encouraged more than a few competitors to enter into multiple events: two-handed, dual-wield, sword-and-board, jousting, knives, unarmed combat. There were also a number of different target skills, ranging from slingshot to spear-throwing to several types of archery. "Give them a fair chance," Commandant Bastard told the Congress of the Royal and Ancient Company of Heralds. "They've come all this way."

The judging Chief Herald began to object, *"With all due respect, Sire—"* Commandant Bastard cut him off, saying "Pick your weapon, Master Herald, and take a turn with me. Then tell me how many more bouts you think you could stand in one day." The offer was politely declined. Three days it would indeed be, the heralds agreed without further debate. The knockout rounds would be completed on the first two days. The Grand Finals would take place on the third morning, to

126

be completed before the Champions Feast—which would begin after the Main Event: Commandant Bastard versus Grell, the Best Bloody Orc He'd Ever Seen.

"It was all I could do not to laugh," Qrysta said. "But it 'doesn't do' to laugh at a Congress of Heralds. That would be bad form." She put down her mug of ale, after a long draught, and wiped her mouth with the back of her sleeve. "I wish I could fight in the damn thing, let off a little steam," she growled.

I knew what she meant. That was where Qrysta belonged: in combat. Sword-dancing, dual-wielding, dodging, striking, free and in her element. But during the Royal Tournament she would be on duty. Esmeralda would be here, there, and everywhere, mingling with the crowds, talking to all and sundry, high and low, commoner or noble. As the Captain of the Royal Guard, Qrysta would be watching her queen's back every second she was in public. And while we knew that the public loved Esmeralda, and that she had them eating out of her hand, we also knew that all it took was one.

"I bet you do," I agreed.

She inhaled deeply and let out a long sigh. "I'll be glad when it's over and we can relax."

"Bet Grell feels the same, eh?" Oller said.

Qrysta grunted agreement.

I said, "You think he has no chance too?"

"Nah, mate," Oller said, with a shake of his head.

"Well, he's got a *chance*," he reconsidered. "Two, in fact: fat and slim. Funny how those mean the same thing, in this instance."

I was beginning to feel sorry for Grell. If Oller, as well as Qrysta, thought that Commandant Bastard was inevitably going to beat him, who was I to argue? They knew Grell better than anyone.

"Well," I said, "he'll give a good account of himself; we all know that."

"He will indeed, gods bless the big lug," Oller agreed.

Once again we had the snug bar to ourselves, a fire burning merrily in its hearth. Sounds carried in through the serving hatch from the main parlor. There were many more of them that evening, and they were much louder than I'd ever heard in The Ship Aground. There were bursts of laughter, and voices, some of them shouting to make themselves heard above all the others that were singing.

As befitted a tavern in a port town, the songs they were roaring out were sea shanties—in more than one language, as far as I could tell. Feet thumped onto the floor, in time to the stamp-and-go choruses, all accompanied by a high-pitched pipe squeaking merrily away. Oller poked his head out through the hatch, and finally caught the innkeeper's attention. "Blimey, it's heaving in there," he said, as he brought another foaming pitcher over to our table. "Mine host says if we hadn't ordered ahead we'd stand no chance of supper; cooks are run off their feet. It'll be here in a minute, and I told him to keep the ale coming." He sat back down as the door opened and Jess hurried in, followed by Evall. Their cheeks were flushed and their eyes were shining. They were excited, as if they had something delicious to tell us. Little Guy emerged from under the table to greet Jess, who scratched his ears while he wagged his scruffy tail, happy to see her.

"What'ch you two scallywags been up to, then?" Oller asked them, sensing their excitement. They were about to tell all when they saw me, sitting between Qrysta and Oller.

Their faces fell, and they immediately became serious.

They stood, politely, looking from me, to Oller, to Qrysta, waiting for some kind of clue as to how to behave.

Who, I could see that they were wondering, was this shady-looking, foreign-looking character …? Should they wait outside? Was this a private occasion, something they didn't belong in …?

"Hello, Jess," I said, in a shady, foreign-sounding voice. "Hello, Evall. How's things?"

They were surprised that I knew their names.

Jess recovered first. "Very well, sir," she said, bobbing a little curtsey. "Thank you, sir."

"Yes," Evall said. "Sir."

"You'll join us for supper?"

They could see that Oller and Qrysta were amused. They couldn't think why and looked from one to the other, baffled.

"Come on, lass," Oller said, chuckling. "What have I been teaching you?! Looking's just the start of it—you need to be *seeing*. Use that sharp mind o' yours, and them sharp eyes. He knows you, it seems? Well, may be as you might know him?"

Evall had spent little time in our company, compared with Jess, so it was no surprise that she worked it out first. Her eyes narrowed, and she looked around for clues. It didn't take her long to see the ordinary-looking staff propped up beside the less-than-ordinary-looking "traveler" that I now appeared to be. Shift didn't look like Shift, any more than I looked like Daxx; but Jess had been with us on Dawn Isle, when we scouted the harbor town in the Cove and I'd made us all blend into the scenery under our Glamours as pirates. She put two and two together quickly enough. *Oller, Qrysta; The Ship Aground; why would they be having a friendly ale with some stranger—and one with a staff…?*

Her eyes grew round in recognition, but before she could say my name, I held up my hand, and said, "And *nobody* must know I'm in town. And that means not saying my name. But, yes, Jess, it's me."

"Wow!" Jess said. "That's incredible …"

"You can tell Evall," I said, "but in a whisper. I wouldn't be doing this if I didn't have to."

Jess nodded. She got the picture. This was serious. She whispered in Evall's ear, and he turned and looked at me, shocked.

"And if anyone comes asking, or says they're a friend o' his," Oller instructed her, "say you haven't seen him. He left town, you don't know where he went, and he hasn't come back yet. The whole town was waiting on the docks with Esmeralda when we sailed in on *The Red Rose*, right? It wouldn't take a good snout long to learn from the townsfolk about you two, and how you're friends of his. And then they go and find you, and ease into conversation …"

Jess and Evall exchanged glances.

"We won't say a word," she said. "To anyone."

Evall nodded, and added, "Promise."

"I know you won't," Qrysta said, with a smile to put them at their ease. "He'll explain when he's ready to. Meantime: Sit yourselves down, and help yourselves to some ale, and tell us what you've been up to."

They sat, and Jess poured two flagons from our pitcher. The serving hatch darkened as the innkeeper and his son loaded trays of food into it, which they passed through to us. Jess and Evall helped Oller bring them over, and we all fell to with a purpose. There was, as I had expected, eel and shoreweed stew, and it tasted better than ever.

The *something delicious* that Jess and Evall had to tell us, between mouthfuls and passing morsels down to Little Guy, was, basically, everything that they'd seen and heard that day, one splendid sight after another, all over town. Jugglers, knife-throwers, stilt-walkers;

performing dogs, fire-eaters, tumblers; fights broken up by the town guards; fishwives yelling at each other and pulling each other's hair; a cook kicking over a rival's brazier and setting fire to a tailor's stall. Overexcited children running riot. An honest-to-gods *duel*, between two lordlings in their finery, one in blue, one in red—"Only they were both terrible!" Jess said, delighted. "Lots of striding about, and posturing, and swishing their cloaks, and swapping insults, and glaring, and preening, but *pathetic* swordplay. The crowd let them know it and started jeering. Then their seconds yelled at the crowd to shut up, and strutted about threatening us. And we all yelled back. And this woman fought her way through, and ran up—well, *waddled*, more like, her big belly about to pop—and accused one of them of getting her up the duff, and the crowd roared, and booed, and his opponent said, 'That's my sister, you—' What was it he called him, Eev?"

"Vile seducer," Evall said.

"And he replied, 'Finally, there'll be a bastard with honorable blood in your miserable family, Uncle Fartface!' And the crowd hooted, and Uncle Fartface attacked, and the woman started beating him—not her brother, the other one, the vile seducer—over the head, and we were all in hysterics."

Evall took over the story. "Then this horse trotted up, only it was two people in a horse costume, and pranced about, and kicked, and got in the way—and then two acrobats, somersaulting in, and doing cartwheels and flinging each other around."

"And the woman gasped," Jess jumped in, "and staggered, and an older woman helped her lie down, and she writhed, and screeched, while it was all going on around her, and eventually the older woman pulled a baby out from under her skirts—only it was a silly-looking hand puppet, bawling. Well, the older woman was doing the bawling for it, obviously. It was mayhem; the crowd was in stitches."

"And then," Evall continued, "a wild, skinny old man with no trousers ran in, holding his hat out, and if you didn't give him a copper he'd turn around, and bend over, and flip his shirttails up, and show you his bottom."

"And everyone he showed it to shrieked," Jess took over, "and then laughed, because he had a demon painted on it. Two big eyes staring at you, with red horns above, and a roaring mouth with a long red tongue sticking out of his—you know what. So they all forked out a copper or something."

"And how long," Oller said, "afore folks noticed they'd had their purses cut?"

Jess's smile faded as she thought about it. Oller had obviously been teaching her the basics of his trade. *There's nothing better than a diversion. When their attention is all looking the other way they won't notice you.*

"No one had, as far as I know," she said.

"Good," Oller said. "Then I won't have to notify the Receiver about them mummers. As long as they keep the queen's peace, they're welcome in Eastbay. Wouldn't mind seeing them myself."

"I 'spect they'll do it again tomorrow," Jess said.

"Hope so," Evall said. "My sides hurt from laughing."

We ate. We drank. We listened to the sea shanties being roared out in the parlor beyond the serving hatch while the piper tootled their tunes. We had to raise our voices to talk over them any time we had something to say. We filled ourselves up with food, and ale, and each other's company. Only two days before I'd been drained to empty, strong though I had been in the Form. Now, I could feel myself recovering. Yes, there were challenges facing me. They could wait, I decided, for another day. This night I would set them aside, and enjoy the company of my friends.

Which was all very well for me to say. It wasn't up to me.

It was Shift who reminded me that my challenges weren't going to set *me* aside. Only when I reached for her, absent-mindedly, did I realize that she had been trying to get my attention. As soon as my hand closed around her, she berated me.

*You have ninety days!*

*Okay, fine, this day's over; I'll deal with that tomorrow—*

*Tomorrow you will have eighty-nine.*

*Give me a break, will you?*

*There is no break, Daxx. You are avoiding the issue.*

*I'm just recharging the batteries! Damn it, I don't even know where to begin! Why are you bugging me?*

*Somebody has to. You have ninety days. Concentrate. Put everything into it. Or you won't have another night like this ever again. Don't take the break before you complete the task.*

"You all right, matey?" Oller's voice broke in on our private argument.

I felt myself jump as I looked up at him.

"Whoa!" he said. "Something on your mind? You were miles away."

I nodded. "Lots," I said.

"Care to share?"

I sighed. "If you can come up with anything, Ols, well, I'd love to hear it."

Shift, in my hands, shivered her approval. *That's more like it.*

Oller said, "Try me."

"All right." I took a deep breath, and began. "I have a task to accomplish. But I don't know what that task is. And if I don't do it, I'm … well. Finished. I have a place to go, to do that task, but I have no idea where that place is. Or how to get there. And I don't have a lot of time. Three months, to be exact."

As I was speaking, the hubbub in the parlor bar, beyond the serving hatch, ceased. Something almost passing for silence had fallen as the last sea shanty ended. Everyone at our table heard what I'd just said.

"What task?" Qrysta asked.

"I won't know till I get there."

"Get where?" Jess said.

I looked at her small, serious face. "Well, that's the thing, Jess," I said, "I don't know. All I know is that it's called the Valley of the Moon."

The name, of course, meant nothing to her.

"And I don't know where it is, or how to find it. Let alone what I have to do when I reach it."

Silence fell at our table.

Evall looked up at me, frowning. "Mondthal?" he said. "Why in the name of any god would you want to go there?!"

I said, "What?"

"That's what it's called, in the old language," Evall said. "Mondthal. Moon Valley."

I felt a jolt of excitement from Shift. I said, "Do you know it?"

"No," he said. "No one does. But we know where it is. Vaguely. I mean, we know where it's meant to be."

"Where?"

"In the Ice Lands."

"In Normark?"

"Yes. Although … well, they're kind of *beyond* Normark. Far to the north. Where the moon sleeps. And …" he tailed off.

"And?"

"And no one goes."

I said, "Why not?"

He seemed reluctant to answer. When he did, he said, "Because no one who does ever comes back."

Normark. Pieces of the puzzle slotted into place, one after another.

Archmage Faldruti had roamed this world over, from the south, heading ever west and north, learning the lores and languages of the realms he passed through. He'd never heard of the Valley of the Moon in any of them. He'd never traveled further north than Eastbay.

Logically, therefore, my destination lay to the north.

Where it was known in another language; one of the many languages that I now knew were spoken in this world. And hadn't I just heard sea shanties being sung in tongues that I didn't recognize?

*Mondthal.*

I'd been surfacing. I'd been looking at what I'd been told; not probing any deeper, into the gaps, at what had *not* been said. Which was where the answers lay.

I felt like kicking myself. I should have known better than that. I was meant to be good at puzzles.

I looked at Evall and said, "How would I get there?"

"Keep going north," Evall replied, with a shrug.

"A long way?"

"I don't know. It's beyond where the maps end. I've never been much north of Sondehafn. There's folk there in town who have; they might be able to tell you."

North, then. Normark. The Ice Lands.

*Well, now,* I thought. *I know where to start.*

Another sea shanty began in the parlor bar, and the din of it soon drowned out our conversation.

I turned to Qrysta, leaned over, and shouted in her ear. "I'll be needing *The Red Rose*. And I'll want her the moment the tournament is over, because I'm not going without you and Grell."

"As if we'd let you!" Qrysta shouted back. "She's all yours. Gelbert's got her crewed and victualed and ready to sail. And you'll like the new captain."

"What's he like?"

"*She.* You'll see for yourself, soon enough. The strange thing is that she's her *old* captain. The crew thought she was dead. Her officers mutinied and threw her out the window of her cabin, and fed her to the sharks—according to her parrot, anyway, who was the only witness. 'Out the window, out the window! Sharks! Sharks!' the parrot had squawked for the rest of the voyage." She laughed. "Of course, no one believed a parrot. But rumors circulated. The crew are thrilled to see her alive after all—if a bit, well … wary. And they're keen to know what happened."

I said, "What's her story?"

Qrysta shrugged. "I expect she'll tell us if she feels inclined. All I know is, Esmeralda sent for me one morning and told me that we had our new captain, and to muster the crew and wait for her. Seems she'd presented herself to the queen and requested a private audience."

I was surprised. "And Esmeralda granted her one?"

Qrysta said, "She's Coven."

"Ah." That explained it.

"It's her ship, and she's her captain," Qrysta continued. "It takes a lot to break that bond. *The Blood Rose*, it was, Gelbert told me, before she took it, and renamed it *The Red Rose*, after herself. Red Rozlyn, people call her. Her hair being the color of flame. So it fits her, and she fits it, though whether that's her real name, or one she chose for the purpose, who can say?"

It all sounded … coincidental. What was it Jewelwright Neva had said to me in Niblunhaem, the day we'd first met?

*I don't trust Mr. Coincidence further than I can throw him.*

I said, "Where did she come from, this Red Rozlyn?"

"Not from around here."

"And she just turns up here, having been fed to the sharks? And breezes in on Esmeralda and immediately gets her ship back?"

"Pretty much. As far as I can tell."

I thought it over. "So?" I said. "Do you want to sail off under her command, trusting everything's aboveboard?"

Qrysta's eyebrows rose, as she looked at me. "You have another ship?"

"Well, no …"

"Then we take the one we do have. Look, we all have our secrets, Daxx."

"Yes, but … I like to know who I'm dealing with."

Qrysta smiled. She leaned forward and patted the back of my hand.

"Well, my friend," she said, "when does anyone ever truly know that?"

I frowned at her, surprised. "I know you, Qrys. And I know Grell, and Oller, and Marnie, and Ez."

She held my eyes, and said, "Do you?"

I realized what she was saying. I admitted, "No, not everything. There are some blanks. Of course there are. But those don't matter, because I know the most important thing."

"Which is?"

"That you've got my back."

She nodded and smiled. "That I have," she agreed.

"That's all that matters, really," I said. "And Ez vouches for her, this Red Rozlyn?"

"She does."

"Then that's good enough for me. So, next stop, Normark?"

"Looks that way," Qrysta said. "Evall will be happy. We can take him home."

"He will," I agreed, glancing at the lad who was deep in conversation with Jess. Their heads were bent towards each other so that they could hear above the noise of singing and carousing coming in through the serving hatch. "Best not tell him yet, though. We need to keep this under wraps as long as we can."

"I gotcha," Qrysta said.

So that, it seemed, was that.

I sat back, and supped my ale, and picked at whatever food was in front of me. I was content, for the first time since I'd ridden out into the Deepwoods. I had a quest. I had a destination. I still had little information, but no doubt I'd gather more on the way.

I'd made a start.

It was a fine evening. I hardly spoke as my friends chatted and sea shanties echoed in through the serving hatch. I listened, and laughed, and wound down, feeling—as we all stood, and said our goodbyes, and went our separate ways—that, at last, I knew what was what. Out in the cool, dark backstreets of Eastbay I stopped. I listened to the sounds of revelry coming from the market square. I inhaled the smells of cooking. Stars shone overhead in the black sky. Low on the horizon drifting clouds obscured the waxing moon. I headed back to Velaryn's house, thinking it all over and wondering what lay ahead, across the North Sea, in Normark and beyond, in the Ice Lands.

I made my way through familiar byways, passing few townsfolk. I had eaten, and drunk, and was thinking as I walked; and my mind was empty, comfortably so, as I came to the back door of her apothecary shop. The lantern above it was lit, as Vel had told me it would be, to guide me home. All I had to do was knock. I reached for the pestle-shaped iron knocker, and something slammed through my back.

I pitched forwards, gasping in shock, my immobilized hand dropping Shift. I looked down and saw an arrowhead sticking out of my right shoulder. It glinted in the lantern's light, white and cold and flecked with my blood.

Another blow punched into my left leg and I slid to the ground. Before I knew it I was being kicked in the ribs, savagely. I could hear my bones cracking under the blows. I was paralyzed, unable to move, stunned by the pain. Strong hands turned me onto my back. A furious, small form knelt across my chest, smacking at my face, forehand and then backhand, its knees pinning me to the ground. When the blows stopped, and my head was no longer being battered, I froze as I felt the point of a dagger at my throat.

"Why?!" Horm shouted down at me, his face inches from mine. "Why'd you do it?!"

Small he might have been but he was far stronger than I was, not just from his position astride my chest, but also from the rage that was possessing him.

I was unable to speak, let alone ask, *Do what?*

His dagger carved a line across my windpipe. I felt blood seep from the wound. In my head I could feel Shift screaming for me to get hold of her so she could defend me, but she was out of my reach.

He leaned in, his mouth next to my ear, and snarled, "You'd better not lie to me!"

He waited. I felt his chest heaving above mine. I couldn't reply, so I nodded, to show that I understood the message. Then I lay there, as submissive and unthreatening as possible, until he made the next move.

He leaned back up, and stared down at me. "You're a fucking healer," he said, lowering the point of his dagger between my eyes, and standing it on my forehead. "If you live, you can heal yourself, right? So put up with the pain and think about that, and pray that you *do* live. And if you don't: Who gives a shit about a few broken ribs? They'd be the least you deserve. I'd break every damn one of them!"

I had no idea, of course, why he was so angry. Or why he was attacking me. Or what he thought I'd done. All I knew was that he was itching for an excuse to kill me.

"I'll give you one chance," he continued. "*One.* And you can't get away until I let you, so make the most of it or you're fucking *dead*, chum! Them arrows I shot into you are silver, and so's this knife!"

Out of the corner of my eye I glanced at the arrowhead sticking out of my shoulder and saw its gleaming point. Among my scattered thoughts, I found somewhere to start. "Silver doesn't matter," I gasped.

He froze.

"I've lost the Gift," I said.

He frowned.

"I'm not a Were anymore, Horm," I explained.

He said nothing.

"*Any* arrow would disable me. You don't need silver ones. Why are you doing this? What do you want?"

I could see the confusion in his dark eyes. "I want to know why you did it."

"Did what?"

"Killed her!" he shouted.

"What?" I said, shocked. "Killed who?"

He stared at me, murder in his eyes. "You know damn well who!"

"Horm!" I said, each word hurting more than the last. "I don't, I really don't. I have no idea. What's happened, why are you doing this to me? I thought we were friends!"

His face recomposed itself. In what little light that was being thrown down from the lantern above Vel's door I saw his eyes narrow, and his expression harden. "So did I."

It was a challenge—as if I had betrayed our friendship. I lay still, knowing that my life was in his hands.

"And you do *this* to me!" he added.

I shook my head. "Do what? Please, Horm, explain. If I've offended you, I'm sorry, just—"

"Offended?" he interrupted. "That's what you call it? *Offended?*" He jabbed his knife into my neck again. I had no idea what it was that he thought that I'd done, that made him think I deserved to die. I knew that I hadn't done anything.

Therefore, someone else had.

So, I needed to divert his anger away from me, before he shoved his blade through my gullet. I said, with difficulty—because it's not easy talking with a knife point in your neck, and someone sitting astride your broken ribs so that every breath hurts almost beyond bearing—"Whatever you think I've done, Horm, it wasn't me. If you kill me, maybe you won't find out who *did* do it. I'll help you if I can. I promise. Like you helped me, leading me into the Deepwoods and handing me over to Urngra."

He'd been relaxing, listening, but when I said her name, he went rigid and snarled, and I could feel his knife arm trembling with tension as he held himself back from the killing thrust.

I knew then what had happened. I could read it in his eyes.

I couldn't say it. He would think that I knew because *I'd* killed her.

I hadn't, of course. But I knew who, or rather what, had.

I wanted to tell him how sorry I was. I couldn't, because he'd think I was apologizing for having done it. All I could do was lie there and wait for his next move.

"Yeah," he said. "I handed you over to her. And you killed her!!"

"What?" I said, feigning surprise. "Urngra's dead? No! Who—it wasn't me, Horm, I swear! She helped me, just as you helped me. I'd *never* hurt her!"

"Yeah? So why are you creeping about town in disguise?!" he challenged.

I said, "I can explain."

"No fucking need!" he snorted. "Trying to fool me—well that's never going to work, pal! Woodfolk eyes see through those cheap mage tricks o' yourn."

He was wriggling about on top of me again, unable to stop himself driving his knees into me. I felt that I was about to pass out from the pain. I couldn't let that happen. He needed answers or I was dead. He needed the truth.

I said, "I wouldn't stand a chance in a fight with Urngra, Horm. She was way stronger than me. We fought on the way to the village."

That shocked him. He stopped kneeing my broken ribs.

"Huh?"

"I Turned. Into the Form. I'd been trudging after her for hours; I was exhausted. I couldn't keep up with her on two legs, so I went onto four. The moment she saw me in the Form she launched herself at me. She beat the crap out of me, Horm! She didn't like Weres. She warned me never to do that again. I couldn't have killed her, in the Form or out of it."

I could see the confusion in Horm's eyes. I could see that he was thinking, *Why was I telling him this, that Urngra and I had fought? Would a murderer admit that?*

I took advantage of his hesitation, and said, "I didn't know until you told me just now that she'd been killed. But I do know who did it."

His eyes widened in surprise. "Eh?"

"I'll tell you everything I know," I said. "And you can make up your own mind. Believe me, or not. Take my staff so I can't use magic against you. I'm as upset as you are to hear she's dead, Horm. I owe her my life. Look—let me up, all right? And we can go inside and my friend will bear witness that I'm telling the truth."

Horm glared down at me. I could see that he didn't know what to think.

"They're my enemies as much as they are yours," I said. "I need to destroy them, before they destroy me."

He studied me, his dark eyes flicking from side to side as he searched mine.

"I'm listening," he said.

He got up off my chest and picked up Shift. He watched as, with difficulty, I levered myself to my feet.

I knocked. Velaryn answered the door.

Her smile of welcome faded as she saw the silver arrows sticking through me.

"This is my friend Horm," I told her, in gasps. "There's been a death in his family. We need to help him."

She stood aside and held the door open for us.

I limped in, Horm following.

Velaryn's apothecary skills soon soothed my pain. She gave me potions, and rubbed my skin with a salve, and eased the arrows out of my shoulder and thigh, while Horm fidgeted, in a state of wretchedness somewhere between fury and guilt. I didn't need Divination to read his thoughts. If I hadn't killed Urngra, he'd made me suffer unnecessarily. But who else could have chewed her poor body like some puppy's toy but a Were? Which would have to be me. Case closed, surely?

As Velaryn worked on my wounds, I asked Horm why I would kill her.

He had no answer, except that *that was what Weres did*. They killed and ate. And Urngra knew that, which was why she'd attacked me and told me never to Turn in her presence again. Weres aren't to be trusted. They may be your friend, on two legs, but in the Form—they wouldn't know you from any other meal.

I told Horm that they had been hunting me, too.

*Who?* he demanded.

I told him.

He listened as I related everything I had been through since he had left me at Urngra's hovel. I was the Wild Hunt's quarry. They had lost my onward trail, but, backtracking, must have found the one that had brought me to the village. That trail had also been Urngra's. They must have followed it to its source, rather than picking up my later trail, which I'd taken every care to conceal as I ran in the opposite direction, north, rather than south, the way I'd come—as the Voice in the vault had advised me.

She'd been found, he said, by Woods Kin, splayed and broken-backed, bitten and beaten and pulped. The limbs of the trees above had been sheared off. Out of the sky, then, she had fallen. The Wild Hunt had tracked her, and seized her, and killed her, and let her drop, the weight of her body breaking the branches as she fell.

Velaryn handed Horm a potion, which he supped without thinking. His thoughts were elsewhere.

We could see him gather them, and focus. "And you know where to find them?"

"Not exactly, but I know where to start looking for them."

He nodded. "Then I'm coming with you."

For some reason, I said, "There's no need—"

He jumped to his feet. "What d'you mean, there's no need?!" he shouted. He glared at me, his hand on the hilt of his dagger. "*Nobody kills my cousin and goes unpunished!*" He held my eyes, daring me to contradict him, his chest heaving with anger.

"Horm," I said, "you're coming with me. And I'll be glad to have you."

He glared from me to Velaryn, and back again, then sat back down. Without a word he handed me Shift, and at last I could cast Heals on myself. *I've got this*, she let me know, as warmth flooded my wounds and bruises. *Gods above and below, are you a mess ...!*

I thanked her as I felt my broken ribs knitting together and the pain of Horm's assault easing away. Velaryn topped up Horm's cup with whatever calming potion it was that she knew that he needed and he drank.

He lowered his cup, and growled, "Right. Where do we find these bastards?!"

# 12

## The Royal Tournament

I didn't recognize Jack Blunt when he walked out onto the Field of Honor the next morning, escorted by a phalanx of heralds. My attention was on them, in their dazzling scarlet-and-gold tabards, and blue-and-purple hose, and white-plumed black hats. Spring was in the air. The sun shone in a cloudless sky. We were surrounded by color, and pageantry, and excitement, so I hardly noticed the large person in black in their midst. Trumpeters, almost as gaudy as the heralds, flanked them—long, beautifully embroidered banners hanging from their instruments. They blew a fanfare, signaling the beginning, at long last, of the Royal Tournament.

The crowd roared its appreciation.

The wait was finally over. *Now* for some fireworks!

As one, the heralds turned on their heels and marched away, in perfect synchronization, to the eight points of the compass, where they halted exactly as the fanfare ended. The crowd fell silent for the Proclamation. As one, at the tops of their voices, the heralds announced *The Commencement; Of the Noble Tourney; Commanded by Her Gracious Majesty, Queen Esmeralda; Under the direction of the Grand Marshal of the Lists, The Commandant of the Royal Army; Whose Word is Law on this Field of Honor; And which None may Dispute; On pain of Disgrace, Disqualification, and Death.*

The crowd cheered—and I looked again at the huge figure at the center of the arena, who was now bowing in acknowledgement. I couldn't believe my eyes. *That* was Commandant Bastard?? He was a completely different shape from the Jack Blunt that I knew. Not only did he seem half a foot taller, which was clearly impossible, but it was also as if his upper body had inverted itself. The broad chest was broader. The formerly bulging stomach was now as trim as a dancer's. He moved with an easy, youthful gait, up on his toes—not the middle-aged, back-on-his-heels stroll that I associated him with. As a raw recruit in the training yard of Brigstowe Castle, I'd learned the hard way that that slow stroll was deceptive, and that Blunt was as fast on his feet as a greyhound when he wanted to be. But now he also *looked* fast, as well as lean and mean—and, when I thought about it, more like a wolf than I ever had.

Perhaps the scariest thing about him was that he was smiling. Commandant Bastard rarely smiled, as far as I could remember. When he did, it was a smile that you really didn't want to return, because he might take it personally and demand to know what you thought you were laughing at. And that would be painful. He was enjoying himself. He looked as relaxed as Queen Esmeralda did. This, he clearly thought, was going to be fun.

"*Whoa ...!*" I heard Qrysta mutter beside me.

She was, as befitted the Captain of the Queen's Guards, in the royal box, seated right behind Esmeralda. The flowers of the realm's nobility occupied the front row to either side of their queen. Esmeralda chatted amiably with her lords and ladies, listening attentively, appreciating, laughing at their remarks, making them all feel like her new best friend and determined to protect her. *The loveliest life there ever was or ever will be,* her fairy godmother had laid the blessing on her, on the day of her naming. It was a life that made all our lives richer.

I was unrecognizable as myself, being under a Glamour as an envoy from some overseas land. I'd taken care to make myself look dull. I didn't want to be noticed, or drawn into conversation. No one had talked to me yet, as I'd been escorted to my seat by Qrysta; but, if anyone were to do so, my plan was to reply with a shrug, and a smile, and a few apologetic, nonsense words, as if speaking foreign. If necessary I would just stand, and bow, and leave—and, I believed, no one would regret my going.

I turned to Qrysta and caught her eye. I could see that she was thinking the same thing I was.

"He's taking Grell seriously," she muttered.

I grunted agreement. I leaned over, and whispered in her ear. "D'you think he'll take it as a compliment?"

"No," she replied, "it'll freak the shit out of him. He'll have had one picture of Commandant Bastard in his head—which was bad enough. Now he'll see this supercharged version. It'll blow his mind."

The trumpeters trumpeted. The heralds heralded. The opening ceremony ended and the contests began, not only below us on the Field of Honor itself, but also in other arenas spread throughout the castle grounds. Just about the only static spectators were the nobility in the front row of the royal box, to either side of their queen. Everyone else, myself included, wanted to wander around, and take in the sights. There were jousts in the lists, and target sports in the butts, and a dozen or more varieties of weapon in single combat. There were hand-to-hand fights using no weapons at all. The fields rang with the sounds of arms clashing and blows landing, and the roars and *oohs* and *aahs* of spectators.

Jess and Evall had egged Oller on into competing in the knife fights. It hadn't been hard. They knew that he was itching to be in the action, rather than sitting it out among the stuffed shirts and the bigwigs.

"Haven't had much practice recently. Hope I'm up to it," he muttered to me, as he chose his blunts from the weapon rack for his first bout. It lasted less than twenty seconds. He and his opponent circled each other, crouching, flicking their knives from hand to hand, twisting them around in their wrists, reversing them, changing stances, ducking and weaving, weighing each other up. The lad facing Oller looked about half his age: big feet, big ears, spindly legs, thin trunk, mean mouth, long nose, cold eyes. Every move they made was slick and calculated.

Everyone watching knew that, when something actually happened, it was going to be a blur. Small, slow motions, we knew, were leading up to big, sudden ones. Feint, stalk; skip, pose; wait, shuffle; twirl the knives around …. Half lunge, forward, back. Nothing, really, had happened, and yet we were all on edge, in suspense.

And then came the blur.

And Oller's opponent dancing and flailing, yelping, wondering what in all hells had just sunk its teeth into his buttock.

143

Little Guy, it seemed, had found the tension more unbearable than any of us and had decided to do something about it. He tore himself free from Jess's grip, shot onto the field, sprang, and locked onto his target—where he hung, shaking with rage, swinging from side to side, snarling wildly, paws scrabbling. Jess ran in after him. Oller shouted at him to let go. The crowd was stunned, for a moment, and then roaring with laughter.

Oller had to shove one of his blunt knives in and lever Little Guy's jaws apart to get him off his opponent. I cast a stealthy Heal at the poor lad, while Oller apologized to him and berated Little Guy, who was leaping all over him, and licking his face, and wagging his tail madly in his pride and relief. *That'll teach the kid, eh? No one messes with us!* Oller surrendered his knives to the marshal and forfeited the bout to his opponent, with a bow and a sympathetic pat on the lad's back. The crowd applauded them off the field, Little Guy trotting at Oller's side, head up, looking around at one and all, alert for any more nonsense from any of them.

"Oh well," Oller said, afterwards. "I felt good, and all. Pretty sure I had his measure. Not that we'll ever know." He looked down and pulled Little Guy's hairy ears. "No thanks to you, you little perisher!"

Little Guy thumped his tail on the ground, and we could all imagine what he was thinking: *Job done. Oller saved. Enemy vanquished. How about lunch?*

It was from Oller that I heard that Grell was training behind closed doors in the castle.

"He's not going to show his face out here until his bout with the Commandant."

I asked, "How's he doing?"

"Grumpy. And running out of sparring partners. Nobody but Orcs will train with him anymore; and if Marnie hadn't sent them her best healers even they'd have packed it in. He's been giving the poor sods a pounding, by all accounts."

"I think I need to talk to him."

Oller eyed me, shrewdly. "Oh, aye? Not going to cast no invisible shield on him, so dear old Commandant Bastard won't land a blow?"

"You know me better than that, Oller."

He grunted. "I've fought along o' you and Grell. What I know is, you'd do anything for your pal."

"In combat, yes. Of course I would. Not in a fair fight, which is what he wants."

Oller chuckled. "Well, there's your difference between TG and GAA!" he said. "Too bleeding honorable for your own good, you casters. We'd have Grell unhittable and Bastard nobbled in a heartbeat, if we could do what you lot can. And all our money quietly on Grello, at the best odds going, and we clean up. Oh well." He sighed at the thought. "Give him my best, eh? Tell him I'm rooting for him. Which I will be. With no expectation of him winning, but you needn't tell him that bit."

In truth I didn't know what I was going to tell Grell when I saw him. All I knew was that, if it had been me about to face a feared enemy, I would appreciate my teammate making the effort to show me support. It would be the least I could do for him.

No. I had to do better than my *least*. I had all night to think about it. Surely I could come up with something.


Jousts need a lot more space than other events. They could not take place on the much smaller Field of Honor, so their championship was the climax of the second evening. Esmeralda, and her court, took their seats above the lists, where the last four knights tilted for the prize.

"Say what you like about heralds," I said to Qrysta, as the victor bowed to his queen, "they know how to put on a show."

"That they do," she agreed. "Although there's nothing I like about heralds. I've had enough of them for one lifetime."

"Ship Aground?" I said.

"See you there. Soon as I've seen Ez back to the castle."

In all that I'd observed, over those two days, one thing puzzled me. I asked Oller about it at our supper that evening.

"What's with all these Mystery Knights? Are they afraid they're going to lose and don't want anyone to know that they did?"

"Nah, nothing like that, Daxxie," Oller replied. "Proper knights know what's what. Show your face, do your best. Win or take your licks and admit you lost. There's honor in owning you've been bested— and paying due respect to the one who beat you. *Well played, sir. Jolly good show. My felicitations.* These effing *Mystery Knights* aren't knights at all. If they were, they'd want everyone to know it. They'd have their emblems all bright and emblazoned on their shields, crests on their helms—all that nob dignity and swagger. No, they're just some fifth son of some back-country castellan, or more likely his swineherd, with no future ahead of him, except what he can hack out of it. And best o' luck to the lad with that, says I. Win, and he's someone, and good for him. Lose, and he's revealed to be just some out-of-his-depth bumpkin, and no one gives a toss. Another peasant, getting above himself. Bugger off back where you belong, son. No. If you're someone, you flaunt it. You don't hide, as if you're ashamed of your name. Blimey, you'd never live that down."

I found Grell's tent easily enough the next morning. Two fearsome-looking Orcs guarded its entrance, arms crossed, scowling. They told me to get lost as I approached them. I wasn't going to speak my name, so said, "Tell Grell a pilgrim has come to see him." They had more to say, all of it rude, threatening, insulting, or all three. When they had finished, I said, "I am a friend of his." It was clear that I wasn't going away, so one of them ducked inside with the message. I waited. He reappeared and jerked his head towards the interior. I went in. The guard Orc went out, closing the tent flap behind him.

Grell was slumped on a bench, looking glum but expectant. He sat back up and frowned at the stranger who had entered. I held a finger to my lips, and shook my head, pointing at myself—and holding out my "ordinary looking staff."

He worked out that it had to be me—and that I didn't want anyone to know it.

"Fuck," he said. "What's that all about?"

"Long story," I said, sitting down beside him.

He studied me, then nodded. "You got a name, pilgrim?"

"Mulden," I said, using the name of the bounty hunter who had captured him.

He nodded. That confirmed who I was.

His expression changed. Before, it had been vacant. Now, it was engaged. "This serious?"

"Very."

"Yeah? So what's up?"

"We're hitting the road."

He liked the sound of that. "Where for?"

"Beyond the back of beyond, from what I can tell."

Grell grunted. "Sounds good to me."

"Thought it would. So, sit Jack Blunt down on his arse, enjoy the champions feast, and we're out of here. We have a job to do."

Grell went still, his face falling. "You know that's not going to happen."

I said, "No, I don't."

"He's out of my league, mate!"

"Then shake his hand when he hauls you up off *your* arse, dust yourself down, thank him for the lesson, enjoy the feast, and we're out of here."

Grell studied me, his hard eyes flicking across mine. "Yeah—well, cheers for the vote of confidence."

"No problem," I replied. "Seeing as you don't have any."

His head jerked up in annoyance. "Eh??"

"Anyone else, you'd back yourself. He knows he's going to win. You know he's going to win. Qrysta and Oller know he's going to win. So, how do you win?"

Grell frowned, and shook his head, and said, "Is this supposed to be helping?"

I said, "You win by not knowing that."

"Huh?"

"Stop knowing he's going to win. Stop knowing he's Serjeant Bastard, who trained you up from a raw recruit. That's his secret weapon. He's got you in his pocket. He's in your head."

"Tell me about it …"

"So, get him out of there."

Grell grunted a hollow laugh. "And how, exactly, do I do that?"

"Put someone else in."

"Now you're *really* making no sense—"

"Pretend he's someone else. Look, Grell: Do you think that it's *never* happened that a student overtakes his master? That the torch *never* passes to the next generation? You're better than him! He's older, slower, tireder. You're in your prime. He's yesterday. And you know what? He'll be proud of you when you beat him."

The smile that had been growing on Grell's face faded again and he shook his head. "I'll never beat him."

"Not with that attitude, you won't," I agreed. "Come on, Grello! Don't you *want* to make him proud of you? His champion student? The 'best bloody Orc' he's ever seen? Don't you think he'd *love* the achievement of having, at last, trained up someone better than him? He could rest happy, knowing that he's passed the torch!"

"Yeah. But."

"No more buts, mate. Okay?"

Grell said, not entirely convincingly, "Okay ..."

I said, "And you know why I'm telling you this?"

"No?"

"Because *I* know that you are going to win this contest."

He stared at me, startled. "How?"

I made mysterious motions with my hands and made my voice sound deep and portentous. "I am a mighty wizard. I see through the veils of time. I know that which is unknowable. Great secrets are entrusted to me, from the higher powers beyond. That which I speaketh, happeneth!"

Grell was scowling at me. Then he chuckled, sourly, and knuckled me in the shoulder. It hurt.

"Jeez, mate," he said. "You're as silly as a bagful of arseholes!"

"That I am," I admitted, rubbing my arm.

"Yeah," he said. "I get it. Thanks, Da—I mean, Mulden. Appreciate it."

"No problem," I said, then added, "One other thing. He's really knocked himself into shape for this bout. He looks amazing, as fit as fuck."

"Yeah, I'd heard ..."

"Which means he has the same problem you do."

Grell frowned at me, puzzled. "Yeah?" What's that?"

"You're in his head. Just as he's in yours."

Grell thought about that. "I suppose that's kind of flattering," he said, sounding wary rather than flattered.

"It's more than that. You know you can't beat your master. He knows that his pupil *can* beat him."

"You think?"

"He wouldn't bother getting into top fighting form if he didn't, would he? So, why not prove him right?"

I let that sink in, then stood up. "Oh, and Qrysta says to tell you she loves you. And Oller to say he's rooting for you."

Grell shook his head, and smiled. "You guys," he said. His voice was warmer and his shoulders more relaxed than they had been when I'd come in.

"Us guys," I agreed. "So, go get him, mate. Make him proud."

There was more heralding, and more trumpeting, and more cheering of Esmeralda as she acknowledged the occasion and gave her Royal Consent for the Grand Finals to begin. There was not a spare seat in the high stands on all four sides of the Field of Honor, and standing room only below them. Thanks to the heralds, event followed event as smoothly as clockwork. Oller told Qrysta and me that he didn't know whether to be pleased or annoyed that his first-round opponent had made it to the last four in the knife fights. "I'd've had him," he muttered, leaning in between me and Qrysta. "I know it."

"What about her?" Qrysta asked, when the big-eared lad was out-classed, in the Championship Round, by a girl no older than he was, and no bigger than Nyrik or Horm. He hadn't laid a blow on her. No one had.

"Nope," Oller said. "Rather him than me. I'm nowhere near that good."

The girl took her prize purse from the scarlet velvet cushion held out to her by a herald and bowed to Esmeralda. Before she left the field, the targets had been set in place for the range-weapon skills. Spears, longbow, crossbow, throwing knives: One after the other the best of the best came and went, and victor after victor took the spoils. The hunting bow came down to a duel between Nyrik and Horm—which was no surprise to me. The herald cried, "Loose!" Horm's ten arrows thudded into the gold. Nyrik, who had lowered his bow, nodded at the tight group, eyebrows raised. He smiled, in appreciation. Horm was confused. The two finalists were meant to shoot simultaneously—what was going on? Nyrik turned, drew, and loosed. Ten more arrows thumped into the gold—in Horm's target.

The crowd gasped, then looked again. Nyrik was chuckling across at Horm, who was glowering back at him. "A hundred points to none!" Nyrik called to the crowd. "A record that will never be beat!" He raised Horm's arm, and smiled, this way and that. The spectators applauded, if somewhat confusedly. What was that all about, they wondered.

I knew the answer to that. Nyrik knew that his friend was in turmoil. He needed a distraction, something to take his mind off Urngra's murder. They'd share the prize anyway, whoever was declared winner—and there were no bragging rights between the two of them. They walked off, Nyrik's arm around Horm's shoulders, as the final four in each of the single-combat events entered, to another fanfare of trumpets, and took their seats on the bench. The disciplines would be staggered, to give the winners time to recover for their finals: so, one category would be followed by another, and then a third, and so on, until only two fighters were left in each class.

And then, each fighter, refreshed and rested, would be able to give of his best in the Championship Bout.

To Qrysta's surprise, one who didn't make it to the final, in the sword-and-board class, was her old nemesis, Lord Rylen of Hartwell.

"That's bullshit!" Qrysta said, as a Mystery Knight defeated him and graciously aided the limping Lord Rylen from the field.

"What is?" I said.

"Rylen's way better than that guy."

I didn't know what to make of that. I suggested, "Maybe not today?"

"Today, every day, any damn day."

"So why did he lose?"

"Yeah. That's what I'd like to know."

Oller, leaning forward between us, said, "He threw it?"

Qrysta grunted. "Only explanation I've got." She pointed at the two contestants leaving the Field of Honor. "You think that's a real limp?"

We looked at them.

"Mystery bugger's the one as should be limping," Oller agreed. "All them blows Rylen landed on him."

I'd watched the fight. Rylen had hit home and hard, often.

A thought struck me.

"Hang on a minute," I said. I took hold of Shift and cast Reveals at the Mystery Knight.

He lit up like a Christmas tree. "Well now, that explains it," I said.

Oller said, "What does?"

"He's under a wall of Shields and has all sorts of buffs on him."

"Eh? *Magic??* That's cheating!"

I said, "I think I need to have a word with the Commandant."

"You most definitely do," Qrysta said. "Using magic in a tourney? That's disqualification, and—well, you heard the heralds …"

Oller said, "Disgrace, disqualification, and death."

He and I made eye-contact. We would let Captain Qrysta make the official decision. We turned to her and waited for it.

"Best to make this go away," she said. "Pretend it didn't happen. We're all here to celebrate, right? This is a festival. We don't need to have some poor hopeful nobody put to death. Okay, he's cheated, and rules are rules, but …"

She looked from Oller to me.

"Right you are," Oller agreed. "We don't want to spoil everyone's fun."

Our decision had been made. We all hoped it was the right one.

Then a thought struck me. "Magic or no magic, that just kept him from a hammering. Rylen landed more blows, and better—at first, at least. Until the one that gave him that 'limp' and he yielded. Why would Rylen throw the fight? He's a noble lord, of a big town. He's got all the money he needs. Lords need reputation far more than gold."

Qrysta said, "My point exactly. Rylen made sure to give a good account of himself—out of pride, you'd think, as much as just wanting to not make it obvious that he lost deliberately."

"Meaning?"

She watched us as we considered what she'd said.

Oller's devious mind got there before mine did. "Oh aye," he said, nodding. *"What's in it for him?"*

It was a good point. What sort of reward could make a proud lord like Rylen agree to lose a duel on the Field of Honor? I looked again at the Mystery Knight as he helped limping Lord Rylen from the arena.

A behemoth in black plate armor was waiting for them. I'd noticed him before, always standing behind the Mystery Knight. Everyone had. He was a head taller than anyone else present, even Commandant Bastard. He nodded, respectfully, to the Mystery Knight, then slung Lord Rylen's arm around his shoulders and half carried him to the healers' tent.

Oller grunted.

I said, "What?"

"Sons o' swineherds don't have squires like that," he said.

The Mystery Knight took his place on the bench to watch the next bout—which would decide his opponent in the Grand Final.

I studied him. I couldn't make out anything unusual about him. Plain, black chainmail. A flat-topped black helm. No crest, no emblem. Decent gear—nothing flashy, but far better than the rusty bits and pieces I'd seen on some Mystery Knights.

Well, I thought. We'll get a look at him soon enough, win or lose. Flat on his back, if he loses, or kneeling in front of the queen if he wins.

He turned, as we all did, to see what had suddenly made the crowd roar with excitement and start applauding.

To a swelling chorus of cheers and whistles, Grell lumbered onto the Field of Honor, flanked by his bodyguard Orcs.

Commandant Bastard was waiting for him at the center of the field. He smiled at Grell and held out his hand.

Grell clasped his arm, and they shook.

Commandant Bastard clapped Grell on the shoulder, and said something I couldn't hear.

Grell chuckled in reply.

Commandant Bastard turned and nodded at the Chief Herald.

The trumpeters blew a fanfare.

Commandant Bastard turned towards the royal box and held up his hands for silence.

# I3

## The Mystery Knight

"Your Majesty," Commandant Bastard began. "My lords and ladies, gentlemen and women, and good people of Eastbay: It is my duty to yield the baton for the next bout, and I do so with some pride. Many of you will have heard of how the son I never knew I had was returned to me—thanks to my friends here, chief among them the warrior I am looking forward to taking a turn with myself soon enough, in hopes of working up an appetite for this afternoon's feast."

He paused his striding around and bowed to Grell, who bowed back, while the crowd laughed and cheered. "My son is no knight," he continued, when the applause died down. "No more than I am—us coming from plain stock. He has no coat of arms, and thus far has fought unnamed—just like the winner of the last bout, who is now into the final itself. Well, *I know* who my son is, even if you don't—and, of course, I can't officiate in a bout in which my own flesh and blood is fighting. That would not be fair on his opponent."

He raised his hands to still the audience's cheers at his words. "Other marshals, unaware of his identity, officiated at my lad's earlier contests; but now, for the final rounds, it falls to me, as Grand Marshal, to appoint a deputy. I can think of none better than my own opponent. If it weren't for him, and the Captain of the Queen's Royal Guard and their crew, my young Jack wouldn't be here now. And I wouldn't be able to step back and watch the lad work—the which I'm looking forward to as much as you are."

He held an arm out towards Grell. "This Orc gentleman, as you all know, is Grell of the Ozgaroos."

A roar arose from the crowd, and cheers, and applause. Queen Esmeralda was on her feet, clapping and laughing with delight, and the arena rose as one with her. Grell grinned, somewhat sheepishly, in reply, and bowed to her.

When the hubbub subsided, Commandant Bastard continued, "Now: some of you might be thinking, why him? He and I are going to be knocking seven bells out of each other any minute—what's this all about? The way I look at it, he's the ideal man, or rather Orc, for the job, because he's the one person I know who ain't going to do my son any favors. You think he'll go easy on my son, so I'll go easy on him? Well, if you think *that*, you don't know me, and you don't know him. And I *do* know him. He's the best bloody Orc I've ever had the pleasure of facing two-handed, and I'm looking forward to our next little go-round as much as you are. And I can promise you, he'll be going hard on me, and I'll be going hard on him—and harder, if I see him favoring my son in any way, shape or form. And he knows that because he knows *me*."

Commandant Bastard paused to let that sink in.

"I am pleased to say that he has accepted my invitation, and will act as marshal in my stead. So, if you'll excuse me," he concluded his announcement, "it is with absolute confidence in my enormous friend here, and not a little pride in my lad, that I yield the baton."

The crowd cheered again. Commandant Bastard handed his Grand Marshal's baton to Grell and walked off to take a seat. The trumpeters blew another fanfare. Young Jack Blunt and his opponent rose from the bench and came forward to face each other on the Field of Honor.

I'd fought young Jack before when we helped liberate him and his mother from their captor. I'd seen how good he was. We hadn't wanted to hurt him, especially knowing he was not our foe. As soon as I could, I'd made sure to Root him to the ground, where, for the rest of our battle, he had stood, immobilized, until we'd finally taken down the monster that he'd always believed was his father. I had talked with him on occasion, briefly, on our voyage home from Dawn

Isle; but our conversations had been short and stilted. That was hardly surprising, I'd thought, seeing as we'd thrown his world upside down. He had no love for me. Why should he? So I'd pretty much left him alone as we sailed for Eastbay. Qrysta had got to know him a little better. Young Jack had watched her sparring with Jess on the main deck. She'd noticed and had offered to spar with him too, if he felt like a workout. He had.

"He's good," Qrysta had said, after their first session, clearly impressed with his swordplay and shield-work.

"You had his measure."

"Had to work hard to keep him off me, though. Sword-and-board, he'd have had me, easily."

"Sure, but—you're crap at sword-and-board, Qrys."

She'd stared at me, shaking her head. "That's not the point, Daxx. Dual-wielding, I'm throwing a lot more at him, stuff he's not used to. I know what a good sword-and-board fighter can do, so I mess with that. He caught on, fast. He adjusted. I'm going to have to be on my toes tomorrow."

If Qrysta had thought he was good aboard *The Red Rose*, she clearly knew he was much better now. And I now understood how his father had come to be in such great shape within such a short time. The whole town knew that Commandant Blunt had been shut away, behind closed doors, with his long-lost wife and their son. Now it was obvious what they'd been doing there.

Father and son had been training. Hard.

"Hell's bells," Qrysta said, watching young Jack stalk his opponent mercilessly around the Field of Honor. "I'd back him against Lord Rylen, let alone that Mystery Knight he threw the fight to. He could probably handle the two of them at the same time."

I could only agree. It was a shorter bout than Rylen's and a much more clinical exhibition—not just of skill, but also of sheer, brute strength. The two combatants were matched for size and weight, so it should have been an even contest. It wasn't. Young Jack Blunt hit harder, and faster, and more often, and more accurately, with both sword and shield. It wasn't so much a contest as a battering.

Grell's job was easy. It consisted of watching and, before long, stepping in between them, arms outstretched, then lifting young Jack's arm in victory as his opponent knelt, defeated, head down, his chest heaving for breath.

"Well," Qrysta said, "we know who's going to win sword-and-board."

"Chip off the old block," I said.

"I'll say!" she agreed.

Young Jack helped his opponent to his feet and clasped his arm in a gesture of respect. Then, instead of removing his opponent's helm, he removed his own.

He smiled around at the crowd, shyly, acknowledging the applause.

*Of course,* I thought. We all know who he is now, so there's no longer any point in hiding it. His opponent took off his own helm, and the two of them left the field—the loser to the exit gate, young Jack going back to the bench. I noticed him look across at the black-helmed Mystery Knight who would be his opponent in the final. He nodded, with a faint smile of respect. The Mystery Knight simply stared in reply, without acknowledgement. Young Jack Blunt's smile faded. He stared a little longer, and a little harder, then turned away to watch the next contest.

Sword-and-board, it seemed, was the most prestigious class of all, in the foot-fights. I couldn't quite see why, myself. Two-handed weapons, such as longsword and battle-axe and maul, seemed much nastier, and would obviously do more damage if they struck home. Dual-wield—especially when Qrysta was doing the wielding—was faster and more lethal.

I asked Qrysta why that was as we watched the bouts below us.

"Tradition," she said. "Knights, and all that. They have their coats of arms on their shields. It's seen as more honorable. No idea why. Something to do with warfare, maybe? Fighting in an army, against arrows and spears, where you'd all need protection? I dunno. The way I look at it, why waste a hand with a lump of wood? As far as I'm concerned, a shield is something I lure out of the way, with a feint, or a couple of raps on it, to get his attention, and then he's wide open with just one blade to my two. Well, that's only going to end one way."

Indeed, I thought. I'd seen her end it many a time. This Royal Tournament, though, was going to end according to tradition, with the sword-and-board championship. It would be an anticlimax, I thought, having seen young Jack Blunt brutalise his last opponent—and having heard how little Qrysta thought of the Mystery Knight who would be facing him. Oh well. It would soon be over, and then we'd be on to the *real* Main Event, for which we'd all been waiting: Commandant

Bastard facing off against Grell, two-handed—with Grell's choice of weapon. Everyone in town knew the story of what Commandant Bastard had replied when Grell's second had gone to him, to ask what they'd be fighting with.

"Whatever he likes, son. It's all the same to me."

I'd had to laugh when I heard that. *First point to the Commandant.* Grell, to no one's surprise, had chosen maul. He'd been campaigning with his Kinfolk-forged maul, Kinell, and had grown to love her. A tourney maul would have no sharp edges but would be as heavy as any other. A tourney longsword, or battle-axe, would be blunt, thus losing most of its purpose. Weight was a maul's purpose. Grell would have his favorite weapon, which would please him.

Learning that his opponent didn't give a damn what they fought with would have pleased him less. I was thinking about all this, trying to work out which of the two of them had the advantage, when a fanfare of trumpets announced the final bout. The sword-and-board championship. Young Jack Blunt against the Mystery Knight.

The two combatants came to the center of the Field of Honor, where Grell and Commandant Bastard waited for them. I'd told the latter what my Reveals had shown me about the Mystery Knight's equipment, so I leaned forward, interested to hear how he handled the matter.

Commandant Bastard addressed the Mystery Knight. "Now then, sir, if knight you truly be."

"He is knight!" the behemoth towering behind the Mystery Knight growled.

Commandant Bastard raised his head, stared up at him, and smiled. "Did I give you permission to speak, friend?"

The behemoth leaned forward to reply, but thought better of it.

Commandant Bastard nodded. "Speak when spoken to, and not before," he said, pleasantly. "Now," he returned his attention to the Mystery Knight, "I'm going to put this as politely as possible. I can't prove anything, and I don't wish to, and I'm not accusing you of anything, sir. You can read into that what you wish. I would just like to remind you that all here fight fair and square, with no trickery, everything aboveboard, and all according to the Rules of Chivalry. You are familiar with those, I take it?"

The Mystery Knight, eventually, nodded.

157

"Good!" Commandant Bastard seemed relieved. "Now, this could get a bit tasty—you two being the best o' your class that we've seen. I wouldn't want any of your nice jewelery to get damaged in the heat of combat. That'd be a shame, eh? So, remove your rings, if you please, and your talismans, and brooches, and suchlike, gents—the both of you."

Young Jack Blunt removed his gauntlets and showed his hands. No rings, no bracelets.

Grell checked his neck and saw nothing hanging there. He nodded and Jack put on his helm.

Grell turned to the Mystery Knight, who had gone still.

Then, slowly, he took off his gauntlets, and his rings, before reaching under his helm to remove his necklace, all of which he handed to his second. Unobtrusively, I lifted Shift off the floor and cast Reveals at him. Nothing showed anywhere on his person. When Commandant Bastard glanced up at me, I nodded. *All clear.* He bowed to Grell and walked off to take his seat.

Grell called the fighters to their marks. They saluted each other and took their stances.

Grell stepped back and the bout began.

Shields raised, swords hefted, young Jack Blunt and the Mystery Knight circled each other. The Mystery Knight feinted. Jack saw it, spotted an opening, and attacked. The Mystery Knight jumped forwards, grabbed Jack around the waist, hooking a foot behind his leg and tripping him, backwards, to the ground. He was on his feet before Jack had recovered from the shock of being the victim of an illegal assault. He was flat on his back, the Mystery Knight's foot on his chest and his sword at his throat.

He froze, as did everyone watching.

"Yield," the Mystery Knight ordered, in the stunned silence.

The first sound I heard was a growl from Commandant Bastard as he rose to his feet.

He strode into the center of the field. From the other side of it, the behemoth in black plate armor came towards him. The crowd was in an uproar, yelling, booing, whistling.

Commandant Bastard held his arms aloft for silence.

"This is a tournament, sir!" he bellowed at the Mystery Knight. "Not some backstreet brawl."

"If this were a street brawl," the Mystery Knight replied calmly, "your boy would be dead."

Commandant Bastard froze. He couldn't believe that anyone would talk to him like that—let alone a knight, on a Field of Honor. I could see that he was struggling to control his temper.

"Which is why we have rules, in tournaments. Or half the fighters entering them would be killed. Are you a knight or an idiot?"

"He is knight!" the behemoth repeated, his voice harsh.

"And you," Commandant Bastard snapped, "are beginning to annoy me. He turned to the Mystery Knight. "Take your foot off your opponent's chest, if you please, and fight fair or forfeit, *sir*," he said, putting emphasis on the word.

The Mystery Knight turned his helmed head towards him and replied, "I fight to win. I won."

Absolute silence fell around the arena.

Commandant Bastard nodded slowly, staring at him. Eventually, he said, "You did not fight *fair*. Therefore, you forfeit. Leave this field."

"Not until I have the queen's prize."

I did not like the way he said that. It was insolent, and insinuating.

I could see that Commandant Bastard was struggling to control himself. "Sir," he said, "I am surprised I need to remind you that the marshal's word is law, on a Field of Honor."

"And I," the Mystery Knight replied, calmly, "am surprised I need to remind you that you are not the marshal, and that your boy is flat on his back with my sword at his throat."

That was the last straw. "Gods above and below!" Commandant Bastard barked. "You hold your tongue, you insolent pup. This match is forfeit, as is your honor. Get your miserable carcass off my field before I beat you off it."

The behemoth stepped towards him. "You do not speak to my master with such disrespect."

"And you hold your tongue, fool, unless you wish to lose it!"

The behemoth unslung his broadsword. The crowd gasped, and went still.

Commandant Bastard stared at the huge man's black plate helm. In a cold voice that made me wince, because I remembered it all too well from my days as a recruit in Brigstowe Castle, he said, "Are you aware of the penalty for drawing a weapon on the Grand Marshal, on his Field of Honor?"

The behemoth did not answer.

The Mystery Knight made a gesture and the behemoth replaced his weapon.

"You are foreigners," Commandant Bastard said, as if the matter were settled. "On which account, I will overlook this breach of protocol. There had better not be another. Marshal Grell?"

Grell said, "Huh?"

"Your decision?"

"They can go again, if they like."

"I do not like," the Mystery Knight said. "I won. I will have the queen's prize."

Again, I did not like the way he said it. Nor did the crowd, which was rumbling with anger.

Commandant Bastard snapped. "You didn't, and you won't. Off you go, you insolent pig, and take your nursemaid with you. Disgrace, disqualification, and death. You've earned the first two, you'd be wise not to push for the third."

The behemoth stepped towards him, saying, "You do not call my master pig!"

"I'll call him whatever I want!" Commandant Bastard roared. "Pig, cheat, dog turd, son of a dockside whore—take your damn choice and get off my field!"

The behemoth unslung his broadsword again. "I challenge!" he barked.

Commandant Bastard laughed, relieved. "Well, thank the gods for that! Means I don't have to waste any more words on a fool. You challenge; I accept. You too, boy. You're in plate, and chainmail, and I'm in marshal's robes, so let's make this easy, shall we? You choose the weapons; I'll choose the armor. Yes?"

The behemoth nodded. "We choose weapons." He lowered his head and conferred with the Mystery Knight in whispers.

"My second will use his longsword," the Mystery Knight said, "with which, let me inform you, he is our champion. And undefeated."

Commandant Bastard snorted. "And let me inform you, sonny, that all good things come to an end. What about you, cheating so-called knight: still going sword-and-board?"

"None here has stood against me," came the reply.

"None here has been me, pup."

The behemoth growled at the insult and drew his broadsword. Commandant Bastard ignored him.

"I will use sword and shield," the Mystery Knight continued. "And for you, I choose knives."

"And I choose no armor. So, get that plate off you, *champion*," Commandant Bastard said to the giant, with mocking emphasis on the word. "And you, scum, out of your chainmail and stand to the mark!"

"I will keep my helm," the Mystery Knight said.

"Can't blame you," Commandant Bastard replied. "I'd be loath to show my face, too, if I'd behaved as shamefully as you. Keep your helm, cheat. Fat lot of good it'll do you."

He strode across to the weapons rack, pulling his marshal's robes off over his head. He chose a cross-harness of knives and strapped it around his bare chest. He returned to the center of the field and stood there, arms folded, waiting for his opponents.

Leaning between Qrysta and me, Oller chuckled. "Oh, *neatly* done!"

I said, "Huh?"

He didn't reply, just looked amused.

I didn't get it. Daggers against sword-and-board—*and* a broadsword wielded by a monster? I looked at the Mystery Knight's second as they removed their armor. He was almost as tall as Urngra. He took off his helm first and stared at Commandant Bastard, giving him, and the rest of us, time to take in his appearance.

It was a huge face, as hard as stone, its features exaggerated: bulging nose, bulbous forehead, jutting chin; wide, narrow mouth, massive neck—and eyes as yellow as a cat's. The most remarkable thing about him, though, was the color of his skin.

It was white.

Not pink, or weather-beaten tan, like most folk of this northerly realm, but as white as paper.

A mutter of fear ran through the crowd. In front of us, Esmeralda, and her noble lords and ladies, gasped.

Commandant Bastard smiled, nodding in recognition of what he was looking at.

"*I* see," he said. "One o' them then, are you? I've killed more than many of you lot, and I'll be doing the world a favor by ridding it of another. So, bred in the pits of Sarmen. Slave and owner. Each worse than the other. If you lickspittles had any balls you'd turn your blade on him, not me."

The giant froze.

"Oh, I forgot," the Commandant said. "They geld you after breeding. Anyone did that to me, I'd put my sword through his skull. And still you chalkers follow them. Pathetic."

"You do not use that word!" the behemoth bellowed.

"I'll use any word I want, chalker! Now, are you two pisspots ready for the beating you deserve?"

They charged.

They stopped before they had gone three paces.

The giant had a knife in each shoulder and each thigh, the Mystery Knight two in his shield and one in each foot. They stood rooted, stunned, gasping, their weapons dropping from their hands.

The crowd, too, gasped.

It had happened too fast for anyone to see.

And then, as one, the audience cheered, and applauded, and hooted with laughter.

"See now?" Oller said. "They're the only sharps on the field, throwing knives! If they weren't, they'd not stick in the target. Walked right into his trap, didn't they, those two twats? *You choose the weapons, I'll choose the armor.* Wily old bugger, eh? *Hehe!* They figured the knives would have too short a reach against their swords. Idiots."

Blunt strolled over to his swaying opponents, and slowly around them, and came back to stand in front of them, arms folded, looking them up and down in contempt.

"Pff!" he said. "Pathetic. Well, there's your lesson, fools. The public shaming you deserve. You are cheats. You are cowards. You are laughingstocks. Call yourself a knight?" he shook his head in disdain; and then reached up, and removed the Mystery Knight's helmet.

In front of us, I saw Esmeralda's back stiffen. "Oh no," she muttered, under her breath. "Not him ..."

Qrysta leaned forwards, and asked, "Problem?"

Esmeralda fidgeted. "I don't know. No. Yes. Nuisance, shall we say. He appeared in Mayport, when you were overseas. He's been ... a bit of a bother."

Well. I thought that I knew what that was all about. He was a dashing enough fellow; young, in his twenties, with flowing, jet-black hair, and a neat black beard, and piercing dark eyes. Though his face was taut with pain, it was a handsome one. And who doesn't fall in love with Esmeralda?

Qrysta said, "Well, the Commandant's put a stop to that. He won't be bothering you anymore."

Below us, Commandant Bastard leaned close and spat into the Mystery Knight's face.

The Mystery Knight recoiled, blinking.

Commandant Bastard pronounced his sentence. "You bring shame to this field, and shame on yourselves."

Between gasps of pain, the Mystery Knight said, "I won't forget this."

Holding his arms wide, to indicate the crowd, Commandant Bastard said, "Nor will anyone here who is laughing at you." He turned to the behemoth, whose heavy, pallid face was contorted in agony. Commandant Bastard stared at him, then added, "You deserve death, chalker, but I won't defile this Field of Honor with your foul blood. If I ever see your ugly face again I'll finish the job. That is a promise."

He turned his back on them and bowed to Esmeralda. "The title is forfeit, Majesty," he announced, "and this tournament is ended."

I could see that she was relieved. She clearly didn't want anything more to do with the Mystery Knight. I really wanted to know more of what she had to say about him.

She stood and we all rose to our feet. "As you wish, Grand Marshal," she said.

Grell said, "Huh? Aren't we going to—"

"No, we are not!" Commandant Bastard snapped, still plainly seething. "I'm not going to take my displeasure out on you, friend Grell. Perhaps some other time. This field has been dishonored. I'll not sully your good name with having to follow that disgrace."

Commandant Bastard stalked off the field, not even glancing at his skewered opponents.

Grell could see how angry he was. And, like any sensible person, he wasn't going to argue.

Commandant Bastard stopped and turned back to Grell. "You can take a turn with this fool and his broadsword, if you need to swing your arms."

Grell looked at the frozen, sweating, chalk-white behemoth.

He shook his head. "I came here to try myself against the best, thank you, Commandant. I've no interest in beating sense into some loser."

# 14

## Out of the Blue

I looked around the Great Hall of My Lady of Eastbay's Castle. The place was packed. There was not a spare seat to be had. Everyone who was anyone had done all they could to secure an invitation to the Champions Feast. The great and the good from all over the realm rubbed shoulders with the townsfolk of Eastbay, all of us crowded together on benches at long tables throughout the hall. Strangers and townsfolk were soon enough toasting each other, and wondering who those two damn foreigners that Commandant Bastard had taken down a peg or two had been.

*Who in all hells did they think they were, to spoil the Royal Tournament?!*
*Well, at least they're gone now.*

Healers and apothecaries had hurried onto the field and removed the knives that were pinioning them. They gave them potions and salves and cast Heals on them. The foreigners had last been seen galloping out of town, being jeered by the guards, and with urchins flinging mud and stones and hooting at them. And *good riddance*, everyone felt. The fools had deserved it. And, because of them, now we'd never know who would have won between the Commandant and Grell!

The castle cooks had been preparing for days and had outdone themselves. Flagons of wine and jugs of ale passed along the tables.

164

Musicians played in the gallery, although it was just about impossible to hear them above the hubbub. Servants bustled in and out with course after course. We ate, and drank, and celebrated.

No longer Glamoured as a "dull envoy," but now an "old soldier companion," I sat opposite Commandant Bastard, who was flanked by his wife and son. You would never have guessed what Jenny Blunt had been through from her demeanour. She was calm, and comfortable, and in good spirits. Marnie and Velaryn's healing had clearly worked wonders on her. Young Jack was less withdrawn than he had been, I thought; but it was obvious that he was still reserved—and, clearly, irked that he hadn't had the chance to punish the Mystery Knight for his insolence.

Oller, on my right between me and Grell, had his measure. "You going to cheer up and enjoy yourself or what, matey?" he challenged.

Young Jack glared across at him.

Oller grinned back. "Tell you what, old son," he said—and they were about the same age; Oller, if anything, being the younger—"we all know he only cheated because he knew he couldn't beat you, and I can prove it."

Young Jack Blunt frowned. "How?"

"How about in the court of popular opinion? You prepared to accept the verdict of the jury?"

"What are you talking about?!"

"I'll show you. And if I can't prove it, well"—he ducked under the table, came back up with Little Guy in his hands, and stood him on the table—"you can have my dog. Deal?"

Young Jack stared at Little Guy without enthusiasm. Little Guy wagged his tail. We had no idea what Oller was up to, but we were all enjoying it. Young Jack clearly didn't want to win a scruffy mongrel. Just as clearly, he didn't like being the center of attention and wanted this to stop—presumably so that he could go back to his brooding.

He glanced at his father.

Who winked at him.

Young Jack got the unspoken message. *Might as well play along, eh?*

He nodded at Oller, and said, "All right."

"Good," Oller said. He got up from his bench and climbed onto the table. He waved his arms at the nearest herald, who quickly signaled the trumpeters to blow for silence.

A few sharp blasts, and silence fell.

All eyes turned to Oller.

" 'Scuse me for interrupting, folks, this won't take a moment," Oller said. "This lad here don't believe what we all know to be a fact. So, would you all please help me convince him?" He turned to young Jack, and said, "Oi, you—up on your feet."

Young Jack stood.

The entire room cheered and applauded.

Jack, looking at first embarrassed, and then gratified, if somewhat sheepish, bowed in acknowledgment.

Oller made a gesture to him that said, *See? Told you so.*

Then, to the assembly, he said, "Anyone who thinks this lad *wasn't* going to win his bout against that son-of-a-you-know-what in the black armor, please applaud."

The happy noises in the hall faded to absolute silence.

Oller let it settle over us all. He waited while we all got the point.

Low rumbles of laughter began as we all appreciated that everyone else in the room felt the way that the rest of us did.

Then Oller said, "And anyone who knows that our lad here is ten times the man that Mystery Knight is—"

The rest of his sentence was drowned out in a storm of cheering and clapping and whistles.

Oller held up young Jack's arm while we all drummed our feet, and raised our mugs, and made as much noise as possible.

"Thank 'ee, one and all," Oller said, when it was all over. "Pardon the interruption, folks; back to your feasting."

He sat back down, and said, "Right, I'll have my dog back."

He retrieved Little Guy, who was polishing off young Jack's plate, and put him back under the table where he belonged. Then he sat back down on his bench and grinned across at young Jack, as mugs banged on tabletops all around us and onlookers cheered.

I could see that Jack didn't like being made fun of. I could also see that he was learning; just as he'd learned from Qrysta, in their sparring aboard *The Red Rose* .... And, no doubt, just as he'd been learning from his father since his arrival in Eastbay.

Jack picked up his mug and held it out across the table towards Oller.

Oller winked at him and held his own towards it.

Instead of clinking and drinking, though, he looked around at the rest of us.

We raised our glasses and mugs towards theirs. We clashed them all together, and drank to the health of the man that we all knew would have won the sword-and-board championship.

Jess and Evall were beside me. They were, thanks to Qrysta, special guests of the queen. Coming from their provincial backgrounds, they'd never been at anything like that grand gathering and were drinking it all in, whispering excitedly between themselves. I was just about the only person they paid no attention to, being, as far as they could see, just a "boring old soldier."

Qrysta herself was on duty, standing behind her queen. Esmeralda was seated at the center of the High Table, much to My Lady of Eastbay's delight. She was bursting with pride at having the young queen as her guest of honor, not to mention most of the nobility of the realm. Of all those who had attended the Royal Tournament, only Lord Rylen of Hartwell was not present. He had gone home, angry at his defeat at the hands of the Mystery Knight and wanting the treatment of his own apothecaries.

I knew that Qrysta would rather have been down here, with the rest of us, enjoying and celebrating. We'd made eye-contact: We'd catch up later. I made a mental note to tell her as much as I could remember of what we all talked about.

Much of it concerned the Mystery Knight and his gigantic second—with whose kind Commandant Bastard, we'd gathered, was familiar.

"They breed them that way," he said, "in the slave pits. Vu-Sant, they call themselves. Means *Born Dead*. The paler, and harder, and bigger, and uglier the better, is how they're judged by their masters. They train at arms as soon as they can walk—boys and girls alike. Those who survive to sixteen have a coming-of-age tourney each year by way of a graduation—the which is a little different from how yours was in Rushtoun, Masters Oller and Grell.

"Some are culled. If they're not big or ugly or pale enough, they won't even get the chance to fight for their lives. They see it as an honor to make it to the arena. And then it's survival of the best. Most die, in combat, between themselves, boys against boys and girls against girls. Win two bouts or die, for the boys; so, if there were four hundred starting, say, a hundred would live. With the girls it's just the one bout, as they're needed for breeding. The girls, and those from the six years above them, are farmed out to the boys, who'll have a dozen or more each to service. Seven years, the girls breed for—still training at arms and the arts of war all the while, of course.

"There's a lot of wastage in the emperor's armies. The ranks always need filling. When his girls are all pregnant, a boy moves down to the night caves, to await graduation, so his skin can bleach out in the dark. Any who don't get his girls in pup is culled, and the girls paired with other lads. Conception Day, they call their graduation ceremony— which is about the opposite of what any of *us* would name it. For a start, it's at the dead of night, not in daytime, and deep underground, in their temple, lit by torches. The boys line up, naked. One by one, they walk to the dais to stand and are castrated; and so starts their long journey from death to life. Each lad's girls draw lots among themselves to see which one of them does the cutting—they're all sitting there, silent, naked, waiting to do their part. Any lads who flinch, or, worse, make a sound, are culled on the spot by the girl wielding the knife—and if she don't do it right off, she's culled herself.

"They take their vows, boy and girl, to their secret gods, and so are consecrated Vu-Sant. Then they are eligible to serve. The boys' superiors in their next round of training are the girls of seven years above them, who have done their breeding, and suckled their babes, and handed them to the Old Mothers to rear. The which is one reason why the boys have their balls cut off. No fornication allowed in the emperor's army. Save your strength for battle.

"From then on they exist to guard their masters, as assigned, for as long as they live—as we would call it, though they consider themselves dead from birth. And when they pass from that existence—what you and I would call dying—they believe that, if they have served faithfully and have protected theirs masters well, they become Vu-Chent. The which means *Dead Born*. And thus they will have deserved the gift of life and, in due course, will have the grace of taking their place themselves, at last, among the living. Their reward at last: reborn as masters, as full citizens of Sarmen—and not in the outlying realms of the empire that the Sarmenids have conquered, over the ages, but in Sarmen itself.

"The best of the best of them will be born into noble rank; mayhaps even royalty. Whatever—beggar, cobbler, merchant—anything would be better than being Vu-Sant. It follows then that the royal princes, of course, must have been the greatest of all Vu-Sant, to attain such high status when reborn. Which means that the emperor himself might look like some scrawny little shrimp, like Master Oller there, and be ninety years old, but inside he's the mightiest of champions."

Oller chuckled. "Born Dead?" he said. "Born Yesterday, is what I'd call anyone as would believe that malarkey."

Jack Blunt, clearly, agreed. "Well, that's what happens to a bairn who's force-fed such stuff from the cradle up, and never gets the chance to step back and question," he said. "They believe because they're told to. Simple as that. Seems clear as day to us sitting here that it's just foreigners' foolishness. But if your mind is fuddled by tradition, and beatings, you do as you're told. *Anything's better than this; there's a way out, with honor, at the end of the rainbow.* What choice do you have? Better luck next time around."

Evall said, "Are there lots of them?"

"Thousands upon thousands, lad. This whole realm would be but a small part of the Sarmenid Empire. And realms don't like being part of empires, so emperors have to station armies in them. Many armies, in many places, throughout many realms. And those armies are Vu-Sant. At least, the foot soldiers are. Bowmen and cavalry are masters—archery and tilting being sports for the yeomanry and the nobs. Officers too, of course. And the generals are always royalty."

Jack Blunt stopped to take a swig of his ale, which gave Evall the opportunity to ask, "How do they get to be that pale, sir?" at the same time as Jess asked, "Where did you fight them before?"

"Diet and breeding, lad," Commandant Bastard said. "Conditioning, keeping them in the dark. Secret recipes, and all that. Rumor is, every meal contains chalk."

Jenny Blunt laughed out loud. "A gut full of chalk? You'd never pass another stool, Jack! You'd burst wide open."

"My own thought too, Jenny love," Blunt replied. "Still, that's how they get their nickname. The which you do not use in their hearing, if you want to live. No Sarmenid says *that* word, if one's around! Petrified of them, the common people are. Even though they know they're being protected by them. They think they really *are* dead, ghouls from beyond the grave. As to where I fought them, young lady," he turned to Jess, "in about the farthest end of the Sarmenid Empire, it was.

"A land named Temuan. The which, as far as I understand it, was an old realm Sarmen conquered centuries ago, and more or less forgot about. My road took me beyond that, to a place no one knew the name of, because no one had ever been there." He turned to his wife, and reached for her hand. "Got to the end of that, and you weren't there neither. So, I turned for home. And much though I wanted to find you, I was glad I didn't find you in *that* particular place. A cruel people, the Sarmenids. I saw things among them that I wished I hadn't."

Jess said, "Like what?"

Blunt looked at her. "I'll not spoil your meal by telling, lass. Things I'd give a deal of gold to be able to forget. Passing through Temuan was where I came up against chalkers. I needed to go where they weren't going to let me. So, one thing led to another. Once you realize their main weapon is fear, you soon see they're not as hard as they look." He grunted, and shook his head. "After all that, my destination turned out to be just another dead end, at the end of another false trail."

He looked across at Grell, and glared at him, as if it was all his fault. "If only I'd known that all I needed to find my Jenny was you lot!" he said. "I'd have stayed home, with my feet up, by my fire, and my mug of ale, pulling my old dog's ears as he slept, while you took care of things."

Grell chuckled. "Oh, I can really see that!" he mocked. "Yeah, *right*: Jack Blunt, snoozing by the fireside, while someone else does his dirty—"

Grell's speech was cut off by an almighty *thump* from outside.

The foundations of the castle shook below us.

The sounds of celebration that were filling the Great Hall died away.

Trails of dust, disturbed by the impact, scattered down from the ceiling.

Neighbor looked at neighbor, wondering what had happened. I reached for Shift under the table, scared that this was the Wild Hunt coming for me. She woke in my hand immediately. *No. This isn't about you.* She sounded more worried than reassuring.

The silence was broken by a loud, harsh bray. It sounded like a challenge, bellowed from the throat of some huge beast—but not any beast that I could identify.

Two more massive *thumps* followed, one after the other, and then two more of those unnerving, raucous cries.

More debris broke loose from overhead and clattered to the floor.

Esmeralda was on her feet, as were many of us.

The doors flew open. Two breathless guards rushed in. They both looked terrified.

"Milady," one gasped, and, "Majesty," the other.

"What is it?" Esmeralda said.

"I ... I ..." was all that one managed.

The other said, "If it pleases you, Majesty, to come outside ...." He was pale with fear, trembling, gulping. He seemed unable to say more.

We stood back to let the queen pass. At Qrysta's command the Royal Guards closed in around Esmeralda to escort her from the hall, accompanied by My Lady of Eastbay and other lords and ladies. We followed them out, crowding awkwardly through the doors. I knew that there was a wide, grassy courtyard between the castle and the gatehouse, where, in times of trouble, the townsfolk could gather to seek shelter behind the castle's high walls.

What I did not know was what I was going to see there.

Three vast, dark shapes loomed against the late afternoon sky. On the ends of long, serpentine necks, bulbous heads moved around, looking this way and that, alert, threatening. Those necks rose from hulking bodies. Clawed feet dug into the turf. Long tails lashed.

On their shoulders, wings.

They were as different from the helldragon that we'd fought under Wester Isle as they were from Vagg's chicken-sized creatures—but there was no mistaking what they were.

*Dragons.*

Their heads were elongated, and lumpy, each shaped more like that of some outsized moose than a lizard's. Their bodies had no bright scales but were dark gray. Their skin looked like rhinoceros hide. It was hard to take in what we were seeing. They towered above us, glaring, chilling, enormous.

They were so large, indeed, that I did not, at first, notice their riders.

A figure, dwarfed by the size of their mount, sat astride each dragon's neck. They stood up, becoming outlined against the evening sky.

Each dragon extended a long wing to the ground. The figures walked down them, towards us.

One of them, I saw—the one in the center, who was descending the wing of the largest and darkest dragon—was wearing a slender gold crown.

He stepped onto the ground; and, as he approached us, I recognized him. We all did.

He was no longer in black chainmail but in bright robes that shone in the evening sun, saffron and pink, shot through with orange and blue and gold thread. He did, without doubt, look magnificent. But, as my father had often said, "You only get one chance to make a first impression." He'd made his first impression on all of us earlier that day, and it hadn't been a good one.

There was no mistaking who he was.

The Mystery Knight.

To one side of him, a pace behind, as before, was his huge second, once again clad head to foot in black plate armor.

On his other side walked a gaunt figure in black robes, holding a staff.

I knew her at once for what she was.

*Sorceress.*

Instinctively, I gripped Shift tighter. I was glad to feel her immediate response. *Ready when you are!*

We would be ahead of the sorceress if she tried to cast anything at anyone—especially at Esmeralda.

It was towards Esmeralda that the Mystery Knight was strolling with an easy, confident gait.

He stopped a few paces away from her.

Instead of bowing, he inclined his head politely, as if to an equal, and smiled.

He looked a lot better than he had when I'd last seen him, his face twisted in pain, with Commandant Bastard's daggers impaling his feet. And he was, indeed, a handsome specimen. Now, in his shimmering robes, he radiated nobility. But, just as before, I did not like his smile.

"Milady," he said.

Not, we noticed, *Majesty.*

His fingers fluttered in a gesture to the gaunt woman in black beside him. "I know your name, Queen Esmeralda. You should know mine."

The sorceress spoke without effort. She did not draw in a deep breath and boom, but her voice sounded loud all around us, bouncing back in echoes off the castle walls.

"His Radiance, Mejnul, Crown Prince of Sarmen."

*Whoa,* I thought, wondering what kind of magic had broadcast that voice at us. Sound Magic, maybe—something akin to the Light Magic I'd learned from Avildor?

Beside me, I heard Commandant Bastard growl.

We waited for Esmeralda's reply.

She said, in acknowledgment, "I am pleased to make your acquaintance, sir."

Prince Mejnul smiled. "I apologize for interrupting your feast, Milady. I mean no harm. We will not stay. Only long enough to ask your forgiveness."

"For what, sir? For despoiling our tournament? For cheating on the Field of Honor?"

Prince Mejnul bowed. "For exactly that, Milady. I am, regretfully, sure that everyone there knew that I am not the fighter that young Master Blunt is. I would that I were! I must concede that there is no way I could beat such a warrior in fair combat. His skills far surpass mine. Sadly, I have other duties to occupy my time than studying the arts of war. I wish it were otherwise and that I were good enough to measure myself against him. I am not."

He turned to young Jack, and said, courteously, "You are the better man, sir. I apologize for my conduct today. The victory should have been—indeed, very shortly would have been—yours, had I not cheated."

Once again, he inclined his head towards young Jack Blunt. It was at the same time an admission of fault and a casual dismissal of a social inferior.

"Unfortunately," Prince Mejnul went on, without waiting for a reply, "it is impermissible for me to allow myself to be defeated. That would have had repercussions. Word would have spread. I could not allow that—as perhaps you, Milady, will understand. My father and I have many realms to rule. I believe you might agree, Milady, that ruling is not a simple task? In short," he shrugged, with a rueful smile, "I could not lose. Yet I knew that I could not win against a superior fighter. So I fought foul and put Master Blunt at my mercy. And so it will be known, once again, throughout our empire, that we always win, whatever the cost. The cost to me today, it pains me to say, was my honor, and a harsh lesson at the hands of my opponent's father. A steep price—but one that had to be paid. No one who hears of this will fail to understand. Our will is law."

He looked from young Jack Blunt to his father, to the rest of us, and finally to Esmeralda.

It was, I had to admit against my will, handsomely said. I could feel the crowd around me relaxing, as if they, too, were now less hostile towards him, now that they had heard his apology and understood his reasons for cheating.

We all waited for Esmeralda's reply.

"If you admit your transgressions, sir," she began, and stopped.

Prince Mejnul bowed, and said, "I do."

"Then that is knightly courtesy," she acknowledged. "And it would be discourteous of me not to accept your contrition."

Good for her, I thought. She's playing this nobility game better than I ever could. Under the cover of civility these two were twisting each other in knots; sticking the barbs in while pretending that they weren't. I began to relax. *She's got this*, I thought. He's come to make good. She's letting him do that—while also letting him know that we all know he behaved despicably. And that, maybe, we now understand why. He had other matters to consider beyond this one, small tourney.

He, or rather his dynasty, has a kingdom to rule. An empire. *Win at all costs.* Leave the Rules of Chivalry on the Field of Honor where they belong. What do those matter, compared with the stamp of authority, without which they could not govern? They did not rule by honor, by the conventions of games. They ruled by force, in the real world. He must appear invincible. He was taking us into his confidence by admitting, candidly, that he'd only done what he had to do.

He had, I thought, made his point well—and done so with a good grace.

"I am grateful, Milady, for your forgiveness. That is generous indeed." Prince Mejnul said, bowing, with another smile.

It was a smile that I liked more, now.

I looked around, and saw other smiles break out in response.

He was winning a tough crowd over.

Shift, though, was trembling in my hands. She did not like the way that this was going. She was nervous, on edge.

"Your fame has spread far and wide, Milady," he continued. "When I heard of you, I could not believe what the reports were saying. *The loveliest life there ever was, or ever will be.* I had to make the long journey to this realm to see for myself. And what I saw turned my world upside down. I saw you holding court, in Mayport, and was amazed to see that you are as wise as you are beautiful. I entered your tournament with the vainglorious idea of winning it; and, as victor, laying my heart at your feet."

He shook his head, with a rueful smile. "That was not to be. A foolish, romantic notion. Much though I would love to be as skilled at arms as Master Blunt, my fate is to rule, not to win glory on the Field of Honor. I accept my limitations. I hope that you can accept them too, as well as my hand in marriage. You will grace my father's court, which, in due time, will be ours. I have seen how your people love you. My people will love you too."

Gasps of shock came from the crowd around me. None of them had seen that coming. Nor would I have, had Shift not alerted me.

Prince Mejnul stood there in front of all of us, smiling, calmly waiting for her response.

Which, I saw, he clearly expected to be a grateful acceptance of the honor that he was bestowing upon her.

Esmeralda gathered herself. "Sir," she said, "I am not yet seventeen."

"Nor was I, when I first wed. She was fourteen. You will like her."

Now the crowd around Esmeralda was grumbling, everyone exchanging looks, none of them liking what they were hearing.

Esmeralda frowned, and said, "How can I marry you, if you already have a wife?

"I have four. You will be my fifth. And, upon my honor as Crown Prince of Sarmen, the foremost among them and my future empress."

That was too much for Commandant Bastard, who bellowed, "You have no honor, boy!"

Prince Mejnul stared at him. "I have torturers," he said, "who will enjoy working on you, old man."

Commandant Bastard sneered. "Do your own dirty work, coward."

Prince Mejnul's smile faded, and his face darkened. He turned to Esmeralda and said, "You allow this commoner to address me thus, Milady?"

"Oh, no one tells him what to do," Esmeralda replied. "Commandant?"

"Yes, Majesty?"

"Perhaps you could hold your peace?"

Commandant Bastard growled; then, bowing, said, "As *you* command." After which he gave Mejnul a filthy look, which, I was glad to see, made him take a couple of steps backwards.

Esmeralda smiled at Prince Mejnul—not entirely convincingly. Clearly she did not know what to say. She did not want to say yes. Nor did she want to provoke him or humiliate him.

She wanted this not to be happening.

She said, "Wouldn't your other wives object?"

Prince Mejnul shook his head and smiled. "They will be as delighted as I will be to welcome you into our Imperial Family."

He waited for her answer.

Eventually, Esmeralda said, "You must understand, sir, that this is somewhat of a surprise."

He inclined his head. "A pleasant one, I hope."

175

She wasn't going to fall into that trap. "You must also understand that the customs of our realms may differ?"

"They may, indeed," he conceded. "There are many realms in my father's empire, and among them many different customs. We make sure to honor them all."

"In ours," Esmeralda said, "we believe that a woman is free to marry as she chooses."

Prince Mejnul's eyebrows rose in surprise. "Really?" he said. "What a peculiar idea."

He appeared to think over what he had heard. "May I have your answer?"

Esmeralda said, "I thank you for your courtesy, sir, and the compliment, but I must decline your offer. I shall choose my own husband, on my own terms."

Prince Mejnul contemplated her, thoughtfully. "Well, I thank you for *your* answer, Milady," he said, with a smile—which was, somehow, not quite as nice as it had been before. "Your realm, your rules."

Esmeralda said, "I'm glad you understand."

"Indeed," Prince Mejnul agreed. "And in turn, I ask you to understand something. When this is my realm, my rules will apply."

The crowd, which had been shifting and murmuring, went still.

Esmeralda said, "*Your* realm, sir?"

"You could save your people a lot of pain by coming with me now," Prince Mejnul said. "You will be treated with the highest honor, as my bride and future empress. Or, I will accept your surrender when I return with an army you can never hope to match." He waved his hand at the three gigantic beasts behind him. "A hundred of these, raining fire and fury down on you from above. A hundred thousand like my bodyguard below, with their swords and spears. Tens of thousands of archers and cavalry. After which, you will be my captive, so I will have no need to wed you. And you, and your realm, will be mine to do with as I please. You saw how I cannot allow myself to be defeated. Just so, I cannot allow myself to be defied. We tend not to have pity on those who defy us. Need I say more?"

"Yes," Esmeralda said, when she had gathered herself. "You need to say how this is honorable."

Prince Mejnul frowned. "It is honorable because it serves my honor."

"And my honor, sir?"

"Your honor is my honor. Your honor is my offer. Or is nothing. You have a choice. Come with me now, or wait for my return. At the head of my Imperial Army."

All eyes turned to Esmeralda. They did not want to lose her. Nor did they want to be at the mercy of a hundred dragons and a horde of chalk-white monsters.

Esmeralda said, "Will you allow me some time, sir, to consider your proposal?"

Prince Mejnul thought that over.

"I will," he said. "I would not like to be thought inconsiderate. You have much to think on. With you ruling as my empress, all here would be safe under my protection. We could spend half the year here, should you wish. It is a pleasant land. If you are happy here, so would I be. Or—the alternative. This realm ravaged, until it surrenders. My regent on your throne. A harsh rule imposed as punishment for your defiance. And," his voice took on a tone of warning, "should you die, Milady, know this: That will be no escape. Your realm will be destroyed and your people put to the sword.

"Do you wish that," he challenged, "on your realm? On your people?"

Esmeralda stared at him, then lowered her gaze. In front of her, her fingers knitted together, in and out of each other.

She raised her head, and looked up again at Prince Mejnul, her eyes moist with tears. "I do not."

He smiled. It was the smile of a victor. He said, gently, "Then you will come with me, Milady?"

Esmeralda said, "I will not."

Prince Mejnul held her eyes and then nodded.

"I will return," he said, "on Midsummer Day. And on that day the choice will be yours."

He inclined his head in farewell and turned away, flanked by his bodyguard and sorceress.

They walked back up the wings of their dragons and settled into their seats above their mounts' shoulders. The beasts spread their huge wings and launched themselves into the air.

We watched them beat their way skywards, their silhouettes dwindling into the setting sun, their harsh cries fading off into the distance.

# 15

## Separate Ways

Not surprisingly, no one felt like celebrating anymore.

Esmeralda, though, was having none of it. Commandant Blunt was murmuring a few words in her ear as I looked away from the black dots that were the disappearing dragons to see how she was doing. *This is so unfair on her,* I thought.

When the Commandant finished, she clapped her hands, and her face lit up in a delighted smile as she jumped on the spot.

"Oh, that's *wonderful,* Commandant!" she said, her eyes shining. "I can't wait to tell everyone! Just say the word."

He bowed, and backed away.

Esmeralda hurried out into the courtyard, then turned around and addressed us all, the smile of a delicious secret on her face. "Well, we've had the bad news. I look forward to telling you all the *good* news! Which I will do as soon as I can—perhaps even tonight? Who knows? Meanwhile: We have a feast to finish," she said. "It would be a shame to let all the hard work that has gone into preparing it go to waste. As to what will happen between now and Midsummer Day: Who can tell? All I know is that I have good advisers, and they will give me the wisest counsel. I also look forward to hearing from all of our noble lords and ladies for their opinions as to what we should do. And I make you this promise, now: I will do what is best for this realm, and for all of you.

"As for this evening: We have champions to toast, and to honor. I, for one, intend to do just that!"

She looked around, from face to face, calm, and confident, her expression radiating honesty and openness. She did not seem in the least downcast, but, rather, as if she was looking forward to what lay ahead and was sure she would enjoy it. I wondered what it was that Commandant Blunt had told her. People moved aside to allow her through, and Esmeralda walked towards the castle, catching her guests' eyes and smiling. She led the way back into the Great Hall, her Royal Guard falling in around her.

It should have been a wake, considering what we had just seen, and what Prince Mejnul had threatened us with. But, pretty quickly, it wasn't. Apprehension gave way to anger. The more we drank, the more defiant we became. "I should've taken Kinell to those damn brutes!" Grell snorted. "Smashed the crap out of their feet till they fell over, then beaten their brains in."

"Might get a bit fiery, Grello," Oller suggested.

"Oh, I do believe we know a mage or two who'd cast Shields on me."

"That we do," I agreed. "And Ice Storm might cool them down a bit. Hail, and snow, and frost swirling round them, and the ground under them freezing them solid into it? I don't think they'd like that."

"Think you could handle three at once?" Grell said.

I felt Shift's anger, and her defiant *You bet we could!*

"If they're close together, like those three were, I don't see why not," I said. "Ice Storm's an Area of Effect attack, so they'd all be caught in it. And I'd maybe send a few Ghouls or Screamers over their heads, to Fear them; and they'd go berserk, and trample their own riders. And, by the way: Shift wasn't the only battlestaff in the crowd. Marnie, and Junie, and their Covensisters, and the Archmage, and others had theirs. We'd have kept them busy."

Yes, we liked the idea of taking the fight to the enemy. We weren't going to roll over for that arrogant show-off. He deserved his comeuppance. We all loved the idea of him getting it.

And then, inevitably, our ardor faded, as we thought about the numbers.

Perhaps several powerful casters might inflict damage on three dragons. But on a hundred? And them not crowded together in a tight space, on the ground, but overhead, flying?

And—what was it Mejnul had said? *Raining fire and fury down from above.*

We tried to keep our spirits up. It was a losing battle—which we all felt, in our hearts, that a battle against a hundred dragons and a hundred thousand chalkers and knights and archers would inevitably be.

We'd be overwhelmed. We'd do our best. We'd die trying.

*We'd die.*

Our realm would be destroyed. It would all be for nothing. And Esmeralda … doomed if she did, doomed if she didn't.

We didn't want to think about it.

I really wanted to hear what Commandant Blunt had to say about it all, but he had disappeared. Young Jack escorted his mother home, after a while. I couldn't think why Qrysta had not gone back to take her position behind Queen Esmeralda at the High Table—or why there were far fewer of the Royal Guard in attendance than there had been when the feast had started. But she, and they, were nowhere in sight. No doubt, I thought, we'd find out in the morning.

We had little appetite for food or drink. Only Esmeralda, at the High Table, did not share our feelings of annoyance, and impotence, and despair. She behaved as if nothing had happened. She laughed, and listened, and discussed, and chatted. She raised her goblet to the champions of her Royal Tournament. She honored their victories, and thanked them for attending, and praised them for their prowess. She rose above the occasion. It was inspirational.

If only we could have been inspired. We knew that we were doomed, as was she. We acted the part of revelers at a royal feast. We convinced neither ourselves nor each other. A celebration that should have lasted into the small hours ended well before midnight. In ones and twos we all left, the thin tunes of the musicians in their gallery echoing down into the emptying hall.

The Royal Assembly would take place the next day at noon, as it did every day; which left plenty of time before it for the Privy Council meeting that Esmeralda had ordered for the hour of sunrise. Those of us who had been summoned rose early, and broke our fasts before dawn, then made our way to the queen's private audience chamber. There were nine of us: only those she deemed both essential and trustworthy. Esmeralda was all business and practicality. What killed dragons? Velaryn did not know. She and her fellow apothecaries would find out all they could.

"If there is a dragonbane," Velaryn said, "we'll find it. If not, we'll mix the deadliest poisons we know of, as powerful as we can, and a lot of them. They'll kill anything that can be killed."

Esmeralda said, "Good."

I remembered Vagg and suggested that the queen send for him. "My friends say he knows more about dragons than anyone," I said. "Very different type of dragon, but still, somewhere to start?"

A royal envoy was dispatched with a summons to bring Vagg and his charges to her court at once.

We all waited for Esmeralda to reveal what Commandant Blunt had told her the previous evening that had made her so relaxed, confident even, in the face of the threat that the realm now faced.

She looked up at us, from face to face. The happy expression that she'd worn the night before, and had kept up all through the feast, was nowhere to be seen.

"I expect you're all wondering what the Commandant said to me last night, that cheered me up so," she said. She paused, then continued, "Well, I hope that everyone else in town is wondering the same and waiting to find out." She gathered herself and shook her head. "What he told me was to buy him time enough to lock the town gates and station soldiers and the Royal Guard everywhere, with orders to let no one leave Eastbay under any circumstances. Which, he assures me, has now been done. Commandant?"

Jack Blunt explained. "I need every man of fighting age the realm has, and every man or woman who can draw a bow or cast a spell, and I need them assembled and ready for battle at Mayport, by Midsummer Day. And that means not letting any noble lords or ladies swear their eternal loyalty to Her Majesty, then scuttle back to their castles and lock their gates, and drop their portcullises, and raise their drawbridges, and keep their armies to themselves, safe behind their castle walls. I'd never have time to lay siege to any one castle in the kingdom, let alone all of them, and they'd all know that. They'll be provisioned for a year, let alone for the few months till midsummer.

"Why should they suffer destruction and ruin, they'll all be thinking, on the queen's behalf? *Much better, for the realm, for her to accept the high honor the crown prince has offered her, and leave, and never come back—and what choice will she have, if there's no army at her back, when he returns at the head of his? There'll be the Royal Guard, who won't fight, because they can't, being just ceremonial, and a few hundred Orcs, outnumbered scores to one by chalkers.*

*"We have no quarrel with Sarmen. Why should the emperor, or his son, bother with this little out-of-the-way realm? And if he does want it, why, we'll open our gates to him, and pledge obedience! Defy him, and he'll not stand for that. He'll unleash his monsters, and that will be the end of our noble families. Work with him, and we'll keep his peace, and our heads, and our castles and lands. The girl will see sense. Either way—vassal state of Sarmen, or free Jarnland—we'll have a new king or queen on the throne, and why should that not be me?"*

Silence fell around the table, as that sank in.

It was broken by Marnie's chuckle. "Quite the performance, young lady!" she said. "Took me in and all, and I don't take in easy." She seemed never to have considered using a more formal address. To her, Esmeralda was as much scullery maid Mabel as she was her queen. I think Esmeralda liked it that way. And, after all, Marnie was her Elder, and Covensister. It must be a relief for her, I thought, not to have to be always in charge.

"You convinced me too, Majesty," Archmage Faldruti said, with a bow.

"Well," Esmeralda said "I don't want to marry Prince Mejnul. So I needed to be convincing. I will marry him if I have to, of course. I won't allow war. Certainly not one that we can't possibly win."

"That remains to be seen," Marnie said. "We're not giving up yet, thank you very much. I don't appreciate threats. Or arrogance. So," she turned to Blunt, "you have time enough to round everyone up?"

"Yes and no," Commandant Bastard answered. "I will muster all the forces I can find. But not every lord or lady came to Eastbay for the tournament. The further west their domains, the more likely it was that they did not make the journey."

"So?" Qrysta said. "How many, do you think?"

"Fifty thousand," Blunt replied. "Seventy at most."

A sizable host, but—against a hundred thousand, with a hundred dragons in the air above them? We would be hopelessly overmatched.

I remembered what the Commandant had told us about what he called *ghoulies and ghosties,* when he was training us as recruits at Brigstowe.

I said, "Special forces?"

"Not their kind of fight," Blunt replied. "They're more suited to skulduggery than open battle. Dirty work, in the dark, underground, rather than in broad daylight, in the open air. I know who to ask, and I will; and they know me, so will be inclined to join us, I believe. We'll not get more than a few dozen though, at most."

We all waited for Esmeralda's decision. She was staring at the table-top in front of her. She lifted her head, and shook it, firmly. "No," she said, "I can't allow this. I'm not more important than anyone else. I'll send to Sarmen, and tell the prince I accept his offer. With … whatever humble and grateful and flattering words I need to say. Appreciation of the honor bestowed on me. And how I am looking forward to experiencing the delights of Sarmen and the Imperial Court. And then, maybe I can keep his gaze away from this realm and he'll forget about it, and leave it in peace."

And that, we all thought, would be that.

Problem solved.

He wins, we lose—but not everything.

Esmeralda is doomed anyway, so why not avoid the collateral damage?

It was Marnie who broke the spell. "Yes," she said. "You can do that, girl. But you don't have to do it *yet*. Mayhaps things'll work out different. You have time. Use it. He'll be thinking about you, as you'll be thinking about him. He's made his move. He thinks he knows how everything's going to go from now on. He doesn't know, any more than anyone ever does. So, don't rush to make an early end of this. Play it long."

Esmeralda said, "What does that mean?"

"His move, your move. His counter, yours. One after the other."

"So, what is my move, Marnie?"

"Same as it always is!" Marnie snorted. "Stay ahead of *his* move. So, down to business: There are two jobs. Prepare, and keep everyone happy."

Esmeralda said, "And how do I do that?"

"*We*. Not just you, girl. You do the second bit. You keep your spirits up, and your chin up, and everyone else will see that and think, *Oh, ah? Queen's chipper, and confident, so things might not be so bad.* As I said, you fooled me earlier, and I don't fool easy. Comes natural to you, that, so you just keep doing what you're good at. Meanwhile, the Commandant will muster the realm."

"I've ordered the troops to horse, Majesty," Commandant Blunt said. "We'll be on our way within the hour. And I'm taking the Orc chieftains with us. No one says no to them. You just need to keep the nobles distracted."

"I'll do what I can," Esmeralda said, "but I don't really know how I'll—"

"Heralds," Qrysta said.

All eyes turned to her.

"Tell the Chief Herald that you wish to see every noble lord and lady in private, for their advice, in strictest confidence. Let them know that you want them to feel free to talk to you, because you trust them, without some other noble lord listening and rushing off to tell his friends. And let it be known that you are taking counsel from every nobleman, or noblewoman, in strictest order of precedence. Heralds love all that stuff. They must tell every noble that he or she is in the second or third tier of precedence, and when they ask who is ahead of them, give them the name of some neighbor or rival that they regard as inferior. That'll infuriate them. The nobles will object, so tell the heralds to be obstructive, and snotty, and to go strictly by protocol. And to talk about lineage, and family trees, and bends sinister, and cadet branches of the family. That'll keep them busy for weeks."

Esmeralda's face broke out in a smile. "That it will."

Amused, I said, "How d'you know all this stuff?"

"It's all I've been hearing for weeks now, while you were gallivanting around in the Deepwoods," Qrysta said. "They drove me nuts. Well, now let them drive everyone else nuts."

Esmeralda said, "Can you see to that?"

"It'll be my pleasure," Qrysta said, getting up and leaving the room. "There's nothing I'd enjoy more than giving our Chief Herald a headache."

As she left, Commandant Blunt said, "I'll have the full force of the realm mustered at Mayport within two months, Majesty, and then I'll knock them into shape."

"Thank you, Commandant," Esmeralda said. A thought occurred to her. "Why d'you think he picked Midsummer Day?"

"It takes time to prepare for war, Majesty. The bigger the army, the longer it takes. And it's a long voyage from Sarmen. Their fleet needs assembling, and victualing. Horses, arms, armor, supplies—all that."

"Yes," Esmeralda said, nodding. "I can see that it would. Well, that gives us time, at least. We must use it. But I won't allow war. Not one that we can't possibly win."

"With respect, Majesty," the Commandant pointed out, "there's no point in not being as ready as we can be."

"True," Esmeralda said. "Still. I can't allow bloodshed on my behalf."

Marnie and Archmage Faldruti told her that they would mobilize Coven and the GAA, and train up every capable caster in both guilds to the highest possible levels in Destruction Magic and Healing. They had, of course, noticed Prince Mejnul's sorceress. As to how many more like her the Sarmenids had, and what they were capable of, we had no way of knowing. Only Jack Blunt had been to that part of the world. He'd told us what he knew, and it was not encouraging.

Silence fell over the Council. We simply didn't know what we'd be dealing with. You can't fight a war without information.

It was Oller who broke the silence. "Right, well, I'd best be on my way."

We all looked at him in surprise.

"You need eyes and ears in the enemy's camp, right?" he said. "You just said that, if not in so many words. Well, you can't tell me you'll find better eyes and ears than *mine*. I can't take Little Guy, though; he'll have to stay here. Dogs attract attention. *Hullo, what's his name, friendly little chap, isn't he?* On my own I won't be noticed."

He turned to me. "He likes Jess. She can look after him, eh?"

I nodded. "She'd love that. And he can look after her while she's a cadet in Mayport. That's perfect. She'll be protected; he'll be sheltered. Any bully tries to bother her, he'll have Little Guy's teeth in his leg. And Little Guy will have a warm bed at night and someone to feed him."

Esmeralda said. "Oller, no, I can't allow it."

"Eh? Why not? I mean, *why not, Majesty* …"

"It'll be dangerous."

Oller looked at her, baffled. "So?"

"What if they capture you?"

"What if they do?" Oller scoffed. "I'm just some wharf rat from somewhere they've never heard of. Deserted from a ship's crew. I'll have a good story. I always make sure to have a good story. Anyway, nobody's going to pay no mind to me. I'm used to keeping my head down, don't you worry about me, lass—I mean, *Majesty*. Trained my whole life in sneaking and peeking, I have. And finding. You need answers found, no?"

No one denied that.

"Well, I'll find them, if there are any to be found," Oller concluded. "I'm good at finding."

Hearing Oller's trademark boast, I couldn't help smiling. He had, after all, lived up to it, many times over. I remembered him recounting to me the tale of how he'd sneaked into the necromancer's tower, up on Aylsmoor, and what he'd seen and done in there, undetected. He'd had the nerve to carry out the grisly task—a nerve I'd never have had. If he could do that, I thought, well, maybe he'd be okay in Sarmen, blending into the background, eyes and ears open. And maybe he'd find something we needed to know.

Commandant Blunt was studying him thoughtfully. "And how d'you propose to get those answers to us, lad?" he asked. "From all those leagues away, across the seas? And in good time enough so we can make use of them?"

Oller replied with a wink and tapped the side of his nose. "Trade secret, if you'll allow me, Commandant. I have my ways; shall we leave it at that? Soon as I know anything, you'll know."

Jack Blunt frowned. He didn't like being in the dark. Then he nodded. "You're as good a sneak as any I've ever seen, Master Oller," he allowed, "and as good a graduate as I ever trained. It was you as got us into Rushtoun, all nice and quiet, when we were stumped outside its walls. My Lord of Brigstowe had the sense not to ask you your methods then. Strikes me I'd be wise to follow his lead and ask no further now."

He turned to Esmeralda. "I'd be inclined to allow him to prove himself, ma'am. He's never let me down yet, and I don't believe he'll let you down either."

I could see that Esmeralda still didn't like it. She didn't want someone going into danger on her behalf. Especially not someone who had already done so before.

"You can't protect everyone, girl," Marnie said, gently. "I know you think it's your job, but that's not the way the world works. Why ... if war's coming here, the lad will be well out of the way, won't he? He'll be safer there in peaceful Sarmen than any of us here in the eye of the storm."

"Oh, I'll be back in time for the fireworks," Oller said. "You can depend on that. I'm not going to miss seeing the look on Prince Mince's face when we put him in his place."

Esmeralda sat back, startled. Then she broke out in a grin. "Is that what you call him?"

"Suits him, eh?" Oller smirked.

"I do believe it does. Just don't call me Princess Mincess when I have to marry him."

"Not going to happen," Grell said.

Esmeralda looked at him. She appreciated his support, but needed to point out, "As the Commandant said, Grell, we must prepare for all eventualities."

"He'll have to marry me, first!" Grell countered.

Esmeralda giggled. "Yes, well. I'm sure he'd love *that* wedding night. But enough foolishness. Although you have cheered me up. Thanks."

"So," Oller said, "where's this Sarmen, then, and how do I get there?"

"South and west," Jack Blunt replied. "And by smuggler, would be best. Nothing official, like. Wharf rats don't sneak off legal ships that report to the Tidemaster as soon as they dock. Westwich, you'll find passage. Fine port for the smuggling, Westwich, and the main port for the empire trade. Ships sail from there to Sarmen all the time. I know who you need to speak to, I'll give you a note for him. I left from there myself, for Temuan. And they didn't set me down in no port, neither. Rowed me ashore in the middle o' nowhere, in the middle of the night, they did—the which suited us both fine. No one saw me come, no one saw me go."

Oller grunted. "Sounds about right."

Archmage Faldruti said, "Our guild will consult with the College of Lore and Learning. We will supply maps, and what knowledge we have. We will examine our archives for anything that might be of help to you."

Oller said, "Thank you, Archmage."

"Not to mention potions, powders …" he added, and then glanced at Marnie, and Velaryn, before continuing " …and poisons."

"Mm," Oller grunted. "Much appreciated. Might be as how I'll be needing those. Best label them clearly, eh? I wouldn't want to get them mixed up."

"We will," Velaryn said.

Oller nodded and turned to me. "So, looks like I'm going one way, you lot are going t'other. Wish I was going with you, mateys. It's more fun traveling together. But sometimes you get more done traveling alone."

I couldn't think what to say. I didn't like the idea of heading off into the Ice Lands without Oller. He was a third of Grell's size, and nowhere near the warrior that Qrysta was; but, somehow, I felt that, with Oller in our team, we were safe. He saw everything, heard everything, gave us all the warning we needed. And no one pulled the wool over his eyes. Compared with Oller, Grell and Qrysta and I were innocents. I was meant to be the one who was good with puzzles; but half the time it felt as if Oller was the brains of the outfit.

On this occasion, though, his skills were needed elsewhere.

It was Grell who found the right words. "We'll be ending up in the same place, Oller mate. Mayport, Midsummer Day. We're just taking different roads to get there."

Oller grinned. "Sooner we take 'em, the sooner we all get back here, eh?"

I hoped we'd be okay without him. I was pretty sure he'd cope just fine without us. I wondered if he'd find anything useful in Sarmen. At least I knew how he'd get the information to us if he did.

We practiced our comms after the Council meeting was over. When we'd explained it to him, in the local TG hideout, Oller had understood the principle of Morse code right away. "All I need is a dot and a dash, eh?" he said. "That should be easy enough."

It was. When he touched his Ring of Blending to his Link of Impartment, it showed a ghostly white on my band and his, obscuring both of them. His star sapphire Ring of Seeking and Seeing shone a vivid blue. "Can't be seen wearing this where I'm going, he said. He took it off and tucked it away in a secret inside pocket. "Gold and jewels on a street scruff? Guards would haul me up. I'll be seeking and seeing, though, so I'll need it with me."

White would be dot, we decided; blue, therefore, was dash.

Touching my Link with a magic item seemed a better idea than casting Damages or Heals at it—those lasted too long and made forming my letters a slow process. My greenfire Masterpiece pendant lit it up green—for dash—and the Lightseek fire opal ring that Avildor had given me made it glow orange, which was near enough to red-for-hot.

"Right, then," Oller said, once that was established. "Now what?"

I said, "We tell you the letters. And the numbers."

"All right. Piece of cake, this! Love it. What are they?"

I looked, Qrysta. "What?"

"Well, go on. Tell him."

"I don't know Morse code."

I gaped at her. "This was your idea!"

"Yeah, well, it's a good one."

"But if we don't know Morse code? You suggested Morse code, and you don't know Morse code?"

"I know SOS," she said. "You?"

"That. And V for Victory; and R for Roger. Which only leaves us another twenty-two letters."

"I also know the numbers," she said. "They have a pattern,"

She showed us, and they did.

"Logical, that," Oller agreed.

So at least we had *zero* through *nine* covered. Which had to be something. If Oller wanted to tell me that the enemy had 150 dragons coming our way, at least we'd understand the *150* part of the message.

We were still a long way from knowing what we were doing, though.

Grell was frowning, deep in thought. "I should be able to remember most of them," he said. "When we were kids, we played with torches at night—what you yanks call flashlights, Qrys. Sending each other secret messages, and that."

It took longer to find a pen and an inkwell than it did for me to write Grell's dots and dashes into my Infinite Notebook. There were only a few letters he couldn't remember, so we just made those up. Writing and reading were essential skills in the TG, Oller told us. You couldn't get inducted into the guild without the basics, and had to be proficient in order to rise up the ranks.

"Important, in our line o' work, to know the difference between *Treasury, Keep Out* and *Beware of the Dogs,*" Oller pointed out. "Not to mention things like *Storeroom, Armory, Wine Cellar,* and such; and if you can read the labels on bottles, you can lift the valuables, and leave the cheap stuff. Remember Urrch? That vamp who took me down into Long Cavern? A phial of his blood, if he was contagious, would be worth its weight in gold. And it would just look like brown muck to you and me, if you couldn't read the label."

He and I sat across the table from each other and sent messages back and forth into each other's Link of Impartment. We soon got the hang of deciphering them. The tricky thing was judging the length of the pauses between letters and words. We agreed on a number of shortcuts, such as *r* for *are,* and *u* for *you.* Two *N*'s would mean *ends.* Then the other would know it was his chance to reply. Three *N*'s would

mean *end of communication, signing off*. In all we had about fifty separate signals, with which, we thought, we could communicate pretty
much anything.

"I'll have lots o' time to get these by heart," Oller said. "It's a long
sea voyage to Sarmen, the Commandant says. Not to mention a few
days overland from here to Westwich."

I said, "You don't have to learn them, Ols. You can just consult
your notes."

Oller snorted. "What do you think I am, Daxx! Stupid? Get
caught, with a code book on me?! No thank *you*. Soon as they found
that they'd know I'm someone they need to take a long look at. And
then I'll be stretched out on the question-master's table, while some
sage or mage looks through my notes, and thinks, *Hullo, I wonder who's
at the other end of this little lot, then?*

"And they send you a message, as if it's coming from me—and
you never the wiser. So they open you up like a nice, fat, unsuspecting
oyster. And they pump you dry. And instead of me supplying you with
anything I might know, you'll tell them everything that *you* do. After
which, well …." He swallowed. "No, that's not a way I want to go, mateys. I've no wish to die as a spy. They ask spies all sorts of things, and
not nicely. And I wouldn't know any of them. Well, that's not going to
satisfy them, is it? So, they'd keep on asking, harder and harder." He
grimaced. "No, matey. I'll be committing this lot to memory."

"I see your point," I said. I didn't like the thought of being tortured
for information I didn't possess.

"And I'm not being caught with this on me neither," he said, taking
off the silver chain that hung around his neck. He removed his Ring
of Blending and pocketed it, before handing the chain, with its silver
key, to me.

I said, "Won't you need it?"

He shook his head. "I'll be spying in Sarmen, not stealing. I'll be
keeping my ears and eyes open, and my nose cleaner than clean. Don't
want no trouble with guards. If I need to open a lock, I'll do it the
old-fashioned way. Besides, if I get hauled up by the guards, and they
find this on me? *All right, chum, what's this fancy key for, then?!* I can
hide my rings in the linings of my clothes, but not this. I don't want to
be facing no hard questions while I'm over there, thanks. No, Jess looks
after Little Guy for me; you look after this."

"I will," I said. I was about to hang the key around my neck when I remembered the agony of silver against my skin over the recent Moon Nights. I tucked it away in the inside pocket of my jerkin.

It was a nasty night as we gathered at the quayside in the small hours. The Tidemaster was waiting for us outside the dock gates, a lantern swinging in his hands. The port was off limits to everyone else, by order of the queen. A cold wind was whipping up out of the north. Sharp rain stung our cheeks.

Wrapped in his cloak, Evall was watching the porters as they carried the last supplies aboard *The Red Rose*. Very diligent of him, I thought. He'd advised us on what trade goods we should take to Normark. He knew the sort of things his father's employer wanted from southern lands such as ours. There had not been enough time to gather the best possible cargo, but, with the queen's authority, we had a valuable load from what was available in the warehouses.

Evall was relieved. What we were carrying should help compensate for the failure of his father's expedition. He told us that Master Bjarnevalt, his father's employer, was the leading authority in Sondehafn, the port town where we were heading. We would need his cooperation if we were to get to where we needed, in the Ice Lands and beyond. Bringing him good merchandise should help us get it.

I said, "You should get belowdecks Evall, and out of this rain."

He jumped as if he hadn't seen me arrive. "Huh? Oh, yes, I will. I was just … waiting for Jess. In case she, you know, um, changed her mind, and came to see us off after all." He turned away and hurried up the gangplank.

He's going to miss her, I thought. And she him. They'd been a comfort to each other after all the hardships they'd both been through.

I wondered if they'd ever see each other again.

And would we, the thought followed, ever see our friends again? Oller, Esmeralda, Marnie, the Commandant?

Only time would tell.

There was no one to see us off. That was the way we wanted it. Slip out, unnoticed, and make our way north and east to Normark. Black clouds blew across the sky overhead, obscuring us from any watching eyes. Even so, I kept looking up, and around, for signs of pursuit. Foul weather, yes, but it was not a true storm, on which the Wild Hunt might ride.

I found the others below deck in the cramped quarters that had been assigned to us. Most of the little cabin seemed to be taken up by Grell, who was already snoring in a lower bunk. Qrysta was curled up in a blanket on the bunk above him. I knew Horm would be there, but was surprised to see Nyrik as well. He was sitting on a bunk, carefully wiping down his hunting bow by the light of a single candle. He gave me a wink and a grin. "Not letting my mate go off on his own, Daxxie," he said. "He gets into trouble without me."

"I don't doubt there'll be trouble," I said.

"Yur, Horm told me what you told him. Well, we'll all get into it together, then."

I felt better for seeing him. "It's good to have you with us, Nyrik," I said.

"It's good to have something to do," he said. "You was the one as advised us to find another line o' work, now that your lovely queen has outlawed our former profession. Me and Horm are thinking we might take up your trade, when this is all over."

I was baffled. "You want to become mages?"

Nyrik chuckled. "Gawds no, not *that* trade, mate. Questing. Adventuring. Take to the road, see what's out there. Seek our fortunes. Never know what you might find, eh?"

"That you don't," I agreed.

The ship moved under us. She was leaving the quayside. Sails slapped as they were run out to catch the wind. Orders were shouted. Footsteps hurried on the deck overhead. *The Red Rose* heeled onto her course. The floor under us tilted, and running water drummed under her hull.

Evall was crouched on a neighboring bunk. He looked exhausted, but, somehow, too anxious to sleep.

I took off my dripping cloak, and sat next to him. "You'll be home soon."

"Yes," he said.

"You must be happy about that."

"Yes," he said.

He didn't seem happy.

Well, I thought. He's young, he's tired, he's overwhelmed. He's lost his father, and is going home to his family, and his employer, to tell them of their bereavement and his losses. He probably doesn't know what to think.

192

"It'll be dawn in a few hours," I said. "You should get some sleep."

He nodded, and climbed up the ladder to the topmost bunk.

Nyrik blew out his candle and the cabin was plunged into darkness.

The familiar sounds of a wooden ship underway came down to us: creaks and groans of timber; wind whistling in the stays; water flowing past her hull; the footsteps of the crew above our heads. I stretched out on my bunk, wondering what lay ahead.

The College of Lore and Learning had found plenty of maps of the Sarmenid Empire for Oller to study. They'd had a map of the coastline of Normark, but none of its interior—let alone the Ice Lands.

Normark.

The Ice Lands.

I turned the words over in my head, along with Eilwen's cryptic lines, which still meant nothing to me. And then what Marnie had said about them:

*It's all there. All we need is the eyes to see it, and the wit to know what we're looking at.*

I was asleep before I knew it.

# 16

## Captain Rozlyn

I'm no kind of seaman. I knew just enough about sailing to realize that this wasn't as bad as our voyage out of Mayport aboard the ghost ship had been. Even so, it was far from a pleasure cruise. We beat north and east through stiff winds, the sky above us gray by day and black at night. We never saw stars.

*The Red Rose*'s hull bucked up and lurched down into heaving seas, which always seemed to be running across our line of travel, and shoving us this way and that, up and around and sideways. Most of the time we lay in our bunks in our stifling cabin. When that became unbearable we made our way above, into the open air, and tottered about on deck. We leaned on the gunwale for support and stared glumly at the horizon, wind and rain stinging our faces, hoping for a sight of land, wondering when the misery would end.

We threw up over the sides. The crew teased us. "Only another week of this, mates," they would say, "or two, if this fine wind drops." They walked with ease, never needing to use the lifelines that we groped our way along. Or they'd be standing out in the rigging far overhead, working the sails, calling, singing, answering. Clearly, this was nothing to them. Clearly, we were just passengers, even though this was our ship, and we were, technically, in charge.

We weren't *actually* in charge, of course. That is never the owner's role when a ship is underway, but always the captain's. Our captain was Rozlyn.

She was a tall, agile, angular creature, green-eyed, her long, red hair tied back above gold hoop earrings under a black headcloth. In her movements she was as lithe as a cat. One of her front teeth was gold, inset with a diamond. She wore a white blouse under a brown leather waistcoat, its loose sleeves ending in lace cuffs, tucked into a red sash above black leggings and seaboots. In foul weather, which was most of the time, she wore a calf-length, black woolen overcoat. A cutlass hung at her hip.

Qrysta had told me that I would like her. I didn't. The words that she said were respectful, but the way that she said them was condescending. *Her ship, her rules,* she seemed to be asserting. *My ship,* I made it clear, *your command.* Her job was to sail it; to get us to Normark, and wait there for our return. I reminded her that she was under royal orders. She conceded that she was, and there the matter rested. I had much more on my mind than Captain Rozlyn; but, when I considered her position, I thought that I understood it. This had been her ship. Now it wasn't. Maybe, I thought, when this is over, we could restore it to her again. If, somehow, we actually got through whatever lay ahead of us, and weren't incinerated by dragons, or slaughtered by chalkers … well, she'd have helped us, and why not spread the rewards around? I had no idea, of course, how any such thing could happen. But if it did, she'd have earned it, and our thanks.

And I was intrigued by her story.

She asked me what I knew of it.

I told her that, according to her parrot, she'd been thrown out of the aft window of her captain's cabin by her mutinying officers. *Out the window, out the window! Sharks! Sharks!*

Rozlyn chuckled. "I trained that bird well," she said. "You'd never find a better liar. Not that he knew he was lying—he just said what I told him. Pity that bastard Moyle sold him in Freehaven. He'll have got a pretty penny for him, I've no doubt."

She glowered, then her face lightened as she grinned. "No, it was a simple trick. First Officer Moyle comes in on my breakfast, and his thugs with him. Well, I'd been expecting it. I was outnumbered. Long story, none of which need concern you. Basically, they're a superstitious lot, sailors. And Moyle used my being Coven as a way to turn the officers. *Bad luck*, I was. *They'd never find plunder with me as captain.* Or, worse, *I'd sink the ship under them, and turn them all into mermen.*

"A lot of nonsense, which I only heard about too late to stop what was coming. They were armed, and I wasn't. If you don't count a teaspoon, which they didn't. And they should have, that being all the weapon I needed. I kept them talking, sat at my breakfast, the aft window open behind me, and a nice fine morning it was too. That bothered them, so they blustered, and spat, and I just asked for a moment to finish my breakfast, gentlemen, if that was all the same to them, and then I'd be leaving. Which confused them; and so they shuffled, muttering. And I scooped out my egg, making sure not to puncture the shell, and ate the last spoonful and a finger of toast. Then I drained my coffee, and picked up the eggshell, and a napkin, and bid them farewell, and jumped out of the window, spelling shell and spoon and cloth to grow as we fell.

"And yes, there were fins aplenty in the water below, but they weren't going to bother me. I remember looking back, as Moyle and his men ran to the window to look out and saw me sailing my eggshell away, with her teaspoon mast and napkin sail. I waved at them, and their faces fell. That was when they knew. They already knew I was Coven and didn't like it, which is why they'd mutinied. But now they knew I'd be coming for them.

"Turned out that I didn't, though. You and your crew did. And made an end of them. For which I thank you. And not many months later, your friend, my Covensister, the queen, returns me to my command. Of your ship. All has worked out very nicely, wouldn't you say?"

Again, it made sense.

Again, I didn't like it.

Oh well, I thought. We'd be ashore soon enough, with more to worry about than a captain who was too pleased with herself by half. And she ran a tight ship, there was no doubt about that. We were in capable hands. I just didn't like them.

I had time enough to get our Morse-ish code by heart. If Oller was learning it, I thought, so should I. Qrysta pointed out that he might get through to me after dark—or when we were underground, somewhere where we didn't want to risk a light, which I'd need if I had to fish out my Infinite Notebook in order to decode what he was saying.

Qrysta and Grell were memorizing it too—which, again, was sensible, in case anything happened to me.

Oller and I had agreed that I wouldn't try to contact him unless it was absolutely necessary. He'd be at his sneaking and peeking in enemy territory, where a band on his wrist flashing red dots and green dashes might attract unwanted attention. He was already going to be in harm's way just by being in Sarmen. The last thing I wanted to do was alert the enemy to him. He'd promised me that he'd try comms once he'd learned the letters perfectly.

We were about a week out from Eastbay when his first message came through. It opened with the sequence that we had agreed on. Qrysta, watching the blue and white glows on my Link of Impartment, translated aloud, to show that she too had mastered the letters.

In w nn ("In Westwich, ends.")

I replied, my Band now lighting up orange or green:

On rr nn ("On *Red Rose*, ends.")

A g u q nn ("All good you query? Ends.")

A g 2 nn ("All good too, ends.")

Ship 2 s 2 nite nn ("Um—Ship to Sarmen tonight, ends")

"I believe so," I answered Qrysta's questioning look.

I tapped in:

Safe jrny nn ("Safe journey, ends.")

T y g l m 8 s nn ("Thank you, good luck mates, ends.")

U 2 o nnn ("You too, Oller, end of communication.")

"Worked well," Qrysta said, as the colors on my Link of Impartment faded.

"It did," I agreed. "Well, I hope his voyage is smoother than ours."

Qrysta grunted. "I wonder how things are in Westwich."

The tone of her voice made me glance over at her. She sounded anxious. That was hardly surprising, considering the circumstances in which we'd left Eastbay.

I knew she'd been reluctant to leave Esmeralda, who would have the weight of the realm on her young shoulders. And there were plenty of noble lords and ladies, not to mention the late King Wyllard's kin, that Qrysta didn't trust. They'd been all smiles and courtesy when the realm was at peace, and the people grateful that Esmeralda had emerged victorious from our campaign against Jurun. With the threat of war, against an enemy as overwhelming as Sarmen, their attitudes had changed.

Qrysta knew how it would be. The noble lords and ladies would argue that the fate of the realm lay in Esmeralda's hands. It was her duty to submit to Prince Mejnul and spare her people any suffering. Why should they lose their lands and castles on her behalf?

Commandant Bastard had told Qrysta not to fret. No one would hurt Esmeralda while he drew breath. And he, and Esmeralda, had told Qrysta that her place was at my side, not kicking her heels in court and worrying about me on my journey into the unknown, feeling she'd let me down.

After several days the weather turned fine, which was none too soon for us landlubbers. The wind lessened but remained favorable as the seas became more or less calm. It was a relief to be out in the open and breathing the fresh, salt-tanged air, rather than being hunkered down in our stuffy cabin. It was with the idea of impressing upon Captain Rozlyn that this was our ship, rather than hers, that I got Qrysta and Grell to spar with the crew. I wanted to see how good they were. They weren't.

Nyrik and Horm wanted in on the action too. Watching them at work with their knives, I thought they'd even trouble Oller. They were lightning fast, both on their feet and with their bladework. Their skills were to the sailors' tastes. Every jack aboard wanted to learn as much as he could from the two Woods Kin—just as they all wanted to avoid tangling with Grell. Their swordplay improved dramatically from Qrysta's tuition. Their preferred fighting style was a cutlass in their main hand and a short blade in their off-hand. Qrysta's dual-wielding skills were a good fit.

Captain Rozlyn was pleased with the progress her men were making.

"They'll be a damn sight better in a boarding now than any other free fleet crew!" she said. We were on the quarterdeck, watching the action on the main deck below us.

I looked at her sharply. "Other?"

She returned my gaze, eyebrows raised in surprise. Then she realized what she'd said. "I'm forgetting," she said, bowing her head. "Old habits die hard. What I mean is: Should any *pirate,*" she emphasized, "be foolish enough to attack one of Her Majesty's warships, they would find her very well defended. Especially any who recognized this ship, and thought we'd be easy prey, with her rabble for a crew."

I raised Shift, pointed her out to sea, and fired off a Flamebomb. It sizzled away across the water, before exploding with a roar—which stopped the sparring on the main deck as all turned to watch, startled. I then threw up a Thundercloud over the spot where it had detonated. Torrential rain poured down.

"No ship would get near enough," I said. "Can't sail without masts."

She eyed me thoughtfully. "What's the rain for?" she asked.

"No need to set their ship ablaze. Unless they insist, of course."

She nodded. "Useful."

She understood the message. *The Red Rose* was Her Majesty's warship, not a free fleet buccaneer.

Now that we'd found our sea legs we also recovered our appetites. Food no longer turned us green just to look at it. What we ate went down and stayed down. It was after one such midday meal that Nyrik stopped me, Horm at his side, as always.

"Need a word Daxxie," he said.

He was, I was surprised to see, holding a lantern, the candle behind its storm panel alight. I wondered what he needed that for, in broad daylight.

"Of course. What is it?"

"It's the lad, Evall."

"What about him?"

"You haven't noticed?"

"No? Noticed what?"

"Tsk, tsk! You townies. Can't see your noses in front of your faces. You didn't see what he just did? What he does most mealtimes?"

"He eats. Same as we all do now."

"That he does," Nyrik agreed. "And he also squirrels food away under the table. Now, why would he do that? If he wanted something for later, he could just pop it in his pocket, right? I mean, would anyone mind? 'Course not. So, we've been keeping an eye on him, Horm and me, to see what's what. Woods Kin eyes, which are sharper than yours. He never knew. You've seen how me and Horm can't be seen when we don't want to be."

I had. I nodded.

"So, what he does is, he takes himself down into the cargo hold, twice a day or more. I couldn't see exactly what he did in there, him opening doors and closing them behind him, so we couldn't follow him. So, I go down later on my own, with a lantern, and what d'you think I found?"

He brought out a small lump wrapped in a piece of rag from under his cloak.

He unfolded it to reveal something brown.

He held it out towards me. It was a turd.

I leaned back, and said, "Er ...?"

"Dry, that is," Nyrik pointed out. "Been there a day or three."

"Well, maybe, one of the sailors—"

"Sailors don't shit in the holds. They use the heads, same as we all do. And bloody scary it is, hanging your bare arse out o' *them* in a stiff wind! I've nearly slid out more than once."

"Also," Horm said, "sailors don't piss against the hull. Not below-decks, not above. And if they did, it wouldn't be below knee height. It's all over the walls down there. Even these winds can't blow the smell away."

"The lad obviously clears up," Nyrik said. "He just missed this one. Townsfolk eyes, like yourn, not as sharp as ours. Brown on brown."

"We've seen him carry rags out, like this one," Horm said. "Food in, shit out. And in the middle of the night, he comes up with a chamber pot, covered up. Empties it over the side when no one's watching."

"Except us," Nyrik said.

"Takes it straight back down below again."

"So," Nyrik said "putting two and two together: Someone uses a chamber pot. Someone else uses the floor. And pisses against the hull. Now who could that be, I'm wondering?"

Well. I could make an educated guess. "You didn't look for them?"

"They don't know us, Daxxie. Scare them, that would. You're the boss, not us. Not our place. It's your decision."

Great, I thought. Stowaways. Just what we need.

"Well," I said, "the sooner we let them out of there, the better. There's no going back to Eastbay now; we'll just have to deal with this. Damn."

Nyrik led us off across the rolling deck and we made our way below.

Outside the door to the cargo hold Nyrik opened the storm panel of his lantern. He held it up and led us inside. The weak light that it threw illuminated barrels, and chests, and crates stacked everywhere. I followed him as he wound his way between them. Eventually, he stopped at a bulkhead door.

He opened it and stood aside for me to go in.

I listened. I heard *The Red Rose*'s hull echoing to the sound of water running along it. I heard each thump as her prow carved down into wave after wave. And then I heard other thumps, small and regular, coming from within a large chest, followed by a quiet, sharp *shush!* And then a tiny squeak. I knew that it was a squeak of excitement. I knew whose tail had done the thumping against the wooden side of the crate.

Little Guy had recognized my scent and had squeaked because I was his friend.

I cleared my throat and said, "It's okay, Jess. You can come out now."

For a while, nothing happened. Then, the lid of the chest opened.

No one emerged.

Abruptly, Jess stood up, an arrow drawn tight on the string of her whitewood bow.

Nyrik held up his lantern to show her my face, and I held my arms out wide, and said, "There's no need for that."

Seeing me, she lowered her bow. Little Guy leaped out of the crate and scrambled over to me, jumping and yelping with joy, wagging his tail madly. Instinctively, Jess ordered him, her voice low and hoarse. "Sh! Little Guy, stop! Quiet!!"

I smiled at her. She must have been terrified, in her crate, but she had been brave daring to stow away in it.

I said, "You don't have to hide anymore. Well, this is a surprise!"

Her lips began to tremble. "You're not angry?"

"No," I said, shaking my head. "You're old enough to make your own decisions, Jess. And if you'd rather be stuffed inside a crate all day and night with a small, hairy dog than living in comfort in the castle … well, I'm sure you have your reasons."

She looked down at the floor. She wiped her eyes, angry that she was weeping, but unable to stop herself.

"I'm sorry," she muttered. "I just had to. I don't have anyone else."

Her frail body started shaking. Good gods, I thought, what this child has been through. We'd rescued her—and then, in her mind, abandoned her, in a strange land, where she knew no one, and was about to be clapped up in a military academy. That must have seemed like a prison sentence looming over her. Qrysta and I had thought it a good solution—a great opportunity for her, a start at a new life. I now saw that it didn't seem like that to Jess.

"These are my friends," I said. "Nyrik and Horm."

Jess stopped sniffling, and looked at them.

"You'll never meet finer archers, and they will make you an expert with that thing."

"Pleased to meet you, miss," Horm said.

"Nice bow!" Nyrik said, and he clearly meant it. "Kinfolk made, that, I'd bet my life on it. Where'd you get that, then, girl?"

"They found it," she answered, in a low voice. "Daxx, and the others. On Wester Isle. Where I was born. And gave it me."

Horm whistled. "Whew! Lucky you!" he said. "Wouldn't mind one o' *them!* Whitewood?? Takes a rare bowyer to craft whitewood. You keep a tight hold o' that, young 'un, or I'll nick it off you."

Jess straightened up and stared at him, alarmed.

"There you go!" Nyrik chuckled. "That's the spirit. You see his thieving hands anywhere near it, you put arrows in them. We'll be off then, Daxx," he added, nodding at Horm. "And we'll see you on deck as soon as you like, young Jess, and show you how to make that beauty proud of you."

They left.

I knelt down and ruffled Little Guy's ears. "It's good to see you, friend," I said. "You too, Jess. Need a hand?"

"No, thanks, I haven't got much."

She climbed out of her crate, carrying her bow, her quiver full of whitewood arrows, and a small bundle tied up in a cloth on the end of a stick.

We went up on deck and I made the introductions.

Qrysta saw Little Guy first, and was confused; and then Jess, and was astonished.

That night, a dream emerged out of the darkness. Pale, scudding clouds and a round, full moon.

In which yellow eyes blinked open and stared at me.

The Voice said, "Where are you?"

"On our way to you," I answered.

"You know where I am?" He sounded surprised.

"Yes."

"Where?"

"In Normark."

I heard no reply.

Eventually, the Voice said, "Perhaps the land has been named such since my long sleep began. And now it is another Moon Night. Do you see, now?"

"No," I replied. "See what?"

"You will," he said. "When you awake."

The yellow eyes closed as the dream faded.

Slowly, my eyes opened. Qrysta, Grell, and Jess were looking down at me, their faces concerned.

"Thank the gods!" Qrysta said, almost as if she'd given up hope.

"Hi guys," I replied, relaxed, well rested, happy to see them all.

Grell said, "Mate, we thought we'd never see you again!"

"What are you talking about?"

"You've been dead to the world for three days."

I said, "Three …"

"We stuck pins in your hand. Nothing. You were a goner."

"Huh? I feel great!"

They frowned at me, clearly unsettled.

"Yeah, well, that's good to hear," Grell said, "but what about the last three days?"

"What about them?"

"What do you remember?"

I thought back. Three days? I'd had no idea it had been that long since I was awake. "Nothing."

"Yeah, well," Grell muttered. "That's not good."

I said, "What did I do?"

"Nothing. You just lay there."

It didn't compute. I tried to work out what had happened to me. I'd lost three days, in some kind of coma?

To be exact, I realized, what I'd lost had been three Moon Nights. Nights when, in Graycote's words, the Form chooses you. But the opposite had happened. I had not Turned. If anything, I had turned inward. Not into a werewolf, but into whatever the opposite of one is. I'd had no mind of my own, no consciousness, even. I did not have the power and speed of the Form to protect myself. I'd been completely vulnerable, wide open to any kind of attack.

I remembered the word that Marnie had used.

*Husk.*

Over the following days, the weather worsened again. *The Red Rose* still had a steady wind at her back but it was now a cold one. The skies above her masts were gray and heavy with rain, and the seas under her hull were choppy. At last, one morning we heard the cry of "Land ho!" from the crow's nest. We gathered on deck and searched the horizon, where a dark smudge lay below a bank of black cloud.

"Normark?" I asked Captain Rozlyn.

She nodded.

"Normark," she confirmed.

"Will we get there by nightfall?"

She looked at me, and smiled. "That depends."

"On what?" I didn't like her tone. I also noticed that *The Red Rose* was no longer underway. Her sails were not sheeted to the wind but hanging loose, flapping. The entire strength of the crew was on deck, and they were all armed. Two of them, I noticed, were operating pulleys to lower a small boat over the side.

Captain Rozlyn answered, "On how well you can sail."

"Excuse me?"

She glanced up at the crow's nest. It, and all the spars above us, were lined with archers, their bows drawn, all of them pointing downwards at me and my companions. Grell unslung his maul with a growl, and Nyrik, Horm, and Jess reached for their bows. Arrows thudded into the deck around them, and they went still.

"Reach for that staff," Rozlyn said, "and you're dead."

I froze. She nodded at two sailors, who unhitched Shift from my back and stepped away. She was furious, screaming curses at them that only I could hear.

I turned to Captain Rozlyn.

"This is our ship," I said.

"Not anymore."

"Then this is mutiny."

"It's not a mutiny if the captain leads it," she said, coolly.

I was furious. I reminded her, "You're under orders from your queen!"

She laughed. "Let me set you straight," she said. "She is your queen, not mine."

Qrysta said, "She gave you this command!"

"And she won't be anyone's queen for much longer," Captain Rozlyn continued, ignoring Qrysta. "Against the might of Sarmen? Well, good luck with that. We'll be long gone. The Sarmenids have enough to deal with already, and now with Jarnland to subdue? They'll be busy. They don't bother with the free ports. I doubt they even know where they are, or who we are. They're the lion; we're just fleas."

I said, "You're her Covensister."

"So?"

"You don't have loyalty to each other?"

She considered the question. "We help one another out. But we're not a team. Each of us is on her own. Coven is us against the world. Most of the time, the world is indifferent. It is busy with other things. Most of the time, we're alone, everyone having to do what's best for herself and her children. Do you know what our main ambition is?"

No one answered.

"To survive. As your queen will learn. She's what—sixteen?"

Qrysta said, "You owe her."

"Yes, I do. I have many unpaid debts, in many lands. You want what I owe you? Come and get it. Or are you forgetting what I do for a living?"

"No," Qrysta said, holding her eyes. "I'm remembering. You're a pirate. And a traitor. And I will remember this, Captain Rozlyn."

Rozlyn shrugged. "Yes, well. My advice: Don't take it personally. These things happen. Move on, get over it."

Grell said, "We could kill the lot of you."

Rozlyn gestured at the archers above us. "You could try," she said. "And if you succeeded, you'd have a ship with no crew. Six of you landlubbers, with no seamanship among the lot of you? You'd have no chance of bringing her into Sondehafn. Do you know what a lee shore is?"

I didn't.

She glanced towards the dark smudge on the northern horizon. "You're looking at one."

I said, "Well? That's where we're going, isn't it?"

"Yes. And where's the wind?"

It was at my back as I looked towards Normark. "Behind us."

"Blowing us towards the land," she pointed out.

"Well, that's good. Means we'll soon be there."

"It's only good," she clarified, as if to an idiot, "if you can avoid being blown onto the rocks. So, we're standing well off. There are a *lot* of rocks around the island—both inside and outside Sonde Bay. Do you know where they are?"

I didn't, of course.

"I'll show you," she said. She unrolled a chart and pointed. "Here, here, there and there. As you can see, there's no straight line through them. And even if there were, how do you judge the wind? Even with our full crew we'd have our work cut out to tack through them. We'd manage it easily enough, but it would take the best part of a day. You six wouldn't.

"So, here's what we're going to do. I am going to complete the task our lovely young queen gave me and get you ashore. In the longboat. Which isn't, as you will see, very long. That is yours. *The Red Rose* is mine again. As is her fine cargo, for which I thank you. It will fetch much gold in Freehaven. You will go your way, and I will go mine. I don't think we'll ever meet again."

"You'd better hope we don't," Qrysta said.

"Enough talk, I think," Captain Rozlyn said. "If you have any skill, you might make it to Sondehafn before nightfall. But you won't if you waste time jabbering." Crew members had brought up our belongings and dumped them on the deck. "Sea's getting up," she continued. "It's not going to be much fun climbing down the rope ladder as it is; pretty soon it'll be downright dangerous. You wouldn't want to fall and break something. I'd get on with it, if I were you."

We did. We clambered down, awkwardly. Our gear was thrown down after us; bows, quivers, arms and armor, and last of all, Shift. I caught her, and could feel that she was still seething. *Let me at them!*

*No,* I told her. *You heard the Captain. We go our way, they go theirs. Sinking* The Red Rose *and killing them all won't help us, even if you could manage it.*

She settled back down, sulking.

Then she suggested, *Ghouls?*

I thought, why not? A little parting gift.

I raised Shift, who sent a wave of airborne spectres after *The Red Rose*, not just Ghouls but also Barkers and Screamers. The alarmed shrieks of the crew came back to us across the water.

Nyrik and Horm were rigid with fear. They didn't like the sea one bit. They hadn't liked it from the safety of *The Red Rose*. They liked it even less in the cockleshell that was the longboat. They had the good sense to hunker down on their haunches low in the hull, wrapped in their cloaks, and keep their nervousness to themselves.

Qrysta, Jess, and I were useless. We just sat, mutely, while our former ship bore away to the south. Evall, though, and Grell, had some experience of sailing. "Easy enough, mates," Grell said, taking the tiller and sheeting out the longboat's single sail. "I spent plenty of time on the water back in Oz. Couldn't have sailed that big ship on my own, but a little boat like this won't be a problem. Provided she doesn't sink, of course."

With all our kit onboard, and the seven of us and Little Guy, the longboat was low in the water.

"I know the bay," Evall said. "I've sailed it with Dad, and my uncles and cousins. Once we're in past the islands, I can guide us home."

As he said that, a black shape rose out of the water and blew out a blast of wet air that stank like rotting fish. Little Guy barked in alarm. The whale arched over and slid beneath the waves, its huge tail churning the surface. I didn't like to think what else might be down there under us, waiting for us to capsize.

We never did—although we came close a couple of times, as we tried to get the hang of what to do when Grell called out the order to tack across the wind. More than one of us got smacked by the boom during those maneuvres, which taught us to look out for it and duck below it as it swung across. Captain Rozlyn had been right about the weather worsening. The waves grew choppier and bigger, making the longboat wallow and judder. Rain came in squalls of cold wind—but it was a wind that was blowing us in the right direction. If we failed to make it into Sonde Bay, and were blown ashore onto the mainland, well, that would be okay with us, as long as we could salvage our gear. We wouldn't need the longboat again, so who cared if she were broken up on that *lee shore* I'd just learned about? As long as we avoided the rocks around the islands, we thought, we'd get to Normark somehow.

And, as evening fell, we did. The wind grew stronger, and the rain colder and heavier, but once we rounded the cliffs into the bay, the sea became calmer. With land visible to three sides of us, and the wind driving us towards it, even Nyrik and Horm began to relax, miserable and cold and wet though we all were. I cast Orbs of Warmth on us when I could, but they don't last long, and they drained Shift.

Grell brought us in to the northwest corner of the bay. The rain eased up and we could see lights glowing ahead of us through the murk.

The longboat crunched ashore, and Evall jumped out and tied up. We followed him—drenched and cold but relieved to be on dry land again—carrying our gear through the now-gentle drizzle into Sondehafn.

It was a quiet little town, far smaller than Eastbay, and there were few people on its streets. Those who were out and about did not seem worried, or hurried, or bothered by the rain. They were just going calmly about their business, none of them keeping a wary eye out for trouble. A peaceful place, then.

As we passed a tavern, the sound of voices singing came from within, accompanied by some kind of musical instrument—although I'm not sure about the "musical." It sounded like cats complaining. But it was clearly meant to be making those strange sounds, and the song it was accompanying was tuneful enough, and filled with longing.

Warmth, I thought, and company. Shelter. We were cold, and soaked to the skin, and exhausted, but things were looking up. At least we weren't being thrown about on the sea anymore.

Evall hurried ahead of us, Jess and Little Guy trotting at his side. We were no more than a dozen turns from the beach where we had landed when he stopped at a small, gabled house in a side street. Lights shone through the cracks in the shutters that covered its windows. He lifted the knocker and rapped, hard, and then harder and harder. We heard voices, surprised, and then hurrying footsteps.

A panel in the door slid open and a lantern was held up into it.

"Ma!" a girl's voice screamed. "It's Evall! It's *Evall!*"

# 17

## Normark

More footsteps came running. A dog barked, low and slow. Little Guy yapped a response. Bolts were slid back behind the door and a crowd of faces beamed out at us. And then froze when they saw Grell looming behind their brother and son.

"It's all right," Evall said, "they're friends. I wouldn't be here without them."

Then it was a confusion of hugs, and kisses, and introductions, and interruptions, and eyes searching for Evall's father; and then faces falling when they realized that he was not with us. The mood changed from ecstatic to uncertain as we were welcomed in and shook the water off our clothes. In the silence that fell, Evall told his mother, and sisters and younger brother, that her husband, their father, was never coming home.

They insisted that we stay. We didn't want to intrude. "My Evall would have wanted it," his widow said. "You brought our son home. Our house is small, but our kitchen is warm, and we'll bring blankets for you while your clothes dry, and my children and I will feed you. And our old dog will be pleased to have your young dog for company. He's stiff, and slow, and can no longer see well, but he knows a friend when he smells one."

That settled the matter. Birgit, Evall's mother, was not to be denied. No doubt, in the last year, she had feared both husband and elder son dead. Now she knew. She felt herself in our debt. We let her know that we were grateful for her hospitality. We stripped off, as decorously as we could, and sat wrapped in blankets in her kitchen, and steamed, while food cooked and the delicious smells of it filled the room. Jess was hurried upstairs by Evall's sisters and reappeared in a neat smock that they had picked out for her. They were intrigued by her battle leathers, and wanted to learn all about them, and where she'd got them, and what she'd done in them, as they washed them clean—with much more attention, I noticed, than they paid to the rest of our travel-stained clothes. It was good to see Jess chatting away with girls of her own age as they all scrubbed and rinsed. She looked more alert and alive than I'd seen her in weeks.

We all did what we could to help Birgit, which was not much, as she kept telling us to sit down and get out of her way. Hengst, Evall's younger brother, placed a stone jar and mugs in front of me. I poured, and we drank, and the tiredness leached out of our bones. The liquor tasted of peaches and fire. It teased my tongue and warmed my stomach. I sat back and relaxed. A day that had begun badly, and worsened by the hour, was ending well.

Grell had been adopted by a girl of about three, who was sitting on his knee and chattering away, asking him all sorts of questions. His responses were mostly chuckles. Another little girl piled bowls high with scraps of meat, and cold cabbage leaves, and lumps of old bread softened in gravy for Little Guy and Mulnd, their old seal-hound, and fussed with their ears as they wolfed it all down. Hengst examined Qrysta's swords, enchanted.

Supper was a rich fish broth, and warm black bread and butter, and half a dozen green spring vegetables, which delighted Horm. I remembered his words, *Nothing pickled.* He was soon deep in conversation with two of the older girls, who, it seemed, disapproved of pickles as much as he did. Which they had to do, of course—the pickling—or the produce of their garden would go to waste. They had a glasshouse, they explained, as all their neighbors did. It was heated by warm springs that bubbled up from deep underground.

That piqued Horm's interest. "Oh, ah? Make your own, do you? As bad as anyone else's, I've no doubt?"

The older girl said, "Well, they're just *pickles*. You wouldn't want to eat them if you don't have to."

"Not when you've got fresh," her sister said.

Horm said, "You're probably right. Pickles, eh? Better'n nothing, but nothing like fresh. Still: I'd be interested to taste them, if that's not an inconvenience, young ladies."

"No, not at all, but—it's not like they're *fresh*," one said.

"Straight out of the ground," the other added.

"Well, no, I know that, o' course," Horm said. "But, if you've gone to the trouble to make them, it'd be a pity not to inflict them on a fellow pickle-hater, now wouldn't it?"

The girls looked at each other and giggled. They ran out into the pantry and returned with several jars, which they opened and placed on the table.

There was a pause as Horm took a knife from his belt and wiped it carefully.

He speared an onion, inspected it, and put it into his mouth.

We all heard the crunch as he began to chew.

As his jaws worked, his face changed. Horm's default expression was something between a frown and a scowl. He nodded, and speared a pickled radish, and ate that, and then a chunk of cauliflower. His default expression lightened, as he chewed, into something thoughtful.

We watched in silence.

When he spoke, his eyebrows had risen almost all the way into his hairline. "Well now. It strikes me, young ladies, as mayhaps I've been wrong about this all along. Mayhaps as I've never had *proper* pickles before. Mine host in The Ship Aground, swanking about how his family recipe was famous, best pickles in Eastbay? Well, I can tell you: They may be famous in a know-nothing port like Eastbay, but they're not a patch on these. Nowhere near. So, eh? *This* is what pickles should taste like, is it? Hm. Well. I begin to see it now. Thank you, young ladies. Thank you very much indeed. I can see that I've been seriously misinformed on this subject."

The girls were delighted. Birgit was delighted for them. We were all relieved to be off the sea, and under shelter, warm, and dry, and eating and drinking and relaxing. Evall, I saw, was proud to have brought us, his motley band of peculiar companions, into his home. Even though there was a sombre note of loss underlying the evening, and even though most of us were strangers to each other, there grew, over that supper, a sense of community, and consolation.

Peaches and fire. Fish broth, new bread, fresh vegetables *and* pickles. Warmth and shelter. Birgit apologized for not having beds for all of us, but we were just fine in that cozy kitchen. Jess found space in one of Evall's sisters' cots. Evall had his own bunk in the room he shared with his younger brother. The rest of us settled down under blankets on the rush-covered floor and were grateful while the fire died down, and the candles puckered out. Grell, Qrysta, Nyrik, and Horm were asleep in no time. The fumes of farted cabbage wafted up from the basket where Little Guy and Mulnd were dead to the world, whiffling peacefully next to each other. An orange cat appeared and settled in between them. Outside, the wind got up and rattled the eaves. Rain drummed against the shutters.

I watched the flames from the hearth dancing on the ceiling and wondered what lay ahead. We had no trade goods. We had no map. We had no way of knowing.

Of one thing, I was sure.

It would be less comfortable than this.

I was wakened by the smells of cooking, and voices whispering, and small feet tiptoeing about. I sat up and the whispers turned into normal conversation, and the tiptoeing into regular footsteps.

I was, I could see, the last one to wake.

Birgit was at the stove where things were sizzling in skillets, her children all helping her. The two oldest girls hauled in a pail of fresh milk between them, which they poured into mugs. It was warm, and sweet, and straight from the cow. As we fueled up for the day ahead, Evall let us know what had to be done.

We needed to get the blessing of Master Bjarnevalt, his father's employer. We wouldn't get anywhere without his authorization.

"If he doesn't sign off," Evall said, "you'll be turned back by the guards. They'll tell you that you have to report to him, so he learns your business. No foreign traders are allowed outside Sondehafn."

Grell said, "How many of them?"

"At the gate?" Evall said. "Two or three."

Grell's eyebrows shot up in surprise.

"That all??"

"Four at most. Normark's not like other lands. We don't have much trouble here."

"Mates, we can fight our way out. A couple of guards aren't going to stop us."

"We could," I agreed. "But, then what? We'd have made enemies. And we'd still be a long way from where we need to get to: the Ice Lands. Enemies behind, chasing us; enemies ahead, waiting for us. And us not having the first clue what's what. We don't need more problems; we need help solving the ones we already have."

Grell shrugged. "Yeah, makes sense. Over to you then, Daxxie."

Evall and I left, wrapped in our cloaks, leaning into the thin wind that was whining through the streets of Sondehafn. We came to the water, which stretched gray and dark ahead of us and out beyond the harbor walls to the ocean. Gulls cried overhead, white against the leaden sky. The few people we saw were hunched within their own cloaks, uncurious about us. This was, I thought, a place where nothing much changed, and no one minded about that.

The house of business where his father had worked his entire life was the largest building on the wharf. Evall was nervous. Their employer, Master Bjarnevalt, had entrusted his father with a large sum of money. Almost all of that had gone. Evall had returned without goods, without trade agreements, without his father, without Master Bjarnevalt's coin. From what Evall told me, it seemed that Master Bjarnevalt was a sour old curmudgeon. Perhaps that's just the point of view of a child, I thought. Well, I'd be seeing for myself soon enough.

A plump little clerk with a shining, bald head sat at a desk by the open front of the warehouse. He was well wrapped up against the cold, from the gloves on his hands to the scarf around his neck. His breath was visible in the morning air. He recognized Evall, and his expression changed to one of surprise mixed with disdain. He barely glanced at me. He jumped to his feet and led us up rickety, wooden stairs to the upper level.

He knocked at a door.

A gruff voice said, "Come in."

The clerk went in, closing the door behind him.

We heard the two of them conferring.

"Send them in," the gruff voice said.

The clerk reemerged and held the door open for us, shooting Evall a hard glance. Evall, clearly, understood the message, and shrank visibly. I put a hand on his shoulder. He looked up at me, gathered his courage, and we entered Master Bjarnevalt's office.

The door closed behind us.

It was a gloomy room, but warm. A fire burned in a large hearth beside a desk where an old man sat, watching us as we approached. A round, velvet hat, embroidered in purple and white and green, sat on his cloudburst of gray hair and side-whiskers. Thick eyeglasses perched on his long nose. Pale eyes peered out at us from behind them. Sharp eyes, I thought. Old he might be, and short of sight, but this one does not miss a thing.

He studied us as we approached.

Evall bowed, and said, "Good morning, Master."

The old man grunted.

"I have brought the report of our commission to the southlands," Evall went on. "I regret to inform you that my father died on our way home. I have his documents and the remainder of the subvention you allowed him."

The old man stared at Evall. "How much?"

"Forty-two gold, sir, and some silv—"

"Forty-two? Out of *six hundred??* You had better tell me that he found me some new trade routes!"

Evall swallowed. "I'm sorry, Master Bjarnevalt, but he did not negotiate any."

Silence fell.

Master Bjarnevalt stared at Evall. "Not *one?*"

"No, sir," Evall admitted.

Master Bjarnevalt nodded, slowly, and leaned back in his chair, examining Evall.

"This is what I get," he said, "for allowing a clerk the chance to prove himself."

"He did not want to voyage, sir. That was not his skill. He wanted to stay here," Evall said, "with his family, doing what he knew how to, his figures, in your—"

"Quiet!" Master Bjarnevalt's hand thumped on his desk. "Do not contradict me, boy, in my own office!"

Evall was cowed into silence.

Master Bjarnevalt stared at him for a long while before he spoke again.

"What he *wanted* is unimportant. Every merchant must know the whole business, not just one part of it. He must know trades, and routes, and lands, and customs, and people. He must know who and what he is dealing with, and where. Entering sums in a ledger is not *trading!*" He waited, until he saw that Evall understood.

Evall nodded.

"Your father," he continued, "was unfit for the task with which I entrusted him. He promised he would not fail me. He knew what the consequences would be. Well. Now they must be faced. Five hundred and fifty and more gold lost, and for what?!"

He stared at Evall, waiting for an answer.

"We have brought back maps, sir," the boy said, his throat working, his face miserable, "and names, and information."

"And not one, single, deal! Trade, boy, is about *deals*. I sent you south with gold and goods. Furs and hides, fruits in spirits, Ice Balm, barrels of salt fish, walrus and narwhal and mastodon ivory; wool, timber, copper, iron. Merchandise the southerners pay handsomely for. And what do you return with? 'Names.' And forty-two gold."

"Your goods were safely delivered to your warehouses," Evall said. "They are all accounted for."

"Well and why wouldn't they be? Thanks to my captain, not to your father. We know what they will fetch down there, and what we can buy to bring home for our people. You were to go where we are *not* known, and find new markets for them, and better prices—and new wares for us here in Normark!"

"I'm sorry, Master. We took samples, and left them, in many new ports, and—"

"And brought back from them, what? Samples of new wares that might interest us?" He looked around, affectedly. "I see no samples."

Evall hung his head. We'd brought a good cargo with us on *The Red Rose*—but why point that out, when we'd lost that as well?

Master Bjarnevalt leaned forward, his elbows on his desktop, and stared at Evall.

"What am I to do with you?" he said. "You are as useless as your father. Why would I think now to train you up as clerk, a position for which any boy in town would fight, when you will clearly never go on to become a merchant? After the opportunity I gave your family! I have ships, and captains, and crews. They leave with our cargoes, and return laden with gold and goods from the south, which I sell on, around this land and into the north. Those who fail leave my employ. They know that. That is what you will do now."

Evall swallowed. I could see that he was trying not to cry. "Yes, Master."

"And you will leave now."

"Yes, Master," he said, getting to his feet. He turned and looked at me, to see if I was coming.

"I will make my own way back, Evall," I said. "I need to talk to Master Bjarnevalt."

Bjarnevalt looked at me sharply, as if noticing me for the first time. "What do you want?" he demanded, as Evall hurried to the door.

"A moment of your time, Master Bjarnevalt."

"My time is money."

"As is mine."

"Yours?" he scoffed. "Then what do we have to trade, sir?"

"I will show you," I said, "when I have told you who I am, and why I am here."

"Will this take long?" he grumbled.

I waited, without replying, until he stopped fidgeting. I knew that he was trying to put me in my place.

Eventually, I replied, "You might as well ask if this will be worth your while."

He frowned. He did not know what to say, but his interest had been piqued. Merchants like to hear what will be worth their while.

"I did not come to Normark simply to bring Evall home," I began. "We were coming this way anyway."

"Why?"

"I have business here."

"Then show me your bill of lading."

"I don't have one."

"You do not even have a ship!" he snorted. "You scrambled ashore by night in a tub. You are no merchant."

"I never said I was. There are other sorts of business than buying and selling."

"Such as?"

"Master Bjarnevalt," I said. "I have come here to seek your advice, not to be interrogated."

216

That seemed to displease him. He snapped, "How can I advise you if I do not know what you want?"

"Evall tells me you are the most important man in town. Perhaps even in the realm."

"This is no realm. We have no king."

"The land, then. If anyone can help me, he says, you can."

"And why should I help you?"

"We brought back your employee's son. He returned you what money there was left in his father's possession."

Master Bjarnevalt was, clearly, annoyed. "The man failed!" he retorted. "If he had lived, he would owe me more than he could earn in two lifetimes! He knew the terms. I gave him a chance that few are ever given. Had he done well, he would have returned rich, bringing new trade agreements, new contacts, new markets, new wares. I *sponsored* him! And his son. Yes, and what do I get in return, I ask you? I get nothing! I am, as you say, sir, a merchant. We do not succeed in our line of business by losing money. I do not *like* to lose money!"

"I understand. What is your loss?"

"Six, *hundred*, gold!" the old buzzard shouted, thumping his fist on the table at each word. "Less what the boy returned; forty-two I believe. Then there is the rent on their house—unpaid for more than a year, four silvers a quarter. I have let the family stay this last year and more, out of the kindness of my heart, the wife having no employment, and the children not yet earning. Well, how will they pay me now, sir, with no breadwinner?! Answer me that! I will have to evict them. The boy has no future in my employ. He is clearly incompetent."

I pointed out, "He was orphaned, in a strange land, Master Bjarnevalt. He survived, on his wits alone."

"Alone? He survived on *my money!*"

"And he brought you back what remained of your sponsorship. He could have run away with it, scared of your anger at his father's failure. I would not call that incompetent. I would call it honest. And diligent."

"It is of no interest to me what you would or would not call it."

I had let him vent his annoyance. Now that he had got his complaints off his chest it was time to take the initiative.

"I may not be a merchant," I said, "but I am wealthy."

He looked over my clothes, a sneer of disbelief on his crabby old face. "You do not look it."

I reached into a pocket inside my jerkin and brought out the cloth-wrapped bundle that contained our six heartstones. I placed it on the table between us. "See for yourself."

Grunting dismissively, he reached forward and unwrapped the cloth.

When he saw what was inside, he swallowed, several times, and, when he could at last speak, whispered, "Where did you get these?"

"On my travels."

I raised Shift, and cast Reveal on the jewels.

Each lit up and gleamed with its own inner light. Red fire and green mist shimmered from the tourmaline. The multicolored points of tiny fireworks burst and glittered around the opal. The sapphire glowed blue, the ruby blood red, the topaz a kaleidoscope of purples, blues, and golds. The olivine shone a deep, steady green.

Master Bjarnevalt tore his eyes away and looked up at me. "These are ruensten!"

I nodded. "Heartstones, we call them."

I waited as he studied the shining gems, entranced.

He raised his eyes to mine, swallowed, and said, "May I …?"

"Of course."

He picked up the topaz, reverently, and turned it over in his hands. The ever-changing colors that swirled in its depths reflected in his old eyes. His lined face softened into a smile. Eventually, he said, "I have never seen a finer."

I said, "It is yours."

He looked up at me in shock.

"If that is the one you choose. As a token of my goodwill," I added.

"You …." He choked. He tried again. "You are not serious …?"

"Completely serious," I said. And then, as if reconsidering, suggested, "Perhaps a trade?"

I saw him switch into merchant mode. This made more sense to him than a gift from a stranger he had been belittling. "For?"

"Evall's family house. This gem is worth much more, I know; but a merchant such as yourself would rather have a bargain than an obligation, am I not right? So, the house is Birgit's. Evall continues his apprenticeship with you. His father's debt is paid—with, you will agree, interest."

Master Bjarnevalt couldn't stop himself nodding urgently. "It is, indeed. Fully paid. My clerk will draw up the papers. I should warn you that the roof—"

"Has been leaking, I know. Birgit told me, and that she has asked you to repair it. That need not concern you now."

"Yes. No. So." He looked up at me, even though he would rather have kept gazing at the topaz heartstone. "But, surely, there must be some other way I can I help you, sir?"

I inclined my head in agreement. "There is. A simple one. Give us your leave to go north."

His expression became wary.

"North? How far north?"

"The Ice Lands."

The blood drained from his face. "Your business lies *there?*"

I nodded.

"Then … then …." He kept looking from me to the topaz, as if he was about to lose what he had just gained. Eventually, he said, his voice no more than a croak, "What do you know of the Ice Lands, sir?"

"Nothing. What do you know of them?"

He swallowed. "As little as any of us here in the south. We know of those who live there. Ogres. Hill Orcs, and Ice Orcs, and Wood Orcs. Sprites and feys. The root folk. Those of the Undergrounds. Of which we do not speak. But we do not have dealings with any of them. We deal only with those who guard the pass." He swallowed, clearly uncomfortable. "The Ice Wights."

I waited.

"We trade with them," he continued. "All they want in trade is livestock. Cows, goats, sheep, fowl. The drovers say …." Master Bjarnevalt stopped, and swallowed, as if he didn't want to go on. He took a deep breath. "The animals are terrified. When they come to the stockade. They have to be hobbled the day before, or they'd stampede. And when the Wights come out …. Many drovers refuse to take another drive. Once is enough. They love their animals, that they have raised from birth—even knowing, yes, that they would eventually go to the butcher here in the south. But, up there …"

He took a deep breath, and gathered himself. "The Ice Wights rush on them. They start feeding straight away. Clamp their jaws onto the neck of some poor beast, wrap their arms and legs around it, even the little children, with a goose, or a pullet, or a lamb, the creature bleating helplessly. And the worst thing …"

219

I thought, *there's worse?* The picture I had in my head was bad enough already.

The worst thing, though, was apparently not visual.

"The sounds they make, while draining the life out of those creatures, are said to be … the stuff of nightmares. I haven't been there myself. I … lack the courage."

I said, "They are vampires, then?"

Master Bjarnevalt shook his head. "They do not make more like themselves, as vampires do. They breed, and have young. They're not undead, just as they are not dead. Although they look more dead than alive. After a meal, they're flushed and pink. And happy. They smile. Their smiles are not pleasant." He grimaced. "It has been conjectured that once, perhaps, they were like us. But that must have been long ago. They were here when our ancestors first arrived in this land, from the south."

He shook his head, as if he did not want to talk about this. But he had more to say about the Ice Wights. "Also," he said, "they steal children."

He let that sink in.

"They leave clues. A shirt, a shoe. The price is fixed. Livestock to the value of fifty gold, within a moon month. Many cannot pay. We help those we can, but … we cannot help everyone. Some winters we do not have sufficient beasts to send."

He swallowed, and continued. "Many believe that the Ice Wights would rather keep the child than the ransom. The blood of a human child is a delicacy, worth more to them than that of any beast. That is why we trade with them. If we do not, more children are taken. Not in the summer months, but in a bad winter, when the whole land freezes. They come down, by secret ways out of the mountains, and raid farms and villages and towns, even to the coast."

I could hardly think of more disturbing neighbors. "What do they trade for your livestock?"

"Ice Balm. It is our most valuable export. In the courts and cities of the south, where the heat is oppressive, it is sought after more than jewels or gold or silks. It cools. Applied to the skin, it turns a stifling day into a mild one. The great ladies buy every drop we can send them, at prodigious prices. Just as a hot pepper will scald the tongue, and bring sweat to the brow, Ice Balm will soften the fiercest heat. They say you can stand out in the sun and never burn, while the Balm lasts."

I could, indeed, see how such stuff would be worth a fortune. "What is it?" I asked.

"We do not know. Any more than where they get it. It could be anything. Our wisefolk think it is the sap of some tree that only grows in the Ice Lands. Or, maybe, an extract from some plant we know nothing of. It could be ichor from the veins of the earth. It could be their own blood, for all we know. They are cold; Ice Balm cools ..." He shrugged, and looked at me. "If you bring me Ice Balm, sir, I will pay thrice its weight in gold. And in thanks for this ruensten, you will have all the equipment and supplies you need: food, drink, horses, furs against the cold, snowshoes, weapons, anything. Horses won't get you beyond the stockade, of course, but they will get you there quicker."

"The stockade?"

"Where the Ice Wights gather, for the trade." Master Bjarnevalt reached into a drawer and pulled out a scroll, which he unrolled on the desktop between us.

At last, I thought. A map of Normark.

He pointed at a line that curved across it.

"That is the Snowline. There, the seasons end, and beyond it is always winter. North of the Snowline the ground is frozen, year-round. The skies bring snow or hail, not rain. The mountains rise to the north, and narrow ahead, as the road climbs up into them. You will come to the pass. It has the wrong name, for those of us from the south. None going north ever pass through it.

"There you will find the stockade. You must bring livestock, or the gates will not open for you. We will supply those, and gold for other goods that will have come down from the north to wait for our coming. The Ice Wights have no interest in those things, and can be trusted with our money. Your escort will bring those goods back, along with whatever Balm the Wights allow us.

He hesitated. "You, and your companions, intend to go ahead ...?"

"They will let us pass? I thought you said—"

"I should have said, no one *in their right mind* passes through. They always seem surprised when anyone asks. They gather around, and look to whoever has asked up and down. Then, one of them says—and from what I've heard their voices are as cold and harsh as the place itself—'Welcome to the Ice Lands.' And those who asked go through ... are never heard of again."

"Any idea why not?"

"Well, there are many dangers up there—many we know of, and no doubt many more that we don't. But we think the answer is obvious."

He waited while I thought it over. "They know you're there."

Master Bjarnevalt nodded. "They know where you go. And know what you do. And know when to make their move." He looked at me.

I could tell he thought of something else, then wondered whether to tell me.

My topaz heartstone, though, had loosened his tongue. "There was a time," he began, "before Normark was as peaceful as she is now. Our few towns and villages quarreled with each other. Feuded. Enemy prisoners were taken and sent north. To the stockade, in trade for Ice Balm. The Ice Wights," he explained, "prize human warmth above all. It was, I think, that as much as anything that made the people of Normark find peace with each other. A truce was called, and a parley. It was asked how we could justify inflicting that death on our own kind, even on our foes.

"So, we stopped fighting and jostling for power. We have no ruler. We live by consent. We have Ealdors—men and women of wisdom who share the care of our land. Some towns have two, some three—some areas have one between several villages. We cooperate. We prosper. We avoid the north. The Ice Wights have what we desire. We have what they desire. It is mutually beneficial. Except for the poor beasts."

I had come looking for solutions and had found only more problems. "Are there many of them?"

"Who knows? The Ice Lands are vast, but they are poor. We doubt they can support many mouths. Not much grows there, except trees—and who can eat trees? But there is game aplenty, in the forests and plains. Seals and walruses on the ice sheets above the frozen seas. Fishes and whales below them. But hunting is hard in such a cruel place, and there are other hunters up there. Orcs, Ogres, sprites, wolves, sabre-cats, bears—both brown and white."

Master Bjarnevalt let me keep the map. His clerk showed me out. He would, he assured me, bring the Deed of Ownership to Birgit's house that very day. I walked back through the town thinking over what I had learned. Tracked by cannibals who know every inch of their territory. Against six of us, and a small dog. How in all hells were we going to prevail against those odds?

The thought of Little Guy made me grunt a rueful laugh.

We'd have a good lookout, at least. No one and nothing would escape his nose. So, we'd have, what, an extra minute of warning before the Ice Wights attacked? A lot of help that would be. We'd also have Nyrik and Horm for eyes, I considered. So, three sharp lookouts. And those two knew woodlands and how to survive in the wild. Maybe they could open trees for us to shelter beneath. Although, of course, the trees up there would not know them, so presumably would not let them in.

The future looked as gloomy as Sondehafn did that day. Mist was drifting through the streets, as if the clouds had descended on the town.

Oh well: could be worse, I thought. I could be in the heat and dust of Sarmen.

# 18

## Sarmen

Oller reached Westwich ahead of the news. The guards at the gate were bored. The town was sleepy. It wouldn't stay that way for long, he knew, as he rode through its quiet streets to the castle barracks. Within days every corner of the realm would hear what had happened at the Champions Feast in Eastbay, and everyone would be worrying about the war to come. Serjeant at Arms Struan smiled when he saw Commandant Blunt's seal on the letter that his corporal handed to him. "Friend o' Jack's, hey?" he said, looking up at Oller. "Sit yourself down, lad, and let's see what the old scoundrel wants from me."

Oller sat.

The corporal left.

Struan slit open the seal and unfolded the letter. He chuckled as he read. There was no mistaking the author.

*Struey, old son, I need a favor. It'll be repaying a favor that Terren, the bearer of this letter, did for me when I was in sore need of one on my travels overseas (the reason for which being well known to you, you being a cousin of my Jenny). Terren helped me out of a tricky spot, without which help I doubt I'd have lived. I'm not about to entrust further details to this letter, lest it fall into the wrong hands. Suffice it to say that he has now, in turn, found himself in a tricky spot in our realm, and needs to leave with all possible speed for Sarmen, where he has business. Important business, involving important people. Don't let his appearance fool you. There's more to the lad than meets the eye, is all I shall say. You'll be doing your old friend Jack a good turn to help him find a fast ship to get him there, and none the wiser for his coming and going. I'll be obliged to you, Struey, and you know how I don't forget those as do me good turns. He has the wherewithal to pay his passage. Your old comrade in arms, J. Blunt. P.S. Best burn this letter.*

"So, now," Struan said, looking up at Oller, "no questions, is it?" He nodded. "Well, if that's the way Jack wants it, that's the way it'll be. Much as though I'd like to hear what he's not telling me. We go back a long way, Jack and I do. Fought alongside o' one another in more than many a scrap. Plenty of which I'd not have lived through fighting alongside of anyone else, I can tell you that." His eyebrows rose as he studied the scrawny youth in front of him. "Helped him out of a hole, did you, lad? That's a tale worth the listening, I'd warrant."

He paused, more in hope than expectation.

Oller said nothing.

Struan understood. "Some other time, eh?"

"Some other time," Oller agreed.

Struan looked back at Blunt's letter. "Sarmen," he said.

Oller nodded.

Struan studied him, and then sighed. "Anyone else, young master Terren, and I'd have a deal o' questions for them. But seeing as it's Jack Blunt, I know better than to ask any."

He pushed himself back from his desk and stood up. "Such as, you're no Sarmenid and, why would you want to go to that perilous place?" He crumpled Blunt's letter and dropped it into the fireplace. "The none of which is my business," he added. Flames licked against the paper, which caught, and burned, and turned black. Struan came around the desk and clapped "Terren" on the shoulder. "So, let's get you on your way, eh, lad? And good luck to you. And mayhaps, one day, you or Jack will be back here to tell me all about it."

Struan led Oller to the quayside office of the Westwich Tide-master. *The Rorqual*, he told them, was sailing on the evening tide, for Sarmen and beyond. Struan relaxed on hearing the news. A reliable captain, he told Oller. Knows all the ins and outs.

Oller knew better than to ask questions. He could read between the lines, and hear what the two officials were not saying. He remembered Commandant Blunt's words. *A fine port for the smuggling, West-wich.* And that was fine by Oller. *The Rorqual*'s captain was summoned. Gold changed hands. Oller slipped aboard, long after dark, shortly before she set sail south and west for Sarmen.

He didn't want a private cabin. That would have made him an object of curiosity. Oller wanted to be a nobody, to blend into the background, so he slept in a hammock between decks with the crew. They were the kind who knew not to pry into anyone else's business, because they didn't appreciate it when anyone was nosy about theirs. They gave him no trouble—apart from one night, when one of them felt his clothes for his purse, thinking Terren was sleeping. He was stopped by a knife at his throat, and a few quiet words, along the lines of, *Try that again, matey, and this goes in.* No one messed with Terren after that.

When, at last, land came into sight, *The Rorqual* hove to and waited the day out. Towards evening her sails were run out again and she headed in. Dusk fell. Soon dim lights could be seen glinting on the water. *The Rorqual* made for them, where three cutters were waiting for her. Half the ship's cargo was unloaded into them, and they turned for the shore, while *The Rorqual* headed the other way, towards the port of Sarmen. No one onboard saw Oller disembark as porters brought out what was left of *The Rorqual*'s cargo—which was all the Imperial Tidemaster would see and value for import duties. No one on the wharf saw him come down the gangplank and pad off into town, keeping to the shadows.

Late night. An unknown city. Oller knew of no safe houses there, so had nowhere to run to and hide in, if the authorities found him of interest. But why should they? He was insignificant: a nobody in a heaving sea of nobodies, any of whom would be far more likely to commit a crime than he was. He was going to keep his hands clean, and stay out of trouble.

He watched. He listened. He hadn't felt this alert in years. How he'd missed this, he thought. Always on the edge of danger, of betrayal, of making some stupid mistake. He was no novice, though. He wouldn't make stupid mistakes. He felt almost lightheaded at the thought of it—the idea of respectfully asking some puffed-up, ignorant guard for directions, and getting a cuff over the ear for his pains.

He stifled a chuckle at the thought. *Careful,* he told himself. *Don't be getting too cocky, now. One misstep and you're on the question-master's table, and you won't feel so full of yourself then.* He focused, and slipped back into his former life as if into old, familiar clothes. He'd never been there before, or anywhere like that hot, stinking, stifling city, but this was where he belonged. In the game. In the life.

He padded through the back alleys of Sarmen, savoring the smells and sights and sounds. He noticed everyone, and everything. Cooks at carts of street food. Strollers looking for custom, or friends, or quarrels, or alms, or victims. He saw who was ahead of whom, and knew that he was ahead of all of them. *You won't catch me,* he thought—*at least, not tonight.* He bought food with Sarmen coppers that he'd exchanged for Jarnland coin with *The Rorqual*'s captain, who hadn't ripped him off too badly, for fear of Serjeant at Arms Struan. He ate as he walked, biting into a fluffy bun filled with what he recognized, with pleasure, as spiced rat. It was delicious. Chewing on the gristly meat in its thick gravy, he made his way to a large market square, where he settled back into the shadows at the alley's exit to watch and listen. No one took a second glance at him. He was just some unremarkable scruff eating a late-night snack.

Oller saw calm, and energy. He did not see alarm, or emergency, or patrols passing at the double and citizens scurrying to their homes to bolt the doors behind them. It was clear to him that they were not worried about the coming war.

He knew that they would know about it. Everyone always does. Rumor loves to tell of war and disaster. In this conflict, those would lie overseas. Some small land that His Supreme Radiance would absorb into his empire was about to feel his wrath. It wouldn't be the first, and wouldn't be the last. Oller judged that the idea of it would make the citizens of Sarmen feel better, not worse. They would be proud of what their army was about to achieve, as if it reflected well on them personally. The emperor would show those ignorant foreigners who was boss. He'd teach them to defy the might of Sarmen.

Good, Oller thought. Life is easier for sneakers and peekers when all is calm, and guards are relaxed.

It was nearing midnight, but the market square that he was observing was filled with citizens of all kinds, high and low. The stalls were still open for business, torches flaming in sconces in front of them, merchants and crafters calling out their wares in loud voices. The night air was hot, and humid, and filled with smells—of cooking food, and animal dung, and the perfumes of the gentry and the sweat of the common folk. Where the gentry strolled, and chatted, and stopped, and bowed to each other, and exchanged courtesies, and laughed, the common folk hurried about their work. They made sure to step out of the way of their betters, squeezing back against walls where necessary, while the lords and ladies in their finery passed by, hardly noticing them.

The gentry were easy to spot, not just because of the bright colors of their clothing, but because always, behind them, group or individual, walked their own looming shadow: a Vu-Sant bodyguard. Male for the gentlemen, female for the ladies. They towered over their owners, the handles of their weapons standing above their shoulders, their chalk-white, rock-hard faces impassive, their yellow eyes alert, missing nothing. Their owners paid them no attention, not even when one stepped around them to nudge some commoner out of the way. Clearly, they were more than just bodyguards. They were status symbols, and nobody who was anybody would be seen in public without one.

The spices in the rat bun had brought a sweat to Oller's face. It was a relief, in that oppressive heat. It would be even hotter under the sun, he thought, which would be fierce overhead, this far south. That was, no doubt, why the gentry did their socializing in the evenings, after dark, when the heat was not unbearable.

He noticed how cool the noblemen and noblewomen all looked in their silks and satins, the ladies especially. From time to time, one would dip a finger into the little jeweled or enameled pot that hung from her belt, and dab something pale and sticky onto her skin, and that of her companions. It seemed to be something that they did automatically—like buying a round of drinks in a tavern: *dab one, dab all.* It was a ritual, repaid with thanks, and compliments, and smiles. Oller was close enough to see them as they passed. There was never a drop of perspiration on any of them, while the clothes of the common folk were damp with sweat. The gentry looked as cool and relaxed as if this were a mild evening back home in Jarnland.

Oller made sure to have turned away, and be looking at something else, when the head of the chalker pacing behind the Sarmenid nobility glanced in his direction. He saw how everyone else avoided meeting those searching eyes.

Oller didn't need to look in order to hear. He had long trained his ears to pick out conversations that no one having them knew he was listening to. Eavesdropping on the nobility of Sarmen could hardly have been easier. Their voices carried clearly over the hubbub in the market square. It was as if no one existed but them. They were confident in their superiority, knowing that no commoner was going to take issue with anything that they said. Those who didn't like what they heard had the sense not to show it. The gentry only conversed among themselves, Oller noticed. No one who was not of noble rank addressed them, unless spoken to first.

A group of highborn girls strolled past him. Their clothing, such as it was, was no more than wisps of the most exquisite silks. Back home, in Jarnland, any girls as young and beautiful as those would have attracted, at the very least, a comment or two. Here, in Sarmen, they were studiously ignored. Oller got the idea at once, and studiously ignored them himself before their Vu-Sant shadow could see him gawping at them, two-thirds naked though they were.

They were so relaxed that they might as well have been at home in their pajamas. Nobody, they knew, was going to bother them. Everybody, they knew, would have noticed them, highborn and lowborn alike. Oller had seen them casting their eyes over other noble girls, measuring their scanty costumes and their allure, while waving their greetings at each other. Gallant young lordlings bowed at them. The girls replied with smiles, and knowing glances, and whispers among themselves— or not at all.

A parade, then. A competition, an evaluation, a fashion show. An exhibition. A game. Common folk girls of their age kept their heads down, busy at their work, clothed in drab colors from head to foot, as their superiors sauntered past laughing and chatting.

Oller slipped on his Ring of Blending and followed them.

"Qu'ara has been posted to the First Division, Prince Vashtenar's," one noble girl, who looked younger than Esmeralda, said to her companions.

"How wonderful!" another responded, clapping her hands and turning back to smile at their bodyguard. "You must be so proud."

"We are, but I'll miss her. She's family, after all. Don't we always say that, Qu'ara?"

The Vu-Sant replied, "Always, milady, I am humbled to say." She glanced around and looked right through Oller, who was a pace or two behind them.

Good, he thought. She didn't notice me.

"But it *is* an honor," the young noblewoman continued. "His Radiance himself made the inspection of her cohort. All the graduates of her year were on parade it was quite the event. He was pleased enough at their turnout to order a march past *and* an Imperial Salute! His royal brother was delighted, as you can imagine. Qu'ara was—oh, I forget the name: the one they line up by. What is it, Qu'ara?"

"Left Dress, milady."

"Left dress?" The friend giggled. "Sounds like something that happens when you've escaped one of His Radiance's parties without your clothes."

"No! You *haven't!*" another girl said, both shocked and thrilled. "Have you?"

"No. Sadly. Not yet. Perhaps one day."

More giggling.

"Why is it called that, Qu'ara?"

"The ranks march while watching to their left, milady, and keep line on the shoulder of the soldier on the end."

"Oh. Not quite so exciting. When do you leave?"

"Not for some weeks, milady. The fleets must gather at the ports. Arms and equipment and supplies have to be transported to them. The regional divisions will already be assembling. It is a long march for some of them."

"Oh, well that's good. You'll be with us until then, that's nice." The girl sighed. "I do envy you, Qu'ara. Voyages, and battles, and such. I wish I could go with you. Or the air division. Imagine being one of the dragon riders, flying through the sky, blasting His Radiance's enemies."

"More exciting than being stuck in Sarmen," one of her friends said.

"A lot more," another said. "My uncle's a provisioner, and he says that they're all gathering at the grazings. Fattening up for the long flight ahead."

"And fight, eh, Qu'ara? I expect you'll have lots of exciting stories when you return."

"I would hope so, milady, but I doubt that I will. This is expected to be a bloodless victory."

"Oh. What a shame."

"Indeed," the Vu-Sant agreed.

"Why, are you hoping for bloodshed, Qu'ara?"

"Of course, milady. Those who defy His Radiance deserve to die."

"So say we all."

Oller stopped tailing the group and the girls strolled on into the crowd, dwarfed by their hulking shadow. He turned over what he had heard in his mind.

Grazings.

Divisions.

Fleets.

Other ports.

Even if he could set every ship in Sarmen docks on fire there would be plenty elsewhere that he could never reach. And the naval base would be heavily guarded, of course. He might be able to sneak in unnoticed, but he'd be spotted the moment he lit even a candle, let alone a firepot. A squad of battlemages might manage the job and destroy the fleet, but it would be a suicide mission. Which would still leave all the other ships, in the other ports.

And he didn't have a squad of battlemages. He was on his own.

Besides, he was there as a spy, not a saboteur.

Keep on spying, then. Look, listen, and learn. He had several weeks in which to do just that. Even if he didn't learn anything, at least he'd be able to let Daxx know when the fleet sailed, via their Link of Impartment.

Oller imagined the mass of ships, heading out of the port, north and east for Jarnland. *Then what?* he wondered. He'd make his way there himself, sooner or later—he was confident of that. But what would he find when he got there?

Cities in ruins.

The land occupied.

Her people subjugated to the Empire of Sarmen.

And his friends? He couldn't imagine Grell surrendering, or Daxx or Qrysta, or Commandant Bastard.

And Esmeralda …?

He shook the thoughts from his head. That was a picture he didn't want to look at. He had a job to do.

He made his way back to the docks, trying to decide his next step. *The regional divisions. Air division.* He needed to find out about those. There would be sentries. Guard dogs too, no doubt. He'd have to deal with those when the time came. First things first, he told himself.

Yes, well, what were those?

Normally, the first thing in any new city was to make his number with the local Receiver.

He smiled as he remembered what he'd been told.

*There's no Thieves Guild in Sarmen. The emperor had stamped it out, and had everyone associated with it executed.*

But Oller knew there is *always* a Thieves Guild.

He didn't think it would take him long to find it. He was good at finding. But checking in at TG was the last thing he'd be doing in this particular town. He'd never use his real name, of course—not that any Receiver would expect him to. Even so, identifying himself as a TG member in good standing, in a foreign city, would immediately have marked him out.

Suppose the Receiver were to get curious and have him tailed. That would be bad. He might be able to lose the tail; but that would only make the Receiver more curious and put more tails on him. Receivers talk to officials, when it's in the TG's interest. And even though the TG didn't officially exist in Sarmen, he knew that there would be officials who unofficially dealt with it. Lines of communication would be open. Officials would be paid off, to look the other way—and tipped off, when there was something TG thought they should know about, such as a foreign sneakthief giving his tails the slip. Oller didn't want anyone to know that he was there, or where he went, or who he talked to. His job was to get in, get the information, and get out, with no one the wiser.

First part accomplished. Now for the hard part: the information.

It was long after midnight when he made his way back to the docks. *The Rorqual*'s captain had recommended a flophouse that was frequented by foreign sailors. Oller had marked it earlier. As he headed there, he turned his situation over and over in his mind. What did he know? What *didn't* he know?

Prince Mejnul. *Crown* prince, son, and heir of the emperor.

Prince Vashtenar, his brother.

An army of chalkers and a horde of dragons.

All gathering to be in Mayport by Midsummer Day.

Well, he obviously couldn't defeat an army all by himself. Nor could he take out a hundred or however many dragons.

What did that leave him? Cut the head off the snake.

No more Prince Mince, no more threat to Jarnland and Esmeralda.

That sounded good—in theory. It also sounded suicidal. He had no idea how he might get close enough to Mejnul to kill him. He was pretty sure he'd never manage to escape afterwards, his Ring of Blending notwithstanding.

Well, there was no rush. He still had plenty of time to look around.

The tavern below the flophouse was still open. A yawning boy carrying a candleholder showed him up to the attic. As they passed along it he could see several lumps on pallets on the floor. One lump seemed too big to be a single person, and was writhing under its blankets, grunting, and moaning. Other lumps snored. Drapes, on sagging ropes, served as makeshift partitions, to give the illusion of privacy.

Oller found a pallet in a corner at the back. Perfect, he thought. The walls left only two sides from which anyone could approach. He tipped the lad with the smallest of his Sarmenid coppers and drew the drapes shut to enclose his space off.

He could afford far better than that, of course, with the gold in his cly; but he wasn't going to go anywhere where a traveler with gold would be noticed. He intended to lie as low as possible. Besides, this gaff was luxury compared with many of the places he'd had to sleep on the streets of Brigstowe. He settled back, knowing that he'd be wide awake before anyone got within three feet of him.

He wrapped himself in his blanket, wondering what else was living in it, and hoping that there weren't too many of them, and that they wouldn't bite too hard.

Once again, he turned over in his head what he'd learned.

Ports.

Fleets.

Chalkers.

Divisions.

Princes.

Dragons.

Grazings.

He was asleep in moments.

# 19

## Into the North

**We** gathered before dawn in the market square of Sondehafn. It was cold, but there was no wind. The livestock that had been assembled there were calm; but then, of course, they did not know what lay in store for them. I did, and tried not to think about it.

I was surprised to see Master Bjarnevalt, wrapped in a cloak, wearing his strange hat, his clerk at his side holding a lantern. He introduced us to Gundur, the head drover. We shook hands. He was tall, and broad-shouldered, and neither young nor old; but the lines on his face told of a hard life. *He has done this before,* I thought. *And he does not like it.*

I introduced Master Bjarnevalt to my companions. He wished us all luck, then shook my hand, and stood back as we mounted the horses that he had provided for us, for which I had thanked him. They were fine animals. The stallion that was to carry Grell was as big as any I'd ever seen. Gundur's men moved the livestock out, gently, with no cries, and no whips, just the nudging of dogs. Our procession passed through the town gates and took the road north, as the sky lightened in the east, and the day dawned. We moved at a walking pace, for the comfort of our beasts.

The road took us through farmland and orchards. The trees and fields were mostly bare, but showed signs of spring, with early flowers and new leaves. There were villages, and farms, and gardens; not hud-dled together, but with plenty of space between them. Each garden had its own glasshouses, their panes fogged from the heat rising within them from deep in the earth. Hedges and ditches lined the road, all well kept and cared for. A peaceful land, I thought. Here, life was lived at a gentle pace, according to the rhythms of the seasons.

We reached the first inn, The Drover's Rest, as evening fell. Gun-dur and his men settled the livestock into their corral while we went inside. We ate, and drank, and said little, and went to our rooms and slept. Before dawn the next morning, we were on the move again.

The second day was like the first, as was the third. Only the weather changed. One day teased of summer. The next reminded us of winter. Our horses were hardy. They were used to the cold and knew this road that wound up and around, taking us into the north.

We rested as much as we could, which was little. The tension we felt was debilitating. We were riding to our doom. We did not need to tell each other that. We soon stopped trying to keep each other's spirits up. It wouldn't have worked. Who were we kidding?

On the fourth night there was no inn—only a charred compound where we set up camp. One harsh winter, Gundur said, when his grand-father was young, the Ice Wights had come down from the mountains. When they had finished with the innkeeper, and his family, and guests, and workers, and their animals, they had burned the building to the ground. "They crave the warmth," Gundur told us.

Despite this being a trade route, and thus potentially profitable, no one had wanted to rebuild it. If the Wights could come this far south once, they could do so again. All it would take would be another hard winter, and those were not rare in Normark.

On the next day, we crossed the Snowline. The path narrowed and led ever up, ever steeper. Snow fell that afternoon, and all the next day. We huddled at night, close to the beasts that we were taking to their deaths. It felt like a betrayal. We spoke little.

Each evening, Horm and Nyrik worked with Jess on her archery skills. Though it was a welcome distraction for them from what we were going through, each session lasted no more than a half hour. Their hearts weren't really in it. Their minds, like ours, were preoccupied with what lay ahead. Qrysta and Grell and I talked, but we really had noth-ing to say, because we did not know what to talk about. *We'll see when we get there,* was the only notion we all had. The anticipation worked on us, and was more tiring than the journey.

On the seventh day, the path wound back and forth across the face of the mountains that reared up ahead of us, becoming ever more narrow and treacherous. The pack horses labored up it. The livestock became nervous. We reached the last staging post that afternoon. Once the beasts were hobbled, and fed, Gundur found us to tell us that we would reach the pass by noon the next day, and would camp back here the next night after making the exchange.

He left. Snowflakes flickered out of the dull sky, as if teasing us. They stopped as the wind shifted, then started again—only to stop again. Everything, it felt, was grating on our nerves. Our little group huddled around our campfire, eating our last meal below the pass. Horm allowed us each a mouthful of Careful Juice. It helped, if only a little.

Tomorrow, we knew, we would be in enemy territory. An enemy that we did not like to think of. An enemy that would be hunting us, to drain our warm blood and then eat us alive.

Nyrik and Horm shook their heads when I asked if they could get us into cellars under trees.

"Doubt it," Nyrik said. "We can try. We have our keys, but …." He trailed off.

"The trees there won't know you," I finished his sentence for him.

He nodded. "Yur."

That was the end of that idea.

We all looked at each other. No one had a clue.

Grell said, "Well, mates: We can always go down fighting."

Though that statement of defiance made us all feel better, knowing we'd have a warrior like Grell leading us, it was still an admission of defeat.

We stared at the flames of the campfire.

"Tomorrow, then," Qrysta said.

We understood.

The Ice Wights would look us over and let us pass; and, sooner or later, they would come for us in numbers, and we'd be fighting for our lives.

A fight that we probably wouldn't win. In their land. Overwhelmed.

What choice did we have? Go big, or go home.

Yeah.

A long silence fell.

Qrysta shook her head and let out a sigh of frustration. "If only we knew the lay of the land up there," she said. "Defensive positions. High ground. Anything, really. Anything at all."

And then Jess spoke up, as she got to her feet. "I could go up and take a look."

We all looked at her.

I said, stupidly, "Go up?"

She was already searching the ground nearby.

"Plenty of twigs," she said, bending to pick some up. "This won't take long."

"What are you talking about?" I said.

She straightened up and looked me in the eye. "I'm Coven."

That was news to us.

I said, "You are? Since when?"

"Since Sister Esmeralda sponsored me. I've only had a couple of lessons, but it's not that hard."

"You can fly?"

She shrugged. "First thing a novice has to learn is how to get about. Coven gatherings are usually a long way from anywhere. Sisters come from all over for them, from dozens of leagues away. If I'm to learn, I've got to attend, haven't I? Same as any other novice. So, I need to know how to fly. I haven't had much practice, but it's pretty easy."

Qrysta and I looked at each other, astonished.

Qrysta said, "Okay, but … won't you need a stick?"

Jess picked up the stick on which her little bundle was tied. "What do you think this is?"

"I meant broomstick," Qrysta said.

"I said, all it needs is twigs," Jess said, continuing to gather them. "About the length of my arm," she told us as we all got up to help. It was a relief to have something productive to do—not to mention something else to think about other than Ice Wights. "Not too thick, not too thin. What you'd need for sweeping."

"Why didn't you tell me?" Qrysta said.

"Novices aren't supposed to tell," Jess replied, as she fished some lengths of twine out of her bundle and started tying the twigs that we'd gathered around one end of the stick. "And I didn't want to upset you. You've done so much for me and wanted me to go to the military academy in Mayport. I know you thought it would be good for me, but—I didn't think I'd fit in. And I was scared. Esmeralda noticed. She summoned me for a chat. And she offered to sponsor me, if I liked the idea of becoming Coven. Which I did. So, she and Marnie took me to the carpenter, for my stick. They're not just any old piece of wood, even though they might look it, you need to have the right one. I mean, I still want to fight two-handed, like you," she assured Qrysta. "And with a bow. But …"

"But what?"

"Coven seemed like somewhere I'd belong," Jess said.

No one said anything.

We all knew it was Qrysta's turn to respond. We watched as she processed what she'd heard. She nodded, slowly, and smiled at her protégée. "I'm not going to disagree with Marnie and Ez."

"Then you don't mind?" Jess said, sounding both relieved and hopeful.

"No, I don't. Jess, I just want you to be happy. I had this idea that I wanted the best for you, so in my mind that meant you should go to the best academy in the realm and study with the best teachers. But, I see it now. You'll learn wherever you are. In school or out of it, whatever you're doing. Right?" She waited for affirmation. "Yes. So, good for you, kid. Why waste all those years in a castle?"

Jess tied off the twine around her new broomstick and smiled. "I should have known you'd understand."

"I should have understood earlier," Qrysta admitted.

It was an awkward moment.

Grell defused the situation. "Yeah, well, better late than never, eh?" he said. Which made both of them chuckle.

Horm, being half niblun, knew his crafting. "I thought that was a nice bit of wood," he said, looking at Jess's broomstick. "That's rowan, that is. Like yours, Daxx."

"Marnie noticed that too," Jess said. "I just picked it because it *felt* right, but I thought that was nice when she pointed it out." She looked up at me with a smile. "And it's a good, strong stick, which Marnie says is what you want, in case you have to whack people with it."

I said, "I didn't know those things were collapsible."

"We don't walk around with broomsticks on our backs; people would notice," Jess said. "Better to be a simple traveler with a simple stick."

I recognized those as Marnie's words.

"Just like you casters, closing the eyes of your staffs so no one knows what you are," Jess went on. "The power's in the stick, not the twigs. The twigs just bring it to life, and the stick then knows, *Uh-oh, here we go.* Like when you open Shift's eye, and she's awake and ready for action." She turned her new broomstick around in her hands and nodded, satisfied. "The twigs are there so the stick knows which way 'round it is, and which way is forwards. So. What am I looking for?"

We told her all that we could think of. Look for cover. Look for places that are hidden from the stockade. Look for Ice Wights—where they are and where they aren't. Look to the north and east, where we'll be heading. Master Bjarnevalt had mentioned secret ways down from the mountains that the Ice Wights used. Look for those, both ends of them, and maybe we could sneak over one of those if you can find one. And don't fly above the stockade—they will be watching the pass. We don't want them to see you.

Jess mounted her broomstick and flew off, not on up the pass, but away from it towards the east. Her black silhouette shrank to a dot against the darkening mountains and then disappeared. Minutes later, it rose against the light of the evening sky, far off to the east, and turned north, at speed.

It was long after darkness had fallen when she returned, hours later. We didn't hear her coming, or see anything above us—not even the sharp eyes of Nyrik and Horm could pick her out against the black night. She dropped out of nowhere, quietly, behind Grell, provoking a quiet *woof* of surprise from Little Guy.

She dismounted and came to join us round the campfire.

"There are some good places," she said. "Plenty of tree cover, some caves, big rocks we could defend. There are more mountains beyond those, and lakes, and rivers. I didn't see any lights anywhere, except in the stockade where there are torches burning—and I went as high as I could, to see as far as I could. It's nothing but wilderness up there in every direction."

That was all worth knowing. It's easier to disappear into wilderness than into a land full of people.

"We don't want to defend," I said. "Even in a good place, where we have the advantage of rocks or whatever. We want to disappear."

"I was thinking," Jess said. "I could fly Nyrik over, and then Horm. The Ice Wights wouldn't know we're there. You could lead them into a trap, where we'd be waiting for them."

239

"You can get two on one broomstick?" Qrysta asked.

Jess nodded. "If they're light. Ez told me she used to take Marnie's sheepdog, Ezzie, wherever they went. She loved it, her ears streaming in the wind. And I'm lighter than Esmeralda, so …"

"Yeah," Grell said. "Remember Oller, telling us how he'd been woken by a tapping at his window at The Wheatsheaf, and it was Ennis with Hob on the front of her broom?"

We all did. Even Little Guy seemed to, as his ears perked up, and he wagged his bushy tail. But that was probably because he'd heard Oller's name.

"What about me?" Qrysta said. "Obviously, you couldn't take Daxx, let alone Grell."

Jess looked doubtful.

"I shouldn't think so," she said. "I dunno—d'you want to see?"

"Might as well," Qrysta said, getting to her feet.

"It'd be dividing our forces, Qrys," Grell pointed out. "Three ahead, three behind—wouldn't that be better?"

"We don't even know if it can take my weight," Qrysta said, straddling the broomstick behind Jess.

"Just relax," Jess told her, "and hold on to me."

Nothing happened. Then, after a few moments, the broomstick struggled a few inches off the ground. Slowly, it moved forwards. Even more slowly, it rose a few more inches, then stopped, and hung there, in front of us.

"Come on, move, you stupid thing!" Jess muttered.

Clearly, they weren't going anywhere.

"Too much weight," Jess said. "It can't lift this much."

"Oh, well," Qrysta said. "Worth a try."

And then it hit me. *Weight. Lift.*

I remembered how we'd met Ironwright Ron, the Orc blacksmith. There'd been too much weight on his cart "for these old shoulders," he'd told us, so he hadn't been able to lift it to replace the broken wheel.

But I had.

"Hold on a moment," I said.

I raised Shift, feeling her jitter in my mind in her eagerness, and cast Levitation on the broomstick. It shot up into the air, and forwards, and out of sight, nearly throwing Qrysta off the back. We heard her gasp of surprise, already high above us. Then Jess let out a quiet whoop, which came from far off to one side. A moment later, she skidded to a halt between us, laughing.

Qrysta looked as if she'd left her stomach somewhere up in the clouds. "Whoa!" she said, tottering off the broomstick. "A bit of warning would've been nice, Daxx!"

I looked at Grell and said, "Next?"

Grell stared back at me. Then he nodded, and got on behind Jess.

I Levitated them.

Once again—but more smoothly this time, because Jess was expecting it—the broomstick rose and flew up into the night.

"A lot less weight than Jurun's throne, with six of us on it," I pointed out.

Nyrik chuckled. "Them ice buggers won't even know we're there."

And that would be just fine by us. We could concentrate on what lay ahead, without having to keep constantly looking back over our shoulders, worrying about what was coming up behind us with the intention of eating us alive.

Jess brought Grell back to earth, and they both dismounted.

"Me first," Horm said. "I've always wanted to fly."

Jess said, "Get your things and hop on."

"Wait," I said. "Grell first. He's the heaviest. Go as far as you can with him before the Levitation wears off, Jess—okay? I had to keep refreshing it all the time coming up from the Undergrounds, and I won't be with you to do that. Leave all your gear, Grello. The rest of us will bring it."

Grell stripped off his armor and dropped everything except his maul, Kinell.

"Not going anywhere without this," he said, and got on behind Jess.

I Levitated them and they disappeared into the night.

I turned to the others, and said, "I need to talk to Gundur."

I found him with his drovers by their campfire, and brought him back over to ours.

I told him what we were going to do.

He listened, frowning, wary. He could see no reason why I'd tell him anything so impossible to believe. But he could not believe it. And then Jess landed beside him, out of nowhere, in silence, and he jumped, startled. He watched as Nyrik got on behind her and we handed him a load of equipment. I Levitated them, and they flew up and off.

"Well, now I've seen everything," Gundur said.

I thanked him for what he'd done for us, and told him that, as far as I was concerned, he did not need to go on and sacrifice his beasts.

He shook his head. "They'll already know," he said. "They'll have heard the oxen lowing, and such. Some believe they smell warm blood from miles away. If we turn back now, without trading, they'll be angry. They'll see it as betrayal. Provocation, even—taunting them with live flesh and blood, then taking it away. There would be reprisals. More childer missing." His expression hardened. "No. We have to go on."

I understood. "If you say so."

"I've Balm to fetch for Master Bjarnevalt, and whatever other goods have been left there for us, to await his gold. Besides …." A thought struck him, and he looked at the place where Jess had landed and then up into the sky. "You want them distracted, so as you can get past the stockade and put a good distance between you and them."

That was indeed true.

"They gorge themselves, see?" he explained, and tried to hide his revulsion at the sights that he'd seen in the stockade. "Eat themselves into a stupor. We don't stay longer than we have to, but ofttimes we have to load up, and that means carrying goods up and down, back to the horses—we leave those outside, or the bastards would be all over them, too. I've had to whip them off our horses more'n once. They can't hold back when the frenzy is on them. So, we go in and out, while they're feeding on the beasts. Several trips, it can take, and some of them are fallen over by the time we leave, sleeping it off, like drunkards who've overdone the liquor. I doubt if any will be out and about for a day or two after tomorrow."

"That *is* good news," I said.

His brows furrowed. He was clearly thinking something over. He shook his head, deciding against it.

"No," he said. "Same as always, is best. I was thinking as mayhaps I'd arrive later than usual. Tell them that a horse threw a plate and we needed to reshoe it. Not that they'd be listening, as they'd be raring to feed. But no, you don't want them annoyed by the delay or, worse, suspicious. I doubt it would buy you any more time, anyway. A day to feast, a day to recover. Then they'll be up and about again."

Two days' head start, I thought. That would be invaluable.

"Thank you, Gundur," I said.

He looked me in the eye. "And I know what you're wanting to ask," he said, "but there's no need. The Wights won't hear of you from me, nor any of us. No man would betray another to those things. There was just us on this drive, and not the six of you."

I took out my purse and counted out ten gold.

His eyes grew round. "There's no need," he said, as I offered him the coins. "Master Bjarnevalt pays well. He has to, or no one would take this job."

"You've earned it, and our thanks," I said. "Buy your men ale and food on your way home."

I waited until he accepted the gold.

"That I will," he said. "We'll drink to your health, every night, and thank you for the kindness."

We shook hands.

"I hope we meet again," I said.

"I hope so too," he said; and, for the first time since I'd met him seven days earlier, he smiled. "If we do, I'll want to hear of your quest in the Ice Lands."

The worst part was the waiting. We had this overwhelming sense of relief that we might have found a workaround, but we wouldn't dare to believe it until we were all beyond the mountains, gathered together, and heading north and east away from the stockade.

After Nyrik, Horm flew with Little Guy and Jess, and more gear. Then it was Qrysta's turn. Finally, Jess and I strapped all that she could carry around her broomstick, and she took to the skies once more.

I waited, by the last embers of our campfire, as the night stretched on, and flurries of snow came and went on the sharpening wind. That seemed the longest wait of all—but perhaps it was because I was alone, the last one to leave.

At last Jess slid out of the night, snow drifting around her. I mounted her broomstick, held onto her waist, and Levitated us. Before I knew it, we were rushing north through the swirling snow. I was wrapped in the furs that Master Bjarnevalt had given us, but even so, the cold bit into my lungs at each breath. I buried my chin in my hood and told myself to relax, not to fight the flight of the broomstick but to go with the flow. Jess knew what she was doing.

Below us, to the west, torches glowed in the distant stockade. Low in the east, the half-moon was dim behind thick clouds. The mountains

243

under us were a long, black, irregular mass. Higher and higher. Colder and colder. And then, a swoop down, and across, and a landing in a small space hidden among trees, where the others were waiting.

We loaded up and headed out.

I could hardly see anything. There was little moonlight filtering down through the clouds and trees, but Nyrik's and Horm's Woods Kin eyes were sharp enough to find our way ahead. We knew that there would be no rest for a long while, and no fires, perhaps for days. But we felt good. We had what we needed. Supplies; warmth, thanks to Master Bjarnevalt's furs; survival gear—our snowshoes.

We traveled hard, and fast, for hour after hour. I had thought that Jess would be the first to need a rest. She wasn't. That was Little Guy. He fell back, behind us, again and again, eventually whimpering. I felt like kicking myself. We had snowshoes, which helped us skim the surface. He had short, spindly legs, which drove down into the snow with every step. When we realized this, Grell slung him across his chest with the rest of his gear. Little Guy licked Grell's face, and wagged his tail, and lay back and slept. We kept going.

We pushed ourselves, but not beyond reason. As the first light of dawn grew in the eastern sky, we rested up. We slept in a hidden fold in a wooded hillside. We woke as day broke around us, and stretched, and ate, and moved on. At about midday we all stopped, suddenly, wondering what we'd heard coming on the wind from far behind us.

We waited. We listened.

There they were again. Faint sounds. Awful sounds.

Then we knew what we were hearing.

From leagues behind us, in the stockade. Animals in terror. Screaming, howling, baying, bleating.

And the shrieking of the Ice Wights in their feeding frenzy.

I hoped never to hear such sounds again.

# 20

## Bumpers or Clumpers

**Some** of the other sounds that we heard over the following days weren't much of an improvement.

That night, it was monstrous trumpetings. Mastodons, Nyrik said, and Horm agreed; there was no mistaking them things. Jess asked how big they were. Horm pointed up. The shadows of tall pines could be seen against the night sky. "I've seen them taller than those trees," he said. "Grumpy buggers, too. You want to stay out of their way. Stomp you, swat you with them great trunks o' theirs—or, if you really piss them off, you'll be fifty foot up in the air impaled on one of their tusks. They're quicker than they look."

The next evening, it was roars—sabre-cats, the two Woods Kin said, definitely: louder and fiercer than any they'd ever heard. Probably, therefore, bigger than the ones back home—and those were big enough. They sounded a long way off though, they judged, so we should be okay. Only, they warned, they can sneak up on you, like any cat; so, if it's your turn on watch, keep your eyes peeled.

It was hard not to doze off when on guard duty. At the end of every day's march, we were exhausted. We weren't used to walking in snowshoes. It's more tiring than it looks. But, without them, our feet would have sunk into the deep snow at every step, and we'd be walking at a snail's pace. Also, we had to carry our gear, which weighed us down, and made the going harder. I tried Levitating us, but you can't walk with your feet in the air. So, it was one step at a time, for a very long time, and it was slow going.

We knew enough not to push ourselves. That was to avoid the one enemy that we could avoid—an enemy that would kill us from inside our own clothing, if we let it: sweat. We had no idea how many other threats there might be, out there in that frozen wasteland—we'd just have to deal with any that appeared and face them as they came. If we sweated, though, we would perspire on the move and freeze when we stopped. Our clothes would turn into the opposite of wetsuits. Instead of an insulating layer of warm water trapped between suit and skin, there would be a sheet of ice, held against you by your frozen clothes. That will refrigerate you to death, no matter how many furs you might have on as outer layers. There'd be no waking the next morning.

I'd heard that freezing to death was a gentle way to go: that the body closes down and the mind sleeps—and never wakes again. It sounded preferable to drowning, or burning; but it was still to be avoided. However comfortable, or otherwise, my end was going to be, I felt that I'd rather it was a few decades off yet. I wasn't ready for it. If I had been, I could have avoided all this, stayed in Eastbay, and slowly morphed into a husk.

The sun circled the sky, varying in color from blood-red to orange. It never shone with the blazing yellow of the south. Night was soon less than an hour of darkness, the season being early spring. Even then, the sky was light blue rather than black. We could see stars, but not many of them, against that never-dark background. Occasionally, to the north, ribbons of green and yellow smudged the horizon, writhing in the distant sky, then fading: the Polar Lights. Guiding us to our destination, I thought. *Where the moon sleeps.*

We walked. We camped. We made fires and ate. We hadn't been able to fly over all the supplies that Master Bjarnevalt had given us, and our reserves had dwindled fast, but Nyrik and Horm supplied us with fresh meat every evening: plump arctic hares; wild goats that were all hair and gristle; geese and ducks. They always took Jess with them, teaching her how to hunt with her whitewood bow. We slept around our campfires, wrapped up warm in our furs; and rose the next day, stiff and cold from the frozen ground beneath us and the merciless, chilling night air. Every morning, any exposed hair would be white with hoar-frost—our eyebrows, Horm's beard, Grell's brown-fuzzed face. When we woke, we'd beat warmth into our arms and stamp our feet to get the circulation going.

On the fourth morning, as we hauled ourselves to our feet in a grove of fir trees, I said to Nyrik, "Pity none of these trees know you. I could do with a night under shelter."

Nyrik grunted agreement. "You and me both!"

And then the realization hit me. "Oh, what an *idiot!*" I growled.

Nyrik, offended, said, "Eh??"

"Not you, Nyrik: *me*. I can't believe how stupid I am sometimes. *Why* don't I ever see the bleeding obvious?!"

I fished out Oller's silver key from my inside pocket and took it to the largest nearby tree. Just as a silver keyhole had appeared in the Tree of Life at the Floor Of The World, so one now appeared in the pine tree's trunk.

I inserted the key, turned it, and a door swung open.

Horm's jaw fell.

"You're joking," Nyrik said.

I grinned. "Want to take a look?"

Sure enough, there was a dry cellar beneath the tree. It wasn't large, but there was enough room for all of us to stretch out.

"Well, now!" Grell said.

From then on, we slept every night underground, warm and hidden. There was no longer any need to set sentries, or to worry about Ice Wights or sabre-cats.

Snow fell. Skies cleared. Winds rose and dropped. North, we walked, and east, day after day, eyes scanning the forest ahead and around for dangers, Jess taking to the skies from time to time to scout out the lay of the land. Sometimes we emerged above the tree line, and surveyed the new vistas that each summit revealed. They were always bleak, always harsh, always winter.

One day, as we descended a wooded slope, Nyrik and Horm held up their hands to halt us as other worrying sounds came back to us from ahead: deep snarls that sounded almost like a conversation. They couldn't think what was making those. It sounded like bears, they said—but what bears wouldn't be hibernating at this time of year, this far north, in weather this cold?

We crept forwards—and saw the answer, as we looked down through the trees at a frozen lake below us. Three enormous white bears were shambling across it—away from us, we were happy to see. They were heading east, presumably towards the frozen ocean, to hunt—what? Seals, walruses, narwhals? We steered well clear, keeping back out of sight.

That evening, Jess was beaming as she and Nyrik and Horm staggered back to our camp beneath the weight of a bristle-covered boar that was bigger than the three of them. A whitewood arrow was sticking out of its armpit, its head buried in the animal's heart. A deadshot. Nyrik and Horm were proud of her.

"Just the one arrow was all it took!" Nyrik said, with a grin. "Oinker dropped dead in a heartbeat."

"Couldn't have done it neater myself," Horm said. "Feed us for a week, this will."

Grell eyed the carcass doubtfully. "I've got enough to carry already. I can't lug this great thing as well."

Qrysta said, "Use your glove of strength."

"Only lasts a couple of minutes."

Nyrik chuckled and winked at Horm.

"Woods oven?" he suggested.

Horm broke into a smile. "Yur!" he said. "*Now* you're talking!" Then, he reconsidered. "Well, I dunno, Nyr. Ground's frozen. We'll never manage."

Nyrik glanced at me. "Him, and his clever stick?"

Horm's eyebrows rose, and he looked at me, and at Shift, and nodded. "Never thought o' that," he said. "Might work, might well work indeed. Hope so. Haven't had a good Woods Roast in far too long."

Horm cut off a foreleg at the shoulder and handed it to Jess, whose job was to get cooking. That would be tonight's dinner. I opened Shift's eye and blasted fire into a pile of branches, and Jess got to work, turning the meat on a makeshift spit. The rest of us collected rocks, and branches thick with pine needles, and more firewood. Nyrik marked out a square in the snow, and told me to make him a nice deep pit.

Shift melted the snow, and heated the frozen earth beneath it, and then blew it apart. When the pit was as deep as they were tall, Nyrik and Horm jumped down into it and assembled the woods oven. At the bottom they laid a mass of firewood, kindling and sticks below thick logs. On top of that, they arranged a layer of rocks. They then scrambled out of the pit, and for the next half hour Shift poured flame into it, while the logs burned fiercely from below.

When the rocks were glowing with heat, the two Woods Kin shoveled dirt on top of them. "So's the branches don't catch alight," Nyrik explained. Then, they laid green pine branches in a crisscross pattern on top of the dirt, to protect the boar, which Horm had gutted and split in half. Each half was laid on the branches, along with the boar's kidneys and liver. More branches were laid on top of it all, and the whole arrangement was covered up with a high mound of earth, which we all patted down to seal the meat in its oven, until no more wisps of smoke drifted up out of it. "Job done!" Nyrik said, dusting off his hands. "Let that cook overnight; we'll dig it up in the morning. Then we'll joint it up, and share the load between us."

"Pity none of us is an Ogre," Horm said. "They'd love these gizzards. Anyone?"

Nobody wanted raw pig intestines. What we all wanted was what Jess had been cooking, which was smelling delicious. Horm walked off into the trees and disposed of the unwanted entrails.

We ate well that night. The moon rose, bigger now than she had been the night before, shimmering pearl-soft light down onto the forest floor. As we gorged ourselves on Jess's boar, we heard the first sounds that Nyrik and Horm couldn't identify. They froze and stared at each other in confusion, as high, mournful cries came down the wind from the mountain range that we'd seen rising ahead of us.

Grell knew what was making them. "Yetis," he said, with a smile. "Klurra and I heard them—back in Jarnland, in the Western Mountains. She loved that sound." We listened, and there was, indeed, something lovely as well as lonely in those distant howls—one calling to another.

It was the next morning that we heard the sound that we had been expecting to hear, in that arctic wilderness, but hadn't yet heard: the howling of wolves. It came from ahead of us, very suddenly, very loud, and very close. One moment the world was silent but for the wind in the branches above us; the next, there burst in on us the cacophony of a pack of them, all giving tongue at the tops of their voices.

They were downwind of us. They must have caught our scent. We stopped and unslung our weapons. They were heading straight for us, at speed.

They were on us almost immediately. Grell strode forward, Kinell at the ready, Qrysta circling beside him, her blades drawn. Nyrik, Horm, and Jess had arrows taut on their bowstrings. I cast glowing green Shields of Healing on all of us, and prepared to cast Traps and Damage Attacks, as the wolf pack burst into sight through the evergreens.

They were in two lines, in harness, galloping at full speed—despite the efforts of something that looked like a black bear hauling for all he was worth on the reins at the back of the sled they were pulling, and roaring at them, "Stop that blasted noise! What in all hells are you doing, damn your miserable hides?!"

No one loosed an arrow, and I did not cast any Damages—more out of surprise than anything.

Then the wolves were all over me: jumping, licking, whimpering, wagging their tails in delight, crooning with joy, scrambling on top of each other to stand up on their hind legs and mob me. Little Guy got into the spirit and joined in, bouncing around them in excitement.

Their bearlike driver stopped yelling and stared at us in amazement, and then back at his ecstatic wolves. There were twelve of them—the smallest of them bigger than any wolf I'd ever seen. If they hadn't surrounded me, and tangled me up in their harness, I'd have been knocked down and buried under them, and probably licked to death.

It was complete chaos. Their driver jammed his anchor-spike into the ground and tied off his reins around his crossbar. He stepped off the sled's runners and strode over towards us. "Down!" he ordered, and "Sit!" and "Leave it, *leave it!* Stop! Gods damn it all, WILL YOU MISERABLE BASTARDS LISTEN??!"

The wolves didn't.

Eventually, I found my voice, which until then had done nothing but splutter and cough, as huge paws scrabbled at my shoulders, and sticky tongues licked my face, making me screw up my eyes and grimace. "Stop!" I gasped.

Instantly, the wolves stopped leaping and licking, and disentangled themselves, and stood around me, looking up at me expectantly with alert, yellow eyes, tails wagging.

The driver muttered, "What th—"

I took a few gulps of air, and said, "Sit."

The wolves sat.

Little Guy sat too.

Silence fell, broken only by the panting of the wolves, their tongues lolling out of their mouths. Long, sharp teeth they had, I noticed.

Well, at least they weren't sinking them into me. Which was good.

I looked at the driver, who was staring at me, a frown of bemusement on his hairy face. And when I say that it was hairy, I mean that all of it was. He was hair all over—just like Grell; but, unlike Grell, most of his hair was long. The only place where it was short was on his face, where a human would have no hair at all. He had a warhammer slung across his back and was wearing leather armor, around which his monstrous pelt sprouted out in all directions. And though it was thick hair—more like a bear's fur, in fact, than hair—he was no bear. His movements were sure on his long, hind legs; the walk of a natural biped, not an awkward, bearlike waddle.

He was an Orc.

And the hairiest Orc—indeed, just about the hairiest anything—that I'd ever seen.

Clearly, he didn't know what to make of me either. "How in all hells did you do that?!" he demanded.

"I … don't know," I said.

"These bastards get that close to anyone, they're *dead!*" he said, still clearly not believing what had happened.

"I can well imagine."

"They don't *like* people! Except to eat. And a total stranger? They don't even like *me* that much, and I've reared them from pups. And look at them!"

The wolves were all sitting, staring at me, rapt—and, I had to admit, as adoringly as Little Guy stared at his beloved Oller.

"They're … very nice wolves," I said.

"Nice?" The bear-Orc said, affronted. "*Nice!?* They're the meanest sons of wolf-bitches west of the Winter Sea! If any one of them was nice, he'd not be in a team of mine! Nice!? Out here!? Out here, nice gets you *killed!*"

I said, "Sorry. I was trying to be … friendly."

The bear-Orc snorted. "Friendly. Nice. Out here in the middle of the blasted Ice Lands." He shook his head in disgust. "I never heard the like!"

He looked around at the rest of us and was, clearly, baffled by what he saw. "Never seen the like of you lot, neither." He turned to Grell, and said, "I presume you're in charge?"

"Er, well … no, he is," Grell said, indicating me. "I mean, we're a team. We work together."

The bear-Orc frowned, as if that made no sense. "You're the only Orc. This is Orc territory."

"Oh," Grell said, "yeah. I see what you mean."

"So, you should be in charge."

Eventually, Grell said, "All right," which could have meant anything.

"What are you, then?" the bear-Orc demanded. "Bumper or clumper?"

Grell said, "Eh?"

The bear-Orc shook his head in annoyance. "Are you," he said, slowly, as if to an idiot, "a bumper or a clumper?"

Grell's eyes were wide with confusion. "I've no idea what you're talking about, mate."

"Huh? What part of *bumper or clumper* don't you understand?"

"Every part."

Now it was the bear-Orc's turn to be surprised. "Really?"

"Yeah. Really."

"Oh. Well …. Mayhaps, you don't know our nicknames for you lot," he said, in a patronizing tone of voice, "although I find that hard to believe, what with us fighting over far less than that for the last few hundreds of years. Are you," he asked, after taking a breath, "a Hill Orc, as they call themselves, for those feeble little bumps they name hills wot they put their strongholds on top of—or are you a Wood Orc, wot builds them in clumps of trees?"

"Oh," Grell said. "Now I get it. Neither, mate. I am Grell of the Ozgaroos."

The bear-Orc frowned at him. "The what-the-fucks?"

"Also," Grell continued, fishing out his pass from Chief Elbrig, "an honorary Stonefields, as are my companions. Allow me to present my papers."

He handed them to the bear-Orc, who took them and looked them over, scowling.

"Never heard of any of them," he said. "And you can't tell me those are Orcs. Couple of them are bloody pixies, by the look of them."

"Watch it, pal," Horm bristled, bringing up his bow; but Nyrik stopped him, quietly. "His realm, mate, his rules," he muttered. "Let the gentleman explain."

Horm grunted and lowered his weapon.

The bear-Orc ignored him.

"*Honorary* Orcs, pal," Grell emphasized. "They're with me. Would you like to know why they are honorary Orcs, of the honorable Stone-fields tribe?"

"What I want to know is," the bear-Orc countered, "what daft chief goes about recruiting bloody pixies. And a dog—I suppose he's an Orc too, right?"

"*Honorary* bloody Orc, you dense twat! How many times do I have to say it? They are *honorary* because they—and *we*, and our mates in the Stonefields mob—saved our realm, and our queen, in a MOAF."

The bear-Orc went still, and his eyebrows, which were even bush-ier than the rest of him, shot up into his scalp. "Oh, ah?" he said, sud-denly interested. "A MOAF, hey?"

"Yup," Grell nodded. "Undead, stone trolls, skeletons, eefrits, ghouls: You name it, mate, we fought it. And killed it. Even if it was already dead. We ripped the crown off the skull of a long-dead king, who made the mistake of coming back to life and being rude."

The bear-Orc glared at him—not in disbelief, I thought, but in annoyance. I wondered what he was annoyed about.

I soon found out.

"Oh. *Well* now. Chief will want to hear about that. A MOAF? We haven't had one of those in years. You lucky bastards!"

I realized that he was annoyed because he'd have liked to have been a part of something like that himself.

Well, that was hardly surprising. He was, after all, an Orc.

Nyrik looked at Qrysta, puzzled. "What's a MOAF?"

"Mother Of All Fights," she explained. "Orc Talk."

"Ah," Nyrik grunted, understanding.

"So, what are you doing up here, and where are you going?" the bear-Orc said. He didn't sound nosy, but more ... hopeful? As if we might be heading towards another MOAF.

Grell said, "That's our business."

The bear-Orc's eyes narrowed as he digested Grell's answer.

"Fair enough," he allowed, "if it doesn't concern us. But if it does concern us, Chief needs to hear about it. Strikes me you and she have plenty to discuss."

"Suppose we don't want to?" Grell said.

"Don't ask me, pal—that's between you and her. You have your dis-cussion; tell each other what you want. How should I know?"

Grell glanced at me and caught my eye. With a slight tilt of his head, he indicated the Orc.

Who got the message at the same time as I did. "I know what you're thinking," he said. "There's only one of me, and six of you." He waited for Grell's reply.

"Er ..."

"Normally," the bear-Orc went on, "I'd point out to you there's actually thirteen of me. And these bastards love a fight even more than I do. You'd need a lot of arrows to take down even a one of them, and the others wouldn't appreciate you shooting their pack mate. As it stands, though," he said, shaking his head at his wolves, who were sitting, quietly, intent on me, "seems to me it's eighteen of you and me all on my own. So, here's my question. Don't you want to know what's up between my wolves and your friend there, as much as I do?"

We all did. Me most of all.

"Thought so. Couple more points. One: Seems to me you're heading more or less in the direction of our stronghold. You may want to keep your business up here to yourself—final destination and all that—and that's fair enough. But you're an Orc, you know the rules. You're on our turf. If one of us says you need to report to our chief, and get leave to go on, that's what you need to do. Besides. It's only polite, right? And two: While you're at it, you get to sleep in a nice warm stronghold tomorrow night after a nice long soak in the hot pools, instead of out here. Might be a pleasant change?"

I had no need to look at the others. I knew that they were all thinking exactly what I was. *Nice warm stronghold. Hot pools, nice long soak.*

That sounded good to me.

"So, now you know who we are," Grell said. "What about you, chum? I expect you have a name?"

The bear-Orc glared at him. "Desmond."

"Of?"

"Well, what do you think?! Way out here, on the Ice Plains? Of the Ice Orcs, o' course. Or thumpers, as we call ourselves, 'cos we're always thumping the shit out of the other lots. What in all bloody hells else would I be? I wouldn't last a winter out here as bald as you ..." he glanced back at Grell's papers " ...Stonefields. Where are they, then, when they're at home?"

"Overseas."

Desmond was surprised. "There's Orcs overseas?" he said.

"There are."

"Well now. That's news to us. Chief needs to hear about that, too. Overseas where?"

"Jarnland."

"Never heard of it."

"Ozgaroo."

"Never heard of it."

"Well, you have now. So yes, if you'd be so kind, Dez: escort us to your stronghold, would you? We'd be happy to report to your chief, fill her in. And, by the way," he added, "we have gifts, if she would be prepared to extend her hospitality?"

Desmond went still, and stared at him, suspicious. Eventually, he said, "You sure you're an Orc?"

"What do I bloody look like?" Grell replied, affronted.

"A softy, bald Orc," Desmond replied. "But if you think we won't, as you say, 'extend our hospitality,' you clearly aren't one. That's what Orcs *do*!"

"Well, when they don't attack you," Grell pointed out.

"There is that," Desmond conceded. "The which is not happening on this occasion: What we need, in order to have our chief's 'hospitality extended' to you and yours, is to get my blasted wolves back to work!"

He glared at me. He waited. Eventually, he hinted, "*If* you would be so kind??"

"Yes," I said. "Right. Of course. Er …." I looked at the wolves, who hadn't taken their eyes off me since sitting obediently at my command. "What do you usually say, Desmond? To get them to, er, whatever it is that you—"

"Mush," Desmond said.

"Mush," I repeated, wondering what tone of voice I should use when saying it. But I didn't need to decide, because I'd already said it, and the wolves snapped into their places ahead of the sled with a smartness that would have earned even Commandant Bastard's approval.

"Hell's bells," Desmond muttered. "Never seen them do that!"

We all looked at the eager, expectant wolves. Ready and waiting.

Desmond was frowning at me. "What in all hells *are* you?"

"It's a long story."

He contemplated me, nodding. "I'll bet it is," he said. "And it's a long way to our stronghold, so you can save it for the chief. No point in freezing to death out here while you tell me, so jump in, and let's be going."

Grell said, "What? All of us?"

Desmond said, walking over to harness his wolves, "They're stronger than they look."

The wolves looked far too strong for comfort already.

We squeezed into the sled and arranged our gear and furs around us. Desmond took his stance on the runners, hauled out the anchor-spike, untied the reins, slapped them gently, and said, "Mush."

The wolves shot forward, slamming us back against each other. Grell, who was wedged up against the sled's frame at the rear of our group, caught the full force of it.

"Oof!" he gasped, as it drove the wind out of his lungs.

It was a nice surprise to learn, as we soon did, that, after days and nights of hard slog after hard slog, traveling in the Ice Lands could be a delight. The wolves ran, fast and silent. Any time that Desmond stood on his skid-brake, or hauled in on the reins to slow them down for a sharp bend or to descend a slope, several of them would turn, and look back at him, annoyed, as if to say, "Oy! Cut that out, we're running here!"

Crowded together as we were under our furs, we were as warm as toast, and more comfortable than we'd been since our last night in Birgit's kitchen. Whatever we were sitting on—Desmond's supplies, I supposed—was soft enough, if a bit lumpy in places. This, I thought, leaning back against Grell, was far preferable to plodding along on snowshoes.

Desmond was a skilled driver. Even so, the sled was thrown about from time to time, over bumps, or around corners. We hardly felt it. All we did was lean into whichever neighbor we were crushed up against. It was exhilarating: the cold air on our faces; the galloping of the wolves; the bright sunlight slanting down through the pine trees. I noticed that my companions all had smiles on their faces.

As if Jess was missing the best thing in the world, Qrysta sighed, and said, "And to think, you could be sitting in a classroom in Mayport Castle, learning etiquette."

Jess laughed.

"No regrets?" Qrysta said.

Jess shook her head and gazed out at the snowscape that the wolves were hauling us through. "None."

After an hour or so we descended a series of awkward slopes, slowly, our sled lurching and twisting—and then we were away, at speed, across a frozen lake, the wolves picking up the pace in their joy of being now, at last, free to run as fast as they could. They clearly loved their work.

"I can let them have their heads now," Desmond yelled into the rushing air. "They know the way from here."

The wind whipped in our faces, cold and sharp, making Little Guy's ears flap. The sled's runners hissed below us on the snow-covered ice. We didn't know where we were going, or what would happen when we got there, but we were all enjoying the ride.

Nobody talked. We didn't need frozen air burning into our lungs. There would be time for talking later. Meanwhile, there was this ride. White below. The wide expanse of the ice lake around us. Beyond its shores, the dark green and black shadows of the endless forest. The gray sky above. Ahead of us, the heaving bodies of the wolves.

It turned out that we were wrong about Jess's boar. It didn't last us a week.

Twelve wolves made short work of every bit of it that we didn't eat that night.

As evening fell, Desmond brought the sled to a halt at the mouth of a cave in a cliffside above another frozen lake. Shift soon had a fire roaring. We spread our furs on the cave's floor, and the wolves settled, while the remains of Jess's boar got their second roasting.

As our supper cooked, Desmond explained who he was and what he did. He was, he told us, a bounder. His job was to patrol the boundaries of Ice Orc territory. He had been three days out from his stronghold, on a sweep that usually took him a week, when he came across us. He wasn't taking us back the way he'd come. He wanted to get us to his chief as soon as possible, so we were heading home by the direct route.

He had a number of duties. He was to note the migration of the herds and birds—mastodon, reindeer, fur-elk, and musk ox; terns, geese, and ducks. He was to keep an eye out for trouble—predators, undead, Ice Wights, and so on. If he had trade goods for the south, he'd drop them off at the depot and pick up anything that had been left for his tribe.

It was all done on the honor system, he explained. "Although you'd not think Ice Wights would have honor. And they'll eat you, if they catch you out in the wild and you can't protect yourself. But they need the trade and don't want what we're sending south, or has been sent up for us. So, the depot's neutral ground, more or less. You rarely see the buggers there. They stay away. All this warm blood—twelve wolves and me? That'd drive them mad."

Above all, he was to make sure that any bumpers or clumpers didn't trespass. Which they didn't need to do, there being far more land up there than any of them could ever use; but still, it was the principal of the thing. This was Ice Orc territory; they needed to stay in theirs. Occasionally, he'd come across the bounders of the other tribes. They'd share a campfire and a meal, friendly enough, but it was never a peaceful night. Their wolf teams would snap and snarl at each other, and he never got much sleep. Our wolves, by contrast, could not have been more placid. All they wanted to do was watch me; and, if I looked at any one of them, its tail would wag and it would lean forward and want to know if there was anything it could do for me.

Jess, with Little Guy at her side, was enraptured. "Can I pat them?" she asked Desmond.

"Eh?" he said, startled. "Are you mad? Do you want to lose an arm?"

Jess said, "They don't look like they're going to bite me."

Indeed, they didn't. They looked as calm as lapdogs.

Desmond didn't exactly say yes, because he didn't want the responsibility for any unfortunate incidents, but he didn't say no, either.

Jess and Little Guy walked over to the docile wolves and made friends with them.

Desmond shook his head as he watched. He turned to me, and said, "What have you done to them?"

"I really don't know."

"No?" he said. "Well, then. I expect you'd like to find out as much as I do."

"I definitely would," I agreed.

"Sylmond will know more'n I do about this sort of thing," he said, as we watched Jess scratching wolf ears and Little Guy sniffing wolf bottoms.

I said, "Who?"

"Our shaman. Chief's grandmother. Although you wouldn't know it to look at her. Live long and look young, do shamans. Until it's their time to go, when the years come rushing back all at once and sweep them away."

What we had been sitting on in the sled had, indeed, been Desmond's supplies. Most of it, the soft bits, were fodder for his animals. "Wolf biscuit," he explained, hauling out a sack. "Twelve wolves, seven days: needs a lot o' biscuit. We're not out here to hunt; we have bounds to beat. If I let these bastards loose to find their own food, they don't come back for days."

"What's in them?" Jess asked.

"Everything. Nothing goes to waste, from gravy to giblets to old vegetables and rats from the traps. Ground up bones and gristle. Mash from the brewings. Stale bread. Moldy yak cheese. They're not picky. The riper it is, the better they like it. The cooks boil it all up, and cool it all down, and when it's set, chop it into chunks."

His wolves were all looking at him hungrily, their tails wagging. Jess said, "Can I feed them?"

Desmond shook his head, chuckling. "And you feasting me on that boar of yours?" he said, handing her the sack of wolf biscuits. "It'll be my pleasure, young lady. Just be sure to spread them evenly; they can be quarrelsome."

Jess fetched a sack from the sled and took it over to the wolves. They sat quietly as she poured out a pile of wolf biscuit in front of each one, and a smaller one for Little Guy, who tucked in as happily as the wolves did.

There was no leaping, no snarling, no snapping. Each wolf ate its ration, and then lay down, its eyes on me.

Desmond watched, shaking his head. "I dunno what's got into them," he muttered. He looked at me. "You've some explaining to do."

"I do," I agreed. "And I'll be happy to tell you everything I can."

He grunted. "And I'll be happy to listen. We've never seen anything like you lot up this way. Turning my wolves into pussycats. Coming up here off a MOAF? Yes. We'll want to hear all about *that*."

The wolves watched us eat. When we'd eaten our fill, Jess fed them, and Little Guy, the scraps. Desmond told us that we wouldn't be needing them. We'd be at his stronghold the next day, where there was plenty of food. The cave echoed with the sounds of chewing and the crunching of bones.

I fell asleep, under my furs, watching the shadows cast by the fire on the cave's walls, listening to the snuffling of the wolves, who had all mysteriously gathered as close as they could around me.

*Danger behind,* I thought, *and no doubt danger ahead, but I'm pretty safe where I am tonight, with this lot for bodyguards.*

# 21

## Iʒvellir

I slept—a deep, deep sleep.

Out of the depths of the night I surfaced to see two familiar, yellow eyes gazing at me from behind passing clouds. *My old friend,* I thought. *How nice to—*

"They know what you are," the Voice from the vault interrupted my thoughts. He sounded weak, and fretful, as if he was fading, as if he was almost out of time.

I struggled to think who they were—then realized that they were sleeping all around me. "Yes," I agreed. "They know that I am Gifted."

"More than that. Much more."

"Care to explain?"

"When you get here," he said, his voice little more than a rasp.

The eyes closed. The moon faded. The clouds disappeared.

The dream ended.

I heard snores around me, and rumbles, and felt warm wolf breath on my face.

The words echoed in my head.

*They know what you are.*

Why had he interrupted my sleep to tell me something I already knew? Or was he trying to tell me something else, something I had not grasped? Instinctively, I reached for Shift. I needed her advice. The sooner I found him the better. Not just for him, for both of us. I was his only chance, just as he was mine.

Shift, as if from the depths of sleep, mumbled *huuhh* …?

No help there, then, I thought. Feeling more on my own than ever, I drifted off at last into an uneasy sleep, worrying about what lay ahead.

That night was the first of the year in which the sun had not set entirely below the horizon. We were underway early. We had, Desmond told us, a long, hard day ahead of us. For most of the morning it was a fast run, over frozen lakes or flat terrain. The further north we went, the fewer trees there were. We had left the great forest beyond the stockade behind us days ago.

We came to the first climb towards noon. Desmond halted, and we got out of the sled, to lighten it for the wolves. They hauled it uphill, the sled lurching and bucking, the wolves straining in their harnesses. At the crest, Desmond reined in, the wolves panting hard, their breath clouding the cold air. He handed Jess another sack of biscuits, which she rationed out among them. Little Guy, who seemed to have adopted the wolves as his new crew, was given his own pile beside theirs.

Desmond didn't know whether to laugh or complain. "They'd normally fight over each other's food and then eat him!" he said. "Can't say as I mind them being this well behaved." He gave them half an hour's rest, telling us that they'd need all their strength for the next climb. "And you folks rest, too," he added. "I don't take this way unless I have to, as we're all half dead by the time we get over it. But with you lot helping, we'll manage."

I said, "Why would you 'have to' take this route?"

He looked at me, his expression serious. "There's no rules out here, friend," he said. "Any number of things might come after me, and not just the other tribes, if we happened to be having one of our disputes."

"Such as?"

"Well, there's not many as would mess with a dozen wolves. Sometimes, if game is scarce, sabre-cats might form a pack. There's enough eating on us to see them through a winter. Ice Wights—you never know with them things. Mostly they stick to their haunts, but those are all over, not just down by the stockade. The wolves smell them, and let me know to get moving. You can sense the difference in them.

They just run like hell, ears flat, heads down, and won't stop until we're behind walls. We have refuges out here that we can hole up in—if we can get to one in time.

"Mainly, though, it's just the weather. I can read the skies as well as any Ice Orc. You can't be a bounder without that skill. But it can change fast in the Ice Lands, and there's not always a lot of warning. One moment it's a fine day; an hour later the whiteout drops, and I can't see halfway down the sled, let alone the back wolves' arses. They know what to do. I tie off the reins, and they trot to the nearest shelter. Which might just be a stand of trees, where we can camp down and defend ourselves if we have to. Then there's nothing for it but to wait it out—the which most creatures up here will also be doing."

He grimaced—at least it looked as if he did, as much as we could tell under all that hair. "Not Ice Wights, though. Whiteout's nothing to them. They thrive in it. I've had more than one scrap with them appearing out of the white. My wolves sense them coming, though, so we're ready for them. Not the best fighting conditions when you can't see more than a foot in front of your face."

I tried to imagine it. It must be like fighting for your life in the dark against an enemy that could see.

Grell, too, had been thinking about what Desmond said. "Wow. Rather you than me, mate."

"You just have to keep them off you," Desmond said. "Or the cold from their grip will stop you, and that's the end of you. Only, they'll have their teeth into you before you're dead. Not a good way to go, chilled to a standstill and drained. But they don't use blades and you just have to get a fire going. They burn, same as anyone."

I remembered what Gundur had told me. "I thought they craved the warmth."

"Warmth, yes; burning alive, no," Desmond replied. "I expect you've not found sitting in my sled all that comfortable?"

"No, it's fine," I said. "I mean, a bit lumpy."

He grinned. "Know what those lumps are?"

"What?"

Desmond waved at the landscape, which was nothing but snow, and ice, and trees. "The last thing you'd think anyone would need to drag around in a sled out here," he said. "Firewood—all dry, and plenty of it. Also jars of oil and cloth for making torches. You don't need a big blaze, for the warmth; just something you can put your torch to, and then shove into an Ice Wight's face."

The others, I could see from the looks on their faces, were thinking exactly what I was. The sooner we got to his tribe's stronghold the better.

After another hour's smooth running we came to the second climb. It was twice as steep and three times as high as the first one had been. "The less often I have to tackle this bugger, the happier I am," Desmond muttered, looking up at the crest above us. I saw what he meant. The path up it, if path it could truly be called, zigzagged around large boulders.

Beside me, Nyrik muttered, "Blimey ..."

It was obvious that Desmond, and his wolves, were going to need all the help they could get. We hadn't told him anything about ourselves, apart from showing him Chief Elbrig's papers. He hadn't interrogated us, that being his chief's business. I did not know how she, or her shaman, would take the news that I was a mage, so I didn't want to volunteer to Levitate his sled. Shift's eye was closed, and she looked just like an ordinary staff. Better, I thought, to keep my cards close to my chest.

But we'd had a day to get to know Desmond, and while we were something between guests and prisoners, he was only trying to do the right thing—by us, as well as by his tribe. So now, I thought, it was our turn. I caught Grell's eye, and mimed putting on a glove. He understood and started searching his inside pocket.

"I normally dump everything I'm carrying," Desmond said. "I have to, or we'd never make it. We should manage, though, with you lot to help—especially another Orc." He turned to Grell. "I'll take front, all right, so I can work the wolves. You be all right at the back?"

"No problem, Dez," Grell said, getting out his scruffy little glove.

"Back *is* the hardest," Desmond pointed out.

Grell put on the glove, which expanded to fit his huge hand, and wiggled his fingers at him with a wink.

"What's that?" Desmond said, frowning.

Grell said, "In case of emergencies." He picked up the back of Desmond's sled in his gloved hand and raised it above his head.

Desmond's eyebrows shot up in surprise. "Eh?" he said, as Grell lowered the sled.

"It doesn't last long," Grell said, taking the Glove of Strength off. "I'll save it until we need it."

"Looks like we'll be all right, then!" Desmond said, smiling. "Right, put your gear in the sled, take a handhold anywhere you can, and listen to my orders, all right? Heave when I call *heave*, hold on *hold*."

We heaved. We held. We heaved again. When we got stuck, Grell lifted the rear of the sled, and the rest of us hauled it forwards. Grell lowered. We heaved. We held. Even with the six of us helping, it was hard, awkward work. I couldn't imagine how Desmond could manage this job on his own.

The sun was warm overhead. We sweated. I could feel it running in rivulets down my back inside my clothes. When I told Desmond, he understood at once.

"Best keep at it," he said. "You'll be indoors by evening, then you can get your kit off, and into the hot pools to warm up." He didn't tease us about being hairless softies. I hoped he was right, and kept climbing, and hauling.

At last we dragged the sled over the crest and stood, panting, and whooped, and smiled, and leaned on the sled to catch our breath. Below us, a longer, gentler slope led down towards the level Ice Plain. "Never done that climb in an hour," Desmond said. "Usually takes at least four. Right, get under them furs before you cool off."

He doled out more wolf biscuits as we settled back into the sled. Desmond took his place on the runners, and clicked his tongue. The wolves ran. The slope took us down to the plain, where they accelerated into a gallop. The sun circled towards the west as they ran, hour after hour. I was warm, if damp from sweat, under my clothes and the pile of furs over us. I didn't want to think about having to sleep out in the open that night, even safe and snug beneath a tree.

We were racing across another ice lake, the evening shadows growing long around us, when Desmond announced, "Isvellir."

Ahead of us, a mountain loomed at the far side of the lake.

It was all white, apart from a dribble of red down its eastern edge. Its top was not a peak, but a basin.

It was no mountain, I realized, as we sped closer. It was a volcano. The dribble of red was a lava flow. Beyond it, the sky—which had been a clear blue for most of the day—was a thick blanket of gray and white.

"Don't like the look of that," Desmond muttered, as he drove the sled up off the ice onto the land. "It's going to be a nasty night."

"Glad we're not going to be camping out in it," Grell said, behind me. "If it's nasty for an Ice Orc …"

The wind was a lot colder now, as the wolves hauled us through a stake-filled ditch and up a narrow path that twisted through trees and around boulders. There would be no chance of a surprise assault on this place. As we neared a high stone wall, Desmond unslung a horn from his belt and blew a signal. Heads appeared over the parapet.

By the time we reached the gates they had been opened and the drawbridge lowered. The wolves towed us into the stronghold and stopped, panting and wagging their tails at their approaching friends. Ice Orcs hurried over, wind whipping at their hair and clothes. They were clearly surprised to see Desmond back from his round so early— and even more surprised to see us as we clambered out of his sled. One 'bald' Orc; two pixies; three humans, and a small dog.

Wolf wranglers were doing what they always did: unharnessing the wolves. The wolves did what they never did. Instead of trotting off to the kennels for their dinner, they came over to me, and gathered around me. Orcs that had been speaking to Desmond, and asking what was up and who we were, fell silent, watching.

The wolves surrounded me as I accompanied them into their compound. My companions went with Desmond into the longhouse. I stayed with the wolves, stroking them, settling them, trying to ignore the cold wind. Shift jumped against my back, letting me know she wanted to be part of this. I unslung her and I felt her familiar shiver of interest as she took in the scene around us.

*What do you think?*

*I think they want to know more about you.*

The wolves snuffled, and nuzzled, tails wagging, eyes bright. *And I think we've found good friends here,* Shift added.

*Good friends*, I thought, *in a dangerous land.*

We made sure to pay attention to each animal. There were other wolves there, ones who had not been harnessed to Desmond's sled. They, too, all wanted to check me out—to get to know me, to have my attention. Some were old and retired from work, now more like pets than working animals. Others were pups, scampering around their mothers.

There must have been more than forty of them. I sat, cross-legged, on the straw-covered ground of their pen, my arms around Shift, and gave them all the time that they needed. I knew that I was being watched by their kennel-master. That was to be expected. What I didn't know was what was going on.

I recalled the Voice's words. *They know what you are.*

The more I thought about it, the less I understood.

*That,* I felt Shift's amused voice in my head, *is because you're not thinking right.*

*In what way?*

*In every way. You're one of them now. They know that. So, think like them.*

Which sounded all very well, but… think like a wolf? It was hard to think when in the Form. Hard to do anything but feel.

*So, don't think. Feel.*

*Yes,* I thought. *Feel. As I would in the Form.*

I ruffled ears. I tickled stomachs. I scratched, and patted. I inhaled their rich, damp breath. Large, hairy bodies leaned into me, pushing me over. I laughed. Tails wagged. I stroked every head that shoved itself towards me. Gradually, my mind opened to them. Each animal, in turn, needed my attention. I gave it. I tried not to play favorites. I loved them all. But I had favorites that I loved more. I fussed with them less than with the others, deliberately. But they knew, just as I knew. They were patient. They would wait.

My caresses, when I fondled them, were gentler, more meaningful. With one in particular I felt a bond as strong as that between Oller and Little Guy. He was not the biggest, or the strongest, or the liveliest, so I don't know what it was about him, but we belonged together. It was a strange, private connection. Shift, I knew, felt it too. *Yes,* she agreed. *That one.* I knew that the next time I came back to that crowd of black hair, and pink tongues, and yellow eyes, I would recognize him immediately. I thought, *I could stay here forever.*

"You want to get indoors, friend," the kennel-master called through the iron gate over the wind that was now howling. "Storm's getting up."

Shift and I must have spent longer with them than I had realized, because when I stood up, I felt my sweat-damp clothes chilling my skin. The cold wind was driving out of the north, and clouds filled with swirling snow had blown down into the stronghold. I let myself out of the wolf pen, and wished them all a good night. The kennel-master accompanied me as we hurried through the gloom toward the longhouse, which I could no longer see, only yards away though it was across the courtyard.

"Put a spell on them, have you?" he shouted, above the wind. It wasn't an accusation. He sounded genuinely interested—as if, perhaps, that might be some new way of controlling them that he could learn from me.

"No. I can't explain it. They just …"

I remembered the words of the Voice in my dream.

*They know what you are.*

"…seem to know me."

"Um," he grunted. "And how d'you think that has come about?"

I said, "That's what we all want to know."

The longhouse loomed out of the murk. I saw, as we approached it, that it was built of stone. Huge boulders formed its base, cleverly fitted together and sealed with mortar, above them layers of smaller stones. Tree trunks supported its steeply sloping, snow-covered roof, from which icicles hung. The top of the roof was hidden by clouds. I was shivering by the time we went inside and out of the bone-chilling wind.

We passed through a small entrance lobby, filled with boots, and cloaks, and sticks, and clutter, into the main hall. A log fire was blazing in a wide hearth at the center of one wall. Torches burned in sconces. Preparations were being made for the evening meal. The place echoed with the rumble of Orc voices and the chatter of scampering Orc children.

The talk died as all eyes turned to me. They must all have heard about the wolves.

Desmond strode over to me, saying, "This way, friend. You want to get them damp clothes off you, sharpish. Can't have you catching a chill."

He led me down a corridor at the back of the hall. Its walls and ceiling were wood-paneled, and we walked on floorboards; but the walls and floor soon became rock. We were, I realized, walking into the mountain itself.

Desmond turned into a side passage, which ended in two doors. "Men left, women right," he said, opening the left-hand door. A swirl of steam rolled out. I followed him into a large bathing chamber. "Leave your clothes on the floor. They need a good washing," he said. "You'll find towels and clean clothing in there." He pointed at another door.

"Hullo, mate!" Nyrik's cheerful voice called out from behind the fog of steam. "Come on in, the water's lovely!"

"I'll leave you to it," Desmond said. "Take your time, supper won't be for another hour. Although there's ale while we're waiting."

He went out, closing the door behind him.

I stripped off, glad to be out of my freezing, wet clothes, and climbed into a large plunge pool, where Grell and Nyrik and Horm were wallowing, grins on their faces.

"Can't believe this place!" Horm said. "Bloody brilliant, how they did this."

The water was almost too hot to bear, at first, but I soon got used to it. The others showed me how everything worked. Boiling water bubbled out of a culvert that emerged from a rock wall and spilled into a trough that ran the length of the room. The trough funneled into a pipe that led out again through the wall into the main hall. "Central heating," Grell said, "courtesy of this volcano we're perched on."

There were two simple sluice gates. One allowed us to divert scalding water into our pool; another was fitted into a tall cold tank.

"Fed by snow, Dez told me," Nyrik said. "They've got a hot pipe up top that melts it, and cold water runs down into the tank. Never going to run out of snow."

There were brushes and bars of soap, and I set about scrubbing myself as clean as I'd ever been. Nyrik and Horm played with the sluice gates so that the dirt that came off me flushed away below, and fresh water flowed in from above. Then, like them, I leaned back on the stone bench that ran around the edge of the pool and felt my muscles softening, the tiredness of travel leaching out of my bones. It was like being up to my neck in a hot spring that was also our own private river. After our hard days and nights in the Ice Lands, it was heaven.

The two Woods Kin had never seen anything like it. They marveled at how the bench had different levels, so that they were as comfortable as Grell and me. "For the kids, I'd think," Nyrik said, and Horm agreed. "Yur, can't have the nippers drowning."

"I'd never have thought this," Grell said, "when we were flogging through the Ice Lands."

"Still some flogging ahead of us, mate," Horm said. "We're not there yet."

"That we aren't," Nyrik agreed. "But it's nice when it gets better before it gets worse, eh? It's usually t'other way round." He looked at me with a grin and shook his head. "If you'd have told me, Daxxie, the day we met, that we'd go all this way together, and end up here …!" He chuckled.

"It's not ended," Horm pointed out. "Job to do, still, Nyrik."

Nyrik splashed him. "No need to bloody remind me, chum. I'm just appreciating the moment. 'Course there's worse to come, we know that. Just saying, couldn't get better than this—I mean, what possibly could be?"

"Supper," Horm replied.

"Fair point," Nyrik said. "No hurry, Desmond said. No need to rush this, eh?"

We didn't.

After half an hour, in which we soaked, and chatted, and went over all that we'd been through on our way there, we finally forced ourselves to get out. We reminded each other that we were guests in Isvellir. We needed to present ourselves to our hosts. In the laundry room we found towels, and clean clothes of all sizes, and dressed in shirts and jerkins and leggings, which were coarse but comfortable. By the door was a chest full of reindeer-skin slippers, fur side in, skin side out. My feet had never been so warm. It felt good to be clean, and dry—things that I had so often taken for granted.

We went back into the hall and joined the gathering. It had grown in our absence. The large room was packed. Qrysta and Jess, also in clean, borrowed clothes, were already on benches at a long table, mugs of ale in their hands, sitting with Desmond and other Ice Orcs, including several children.

They waved us over, and we went to join them.

"Good timing," Desmond said, and we could see trays of delicious-smelling food starting to arrive from the kitchens. "First things first, though." He drained his mug and stood up. "You others make yourselves at home," he said. "It's Daxx the chief needs to see."

"For the chief," Qrysta said, pushing two large, stone jars towards me across the table. I knew what they contained: peach brandy, from the supplies that Master Bjarnevalt had provided us with. I nodded and picked them up, while Grell, Nyrik, and Horm sat down to join the group.

As Desmond escorted me to the high table on the dais at the head of the hall, the chatter in the room died away to a murmur. Everyone wanted to hear this.

Chief Izmond sat at the high table's center, staring at me as we approached. An old, gray-haired Orc sat on her right, staring into space. His eyes were white, I saw, clouded with blindness.

A young woman sat on her left. She was slender, and graceful, unlike everyone else in the hall; but, just like everyone else in the hall, she was more or less all hair. Where Desmond's hair was coarse and black, hers was a cloud of chestnut brown. It made her look as if she was enveloped in some delicate aura.

I caught her eyes and felt a jolt run through me. I realized at once who she was.

Sylmond. The shaman.

She was twice her granddaughter's age, but she looked less than half of it.

I felt Shift quiver on my back and knew that she too had identified a fellow mage. I unslung her and saw Sylmond glance at her. It was a glance of understanding.

Sylmond, I knew in that moment, was the reason that my path had brought me there. She never took her eyes off me as Desmond introduced me to his chief and to her blind father.

In a quiet voice, which carried to every corner of the hall, Chief Izmond said, "You are welcome, sir, in our hall."

The words echoed off the roof and walls. The way she said them, they did not sound very welcoming.

I said, "Thank you, Chief Izmond. We are grateful for your hospitality. This is no weather for sleeping out in the wilds. Please accept these jars of peach brandy, with our thanks."

She inclined her head in acknowledgement. "A generous gift," she said. "No peach can grow this far north, not even in our hothouses. I look forward to sharing it with one and all after we have eaten. First, though, I have some questions for you."

"I will be happy to answer them."

She grunted, as if she wasn't sure about that. "What have you done," she said, her dark eyes fixed on me, "to our wolves?"

"I don't know," I replied. "I wish I did."

She turned to her grandmother. "Can you grant that wish, Grandmother?" she asked.

Sylmond said nothing.

Chief Izmond looked back at me. "What are you doing here?"

"Passing through. With your permission, Chief Izmond."

"Passing through to where?"

I hesitated. Something held me back from revealing my destination. "To the north," I said.

"What business," she said, "does one such as you, from the warm south, have in the far north? This land does not suit you. What do you seek, in the north?"

Shift silently provided me with the answer.

I replied, "Knowledge."

It made no sense to any of the others listening, but I saw Sylmond stiffen.

Chief Izmond probed. "Knowledge of what?"

"Of what is there. Of these lands. Of their inhabitants. We have no maps of Normark."

I felt a stirring all around me, and heard growls.

"We do not use that name," Izmond said.

"I had never heard it myself, until recently," I said. "That is what the folk south of the Snowline call it."

"They are incomers."

"And we are explorers. We wish to make maps."

"Why?"

"We do that with every new land that we discover."

"Why?"

"To know them."

"Why?"

She was becoming more and more hostile. I knew that I needed to deflect the issue. Once again, Shift cued me with the right words:

"So that we might trade with those that live in them."

Chief Izmond was about to reply when her grandmother rose to her feet. Once standing, she looked as graceful as a young woman in the bloom of her youth. The movement that unwound her and brought her upright, though, had been slow, and stiff.

Sylmond, the shaman, the chief's grandmother, looked down at me, and smiled. "And what," she asked, her voice as gentle as her gaze was sharp, "do you have to trade?"

I held her eyes. I realized what was happening, and relaxed. She and I were in a private conversation; one that involved nobody else.

I smiled back at her. "Like for like." I said. "Knowledge."

The hall around us was utterly silent, apart from the crackling of the logs in the hearth, as all ears waited for her reply.

Slowly, she nodded, and said, "We will talk later. Now, as our chief has asked, you need to tell us what you have done to our wolves."

I hesitated. I had no idea how these Ice Orcs would react if I told them I had been Gifted. As far as I knew, no one wanted anything to do with Weres. I remembered what Horm had told me, that night in The Ship Aground. *The only good Were being a dead Were, as they see it.*

"I have done nothing to them," I said. "Just as they have done nothing to me."

I saw a flicker of understanding in her shrewd, dark eyes. She could read between the lines. Normally, as Desmond had told us, his ice wolves would attack a stranger. They hadn't attacked me. Far from it.

This was not, she saw, a matter to be aired in public. "Then we will talk about that, too," she said, "but not on an empty stomach."

She sat back down—and that, for the time being at least, was that. Chief Izmond seemed satisfied with her grandmother's response to my presence. This was shaman business, which the tribe's shaman would handle. And she would later inform the chief of what she had learned.

The Ice Orcs, who had been listening intently, turned back to each other and began to talk among themselves—and with Nyrik, and Horm, and Jess, and Qrysta, and Grell, who were all in great demand. Little Guy, as usual, made friends everywhere he went—and got fed scraps by one and all.

We'd dined with Orcs before. We'd seen that they knew how to lay on a spread. The food came, and kept coming. The drink flowed. There was ale—brewed, they assured us, from barley malt—but it was unlike any ale that I'd ever tasted. Arctic barley, I thought, must be a hardy crop. The ale was also warm—not room temperature warm, but blood-heat warm, as warm as I was. It took some getting used to but, like all good things in life, was worth the effort. Desmond was baffled when I asked him how they got it that way. He called the brewmaster over.

"The wort stays warm," the brewmaster said. "It needs to, in this climate. We run it off into barrels, and they don't cool. It's always warm, in the brewhouse. If a barrel gets cold we know it's off. We give that to the wolves, before it freezes."

"They love it," Desmond said. "But you just try harnessing them the next morning, when they want to sleep it off! They're snappy enough at the best of times."

Neither of them could imagine drinking *cold* beer. The idea made them wrinkle their noses in disgust. The food was hot, too: a thick, brown stew, spiced with ferocious peppers. I'd never eaten seal before. Nor snowpeppers. I'd always associated hot peppers with hot climates.

That made no sense to Desmond. "They have to be hot," he said. "How else would they survive up here?"

Floating in the seal stew were chunks of vegetables, some of which I recognized—beans, green peas, potatoes, carrots, beets. Others were unknown to me, as were their names, which rang no bells.

"They're tended by the root folk," Desmond explained. It was an explanation that demanded further explanation. Spread around the stronghold, he told me, were hothouses, heated by the thermal springs that bubbled up around Isvellir.

The root folk lived underground. They knew their roots. Thanks to their help, the hothouses flourished. The Ice Orcs traded with them— forged iron and steel and gemstones coming up, ale and food and tools and skins going down.

"Who are they?" I asked.

Desmond shrugged. "Undergrounders," he said. "But decent ones. Not like most of them."

"Do you go down there?" I asked.

"Not if we can help it." He clearly didn't want to talk about it.

I knew the feeling. We didn't belong in the Undergrounds. The Undergrounds didn't want us coming down into them. Whatever was down there was trouble.

Dessert was ice cream—yak cream, which was sour and sharp and sweet at the same time, but delicious nonetheless. Snowberries and bilberries and whortleberries accompanied it, as did cupfuls of peach brandy—which Desmond, and the brewmaster, and their fellow Orcs, pronounced excellent.

Toasts were exchanged.

"You can bring more o' this anytime you're passing!" Desmond said. "Fine stuff, this! And this a finer night than I'd be having out there in the whiteout this minute, if I hadn't run across you lot."

Jess was surrounded by Orc children of her own age and younger, Little Guy at her side. Grell had a rapt audience as he told of his Orc Quest with Klurra. Nyrik, as usual, was chatting nineteen to the dozen with anyone and everyone, and Horm was as loose and comfortable as I'd ever seen him. I was glad that the evening was taking his mind off Urngra.

Qrysta and I watched, and listened, and answered any questions that came our way. It was promising to be a nice night's relaxing and chatting, when I felt a tap on my shoulder.

I turned around to see Sylmond standing behind me.

Next to her, holding her hand, was a small Orc boy, perhaps four years old, his eyes wide, his face solemn.

"Come," the shaman said.

I picked up Shift from her place on the bench beside me and followed shaman Sylmond out of the hall.

# 22

## Sylmond's Tale

Sylmond took a torch from the wall and led us through a door at the back of the hall.

She closed it behind us, stopped, and said, "This is Kalmond, my great-grandson. He has the gift. His sisters do not. It is shown to each of us, when our successor is born. The years will come for me, when he is of age; by when he will know all that I know, and what my forbears knew before me. Some of which we must now share with you."

She smiled down at the child, who continued to stare up at me.

"It's nice to meet you, Kalmond," I said.

He looked from me to Sylmond. Her eyebrows rose, as if to say, *You know what to do.*

He dropped her hand, and held his out to me. "Hullo," he said, quietly, as I shook it.

He released my hand and reached again for Sylmond's. She patted it, and I fell in beside them as she turned down another long corridor that led into the mountain, its walls paneled with rough wood planks. Doors were set into both sides of it. The air grew warmer and staler as we walked on. I could hear, almost below the edge of sound, a faint, deep rumble coming from ahead of us. It receded, before fading into

275

silence; and then, moments later, returned. The roof above our heads changed from wood to rock.

"Does the volcano erupt?" I asked.

"Occasionally," Sylmond replied, as matter-of-factly as if I'd asked her if it ever snowed.

I thought, if I lived on, indeed *in*, a volcano, I'd be nervous.

"Doesn't it bother you?" I said, as we came to a fork in the passage. A dull, red glow shone at the far end of one long tunnel. The air that came down to us along it carried a whiff of sulfur.

"We don't bother him," she replied, "so why should he bother us?"

I tried to work out that logic. I wasn't sure that I could.

We took the other, shorter tunnel. She stopped at a door where the corridor ended, and turned to look at me.

"If Isvellir wanted us gone, we'd go," she said. "We believe that he likes us here. Appreciates our company. We appreciate his. His warmth, his protection. We are his people. The Wood Orcs have cellars beneath their trees. The Hill Orcs have their buried halls. We have Isvellir."

She opened the door and we went inside.

I'd been expecting a small, cramped room, after the narrow corridor we'd come down. The space I found myself in was anything but. It was large, and an irregular shape, its high ceiling arching above us. It was not a room, I realized, but a natural chamber formed inside the volcano. Its walls were lined with bookcases and shelves and cabinets. There were several tables, most of them cluttered with scrolls, and books, and packages and boxes. Sylmond moved among them, her torch throwing light on strange objects as we passed. Everywhere I looked there was something that caught my eye: instruments, contraptions, stones, boards of diagrams, charts of arcane symbols. Taxidermized creatures stared out from glass cases: a pine marten, a wolverine, a treecat, a pit elf—and some other gaunt, gray, tall thing, in scraps of fur, its face as bleak as the heart of winter.

I stopped in front of it, staring. Long arms, its hands ending in talons. Legs that seemed nothing but skeleton and sinew, above bony feet that had black claws for nails. Hanks of hair hanging to its shoulders out of a bald, corpse-gray scalp. An elongated, narrow skull, bulging above, and pointed below. Yellow teeth, the sharp incisors unnaturally large. Cold, cruel eyes. Neither human nor… what? I wondered. *Other.* What "other"? Not wolf, as was my *other*. Something colder. Something bred of these bleak Ice Lands. Something to be avoided.

Sylmond, beside me, confirmed what I had suspected. "Ice Wight."

I studied the thing in the glass case. "Are there many of them?"

"We do not know. But just one is too many."

I couldn't take my eyes off it. It had been mounted so that it seemed to be striding towards us. "What are they?"

"Beings that have learned to live in this land," she said. "It is harsh. Even for us. But we love it. They hate it. We belong here. They do not. Can you imagine?"

I considered what she had said. I tried to imagine hating my world. I tried to imagine hating what, and where, I was.

My imagination failed.

I shook my head. "No. It must be awful."

"It is. They are. We kill them, whenever we come across them, just as they kill us. But we do not eat them alive, as they do us."

At which, my imagination came to life again. Desperate battles, far from anywhere, in the mists of the frozen forests. Ice Orcs against Ice Wights. Hand-to-hand combat. Fights to the death. A harsh land indeed.

I said, "How did they get that way?"

She turned to me, and I looked away from the corpse of the Ice Wight and into her eyes.

She said, "We have often wondered. We have tried to scry out their secrets, but their minds are closed to ours. Unlike yours."

"Unlike mine?"

"I have studied it. And a very interesting mind it is, young Mastercaster."

She saw my look of surprise. "It is a good name that she gave you, Sister Marnie."

*Wow*, I thought. She could read my mind as clearly as Marnie could.

She smiled, and nodded. "I can," she agreed.

I wondered what else she had learned about me, while I had been unaware that she was even looking. I wondered, also, what magic skill she was using—Awareness, like Marnie? Insight, like Avildor?

I said, "You're Coven?"

"In a way. Not formally. Our shamans are male and female. Coven is only for women. We are, shall we say, associates." She left it at that, and walked away.

At the end of the chamber a tapestry hung between two stone columns. Woven onto it was a strange scene that at first seemed almost childlike in its simplicity. Crude, sticklike trees stood white against a black background. Below them a tiny archer aimed an arrow at a full moon hanging in a black sky. On top of the moon a wolf sat, head back and vertical, mouth open, as if howling. Behind it, stars, constellations, a comet trailing white fire.

She waited, letting me study it.

The more I looked at it, the richer and more filled with detail the scene became. I noticed figures among the trees: animals, creatures on two legs, birds. I recognized some of the constellations above them: the Demon, the Fisher, the Willow Tree, others.

*There was meaning there,* I thought. *A story. Meaning I should work out. A story I should know.*

"There is," Sylmond agreed, once again reading my thoughts. "Which I will show you." She drew back the tapestry and stood aside for me to enter the little space that lay beyond it—a dark grotto behind the large cavern.

She followed me in with her torch, which she set into a sconce on the wall. A round table took up most of the grotto's space. We sat opposite each other on chairs while Kalmond clambered onto a high stool between us. The torch's flames threw shadows that danced on the walls around us.

Sylmond leaned forward, one hand taking hold of Kalmond's as her other reached for mine—which was holding Shift. I felt Shift's mind opening to hers in a surge of warmth.

*You trust her,* I thought.

*I do.* My rowan staff was interested, eager to listen and learn. Reassured, I settled back as Sylmond said, "Now, tell me everything."

"Can't you just read my mind?"

She smiled. "I need more than just glimpses. You have a long tale to tell—as do I, when you have finished yours."

*If she is to help us,* Shift added, *you need to help her.*

Just as I had with Marnie and Velaryn, I began with my encounter with Graycote in the wilds of Mourvania, and how he had Gifted me. I told Sylmond of my trek into the Deepwoods with Urngra. I told her of the wolf dream that Byrneth's potion had shown me; of how I had fallen into the vault below the village, and met the Voice, whose presence I could feel but not see—and of what he had told me that I must do.

I told her of how I had run for my life, and heard the Wild Hunt overhead as I cantered the long way around back to Eastbay. I told her of Urngra's death, which was the reason for Horm and Nyrik accompanying me. I told her of Evall, who knew of the destination that I needed to find, which was here, in the Ice Lands; and I told her how every day brought me closer to annihilation, as I sought the Valley of the Moon.

She listened, watching me closely, saying nothing until I finished.

She nodded, considering everything I'd told her.

"I've probably left some things out," I added.

"If I need to hear them, you will tell me." She opened a drawer in the cabinet behind her. She found what she was looking for and placed a vial, a small chest, a pitcher, and three cups on the table between us. She opened the chest, and began to sort through its contents. "Well, now we know what you have done to our wolves. Shown yourself to be one of them. And they love you for it." She looked up at me and fixed her eyes on mine. "We do not."

She let that sink in. "We will speak of that later. You started from your beginning. I will start from ours."

Good, I thought. I needed to learn what she had to tell me.

Sylmond lifted out shallow wooden trays from the chest and placed them on the table. Each tray was divided into nine compartments, all containing powders, or lumps, or seeds, or leaves. Ingredients, I assumed.

Ingredients for what, I wondered, as Sylmond added them to the pitcher, pouring liquid from the vial over them. A sweet odor rose from the mixture.

She poured three cups, handing one to me and another to Kalmond. "He will remember," she said, "as we shamans all do. We remember everything, not just our own memories, but also the memories of those who have come before us. Think of it, Daxx: Your tale will be told down the ages, generation to generation. It will come alive, time after time, for those who will follow—to watch, and witness, and explore. Just as the tales of those who came before will now come alive for us."

She raised her cup. "Close your eyes and drink."

We drank.

I had been expecting a vision. Something shadowy, and imagined: a tale from long ago, such as I had lived in the wolf dream in Byrneth's library. What I saw, when I opened my eyes, could not have been more immediate, or more colorful, or more different. We were in a crowded market. The midday sun was high overhead, its heat beating down. Smells assaulted me: sweat, food being cooked, dung, fruits on stalls, the stench of animals, the sharp perfumes of the gentry in their brilliant, silken robes. Noises ebbed and flowed in my ears: the cries of vendors, the orders of guards, the cracking of whips; donkeys and camels braying, beggars calling, children squealing and laughing.

We wove our way through the crowd, which parted before us. No one looked at us. *They do not see us,* I thought. And there, lurking in a corner, where no one but I would notice him: Oller! I went over to him, happy to see him. "Hey, matey," I said, quietly, so as not to draw attention to us. "Fancy meeting you here. How's it going?"

He didn't respond.

All he did was frown slightly, then glance at his left wrist. He put his right hand over it to shield his Link of Impartment from prying eyes, then, with his thumb, pushed his sleeve up just far enough up so that he could check it. It was not glowing orange or green, so he looked back up at the scene that he was surveying and locked his eyes back on his target. He had work to do. His target moved on and Oller followed him. I tried to go with him—but couldn't. Oller slipped into the crowd, unnoticed as always, and disappeared; but I stayed where I was, beside Sylmond, as the shadow of her grotto intruded between us and the marketplace of Sarmen. Her left hand still held onto mine, but her right was now over the Link of Impartment on my wrist. "Be with me," I heard her say. "No one else. There must be but one connection." She slipped the iron hoop off my wrist and laid it on the table between us, before reaching again for Kalmond's hand.

Sarmen vanished. The shadow of her grotto faded, and we were in winter.

"Our beginning," Sylmond said.

Far below us, ice and snow and forest stretched in all directions. "What do you know," she enquired, as we began to descend from a great height, "of our beginning?"

Mountains rose, close and far, until they circled every horizon, growing higher and higher as we neared the ground towards them. I thought of what Grell had told me: Murruk's tale of the origin of Orcs.

"In the Ice Time," I replied "a tribe of men and a tribe of Ogres put aside their differences, and pooled their resources. Together, they survived. When that long age ended, there were no men, in that place, and no Ogres: only Orcs."

Wisps of smoke rose through the whiteness below us. Down and down we went. A snow-covered roof came into view. A chimney. A longhouse. An enclosure, fortified, at the edge of a frozen lake. Pens for animals. Bare trees in rows. Frost-covered fields. The seasons cycled as we descended. Trees blossomed, and fruited; fields sprouted, and cropped; livestock birthed, and grew, and were butchered, as the short summer ended and the monthslong night closed in. We passed down out of the darkness through the roof and into the light of the feast-hall.

"They survived," Sylmond took over the tale, "because they shared. They shared everything—more than just what was needed to fend off death. In those long winters they learned each other's lore. From the Ogres, men learned the old lores: plant-lore, and beast-lore, and sky-lore. They learned what cured and what killed, what healed and what harmed. They learned the cycles of migrations of the herds. They learned of predator and prey. They learned the histories of the skies. They learned the patterns of the weather and the stars, which told of what was past, and passing, and to come. From the men, Ogres learned the new lores: fire-lore, and water-lore, and earth-lore. They learned the secrets of the lakes and seas and rivers, of fish and seals, of fresh water and foul. They learned of sowing, and growing, and tending, and reaping.

"Together, they learned to brine, and preserve their stores. They taught each other how to brew, and to cook, and to distill, and to forge. With their tools, the men built hives for the wild bees that the Ogres brought from the forests; and, in the warmth of those hives, the queens that were hibernating quickened, and woke, and bred their swarms, which pollinated their crops. And in the long night months, men and Ogres told each other their secrets. They knew that there was no point in hiding them from each other any longer. They were going to die out, as all folk were, in that endless winter. They might as well talk, and listen, and contemplate, and learn—even if there would be no one left after them to tell the tale."

She sighed, then continued. "But they did not die. The Ice Time ended. And the Orcs, which is what they had all become, survived. We who stayed here in the north call ourselves *mondkin*, meaning Moon Kind in the Old Language—hence the way we make our names. Others moved away to seek new lands, east and south and west, leaving us here with the lore of our ancestors. Which is a muddle. What else would you expect, from the merging of the beliefs of men and Ogres?

"It was not all farming and fishing, and hunting and feasting. As the years passed, there was time enough for broaching every subject under the sun. As well as lore, there is learning; and as each learned the other's lore, they explored it. Discussed it. Argued it, embellished it, mined it for truths and revelations; tore it apart and put it back together, better, and richer, and more filled with meaning. And just as men and Ogres merged, so did their lores.

"But not all of those lores sat well with each other. Where man and Ogre had been able to adjust, their conflicting lores were not. *We know best*, each lore said. And to this day, we, their children, have had to live with that. We are not men. We are not Ogre. We are Orc. Which means that we do not know what we are, in one way; but in another, we know that all that old nonsense needs to go away. We are what we are.

"Can we help how we got here? Of course not. No more than any-one can.

"So we turned our back on those traditions, taking what we deemed useful from both, and consigning the rest to history. That was then, this is now. We are a practical people."

Sylmond gave me a wry smile. "Well, who were we to reject the wisdom of our forebears just because we could not reconcile them with each other? But what, on the other hand, were we to do when those beliefs clashed? Contradicted each other, fought with each other?

"We saw that there was no answer. So we just ignored the whole question. As I said, we Orcs are a practical folk. Beliefs, legends, gods, spirits, origins, meanings: no. We just get on with the business of living. We don't need a reason for doing so, an explanation. It seems self-evident. The meaning of life is: *the state of being alive*. What more do you need?" She shrugged. "We don't. Does it have to add up to something? Why? What makes us think that we are so important? We come, we go. And there's an end."

She shifted on her chair. "Which, of course, is simply us 'practical Orcs' avoiding the subject. We cannot do that forever. You, and I, and my tribe, and your people, may indeed be of no significance whatso-ever. But what if we are? Would we not want to know about it, and where we fit in, and what our role is in the great scheme of things—if, indeed, there is one?

"So, as I said, we will begin at the beginning. Not our beginning, of which we just saw a glimpse, of men and Ogres becoming Orcs, but the first beginning itself."

She stopped speaking and bowed her head.

Kalmond and I bowed ours.

Sylmond waited, until she sensed, through our linked hands, that our minds were empty, and open, and ready. "This lore was learned from the Ogres. They were here long ages before men. Ogres were the first in this world, and, they believe, will be the last. Watch."

The winter feast-hall of the men and Ogres faded. The night sky filled my field of vision. At its center the full moon shone, white and luminous. Around her the heavens wheeled slowly in the silent vastness of space. There was so much to see that I did not know where to look. Wherever my eyes rested, they were drawn in, to search, to discover and learn. I explored detail after detail, entranced, until I realized that the scene in front of me was, imperceptibly, morphing into something else.

I watched the vision settle into its new form.

No longer was I looking at the sky itself.

Spread before me was a star map.

I recognized it. I had first seen it in an old book in the study of the Arch Historian of the Faiths, Eldress Quen, in Mayport Priory. Later, after our stargazing session on the Tower of Light, Elun, Avildor's wife, had given me my own copy.

I watched as the constellations rotated slowly before me, now in their familiar pattern. Each was outlined in white lines that joined their stars to one another, depicting the symbols they were held to represent. Most I recognized. They had become familiar sights overhead in the many nights I had traveled in that world. I knew their names. The Swallow. The Thief. The Dancer. The Urn. One, though, was new to me.

As I explored them, Sylmond spoke. "At the beginning of time, when the world was young, the Moon rose and shone her light out into the night. The Hunter saw it, and she dazzled him. He longed for her, and so he stepped out of the sky, to seek her out, and lay his gifts and his heart at her feet."

As she spoke, the constellation that was The Hunter moved. He walked, bow in hand, his head turned towards the Moon. He stopped, and gazed at her, as if enchanted.

"But he was only a humble hunter, while she was the light that shone for all the world against the darkness of the night. *I will bring her the greatest prize I can,* he decided, *to lay at her feet along with my heart;* and so, he hunted the Great Wolf, night after night, and shot him with his starsilver arrows, which at last pierced the Great Wolf's hide and found his heart. And the Hunter skinned him, which is why there is no longer a Great Wolf in the sky, but only what is left of him."

I watched, as the constellation that I had not recognized changed above me. What had been the Great Wolf's stretched foreleg, as it ran across the sky, was now the familiar, lowered head of the Lamb.

"And without his tail, and his neck, and his head with its sharp ears, and open jaws," Sylmond continued, "what is left of him was reduced to a meek, grazing lamb, which is why that constellation now stands in the heavens in his place.

"And as the Wolf became the Lamb, so the Hunter stood in the sky in a new form. Before, the great arc of his bow had been drawn to his ear. Now, he was raising his hunting horn to his lips, to announce his arrival at the Moon's tower, bearing his gift. And the Moon accepted the Great Wolf's hide, and gave her hand and her heart to the hero who laid it at her feet.

"In time, a child was born to the Hunter and the Moon—a boy—and their happiness was complete. They scried his destiny, and saw that he would sire many children, and that the line they had founded would spread throughout this world. Mighty hunters they would be, and adepts of the Moon Magic that she shines upon her children to this day, and their son would be the mightiest hunter of all. They were thankful for their good fortune, and they covered the babe in his crib with the wolf hide, so that he would be warm while he slept.

"And that is where their good fortune turned evil, for in the night, the Great Wolf's hide worked on the boy that lay inside him, and when they came for their child the next morning, he was no longer their son, but a wolf cub, his pelt as black as night and his eyes as red as hot coals. And they were filled with horror, for they knew then what they had done. They tried all they knew to rescue their babe, but all their arts were to no avail, and the cub grew and grew, until they saw

284

what they must do, before his power outgrew theirs. They could not kill their own child, for such a crime is forbidden in the heavens as it is on this earth. And besides, what parent does not love their child? They had loved him from the moment they set eyes on him. In their despair, they saw that they had no choice. So they bound the creature, and the boy lost within him, and sealed him away. It is a seal that will hold until the time comes for the world to end, and the Great Wolf takes to the heavens again and hunts the Hunter, and devours the Moon, and the stars, and at last the sun himself, and universal darkness covers all."

As she spoke, the Great Wolf rose out of the Lamb, and grew and grew as he chased down and ate every point of light in the night sky, until only he was left. He slowed, and stopped; and, one by one, the stars that glowed in his outline blinked out into nothingness.

"And that," she said, "is why wolves howl at the full moon. They howl for their lost lord, who has been taken from them, but whose time will come again. They howl for the mother, who they never grew to know and to love."

Silence fell between us in the little grotto behind the tapestry.

I thought over what Sylmond had told me. I had heard much, learned much. I still could not see exactly how it helped.

"Nor can I," Sylmond said, once again reading my mind. "The answers lie ahead. What do you know about Ogres?"

"A bit," I said. "I've traveled with one. But … I didn't exactly get to know her."

She chuckled. "No one 'exactly knows' them. Interesting folk. Very different from the likes of us. You'll need to have your wits about you when dealing with them."

"Will I have to?"

"You won't get to the Valley of the Moon without going through Ogretzk. We'll give you papers, and so on, to show them. So at least you'll have a chance to make your case. Don't worry. They're not as bad as they look."

There was, it seemed, no more to be said.

I did not let go of their hands. I needed to think about all that had happened, and been revealed to me, in that little room.

Yes. I had learned. But I had more questions now than before we'd started. I knew that the answers were out there somewhere. Just as I knew that they were contained, if hidden, in Dean Auditory Eilwen's cryptic lines.

*We've been told.*

Okay. But told what? What *wasn't* I seeing?

I said, "I think I need your help."

Sylmond squeezed my hand, and smiled. "I will give it, if I can."

And so I told her of the Conclave, at which Eilwen had spoken her verses; and how, after weeks of turning them over in my mind, I still could not make sense of them.

"Tell me," she said; and I did.

*Run and hide*
*Hide and run*
*Don't assume*
*Dead reborn*
*Wield the broom*
*Sweep the sky*
*Sound the horn*
*Hue and cry*

*Unlock the rune*
*Observe the moon*
*Assume the form*
*Unleash the storm*
*In fire and flood*
*And turn the tide*
*Divide the blood*
*Devour the sun*
*Let darkness fall*
*And end it all*

"And what," Shaman Sylmond said, breaking the silence that had fallen in the little room, "does that tell you?"

"I think it means I have to do these things."

She nodded, and smiled. "Then what is stopping you?"

I looked up at her, confused. I couldn't see how to do any of them—let alone where, or when.

She leaned closer and held my eyes. "Tricksy things, words," she said. "Twist you around in knots, words will, if they can, so you need to untwist them. There's many a word has more than one meaning. Put them together, and who knows what they hide?"

She waited for me to understand.

When I saw it, I said, "The truth."

She nodded, and smiled. "And there you have it."

The truth, I thought. Hidden. Deep beneath the words. "I have been looking," I said. "I haven't been seeing."

"Because," she suggested, "perhaps you have been looking in the wrong place?"

I didn't understand.

"Look *out*, Daxx," she said. "Raise your eyes, look out and about. Not down and in, straining against those teasing words. You've heard them, you know them, they'll tear you apart if you worry at them forever. Keep your eyes open, and your mind. See what's out there that answers to the puzzles they pose."

She had not been specific—any more than Dean Eilwen's lines were specific. But, somehow, I felt that she had set me on the right path. Dean Eilwen's lines weren't answers. They were clues. Hints. The answers were out there, in the world around me. I would find them, on this quest to the Valley of the Moon, or die trying.

Yes, I thought. That makes sense, in general. But … specifically?

Sylmond sensed my doubt. "You'll know them when you come to them," she said. "Just because you haven't seen them yet doesn't mean you never will."

"You're right," I said. "Thank you."

"And you're not alone," Sylmond continued. "You may have enemies—enemies ahead, enemies behind. You also have friends. Both here and elsewhere" She looked down at the Link of Impartment on the table between us and picked it up to study it. "Who was that, in the marketplace?"

"One of my team," I said. "He's overseas."

She turned the plain metal hoop over in her hand. "Interesting," she said. "Useful."

"We hope so."

"So, what's he doing there?"

"Finding," I said.

"Finding what?"

"Knowledge."

Sylmond slipped the band back over my wrist and smiled. "Aren't we all?"

# 23

## Whiteout

That night, the Voice in my dream said, "I had forgotten."

He sounded far away, and unutterably sad.

"Forgotten what?" I said.

"Forgotten what I was. That she showed you."

I waited.

"Just a babe," he said, his throat dry, and hoarse. "An infant. I remember now. I have grown since …." He sighed. "You will understand, I think. To be bound in the hide of something that you are not. Confused, and distracted this way and that. Does that sound familiar? Sounds, and smells, and sights that pour in and overwhelm you, for which you are not prepared."

I did understand. That was how it was, in the Form.

"But he must be contained. Or he will do what he is destined to do. You cannot imagine the power that he now has. He cannot use it as long as I lie here, bound to him and sealed. And in that time, mortals will be born, and live, and die, as the world turns and the years pass."

He sounded resigned, as if he now, at last, understood what was happening.

I said, "And where do I come in? What can I do?"

I heard another long, weary sigh. "I no longer think you can do anything, my friend," the Voice said. "I have brought you here on a fool's errand. If you were to unbind me, then what? You would also free him, to whom I am bound. No. I must sleep here still. The sleep of eternity, only to reach you in dreams."

The thought appalled me. All the ages of history behind him, eons ahead of him, suspended in that endless sleep …

It was a timescale that I could not get my head around. Whereas I only had another month to live.

It seemed selfish, and petty, compared with what he was going through, for me to ask *what about little me down here?* But I had to. So, how to put it? Without seeming callous?

"Maybe I can't help you, after all," I said. "I wish I could. But you said you could help me, so—will you?" I hesitated. "I have friends who need my help," I continued. "Which I cannot do if I turn into a husk." He did not reply. "Should I just turn around and go back, and, well … fizzle out?" Again, I got nothing back. "I'll help you if I could, but you say you think it would be a mistake for me even to try. You're bound by magic—I'm a mage. Maybe I could break those bonds. Who knows? I'd give it my best shot. Only you think that's a bad idea."

It was a hard thing to say, but I knew I had to say it. "I can't imagine," I went on, "what you're going through. I can't imagine what you have to face, from here to eternity. I may not be able to help you—but if you can help me, I can help my friends. We only have a few years of this life ahead of us, which I know is nothing compared to what's facing you. And we're nothing to you, really. There's no reason you should help us; I mean, why should our little problems be of any concern to you? Of course they aren't. It's insignificant, what I'm asking. We're insignificant. All I can say is …"

I couldn't think what that might be. What I came up with seemed pretty lame. "What would you do, if you were me?"

The sounds of my own words echoed around the silence in my head.

As if reawakening from slumber, the Voice muttered, "I do not mind."

"Mind? Mind what?"

"I asked you to find me. To help me. Release me. In return, I promised that I would release you from the sentence that is consuming you. You have sought me. Your journey has been hard. If you manage to find me, you will have fulfilled your part of our bargain. It is only right that I fulfill mine. It would be dishonorable not to." The Voice sighed. "It has not turned out the way that I thought it would, but what of it? Now we know better. I will stay, bound and in my sleep—but that will be my choice. The choice that I now see I must make for the good of all. I will be glad to free you, mage. Indeed, it will give me peace—to know that one of us, at least, has been released from this curse."

I felt a huge rush of relief and gratitude. "Thank you."

A rumble echoed in my bones, as if the Voice was chuckling. "You are welcome, my young friend. This gives me happiness—which I have not known for so long. And I look forward to welcoming you to my less-than-ideal quarters, should you manage to make it here. Which, I should warn you, will not be easy."

"Thank you," I said again. And then, I added, "Well, it's not been easy so far."

"Indeed," the Voice agreed. I heard another deep sigh. "We've shared much, you and I," he said. "It has been a pleasure getting to know you."

"You too," I said.

"I wish you good luck, on your journey here." The Voice tailed off. But, somehow, I knew that more was coming. "Tell me about your friends," he said.

I did. I told him of Oller, in Sarmen; and Marnie and Esmeralda and Commandant Bastard, in Jarnland; and of those who were with me in the longhouse of the Ice Orcs on Isvellir. As I spoke, I heard grunts of acknowledgement, and amusement, and wariness. He was taking it all in.

Until his tired yellow eyes closed, and the passing clouds and the moon and her tower faded.

He was gone.

I sank back into sleep. And a long, fine, refreshing sleep it was.

I emerged from it late the next morning and looked up to see Grell smiling down at me. He was perched on the end of my bed in the room we'd been given the night before.

"Hey, Grell," I said, as my eyes cleared. "What's up?"

He chuckled. "Absolutely bloody nothing, mate," he said. "You can sleep another ten hours, if you like. No one's going anywhere."

"Huh?" I said, still groggy from sleep. "Why not?"

"Come on outside and I'll show you."

I roused myself from my bed and dressed, throwing my travel cloak over my shoulders. Grell led me through the hall and its entry lobby and opened the door.

Thick, white mist rolled in. I could see nothing beyond it.

"Whoa!" I said.

"Yup. Whiteout." He took hold of my hand and led me outside.

We were a yard from the door. We'd only taken one pace. I was holding Grell's hand. I could not see him. "This is …"

"Yeah, ain't it, mate!" he agreed.

I knew that the longhouse was only a few feet behind me, but I was anxious that I might not be able to find my way back to it.

"Put your hand up," Grell said, "arm stretched out."

I did. I could not see my own hand at the end of it. I was completely out of my comfort zone. "Imagine being out on the ice in this."

Grell chuckled. "Yeah. Would scare the crap out of you. Close your eyes."

I did, thinking it would make no difference.

Grell seized my shoulders, and twirled me around, again and again.

When I opened my eyes, I could not see him. Or the longhouse. Or anything.

Well, I wasn't going to move. I just stood there, swaying.

Grell's voice came to me out of the white murk. "Where d'you think I am, Daxxie?"

I couldn't locate him. "Listen, Grell, can we please stop this?"

I heard his familiar gurgle of a laugh. His giant paw gripped my elbow. "So, we're not going anywhere till this lifts," he said, steering me back inside the longhouse. "Which the Ice Orcs say will be several days. They're a fun lot; it'll be good getting to know them."

I had a problem. I was looking forward to spending time with our hosts, and learning about their way of living. But the Moon Nights were almost on us. When they came, I'd be catatonic. I explained this to Sylmond and she understood.

"Best stay here, then," she said. "It'll pass, and you'll have one last month to do what you need. We'll look after you while you're away."

I thanked her. "And we'll use the days until then to trade knowledge."

"We will indeed. We don't get many such as you up here, and I want to get as much out of you as I can."

That afternoon, Fjernmond, the kennel-master, led me across the courtyard through the whiteout to the wolf pen. They were all lined up against the fence, eager to see me. He told me about all of them, and which of them did what. The one that I had picked out as my favorite was, he told me, named Nostë. Nostë was his best herder.

I could feel Shift drinking him in, getting to know him in her own way, as I scratched the wolf's ears. His wrangler told us about him, and about herding, and guarding, and other wolf skills. Nostë and I looked into each other's eyes and nothing else mattered. He was the best herder, the wrangler told me, because he understood the herd, and the herd understood him. He never needed to hurry, or to howl. *This way,* he showed them. *Don't do that.* They trusted him. He knew his job. They knew theirs. He would lie down and watch. They liked that. So did he. He'd kill anything that came for them.

"Even sabre-cats?" I asked. "Or polar bears?"

"He'd howl for backup," Fjernmond said. "Cats don't come near the stronghold. They're only a problem when the herd's away in the summer pastures. Which is why the herders will take the pack, to guard them. The cats smell them, and steer well clear. There's plenty else for cats to eat out there, especially in summer. Reindeer, musk ox, fur-elk. And the white bears prefer things that swim. It's Ice Wights the wolves need to watch for. They follow the herd, in the hope of snatching a laggard, or a newborn. Haven't lost a one on Nostë's watch," he added, ruffling the wolf's ears. "Have we, eh, lad?"

Nostë wagged his tail.

I remembered how I had felt, in the cave two nights before, surrounded by wolves. *Bodyguards.*

In the weird murk of the whiteout, when I could barely see his head, let alone the rest of his body, Nostë and I reaffirmed our friendship.

"He likes you," Fjernmond said.

"I like him."

Fjernmond chuckled. "Once this clears, I'll show you him working. Nostë can get half a hundred yaks doing what he wants without them even knowing he's asking. Their best friend, he is."

He reached down and scratched Nostë's ears. "He's a good one, this."

I patted the wolf's head as his yellow eyes stared into mine.

I spent a lot of time with Sylmond. Could I, she wondered, teach her any of my skills? I didn't see why I couldn't at least try. I'd seen

Qrysta mentoring Jess, and Nyrik and Horm showing the crew of *The Red Rose* advanced knifework. Grell, in his training for his bout with Commandant Bastard, must have taught his sparring partners plenty. Marnie and I had traded knowledge, and honed our abilities. Our duels on the hillside behind her cottage had battle-hardened both of us.

I'd never really thought about how someone "becomes" a mage. I assumed that it would be through the same process that anyone undergoes to become anything: study, learning, practice.

There was only one way to find out. "First," I said, "you'll need a staff."

Kalmond, who seemed never to leave his great-grandmother's side, said, "Can I have one too?"

I looked at Sylmond, who looked down at the lad, thoughtfully.

"I don't see why not," she said. "As long as you realize it's not a toy."

Kalmond nodded solemnly.

His grandmother added, "I'm not having you turn your sisters into frogs, young man."

Kalmond looked startled. Then he looked at me, seriously impressed. "Can you do that?"

I shook my head. "No," I said, "I wish I could. That would be useful in a fight, eh? Turn your enemies into frogs. Come along, then. You two have staves to pick."

The lumber stores in the compound were enormous. Every summer, Sylmond told me, teams went into the forests to fell trees. Once the autumn snows began and settled, sleds hauled the logs back to the stronghold. The best wood was sawn and laid up to season, for years, until it was needed for building or carpentry. Firewood filled its own huge sheds. Even with the thermal heat provided by the volcano, the Ice Orcs got through a lot of firewood. I knew that we were safe within the compound, and that I could hardly wander off into the wilderness, but I still found walking in the whiteout unsettling. Sylmond sensed my unease and held my hand as we walked through the blankness to the woodsheds, where timber was resting on racks of various sizes.

"Let the woods choose you," I told them. Even though the whiteout was down, and the light was weak, we were in the perpetual daylight of the arctic spring. "Close your eyes and feel for them, and they will feel for you. Bring out as many as you'd like to choose from. Take your time."

I left them to it, and felt my way back along the stronghold's buildings to the longhouse.

Nyrik was where I expected he'd be—in the main hall, chatting with his new friends. It took us a while to find Horm. I knew little about wood, and between them, those two knew everything. I wanted to know what Sylmond and Kalmond had chosen and the properties of those woods. We tracked Horm down to the stronghold's forge, where he was discussing arms and armor with the tribe's ironwrights. Horm, being half niblun, considered himself a master smith—indeed, a master of all types of crafting. He was demonstrating niblun techniques of tempering and sharpening, which he was using to finish two knives he had forged. The smiths did not mind me borrowing him for a few minutes.

"Just keep doing that," Horm instructed them, taking off his leather apron. "Remember to let them rest well, between each pass at folding the steel. Couple of days, those things will punch through rock."

I could see the skeptical looks on the smiths' faces. Horm noticed it too. "Now, I don't know if you're a betting man, but I'll wager gold on it."

The Ironwright shook his head. "I've learned a deal from you already, son," he said. "I'm not going to learn I'm a fool as well. I don't believe you, but I've a feeling that two days from now I will."

Horm chuckled, then accompanied Nyrik and me back to the longhouse.

We waited in Sylmond's chamber until she returned. Nyrik and Horm didn't like the look of the mounted Ice Wight in his glass case one bit. "The longer we don't run into any of these, the better," Nyrik muttered.

Horm stared at it, with furrowed brows. "How's all this add up?" he said. "Fuckers in the sky killing my cousin. These things, creeping about down here. You hearing voices in your sleep."

I thought, *What can I say?* Shift suggested, *Tell him that's what we're hoping to find out.*

I did. Horm grunted. "Yur, well. Let's do that." He was, I could tell, itching for a fight.

Sylmond was carrying four staves when she returned, Kalmond just one. "Made his mind up the moment he laid a hand on it," she said. "I told him to look around for others, but he wasn't interested."

"It's this one." Kalmond showed his choice. It was a fine piece of wood, but twice his size.

"Oak," Nyrik said, approvingly. "King of the trees, in my not so humble opinion. Bit big for you, young 'un, but my mate here will cut it down for you. Best carpenter you'll ever meet."

Kalmond shook his head. "I'm growing," he said.

Nyrik's eyebrows rose, as he considered that. "True. Best you grow into it, rather than out of it, hey?"

Kalmond nodded.

"Yur," Horm agreed. "Be just the right fit for you one day. Good choice, lad."

Nyrik turned to Sylmond. "He's got a wise old head on them young shoulders. Now, then: Let's see what you've come up with."

Sylmond placed her four staves on the table. Shift, in my hands, jittered with anticipation. She wanted to see this as much as I did, so I opened her tourmaline eye to let her inspect them.

Horm named them. "Alder, pine, spruce, fir."

Sylmond picked up the alder stave first. "I'm almost sure this is the one," she said. "But there's something about the others."

Horm said, "What?"

"When I hold them, it's faint, but they each have something different," she said. "Something I'd like to know."

Horm grunted. "So what's the hurry? You're just starting out at this. When you've gone as far as you can with your alder, move on to another. You'll know more what you're doing by then. Don't run before you can walk, eh?"

Sylmond nodded. "Mm. Makes sense." Her hand kept moving back to her alder staff. Every time she touched it, she smiled. It was clear that the matter was settled.

I asked Horm, "What's the right stone, for alder?"

Horm frowned. "He's an odd one, alder. Not like other woods. Slow, but steady. Takes his time, but always comes through. Give him a job, he'll get it done, however long it takes him. Reliable, is alder. A healing tree. You can trust him. Not mischievous like your rowan. She'll play all sorts of tricks on you, if the whim takes her—*Oww!!*"

Shift, unbidden, had hit him with a warning sizzle. *Stop that*, I told her, as Horm tucked his singed hand under his armpit, glaring at me. *I don't like being cheeked*, Shift let me know. *He needs to mind his manners.*

I raised her and cast a green Orb of Mending around Horm, who relaxed under its soothing influence. "Sorry, Horm. She won't do it again."

He grunted. "Yur, well, I won't give her reason to, I'll be sure o' that!" He bowed to Shift. "You have my apology, my lady. I'll save my disrespect for our enemies."

Shift glowed warm in my hand, and the green Orb around Horm bloomed richer and brighter. *Apology accepted.*

"*Whoo,*" Horm said, as he turned his attention back to the alder stave that Sylmond had chosen. "I almost feel sorry for our foes. Purple, that's what this fellow needs. Or blue. Amethyst or lapis lazuli."

I felt pieces fitting together. "And these other woods?"

"Emerald, crystal, turquoise."

I reached inside my jerkin for the soft leather bag of heartstones that I carried in my inner pocket and turned to Sylmond. "None of which I have," I said. "But it so happens ..."

I opened the bag and laid the jewels on the table.

I picked up the glowing purple amethyst, holding my hand out for Sylmond's alder staff. "May I?"

She passed it over to me. I felt along the stave's head, my thumbs exploring for the space that I knew should be there. Among the dark flecks in the alder's grain, I soon found it. I eased it open, the way that Marnie had taught me, and fitted his amethyst heartstone. The wood of the alder shrank back round it, sealing it in place.

"And there he is," I said. I handed Sylmond back her staff.

She stared at it, lost for words.

"And now," I continued, "we need to know if he can do anything. Well, you and him both."

I held Shift towards the alder staff, her tourmaline heartstone above his amethyst.

They began to glow, one red and green and strong, the other purple and tentative. The lights inside them flowed out, and into each other, and danced around each other. She was informing him, I knew. He was drinking in her wisdom, her knowledge. I could tell that Shift was enjoying it. Her merry laugh sang along my arm. Where she was quick, and skittish, the alder was, as Horm had told us, slow, and patient. He listened. He learned. He absorbed. I could sense Shift urging him *get on with it, what's so hard?* He didn't want to miss a thing. He took his own, sweet time. At last, the purple glow around him grew, until it was as bright as Shift's reds and greens. Eventually it dulled, and Shift's colors separated from his, and gathered back home into her tourmaline.

I said, "Now let's see what the two of you can do."

Sylmond said, "I don't know if I can do anything ..."

I said, "Neither do I."

She frowned, staring at her new staff. "How do we find out?"

I was reminded of my first moments with my new and improved Shift, in Farnz's cottage in the village. That hadn't been a place to try out any attacks. There had been no need to destroy his house with a Flame-bomb, so, I'd cast Reveal Hidden Life, which had led me to the ball of light, hovering in the woods ... and, eventually, here to Sylmond's chamber within Isvellir. We could try that again, I thought—but, somehow, Reveal Hidden Life didn't seem the place for Sylmond to start.

What did *she* need, I wondered. I remembered what Horm had said. *Reliable, is alder. A healing tree.*

I said, "Let's see if he can do what my staff did." I raised Shift, and cast another Orb of Mending around Horm, then another around Nyrik. The two Woods Kin relaxed and smiled. "I love these," Nyrik said. "I felt fine before. Now I feel even better!"

Sylmond studied the green blooms that surrounded them.

"Those are Orbs of Mending," I said. "They are also Shields, which will stop a lot of damage hitting them, and will heal what does manage to get through. They don't last long, so you have to keep refreshing them; but they're powerful, and effective. Let him learn them, and you will too."

She held her alder staff towards the Orbs, and concentrated on them.

After a while she turned to me and nodded.

I said, "Got it?"

"I think so."

I cleansed the Orbs off Nyrik and Horm and told her, "Your turn. Let them do the work. Stick and stone know how; you just let them know what it is that you want them to do."

"Out loud?"

"Just think it. They'll do it."

Sylmond raised her alder staff and closed her eyes.

"No no," I said. "Look at your targets. Aim your thoughts through your staff at them. That's how he will know where to hit."

She took a deep breath and pointed her staff towards Nyrik and Horm. For a while, nothing happened. Then, a faint, green mist glowed around them. It glimmered for a few moments, and then faded.

Sylmond looked at me. "Would that ... be any good?" she said.

I smiled. "It will when you've worked on it. It takes time. And I have nothing better to do while this whiteout lasts, so I'll be happy to help you practice."

She frowned, indicating Nyrik and Horm. "But there was nothing wrong with them that needed mending. How do we know it would have done anything for someone hurt?"

We weren't in combat. I didn't have teammates taking damage, who I needed to heal. I didn't have a tiring Grell, who needed a boost to his stamina, or a Qrysta who'd been hit by enemy steel, and needed her wounds closed and her health restored. So, I couldn't show Sylmond any of my battlemage skills.

I had others, though.

I didn't see why I could not use them in peacetime.

"We don't," I said. "So let's find out."

I made to leave, but Kalmond stopped me. "Do you have a stone for mine?"

I said, "I wish I did, Kalmond. But your oak staff needs a diamond heartstone. And they're rarer than rare."

"Diamond," he said, nodding. "The root folk will find me one. I saw how you fitted Granna's. I'll be able to do that, when I get it."

"And her stone will teach yours," I said.

"Yes," he said, and we left the chamber.

Sylmond's son was sitting at his fireside, in the company of his daughter, Chief Izmond, and her husband and their daughters, his head resting back against his armchair, his white eyes staring at the ceiling. His lined, old face looked contented, as he held Izmond's hand while they talked. His head lowered and turned to us on hearing us enter, and his smile broadened as Kalmond ran in and showed his sisters his oak staff.

"Look what I've got!" he said.

His eldest sister scoffed. "A stick?"

"A *staff*," he corrected her. "A magic staff. It's oak!"

The girls giggled.

"Go on, then," the other sister said. "Do magic with it."

"I can't yet," Kalmond said. "I haven't learned."

"I can," the older sister said. "Give it me. I can turn that oak into ash, just by putting it on grandpa's fire."

She grabbed it, and a tussle ensued, which Sylmond quickly stopped. "Watch, children," she whispered.

They went quiet as I raised Shift. I cast Lingering Mend on the old chief, and then Heal All.

We watched, and waited.

He was not aware of what I had done. But after a few moments, he stirred. "What's going on, Mother? What's happening?"

Sylmond knelt beside him, and took his free hand in both of hers. "What do you feel?"

"I … I don't know. It's … tingling."

"What is?"

"Everything. My arms. My *eyes* …"

Sylmond glanced at me, and then back up at her son.

He blinked. His face screwed up, his jaws working, his eyes closing tighter and tighter in confusion. He dropped his mother's hands, and began rubbing his clenched eyes, first with his knuckles, then with his fingers. He leaned forward, as if struggling to stand up.

"I'm … I'm …" he said.

I cast Calm on him, and his nervous movements slowed. His tense shoulders softened. His lips pursed and he swallowed. The lines on his brow cleared. His scalp relaxed. He took a deep breath and inhaled.

He lowered his hands from his eyes, which slowly blinked open.

Izmond gasped. "The whiteout …"

The clouds in her father's eyes were fading. As we watched, they dissipated, and were gone.

He looked around, and then down at Sylmond, kneeling beside him. "Mother?"

She nodded up at him and smiled.

Tears were rolling down his old cheeks. "I can see you." He looked from face to face of his assembled family. "I can see you all!"

# 24

## Sidetracked

**After** that there was nothing that the Ice Orcs wouldn't do for us. We were guests of honor, not to mention the most remarkable thing that had happened to them in years. We were friends. We were allies. Our interests were aligned. We swapped tales, and ideas, and one thing led to another—but not right away. For when I say "we," I mean Grell, and Qrysta, and the others, while I was blacked out under the next three Moon Nights.

As the sun set on the first of them, the evening after I'd cured the old chief of his whiteouts, Sylmond promised me that she'd watch over me while I went through them. I was already feeling my strength draining from me, even though the moon herself had not yet risen. Sylmond and her little great-grandson helped me into bed, where I lay back, each of my hands held in theirs.

And then I dropped, as if from a high cliff into a black sea, into darkness.

Sylmond was the first thing that I saw on emerging three days later. The second thing, on the other side of my bed, was Kalmond, his solemn eyes fixed on me. I tried to smile at him, to reassure him, but my mouth wouldn't work.

Each blackout had been worse than the previous month's. This one had been nothing short of a coma. I knew that I would never re-

300

emerge from the next one. After three days in that deathlike sleep I was weak and confused. They had been anything but three days of rest. I felt as if I had been drained by Ice Wights.

Sylmond had a healing potion ready for me. She and Kalmond helped me to sit up, and held the cup to my lips. I was so weak that I could hardly drink. I sipped at the warm liquid, and just wanted it all to end. I was hanging by a thread. After a while, thanks to her potion, it seemed that maybe I was hanging from two.

"Thank you," I managed, at last.

"How was it?"

There were no words for it. "Nothingness," I said. "The end of everything."

She squeezed my hand. "Did he talk to you?"

"I don't think so. I have no memory of it."

"Then perhaps he has done all that he can for you."

That was hardly an encouraging thought. I struggled to understand where I was, and what lay ahead of me, as I tried to distance myself from the ordeal I'd just been through. I'd never been so exhausted in my life.

I had another month.

And then: oblivion.

I had learned more, this last month. I had also discovered more unknowns. It was like taking two steps forwards, nine back, and four sideways. Where was I, in all this? Why was the puzzle always more confusing, the more I saw of it? What was I not seeing? Would I kick myself for my stupidity when it all became clear? *Duhh—of course! Idiot ...*

That was assuming that "it all" would actually become clear. Of which, I had no way of knowing if it would.

I tried to put all those questions that were crowding in on me aside. There was only one way that I'd come to any answers:

*Keep going forwards.*

The thought disheartened me. I knew that I couldn't stand, yet. How many days would it be before I would be strong enough to resume our journey?

Sylmond could see me fidgeting, and laid a warm towel on my forehead. "You'll need to rest," she said, "and not fret. The whiteout has lifted. The sky's clear, the winds are soft, the sun is shining. Your road is ready and waiting for you, as soon as you're fit to take it."

She laid Shift in my hands, and said, "Now, do for yourself what you did for my son. I've been studying you, young Mastercaster, your mind and powers and all that's in that notebook of yours, and all I can say is: I would rather have you with me in a fight than against me. I'd prefer to be on the receiving end of your Healings than your Damages, thank you very much. I'll take an Orb of Warmth over a Shock Blizzard any day. So, let your friend there take care of you, the way she knows how."

I took Shift in my hand, which hardly had enough strength to grip her. I felt her concern immediately. It was not a time, she knew, for her usual cheery teasing. She was careful to work her Heals on me slowly. I was too weak to withstand the impact of a rush of remedies all at once. I lay back and left her to it. Eventually her Auras of Reviving grew around me—and also, I saw, bloomed around the two of them.

"Well now," Sylmond said. "If you feel a tenth as good as we do, you're on the mend!"

I was, indeed, feeling as if I was now hanging from several threads, and that they were not, after all, going to snap. I drifted off, contented, as the green bubbles that enveloped me worked their magic, knowing that when I awoke, I would be stronger.

I was.

I was also surrounded by people.

Qrysta was the closest, I saw, as my eyes blinked open. She was sitting on the side of my bed in the small, crowded room, holding my hand. I smiled as her face swam into focus. She was so beautiful, so reassuring, so … everything. She smiled back at me in return, and the warmth of her smile filled me with comfort, with confidence. Whatever happened over the next moon month we would face it together, all of us—and we had never let each other down yet. Beyond her, I could see Grell, and Nyrik and Horm, and Jess, and a number of Ice Orcs. They were all staring at me, as if something important was in the air.

"Hey, Daxxie," Qrysta patted my hand. "How are you feeling?"

"All the better for seeing you. All of you," I added quickly.

That appeared to be the cue for Little Guy to jump onto the bed and start licking my face. Jess made to pull him off, but I put my arm around him.

"Hello, Little Guy," I said. "It's good to see you too, my friend."

He wagged his bushy tail, turned around, and sat under my armpit, looking out at his audience.

I saw Chief Izmond; her father, Orvenmond; Sylmond, Kalmond, Desmond, and various other … -monds, I presumed: all looking down at me, expectant, and—it seemed to me—anxious, but trying not to show it. Quite a crowd, I thought. I wondered what they all wanted.

"We have a proposition for you, Daxxie," Qrysta said. "Or rather, our hosts have a proposition for us, which we'd like to run by you."

"Which is?"

She smiled. "A side quest."

I hadn't expected that. "Okay …"

"I think you're going to like it," she said. "It's your choice, though. You being the one with the … problem. I mean, knowing you, normally you'd leap at it. But this isn't normally."

I said, "You can say that again."

"Now, I know what you're thinking: *We don't have the time,*" she continued. "But it won't take long. We'll be going that way anyway—this'll just be a detour, it won't take more than a day. It'll be a busy day, but worth it. These folks are all up for it; they've been itching to solve this particular problem forever. And it's on our way, pretty much."

"What is it?" I asked.

"Clear out the Ice Pits."

I heard growls, and large bodies behind her shifting from foot to foot.

I said, "What are those?"

"Basically, the lair of the Ice Wights."

Well, I thought. That sounds like a challenge.

Chief Izmond, who was standing behind her, came forward and unrolled a map, which she spread on the bed, on top of my legs.

"We're here," she said, pointing at a little snow-capped mountain with a red stain down one side. "Isvellir. To get to Mondthal, you have to go through Ogretzk." She pointed to what looked like a few sticks, between mountains and a large ice lake.

I said, "Why 'have to'?"

"Two reasons. One, you need permission from the Ogres. Two, there's no way around it. Well, there is—across that lake—but there's no cover on it, obviously. There'd be no trees to hide behind on a lake, and the Ogres will see you. And come after you. They'll want to know who the hell you think you are, trespassing on their land. And if I know Ogres, which I do, I'd expect them to attack first and ask questions afterwards."

That didn't sound good. "Could we handle them?"

Chief Izmond glanced at Qrysta, who said, "You're the only one of us who's fought an Ogre, Daxx. What do you think?"

I remembered my struggle with Urngra. I'd been way over-matched, even in the Form. And that was just one Ogre. I hadn't had Shift, so hadn't been able to unleash my destruction attacks, and my Heals; but even if I had, would I have been able to outfight her? I had no way of knowing. And if there were more of them, we'd be only a few against …

"How many?" I said.

Chief Izmond said, "A couple of hundred. And there's more in their strongholds beyond Ogretzk. You'd have to deal with them too."

Not, I thought, a great prospect.

Qrysta said, "So, what do you think? It's obvious, right? Running for our lives, pursued by a mob of Ogres, or get their by-your-leave, and save our strength for, well … the End Boss, by the sound of it. We'd hardly want to be trapped between the two."

"I don't know if there *is* an End Boss in this case, Qrys." I said. "He's bound and sealed and powerless, he says."

"He may be," she said "but what about *her?* This 'she' that he mentioned, more than once? Anyone who can do binding and sealing like that has to be pretty powerful."

"True enough," I admitted.

"Could be that we have to go through her, to get to him," she pointed out. "Which would mean a Boss Fight."

It sounded plausible. Again, though, I had no way of knowing. I said, "We'll just have to get there and see."

"*Keep going forwards,* right?" Qrysta said. "In which case, the fewer distractions the better, I'd have thought. And a pack of angry Ogres chasing us would definitely be a distraction."

"That it would," I agreed. I looked down and followed the map north to Mondthal. "How long from Ogretzk to The Valley of the Moon?"

Chief Izmond said, "Less than a week."

"And how long from here to Ogretzk?"

"Three days in a straight line, four with the detour."

I thought, *plenty of time, then, before …*

A sour laugh escaped me.

Qrysta said, "What?"

"Plenty of time before my deadline."

Qrysta understood. She gave a wry smile. "Yeah. We want to make sure you hit that."

"We do indeed."

Everyone in the room, I could see, was waiting for my decision.

"So?" Qrysta said. "When d'you think you'll be strong enough to travel?"

"One more day of rest and I should be okay," I said. "We can leave the day after tomorrow."

"So, we could take in this side quest."

"We could, but …. You haven't explained why we should."

Qrysta's eyebrows rose. She gestured at the crowd of the Ice Orcs. "Oh, like what have they done for us lately? We'd still be sleeping out there in the Ice Plains, in the whiteout. And you catatonic for three days and nights."

She was right. We owed them.

Qrysta turned to Izmond, and said, "Chief?"

Chief Izmond said, "It's where the Ice Balm comes from."

Then I understood. A rich prize indeed.

"Worth three times its weight in gold," Qrysta reminded me. "And that's to the middleman. What d'you think Master Bjarnevalt sells it for, in the southern markets?"

I saw her point. "A *lot* more."

She nodded.

Chief Izmond sat on the other side of my bed. "It's hard enough out here, even without the Ice Wights," she said, "but those damn things make it a whole lot worse. Everyone in this room has lost someone to them. You won't find an Orc, here or overseas, who's feared of dying, Daxx, you know that, but none of us wants to go *that* way. As long as we can remember, we've wanted to be rid of them. It's not like our spats with the bumpers and clumpers—those don't mean no more than bragging rights. We kick their arses, they kick ours. Orc stuff. Keeps us all on our toes. The Ice Wights, though …" she stopped, and regathered her strength. "They're bad. And they're getting worse."

I said, "In what way?"

"Bolder. More numerous. When our team goes down to the depot, they don't keep away like they used to. They lurk, watching, while we drop off our goods, and pick up the trades. It's like they're eying us up. Planning. We don't trust them anymore. Not that we ever really 'trusted' them, but they knew the rules. The depot is neutral ground. Trade and truce. It's as if the truce won't be holding much longer. And they'll be the ones as will break it."

"So what the chief is saying, Daxx," Grell spoke up, "is, let's get our retaliation in first."

Nyrik appeared at Qrysta's side. "And you might be thinking, what's in it for us, eh?" he said. "I'll tell you. And I'll tell you because it was your goodself, Daxx, as advised Horm here and me to find ourselves a new profession, if you remember? Now that our lovely but bafflingly soft-hearted young queen has outlawed our old one. I do believe, you being a gentleman and a friend, that you'd like to see us nicely established in a lucrative new trade?"

I reached for his hand, and patted it. "So, what are you up to, you old scoundrel?" I said.

"Looking after everyone's best interests," Nyrik replied. "In a nutshell, mate, while you've been catching up on your beauty sleep, we've been putting our heads together. To summarize: Our hosts have heard how we've come here off a MOAF. Therefore, we do MOAF's, right?"

"That we do," I agreed.

"And it just so happens that they have a MOAF they've been itching to get stuck into for gawds know how many generations, only they lacked the firepower, so to speak—and here we turn up out of the blue, MOAF experts. Well: answer to their prayers, eh? So, we MOAF the crap out of these Ice Wights, then we get to control the source of the Ice Balm trade while simultaneously relieving these fine folks of their problem." He beamed at me and squeezed my hand in return. "Tell me what's wrong with that proposition."

I said, "By 'we,' you mean …?"

"All of us." He turned to Izmond. "Chief?"

"There's a lot we need from the south, up here," Izmond said. "Glass panels for our hothouses. Fabrics, rope, paper, so much more, but above all—fodder. Hay and silage for our herds. The grazing up here is poor, and while our yaks are accustomed to it, there's never enough to be sure we'll last the next winter. There's competition for it, from mastodons and reindeer and musk ox and fur-elk. We send down ingots, and ivory, and furs, and resins, and get back glass and grass, and are grateful. We know how plentiful and cheap those are, in the south. And we know what the folk overseas will pay for Ice Balm."

"The which funds," Nyrik said, "Horm and me will make sure flow north to our friends here."

I said, "You'll be living here?"

"Up here, down there in Sondehafn. We'll get it all set up to work smoothly, oversee things. Work hand in glove with Master Bjarnevalt. Wouldn't he like to have all the Ice Balm he can handle, at less than what he's paying now? And wouldn't Chief Izmond like all the glass and grass and other things she needs, at a tenth of what she's paying?"

I saw the picture. "And wouldn't there be a nice cut for you?"

"There you go!" Nyrik beamed. "Everyone wins. And we like it here, me and Horm. Plenty of forests, full of fine trees to get to know. Good hunting."

Yes, I thought. It all fits together. "Okay, What's the plan?"

A rumble of excitement ran around the room. We were in.

"First, clear the Ice Pits," Chief Izmond said. "Then, we form an alliance with the bumpers and clumpers, head south from all directions, mount a raid on the stockade, and kill every Ice Wight we find there. We'll set it up with Master Bjarnevalt. We have ways down out of the mountains to the southlands that folk down there don't know about, same as the Ice Wights do. We'll send Nyrik and Horm down them to get him to delay sending any more livestock up north until the Ice Wights are desperate, which will mean they'd be gathered there in numbers.

"We'll also ask Master Bjarnevalt to send up an escort of archers, armed with fire arrows. When the stockade gates are opened, for the animals to be driven in, we'll fall on the Ice Wights from behind, while the archers attack from below. They'll be easy to pick off when they're stuck full of burning arrows. Then we'll garrison the place, build it up against attacks from behind, and control the trade route with the south."

"Cutting out the middleman," I said. "Or middlewight."

"Exactly," Nyrik said. "Master Bjarnevalt gets all the Ice Balm he can use, at a much lower price, and goods and gold flow into the north. Win-win."

It did, indeed, sound good for everyone. Except, of course, for the Ice Wights.

Horm appeared by Nyrik's side. "That's all for later. We've a job to do first."

"That we do," I agreed. "Sounds like a plan, though."

I looked up at Chief Izmond, and said, "Why haven't you done this before?"

"Many chiefs have tried," she said. "They mustered armies, and went in—well, if you can call them 'armies.' Just a few dozen warriors at most. There aren't many of us up here. They were always defeated. Most of them never came back. Then for years afterwards we were so weakened that all we could do was fall back and defend our strongholds. We … don't like the Undergrounds. We don't belong down there. We're Orcs, we fight fair and square, out in the open. We don't do well in the dark."

Shaman Sylmond came to stand behind her granddaughter and put her hand on her shoulder. "Which now we can take care of, with your Glows."

I said, "Have you been working on them?"

She nodded. "Them and more."

"She set a wolf on fire," Kalmond said, appearing beside her.

"Sh!" his great-grandmother said. "It was a mistake. And it wasn't 'on fire,' it was just a little bit singed. I don't think it even noticed. I cast a Heal on it. I'm not very good at any of it yet, but I'll keep practicing."

I said, "It takes time."

She nodded, then said. "The point is, Daxx: We've never had any battlemages, to heal us, before. And now you're here."

By late that afternoon I was walking fairly steadily. I could feel my strength returning, hour by hour. What I needed, Sylmond said, was fresh air, and to stretch my legs. It was indeed, as she had said, a fine day, as we stepped out into bright sunshine, under a cloudless blue sky. The stockade was a hive of activity. Orcs were training, drilling, watching Grell in action as he went through moves with them. Sometimes he would stop to explain things, then he'd be sparring again, working several opponents at once. I could see how impressed they were by his skills. It was clear that they'd follow him anywhere.

As we passed through, Sylmond cast her Heals on anyone who had been injured in training. They weren't much, I saw, pretty weak casts really—but they were a lot better than nothing. I topped them up with an Area Heal All, and refreshed the fighters with a Stamina Boost. A wave of fresh energy washed over them, and they charged at each other again. The forges were ringing with the sounds of armor being mended and blades sharpened. There were racks of brutal looking warhammers, and a number of battle-axes and longswords—more, I thought, than there were Orcs in Isvellir.

"Chief Izmond has summoned the clans," Sylmond said. "Messengers went out, calling them to gather at the refuge, every fighter worth the name. We promised them weapons. And a chance to make history. Who isn't going to want to be part of the legend?" She grinned. "The Battle of the Ice Pits. No one who can lift a hammer will be missing that."

"Bumpers and clumpers joining in?" I asked.

"No—those are *tribes*, Daxx. They'd take forever to bring round to the idea, there'd be a lot of arguing. The clans are other Ice Orcs, up in the outer strongholds—Thangvard, Eldholm, Helspittyr. All built on volcanoes, like ours here. We won't hear back before we all rendezvous at the refuge, but we think we could be near a hundred and twenty, all told. Forty-odd from here, the rest from the smaller holds."

"Against how many Ice Wights?"

"That we have no way of knowing. But you never see many of them at a time, even at the stockade when they're expecting livestock."

I thought, just because you don't see many of them, that doesn't mean there aren't many of them. I didn't say it.

Horm was working with the carpenters, who were also the tribe's bowyers and fletchers, making as many arrows as they could. Ice Orcs needed to be good shots, Sylmond told me, if they were to survive in the far north. "Without hunting," she said, "we'd never have survived in the hard land here. It's a skill we all learn, from childhood." There was a crowd around the archery butts, where Nyrik and Jess were practicing along with Desmond and other archers. Little Guy saw me and trotted over, joining us as we came to the wolf pen. Nostë was waiting for me, his nose pressed up against the iron bars of the gate, as other hairy black heads jostled around him.

"He's been waiting for you," Fjernmond, the wolf wrangler said, as he let Nostë out. "Ready to show you his stuff, he is."

The black wolf ran to me, tail wagging, eyes shining. I ruffled his ears, and patted his head and shoulders. Fjernmond clicked his tongue, and Nostë fell in beside him at heel, looking back at me to come along too. I took his other side, with Little Guy and Sylmond, and together we walked down towards the stockyards. They were empty, the yaks having been herded into the pastures, where they could get in a whole day's grazing. A sled was waiting for us, its team of ten wolves harnessed and ready to run. We climbed in. The driver flicked his reins, and we were off across the snow, Nostë cantering beside us.

I forgot about everything else, that evening, as we watched Nostë at work. Like all the Isvellir wolves, he was enormous, but he was dwarfed by the yaks he was tending. Fjernmond stayed with us as Nostë trotted down towards them. "He knows what to do; he don't need me," he said.

The wolf moved at an easy pace, checking every animal as he passed. They all greeted him, nuzzle to nuzzle, before resuming their grazing. If he spotted something, he'd nudge the animal towards us, and it would lumber over for Fjernmond to inspect. He checked hooves, dosed them with boluses, put his head to their flanks and listened to their heartbeats and their breathing. Mostly, though, it was not much happening, slowly; and how good it felt, to be under that cloudless sky, in that wilderness, at one with the rhythms of the world. War and worry seemed far away. At last, Fjernmond gave a whistle, and Nostë began to circle the herd, trotting calmly. The yaks gathered, and headed home, the great black wolf walking behind them, guarding their backs.

The sun was low in the west above Isvellir as our sled came to a halt, the evening light sparkling in the snowscape. The yaks were milked, and tended, and settled in their stockyards, where hay bales had been broken out for them. They ate, and lay down, and began chewing.

"That's their supper taken care of," Fjernmond said. "Now for ours, eh?"

"Good idea," I said. After a day in the open air, my appetite had returned and I was famished.

"When you come back, Daxx," Fjernmond said, as we walked back to the longhouse, "we'll take you on a hunt. It's something, seeing wolves work a big herd of reindeer. Just takes a few of them. Not even five or six, is all it takes to drive hundreds. They always know which ones to cut out for us to bring down. Nostë could probably do it all by himself," he added, with a chuckle.

"I'd like to see that," I said.

I didn't tell him that I doubted I'd be coming back.

# 25

## The Ice Pits

It was a two-day run to the refuge, and we were underway before dawn. Every available sled was filled with fighters, weapons, and supplies. Every able-bodied wolf was harnessed to them. There were five sleds, three with eight wolves hauling them, two with ten. It was flat terrain, and a fast, easy run, through scattered trees and across frozen lakes, under clear skies.

We had no idea if we'd be able to take the Ice Wights by surprise, because no one knew how they communicated with each other. We had no idea if they were watching us, as we ran north and east towards the refuge. The only lookout we had was Jess, our eyes in the sky. Every hour or so she'd take off and scout ahead and to either side. She saw nothing, but the first time she mounted her broomstick and flew away she created a sensation among the Ice Orcs. If these peculiar southerners could do that, they thought—well, what else could they do? *At last,* they were thinking, *we can rid ourselves of the wretched Ice Wights forever.*

Even though Jess had seen nothing, we lit no fires when we camped out the first night, as a precaution. We soft southerners were given the sleds to sleep in, under piles of furs, while the Ice Orcs bedded down with the wolves. They'd all done that before, any number of times. Late the next morning we spotted a black dot in the sky heading back towards us, and reined in to a halt.

"Sled's coming," Jess said, as she dismounted.

We soon saw it speeding towards us over the snow. It was one of Chief Izmond's messengers, reporting that the other clans were already gathering at the refuge, and in numbers. Our group cheered the news.

Some hours later, as the evening shadows lengthened, high stone walls came into sight. Our sleds drove in through open gates, which were pushed shut and barred behind us. We were the last to arrive. We could barely all fit inside the refuge's crowded courtyard. The rooms in its small tower were little more than barracks. None of them had anything like the space we needed for our Council of War, so we held it in the open, after the wolves had been fed and settled.

Chief Izmond introduced us, and told the warriors of the other clans of our achievements. They looked at us warily, more in mistrust than hope, I thought.

She handed over to Grell, who stepped forward to lay out our strategy.

He stopped in front of a very large, very suspicious-looking Ice Orc, who was staring at him, a huge warhammer slung on his back.

Grell said, with a smile, "Got a name, mate?"

"Zeygmond," the Ice Orc replied, with a scowl.

"Nice to meet you, Zeygo, I'm Grell of the Ozgaroos. I expect you know how to use that thing?"

" 'Course I bloody do," the Ice Orc replied.

"Glad to hear it," Grell said. "Do us a favor, and give us a whack, eh? Not in the head, as I don't have my helmet on and would rather not be brained."

Zeygmond hefted his warhammer and hesitated.

"Come on," Grell said. "I'm not going to hit back. I just want to show you something, and I need a volunteer from the audience for my demonstration. So—you up for it?"

Zeygmond nodded, a little warily.

"Give it a good swing, middle of my chest. Off you go then."

Still not quite sure what was going on, the Ice Orc, soon enough, did as he was told.

He swung his warhammer in a wide arc, and slammed it into Grell's chest.

To his surprise, and everyone else's, the hammer rebounded with a metallic clang, nearly throwing Zeygmond off his feet.

"Nice work," Grell said. "Thank you, Zeygo. What this is," he explained to the startled assembly, "is Kinfolk armor. I know you've never seen anything like it because neither had I. Made it for me specially, the Kinfolk did, in preparation for a little job they asked me to do for them, and I'd have died any number of times without it. It helped me survive to get the job done for them, I'm glad to say, so I was able to justify their faith in me. Harder than rocks, light as a feather." He shook his head with a smile. "No idea how those little geniuses did it. Knocked it up overnight, and all.

"So. If friend Zeygmond here can't scratch it with his fucking great warhammer, no Ice Wight's going to get through it and get his teeth into me. All of which I'm saying for this reason: Sadly, none of you are in Kinfolk plate—I wish you all were; it'd make this jaunt a breeze. My job tomorrow is to have them all attack *me*. Not you, me. Got that? I may be swarmed by the things. You might not even see me under a pile of them for all I know, but that's good. I'll be challenging and taunting them, keeping them focused on me, while my Kinfolk plate soaks up the punishment and our battlemage here keeps up my stamina and heals any damage I take. So long as they focus on me, your job is simple. Smash 'em to bits!"

Growls of approval ran around the courtyard.

"Think you can do that, lads?" Grell said.

The Ice Orcs answered with a roar.

Chief Izmond tapped Grell on the shoulder, and said something in his ear.

*"Oops, excuse me," Grell said, holding up his arms.* The din subsided. "I should have said, *lads and lasses.* If my girl Klurra was here now she'd have clipped me around the ear for that. I've told the Isvellir folks what she and I got up to, back near her tribe's place. Quest and a half, that was. Fight of our bloody lives. This horrible little goblin turned into a bloody great winged demon—we only survived by the skin of our teeth. Shaken to bits, we were. Right, apologies to all lady warriors present, and how about we make tomorrow the fight of *your* bloody lives eh? Wipe out those bastards once and for all—"

His voice was drowned by more roars of approval, and cheers, and whistles.

"One more thing, Zeygmond, mate," he said, reaching behind him for his Kinfolk bow. "I expect you know how to use one of these too?"

He held the bow out to the Ice Orc, who growled, warily, "I should do."

"Kinfolk made this too. The bowyer who crafted it said only an Orc would be strong enough to draw it, so show us what you've got, laddie. No need for an arrow."

Zeygmond, looking a little bashful, took the huge bow. I could see he was worried that he'd embarrass himself by not being able to draw it. He raised it, set his feet in an archer's stance, and hauled on the thick wire that was its bowstring. Clearly, he knew what he was doing. The bow bent until its string was all the way back to his ear.

"Knew you could!" Grell chuckled. "Okay, Zeygo, loose!"

Zeygmond released the bowstring, and a deep metallic *whrunnnggg* echoed around the courtyard, stirring murmurs of appreciation. Orcs know a good bow when they see one.

"Have fun with that tomorrow, eh, mate?" Grell said. "It'll put a bodkin into granite, and so hard you'll never get it out again. I know that because I made a ladder up a cliff face that way. Had to leave my Kinfolk-made bodkins behind, which was a shame, but they were stuck in that wall hard enough to take my weight as I climbed up. So, you can bet that even ordinary arrows from it'll make a mess of anything they hit. They'll go through one Ice Wight and half a dozen of the ones behind it, I shouldn't wonder. See if you can make yourself some nice Ice Wight skewers tomorrow, eh, Zeygo? Fire every shaft you've got, then bring that hammer of yours in for the fun."

Zeygmond nodded, still in awe of the weapon he was holding. "I will," he said, "but don't you need it?"

"I'll be tanking, mate." Grell saw the puzzled looks on their faces, and improvised an explanation. "That's what we call what I'll be doing, because I'll be standing there like a bloody great water tank, with everyone trying to spring leaks in me."

"Thank you, Grell," Zeygmond said. "It'll be an honor."

"You're welcome." Grell clapped him on the shoulder and turned to the others, a ferocious smile on his face.

"And with them bastards otherwise occupied trying to get at me—well: You're *Orcs*. You know what to do!"

He turned away to rejoin us, and his audience laughed and growled, everyone clearly eager to prove him right.

There was more to our tactics than that, of course; but as a general strategy, it was pretty much the whole plan. Grell on tank, everyone else on damages, range attacks until the arrows run out, then in for close-quarter work. Sylmond and I explained how we'd be illuminating the Undergrounds with Glows—which we demonstrated. The Ice Orcs smiled on seeing them floating over their heads and lighting up the courtyard. Nyrik, Horm, and Jess would be with the archers, along with Desmond and Zeygmond. I explained how my Area of Effect attacks worked, how they'd be trapping and immobilizing the enemy, as well as burning or shocking them. Sylmond and I also demonstrated healing by casting Shields of Mending and Protection on them. We would be watching out for them all, and doing everything we could to keep them refreshed and alive.

"And this is Little Guy," I said, hoisting him up for all to see. "These battle leathers he's wearing are speed-imbued. He'll be charging around creating mayhem. You probably won't see him—he moves so fast—but you'll see whoever he sinks his teeth into, so hit 'em while they're dancing around trying to see what just bit them in the arse."

The assembled Ice Orcs chuckled. Little Guy wagged his tail. He liked being the center of attention. He looked around happily at all the new friends who'd be feeding him scraps that night.

A thought struck me. "What about your wolves? Will they fight?"

Fjernmond said, "You just try and stop 'em!"

"Hate Ice Wights as much as we do," Desmond said.

The council broke up. We ate and settled in for an early night. We wanted to be well rested for the fight ahead.

Sleep, though, didn't come easily.

It was a clear, cold night under the midnight sun. Lying back under my furs in our sled, I watched the clouds of my breath drift up and away. Snowflakes began to fall. It was so serene, so peaceful. Apart from the snoring of a hundred and forty Ice Orcs all around us.

I knew that Grell wasn't asleep because he wasn't snoring too.

I said, "What are you thinking, Grello?"

He grunted. "Busy day tomorrow." He shifted around under his furs.

"I expect so," I agreed.

"Yeah," he said, "and that's the thing, isn't it?"

"How d'you mean?"

"You *expect*. We don't know *what* to expect. Apart from Ice Wights. We've done this before, haven't we, Daxxie? Any number of times. It's never just one thing, is it?"

He had a point.

"The harder the delve, the more it throws at you, right? We all know this is going to be a tough one. The Ice Orcs've tried to clear these Ice Pits before, and never got far in before getting their arses kicked all the way back to Isvellir. If it was easy, they wouldn't need us and all the clans, would they?"

"True," I agreed.

"Well. We know what we've got," Grell continued. "A hundred and forty tough-as-nails Ice Orcs, all of them good archers, so a decent amount of firepower to go along with your Damages. About the same number of wolves. Shields and Heals. Teeth and nails. Which is all very well and good, Daxx, but we don't know what *they've* got, do we?"

"Apart from Ice Wights," I pointed out.

"Yeah, that's exactly my effing point! Apart from Ice Wights—what *else* is down there?"

I considered what he'd said. "With luck, nothing."

Grell snorted. "There'll be something, mate. You know that. There's always something."

After four hours of running, crags rose ahead of us, bleak and forbidding against a heavy gray sky. The wolves hauled our sleds up the long slope towards them. There was no point in trying for a stealthy approach. There was no cover to speak of, just the occasional stunted tree that was somehow managing to survive in the frozen hollows. At the heart of the cliff that we were heading for, a black shadow loomed, forbidding.

The mouth of the Ice Pits.

We raced up the incline and halted. Within minutes the wolves were all unharnessed, a leash around each great black neck, and we were formed up, armed and armored and ready. A cold wind whipped around us. Nyrik and Horm trotted ahead and disappeared into the dark cave. They knew how not to be seen. The rest of us didn't. They'd wait for us if they saw, or heard, anything.

The Ice Orcs were grouped in companies, each with its own leader, who gathered around me as I walked us all through our plan again. It was simple enough, but I wanted to impress on them the importance of my signal flares. Green, *move on.* Two greens, *attack, everyone for themselves.* Red, *stop—nobody move, and that means nobody.* Orange, *archers light up and fire.* Yellow, *retreat.* Not *run: Retreat in order, back up, facing the foe.* Two yellows, *run like hell.*

"If we don't obey the signals, we're not an army, we're a rabble," Chief Izmond told them. "These folks have done this before, remember? This may be our territory, and our fight, but they've got the experience, so they're leading."

They'd all, by now, heard of our exploits, at Niblunhaem, and the Floor Of The World, and in Mourvania.

I saw nods, and heard grunts of agreement.

"Right," I said. "Gear check, and form up."

The leaders went back to their groups. Weapons were readied, lanterns lit.

Every archer carried either a lantern or a jar of oil. Six Orcs had large earthenware jars on their backs—"Just in case," Chief Izmond had said. If all went well, they'd be filling them with Ice Balm. "Be a shame to come back empty-handed," she'd pointed out.

I waited for each leader to give me the nod, and said, "Move in."

The scouts and archers went first, disappearing into the dark of the cave's mouth. I followed with Grell and the others, throwing Glows up overhead to light our way. The way led down, gradually at first, and then steeply. The tunnel's ceiling was high. Cold, stale air drifted up to us from the depths. Our force advanced in order, fast, and surprisingly quietly for Orcs. Even so, we all knew that the Ice Wights knew we were coming. The faces around me looked tense, and on edge, as I would have expected; but nowhere did I see fear. The overhead Glows that traveled down with us were giving the Ice Orcs heart. *We don't like the Undergrounds.* They disliked them less when they were well lit.

We went on down for five minutes; ten; twenty. Down and down. The air colder and colder. Our way took us through winding tunnels—some wide, some narrow, some steep and unstable, others gentle and smooth—and out into large caverns, where phosphorescent mushrooms shone pale in the ceilings high over our heads. There were occasional ice streams, and clumps of stalagmites and stalactites, glistening yellow and brown and white in the light of our Glows. There was no sign of life.

Cracks ran across the floor of one large cavern, which we had to avoid. The hard stone floor, between the cracks, looked polished, as if

from constant use by many feet. We all noticed. Past the cracks, the walls
and ceiling of the cavern narrowed down towards the mouth of another
tunnel. Nyrik and Horm were crouched at either side of it, peering into
the darkness beyond. I popped up a red flare, and everyone halted.

Qrysta and I hurried over to Nyrik and crouched beside him. Little
Guy, curious as always, trotted up to join us.

I whispered, "What is it?"

"Listen."

Faintly, from the tunnel ahead, came the sound of rustling. It was
not a sound that either of us recognized.

Qrysta said, "Any ideas?"

Nyrik shook his head. "It's not getting nearer. It's been like that
since we got here."

We fell silent, and listened again.

Little Guy, sniffing the air coming up to us from ahead, growled gently.

I looked down at him. His ears were flat, back against his skull.

"He don't like it no more'n we do," Horm grunted across at us.

I cast Reveal Hidden Life into the darkness. The cavern ahead lit
up like a bonfire.

Stretching from wall to wall across it, a mass of fuzzy outlines
merged into one great line of red. "There they are."

"How many?" Qrysta asked.

"Impossible to tell. There's a cavern down there, and they're standing across it. I can't see where one body ends and the next begins."

"Hm," she said. "Going to make a stand."

"Looks that way," I agreed.

"Any movement?"

"No. None. They're just waiting there."

"Seems as they're expecting company," Nyrik said.

Horm said, "Be a shame to disappoint them."

Nyrik grunted a sour laugh.

"I'm not risking a light," I said. "They can probably smell us, going
on what Desmond told us about them; but even so, I'm not sending
up another signal. Qrys, can you report back to the chief and get her
to bring everyone here?"

"Roger," she said, and vanished.

I heard Nyrik chuckle beside me.

I said, "What?"

He said, "Roger? So, Daxx is a nickname, eh? Always thought it was a funny bloody name."

I snorted. "I'll explain later."

"Whatever you say, Roj."

I saw that I needed to explain there and then. "It's code," I said. "*Roger* means right. *R* for *roger*, *R* for *right*; but *right*'s a common word, which can mean all sorts of things. Left, right, wrong, right. It's too vague. *Roger* isn't, it's precise. It means, precisely, *message understood*. So, if you say *roger*, I'll know you've got it. We have to keep our comms clear, okay?"

Nyrik said, "Comms?"

"Communications. Particularly, *combat* communications. So, don't roger me unless you mean *yes, message understood, I'll do it*."

Nyrik said, "Whatever you say, roger."

I sighed, and said, "Just *roger*, Nyrik."

"Roger," Nyrik said.

"Good."

Nyrik chuckled.

We heard the sounds of our force starting to arrive behind us.

"Glad you wasn't talking to me just then," Horm muttered.

"Huh?" I said. "Why?"

"Just roger, Nyrik? No thank you. Not my type."

"In your dreams," Nyrik said.

"Fuck off," Horm said.

Nyrik said, "You fuck off."

"No, *you* fuck off!"

"Guys," I said. "We're here to fight Ice Wights, not each other."

Nyrik, crouching beside me, dug me in the ribs. "Don't you worry about us, Daxx. Best mates, me and Horm. Aren't we, eh, Hormy-warmy, darling? Come on over, give us a nice wet kiss."

"Fuck off."

Nyrik chuckled. He clearly got a kick out of needling Horm. "Not roger off?"

"That too," Horm said. "Prat."

Our fighters had all gathered behind us. Orders were passed along the chain of command, and we filed forwards into the blackness of the cavern. Companies spread out to either side of me. When they were all in place, I gripped Shift, and felt her, *Well, here goes—best of luck to us...* Once again I cast Reveal Hidden Life, which showed that our forces also stretched from wall to wall of the cavern behind me. I couldn't see how deep the ranks of the Ice Wights ahead of us were, so I couldn't count them, but maybe we wouldn't be badly outnumbered.

Well, here goes, I thought.

I raised Shift and blasted several dazzling Area Glows up, and, for good measure, shot some Barkers and Screamers down into the cavern to wreak havoc overhead, and Fear them.

The Ice Wights, startled, looked up in panic at the bright lights above them, shuffled, cried out in alarm, and broke and ran.

With a roar, the Ice Orcs set off after them, some grabbing for the two-handed weapons at their backs, which meant that several wolves broke free and streaked ahead of them after the fleeing Ice Wights.

"Damn it!" I shouted, sending up a red flare. "Wait for the signal!"

The Ice Orcs stopped, but the half dozen or so wolves that had been released didn't. They charged after their prey at top speed, howling. The Ice Wights flowed down the slope away from us and disappeared into the mouth of the lower tunnel.

Silence fell.

We stood, listening, as the howls of the hunting wolves grew fainter—then turned to whimpers of fear and squeals, which were quickly cut off.

I cast Reveal Hidden Life again.

At the end of my cast's range, a few faint, red wraiths shrank into the distance and vanished.

I glanced at Shaman Sylmond.

She shook her head briefly. She had nothing.

Well, *now what*, I thought.

We had no idea what was ahead of us, so there was no point in trying to guess what there was down there. We had a choice. Turn around and go home—or *keep going forwards.*

We hadn't come all that way to quit without a fight.

On the other hand, what was that all about? The Ice Wights, crowded into the cavern, waiting for us, then turning tail and fleeing? On their own turf?

I'd Feared them, but Fearing only lasts for a few seconds. I'd have expected them to regroup and attack.

Scared of a few Glows and some noisy distractions?

I didn't think so.

They *wanted* us to follow them.

And those few wolves who had chased after them, howling with the joy of the hunt, but were now silent?

I turned to Sylmond, and said, "What do you think?"

She nodded and turned away. Facing forwards, she closed her eyes, and raised her staff. Its amethyst heartstone glowed purple. She breathed, in and out, long and slow, searching for an answer.

Eventually, she opened her eyes. "They did not fight us here," she said. "They may not fight us further down."

"And they might be luring us into a trap," I pointed out. "Whatever happened to those wolves, down there, might happen to us."

She nodded. "It might indeed. As it might not."

I looked down into the dark mouth of the tunnel ahead of us. "So, what do you suggest?"

She looked me in the eyes. "I suggest that you make the correct decision."

She wasn't being glib, I knew that. She was just pointing out that this was my decision to make. She'd told me all that she knew. The buck had to stop somewhere.

Still, it was an interesting point, I thought, as I mulled over our two options—*head home, or keep going forwards*.

If we turned back, we'd never know if we'd made the correct decision. Which we would if we kept going forwards. Even if it was the last thing we ever knew.

Yes, I thought. It seems like a choice, but it isn't one.

*Let's find out.*

I raised Shift and was about to pop up a single green Flare to signal the advance when there came a humming from ahead of us, a sound so deep that it was almost below the edge of hearing.

We listened, wondering what it was. The noise grew. It was a long, low rumble, as of something waking.

Something large.

The sound went on and on, growing louder, until the whole cavern was vibrating. I cast Reveal Hidden Life again, expecting to see an outline as huge as the sound that was coming from whatever creature was making it—but saw nothing.

The sound subsided and faded into silence.

Nothing for it, I thought.

I refreshed the Glows overhead, and cast up a green Flare.

We moved on down into the tunnel.

# 26

## The Book

The tunnel curved, and widened. Shapes were scattered on the ground ahead of us. The remains of our wolves lay in pools of their own blood. They had been torn apart and chewed on. A larger, moving form lay at the mouth of the tunnel: an Ice Wight, still clamped around a dying wolf, feeding on it, its body working like a pump as it drained the last drops of blood from its prey.

It turned to look up at us, its eyes and jaws red. Grell smashed its skull in. Fjernmond knelt down and tended to his wolf. It struggled back to consciousness, and, at last, knew him. It smelled his hand, and licked it. The wolf's tail rose, weakly, and fell, twice. Its eyes closed, and it died.

We emerged into another cavern, the lowest level. Its floor was pitted with small, bubbling pools. The liquid in them was not water but a thick, gray sludge. Mist hung over their surfaces.

The Ice Pits.

I cast up several Glows and the cavern filled with light. I did not need to cast Reveal Hidden Life.

Beyond the Ice Pits lay a lake. Beside it, against the high wall that was the back of the cavern, a mass of Ice Wights waited, facing us. There were far more of them than us.

We were good in a fight, I knew that. And we had the Ice Orcs and their wolves with us. But we were hugely outnumbered. I could Incinerate, or Blast, or Shockfield from below, or pour down Hellfire from above, but they were too many. If they attacked, more than enough of them would get through to overrun us. I did not want to imagine that overrunning. I'd just seen one Ice Wight clamped onto the neck of one of our wolves. I'd heard the sounds of them feeding on the herds that we'd driven up to the stockade.

That was not the way I wanted to go.

I remembered what Gundur had told us.

*They crave the warmth.*

We were warm. There was a mass of us. Gundur had also said that they could smell us from afar.

This close to us, the smell of our warm blood must have been unbearable for them.

So why weren't they attacking? Why weren't they swarming all over us, to get at our warmth? Wouldn't it be obvious to them that we were there for the taking?

Perhaps not. Perhaps they didn't think like that.

But what predators don't know when to attack, when the odds are in their favor? It is instinct. Charge, or run away. They were doing neither.

Therefore …

…instinct didn't come into it.

Something else was going on.

*What* something else?

I looked for guidance to Sylmond, and to Chief Izmond, and Grell and Qrysta, and Nyrik and Horm. I got nothing back from any of them. They had no more idea than I did. I looked around the cavern, with its mist-covered, bubbling Ice Pools, and its gray, sludge-filled lake stretching off into the distance. I got nothing there either.

I approached the nearest Ice Pool. Its surface, I saw, was stirring, as if something was moving beneath it. The other little pools around it were behaving the same way. Ripples came and went, and stilled. Then thick, sticky bubbles arose, forming on their surfaces, swelling—and, eventually, bursting, releasing a sour, noxious smell. The pools plopped, and burped. There was something in them, though whether it was volcanic gas leaking up from beneath, or something living, I could not tell.

As I watched, a curling, pale shape broke the surface and rolled slowly forwards, before sinking back down again.

Something living, then. Something that almost filled the entire pool, and also seemed to have no head or tail. Pale shapes rose, and rolled, and sank again in the other pools. I tried to think what they, and this strange layout of small pools, reminded me of. There seemed to be only room for one of each creature in each pool.

Then I realized.

Grubs. Growing in cells. Being nourished by what those cells contained.

I knelt down and dipped a finger into the greasy liquid in the nearest pool.

I drew it across the back of my hand.

After a moment, I felt the warmth evaporating from the skin where I had smeared it.

*Ice Balm.*

I wiped it off quickly. That was the last thing I needed on me, in air this cold.

Well, we knew that these Ice Pits were where the Ice Balm came from. Now we knew exactly where it was found, and harvested—and now we also had some idea of what else was in these pools.

I beckoned Chief Izmond over. When she realized what the pools contained, she waved for the Orcs to bring the six earthenware jars over. They filled them quickly and set off at a run back up the tunnel.

So, if Ice Balm was some kind of nourishment, the equivalent for these grubs of honey, or royal jelly, what creatures had gathered it for them? And what would those larval forms, growing in these pools, hatch into?

It could be anything. Caterpillars become moths. Grubs become insects. I had a sudden, nightmare vision of all these pools spewing forth scaly things with teeth and claws and stingers, all at once, a mass of them converging on us.

There was no sign of anything happening, let alone that. But, if it did, we'd just have to run like hell.

I realized that I was ignoring the elephant in the room—or, more accurately, in the cavern. Surely the important question was: What kind of queen had laid her eggs in these spawning pools? And where was she?

*Elephant in the cavern,* I thought. She was probably going to be large.

I could not tell if there were further tunnels in the wall beyond the horde of Ice Wights. Were they massed in front of the queen's lair? Ready to take a stand, to keep us out, to protect her?

Then—why hadn't they taken a stand earlier, before we found out where she was?

I knelt by the nearest Ice Pit and looked down into it, waiting for another pale shape to roll to the surface. When one did, I saw that its shell, or carapace, was faintly translucent. There was a shape within its shape. Something was in there, protected, growing. When it surfaced again, I knew it for what it was. A larva. An embryo. Something that would hatch and become an Ice Wight. Neither human nor animal, but a merging of both. This, then, was a nursery. A breeding chamber.

I stood up, and backed away, and looked around. Lake. A mass of Ice Wights, jostling against the cavern wall. Us.

"What are you thinking, Daxxie?" Qrysta said, quietly.

I said, "I'm thinking they want us here."

"Any idea why?"

"So we can see this?" I suggested. "Their nursery. Pools full of Ice Balm, each with a grub growing in it."

"They've never let anyone see it before," she pointed out.

"Maybe they thought they couldn't stop us," I said. "There's never been a force this size down here before to confront them."

Grell said, "Don't forget that growl we heard."

"I haven't," I replied.

No one said anything, because none of us could think what to say.

We looked at the spawning pools, at the lake, at the waiting mass of Ice Wights, at each other.

Standoff.

Clearly, though, it was our move. And it was up to me to make it.

I'd never been faced with a situation like this before. I was used to heading into delves and fighting foes on the way down, and confronting an End Boss or two, and whatever additional forces they summoned to unleash on us. Then it was just tactics. Our battle skills against theirs. What we had here wasn't a fight. We didn't need tactics. We needed a strategy.

A solution.

Yes, I thought, but: What is the problem? What is the puzzle that needs solving?

Attack the Ice Wights, because we can't think of anything else? When they don't seem to want to fight, and get their teeth into our longed-for warmth?

*What wasn't I seeing?*

Can't see without light, I thought, and popped up Glows everywhere I could send them—above, ahead, to either side. They lit up the pools, and the cavern, and the lake—in which, something glinted.

I threw more Glows across in its direction. I strained to see. My Glows illuminated a small, dark shape on the lake's surface. Something was standing up on it.

I beckoned to Nyrik, who trotted over. His Woods Kin eyes were sharper than mine.

I said, "What do you see?"

He squinted, peering into the distance. "Island," he said. "Something on it."

"Any idea what?"

He peered. I threw more light in that direction. "Stand."

I said, "What?"

"Like one of them things you put a book on, so you can read to people."

"Lectern?"

"Is that what you call it? Yeah. A stand with a book on it."

A book.

Books contain information. Information was exactly what I needed.

How to get at it, though? I wasn't about to swim through that chilling gray sludge. I'd be dead before I'd gone a yard.

On the other hand ...

I looked back at Jess and she joined us. "I need you to fly me over there."

"Okay." She unhitched her broomstick from her back. "Hop on and Levitate us."

I did. We rose into the cold air. Jess ferried me over to the island. It was tiny, no larger than a table. At its center was a book on a lectern.

We dismounted.

The book was large, and thick, and bound in black. On it, in dark red letters, was one word.

*Warning.*

I heard Jess, beside me, suck in her breath sharply.

Did I want to read it? No. Did I *not* want to? Yes.

Could I get Jess to fly me back to shore? Yes.

Would that answer anything? No.

I reached for the book, and opened it.

It wasn't a book. It was a box that just looked like one. A box that was empty.

I thought, looking down into it, *Well, what's the point of that?*

I soon found out. The box emitted an earsplitting screech. Jess and I covered our ears and stared at each other in shock. Her eyes were screwed up in pain. The screech continued, giving no sign of letting up. Then I saw her eyes grow round. She was looking at something behind me. I turned to see a monstrous worm rearing out of the lake, higher and higher, segment after segment of it writhing upwards.

I cast Shields on us, and threw up another Glow, so that I could see what the hell the thing was. It was corpse white, with small pink eyes, and a long, pointed head—which it aimed down towards me. It opened wide and was on me before I could do more than fire off a Flameball, which merely lodged in its maw and fizzled out in the wet folds of its throat.

Then I was inside it and in the dark. I heard Jess's scream suddenly cut off as the worm's mouth closed. I was thrown from side to side as the creature changed course. It arced back into the lake. All sound ceased, except for a low, constant growling that vibrated all around me. Down and down we went, my protective green bubble shrinking ever closer as the increasing pressure crushed it around me.

I raised Shift, intending to see if I could blast the worm apart, but her warning was instantaneous. *Don't even think about it! You wouldn't survive, Daxx! You'd freeze solid and sink!*

She was right. Shield of Mending and Protection around me or not, I'd just sink to the bottom. Dispel the Shield and try to swim through that icy sludge? No chance. I'd never make it to the surface. I looked at the long rows of large teeth that surrounded me, clenched together. One flick of her tongue, one crunch of her jaws, and I'd be pulped. I was assuming this worm was a she—that she was the queen that had laid her eggs in the spawning pools. I was also assuming that the crunching would begin any time she wanted her nice, warm meal.

I racked my brain to think of a plan of action. I knew that I needed something fast, before I became worm food. I went through every skill that I had, looking for anything that might help me. My ears popped as we went deeper and deeper. I held my nose and blew into it, to equalize the pressure inside them. The air inside the bubble that was my Shield was getting staler with each breath that I took. Suffocation; drowning; being mashed by those giant teeth—each of those deaths seemed likely, and imminent.

The inside of the worm's throat bulged as she twisted her way into the depths. I kept my eye on her teeth, waiting for them to open, which they would have to do if she wanted to start chewing on me. Shift, I could feel, was also out of ideas. *Might as well take her with us*, she suggested.

*Yes*, I thought. *If we're finished, this worm is going too.* I would max out my Shields, blow the worm apart with my best shots, hit myself with Levitate, and hope that it would work under this lake of Ice Balm. And that I would, by some miracle, rise to the surface before I ran out of air. *That would be nice*, Shift agreed sardonically.

The air grew staler. My breathing grew shallower, and faster. I did not have long before I suffocated. I wondered why she wasn't grinding me into pulp already. She was waiting for—what? A nice, quiet spot where she could rest up and have a leisurely meal?

Well, how could I know what she thought, or was doing? All I knew was that I didn't have much longer. Cold sweat was running down my face and my back. Every breath that I inhaled held less oxygen than the one before it. I could feel my concentration drifting. I was losing my grip. I raised Shift, ready to end it all, my ears squealing, as the pressure inside them changed again, when her urgent warning stopped me. *Wait, Daxx! We're heading up ...*

I couldn't think straight. I cast Heals on myself, but I wasn't injured. I didn't need healing. I needed air. I choked, and swallowed, and felt a bump, and then a lurch, and then a rush of air as the worm opened her mouth and belched. She spat me out in my green Shield, which somersaulted through the air and bounced me across a shore of gray sand, until it hit something and burst.

Cold air swirled around me.

I gasped, and inhaled, and rolled to a halt. Winded and befuddled as I was, I knew that I needed to gather my wits about me for whatever else was coming. The damn thing was still behind me. I had to deal with that first. I scrambled to my feet and turned to face it, raising Shift in order to attack, my chest heaving for air.

The Ice Worm was already sinking back into the smoking, cold gray sludge.

I stood there, panting, watching her go. No need to launch attacks at her, then.

The last thing I wanted was to enrage her, and have her change her mind, and come back after me. Instead, I popped up Glows, so that I could see where I was.

I was standing on dark sand, in the mouth of another tunnel, that led up and away into the distance. The thing that I'd hit, when the worm belched me out, was another lectern. On it was another book.

Both book and lectern were identical to those on the island where Jess had flown me. Same black cover. Same one word on it.

*Warning.*

I hesitated. I'd opened the book on the island and had been attacked by the Ice Worm. I didn't want that happening again.

Only … how could I not open this book? How could I walk on, and up, and towards whatever was waiting for me up there, without knowing what I hadn't read and learned?

And anyway, was I right about what had happened before? Had I really been attacked by the Ice Worm as it had felt like? After all, she hadn't killed me and eaten me, as a predator would have done. Why not? What was I not seeing?

The Ice Worm had taken me and brought me here.

Perhaps it had been summoned by my opening the book?

As always, I thought, I needed information. I needed to know the warning that this book contained. I wouldn't get anywhere just standing there and speculating.

Hoping for the best, I reached out and opened it. No alarm screamed. It was not an empty shell. It was a real book, with real pages.

I leaned in, and began to read.

*This is the record of my discoveries, and of the results of my life's work. I have written them here in the hope that this volume will one day become known to the Conclave of the Guild of the Arcane Arts, and will serve as both a source of knowledge and a warning. I acknowledge that, in my arrogance, I chose to explore ways that are forbidden. I admit my transgressions. They have cost me a price that I pray to all the gods no other mage will ever have to pay. My suffering will be long, if not endless. I know that now. I accept it. If it is to end, it will be because this book has been found, and some fellow mage will take my warning to the Conclave, and I will at last know the release of oblivion.*

*These are the spells that I have cast. They hold me here, waiting, embodied as I am in a monstrosity. I will wait, if necessary forever, because what I have done must be known, so that no one is ever so foolish as to do it again. Though I am lost, all is not lost. What I have learned is recorded here. I sought to save and to serve. I sought life, for those who depended on me, and who faced death. Instead, I live a death everlasting. I pray that you, who find this, will learn from my mistakes, and in turn will pray for me.*

I turned the page, and, before I had drawn it back, it overtook me. No longer was there a page in front of me, or a book, but a scene, which pulled me into it. I was walking into a chamber, its walls stone, its roof thatch above dark wood beams, a log fire burning in the hearth.

Beside it, at a long table, an elderly mage was waiting for me, seated on a bench. He looked up at me as I approached, and smiled. "Welcome," he said. "Please, take a seat."

I sat opposite him.

"My name is Tolmeth," he continued. "Or, rather, was. Yours does not matter. I cannot hear you, or see you, because I am long gone," he said. "Not dead, but not here. So there is no need to say anything, or to ask questions, because I can neither hear nor reply. What you will see now is all that I have left. I have left it for you. If you have had the skill to get yourself here, you may have the skill to take this knowledge with you. Use what I have found. I was wrong. Let that be learned."

He made a gesture in the air. "Watch," he said.

The scene around us merged into another one. I saw a harsh winter, starved people hunched against a snowstorm, laden down with burdens, driving their beasts into a stockade behind high walls of felled trees. I sensed their exhaustion, their despair.

"When the Ice Time came," the mage's voice said, as I witnessed the unfolding tale, "we faced annihilation as so many in this world did. My family, my household, our dependents. They relied on me, all of them. They believed that I had the knowledge to protect them, that I would guide them through the hardships that lay ahead. I believed that too.

"I was both right, and wrong.

"I had long worked with the dead, in ways that are forbidden—which is why we had come here, to the far north, where there was no one to tell me what I could or could not do. In another land I would have been confronted, and tried by my peers, and found guilty

330

of abominations and put to death. The Guild has no tolerance for such as me. But in those bleak years it seemed that my work could be the saving of us. I had noticed how ice preserved the dead. Could it, I wondered, be used to preserve the living? In the end, after much trial and error, and much suffering for my subjects, I found the answer.

"It is both yes and no.

"You will no doubt have heard of how Orcs are the merging of men and Ogres. Just as Orcs are the result of the Ice Time, so are Ice Wights. They live, but they live like the dead. They are cold, and putrid—and they are both less and more than human. This is the result of my work. They walk like men, and resemble men in appearance, to an extent. But they do not breed like men. It was not the most desirable of outcomes. But those were desperate times, that called for desperate measures. We survived. You may not think it much of a life, but it is all that we have.

"Our hunters went out into the wilds, more in hope than expectation. The herds of game had vanished. None came back with meat. Starvation threatened. Our supplies dwindled; but, one day, two of them returned with news. They had found a cave. They had not dared to explore far into it, but they had seen how it was large enough to be a refuge, for all of us, men and beasts alike.

"More of my people died on our way here. Each death was a knife to my heart. My wife and two of our children perished, among so many others. Few of us survived to reach this shelter. And now we are many. We are many because of what I did. It saved us, and doomed us. I left this life with so many regrets. I would not do again what I have done.

"You will see it all, in the pages of this book. It is a tale that ends badly—not just for my people, but for me. For me, most of all. They are born, and live, and die, and return whence they came; but I remain, neither living nor dead, nothing more than a memory that passes down the generations, queen to queen, Ice Worm to Ice Worm. I live on in them, in the hope that you will come and bring an end to my part in this story. It is all written in my book. It will take time to study, and to learn what became of us, and of me. Take it with you. Pass it on to the Conclave.

"What I discovered, what I did, could destroy us all. May that never happen. May minds wiser than mine see this, and know this, and be forewarned, so that when another such as I comes to challenge them,

331

they will have the knowledge to defeat that threat. That is the only hope I have for my vindication. You may be at peace now, but peace is fragile. Ambition is ruthless. If there is one thing I know, it is that such as I always come, to challenge the old order.

"In short, mage: We explored these caverns, and came to the lair of the Ice Worm. My research on her is all there, in the pages of my book. At last, it seemed to me, the hidden meaning that I had been seeking in my work was revealed to me. Ice, that preserved the dead, could preserve the living—for she lived in ice, *was* ice, was incomparably strong, where we were weak. She was suited to her world, where we were lost in it."

He paused, and shook his head, and sighed.

"I Bound myself to her. Where there is a Binding, there can be an Unbinding. When you take this book, it will begin. I implore the sages of the Conclave to study it to its fullest. It will take time; but time is something that you, now, do not have. You must leave this accursed place while you still can. When the Unbinding is complete, my grip on her will no longer hold. I am her, and she is me, now, but there is little left of me after all these ages, and she is the stronger. My presence confuses her, distracts her. I will hold her for as long as I can. I hope that is time enough for you to escape. Without her, I will die. I long for that. But without me, she will release our children, and they will hunt you up all the tunnels of this refuge and kill you and feed on you—and, if you are not alone, kill and feed on all who are here with you.

"Leave. Leave now. You have freed me, mage, from a life-in-death that is insufferable. I owe you not just my thanks, for this blessed release, but also the chance to escape. My children will live on, in their wretched form, in this wretched land. When their lives end, they return, and stand for her at the broodlake's edge, to wait for her to emerge and consume them. And so they feed her and become her seed. The eggs are laid. The grubs are fed, and hatch. The cycle turns. At last, I can leave it. Take the book, go up, always turning to the right. Gather your companions, if you have any, and flee. My hold over our children will weaken, just as that of any parent must do."

The vision faded.

I took the book from the lectern and ran up the tunnel. A booming, low growl, as of some sleeping creature struggling in its sleep, echoed up out of the lake behind me. As I ran, I raised Shift and Absorbed everything that the book contained into Marnie's Infinite Notebook, inside my jerkin. Better to have a backup copy, I thought, than not. I could feel my staff's interest as she studied and copied Tolmeth's archive. I cast up more Glows, refreshed my stamina, and ran like hell. The tunnel branched, again, and again. I took the branch to the right every time. Each led upwards. At last I saw the mouth of the tunnel ahead of me. I reached it, and stopped, and looked down.

Far below me, a huge crowd of Ice Wights heaved against an invisible barrier.

A barrier, I thought, that was weakening and would not hold for long.

Facing them, beyond the spawning pools, our forces waited.

I looked at the drop in front of me. There was no way down. No handholds. I had no rope.

I could not possibly jump. The fall would kill me—or, if it did not, the Ice Wights would swarm all over me.

I could not fly.

But Jess could.

I lit myself up as brightly as I could with Glows, so that my friends far below could see me.

I threw up three orange Flares, then three greens, then three more oranges.

Qrysta and Grell should be able to work that out, from the bastardized "Morse" code we'd memorized, so that we could communicate with Oller via the Link of Impartment. *Orange, hot, equals dot. Green therefore means dash.*

SOS.

The mass of Ice Wights below me was stirring like a hornet's nest. *He can't hold them for long*, I knew. We needed to get out of there. While I waited, I fired down some Whizzbangs into the Ice Wights, to keep them distracted.

Far below me, I saw three answering, weaker Glows rising above our force.

Shaman Sylmond was responding in kind, as best she could.

They'd seen me.

I peered down into the darkness, searching for Jess.

I saw no movement in the air below, between me and my companions.

The Ice Wights were becoming more and more restless. I could hear them croaking and hissing, working themselves up to break through and attack.

Out of nowhere, Jess appeared beside me, making me jump. "Sylmond knew you weren't dead," she said, turning her broomstick beside me. "We all saw that thing swallow you, but she told us to wait. What happened?"

I got on behind her, and Levitated us. "I'll tell you later," I said. "We have to get out of here."

# 27

## Run Like Hell

Grell and Qrysta and I had been in combat any number of times, back in our previous lives. The better we'd become, the more times we'd won, and the fewer times our avatars had died and we'd had to re-spawn somewhere safe, where we could recover and figure out what we'd done wrong. Then we'd discuss what we'd learned, and rethink our approach, and try again, with better skills and upgraded gear. That was then. This was now.

On this new rock there was no respawning. There was only sur-vival: survive by winning, or survive by not losing. Never, in all our campaigns together, had we fought a strategic retreat like the one we fought that day in the Ice Pits. We were outnumbered. We were over-powered. We had allies—good allies—but they were up-and-at-'em Orcs. Orcs don't retreat. Orcs stand their ground and fight till they drop. Long after other fighters are exhausted, Orcs are still roaring and swinging, and swearing, and singing.

But even Orcs can be overwhelmed by sheer force of numbers. And when those numbers are Ice Wights, no longer restrained by some invisible hand from tearing into our warm flesh for the warm blood that they long for—well, there's no point standing and swinging if you want to live. Before you knew it, there'd be a dozen of the things clamped onto you, feeding, and you'd freeze under their cold grasp, helpless, until you were drained and dead.

The Ice Orcs didn't know what was coming. All they saw was their ancient foes and a chance to finish them off. I knew that we could never finish them off. I knew what was coming, from what Tolmeth had told me. I wanted us to live.

I didn't have time to explain. Jess landed her broomstick by Chief Izmond and I jumped off. "We need to leave, *now*."

Chief Izmond, of course, began, "What are you—"

"*Later*, Chief!" I cut her off. "We don't have time! We have to run for our lives or we're all dead. They're held back for the time being, but they'll break free any moment. When that happens, we all have to turn and face them and make a fighting retreat."

"Retreat?!" she began again, insulted, and I had to shout.

"You want a fight? It's coming! You want to live? *Do as I say!*"

Everyone, I knew, could hear me.

"You'll be killing as many of these bastards as you could ever want, any moment now, because they'll be all over us," I said, "but if you want to live, and you want your people to live, *do as I tell you!* Obey my signals, and if we're lucky we'll make it to the surface. I'll stay here until the spell that is holding them back wears off and they break free. When that happens, I'll lay down traps that will slow them, and then I'll catch up with you. Our only hope is to make it to the open and get into the sleds."

I gave that a moment to sink in, then hurried on.

"When you see my flare, stop and turn and form up. Archers, have fire arrows lit and on the string—you too, Jess. We'll burn as many as we can, then it'll be hand-to-hand fighting—fighting for our lives, on the back foot. There's *no second chance at this!* They're thousands, we're not, but they're a rabble and we're an army. We've got discipline, we've got range attacks, we've got magic, Heals and Damages, all of which means we might just have a chance. But only if we work together. Everyone got that?"

Around us, Ice Orcs were staring at me, and at Chief Izmond, unsure. She nodded.

"Good," I said. "Now, run! *Run like hell!*"

They did.

I backed up past the spawning pools to the tunnel's mouth, watching the Ice Wights. I could see the mass of them straining against the invisible barrier that held them back, struggling to break through.

They did so in less than a minute and poured towards me, hissing and screeching.

I threw every slowing attack I could think of at the ground between us: Flamefields, Earthgrips, Ice Traps, Consuming Slimes, Shockwaves. I didn't wait to see how they worked. I turned and ran, casting a Speedburst over myself. I was through that tunnel and the cavern beyond it in no time. When I saw Shaman Sylmond's Glows in the air ahead of me, in the next cavern, I fired a yellow Flare through them. The jogging mass of Ice Orcs stopped and turned, and fanned out across the cavern, facing down into its depths. We waited, in silence, watching the dark mouth of the tunnel below us.

Sylmond's Glows hovered above it.

I was letting Shift rest, to gather her power for the assault that was about to come. Privately, I let her know: *We're going to need everything you've got, my friend.*

Her reply was a wary, *No question about that …*

Something large pushed up beside me. I glanced down to see Nostë. The presence of the huge ice wolf gave me heart. I heard his low growl as shapes moved in the shadows—and then, with a rattling of claws on the tunnel's floor, a horde of the things burst out of the darkness, desperate to feed on us. I fired up a green Flare. The archers loosed their fire arrows. I laid down Flamefields, and Earthgrips, and sent Shockwaves into the Ice Wights, knocking them back into each other and into a quagmire of Consuming Slimes that they could not escape. Sylmond and I blew in every fire-based attack that we had in our arsenal. The Ice Wights struggled, and shrieked, and burst into flame, and died—and kept on coming, wave after wave of them, always more and more and more.

The other wolves, who should have been one of our best weapons, proved to be our greatest liability. They had no idea how to obey orders, or to understand tactics. They only saw enemies. They only wanted to attack, and sink their teeth into their foes. When one broke free, it would charge, and kill, and be overwhelmed, and die. Its handler might run after it, and meet the same fate. We did not need to kill in ones and twos. We needed to survive, and get to the surface. To do that, we needed all our warriors fighting, not wrangling war-maddened wolves.

*They'll get us all killed,* I thought.

I shouted at Sylmond, "I need Fjernmond here. Now!"

337

She nodded, and hurried off to find him.

In half a minute he was at my side and I explained what I needed him to do.

He ran back up the cavern, gathering the other wolf wranglers on his way. I turned my attention back to the mayhem below us—a mayhem that was getting ever closer. Ice Wights were dying by the dozen, on fire, blown apart by my casts or Sylmond's, but the horde kept on coming.

*Soldier ants*, I thought, remembering the grubs that their larvae resembled. Relentless. Not even Grell in his Kinfolk plate armor could stride forward into that swarm and survive. He was waiting beside me, Kinell in his hands, ready to take the fight to the enemy when I gave him the signal. I wasn't going to do that. It would be sending him to his death. We needed to keep the brutes as far away from us as possible.

They got nearer and nearer, second after second. We poured fire and fury into them. They kept coming. We could see their faces, mouths wide, teeth bared, eyes wild and ravenous. I kept glancing back up behind me for Fjernmond's signal. At last it came. The wolves were in harness. I aimed Shift back at them and Feared them. They ran, yelping with terror, dragging their handlers after them. Only Nostë stayed, glued to my side, ready to kill anything that came for me.

At least some of us will be safe, I thought. They'll make it to the surface and hitch the wolves to their sleds. And if the Ice Wights overwhelmed us, and poured out of the cave's mouth, those few survivors would run like hell for Isvellir. Which would mean that not all of us were going to die down here in the Ice Pits.

I felt a sense of relief as I turned back to the fight. We could well lose this battle, but some of us would live to fight another day.

My sense of relief didn't last long. Unlike the fight. That lasted far longer than I could have imagined. Every yard that we took—backing up, facing our foe—was hard fought. With another hundred mages, or another thousand fire archers, it would have been easy. We could have held them off, and anchored them down, and blown them apart. We were two mages, one of us a novice, and a few dozen archers. Our archers ran out of arrows. Our staffs exhausted their power. I had to balance my Heals with casting raps and barriers, and the occasional Area of Effect attack, which finished off any of our foes that stumbled into them.

Whirlwinds worked well in those enclosed spaces, each carrying off several Ice Wights and smashing them against the roof of the cavern. And then another wave would be on us, and we'd be fighting toe-to-toe, hand to hand, our blades against their teeth and claws. Again and again Grell was at the center of the action, swinging Kinell around him and splattering Ice Wights to pieces, throwing them in every direction. Other Ice Orcs stood shoulder to shoulder with him, battering and hacking. Nyrik and Horm worked in the shadows, slashing and slicing at enemy legs and dropping them for Orc warhammers to finish off. Little Guy tore through the mob of Ice Wights, a brown blur in his speed-imbued niblun battle leathers. Shift and I hardly had time to breathe as we cast Shields and Heals. Sooner or later she would be drained, and I'd nod at Sylmond beside me, who would fire up a yellow Flare, and the fighting retreat would start once more.

Grell and our surviving warriors would fall back. I'd paste the ground with every slowing and trapping Area of Effect I could manage. We'd all run, or rather stagger, back up the slope, through the next tunnel, and into the next cavern—where we'd form the line, and the chaos and mayhem and murder would start all over again.

The time that we had to recover between each clash became shorter and shorter. Sylmond, I could see, was limping and breathing hard. She was, I remembered, far older than she looked—and though she was only a low-level caster, we could not afford to lose her. We needed all the Heals we could get. Qrysta caught my eye, as she so often did in combat. We had fought together so often that we could almost think for each other. "Protect the shaman!" I shouted. She nodded, and a moment later was at Sylmond's side, her twin blades working tirelessly. I could see that Sylmond's staff was being drained of power sooner and sooner, as was Shift. I used every one of Marnie's magic boosting potions that I had. Too bad if I was going to need them later. If I didn't survive this, there would be no later.

More times than I could count, the pattern repeated itself. I'd Trap, and Incinerate, and we'd retreat, backwards, exhausted, up and up, never seeming to get anywhere but into another damned cavern, into which the Ice Wights poured once my Traps had worn off and they'd struggled free. Then they'd charge us, again, and again, and again. And I would cast Area Heal Alls, and Shields of Mending, and they would die by the dozens, and we'd die by ones and twos, and our numbers shrank.

If we hadn't been Orcs, I doubt we'd have made it to the surface. I refreshed their Stamina as often as I could, but if they'd needed it as much as the rest of us did, Shift would have been empty long before we saw the light of day over our shoulders behind us. Seeing it, we all got a last burst of energy from the hope that it gave us. We broke ranks and ran, stumbling out of the cave's mouth, into the driving snow, the Ice Wights streaming after us, then struggling and shrieking as they were held in the last Traps that I managed to throw at them. I looked around, to see who had made it—and then, from the black mouth of the Ice Pits, a shapeless form emerged, stumbling towards us, Ice Wights clinging to its back and legs—

Nostë. Why wasn't he savaging them with his great teeth, as I had seen him do in the Ice Pits, and tearing them off him? There was, I saw as I raised Shift to blast the Ice Wights off him, something in his mouth.

Something small, and hairy, and still.

Shift's last shred of power blew the Ice Wights away as I hurried over to Nostë and half carried, half dragged him back to the sled, where Grell reached out and hauled him and his sad little bundle aboard. I tumbled in after them, the sled already running. Qrysta found my hand, and helped me to upright myself. The shrieks of the Ice Wights faded behind us. I stared back as they disappeared into the blizzard, scarcely believing that we'd survived.

Beside me, Grell said, quietly, "Mate …"

Nostë was licking at the limp, bloody mess that was all that was left of Little Guy.

When we made it back to the refuge we were too exhausted to count the cost. We knew it would be bad. The gates were barred, and the wolves fed and settled. Sylmond and I tended to the wounded. The bites and scratches from the Ice Wights were deep and cruel.

Jess never left our side, watching everything we did. Sylmond noticed, and handed her bandages, with which Jess bound wounds as neatly as Sylmond. Nyrik and Qrysta brought us food, which we ate as we worked on the wounded. Horm appeared beside me with his flask of Careful Juice. "You need a nip of this, mate," he said. I took a mouthful, and got a recharge of energy that kept me going longer than I'd have thought possible. Horm handed the flask to Sylmond, and I heard her grunt as she swallowed.

340

It was a long, hard night. We saved some of the injured, but too many died. The wounds that the Ice Wights had inflicted on them festered quickly. The rot soon spread, and more often than not was fatal. Over the years that we'd run together, I'd seen Grell take any number of brutal batterings. This one had been as bad as any. He hadn't actually been bitten, thanks to his kinskin plate armor, but he'd been slammed around inside it, and was covered in bruises as well as exhausted. Eventually, after my Heals had revived him, he hauled himself upright, and shambled off to find a place among the Ice Orcs he'd fought alongside. They hardly said a word to each other as they ate and drank.

Little Guy had lain still and unmoving all the way back to the refuge, warm in a green Orb of Mending—but, as far as Shift and I could tell, showing no sign of life. I dreaded having to give the awful news to Oller. I wondered how he was getting on in Sarmen. Was he safe? Had he learned anything? I glanced at my Link of Impartment, wondering when he'd let me know. I couldn't risk contacting him to ask and having his band light up unexpectedly, in a dangerous land. That might get him noticed.

Grell appeared at my side and held out something towards me. "Just in case," he said.

It was a sausage.

I put it down on Little Guy's blanket, by his nose. He didn't react. That, we both felt, was finally that.

By the time that we'd done all that we could for the wounded we were drained.

I stretched out in a sled, under a mound of furs, and slept like the dead, Little Guy beside me. When I woke the next morning, the sausage was gone. Little Guy was fast asleep, his breathing slow and deep. I felt a rush of relief as I reached out to stroke his scruffy head. His legs twitched in response. Shift was as surprised, and pleased, as I was. Perhaps, we thought, there was some curative power in his niblun battle leathers. However it had come about, seeing Little Guy alive after all filled me with hope. We may have taken a mauling in the Ice Pits, but we'd lived to fight another day.

The butcher's bill was brutal. We'd lost half of our warriors. We'd lost a third of our wolves. In exchange for those lives, we'd gained a book, six jars of Ice Balm, and some knowledge of the Ice Wights—how they'd originated, and what they were. The Ice Orcs kept glancing up at the sky. They didn't like the look of the weather that was coming.

A cold wind was whipping around the courtyard as Chief Izmond addressed us all. "We have lost our kin," she said, "and we lost the battle, but we didn't lose the war. We would have been wiped out without our friends from the south. This was not their fight. We asked them to come with us into the Ice Pits. They did so to help us. Our losses are on us, not on them. We will be forever grateful." She stopped.

Around us, the Ice Orcs fidgeted, and grunted acknowledgement. No one feels good after a defeat.

"They have a quest to complete," Chief Izmond continued. "So they're going on, and we're going home; but they will always be honored guests in Isvellir."

The Ice Orcs managed a ragged cheer.

We appreciated it. We'd been through hell together.

Chief Izmond stepped aside, so that I could address them.

I did not know what to say. I knew I had to say something. Every word that came to mind sounded insincere, or glib. They didn't deserve any of that. They deserved the truth.

We hadn't won. There was no point in pretending that this was anything but a defeat. We'd been routed. They knew that, and I knew that.

They waited. The words came hard.

All I could think of to say was, "We'd have died out on the Ice Plains if it hadn't been for you. We'd have died in the Ice Pits if you hadn't fought so well."

I looked around at their strained faces. Most of them looked down, or away. We'd survived, but we'd lost. That was all I had. I had to do better than that. For their sakes, more than mine.

"We owe you our lives," I said. "We'll never forget that."

That seemed to land. I saw nods, and heard grunts of agreement, but no one wanted to look anyone else in the eye. Yes, we were still alive, but we'd taken a hammering.

Grell pushed past me and stood before the dejected crowd. "Mates," he said, "I'm not going to lie. We all know we lost. I'm not going to pretend any different. We lost friends. You lost kin. It was a shit show, no two ways about it. And I've been in more than a few shit shows before, so I know what I'm talking about. That was as bad as any. But you know what? We weren't wiped out. We could easily have been. By all rights we should have been. A hundred odd of us, against thousands of them? Just Daxx and Sylmond to heal us? If we'd known what we were up against beforehand, we'd never have gone in there, not in a million years. By rights we should all be lying dead down there.

"But we're not. And we're not because of you. So, yeah, this hurts. It hurts like hell—of course it does, there's no way it couldn't. But I just want to tell you this." He looked from face to face of the crowd in front of him. Their heads had been downcast before. Now they were all raised, and looking up him, wanting to hear what he was saying. "It was an honor to fight alongside you. Every single damn one of you. And I'll be telling of the Ice Orcs, and how we made our stand, and fought our way out of the Ice Pits, and how if it hadn't been for you, I wouldn't have lived to be telling the tale."

We left quickly, the skies to the west thickening by the minute. We all knew that the Ice Wights would be hunting us, looking for stragglers. If the whiteout came down, they'd be in their element. We needed to get to where we were going, and fast. The sleds from the outlying clans headed out for their strongholds. Six warriors were left to garrison the refuge, with eight wolves to tow their sled. They closed and barred the gates behind us as we left, four sleds turning west for Isvellir, Fjernmond driving ours east and north for Ogretzk.

Our goodbyes had been brief. We hoped, and the Ice Orcs expected, that we'd be returning that way, via Isvellir, because what other way was there, back to the south? Sylmond offered to take care of Tolmeth's *Warning* book for me, if I didn't want to be burdened with it. Everything in it had been Absorbed into the Infinite Notebook that Marnie had given me, so I handed the book itself to her, with thanks. I told her that I looked forward to discussing its contents with her on my return to Isvellir. I didn't tell her that I was far from sure I'd be seeing her again.

The storm that was bearing down was coming out of the west—a problem for the others, who were heading back into the teeth of it, but less so for us, as we were running ahead of it. Fjernmond thought we'd reach Ogretzk before the worst of it hit. Even so, he kept looking back, over his shoulder, at the darkening sky behind him, and drove the wolves hard. Not that they minded. They only minded when he steadied them, so that they didn't take a downslope too fast, or when he needed to steer them through patches of trees. Then, as always, they would look back, puzzled, tongues lolling, as if to tell him to stop that nonsense, and let them have their heads.

Nostë was on lead, front left. My eyes kept returning to his arched, black-haired, rolling back as he ran, straining at his harness. After about four hours of hard running, Fjernmond reined the wolves in, and halted. We got out to stretch our legs while he fed them. Nostë inspected Little Guy thoroughly as he shared their food, checking him over for damage. Their tails wagged. Our tough little mutt was, clearly, on the mend.

I strolled among them, scratching heads and pulling ears. They gathered as close to me as they could. It was a pleasure to stroke them, to watch them crunch mouthfuls of snow and swallow it to rehydrate themselves, to see them nuzzling each other.

They were ready to go before I was. At Fjernmond's whistle, they trotted back to their places, and he hitched them into their harnesses. "Best be going," he said. "We don't want to be out in this tonight."

I looked back to the west. The sky behind us was thick and dark. The horizon ahead was obscured by cloud.

Fjernmond *mushed* his team, and the sled leaped forward. We huddled under our furs. Soon enough, the wind blew in sharp and cold from behind us. Snow overtook us, swirling. The wolves bent their backs and galloped.

Sledding across a winter wonderland is one thing. We'd done that, with Desmond on our way to Isvellir, the sun shining in the bright sky, the snowfields sparkling as far as the eye could see. It is beautiful, romantic. Lurching through cold fog as needles of ice drive into you is anything but. The sled threw us from side to side, jolting us into each other.

Fjernmond slowed the wolves to a trot. They knew the way, but couldn't see it, so he couldn't risk letting them run. Eventually, the whiteout dwindled into twilight. No one said anything for a long while, because no one had anything to say that didn't sound like a complaint—until, suddenly, Horm got to his feet, and cupped his hands around his mouth, and bellowed *"Gwlllluuuuuurhnghmmm!!"*

I was not the only one to be jolted upright. *What??*

And then, our sled passed a large, blue figure, who seemed to be heading vaguely in our direction. Horm's sharp Woods Kin eyes had spotted it through the snowstorm.

It stopped, on seeing us, and rumbled, "Hnurfflclarp," in ac-knowledgement, before setting off again, and vanishing behind us into the murk.

"Bleeding Nora!" Nyrik said, "What in all hells was that?!"

Horm chuckled. "Sentry," he said. "We're there."

Fjernmond frowned at him, and said, "You speak Ogrish?"

"That I do," Horm said.

# 28

## Ogretzk

The walls of Ogretzk rose before us, boulder piled on boulder, stretching left and right and up into the gloom, with no ends or top in sight. We couldn't see much of it, and what we could see looked weird, but at least it promised shelter. The storm that had chased us all day had overtaken us. Snow was blowing around us in a bitter, cold wind that we all wanted to get out of.

The gates were closed. The wolves stopped in front of them, panting.

"Over to you," Fjernmond said.

Horm turned to Grell, and said, "Lend us a hand then, mate?"

Grell grunted and followed Horm as he clambered out of the sled. Horm walked towards the gates, his short legs sinking into the snow with each step, Grell striding along beside him.

Horm pointed at something above his head. Grell looked up and nodded, then lifted Horm up so that he was standing on his shoulders. Horm reached up and grabbed the end of a rope. He pulled.

Behind the walls a bell clanged. It kept clanging, as Horm kept pulling.

After a while, the gates inched open.

Horm stopped heaving on the bellpull.

An enormous form stepped towards him out of the darkness. Its cannonball of a head was only inches higher than Horm's.

"Hnyyuurrrrrnghghgngggggnnn?!" it enquired.

"Klangfnappn hanggung urmf, an egggengnegrrruvvv-umbum-bruggle!" Horm replied. "Sa flavvaflunkujj urdunquerg! An nevvum-munnunumfing glup, orait?"

The Ogre leaned back, surprised and interested. "Fnur?"

"Ugging fnurr!!" Horm confirmed.

"Glujun um. Oodafunggung thor …" the Ogre muttered, turning away and hauling the gates open.

Fjernmond *mushed* the wolves, who trotted on, towing us into Ogretzk.

Everything about Ogretzk was enormous. Especially its inhabitants. And the noises they made. Ogres don't speak so much as bellow. Seeing one huge creature turn to its neighbor, scowling, and barking out what could only be a string of horrendous insults, and the neighbor replying in kind, louder and longer—well, we kept expecting a brawl to break out at any moment. And then, we'd understand what had happened, as the neighbor helpfully passed the salt he'd been asked for.

*Gagrwarfffnaaahuuuurgnblagkkkapf!* (Pass the salt, eh?)

*Fnaggnngrooommfnthhnnogggglllfuggabuggaviiiirrrmmm!!!* (Here you go, mate).

We had to work things out for ourselves. Horm was up at the high table, beside the chief, bellowing and roaring away with the best of them. Apart from the mayhem, though, our dinner that evening was excellent. Fjernmond was the only one of us who'd eaten mastodon before. His eyes lit up when he saw its limbs rotating on spits by the—of course—gigantic fires.

"*Ooh,*" he said. "Trunker! This *is* a treat."

The smells coming from the fires were indeed delicious. I could feel my mouth watering.

"The soup's a bit of an acquired taste," he advised us, as a large tureen of it was dumped on our table. An exotic aroma arose from it, and I could hardly wait to get stuck in. I was famished after our hard day's traveling. There were no spoons, I saw, only wooden bowls. All round the hall, Ogres were plunging their bowls into the nearest tureen, and then inhaling what they'd scooped out.

"Why's that?" I asked, filling a bowl.

"It's mainly gizzards. The Ogres love them, though, so the more of those you leave for them, the happier they'll be."

I looked around at the others. Their expressions were unambiguous. "We'll be leaving the gizzards," I said, tilting the bowl I was filling so that it held no long, slimy things.

"Good," Fjernmond said. "They'll regard that as a politeness."

*Politeness?* I thought. We were in a hall full of bellowing, almost naked, blue-furred monsters, who were eating soup with their fingers, or rather talons, while quarreling at the tops of their very loud voices. Occasionally one would empty his—or her, it was hard to tell—bowl over his, or her, neighbor's head. Which was the cue for other diners to grab the good bits off said neighbor's head. Those good bits often being mastodon intestines, which are long and stringy, a tussle would usually ensue, an Ogre at each end of the disputed intestine doing his, or her, best to get it all for him, or her, self. They did that by shoveling it into their mouths, and then chewing their way back along it towards their opponent, and trying to push him, or her, off it. Punches to the gut were clearly the best way to get someone to cough up. It seemed to be an all or nothing proposition. Ogres did not appear to understand the concept of sharing.

"This is just the starter," Fjernmond said. "They're hungry. When they've lined their stomachs, things'll calm down for the main course."

Soup was flying on the high table. Horm, standing on his chair next to the chief—because if he'd been sitting, his head would not have reached above the tabletop—suddenly responded to something that we had no idea about. A challenge? An insult? A toast? In an instant he was on his feet on the table, roaring, chest out, arms flung wide— and then his head ducked down and plunged into the nearest soup tureen, which was bigger than he was, and emerged dripping, greasy, and with one end of a mastodon intestine in his mouth. He glared at his opponent, snarling an acceptance of the challenge through his nose—*Right, you bastard, come on if you think you're hard enough!*

The fight was on. A blue behemoth across from him rose to his feet, leaned down into the bowl of soup, clamped his teeth around the other end of the intestine and started swallowing. Horm, who was a third of the thing's size, made up in technique for what he lacked in stature. The Ogre clearly underestimated him. He was also hampered, on his feet, behind all the other Ogres, while Horm had the whole length of the table to work with.

Obstructed, the Ogre lumbered. Horm danced, sideways, back-and-forth, dodging plates and bowls and mugs. I couldn't see that he stood a chance in that tug-of-war against something nine times his weight. That was because I didn't understand what he was doing. He was timing his opponent's moves. The Ogre leaned forward and shoveled intestine into his mouth, and leaned back and swallowed. Horm played him like a matador outmaneuvring a huge but predictable bull. As the intestine was stretched between them, almost to breaking point, he timed his move to perfection. He ran in. His opponent, sensing victory, leaned in to grab another armful. Horm leaped. His feet landed on the back of the Ogre's head as it was lowered over the tureen, driving it down into the soup. Horm gripped the edges of the tureen, and braced his legs stiff, and hung on for dear life, while the Ogre spluttered, and thrashed, and kicked, and bubbled, and, eventually, went still.

Horm stepped off his head and acknowledged the cheers and roars, and bowed to one and all. The limp Ogre was hauled out of the soup tureen and dragged over to the hearth, where other Ogres beat him on the back until he coughed and blew a lungful of soup into the fire, and looked around in confusion, and demanded to know what in all hells had happened.

That broke the ice on our table. We had no idea what the Ogres around us were saying, but we could tell from all the roaring and back-slapping that they thought we were fine entertainment, and fine fellows one and all. Before long we too were roaring and backslapping. This was because of the sproj. Our hosts filled our mugs as fast as we could drink. That was not very fast, because sproj is hard stuff to swallow. It tastes fine, but smells horrible. It is difficult to drink anything without smelling it. Sproj also hits like an Orc warhammer. Our heads were swimming and our sides aching with laughter by the time Horm made it back to our table. It took me several moments to work out who the out-of-focus, black-bearded face frowning across at me belonged to.

"We've got a problem," Horm said.

"Ha ha ha!" I laughed.

Horm sighed and emptied a pitcher of water over my head.

I stopped laughing and gaped at him.

"No more sproj, Daxx," he said. "We've got a problem."

The others, by now, were, if not exactly sobering up, at least paying attention.

"What problem?" I said.

"They won't let us through."

"What? Why not?!"

"How should I know, mate? They're bloody Ogres. Logic don't come into it. Their realm, their rules. I told them we was looking for the bastard who killed my cousin, who was one of them—an Ogre—but that made no difference. They didn't know her. And they never go to the Valley of the Moon, so they don't see why anyone else should."

"Yes, but—we're not doing them any harm, we're just passing through."

"No, you're not. Not if they say you're not."

"But, well …. What will it take to convince them? Change their minds?"

Horm shrugged. "Buggered if I know."

"Can you ask?"

"I already did. Chief told me to sod off."

"What? I don't get it. We're their guests, they've been very hospitable. We're all getting along fine."

"*Ogres,* Daxxie. They don't think like us. Chief says no go, that's it."

I was, by that point, sobering up fast. I had to get to the Valley of the Moon. There was no other way there than through Ogretzk. "There must be something they want, surely?"

"Probably," Horm agreed. "Everyone wants something."

"Any ideas?"

"No."

I looked at the others.

"Single combat?" Grell suggested.

Horm shook his head. "They don't do single. One in, all in, is how they work. Peaceable lot for the most part, Ogres, but piss one off, piss all off. They'll all be piling in. This mastodon we're tucking into took only a dozen of them to bring down."

There were several dozen in that hall. And our party was a lot smaller than a mastodon.

"Unarmed," Horm added.

A dozen. Taking down a mastodon with their bare hands.

Clearly, we would not be fighting our way through Ogretzk.

"Well," he added, "unarmed if you don't count boulders. Some fling, some flail. Urngra was a flinger and a damn good one. Trained up from girlhood. I'd put an arrow into a tree a hundred paces away, and she'd hit it with a thirty-pound rock. Never missed. I sat on her shoulders more than once as her lot took out trunkers. Them talons o' theirs slice through tendons like they was string. Trunker drops, and that's the end of him."

That, I considered, was hardly helping. I tried to think of magic skills I had that would give me any ideas. I couldn't. "We have gold."

"Don't use it," Horm said.

"So, what do they like?" Qrysta asked.

"A challenge. You saw."

A challenge. None of us wanted to challenge even one of them. Especially not if all the others would all pile in on us.

Silence fell, as we considered the situation.

Qrysta said, "Did the chief say why they never go to Mondthal?"

"No," Horm said. "He just growled like it was trouble."

I needed to know about that. What kind of trouble? What did they know about what was up there, that they were avoiding? I knew nothing about it, and they lived here, within a few days of the place.

Where I'd never get if they didn't let us through.

Grell said, "You're up, mate. *Daxxie, the puzzle king.* How are you going to crack this one?"

I had no idea.

Okay, I thought. What do we usually do, when faced with a problem? Turn it around, and peer up its backside until we see daylight.

I turned. I peered. I saw nothing. I looked at the others. They saw that I was out of ideas.

Nyrik rose to his feet. "Right," he said, nudging Horm, "come with me, old son. I'll need you to translate."

He and Horm walked over to the chief's table, and climbed up onto it.

Nyrik muttered into Horm's ear.

Horm nodded, and bellowed a cartload of syllables.

The chief bellowed back.

The conversation began.

We ate, and drank—water, no more sproj for us—and listened.

Horm translated for Nyrik.

Nyrik said things to Horm, who roared them in Ogrish at the chief.

The hief roared back, while those around them filled out the soundtrack with background noises.

It was a long discussion. It involved a lot of table-thumping, and snarling, and jeers. Despite all the huge heads scowling down at him,

351

Horm stood his ground. He was, it seemed, at Nyrik's prompting, mock-ing them. Insulting them. Whatever he was saying was met at first with disdain. Then with annoyance, as if their pride had been wounded. At that point, the argument really got going. Back and forth they went, neither Horm nor the chief backing down. Half the Ogres were on their feet, gesticulating and roaring. We had no idea what was being discussed, but after a while, one word started getting repeated—a word that the chief had thrown back at Horm in response to his insults.

*Fnyarrrrghh.*

Before much longer, every Ogre in the hall was roaring it—to, it seemed, universal approval.

It appeared that some sort of consensus had been reached. And that our hosts were enthusiastic about it.

The Ogres were shouting *Fnyarrrrghh! Fnyarrrrghh! Fnyarrrrghh!* while banging their fists on the table in time.

The chief glared down at Horm.

Horm, hands on hips, glared back up at the chief.

The surrounding Ogres stopped banging and *Fnyarrrrghh*-ing, and waited for his answer.

Horm clearly wasn't too happy. He pointed back at us, and made some Ogrish noises, which sounded like objections.

He was overruled, in a barrage of thunderous *Fnyarrrrghhs*.

Horm held up a finger, in a *give-me-a-moment* gesture. "War-gagrarg," he requested.

"Grarg," the chief consented.

Nyrik and Horm climbed down from the table and came back over to us. They took their places on the bench across from us.

Horm shook his head, scratching his beard thoughtfully. "I dunno about this, mates."

"What is it?" I said.

"They've challenged us to a game of Fnyarrrrghh."

"What's that?" Grell said.

"Their national sport," Horm said.

"How d'you play it?" I asked.

Horm shrugged. "No idea. Urngra's mob never played it—at least, not that I ever heard of. Must be some local game they do up here."

Nyrik said, "Look, this is all we got. We were getting nowhere. They were adamant. The Valley of the Moon is all nice and peaceful, has been for ages. It doesn't bother them, so they're not going to bother it. They don't want no foreigners going there and stirring up trouble— could make things uncomfortable for them. Who'd be the first to get the fallout? *They* would, being the nearest. Well, that's no good to us, is it? So I thought, let's keep needling them. We had to prick them in the pride. We told them we'd crush them in any challenge they threw at us. Not only that, we'd go back and tell the Ice Orcs how we kicked their great blue backsides."

"Didn't go down well," Horm said.

"So, Fnyarrrrghh it is," Nyrik said.

"At which they're experts," I reminded him. "And we're noobs."

Nyrik frowned. "We're what-nows?"

"Complete beginners," I explained. "Total amateurs."

"Yeah, well," he said, with a shrug, "there is that. But nothing else was working. We got a result. Beat them at Fnyarrrrghh, and we're on our way. You'll figure it out, Daxx, with that fine head for puzzles of yours wot Marnie talks about. If you want them to let us through."

I definitely wanted that; but, so far, I had nothing to go on. I looked around at the others.

"Doesn't sound like we have a choice," Grell said.

I said, "Okay, well … if you can find out the details, Horm, that would be good."

Horm grunted, and got down from his bench, and went back over to talk to the chief.

More barking and bellowing ensued.

Eventually, Horm and the chief bumped fists, to seal the bargain.

Fnyarrrrghh it was, then. Whatever Fnyarrrrghh was.

Horm came back to our table, and climbed back up onto the bench across from me.

I said, "So?"

"I told 'em you've never played Fnyarrrrghh, so it would hardly be a fair fight," he said, his dark brows furrowed. " 'Specially when chief told me Ogretzk are the national champions. They haven't lost a game in three years. I said, 'Against beginners? They won't stand a chance.' He said, (a) it would be a valuable learning experience for you, getting a taste of Ogre culture firsthand; and (b) it would be a good workout, toughen up you soft southern wankers for what lies ahead of you in the Valley of the Moon, in the unlikely event that you get past Ogretzk, the which they don't think you will; and (c) you could spread the word, take the game back to Jarnland, maybe get a league going among the Ogres there, and then they could play internationals. They've always wanted to play internationals, only as far as they know, no other realm plays Fnyarrrrghh, so if you could get one to, that would be great. We could get niblun silversmiths to make us a magnificent trophy, and have a Grand Final, your place one year, our place the next—it'd be the high point of the season, that would; and (d) it's not the winning or the losing that matters, it's the taking part."

When I'd taken in as much as I could of what that meant, I said, "Ah. Well, I suppose, if we have to."

"All right," he said, getting to his feet, "I'll go and tell them you're on."

"Can you ask them for the rules and stuff?" Grell said. "So we can find out what we're in for?"

"Sure," Horm said, and headed back over to the chief's table.

Horm bellowed his question.

"Whagathbunkl urmffun grulg—" an Ogre started to explain, but was immediately interrupted by another Ogre, who said, in Ogrish, "That's bollocks, mate! *First* ... "

An argument broke out immediately. Soon they were all roaring at each other, and pointing, and frowning, and gesturing.

We all watched diminutive Horm being flooded with contradictory information from a cluster of bellowing Ogres. Eventually, the discussion wound down and he came over to report back to us, while behind him, Ogres poured each other more sproj, growling.

I focused on the task. "So?"

"They'll show you tomorrow," he said. "They say the whiteout's going to clear and it'll be a fine day. No idea how they know that, but Ogres are usually right about the weather. So, here's the deal. We get a trial run, us being novices. If we think we're up to it, after that, we have to make a challenge."

I said, "What kind of challenge?"

"We want to go on, right? To the Valley of the Moon. They know that. What's that worth to us? There's nothing in it for them in beating a bunch of poxy southern wankers at their national sport. They expect to do that in their sleep. They'd be insulted if we even *thought* we stood

354

a chance against them. Which, in their view, we don't. So, we've got to put up, or shut up and fuck off back to Normark."

"Put up what?" I said.

"Something that would mean as much to them as getting through means to us."

We all looked at each other.

None of us had any idea what that might be.

# 29

## A Game of Fnyarrrrghh

**We** had a fine night's sleep, in enormous beds. We ate a fine breakfast, from enormous bowls, of what Horm told us was goatmeal—oatmeal, soaked in warm goat's milk and slathered with honey. It was, indeed, a fine, clear morning as we trooped down to the ice lake that wrapped around Ogretzk and stretched off into the distance. The lakeshore was crowded. No Ogre was going to miss this. Their strongest players against a single Orc and a handful of tiny southerners? This was going to be a massacre.

They stared down at the motley bunch of us that had come to face them. There was a lot of amused gurgling. It was plain that they didn't think anything of our chances. Out on the ice itself, teams of Ogres were erecting two long structures, a couple of hundred yards across from each other.

It was time to learn what we were in for.

The chief, flanked by his team, explained.

We studied them, as Horm translated. We knew that only the biggest, strongest, toughest Ogres made it onto the Fnyarrrrghh team. It was an honor that they all craved, and competed for. The five who loomed behind the chief, their captain, were not a pretty sight.

The concept soon became clear enough.

Fnyarrrrghh, it seemed, was a lot like hockey, only with Ogres. And boulders.

The structures that were being assembled out on the ice were the goals, which were sixty feet wide and twelve feet high. Instead of nets, banks of snow were piled up behind them on the three sides where the net would have been. Beside the snowbanks were stacks of boulders.

Whatever they might be—and, despite the time I've spent among them, I really have no idea what that actually is—Ogres are far from stupid. Loud, large, lumpish, yes, *many* times yes, but, somehow, as Byrneth had said about Urngra, always right. So it will come as no surprise to learn that Ogres have a deeper insight into hockey than we do. For a start, they see through all that nonsense about sticks and pucks. They don't bother with those. The essence of hockey lies in the brawls. Off come the gloves. The umpires circle, pretending to be in charge, and two or more enforcers beat the crap out of each other while the crowd roars them on. Eventually, whistles blow and the fun stops. The enforcers are sent to the sin bin, and the dreary old skating and passing and shooting stuff starts again.

Well, that's where hockey ends, and Fnyarrrrghh begins.

In Fnyarrrrghh, the brawling is where it starts.

And then it's simple.

First, get another player down.

Second, hurl him, or her, off—to a teammate, or into the goal, or into the distance.

Hurl someone into the goal, and that's a score.

That was pretty much all there was to it.

In hockey there is the icing rule—you can't pass the puck over the two red lines on the rink. Fnyarrrrghh differs in that you can't hurl your *hurlee* over them—however hard you try. You can hurl him, or her, as far as you can, in any direction, and you still won't get whistled for icing—for two reasons: one, because there are no lines on the Fnyar-rrrghh ice—which is far bigger than any rink, seeing that it is played on a frozen lake the size of Ontario; two, because there are no whistles, and no umpires. Ogres haven't yet invented the whistle. No whistle, no umpire. They have, however, invented Fnyarrrrghh; and I'll take Fnyarrrrghh over hockey any day of the week.

Another difference between the two games is that where there is only one puck in hockey, there are several opponents in Fnyarrrrghh.

So, there is an overabundance of bodies slithering the length and breadth of the lake, howling, propelled by gigantic, blue arms, which belong to gigantic, blue bodies that are juiced up to the eyeballs on sproj. There are no drug tests in Fnyarrrrghh. If there were, anyone whose blood level showed sobriety would be ejected from the game in disgrace and banned for life.

We learned, the hard way, that there are two stages to scoring in Fnyarrrrghh. First, you have to get your opponent flat on his, or her, back, or stomach. As in a hockey brawl, this starts with both players upright, flailing, and raining blows; and then grappling, and, if one player hasn't managed to knock the other senseless, attempting to throw each other onto the ice. A successful throw achieved, the thrower grabs whatever parts of the throwee he, or she, can, and hurls him, or her, off into the distance.

We were well out of our depth; we soon saw that. Grell was the only one of us who could go toe to toe with an Ogre. Qrysta and Horm and Nyrik and I were outweighed and outmuscled. Without her twin blades, Qrysta was as much a liability as the two little Woods Kin. Two-handed, she was lethal. Empty-handed, she was useless. Anytime I saw her, she was flat out and spinning away at speed across the ice. Nyrik and Horm, being lighter than their usual opponents, could be hurled far further than any Ogre. They were quick on their feet, once they managed to struggle back up onto them; but what then faced them was a long, slithering run back into the melee, while the rest of us battled with half a dozen Ogres; and when they got back into the action, they just got flattened and hurled again. Jess had never stood on ice before and didn't know how to stay on her feet. The only one of us who was any good was Little Guy. He charged around, in his speed-imbued niblun leathers, having the time of his life, sinking his teeth into anything blue and huge, yapping his challenges, and distracting our opponents so that we could get upright again and back into the game.

Clearly, we were way overmatched. Our only man standing was Grell, and, good though he was, even he couldn't hold out against a team of roaring Ogres forever. Besides which, there were the boulders. They seemed to crash down out of nowhere, at random. We soon realized that random didn't come into it. They were being flung by the opposition goalie. Some she threw high, to drop down out of the sky and wreak havoc. Others she bounced across the lake, like huge bowling balls, scattering everyone in their path. Understandably, I spent most of my time healing my teammates, because we were all taking a battering.

It was mayhem. Bodies skidded off into the distance, or hit nearby trees, before getting back to their feet and slithering back into the fray. Grell did his best. He downed the occasional Ogre, and hurled it towards the goal. The Ogretzk goalie dealt with those rare attacks with ease and went back to her boulder-flinging. Jess, our goalie, couldn't have picked up even the smallest of the rocks behind her goal, let alone hurled it. Besides, she was busy trying to keep out all the bodies skidding at her. She usually managed to stop Nyrik and Horm, as they hurtled her way, but the bigger bodies knocked her back into the goal that she was guarding, along with whoever had been slung at her.

That was another interesting wrinkle about Fnyarrrrghh. You could sling anyone at the opposing goal, friend or foe. As long as you knocked them down, and got them flat, they were yours to sling. That was the only thing that saved us. Our opponents were often so busy brawling with each other that no one was firing any of our team's bodies at Jess. If Ogretzk had had a coherent game plan, we'd have been twenty goals or more down at the end of the first period, instead of a mere nine.

Nine goals to zero.

We weren't even on the score sheet.

We gathered on the lakeshore, exhausted, bruised, and panting. I cast Orbs of Reviving on us all, and boy did we need them.

Qrysta, doubled over, and as out of breath as the rest of us, held up her hand, as if to stop anyone saying anything.

When she could talk, she said, "I know how to fix this."

"You do?" I said. "How?"

"I've seen enough. We've got this."

We all stared at her, our sides heaving as we gulped for air.

We'd been completely outclassed. What in all hells was she talking about?

Grell said, "Are you nuts? We don't stand a chance against this lot!"

Qrysta, now standing upright and able to breathe normally again, smiled at him.

"Come on, now, Grello. You can do better than that. What's missing from this picture?"

Grell scowled at her.

"Competence?" he said. "As in, *we don't have any, and they're experts?*"

Qrysta shook her head, amused.

"I love you, Grell, but you can do better than that. So," she turned to Horm. "Here's what we do. We thank them for showing us how the game is played, which as they know was new to us. We tell them we've got it now, and that we don't need any more practice. We've seen what they can do, and we're not impressed, so let's eat, and get stuck into the sproj, and have a fine old night, and tomorrow we'll hand them their asses on a plate."

Horm froze.

He stared at her. "Are you serious?"

"Completely."

"What the fuck, Qrys?" Grell said. "I was the only one standing! The rest of you were useless. What chance do we have?"

"Every chance," Qrysta said, calmly.

"Yeah? Right? How?" he challenged.

Qrysta said, "We use our secret weapon."

We all thought, what 'secret weapon'?

"And what the fuck is that when it's at home?!" Grell demanded.

"Horm," Qrysta said.

Horm, his head snapping around to frown at her, said, "Eh?"

Qrysta nodded at him, and smiled. "Like I said, Horm," she said, "we've got this. Now, go tell them."

Horm looked around at the rest of us for help. "How am I your secret weapon?!"

"You're niblun, right?"

"I am," Horm agreed, warily. "On my mum's side."

"So, you can make anything."

He nodded. "I can, yeah. Pretty much."

"Exactly. Now, tell the smiths you'll need the forge tonight. Say we have repairs to do to our gear. They won't mind, right?"

Horm shrugged agreement. "We're their guests, of course they won't."

"Good. So go to the chief, and lay down the challenge. Tell him we very much appreciated the chance to get the hang of the game, which we now have mastered. It could hardly be easier, and we are all looking forward to kicking their butts tomorrow. And when they go *oh yeah*, say, *oh yes, and we'll put our money where our mouth is.* And they'll probably scoff and say, *we don't need your money,* and you just say, *maybe not, but you'll want this.*"

"Want what?"

"Tell him we'll show them tonight."

"Eh? I dunno," Horm said. "They're not going to like that …"

"Listen, they don't get many like us up here, right? We're something new, the sensation of the year. They're bound to want to know what we're up to. Right? Just as you all do."

That made sense. I, for one, couldn't wait to see what she had in mind.

"Let it fester," Qrysta continued. "Let them speculate, talk among themselves, rack their brains, come up with theories. Get them on the hook."

Horm looked doubtful.

"All right," he said. "If you insist …"

"Tell them we'll be putting up something, as a stake, that will blow their minds. Something they'd happily put up their most prized possession against, if they had to."

She waited, while we all tried to figure it out.

"Exactly!" she said, when we all realized that we couldn't. "On the hook, right? Want to know?"

We did indeed.

"And that's what we want *them* feeling. There's no way we can win the way we just played, is there?"

"None," Horm agreed.

"They know that. So, they'll accept."

I said, "I hope you know what you're doing, Qrysta."

She turned to me, as if she was surprised that I hadn't worked it out for myself.

"And you the one who's meant to be good at puzzles," she said, shaking her head, her eyes shining with secret mischief.

Not for the first time, in recent weeks I couldn't think what I wasn't seeing.

Qrysta winked at me. She was enjoying my confusion. "Off you go, then, Horm," she said.

Horm, clearly, was unsure. "Well," he said, "I dunno …"

"Did you enjoy being slung around the ice all over the place just now?"

"I did not."

"Would you enjoy giving them a taste of their own medicine?"

Horm stared at her.

Slowly, he nodded. "That I would."

"Then talk them into it, Horm. Challenge. Hit them where it hurts, in the pride. You know how to do that."

"Yur. That I do."

"So. Do it."

He hesitated. "We're going to look pretty stupid if this doesn't come off."

"If this doesn't come off," Qrysta said, "you're not going to get to avenge Urngra."

Horm's face darkened. "Right," he said, and went off to talk to the chief.

Or rather, to roar at him, and be roared back at.

It was agreed soon enough. Clearly, the prospect intrigued them. *Tonight, the challenge. Tomorrow, the game.*

They were fine with that.

We all trooped back to Ogretzk.

None of us knew what was going on, apart from Qrysta.

We gathered in our room, and she explained.

Nyrik, Horm, and Jess had no idea what she was talking about. Grell and I, though, saw that her plan might indeed work—if we, meaning Horm, could pull it off.

Frowning, and scratching his bushy black beard, he listened to what Qrysta told him he needed to do.

Pretty straightforward, really, he said—even if he didn't understand what the things were that Qrysta wanted him to craft. He wasn't a one to ask questions. He, just like our Ogre hosts, liked a challenge. Once he got the idea, he worked like a demon. We were all there in the forge with him, to assist him, but he hardly needed us. Sparks flew, as he heated, and beat, and shaped, and tempered. I was able to help, with some of my magic skills, which saved him so much time that our new items were ready well before dinner. As he worked, Qrysta laid out her whole plan—what we should do that night, and our tactics for the game in the morning. She'd got it all figured out. Nyrik, Horm, and Jess were confused, because what Horm was making was new to them, but they saw that Grell and I were believers.

"It's a genius idea, Qrys," I said. "I just hope it works."

"Oh, it'll work."

Nyrik couldn't help teasing me. "So much for that clever head o' yours, Daxxie," he said. "Strikes me she's the one with the brains."

"No doubt about that," I agreed, as we inspected our new Horm-crafted gear.

"What d'you do with these, then?" Nyrik asked.

He listened in growing disbelief as I told him.

"Seriously?" he said.

"Seriously."

"Well," he said. "I'll believe that when I see it."

"They're getting impatient," Horm muttered. We were well into the evening meal. Food was flying. The fires, and our hosts, were roaring. Sproj was flowing—on every table but ours. We wanted to have clear heads in the morning. We knew that they were all waiting for our challenge. The longer they waited, I thought, the more impact our stunt would have. We were all smiles and confidence, chatting, via Horm, with the Ogres sitting near us. We had, by then, learned that there was a big difference between the way they looked and the way they were. They, like Urngra, looked terrifying, with default expressions that could chill the blood. Behind those scowls, though, lived all sorts of interesting personalities. They were eager to learn about us, and had a wealth of knowledge about any number of subjects. The only one they wouldn't talk about was Mondthal. Mention of the place turned their friendly chatter to wary growls. "Best change the subject," Horm said, the first time I asked what they could tell me about it. "Chief'll tell us if he wants, is all they'll say."

Eventually, as we had planned, when the evening was in full swing Horm and Nyrik got into an argument. Voices rose. Abuse flew. Insults were hurled. Fingers were jabbed, and chests pushed. There was only one way to settle it: arm wrestling. They made a meal of it, each winning one round, and drawing out the decider as long as they could—all to the delight of our hosts. Eventually, after much straining and sweating, Horm wore Nyrik down. Nyrik grinned. They shook hands. Nyrik, the gallant loser, held up Horm's arm as the winner, and the hall echoed to the rafters with cheers. When the sounds died down, Horm said, pointing at Nyrik, "Vungruff hargnud oomberfuggl." We knew, because we'd rehearsed all this, that he was saying, "The little sod's tougher than he looks."

The Ogres laughed.

At which, Horm frowned, as if insulted.

"Klaggen effumprerp zegg?" ("Don't believe me?")

More chuckles, and shakes of large, blue heads.

And then, to the largest nearby Ogre, "Gurnen, favpraggeh jur-vumjiv!" (Go on then, see for yourself.)

The Ogre's shocked reply, was, "Huh?"

We could translate that for ourselves.

"Fuvnunt dostur glurp kloggl?" (Don't tell me you're chicken?")

"*Kloggl??!*"

"Kloggl. Ognog ugging *kloggl*."

"Kloggl orfundrubstut blurp varnhar aggenflaggenpaggen?"

Horm turned to Nyrik, and said, calmly, "He called you a feeble little pile of weasel shit. And says he's not scared of you."

Nyrik chuckled, and looked up at the Ogre with a smile. "Tell him to prove it."

Horm did.

"Hwwwaaaaaaahhgggh???!" The Ogre roared, affronted.

Insulted, he sat, glowering across the table at Nyrik, set his elbow down on it, and held out his massive paw.

It was so large, and on the end of an arm so long, and Nyrik's arm by comparison was so much shorter, that it took longer to arrange the opponents than the contest lasted. The Ogre almost had to lie down in order to be able to grip Nyrik's hand. Nyrik had to stand on the bench opposite him. The difference in size between them was comical. There could, of course, be only one winner. We all knew that, just as the Ogres crowded around us knew that; but they didn't know what we knew, which was that they were wrong.

Horm, standing on the table as referee, called, "Plarhdd!"

The Ogre attacked with all his strength.

Nyrik held his eyes, smiling.

His arm didn't budge.

The Ogre strained, and sweated.

He looked across at Nyrik's calm, teasing smile.

He roared, and tried again, putting everything he'd got into it.

Nyrik's arm held rock steady.

The Ogre looked up at him, baffled.

Nyrik winked.

And slammed the Ogre's hand back on the tabletop with such force that it threw the rest of him off his bench and onto the floor, gargling with surprise.

A shocked silence gripped the onlookers. They couldn't believe what had just happened.

I'd seen Nyrik's sleight of hand before, at The Wheatsheaf, when he'd produced a sheepdog puppy out of nowhere, to the delight of the innkeeper's twin daughters, so I knew how good he was at misdirection. No one thought anything of him casually removing the scruffy little glove he'd been wearing, and tucking it into his pocket. He knew that the less time he wore it, the less of its power he'd use up. He was pointing at Jess as he did it, and saying, through Horm, that he bet she could beat anyone in the room. Jess was taller than Nyrik, but lighter, and skinnier, and had arms as thin as twigs.

His audience was shocked at the suggestion. *Her?* It was unthinkable. But they'd just seen the unthinkable. Jess beating any of them was even more unthinkable. But who wanted to risk being beaten by a skinny little shrimp like her? He'd never live it down.

It was time to make our move.

"Let's go and see the chief," I said.

He wasn't far away. He was standing on a nearby table, where he'd come to get a good view of the arm wrestling. The wall of Ogres parted to let us through.

Horm greeted him and gave him our proposal.

Which was this: If we won the game tomorrow, he'd let us continue through to Mondthal. If we lost, Horm said, holding up the scruffy little Glove of Strength, he would win this.

The chief's reply, as he peered at the tatty thing, was the only word of Ogrish that we all understood.

"Huh?"

Horm explained, with his prepared speech. "We know what you're thinking, Chief, why would you want that? We will show you. All right?"

The chief grunted a wary "okay" noise.

"Feet together, arms by your side. Stiffen up, and don't move," Horm told him. He handed the Glove to Jess, and the chief did as Horm instructed. Jess knew what to do. She'd practiced with Grell that afternoon. She put on the glove, and it shrank to fit her small hand. She got up on the table, crouched down behind the chief, took hold of his ankle with her gloved hand, and stood up, effortlessly, holding the rigid chief above her head.

Four-and-a-half-foot tall Jess rotated twice holding up the nine-and-a-half-foot Ogre Chief, to display him to all corners of the hall, smiling calmly while he was barking with surprise—as was every other Ogre present.

Jess put him down again before the Glove began to lose power.

After that, it was just a matter of explaining. Jess showed that, without the Glove, she couldn't even lift Horm. Strength is a quality that Ogres prize above any other. The chief, of course, had to have it. He longed to try it there and then, but Horm said no, he'd have to earn it.

Our proposition was eagerly accepted.

After all, he'd seen how useless we soft southern wankers were at Fnyarrrrghh.

It was another fine morning as we gathered on the lakeshore the next day and kitted ourselves up in our new, Horm-crafted gear.

"This is going to be quite like the old days," Qrysta said, as she and Grell and I laced up our skates. Horm had fashioned their blades from the large selection of knives in the Ogre armory beside the forge. He'd reinforced our boots with an extra sole of rck-hard yak leather, half an inch thick. He'd never have been able to cut it in time, he'd said, if I hadn't cast Soften on it. Grell had been given the job of screwing in the plates that Horm had forged the blades into, and it had taken all his strength. There was no way that those skates were coming lose.

"What old days?" Jess asked.

"I started doing this when I was half your age," Qrysta replied. "Quite the teen ice queen I was, back in the O.C. Won all sorts of trophies. I didn't play much hockey. I was too busy training—just joined in a few games for a laugh, when there was the chance. For me, it was mainly ice dancing, solo and pairs. But you don't *play* for the Stanley Cup, do you, Daxxie, right? You *skate* for it. And I," she said, as she got to her feet, "could skate."

She took a couple of paces to test her balance. Horm had fitted steel rods into our boots as ankle braces, to hold our feet rigid.

Qrysta liked how they felt.

"Nice work, Horm," she said. "Won't turn an ankle in these. Okay, let's do this."

Horm, Nyrik, and Jess had never skated before, so there had been no point making skates for them. They'd be on foot, but they all had sticks just as we did. They knew what to do with them, and were looking forward to a little payback for the hammering they'd taken the day before. I'd skated a little as a child, and, later, used inline skates with my nephew. Grell had said that of course he knew how to skate; kids do every sport in Oz—although it had been a few years since the last time he'd laced up. We clumped awkwardly downhill and stepped onto the ice, and then tried to remember what to do.

It soon came back. "Like falling off a bike, eh?" Grell said, with a grin. "You never forget how." He and I were pretty ungainly as we tried out our new skates, but we were soon enough getting around just fine. Qrysta, by contrast, was utterly transformed. She wove in and out of us, at speed, laughing, twirling, forwards and backwards, leaping and spinning and landing on one foot, backwards, the other stretched out behind her. Grell and I drifted over to our opponents, who were all watching us in amazement, Little Guy trotting along beside us, tail wagging.

We stopped in front of them, and smiled.

Qrysta skidded to a halt between us, ice flying from her skates.

I said, "Ready for hurl off?"

They were. But they weren't prepared for what came next. In order to hurl us, they had to catch us. They couldn't. They couldn't not only because they weren't fast enough, but also because we were working our new sticks to good effect. We'd seen how tripping was not just allowed in Fnyarrrrghh but was essential to the sport. Our Horm-crafted sticks wouldn't have been ideal for hockey, being built for sturdiness rather than strike-power. They were perfect for Fnyarrrrghh. Little Guy was everywhere at once, as before, harassing and confusing. It was easy to pick off our distracted opponents—stick between legs from behind, heave and lever, down they go. Grab a leg, skate for goal towing your opponent, spin, and release. Grell had power and could hurl with accuracy. Even so, his shots on goal, and mine, weren't too hard for the Ogretzk goalie to deal with. Qrysta, though, could spin like a whirlwind, building up enough momentum to blast her projectile either past or straight into the goalie, several times hammering her into the snowbank at the back of her goal.

Grell and I soon started passing to her rather than shooting—unless the goalie was concentrating on her and we could aim at an empty part of her goal. Nyrik and Horm were in and out of our opponents' legs as best they could, working their sticks. We didn't bother with a goalie ourselves, after a while. Our opponents didn't have a single shot on goal in the first period, which they'd spent being hurled rather than hurling. So Jess came out to join the mayhem, tripping Ogres as gleefully as Nyrik and Horm. We'd decided on a spectacular finale. Our opponents had started out confident, and then become confused, then angry, then, finally, exhausted. When we'd seen that the fight had gone out of them, Grell skated over to the boulders behind their goal. He put on the Glove of Strength, picked the biggest boulder he could find, and hurled it skywards. All eyes watched it vanish above us to a dot.

And then come back down, faster and faster.

The players on both teams, and the nearby spectators, had the sense to scatter.

The boulder shattered the home team's goal, and smashed a wide hole in the ten-foot-thick ice.

A geyser of cold water blew back up out of it, drenching anyone in the vicinity.

The final score was twenty-six goals to zero.

Grell contested that as we removed our skates.

"Twenty-seven, mate," he said. "You're forgetting the one I hit with my boulder."

# 30

## The Grazings

Oller waited in the shadows, his eyes on the end of the alley ahead of him, listening to the night sounds of Sarmen. They were few that late in the small hours. Furtive things scuttling in the dust. The hoot of an owl. A cat whining. More sounds came as the first deep blue of dawn grew in the sky above the city walls. Eventually he heard the noises he was listening for: the creaking of wheels, the grunting of oxen, the flicking of reins.

The first cart trundled past, on the street that led to the city gates. Before long, another. He watched them go by. He knew what he was looking for. Or, rather, smelling for. And there it was, coming down the breeze towards him. The odor of the backstreets of Sarmen was bad enough already. It was nothing to the stench that was approaching.

Oller edged to the mouth of the alley. A large, slow shape appeared out of the gloom: two oxen, dragging a wagon piled high with excrement—animal dung from the streets and stables, stacked around open fetid vats of human waste from the night-soil dumps. A single driver, hunched up on his bench.

Perfect. Two drivers would mean more questions. Oller didn't want questions. He wanted answers. He fell in behind the night-soil wagon as it passed. He didn't mind the smell. He'd known the night-soil drivers

369

back in Brigstowe. Good folks, for the most part. They were usually pleased to have company on a journey. Not many travelers wanted a ride on a night-soil wagon—just as not many guards wanted to go through its revolting load looking for contraband.

*Runners,* the night-soil drivers were known as in the Thieves Guild. *Slow, stinking plodders* would have been more accurate. The night-soil ox-wagons never went above an amble. But they could ferry goods in and out of anywhere—people, too. He'd taken the night carriage out of Brig more than once, when the guards were turning the town upside down looking for him. It was comfortable enough, in the narrow box under the false floor. All he had to do was remember to bring plenty of handkerchiefs and what the TG nicknamed "night oil": phials of strong herbal extracts to soak his kerchiefs in—mint, and sandalwood, and lavender, which would mask the stink of the load that surrounded him. He needed food and water too, of course, but there was no problem with relieving himself, however long the journey. There was no chance of the smell of anything he had to pass giving his presence away.

The driver hauled back on his reins and muttered a quiet, "Whoa …"

The cart stopped.

Oller padded round to its front.

There were four other carts waiting ahead of it.

The guards at the gate were stirring. They didn't want this stench near them any longer than necessary. The gates began to open.

"'Ere, mate," Oller said, looking up at the driver, "you dropped this off the back." He held up a shovel.

The driver shook his head. "Not mine."

"Eh? You sure?"

"Yup. I'd remember a shovel as nice as that. Better'n my rusty old things."

"Oh," Oller was crestfallen. "I could've sworn I heard a clatter." He looked around in bewilderment, at the shovel, at the gates. "Maybe you just run over it, was all, and that made it clonk. Well, it's no good to me, d'you want it?"

"Eh?" The driver's eyebrows rose at the prospect—then fell again as his eyes narrowed in suspicion. "How much?"

"Wot? No, mate, nothing. I don't want no money. I was just returning it to what I thought was its rightful owner."

The driver ran his expert eyes over it. "Shovel that nice is worth a bit."

It takes a professional shoveler to know a good shovel.

"Is it?" Oller said, with a shrug. "I wouldn't know. It's no good to me. It's yours if you want it."

The driver reached for it, then hesitated. "How do I know it's not stolen?"

"It isn't."

Indeed, it wasn't stolen. Oller wasn't going to risk stealing anything while in Sarmen. However good a thief you might be, someone might just notice you filching something. Especially something as large as a shovel. He had no intention of risking arrest by the guards, which might mean ending up on the question-master's table. Besides, he'd wanted a good quality shovel, which would buy him his passage. He'd paid well for it, in the market square, and had enjoyed haggling the price down with the Ironwright who'd crafted it.

"I found it, like I said," Oller continued, then chuckled. "Blimey, mate! If I'd stolen it, I'd be selling it, wouldn't I? And I'm not. I'm giving it. I'm not going to carry a bloody great shovel all day. Why would I want to do that?"

The driver thought over what he said. "For digging?" he suggested. "When you get where you're going. Might be as you'll have some digging to do."

"Well, I don't have no digging to do. I'm a corder, not a farmer, or a gardener. Don't need no shovel to make and mend ropes. I'll just leave it here, then," he said, turning away to drop it at the side of the street.

"No, no, don't do that!" the driver stopped him. "I'll take it, and be glad of it. Just can't be too careful—wouldn't want to be caught with no stolen shovel. Guards'd do you over for that." He held out his hand, and Oller passed him the shovel, which he inspected in the growing light.

"Beauty, this!" he said, appreciatively. He nodded. "This is what I call a shovel. Much obliged to you, lad." He placed the shovel in the toolbox behind his seat.

"Glad it's found a good home," Oller said, with a smile. "See you, then."

He turned away.

Behind him, the driver said, "Where you heading?"

"Grazings. Plenty o' work for a good corder there, is the word."

Oller, trained as he was by the TG's masters, was as fine a corder as any. Thieves need to know their ropes.

"That's where I'm bound." The driver seemed pleased at the coincidence—which was, of course, nothing of the sort. "If you don't mind the smell, I won't mind the company."

"Oh," Oller said, as if the idea had never occurred to him.

He appeared to think it over for a moment. "Well, I must say my feet would be grateful," he said. "*Holes in your soles, and stones bite your bones,* as they say!"

"That they do," the driver agreed.

"That's a handsome offer, friend," Oller said, "and I'll be happy to take you up on it."

The driver held out his hand, and Oller reached for it. "Up you get, then."

Oller climbed up and sat on the bench beside the driver, who clicked his tongue, and flicked his reins.

The oxen grunted, and pulled, and the night-soil wagon creaked forwards.

"Who'd a thought it, eh?" Oller said, looking around with pleasure. "Riding out o' the city in style!"

The driver chuckled. "There's not many as would call a trip on a shit-wagon 'riding in style'!"

The guards, holding their hands over their noses, waved them through impatiently. "Get on with you! Bloody move it!" one of them ordered, his voice muffled behind his hand.

"Yes, sir!" the driver said. He cracked his whip and the oxen lurched forwards and shambled through the gates, before slowing back to their usual stolid pace.

The night-soil wagon rumbled out of the city on the road south and east. The cloudless sky ahead of it glowed red, and then orange, as the sun rose above the horizon, revealing a flat, parched landscape. It was going to be another hot day. Oller wondered how many more of them there would be before he got to the Grazings. Not that it mattered. He was in no hurry. You don't learn much when you're hurrying. If you want to learn, you slow down and look around, and see what there is to be seen, and hear what there is to be heard.

The driver looked over at him, as the light grew around them, to get the measure of his passenger. Oller's face was tanned and weather-beaten, and far from at its cleanest, but his skin was not the olive complexion of the common folk of Sarmen.

"Foreigner are you, then, laddie?" he asked, with a smile.

Oller grunted. "I get that a lot," he said. "No, matey: Sarmen born and raised, me. Mam was a local girl; my Da, who I never met, was a sailor, is what she said. Sailed away afore I was born, never to be seen again. Although from what I heard about him, smuggler or pirate might be more like it. Never spoke of him without a smile, did my mum. Said he was a handsome devil. Just like me, eh?"

The driver glanced again at the scrawny little specimen beside him and chuckled.

"Just like you."

"Yeah," Oller agreed. "Often wondered where he came from. One o' them northern parts, I would think. You ever take to the seas?"

"No thank *you*!"

"Me neither. Keep my feet dry and my nose clean, is my way o' thinking."

"Who needs storms, and pirates, and krakens, and whirlpools and such, and mermaids what'll sing you overboard and drown you, when we've got warm beds, and roofs over our heads, and enough toil and trouble already on dry land, thank'ee kindly?" the driver said.

"Not me," Oller replied.

The driver chuckled in agreement. "Name's Aril. Arilmahnj for long, but I go by Aril."

"Korv," Oller said, extending a hand, which the driver shook. "Short for Korv. The which was my Da's name, Mam said, or at any rate the name he gave her."

The driver nodded. "Sounds northern, that."

"That's what folks say," Oller agreed. "Wonder where, up north."

The driver grunted. "Who knows, with them foreign places? Well, if he's alive, I hope for his sake it's not where our army's heading."

"Yur," Oller said. "Poor bastards."

Then he added, more cheerfully, "Well, they'll all be a part and parcel of the empire soon enough, and blessed to see what they've been missing."

"That they will," the driver quickly agreed, then added, "those as live, that is to say."

"Must be a privilege to see that," Oller mused. "The grace of His Radiance's bounty being offered to …" he hesitated, as if unsure what to say. "To—well, I don't want to speak ill of my own kin, if such they might be, and I've never met a one of them, but—everyone's barbarians if they're not empire, aren't they?"

"That they are." The driver nodded. "That they are."

Silence fell between them.

The oxen plodded on.

They both understood what had not been said.

*You won't catch me saying a word against the emperor, chum. So, if you're one of those who'd sell a stranger out for a few coppers, you're out of luck.*

In the days that he'd been in Sarmen, Oller had quickly picked that up. Nobody trusted anyone. There were snitches everywhere. The emperor's spymasters paid well for information about traitors. So well that people invented charges against their neighbors, their family, their co-workers, their friends.

Oller and the driver didn't need to say more.

They were loyal subjects of the emperor, both, and proud of it.

Oller looked up at the road ahead. It was good and wide, and in better shape than most roads in Jarnland. A level surface, evenly spread with gravel. Few ruts. Well-trimmed verges. Deep, weed-free ditches to either side, beyond which grassland led away to the horizon, hills to the left dotted with trees, an endless plain sloping down to their right. Cottes and farmsteads stood alone, or huddled in groups around farmyards.

Poor land, Oller thought. Thin grass, brown rather than green, even in springtime. Few animals. No crops that he could see. No sign of a stream or a river. A bright, clear sky above, the sun ahead blazing brighter by the hour. Water would be the problem, he saw—or rather, the lack of it. They passed a cluster of low buildings, the corral between them nothing but dirt.

"Looks like folks here could do with some of your load," Oller said.

Aril snorted. "They could, and they'd love to get their thieving hands on it. And if they did I'd lose mine within the month."

Oller knew better than to ask questions. He just turned to Aril in surprise and waited.

"Emperor's shit," Aril elaborated. "If I turn up with anything less than a full load, I'm a hand short. Any night-soil carter sells so much as a cupful on the way, well, someone'll snitch on him, for the silver. Steal from His Radiance, and you'll be chopped come next punishment day. I like my hands just where they are."

Oller nodded, and pretended to be a little shocked, and scared, when he said, "Emperor's … you know what? You're not afeared to say that?"

"Everyone calls it that. Not just us nightsoilers—guards, grazers, stable hands on the way. And not disrespectful, like. All know it's needed for the imperial cattle. They'd eat the Grazings bare if it weren't for our loads feeding the land. Greedy buggers, and whole bloody great herds of them. You wouldn't believe what they eat in a day. The which is why we cart it all that way, rather than sell it nearer and quicker. *No-one* sells the emperor's shit. I get paid for my time, not my load. Imperial clerks pay the night-soil collectors in the city, and the stables for their cleanings. They load me up and the cattle-master pays me when I deliver, and pays well. It's a good living, if you don't mind the smell."

Oller thought about what Aril had said, and frowned.

"Highwaymen must know that, Aril." he said. "You not worried about getting robbed on your way home?"

Aril chuckled. "Yes, they knows all about it. And they steer *well* clear. Robbing the emperor's servant? That would be asking for trouble. His Radiance wouldn't take kindly to that. No, they don't want no squad o' chalkers hunting them down. Those bastards never give up. And when they find you, well …. Let's just say they have a cruel sense of fun.

"Anyway, they also know that when I say *pay*, I mean cattle-master gives me a chit, signed and sealed, and I take that back to the clerks in the city for my coin. Made out to me, and the clerks know me, o' course. It'd be a rare fool as would walk into the counting house with someone else's chit."

He shook his head at the thought, and turned to Oller. "So, you know what else you've saved, lad, apart from shoe leather, by riding along of me?"

"No? What?"

"Any valuables you might have about you, should them scoundrels think to rob you. No one's going to touch you up here."

"Good to know," Oller said.

"Safe as houses, sitting along of me." Aril chuckled.

Time, Oller thought, to show his appreciation. He reached down for his pack and lifted it onto his lap.

He brought out bread, hard cheese, and an onion. He cut the cheese and onion onto a slice of bread and handed it to Aril. "Share and share alike." His smile faded as he saw Aril staring at him.

"That's no cheese knife," Aril said.

An elementary mistake, Oller thought. Hard cheese needed work to cut. His niblun blades were no kitchen tools. *Should have been more careful, and made the cutting look like more of an effort. Won't do that again.*

He winked at Aril. "Don't need no cheese knife on the road, matey—you know that. Not if them highwaymen fancy shaking me down."

He held out the offering to Aril.

Aril relaxed and took it. "Might be as they'd get more than they expected from a little feller like you."

"Got to look out for yourself in this world," Oller said.

"That you do," Aril agreed. He took a bite and chewed. "Mm. Very tasty. Much obliged."

Oller ate his own bread and cheese, and settled back to view the passing landscape. He wondered how far they'd get that day, and where they'd spend the night.

The companionable mood lasted less than a minute.

"Shit!" Aril said, putting down his bread and cheese, and grabbing for the reins.

Oller saw what had alarmed him, but didn't know what it meant.

On the horizon, a plume of dust was rising from the road ahead of them.

Aril was looking around frantically—not just ahead but at the steep ditches on both sides of the road. He reached for his bullwhip and cracked it again and again into the backs of his oxen. They bellowed and lurched forward. Aril kept whipping and whipping, making them run as fast as they could—which wasn't very. He kept muttering, "Shit, shit, *shit!*"

Oller, being thrown about on the seat beside him, said, "What is it?"

"Chalkers! Can't turn my oxen around, road's too narrow—Gods above and below." Aril was whimpering. "Somewhere, *anywhere* ...!"

Oller looked up at the cloud of dust bowling towards them. "Tell me what I can do," he said. He knew better than to ask what was happening. Oller knew panic when he saw it. Panicking people need help, not questions.

"Get ready to run for your bloody life!" Aril shouted. The oxen were bellowing with pain and fear. Blood was seeping from the wounds that his bullwhip was cutting into their flanks. "Please, oh please ..." Aril was saying, his voice thin with fear.

The dust cloud rolled towards them, blocking out the light of the rising sun.

Oller could hear sounds coming from inside it. Regular sounds, as of drums—no: feet, stamping on the ground. Feet that were not marching, but trotting.

"Thank fuck!" Aril gasped, and hauled on his left rein.

The oxen swerved off the road and onto a lane that led over a tunnel across the ditch and up the hill to a farmstead. It was a miracle, Oller thought, that the heavily laden wagon did not overturn, taking a sharp turn at such speed. Aril, clearly, was a skilled driver. Even though he was off the road, he kept flogging the oxen, driving them up the lane, desperate to get as far up it as he could before whatever was in the dust cloud rolled past them.

Oller was torn between looking ahead and looking back to see what was coming.

The din of thumping feet bore down towards them. Aril cracked the bullwhip again at the struggling, bellowing oxen. There must already have been twenty yards between them and the road, but that, apparently, was not enough for Aril. The stamping of boots, in double time, reached the end of the lane behind them. Oller looked back and saw the first Vu-Sant emerge out of the dust cloud, and pass, jogging. File after file of them followed, relentless, in perfect formation, huge and implacable, their stone-white faces hard, their steps thundering on the road, dust billowing around them. They were in black armor, leaning forward as if at the charge. Each carried a spear and had a longsword slung behind them.

Aril hauled in on the reins and the wagon stopped. They watched, as the long column thundered past in a turmoil of brown dust. It wasn't until the last of them had tramped on down the road that Oller realized that he'd hardly been daring to breathe, or to move.

He shook himself into action. As well as food in his pack, he had a leathern flask of Sarmen firewater. It was cheap, sharp liquor, but it hit the spot. He uncorked it and took a swallow. He wiped his mouth and handed the flask to Aril.

Aril nodded and drank.

They were both sweating, and not just because of the heat.

Eventually, Aril gasped, "Thank'ee, friend. I needed that."

"Me too," Oller said.

Aril took a deep breath and exhaled. "They don't share the road with no one," he said. "They'd've barged us over into the ditch, killed our kine with them spears o' theirs, and us too if we didn't scarper. Anyone as gets in their way is dead meat." He handed the flask back to Oller.

Oller knew where the Vu-Sant were going, to the port of Sarmen, just as other divisions were heading to other ports all over the northern coasts of the empire—from which they would take sail for Jarnland. Tens upon tens of thousands of them.

Oller stared at the vanishing dust cloud.

He took another swig of Sarmen firewater. Hand shaking, he handed the flask over to Aril, who did the same.

Aril was well known in the taverns on the road to the Grazings. Guests and staff alike knew to give his wagon a wide berth, and not just because of the stink. No one wanted to be seen near the emperor's shit. His oxen had all the hay they could eat, best quality. Ale and food was brought out to them. Aril explained that he never let his wagon out of his sight. They slept on pallets of straw, under old blankets, one each side of the wagon—"Two sets of eyes being better than one," Aril said.

"No one gets near me when I'm asleep, mate," Oller told him.

Aril remembered Oller's knife and nodded. He'd had trouble, on occasion, during his many nights in these tavern stables, from locals trying to steal from his load.

They had none on that journey. None, that is, that he knew of. Oller woke a couple of times at the sound of soft footsteps approaching. They stopped when they saw the glint of his knife. Oller saw no reason to say anything to Aril.

They rose in the small hours, harnessed the oxen, and were on the road before dawn. On the fourth day the scenery around them changed. There were more trees. The grass was greener, and lusher. Streams ran down out of the hills to the east. Towards evening, they came to a wide river. A five-arch bridge spanned it. "Journey's end tomorrow," Aril said, as the oxen hauled the cart across it. Beyond it, between the road and the river, was their last port of call before the Grazings: the Bridge Inn.

It was bigger and grander than any of the taverns they'd stayed at before. The food was better, the ale excellent. The water in the river was clear and inviting. Oller was tempted to plunge in, to cool off and get clean. He decided against it. The grubbier he was the less he stood out. The landlord was an old friend of Aril's. He came out for a chat and to hear news from the city. It was the same news they'd been hearing from all over. Chalkers mustering at the ports. Press-gangs scouring the land for hands to man the ships. Crews assembling. Fleets loading and readying to sail.

"It'll be all over come Midsummer Day," the landlord said. "And His Radiance bringing his new bride home. Bards have been singing of nothing else, and how she's the loveliest maid in the world."

"And the luckiest," Aril said.

"That she is. She may be queen of her own little land, but what's that to being empress?"

"Empress-in-waiting," Aril quickly corrected him.

"Of course, of course, and may she wait many years yet. I trust you'll join me in raising a right royal health to His Radiance, His Bride, and our Imperial Father?"

"That we will," Aril said, "with a will! Royal and loyal!"

"Loyal and Royal!" the landlord replied.

They clinked mugs, and drank.

Oller thought of Esmeralda and sighed.

The other men noticed and stared at him, shocked.

*Hells, I'm getting sloppy*, Oller thought. *Another stupid mistake.*

He shook his head, with an apologetic shrug. "I loved a lass once," he said. "Married a baker." He grinned at them sheepishly. "I'm no crown prince, me."

Aril and the landlord relaxed.

"That you're not, lad," Aril said.

"Royal and loyal, loyal and royal!" Oller raised his mug and the awkward moment passed.

They drank.

"Cattle arrived yet?" Aril said, wiping his mouth with the back of his hand.

The landlord shook his head. "Any day now, I'm hearing."

"It's been a good long fallow, then. Grass will be as tall as they are."

"Yup. Crop was feeble only a month ago. Cattle-master was tearing his hair out. If they came to the Grazings that poor, he would have been lucky to keep his head. Then it rained for a fortnight, and everything shot up. He won't be hearing no complaints now. There's enough for the herds to fatten up to bursting, and then it's off to war."

Aril said, "All say it won't be much of a fight."

They reached the Grazings a little after noon the next day. Aril put in a word at the stables for Oller, and a lad was told to take him to the rope yards for appraisal. He and Aril only had a moment to say goodbye. Aril thanked Oller for his company, and Oller thanked Aril for the ride. "See you in a week or three, with my next load!" Aril said, and Oller said, "Look forward to it, mate!" He didn't think he'd be anywhere near the Grazings the next time Aril made a delivery.

A foreman at the rope yards gave Oller some ends to splice together, which he did neatly and quickly, and then some cords to braid into rope. The task didn't take Oller long and the result passed inspection. He was put to work immediately.

The place was a hive of activity, in expectation of the imminent arrival of the cattle, which was all anyone talked about. They did so warily, with a nervous energy, as if on edge. Oller kept his head down at his work, and his ears open. It was late afternoon when a large shadow swept across the open field and cheers broke out all around him.

Oller looked up in time to see the dragon land, with a heavy thump that he remembered all too well. The grass was, indeed, so high that the huge beast was nearly swallowed up by it. Its rider descended its wing, disappeared, and then emerged from the long grass, where the cattle-master and his foremen were waiting. They all bowed low the moment they saw him.

*Lordling*, Oller thought, as the magnificently robed dragon rider clapped the cattle-master on his back and smiled broadly. He heard laughter from the group around them. The rider chatted with them, then sauntered off, leading the way to the barracks.

Beside him, Oller's fellow workers were anxious. He wondered why.

Word spread quickly, and with it, a sense of relief.

The herds would be arriving at the end of the following week.

The tension that he'd been feeling dissipated at the news. Two weeks! Two whole *weeks!* There'd be more grass than the cattle could ever eat in a year by then—what with the good rains continuing, if the skies weren't lying—and cartloads of the emperor's shit arriving by the hour.

Relief turned to excitement. It was as if everyone had been reprieved.

Two weeks, Oller thought. Plenty of time to listen and learn.

# 31

## Unsaid, Unseen, Unheard

**Every** morning since we'd sailed from Eastbay, when I awoke I tried to remember whether the Voice in the vault had come to me in the night, with help, with guidance. Since his last, sorrowful realization that there was, after all, nothing that I could do for him, I hadn't heard from him. It was as if he'd resigned himself to his fate. He had left this world for the rest of us to squabble over, while all he could do was watch, impotent, from his bondage, for eternity.

His absence had left me feeling adrift. He'd been my reason for undertaking this quest into the far north. I felt so much more alone without his presence. I worried—not just for myself, but for him. *Was he all right?* Stupid question. Who could possibly be 'all right' in his situation? His silence made me wonder if he was even still alive. If he weren't, well, without his cure, I too would soon be gone.

Perhaps some small part of me would remain, to totter along beside my companions and bewilder them. *A husk.* I'd never know. I wouldn't be there to see how they dealt with it, and how it all played out. I would never come to understand this mystery that I was currently embroiled in.

There were answers that I wanted to know. To find them, I had to live. The world around me was bright and cold and clear; Ice Plains

381

and forests and mountains stretching to the horizon—sun above, snow below. Inside my head, my mind was darkness and confusion.

*What wasn't I seeing?*

I hadn't seen the missing skates and sticks that Qrysta had seen. Which seemed so obvious now, looking back.

I hadn't looked into the gap in Archmage Faldruti's tale. He had told me of how he'd traveled everywhere from the far south all the way to Eastbay, and had never heard of the Valley of the Moon. Again, I hadn't seen the obvious: that I should start researching where he *hadn't* been. If my chance remark in The Ship Aground hadn't led Evall to tell us that he knew where it was, I might well still have been none the wiser. Nyrik had figured out how to challenge the Ogres so that we could earn our way on from Ogretzk. And what about Dean Eilwen's pronouncements? *We've been told*, Marnie had said.

Told what? The answers were there; Marnie had been convinced of it. I couldn't see them. If she was right, the answers lay in the gaps. The more I stared at the few pieces of the puzzle that I could see, the more the whole picture eluded me. I was used to seeing answers quickly. But with this puzzle I'd been lagging behind everyone else so far, it seemed to me, and only getting anywhere thanks to them.

So it was a relief to me when I woke the next morning with a clear plan of action that had come to me in the night. It wasn't much, but at least it was somewhere to start.

I knew what I needed to ask the chief.

*Yes*, I thought. *Of course.*

It was a simple enough question, but one that Horm's explanation hadn't answered.

*"They won't let us through."*

*"What? Why not?!"*

*"How should I know, mate? They're bloody Ogres. Logic don't come into it.*

*"Yes, but—we're not doing them any harm, we're just passing through."*

*"No, you're not. Not if they say you're not."*

*"I don't get it …"*

*"Ogres, Daxxie. They don't think like us. Chief says no go, that's it."*

That was, I now saw, a lazy answer. It might have been good enough for Horm, but it wasn't good enough for me. He was saying that Ogres had neither rhyme nor reason for doing what they did. That might be the case—but how was I to be sure of that? Horm knew a lot more about Ogres than I did, yes, but it wasn't very deep thinking. Horm took people as he found them. He was straightforward. He didn't pry. I needed to pry. Most of us do things for a reason, whether we know it or not. Why wouldn't that apply to Ogres?

Might as well ask, I thought.

What could be the harm in it?

Nothing impresses Ogres more than strength. They had been astounded that a threadbare glove could give its wearer such power. Nyrik's arm wrestle, and Jess's hoisting of the chief, and Grell's moon shot with the boulder, were the talk of Ogretzk. Everyone wanted to see the remarkable object. Horm was happy to show it to them. They all wanted to try it out, of course, but Horm wouldn't let them touch it—not even the chief. I told Horm to say that he had to defer to me, and to drop wary hints about Forbidden Arts. I was the mage, he was to tell them. Anything magic was my department.

What I said went. And I wasn't saying no, but I wasn't saying yes. *Yet.*

It was all nonsense, but it kept them on tenterhooks.

Preparations were underway for our departure, but I could see that they really didn't want us to leave. Any time that I came into the hall all eyes turned to me, to see if I'd changed my mind. They, clearly, didn't know quite what to make of me. They'd seen how the Isvellir wolves adored me, and would gather around me, as docile as lambs, eyes shining, tails wagging. They snapped and snarled at any Ogre who came near them. They hadn't wanted to leave without me, even when Fjernmond had them strapped into their traces. It had taken several flicks of his reins, and a lot of sharp Ice Orc commands, to get them, reluctantly, going. They kept looking back at me wistfully as they hauled Fjernmond's empty sled south and west out of Ogretzk.

I was going to miss them, I knew. Well, with luck I'd see them on the way home.

The Voice in the vault's words came back to me.

*They know what you are.*

They still puzzled me.

What was I? I was no longer Gifted.

I could hardly ask the wolves.

I knew that the answer lay ahead, in the Valley of the Moon. To learn it, we had to get there. We'd won our passage, so would be free to go on from Ogretzk. But, that morning, as I awoke, I thought that I had found a missing piece of the puzzle.

The chief agreed at once when Horm told him that I needed to speak with him in private.

We gathered in his bedroom. It was paneled with rough planks of raw wood and hardly bigger than he was. Most of it was taken up by his bed, but we could all fit on that, just about, sitting side by side, while the chief folded himself into a wooden armchair made of logs beside the hearth, his head looming up against the raftered ceiling. I'd made sure that Grell had the Glove of Strength visibly tucked into his belt. The chief could hardly keep his eyes off it.

Horm explained that I needed my group to hear what we were going to discuss, as it was quite possible that I might not survive the trials that lay ahead of us.

The chief looked at me sharply when he heard that.

Good, I thought. He wants to know what is threatening me. I have his attention.

I began.

First, through Horm, I told him how grateful we were for his hospitality, and his help. We were going off into the unknown—at least, to places that were unknown to us. I said that we would really appreciate any advice or information he could give us.

He knew what was coming. In his rumbling reply, we could pick out the word easily enough.

*Mondthal.*

He didn't seem keen to talk about it.

Horm looked at me and I nodded. We'd discussed how to approach this. He knew what to say next.

"On our way back," Horm told him, in Ogrish, "as a token of our gratitude for everything that you and our new friends here in Ogretzk have done for us, and as a sign of respect, we would like to make you a gift."

He nodded at Grell, who took the Glove of Strength from his belt and handed it to me.

The chief's eyes grew round in surprise.

"You've seen what it can do, Chief," Horm said. "And it's a thing the like of which none of us have come across before. We don't know its limits. We've said Grell here could lift a mastodon, wearing it. Who knows? That was just our idle talk. An *Ogre* wearing it? Hurl a mastodon a mile along that lake of yours, mayhaps. Thing to remember, though, Chief, is: It don't last long. Its power fades after a couple of minutes. It slowly recharges, once you take it off your hand. It's good to go again in an hour or so, although you'll only get a few seconds out of it. We reckon it gets back ten seconds an hour, so, be sure to take it off and leave it overnight, and it'll be fully charged again. We're telling you this so you don't wear it all the time and think it's no good, suddenly, and that we've cheated you, when its strength runs out."

The chief grunted, nodding.

"Obviously, we can't give it to you now, Chief, much as we'd like to, 'cos we don't know as we won't be needing it, in what's to come where we're going," Horm continued. "Glove of Strength might just save our lives, up there, against whatever's facing us. But we'll be coming back this way, right? I mean, there's no other route south. Is there?"

The chief shook his head.

"So," Horm said, "we're hoping as mayhaps you can answer a couple of questions we have? That might make it so as some of us survive and get back here?"

The chief understood. It would be in his interest for us to make it back to Ogretzk and present him with the Glove of Strength. Even so, he seemed reluctant to help us.

Horm had dropped the hint neatly. *Whatever's facing us.*

That was what we wanted to know about.

The chief might not know everything about what lay ahead of us, but he had to know more than we did. He turned his huge head towards me and studied me as if trying to make up his mind.

He muttered something and Horm translated. "Ask."

I said, "Why didn't you want to let us through?"

The chief stared at me. The logs crackled and spat in the hearth. Eventually, he shifted on his armchair and replied. Not with an answer, but another question.

Horm translated. "He wants to know why we're going there."

So, I told him, with Horn translating for me.

I told him everything: my Gifting by Graycote; my conversations with the Voice in the vault; my flight from the Wild Hunt; Urngra's death; my Form on the Moon Nights aboard *The Red Rose*, and a month later in Isvellir; our journey to Mondthal—and that I might have less than a month to live.

385

It took a while. I tried to keep my expression neutral and my voice level. If the facts of my case didn't persuade him there was no point in trying to sell it, I thought. That might just annoy him. His own face was unreadable as he listened, his yellow eyes more on me than on Horm, even when Horm was speaking.

When Horm stopped translating the chief turned away, and gazed into the fire, his face thoughtful. Eventually, as if he'd made his decision, he nodded.

He looked back at me and held out his hand.

Not for the Glove, I realized, but to seal the agreement.

I reached out for it, and we shook.

Slowly, the chief began to talk, Horm translating for us as he went along.

"Mondthal," he said. "It was here before we were. It was here before the Orcs, and the Ice Wights, and the root folk. We have our dealings with each other. We have our trades and our quarrels, which we settle as best we can. None of us dispute with Mondthal." He stopped. He stared at the fire.

He gathered his thoughts and continued. "At its center stands a tower. Who built it, we do not know. The pale light that shines atop it can be seen from the peaks of fire that rim that valley, which we do not enter—neither Ogre, Orc, root folk, nor Ice Wight."

He paused. "We have forgotten why. Long ago, a pact was made, the lore that has been handed down from our ancestors tells us. We swore, she swore. Our ancestors were relieved at the bargain. Our lands and our lakes were to be ours from then on, to have and to hold, just as that valley is hers. We built our stronghold, here, where you are now, and our outlying settlements. It is hard, in these lands. We are at peace. We do not need enemies. Least of all enemies more powerful than us."

He looked at me as Horm translated that last sentence. "You have seen how we value strength. We are strong. *She* is stronger. Should she come for us, we would perish."

I said nothing and waited.

The chief continued. "Which she might do, if she believed that we had broken the pact. We are Ogres. We do not break our word. She is other. She may not know that about us."

*She,* I thought. The Voice in the vault had talked of a "she." "What can you tell me about her?"

The chief frowned. "She is the moon."

"And?"

"And? And we are mortals! The moon is divine. She circles the sky, night after night, age after age. She guides us. She throws her light on our prey, so that we may hunt, and live. She is our protector. She moves the tides. She changes the seasons. Without her, we are nothing. She returns, by day, to sleep, in her tower. Its light waxes, and wanes, as the moon does. We do not go near her valley."

Before I knew what I was saying, the words were out of my mouth. "And their son?"

He was instantly on alert. "What do you know of him?!"

"Little," I lied.

He bristled, studying me. Eventually, he spoke again. "She is life. He is death. She is light. He is night."

I waited.

He did not continue.

"What does that mean?" I said.

He stared at me, for a long time. He took a deep breath and sighed. "We live. We die. They do not. We do not remember …." He tailed off.

I prompted, "Remember?"

"Anything. Before. Before we were here. We wonder why we are here. Our tales do not tell. Some of us believe that we are no more than gatekeepers. We do not allow anyone through. We do not know why. Some pass, across the lake. If we see their tracks, over the ice, we follow. Few evade us. Of those that do, none return."

Before I realized what I was saying, the words were out of me. "We will return, Chief. And this gift will be yours, with our thanks."

He frowned at me, as if not knowing what to make of my certainty. He spoke again, and Horm translated. "Others of us believe that we have been misled. Lied to. Played for fools. Why should we not go there, to the Tower of the Moon, and learn what is to be learned? Are we just her servants, guarding her realm? If so, why? We would like to know." He paused. "We have never dared. We are at peace, with Mondthal."

Grell muttered, "Let sleeping dogs lie."

The chief wanted to know what he'd said. Horm translated. The chief froze, and glared at Grell. "He is no dog!"

Grell shifted on the chief's bed. "Just a figure of speech, mate. Meaning, leave well alone. Nothing more than that."

Clearly what Grell said had upset the chief.

I said, "He?"

The chief growled, and shook his head. He didn't want to talk about it. But he did. He grunted two words. "Urmfngn Dvrrhhk."

Horm's eyes grew wide with surprise. "The Great Wolf."

Silence fell.

We waited.

The chief spoke again. "The wolf that walks the sky. He who hunts the Hunter, his father. He who will devour his mother, the Moon, and the sun and the stars, until all is darkness. He who is the end."

Dean Eilwen's words echoed in my head:

*Let darkness fall*

*And end it all.*

Something clicked in my mind.

I heard again the words of the Voice in the vault:

*He is a monster.*

And it was him that I must find, if I was going to find my own salvation.

A thought occurred to me. "Have you seen him?"

The chief frowned. He shook his head. "Has anyone?"

No. "Then how do you know all this?"

"It is what has been passed down to us. It has always been known."

Old lore, then, I thought. There were still gaps in it.

The gaps, I had now learned, were where I needed to look. "What else can you tell us?"

He shrugged, as if he wanted the conversation to be over. Then a thought struck him. "We stop those that we can, but no one can stop Rumour. Rumour comes and goes as she pleases. And from time to time they come this way, those who seek the Valley. Southerners, such as you. Many are exhausted, after much hardship, and fit to go no further. Yet all are driven, as if by a fever. They must go on! We ask them, why? Their answers are often wild, incoherent. A great treasure is to be won there, or forgotten knowledge. Some had lost their true loves, and believed they would find a spell, or object of power, that would return the dead to life. Others yearned for magical weapons that could slay any foe. We concocted a story. We told them that they had been misled: A demon was luring them to him, with falsehoods, so that he might drain their souls, and they would die in torment. Some believed us, and turned for home, both disillusioned and relieved. Others pretended to, but doubled back, and tried to evade us. Some succeeded. None returned."

And that seemed to be the end of it.

I looked at the others. I could see that none of them had any ideas. They were thinking what I was thinking. *None returned.*

I looked back up at the chief. His yellow eyes were dulled, sorrowful. He *knew* we weren't coming back.

And then the weirdest thing happened …. I was looking down at me. At my own physical form.

The chief looked back up out of my face at me, seeing himself through my eyes, as baffled as I was.

I was completely disoriented. I could do nothing but stare down at … *him? Me?*

Neither of us knew what to think. We stared at each other, frozen.

I could hear voices, very faint, as if muffled and from a long way away—the others asking if we were okay and what was up.

And then we jerked apart, back in our own minds and skins again.

The chief lurched away from me on his chair, his eyes wide with shock, gargling a stream of Ogrish.

"He wants to know what is happening," Horm said, "and how did you do that?"

I was gasping for breath myself and trying to recover. "I didn't," I said. "I don't know what that was."

"What was?" Qrysta asked.

"I … it …" I didn't know how to explain. "We swapped places. I was looking down at me, only it was him. Inside. He was looking up at me, where he should have been."

The chief was on his feet and roaring at Horm, who was doing his best to placate him, while translating for us.

"He says you're a mage, so of course it was you! Who else could have done that?"

"I don't know!" I said. "Please, assure him I have no idea what happened. I'm as in the dark as he is."

It took a long time for Horm to calm the chief down. Once he was more or less settled back down in his chair, muttering to himself, Horm ushered us out of his room, offering apologies.

"Bleeding hells, mate!" he said, staring up at me. "He was about to kill the lot of us!"

No one questioned why. We were all shaken.

All I could think of to say was, "Thanks, Horm."

"You going to explain?"

I looked down at him. "I wish I could."

Horm glanced at Nyrik, who shrugged.

"Best make ourselves scarce tonight," Nyrik said.

"Yur," Horm agreed. "This will upset them. They have rules of hospitality. Their roof, their rules. We're safe here, while we're under it, but ....
Good thing we're leaving on the morrow."

We retired to our guest room in silence.

Bowls of food and mugs of ale appeared, handed to us by Ogres who glared and said nothing.

It was clear that they wanted us gone.

Why was it, I thought, as I turned over in my mind all that I'd been through, that there were always more questions than answers?

Perhaps there weren't. Perhaps I could only see questions because I kept failing to see answers. Answers that were staring me in the face.

That evening, at last, we heard from Oller.

My Link of Impartment glowed white twice—our code for "okay to talk?"

I tapped it twice with my greenfire pendant. Two green glows would let Oller know that it was.

We watched, waiting to see what he had to tell us.

# 32

## What Oller Learned

People flooded into the Grazings by the day: workers, suppliers and specialists of all kinds, not to mention lords and ladies, and rich merchants, and camp followers, until the place was heaving. Oller kept himself to himself. He didn't want to make new friends. Friends would notice that he was gone when he left. He didn't need to ask questions, which was fine by him. Asking questions can raise suspicions. All he had to do was keep his ears open, while he was at his splicing, and tying, and knotting in the rope sheds.

There was a mountain of work for the corders and not enough hands to do it all. Once the foremen had seen how quick and neat he was at his tasks, "Korv" was left to get on with it, while everyone around him talked of little but the coming war. Oller listened, and learned. Ten divisions were assembling at the ports: the seven imperial Vu-Sant divisions, the rest knights, archers, and engineers. The fleets were refitting and taking on stores. Nobles, in their fine robes, talked openly, paying no attention to the common folk hurrying and toiling around them, swapping news of commands being assigned to the great lords, and what that might mean for their own possibilities of a commission.

All who stood a chance of going to war were eager to take part. It had been years since the empire had sent its forces out on a real campaign of conquest. None of what Oller heard was good news. Just like everyone around him, he didn't see how his little realm stood a chance. There was no point in getting in touch with Daxx simply to tell him that, he thought. *He'll be worried enough already. Besides, he has his own problems. No, I'll just sit here, and see what I see, and hear what I hear, until it's time to make myself scarce.*

And then what? Back to Jarnland, in time to die along with everyone else?

Well. If it came to that: yes. He'd never had friends before. Now he had Daxx, and Grell, and Qrysta, and Esmeralda—the queen, no less—and Marnie, and Jess, and Little Guy. Not to mention Commandant Bastard. Who was not exactly a friend, as such, but was definitely someone Oller wanted to think well of him. He imagined the Commandant glancing down at him, as they faced a horde of chalkers, and giving him a nod of approval for being there, at his side, weapons drawn.

He'd rather die with that than live without it.

Especially if it meant living in a place like Sarmen, with its noise, and heat, and poverty, and cruelty, and spies, and fear. He was sure he could survive there. Oller was a survivor. He'd be fine. But he'd rather be somewhere else. Where? Make his way to the Morning Isles, perhaps, settle in Freehaven?

While his friends died in Jarnland.

And they weren't even *from* there. And he was.

No. He wanted to see how this ended. Even though he couldn't see it ending any way but badly. It made him chuckle when he realized that he wouldn't be able to live with himself if he didn't go home to die alongside his friends.

When his shifts ended, he'd leave the rope sheds and head back to his bunkhouse, with its mess hall, where he'd eat, and listen, and sip water, and listen, while all around him drank ale, and talked. He knew how to play the part that he'd assigned himself. Crouch over his work; avoid eye-contact; stutter when spoken to; let people think him simple. There was too much going on for anyone to have the time to be anything but run off their feet—let alone be bored and looking around for a victim to persecute. Besides, they'd all seen how Korv's foreman, Master Ildrutj, approved of his work. Ildrutj was large, and evil-tempered, and carried a rope's-end that he was quick to lash out with. No one was going to pick on anyone *he* approved of and risk a beating.

After his evening meal, Oller would go out into the dark, and slip on his Ring of Blending. He could stand inches away from anyone while wearing it, and they never knew he was there. If he stood still, and they turned in his direction, they would look right through him, and carry on as if sure they were alone and unobserved. The workers at the Grazings were hearty eaters and drinkers. That, combined with their excitement about the coming campaign, made them expansive. They talked as openly as if they were living in a land that was not riddled with informers. No spy was going to hear them say anything disloyal, or unroyal. They were all for this war, and all for their emperor. They were in it together, and would do all they could for His Radiance's glory, in which they would bask with reflected pride.

So Oller drifted from group to group, in the warm darkness of the nights of that southern springtime, and listened, and learned. He learned what the peculiar contraptions that he had been roping together were. They were harnesses, to go on the backs of the dragons. Long slats of wood that would run along the dragon's back were suspended a couple of feet below each other. The lowest slats on either side supported wooden troughs, a foot wide and deep, their outer edges hinged so that they could fall open. Each trough was divided into compartments. A complicated rigmarole of ropes spread throughout the harness, as elaborate as the rigging of a ship. Brass hoops, hanging from leather straps, hung at intervals from the slats. Ropes passed through them, and looped behind and under the troughs, and tied off into a line of hooks in their outer edges. The ropes gathered forwards to what was termed a "collar"—a hoop of wood, into which notches had been cut. The collar would sit above the dragon's neck, behind its driver. The front end of each rope was knotted, and slotted into the collar.

The whole arrangement baffled Oller. They looked, when finished, very pleasing, he thought, like intricate spiderwebs. He couldn't think what on earth they were for—until he heard the words, "the crew." He listened, and learned how this was all arranged for the crew's convenience, so that they could be ready to jump into action when ordered.

His heart sank as he worked it out.

Rigging. Ships. Crews. The *boarding* crew.

Chalkers, flown in from above, their feet braced in the troughs, which were opened as they landed behind enemy lines, freeing them to jump down, and charge into their foes from the rear.

Chalkers in front. Chalkers behind. Dragons raining fire and fury down from above. What hope did they have? He couldn't see any.

The more he listened, the less he liked what he heard.

He wasn't going to give up, though. Just as he wasn't going to Impart anything doom-laden to Daxx. He'd just turn up in Mayport, in time for Midsummer Day, and if he didn't have anything helpful to say, well, he just wouldn't say it.

One evening, as the stars emerged beyond the sinking sun, he noticed foreman Ildrutj chatting with a man he hadn't seen before—a newcomer, dressed in strange, shabby robes. Campfires were burning around them, throwing firelight on their faces. Camouflaged by his Ring of Blending, Oller moved close to them.

The newcomer was a spindly man of middle years, his hair and beard a white cloud around his face, his eyes mild but alert. Oller was surprised that Ildrutj, a stickler for correctness and precedence, was conversing respectfully with this unimpressive, otherworldly character. He was treating him as if he was a superior. Oller studied the man with interest. He seemed unthreatening—dreamy and vague. Master Ildrutj was not known for his patience, yet he had all the time in the world for this newcomer, with whom he was not his usual bullying self. Rather, he was all smiles, and deference.

*Interesting,* Oller thought. *Wonder what this is about.*

"We have high hopes," the newcomer was saying, his voice light and reedy—a contrast to the gruff tones of the foreman. An educated man, Oller thought. And one who was clearly longing to divulge a secret that it was torturing him to have to keep to himself. "We pray that His Radiance will be as astonished as we were."

"As do we, doctor," Ildrutj agreed, quickly.

He waited. The "doctor" said nothing but merely hummed happily to himself.

Ildrutj could resist no longer. "Be better than last time, then?"

The newcomer stopped humming, and his face fell. He coughed and shuffled his feet. "Yes, well," he said. "That was … unfortunate."

"That it was," Ildrutj agreed.

The newcomer cleared his throat. Eventually, he said, "It was a lesson I shall always value. His Radiance's justice is both terrible and merciful. I meditated upon it, as I watched my predecessor's punishment. Had it been over quickly, I do not believe that I would have come to understand what I see now. He was my mentor, a man I had learned much from, and for whom I had the greatest respect and affection. Until he failed in his duty. His death was an example to us all. His Radiance will spare me that fate, if I so deserve."

"As he will me," Master Ildrutj concurred.

"And if I do not so deserve, I do not deserve the joy of serving the empire."

"That you do not, Doctor Nims, no more'n any of us."

After a thoughtful pause, Doctor Nims said, in a more practical tone, "Were you aware, before the accident, of how much fat the beasts have on them?"

Foreman Ildrutj shook his head. "That we were not, doctor. We'd never seen a one of the buggers on fire before. Burned for two days, it did. Makes sense, though."

"It does?"

"Their humps. Full o' fat. That's where they store their fuel. They can keep going for days without taking on food or water. Without sleep, even. Camels of the sky, they are."

"They are remarkable creatures."

"That they are, doctor. That they are."

Oller waited, through another contemplative pause in the conversation.

"O' course," Ildrutj continued, "that one was full to bursting. He'd been gorging himself for days. Had humps as big as his hips on him. So when your pots cracked—"

"My *predecessor's* pots," Doctor Nims corrected him.

"Your predecessor's pots, indeed," Ildrutj acknowledged. "Well, it was like oil on a bonfire. Poor bastard didn't stand a chance. Up in flames, roaring his head off. Sight I'll never forget. So, no. You don't set fire to His Radiance's chattels and go unpunished. Far more valuable than you, the beasts are."

"Indeed, indeed," Doctor Nims agreed. "A mistake that our guild won't be making again. As you will see with your own eyes, before much longer."

"I look forward to it."

Doctor Nims was smiling again, Oller saw, and once again excited by his Big Secret that was bursting to get out.

"I beg you to keep this to yourself," he said, to the foreman. "The more of a surprise that this is, for His Radiance, the better it will go for us."

"My lips are sealed, doctor," the foreman assured him.

"And by 'us,' of course," Doctor Nims added, "I do not just mean us Alchemists. I mean all of us here at the Grazings. Masters, men— and *foremen*."

Ildrutj smiled, and nodded. "I appreciate your confidence, doctor."

The Alchemist bowed. "And I appreciate your discretion, Master Ildrutj. At the demonstration," he added, lowering his voice, "make good note of the pots."

"The pots?"

Doctor Nims drew back and tapped his nose. "I shall say no more, sir. I have said too much already. Fortunately, I know that I can count on your silence."

"That you can, doctor," Ildrutj assured him. "That you most certainly can!"

The news was all over the Grazings by morning. *The Alchemists have got another one! It's going to be better than last time!*

*Well, it could hardly be worse.*

*They wouldn't be bringing it if it was, would they? They're not stupid. Who wants to be bound to a stake and worked on by His Radiance's question-masters, with everyone watching? Not me, thanks! No, if the Alkies have got something, it's going to be good.*

When he saw it, even Oller had to admit that it was.

Well, good for them.

Bad for us.


A hundred harnesses were needed, and fast. There were plenty in the quartermaster's stores, but most of them were in poor shape, as they hadn't been used in years. Rope and leather and wood rotted fast in that hot, often humid climate. Some harnesses were restored, others cannibalized for parts. More than fifty had to be built from scratch. The crafters had everything they needed except time. So they worked around the clock, from before dawn to late at night, against the day when the crown prince and his court would arrive.

Well in time, a hundred perfect harnesses were laid out in ranks, ready to be fitted to their mounts. A dozen spares stood to one side, in case they were needed. The foremen inspected them, again and again, ordering polishers to buff up the leather, and grease the rings, and carpenters to apply more coats of varnish. They were all proud of their work, and content with what they had produced.

They were also nervous. Each harness was marked with a number. Should any fail to please the air-masters, or fail to work smoothly, or, gods forbid, come apart during maneuvres … the foreman responsible would be answerable. He could not expect mercy. Any who failed His Radiance knew the inevitable penalty. Good workers being scarce, his crew would be let off with no more than a flogging. That would be the replacement foreman's first duty to administer to them, in person. But they were cautiously hopeful that it would not come to that. They all, hands and masters alike, expected, if a little nervously, that things would go well. And that would mean feasting, and bonuses, and pride in a job well done.

Old hands told of the last campaign, when they had cheered the air fleet off to war, two decades and more before. The celebrations had lasted for days. And talk about *anything goes!* Every man jack and woman jill had lined up for their bonuses, doled out by the Imperial Clerks—more gold than most of them had ever seen. *It'll be the same this time,* the old hands said, *you mark my words! His Radiance is generosity itself to those who please him.*

The heavy thumps began in the middle of the night, waking Oller and his co-workers. They all hurried outside to see huge shadows descending out of the moonlit sky into the tall grass of the Grazings. The herds were gathering at last. From all directions they came, in handfuls, or by the dozen. They'd been feeding elsewhere, Oller knew, so as not to exhaust resources. This was the last stop on their journey. They were here to fatten up before leaving for the coast, where they would rest before the long flight overseas, and to war.

Maneuvres would start at dawn. The moment they'd all been working so hard for had come at last.

It took ten men to run each harness from the sheds to the herds, five each side, carrying the awkward frames above their heads. Foremen shouted orders and called out their steps, *left, right, left, right,* as they hurried downhill at the double, making every effort not to twist

397

the contraptions they were carrying, and so perhaps weaken them. And then there were the ramps that they had to walk the things up, one each side of the dragon, starting at its tail. It was like inching the roof of a house onto its frame, Oller thought, only the "house" was a massive, gray, leathery creature, squatting there, grumbling ominously, while its rider menaced it with his whip. To his relief, everything went off without a hitch. His team got their beasts harnessed and retreated back up the slope to watch.

He squatted on his heels, arms wrapped around his knees, studying the scene below. Around him, workers gossiped about the notables gathered on the grandstand.

Oller made a mental note of the names he heard. Mejnul, he knew, was the eldest son of the Empress Prelajnul, and thus crown prince. Surrounding him were his younger brothers, Karjnul and Feyjnul, and his half brothers, sons of his father's lesser wives, Orynmar and Heirnuq. Barthuq, Reyyuq, and Vashtenar, he learned, were older than the crown prince, Eilmar and Irmruq younger.

Oller watched them all carefully, noting their body language as well as the expressions on their faces. They all carried themselves with the arrogance of those used to absolute command, but made sure to bow when Mejnul addressed them, and reply with deference. They were all teeth and smiles, he thought, masking their true feelings. None of them carried weapons, or had Vu-Sant bodyguards, while Mejnul's enormous champion stood behind him, as always. An interesting dynamic. Oller wondered how what he was seeing could help them.

He listened, and learned.

He learned that the generals who commanded the Imperial Divisions of ten thousand Vu-Sant each, were always of royal blood. They spent their careers stuck out in the provinces, keeping the natives under the emperor's thumb, chasing bandits, or leading the occasional punitive expedition into neighboring lands when cross-border raiders became too bold. Their duty was to guard the empire that one day their favored brother would inherit.

*And why him? Why not me?* They'd never say that, of course, or they'd lose their heads. But everyone knew. That's just the way it was. His Radiance didn't want his brothers at court, gaining influence and followers. It was a rare occasion to see them all gathered in one place.

Lesser generals led the three support divisions, of cavalry, archers, and engineers, that would make up the numbers of the invading force. Crown Prince Mejnul himself commanded the air fleet. Oller's eyes kept returning to the huge beasts gathered on the field below. They were as neatly arranged by rank and file as the palace guards at Mayport.

Oller's heart sank as he looked down at them. A hundred massive dragons, in parade-ground order, ready to obey their masters. How had they done that? How were those monsters tamed and turned from threats into weapons?

Only one dragon was not harnessed: the largest and darkest of them all, a gray so dark it was almost black: Prince Mejnul's mount, his Nightshade. His co-workers spoke of it with awe: "Rarer than rare, Nightshades. No one else is permitted to ride one. Reserved for Their Radiances, Nightshades are—the emperor and his heir. His Supreme Radiance was a fine rider in his day. Too old to ride any longer, may the gods preserve and protect him. Shame, the state he's in, the word is. Can't properly speak, can't walk unaided. It'll be Emperor Mejnul within a twelvemonth, as I hear it. As we all hear, he can't wait for the day.

"Unlike his brothers. Yur, that'll be their lot, and they know it. They're only alive now on account of His Radiance's wives pupping nothing but girls. He won't need his brothers to ensure the bloodline once a son comes. Mayhaps this new foreign bride of his will give him some.

"The day that happens, their own chalker bodyguards will finish those fine princes off. Unless they manage to slip away and join the outlaws they've been rooting out for years.

"Yes, gold can make a difference when a man changes sides. And are those outlaws not led, rumor has it, by their own uncles and cousins, who fled the same fate a generation ago?"

Carts drawn by oxen trundled into the field. Oller was puzzled as he watched them pass below the jaws of the dragons, as if unconcerned. He could not imagine the power that so held the dragons in thrall that they did not even appear to notice slow, plump, juicy oxen plodding just below their noses. *If they can do that*, he thought, *what else can they do? Control dragons? And ones this big? Even Vagg could hardly handle his little chicken-sized ones, and he's the best in our land.*

*We're completely out of our depth*, Oller thought. *It just gets worse and worse.*

Alchemists and their apprentices jumped off the ox-wagons and began to unload them. The Alchemists, in their dark robes and pointed hats, gave orders. Their apprentices, in their gray ones, ran carrying stones, as instructed, from the wagons to the dragons.

Stones?

Oller peered, but could see nothing special about them. They were just lumps of rock, all more or less the same size—about as big as a human head. *What's all this?* he thought. Masters hurried about, instructing the apprentices where to put their stones. Each stone, he saw, fitted into a slot in the troughs on the dragon's harness. The apprentices ran back to their carts. Their masters gave them fresh orders. The apprentices got more stones, but this time, very slowly, and with exaggerated carefulness, as if they were as fragile as eggs, carried them to the harnesses, where they lowered them into place, much more gently than before. This was repeated, again and again, almost in slow motion, until every slot in every harness held its own stone.

A lump of rock.

Lowered into place as tenderly as if it were a newborn child.

Oller was baffled. What in all hells was he looking at?

When all the dragons were fully loaded a horn sounded. A voice called out, from the driver of the leading dragon. The dragons lurched to their feet, and waddled, and beat their wings, and took to the air.

Once aloft, they were graceful. They soared. They were not land animals, Oller understood, but creatures of the air. For a while they drifted around overhead, rising and dipping, stretching their giant wings, occasionally mooing to each other as they flew off into the distance. Then, in response to some signal that he hadn't registered, they were in formation again, far off in the sky, facing back in the direction from which they'd come.

Before he knew it, the first run was underway.

They came in formation, climbing high, then dropping lower as they approached, gathering speed. A cheer went up from the crowd around him as the first rocks dropped. Every harness worked perfectly, the two-man crew on each dragon releasing the ropes held in the collar behind the driver to open the sides of the troughs. The target area in the field puffed with jets of dirt as the rocks landed. Once its load was away each dragon soared skywards again, leaving the approach path clear for the ones coming in behind it. Then they circled, lazily stretching their wings, and glided down, the thumps of their landing reverberating through the ground.

His co-workers were delighted.

Not a single hitch. Everything had gone off perfectly.

Oller still couldn't think what he'd been watching. What on earth was the point of dropping a few small rocks on your foes? We built complicated harnesses just to do that?

He didn't get it.

Then came the climax.

Another cart trundled into the field below them where a single dragon waited. All the others had been herded aside into the long grass, where they settled, their long jaws working as they chewed placidly.

Alchemists ordered apprentices.

Apprentices, very carefully, carried pots from the cart to the dragon's harness.

Oller recalled the conversation he'd overheard between his foreman and Doctor Nims. *Make note of the pots.* He craned forward to study them. The pots, he saw, were painted either black or white. Each black pot was roped to a white pot. The apprentices loaded the paired pots into the troughs on the dragon's harness.

Okay, he thought. They've done the runs for weight and accuracy. Everything hit the target area. So now what's this?

The dragon was loaded. The apprentices were shooed away by the Alchemists. A silence fell over the crowd as the driver whipped his mount forward. It waddled a few paces, then unfurled its wings, and took to the air. Once again awkwardness turned into grace. The great creature soared and dwindled into the distance. When it was no more than a distant speck in the sky it turned and began its approach.

Oller could feel the crowd around him holding their breath. The dragon rose, and rose, and dropped, accelerating. Its crewmen loosed the ropes from its collar. The pots dropped from either side of its harness. They hit the bare earth of the target area from a height of no more than a hundred feet. The dragon bellowed as its driver hauled back on his reins and whipped its flanks. It beat its way skywards and away.

In the target area, the pots shattered.

The contents of the black pots and white pots merged.

And exploded.

A roar went up from the watching crowd as spouts of flame erupted, one after the other, blasting into the air, while a flood of fire swept across the ground.

People were cheering, and clapping, and whistling.

*Dear gods,* Oller thought. No one caught in that inferno would stand a chance.

Prince Mejnul, surrounded by his brother princes and the great lords and ladies of his Imperial Court, was clearly delighted.

Oller watched as, below him, Doctor Nims was summoned to pay his respects.

He walked towards his prince, and knelt, and then prostrated himself.

Silence fell.

Oller noticed the sorceress beside Mejnul raise her staff and point it at him.

When he spoke, his voice carried to all corners of the arena, as clearly as it had carried within the walls of Eastbay Castle.

"Rise, doctor," Prince Mejnul said.

Doctor Nims got to his feet.

"I am relieved," Prince Mejnul said, "that you did not cost me a valuable dragon this time."

"As am I, Your Radiance."

The prince smiled.

His court laughed.

"Nor," Prince Mejnul added, reaching out, and placing his hand on the Alchemist's shoulder, "a valuable servant."

Doctor Nims bowed, and clasped his hands in thanks, and backed away, bowing with every pace.

The crowd cheered.

Oller made a point of shadowing Doctor Nims that evening.

"Black ones and white ones, eh?" Foreman Ildrutj said, when he and Doctor Nims were alone, once again under the starry sky, and once again watched by Oller.

"Indeed," Doctor Nims acknowledged. "So you will have seen the answer."

Ildrutj shook his head. "I don't believe I have, doctor, no."

"The mixture, as you saw, on that unfortunate, earlier occasion, is highly volatile," Nims said. "It is its strength, and also its weakness."

He looked at the foreman for a reaction, eyebrows raised, a teasing smile on his lips.

"How is that, then, doctor?" Ildrutj asked, knowing that it was expected of him.

"It is simply for the reason that it is what it is: a *mixture.* It took us months to see the simplest of explanations. We had created an incendiary far more advanced, and more volatile, than any known before—a weapon of astonishing power. We could not wait to demonstrate it for His Radiance. Sadly, as you saw, Master Ildrutj, we were not in full control of that power. One cracked pot, its mixture exposed to the air— and an immediate conflagration. His Radiance's fury was justified. No doubt you remember his words?"

*"You are to destroy my enemies, not my dragons,"* Master Ildrutj said.

"And those words we took as our orders. Do you know how a mixture is made?"

"I am no Alchemist, doctor ..."

"Guess."

Oller saw the foreman scratch his beard, frowning.

"By ... mixing things?" he guessed.

"Exactly!" Doctor Nims cried, and patted him on the back, chuckling. "Dear me, sir, it took our guild *months* to see what you have seen at once. Sometimes being an expert is more of a hindrance than a help. The black pots hold one formula. The white pots, another. Each, when mixed with air, is inert. Should one crack, there will be no reaction, no conflagration. We make the pots sturdy, to avoid accidents, but ... well, you saw. Accidents will happen. And they must break when hitting the ground, of course. And now, when that happens, both formulae are released, from black pots and white, and mix together, and form—the mixture! Which, on contact with the air, engenders fire and fury indeed."

"An ingenious solution, doctor. We all saw how His Radiance approved."

"I was gratified and humbled," Doctor Nims acknowledged.

Oller couldn't sleep that night. He lay in his bunk, staring into the darkness above him, thinking about everything that he'd seen. It looked hopeless. Their cause was doomed. They were overpowered, outmatched.

He couldn't let himself think that.

There must be *something*, he thought.

He knew that he'd be leaving the next day. He could sneak out at night, and no one would see him, but perhaps someone would notice his empty bed in the morning, and think, *hullo.* By day they'd all be busy about their tasks—the most pleasant of which would be collecting their bonuses. Oller would leave after getting his. He didn't need the coin, but the empire owed him. It would feel like a small victory to take its gold.

The celebrations began at the midday meal. Early in the afternoon he was on his way, unnoticed thanks to his Ring of Blending. He set off northwards. He kept to the open countryside, avoiding the roads. He knew that he could slip past any humans he came across. Dogs might be a problem. He had plenty of time to make his way around any places he didn't like the look of. The land was hilly, and wooded, and deserted. Eventually, he'd reach the coast, and find a ship for home. The captain of *The Rorqual* had told him who to look for, in the ports and smuggling havens. As he walked, he turned over in his mind everything that he'd seen and heard while in Sarmen. Sooner or later, he was going to have to use his Link of Impartment to communicate with Daxx. He couldn't bring himself to do so when all he had was bad news. On the third night, wrapped in his cloak, and gazing up at a sky filled with brilliant stars, something clicked in his head.

The more he thought about it, the more he felt he might have found something. It was a long shot, he had to admit it to himself. He had no idea how Daxx could bring it to fruition; but Daxx was a mage, and this was an idea that would need magic to make it work.

He tapped the Link of Impartment with his Ring of Blending, and saw it glow pale white, and fade.

He gave it another tap, and it glowed and faded again.

He waited.

Within a minute, it glowed green, twice, as Daxx replied.

# 33

## Mondthal

"Well," I said, when Oller had signed off, "what do you make of that?"

"You're the bloody mage, mate," Grell said. "Sounds like your department."

"I can't see how we'll do it," I said. "I mean—a hundred of the things, flying around up there? How am I meant to hit a single one, let alone all of them?"

"You'll have help," Qrysta pointed out. "Marnie and Coven. The GAA."

I couldn't see it. The mismatch was absurd. Lone women, on broomsticks, weaving in and out of an air fleet of dragons, popping off whatever they could at them? And the mages of the GAA would be on the ground, firing upwards, with flame bombs dropping all around them. They'd be as likely to hit friend as foe. If any of them got lucky, and smacked a fireball into the tiny target of two pots tied together: well. That might blow one dragon out of the sky. But, so what? There'd be ninety-nine more of the things, working in concert, doing with military precision what they'd been trained to do. And they were aerobatic. They could probably grab Coven flyers out of the air with their claws, not to mention blasting them with fiery breath. The ones we'd seen when Prince Mejnul landed at Eastbay were far bigger than the helldragon, and she'd sprayed fire around in long spouts wherever she pointed her head. So you'd have to expect the Sarmen monsters would hit hotter, and harder, and further.

And it's not as if we wouldn't have our hands full on the ground.

Seven divisions of chalkers, of ten thousand each? Three of knights and archers and engineers?

We would be otherwise occupied.

I shook my head. I couldn't see it.

I scowled as I thought those words again. *What* couldn't I see? What was I missing?

*We've been told. It's all there, even if we can't yet see it.*

What was all where?

We left Ogretzk early the next morning. As far as the Ogres were concerned it wasn't early enough. They were glad to see the back of us—although their faces didn't look glad. We got nothing from them but scowls and grunts. Horm asked the chief if there was any chance of a guide. There wasn't. "He says we can't miss it," Horm reported back to us. "Just go north. We'll get to the Ring of Fire in a few days. Valley of the Moon's in the middle of it."

It sounded like we shouldn't have much trouble getting there.

The trouble, I was sure, would be waiting for us in Mondthal.

It was a long trek, and a cold one. More ice. More snow. Fewer trees by the day, none of them large enough for us to unlock with Oller's silver key and sleep beneath. Days that lasted twenty-four hours. The sun circled the sky, never sinking in the west. The weather changed on a whim. One moment it would be fine, the air calm. The next, snow had driven in and was swirling around us as we trudged into it, head down, barely able to see the person ahead.

We were well equipped, though, and well provisioned. If the going got bad, we simply stopped going, and hunkered down in our furs and cloaks, and slept until the skies cleared and we could move on again. Little Guy always tucked himself inside Jess's cloak and slept with her arms wrapped around him, his nose poking out from under her furs. Shift and I could keep everyone reasonably warm and dry, in protective bubbles, and we could march long hours as I refreshed everyone's stamina.

There was little cover. We stood out against that wide, white landscape. Anyone with eyes to see would spot us coming from afar, so there was no point in trying to conceal our presence. When we halted, we lit fires and gathered around them, and ate, and discussed what little we knew, and what might lie ahead. Nyrik and Horm twice brought down snow geese, which we spitted and roasted. They were delicious. We were anxious, of course, and underinformed, but, all things considered, in good shape and good heart. We knew that we hadn't seen anything yet, and that the worst lay ahead, so we weren't fooling ourselves, but we were far from despondent. Nyrik and Horm kept our spirits up with their banter at us and each other.

Qrysta and Grell and I agreed that this wasn't anything like as bad as our descent to the Floor Of The World had been. By the time we'd reached that, we'd been running on empty. And we'd had to fight our way down, each battle more exhausting than the one before it. Nothing attacked us on our way to the Valley of the Moon. We saw reindeer, and musk ox; fur-elk, and wolves, and bears, and the occasional mastodon. We avoided them. They avoided us. The further north we went the fewer there were, until, it seemed, the land was empty, and we were the only creatures on it.

On the sixth day a red glow, faint at first, grew ahead of us, as if the sun was rising in the north—or rather, several small suns, at intervals. As we walked, the red lights leached up into the sky above, turning it orange. At last, peaks emerged above the horizon, some white with snow, others crowned with splashes of crimson, which burned bright, then faded, then burst high, and fell back, and flowed down the mountainsides in rivers of lava.

The Ring of Fire.

There was no end to it, that we could see, neither east nor west. We could not have gone around it even if we'd wanted to.

Which we didn't.

We wanted to get over it, or pass through it, into the valley that lay within.

We made camp that night under the shadow of those mountains. We needed to be well rested for whatever lay ahead. Ahead of us, far above, volcanoes belched and boomed. The smell of sulfur came down to us in gusts of cold wind. It was spectacular, awe-inspiring. It made us feel small and vulnerable.

"Nearly there, eh?" Grell said, as he settled down to sleep.

"Nearly there," I agreed.

That night, I turned everything over in my mind.

*Nearly there.*

407

Grell's words echoed in my thoughts.

For days the feeling had been growing on me that a revelation was imminent, just out of my grasp. I had no idea what that feeling was based on, but it kept me alert. My mind felt sharper than it had since the village. *Nearly there.* I was sure of it. Whatever I realized next, I was convinced, would be crucial. *We've been told. It's all there, even if we can't yet see it.* Everything I needed to know I knew already, but I … just didn't know it. I was the puzzle king, and I couldn't see which twos and twos to put together to make fours. I circled all the information I'd been given, around and around, testing every point of it, until I felt my mind cracking. I fell asleep before I got anywhere.

Clouds scudding across a full moon. A pale tower in a white plain. Yellow eyes opening.

The familiar Voice. Weak, and defeated, and tired. *You have come.*

*Yes. I promised that I would.*

A silence.

*I am grateful. It will be a nice change to have company, if only for a little while. Someone warm. And generous. The company I share is … anything but.*

*What must I do?*

*Cross the barrier. No human can. She made it so. But those who have been Gifted are more than human. You were my last hope. Even though I have lost all hope now, and there is nothing you can do for me, I will give you what you need. You have my word on it.*

*Can I not free you?*

*Not without freeing him. That must not happen. He is the end. I am the price that must be paid to forestall it. I see that now. Come and be cured, mortal, and leave me to my fate. It gladdens me that you have tried to help me. I laid a plan, long ages ago. Should one who has been Gifted and is skilled in magic come to the village, my salvation would be at hand. I was wrong. It was not to be. She is more powerful than I knew. No doubt she knows best. After all, she is my mother.*

He was resigned to his fate.

A fate that I could not imagine. Bound to a monster forever and sealed in a cavern beneath the ice.

There must be something I could do, I thought.

I thought again, *Must there? Who says?*

If there were, I decided, I would do it. Of course I would. I would be face-to-face with him soon enough, beyond the barrier that no human could cross. Then I would receive my cure, and see what I would see, and do what I could do for him—even though, from what he had told me, I assumed that there was nothing—

*Assumed …*

The word echoed in my mind. I recalled Dean Eilwen's line:

*Don't assume.*

*Yes,* I thought. Maybe I *would* be able to help.

The dream faded. The clouds, and the moon, and the tower, and the scudding clouds, and the yellow eyes drifted out of my sleeping mind.

*We've been told.*

*It's all there, even if we can't yet see it.*

The chief had been right. We couldn't miss it. A path led towards the Ring of Fire. We followed it the next morning. It climbed higher by the hour, but not nearly as high as the snow-covered mountainsides that reared either side of us. It was, clearly, leading us through a pass between two high peaks, one leaking red lava that flowed past us, steaming and hissing as it ate into the snowfield.

The wind got up. Snow swirled. Clouds descended, obscuring everything. The path ahead of us disappeared into them. We climbed on and up. We had intended that Jess would take to the skies and scout out the lay of the land, but there was no point in her going up into that murk. She wouldn't see anything, and might well not be able to find her way back to us.

False crest followed false crest. We kept thinking that we'd come to the summit of the path, and that we were starting our way down, only to start climbing again. The wind blew stinging snow into our faces. We could hardly see each other, as we trudged on, and up, heads down, our cloaks whipping about us. Our blindness kept us on high alert, anxious to spot any threat that might appear out of nowhere. None did, but the tension was as exhausting as the climb.

Eventually, although we did not know it, we came over the last crest. No more climbs interrupted our descent. After a while we all realized that we were finally on our way down. We stopped. We wanted to see what lay below us, from as high a vantage point as possible. There was no more up, only down.

We would have to wait, to see what we could see. Another halt, then. But not another fire. We would not have lit one even if we had been able to find wood to burn. We did not want to warn whoever was below of our approach. We expected a tower. We expected its inhabitants would be vigilant. Someone—some*thing*—would surely be on watch.

We wrapped ourselves in our furs and our blankets, and huddled close to each other, and I cast what Sheltering and Warming I could over us. It was a bleak "night," in that perpetual daylight, shrouded by thick clouds and obscured by driving snow. None of us slept well. We each took an hour on watch, but we all kept waking up and looking around for trouble, before dozing fitfully back off again.

The wind lessened. The snow stopped falling. The clouds thinned, and lifted.

The horizons cleared, and we looked down into the Valley of the Moon.

It was a desolate prospect. An empty terrain, on which nothing grew: stony ground; ice fields; snowdrifts; scatterings of boulders that had slid off the mountainsides. Above us, snow caps, and soaring peaks of fire, the echoes of their eruptions rumbling and fading in the distance. Lava snaked down into the valley floor, curdling in long, gray rivers of slowly congealing molten rock. A grim place. A dangerous place.

And at its heart, a pale tower.

Its circular wall was riven by black slits, which spiraled up to a single, wide window, in which a dim light shone. A crenellated parapet flared out above the window. Wisps of cloud drifted past it.

*Mondthal.*

Our destination.

Grell grunted. "Yeah," he said, nodding. He turned to look at me. He had no need to say what he was thinking. *This is it.*

I could only agree.

Beside me, Horm growled, "Is this where the bastards are, then?"

I grimaced. "I think so."

"Good," he said.

I looked down at him. The expression on his face gave me chills. I'd seen it before. It had been on his face when he was astride my chest, about to slit my throat, in the back alley outside Velaryn's house in Eastbay, his silver arrows in my shoulder and leg.

Seeing that look again also gave me strength.

We were there with a purpose.

I thought, *Forget about what we don't know. Let's just see what we have, in front of us, and maybe we'll find out.* I said, "Jess, can you go up and take a look?"

"Sure." She unhitched her broomstick from her back.

"Don't get too close. You don't want to be seen, but anything you can spot through that top window could be useful."

"I'll be careful," she said. She straddled her broomstick and shot up into the sky.

We watched her fly up, and around, as she scoped out the Tower of the Moon far below us.

First, she descended onto its top, and hovered around it.

Clever, I thought. There are no windows up there for anyone to look out through, but there might be an observation platform, for viewing the stars.

Next, she rose again, and widened her flight into circles as she looped around the tower. When she dropped to the level of the high window, its light shone out on her, turning her from a black dot against the sky to a gray one.

She circled. She reversed direction. She went in closer.

The nearer she got to the window, the tenser we became.

At last, she was hovering right outside it.

She must be looking in, we thought.

*Nothing has alarmed her yet, but surely, this was a risk …*

Abruptly, she wheeled away into wide loops around the tower.

She circled, lower and lower, almost to the ground. Then she shot up into the sky and turned back towards us. She landed and dismounted.

Little Guy padded over to her, tail wagging.

"There's no one in there," she said. "There's just a light. I couldn't see where it was coming from."

I said, "What sort of room is it?"

"Big and empty. Just something big in the middle, where the light was, like a big box maybe. I tried to look through the slits as I flew down, but I couldn't see anything; it's dark inside. I didn't see any signs of life."

Well now, I thought. It seems that we'll be the first in quite a while to enter the Tower of the Moon.

And then I thought, there's probably a reason no one else has gone in.

They had the sense to avoid the place.

We hadn't come all that way to do the same.

I said, "Nice work, Jess."

She grinned, and slung her broomstick on her back.

Qrysta, and Grell, and I caught each other's eyes.

We had a feeling that we knew what was coming.

*Boss Fight.*

Horm said, "Are we going to kill these fuckers or what?"

Yes, I thought. It will probably come to that.

I nodded, and said, "Let's go."

The descent was much easier than the climb had been. After a couple of hours, we reached the valley floor. Ahead of us the pale tower stood sentinel against the surrounding white and red peaks. It looked farther away than it had from the pass through the Ring of Fire. Clearly it was a lot taller than we'd thought.

We'd been marching in silence for a while, and had just passed through a field of snow-covered boulders, when Qrysta said, "Hold up, guys."

We halted.

She was looking around, clearly puzzled by something.

Grell seemed curious. "What's up?"

Qrysta turned to him. "Where are the bodies?"

"What bodies?"

"People who evaded the Ogres. You heard the chief. *None return,* right? So, where are the bodies?"

We couldn't see any.

I said, "Maybe they're still alive."

Nyrik muttered, "Now, why does that sound worse?"

Qrysta got her answer not much later.

When we were within a mile of the tower, we saw the first of the corpses. They were lying on, or near, the path. They hadn't been eaten by scavengers. They still had their eyeballs, which stared up at us out of rigid faces. It seemed that even crows and ravens avoided this place. They had been preserved by the cold, but there were plenty of creatures that would feed on frozen flesh—rats, foxes, wolves, bears. Also, their feet were pointing towards the tower, not their heads.

They'd been running away from it.

Nyrik knelt down by one and inspected it. He pulled off its cloak and held it up to me. Its edges were ragged and blackened, and the whole thing was covered in burn marks. "Wonder what did this."

Grell said, "Let's find out."

He trudged forwards and we followed him. More corpses, in various stages of decay, lined the path. "Why'd they keep going?" Nyrik muttered. "If they see this lot dead all around them, wouldn't they think, *Hang on a minute, might be a good idea to turn around and make meself scarce, before that's me down there along o' these other poor sods?*"

"You'd think," Qrysta agreed.

Something clicked in my mind. I said, "Maybe they couldn't?"

"Eh?" Nyrik said. "Couldn't what?"

"Think," I said.

He frowned up at me, not understanding.

"Think for themselves," I elaborated. "Someone else was doing the thinking for them. What I mean is, they couldn't help themselves. Not anymore. They'd been taken over."

He said, puzzled, "Where d'you get that from?"

"Something lured them here, right? You heard the chief. Whispers of magical items, weapons of power, treasure. Well: Who was doing the whispering?"

"Rumour," Nyrik replied. "Is what the chief said."

"Maybe," I allowed. "That's what Rumour does, yes. But what if she's just the messenger? Who sent the messages? And why are there many of them, not just one?"

Nyrik said, "Well? Why?"

"Someone *wanted* them to come here."

He looked at me thoughtfully. "Just so he could kill them?"

I considered that. It did indeed seem pretty pointless. So maybe that wasn't the point. "To test the defenses? Make sure they were still working, and that nothing could get through?"

Nyrik frowned. "Anyone else got any better ideas?"

None of us had.

Eventually, Horm said, "I do."

Nyrik said, "What?"

"Find out what killed them and kill it." We all looked at him. "Well, we're not going to find out why if it kills us, are we? So, we kill it. Then we'll find out why. Or not. But it'll be dead, and we won't be. Unlike these poor sods."

Grell said, "Makes sense."

He turned towards the pale tower and we followed through a sea of corpses.

413

I felt Shift's apprehension as she shivered on my back. She, like me, has never trusted the dead. They're misleading and unreliable. They can't tell you much, and you're never sure if it's truth or lies. And you can't always rely on them to stay dead. These ones didn't. We'd almost got used to them, lying all over the place, behind, ahead, all around. They were hardly a pleasant sight, but it wasn't as if they were giving us any trouble.

Until they did.

Grell was leading, followed by Qrysta and Jess, with Little Guy trotting at her heels. He suddenly turned and started yammering, his ears flat back against his skull.

He was fixed on something behind us.

Or rather, some *things*.

The corpses that we'd passed were on their feet and following us down the path. Others were rising all around us and closing in on us.

As were those *ahead* of us.

"This way!" Grell roared, and he charged, whirling Kinell around him.

I couldn't think what he was doing as he carved a path through the undead ahead of us. We were in a trap, hemmed in on all sides, our foes closing in. We were unable to take positions as we'd have liked to: tank ahead on point, drawing enemies towards him while our damage crew worked from the best vantage points: Qrysta and Little Guy darting in and out of our attackers, tearing holes in their ranks, Horm and Nyrik and Jess shooting arrows from positions of safety, as I laid down Area of Effect attacks and spammed Heals on us.

And now here was Grell smashing his way forwards, splattering any undead who came within striking distance of his maul, leaving the rest of us to fend for ourselves. My thoughts flashed through my mind at hyperspeed. *He's been taken over, like they were*, then, *we're surrounded*, then, *of course!*

"Run!" I yelled. "Backs to the wall!" I set off after him, Shift raised, casting Shields and Area Heal Alls. The archers stopped shooting as they understood, and sprinted down the path that Grell had cleared for us. I laid Earthgrips and a Flamefield around us, and we ran through it. With our backs to the tower, we turned, and faced the onslaught as a horde of undead closed in on us. Now, though, we stood a fighting chance. They couldn't get behind us.

Grell waded out into them, taunting and challenging, and they closed in on him. I boosted his stamina, and kept his Shields up, and threw up Thunderclouds to strike down on them from above, and turned the snowfield below them into a morass of Consuming Slimes that glued them to the spot and digested them where they stood. Our archers picked them off from safety, behind my traps. Little Guy harassed, and bit, and distracted, and Qrysta's blades stabbed and hacked as she danced.

It was a long fight. Nyrik and Horm ran out of arrows soon enough, and ran in with their niblun knives. We knew that the enemy would just keep coming, because that's what undead always do. Attack, until dead again.

We also knew that we were going to win. A mob like this would be too much for a few misguided adventurers, lured by tall tales, who would be overwhelmed and die—and rise again, to take their places by the path, ready to defend the way to the tower.

This lot wasn't going to overwhelm us, however many there were of them. There were more than many. We didn't bother to count the corpses when the last of them dropped.

Grell lumbered back towards us, slinging Kinell on his back, breathing hard.

"I needed that," he said. "Fed up with bloody walking, couldn't wait to swing my arms again."

Qrysta looked around at the carnage.

"Damn undead," she said. "Think they'll be waiting here for us, when we come out?"

Good point, I thought. "Not if I can help it." I raised Shift and cast a Flamewall on the charnel field around the tower. The corpses caught fire and began to burn. I was about to cast more, when Jess said, "Hang on a minute, Daxx."

She raised her bow and shot arrow after arrow into two nearby corpses.

When they had so many arrows in them that they resembled hedgehogs, she nodded at Nyrik and Horm, and said, "You might need those."

"Good thinking, lass!" Horm said. They hurried over and filled their empty quivers. Jess's own doeskin quiver was, as always, magically full.

I flooded the ground with Flamefields, and refreshed them, again and again, until every one of the corpses around us was reduced to ashes.

"So, what do you think that was all about?" Qrysta said.

"Someone wanted to keep the riffraff out," Grell said.

We all turned to the tower.

The only light coming from it was the pale gleam behind the wide, curved window at its top. There was nothing but darkness behind the slits that spiraled down around its circular wall. The lowest of them was twenty feet above our head.

There was no door.

# 34

## The Tower of the Moon

Our destination. After all that traveling. We'd come this far. We needed to get inside.

There was no way in.

"Wonder if any of the riffraff *did* make it inside," Nyrik said. "It'd be nice to know how, if they did."

Indeed. Without a door.

Qrysta leaned back and looked up towards the glowing window high above us under the battlements. "We could do with Oller and his stickies."

Grell said, "Even Ols couldn't sneak in through those slits."

I thought, *Just because we can't see it, doesn't mean it isn't there.*

I raised Shift and cast Reveals at the tower.

The outline of a simple, arched door appeared.

I smiled. "Easy when you know how."

"Makes a nice change," Grell muttered. "Usually, it's one damned thing after another."

I walked towards the door, bringing out Oller's silver key from my inside pocket. A silver keyhole glowed to life in the door as I approached.

I never got there.

The key stopped, a yard from the tower.

I felt around it, as did the others. We were up against a barrier. We couldn't see it. We couldn't really even feel it. Our hands simply wouldn't pass through what was solid air.

"Yeah, right," Grell said. "What did I tell you?"

The barrier was impenetrable. I couldn't get rid of it with Cleanses or Negates. I blasted every attack I could think of at it, Thunderbolts, Fireballs, Ice Shards. All they did was light it up briefly where they hit before fizzling out. I laid down Flamefields, which lapped up against it before fading away. I threw up Stormclouds, which blew down rain and hail and lightning. They just illuminated the barrier from above, wherever they struck. It hung around the tower, all the way down from the battlements, glittering where my attacks hit them. Nothing was making any impression on it. It was as if the barrier was standing there, unbothered, saying, "Is that all you've got?"

It was. I gave up throwing ineffectual Damages at it and wondered what to do next.

The high window was still gleaming. That, too, was protected by the barrier, which sealed itself off at the battlements.

A shield, encircling the tower from the ground to its highest level. One that nothing I hit it with could penetrate.

The others, I knew, were looking at me and all thinking the same thing that I was. *So now what?*

Yes. Good question.

I had no answer, so ignored it, and moved on to more practical ones.

*What's the problem?* Barrier. This was not *the* barrier that the Voice had told me about. I'd been Gifted, I'd be able to get through that. There was no way through this one. *How about around it?* It encircles the tower. There are no gaps. *So where does it begin and end?* At the ground, and at the battlements.

I considered the options. "Jess, you didn't happen to see a trapdoor up there on the roof, did you?"

She shook her head. "No. It's just flat."

"I need you to take me up."

"All right." She unslung the broomstick from her back. I Levitated us, and we rose into the air.

The barrier did not extend to infinity. It stopped at the battlements. Jess flew me up, and moments later we were over them and landing on the parapet within.

Its surface was, just as Jess had said, flat.

I dismounted and took a look around.

It reminded me of Elun's observatory on the Tower of Light—the high platform where she would go to study the heavens.

There was no need for this, I thought. Why are all these crenellations here, as if dozens of archers are going to be shooting down through them? Just to make the tower look imposing?

Look imposing *to whom?*

There's no one out there, in this frozen wasteland way up at the roof of the world, for these fortifications to impress.

Okay, I thought, let's look for an answer.

I raised Shift and cast Reveals.

Something glowed into life in the center of the parapet. It was a symbol. It consisted of five pale, jagged lines.

Three of them were upright, and of different lengths. The tallest upright was on the left, the shortest on the right. The other two lines were diagonals that sloped down. One slanted across from outside the top of the left leg, to cut just through the middle of the center one. The other one did the same from outside the top of the center leg, down through the middle of the right one.

It was stark, and clear—and, obviously, not there by accident.

I'd seen such things before: Wards, set in place, to protect and repel. They are often also warnings of dangers that wait beyond them.

Barrier below. Ward above. *Enter at your peril.*

I thought, why a Ward up here? Who is it meant to warn off, or keep out—when anyone who couldn't fly couldn't get up here anyway?

I couldn't make head or tail of it.

I studied the symbol, walking round it, to see it from every angle. It was a round tower, so who knew what the "correct" angle to view the symbol from was? What was it meant to look like, when it wasn't on its side, or upside down?

I looked up and around. If it were dark, I'd be able to see where due north lay, by finding the Axle in the night sky. But it was early summer, so no stars could be seen. The midnight sun was low in what must be approximate west. Opposite it, the waning moon hung high off to the north and east.

I walked around the symbol again, checking my position with the sun and moon. When I stood opposite the moon, with the symbol between us, it resembled a stylized letter.

ᛗ

Once again, I heard Marnie's words:
*We've been told. It's all there, if we have the wit to see.*
I closed my eyes and cast my mind back to Conclave. Once again, Dean Eilwen's pronouncements echoed in my head, line by line:
*Unlock the rune.*
Pieces fell into place.
*Mondthal.* Moon Valley, in the old language. *M in the old script.*
It wasn't a Ward. It was a rune.
The question wasn't. "Who could fly up here?" It was, 'Who can come down here?'
I looked up at the moon.
This was her tower. She wouldn't come and go at ground level. She'd use the skyway.
*Unlock the rune.*
I took out Oller's silver key and approached the rune on the parapet's floor.
A silver keyhole emerged at its center, halfway up its middle upright. The key grew to fit it. I inserted the key and turned it. I felt a click as something within the rune unlocked. I completed the rotation and pulled out the key.
Nothing happened.
Beside me, Jess said, "Daxx ..."
I looked up at her. And then behind me, at what she was pointing to.
A shaft of pearly light was gleaming out from below through a rectangular opening in the roof.
We approached it and peered inside.
I could see nothing but the light, and the shadows that it cast. Shadows that were thrown by the stairs set into the tower's wall.
Our way in. Our way down.
I said, "You need to go and get the others."
Jess nodded and mounted her broomstick. I watched as she flew down. When she had her first passenger behind her, Horm, I cast Levitate down at them. One by one they arrived, and saw the silver rune, and the light gleaming up through the open rectangle.

While Jess had been ferrying them up, I'd been thinking—and putting more pieces of the puzzle together. The memory of Elun, and her observatory on the Tower of Light, had reminded me of Avildor. Avildor had initiated me into his skill line of Light Magic. I was a novice at it, but at least I knew the basics. Light, that I suspected was moonlight, was pouring out of the opening. I needed to find out about it. What was its source?

I would use Lightseek. I closed my eyes and Sought for it.

It could hardly have been easier to find it. It hit me like a dozen searchlights, all coming from the same place. Even with my eyes closed I was dazzled. I shielded my eyes with my arms and turned my back on the light source, and, eventually opened my eyes. The searchlights faded. When, after a few moments, my vision returned, I realized that, actually, it had been … fascinating. A kick in the head, yes—but this was something that I wanted to understand. I was tempted to try again. It was an effort to stop myself. *You've found the source*, I told myself. *You Sought the Light, and there it is, right below you. You're no Avildor, don't get above yourself.*

Avildor.

What had he taught me?

*No mortal shines with the pure white light of the divine.*

So, what was down there, radiating this white light, was no mortal.

We'd wrangled with this world's divinities in Mourvania—and above it, in its heavens. I'd been way out of my depth.

And now, here I was, perhaps about to deal with them again.

I remembered my task, from the dream I'd had at Velaryn's house.

*There was something down there. Something that I must find.*

Soon, I thought, we'll be getting answers.

When we were all gathered on the rooftop, Qrysta said, "So, what's the plan?"

"I'll go first," I said.

Nyrik frowned up at me. "No scouts?" he said. "Daxx, if you don't mind my saying, mate, you're a bit bloody obvious, the way you clump about."

"This is mage business," I said.

"Yeah, but, it's not as if you can mage yourself invisible."

"This isn't a sneak job, Nyrik. There's no sneaking past."

"Past what?"

I nodded over at the moonlight pouring out of the opening. "That."

They all looked over at it.

I said, "We're going to walk down. Not sneak, like thieves in the night. We're going to enter like invited guests, to present ourselves to our hostess."

Nyrik straightened up. "Oh," he said. "D'you think she's going to be pleased to see us?"

"No."

"Then, why—"

I sighed. "Because she might listen."

"Might?"

"Rather than attack us as intruders."

Nyrik, and the others, thought about that. "Mm. I see what you mean."

Horm said, "Listen, if these are the bastards that killed Urngra—"

"*If,*" I interrupted. "We don't know, Horm. We need to find out, right? We don't need trouble with anyone else. We need answers. I'm hoping that our hostess will provide them."

"Well, what sort of answers?!" he demanded.

I said, "How about, '*Who are the bastards who killed Urngra, and where do we find them?*'"

He grunted and then said, "Yur, be good to know."

"So, we're going to go in nice and friendly, weapons not drawn, bows unstrung, and giving off the right signals. *Nice place you have here, how kind of you to allow us into your lovely home, if there's anything we can do for you, please, all you have to do is ask.* How does that sound?"

Grell gave me a puzzled look. "I dunno, Daxxie. Six strangers and a dog stroll into your house uninvited, what are you going to think?"

I said, "I'm going to think, *They didn't sneak in, so I don't need to atomize them.*"

Grell said, "Atomize?"

I nodded.

"We're outgunned?"

"Almost certainly."

Nyrik was puzzled, "Out what-now'd?" There were no guns in his world.

"Outmatched," I translated. "Out of our depth. She's more powerful than all of us put together."

He said, "Who is?"

I pointed up at the moon.

The others glanced up at it and then back at me.

"You know where we are," I said.

Nyrik frowned. "Yes, but …"

"The Tower of the Moon."

"The moon's up *there!*"

"*And* shining out of that trapdoor."

"How can she be in two places at once?"

"I have no idea. She's divine, I'm not."

Eventually, Nyrik muttered, "I dunno about this."

"Nor do I," I agreed. "We're here to get answers, right?"

He thought that over, and then nodded. "Yeah."

"Nice and steady," I reminded them all. "Respectful. Are we ready?"

We weren't, but no one said no. We'd come this far. We needed to get inside. I led the way towards the rectangle of light.

And into it.

A stone staircase ran around the tower's circular wall. We walked down it, calmly, slowly. We were allowing plenty of time for anyone to see us coming. We said nothing. We listened. We looked around. There was nothing to see below us but the pale light coming up at us. We couldn't see into it, or through it. It was like descending into a pool, I thought, but not one of water.

On down the stone steps around the wall, my feet descending into the light.

I followed them down and the light enveloped me, legs, and waist, then shoulders, and arms and neck and head.

And then I was *underlight*.

It was like being underwater, only … stranger. And I wasn't wet. And I could breathe. And I was treading in a cloud of light that somehow stopped me seeing in any direction. All I knew was that my feet kept finding their way down, stone step by stone step. *Keep going forwards.* I had no idea what we were doing, but I wasn't worried. I had unlocked the rune. Another one checked off Dean Eilwen's to-do List.

We were doing what, in Marnie's words, we'd been told.

Diving, feet first, into a fog of pearlescent light. It was silent, and eerie, and beautiful. I could not hear my own footsteps, nor those of the others as they followed me. I was anxious, but, somehow, not very. I knew that I *ought* to be worried, about what unknowns lay ahead, but I didn't feel worried. My busy mind wanted to know why not. *What are*

423

*we getting into?* I had no answer. *What we came here to get into,* I told myself. I decided to ignore my busy mind, and to go with my feelings. In the fog of pale light that enveloped me, I couldn't see my left hand that was stretched out touching the wall. I couldn't see below my waist. Until I could. The glowing fog thinned below. Shadows moved beyond it as I walked on down. Those shadows became my feet, their outlines clearer by the step. And then the rest of me. I emerged below the cloud of light and saw the room around me.

It was a bedchamber.

At its center stood a tall, four-poster bed. Drapes hung around it, as pale and wispy as gossamer. The source of the light was coming from within.

Beyond the bed, the chamber's walls were dark. It took me a moment to realize why that was odd. From below, we'd seen light gleaming out from this topmost room.

No light penetrated in through its long window. And, outside, it was the summer sky of the north, permanent daylight.

I thought, *Where the moon sleeps.*

In the comfort of darkness.

One by one the others appeared down the stone steps and followed me onto the chamber's floor.

No one spoke.

We gathered around the bed, listening to the silence, wondering what lay within its gauzy drapes.

Horm's hands were on the hilts of his knives. He caught my eye, and removed them when I shook my head.

There was no need to cast Lightseek again. We knew where the light source was.

What we didn't know was *what* it was.

I unslung Shift from my back and felt her come alive in my hands. *Whoa! What have we here?*

*Exactly what I want to know.*

I raised her and cast Reveal Hidden Life.

A white sphere was hanging in front of me. If it had been alive, it would have been outlined in fuzzy, unstable red.

*The pure, white light of the divine.*

I was none the wiser. No answers, just more questions. Shift let me know that she could sense no threat.

There was only one thing for it.

I nodded at Qrysta, and, together, we reached for the drapes and drew them aside.

A ball of light filled the space within the four-poster bed. It was as cold as the moon, and as beautiful. It was just like the one I'd seen hovering in the woods behind Farnz's cottage in the village, only larger.

Below it lay a woman. Or, rather, what remained of one, which was not much more than a skeleton. The long tendrils of sparse hair that hung from her scalp were white. Her skin was almost entirely rotted from her skull. She wore a frayed, white robe. Her hands were nothing but bones peeking out of her sleeves. Her left hand lay across her stomach. Her right was dangling off the side of her bed, its bony forefinger pointing at the floor, the other fingers curled up.

And then, pieces of the puzzle clicked into place, as several realizations coalesced in my mind.

*Where were we?*

*The Tower of the Moon.*

*So who is this, then? This woman? She looks like she belongs here, on this bed, below that pale, shining light.*

*If this is her tower, then she is the moon.*

*Observe the moon,* Dean Eilwen had said.

I'd been doing that night after night, month after month. I'd learned nothing, staring up at her as she passed across the night sky, waiting for her message. None had ever come.

I studied the dead, luminous woman.

*Dead reborn?*

She showed no sign of coming back to life. We'd been through *dead reborn* outside. Maybe that line applied to them rather than her.

I wondered what to make of her.

*Observe the moon.*

Eilwen hadn't said *study.*

She'd said *observe.*

Observe means watch, look for behaviour. See what she does.

She's dead, she's not doing anything.

Yes, she is. She's pointing. At the floor.

There was nothing on the floor. I cast Reveals. Nothing showed up.

Something beneath the floor, then?

*There was something down there. Something that I must find.*

Time to go and find it.

425

# 35

## Bound and Sealed

I caught Qrysta's eye and we closed the gauze drapes. The others followed me to the stairs and down into the room below. It about twice the height of the bedchamber that we'd just left, and the stone steps around its wall were steeper. It was empty, and dark but for the moonlight glowing down through the space behind us. The entrance to the next level was across from the opening we'd come down through. There was almost no light in the chamber below, so I popped up a soft Glow, to travel along with us as we moved down.

We were on high alert, of course, but I didn't think we'd encounter anything waiting for us. We didn't. There was no sign that any "riffraff" had managed to enter the tower. No corpses, no skeletons. Nothing that might reanimate and attack. All the same, I kept Muffles up on us all the time, so that our footsteps made no sound. There was also no sign of any possessions. No furniture. No containers. Nothing hanging on the walls. The only object that we'd seen had been the four-poster bed.

Grell was thinking what I was thinking. Under his breath, he said, "You'd have thought there'd be good loot in a place like this."

"You would," I agreed.

I cast Reveal Hidden Life and Show Traps before we entered every floor. Nothing appeared, not even the fuzzy, red outlines of mice or rats

426

below the floorboards. We went on down. Each chamber was larger than the one above it. After five levels, we were so used to seeing each chamber exactly like the one above it—quiet, dark, and completely empty—that we had stopped looking around for anything when we descended into the sixth. It was only when we were halfway down the stone stairs, on our way to the opening to the lowest floor, that Nyrik noticed something and stopped.

"Hang on a moment …" he said, looking across at the wall opposite us.

We looked where he was pointing. Something over there was glinting in the soft light of our Glow. We all strained to see it.

"Well, now!" he said.

His Woods Kin eyes were sharper than mine, I knew.

I said, "What is it?"

"A little more light?" he suggested.

I sent a brighter Glow towards it. It glided across the chamber and hovered above a gleaming, curved shape that was hanging on the wall, high up under the ceiling.

Whatever it was, it wasn't very big. When we got closer, we could see that it was a small bow, perhaps a quarter the size of Jess's. An emblem, perhaps, rather than an actual weapon. Which was also odd, as it was the only decorative item—indeed, item of any kind—that we'd seen since the topmost chamber.

It was not, it seemed, made of wood. It shone with the same pale light that we'd seen within the four-poster bed. Here and there along its length seven sharp points glittered brighter, as if it was inlaid with stars.

Horm whistled. "Ain't *she* a beauty!" he breathed. "A masterwork, that, if ever I saw one."

There was no way that we were going to leave it there—unless, of course, we couldn't prise it off the wall. The only problem with finding out if that was possible was that it was several yards above our heads. Jess mounted her broomstick, only to find that it was unable to fly inside the tower. That baffled her, and made the rest of us doubly determined to get the bow if we could. If someone had protected it by preventing anyone flying up to it, it must be valuable indeed.

And that was how we came to build a human ladder. It was not something we were skilled at, so there was a good deal of grunting, and confused orders, and swearing, and bumps and bruises; but we made it, in the end. Grell stood with his back against the wall, and cupped his hands. I propped Shift against the wall and clambered awkwardly up him, until he hoisted me onto his shoulders. I stood there, my face to the wall, arms spread wide, trying not to look down. Grell clamped his hands over my ankles. Horm climbed nimbly up both of us and stood on my shoulders. Qrysta, who was taller than him, had wanted to go third, but Horm told her that he was stronger than he looked, and that she should go after him. She took the longest of all of us to get in position—mainly, I think, because of the swaying of the three of us below her. Finally, when she was set, with Horm gripping her ankles, Nyrik shinned up the four of us in no time, and reached for the bow, saying, "Here's hoping …"

It lifted easily off the wall. Nyrik tucked it into his belt and was back on the floor in seconds. Qrysta followed, with some difficulty, and Horm was down beside her a moment later. Grell lifted me up, slid me down and stood me upright.

Nyrik and Horm were appraising the bow.

"What's it made of, Horm?" Nyrik said. "Silver?"

Horm shook his head. "Starsilver. Rare as rare. There's not a lot of this about. And what little there is, is well guarded. Worth a king's ransom, this!"

I said, "Why's it called that?"

Horm, being half niblun, knew his crafting and his materials. "Story goes as the first miners to find it thought it was silver, 'cos of the color, which it's very like," he said. "It's not. It's far more valuable—and far more powerful, if Imbued right. An enchanter can spell all sorts of secrets into starsilver." He turned the little bow over in his hands to examine it. He shook his head and whistled. "Beauty this. Worth ten times what gold is. And like gold, it don't tarnish neither—not ever—unlike silver, which needs polishing regular. As for the name: Daxx, kill that light o' yours."

I retrieved Shift in order to extinguish the Glow that hovered above us, and felt her jolt of interest in the little bow that Horm was holding. As the Glow disappeared it began to gleam silver in his hands.

"See that? It drinks in the light and shines it out again. It'll shine for an hour or more before it fades."

The soft light coming from the bow lit our faces as we gazed at it.

Horm sighed. "Beautiful, ain't it?"

It was, indeed.

428

He was turning the bow over in his hands as he spoke. "And look at these." He pointed to the jewels that were set along its length. They, too, were radiating light—a whiter, sharper light than that emanating from the starsilver of the bow itself. "Those ain't there by accident," he said. "I'd dearly like to meet the wright who crafted this. What do you think, Daxx?"

"Diamonds," I said.

He snorted, and shot me a look of contempt. "Well, I know *that*. What d'you think I am, a novice? *Course* they're diamonds. What I want your expert opinion on is what *kind* of diamonds. The ordinary kind, or the kind like that tourmaline, in that staff o' yours."

*Definitely my kind*, Shift affirmed. I said. "Only heartstones glow like that."

Horm nodded. "My thought exactly."

I wondered what magic they, and the bow they were set into, were Imbued with. Shift, I could tell, was examining it, as eager to learn its properties as I was. She couldn't. I sensed her withdrawing from it, baffled, respectful—as if she had seen that she did not have any right to enquire. *The white light of the divine*, I thought. Its secrets, clearly, were none of her business.

I knew that it must have a purpose—this emblem, or artifact, or whatever it was. It had heartstones set into it. And *seven* of them! Shift packed a punch with just her one heartstone. But this bow was too small to be an actual weapon.

At least, it was until Horm gripped it to draw back its tiny silver bowstring.

As he did, the bow grew until it was exactly the right size for him. Its diamond heartstones, too, had grown in proportion.

This was magic that I knew nothing about.

"Bleeding hells!" Horm said. He drew the string tight to his ear. When it was fully taut, a matching, starsilver arrow appeared between his hands, nocked to the string. "Whoa!" He relaxed the string in surprise, staring at the arrow.

Which faded out of existence.

He turned to Nyrik, his eyes wide. "What d'you think, Nyr?"

"I've never seen a bow made of metal. Didn't know it was possible."

"Nor me," Horm said. "But it draws good and hard. Feel the power in that." He handed the bow to Nyrik, who drew it until an arrow appeared between his hands.

"Like a coiled spring!" Nyrik said. "This'll hit like the devil's own hammer."

"I'll say," Horm said. "And look at the size of it. It's worth *four* kings' ransoms now. Hang on a bit," he added, as a thought struck him. "Give it to Grell."

Nyrik did.

"Make that eight," Horm said, when the starsilver bow had grown to Grell size.

I said, "Good enough loot for you?"

"Eight kings' ransoms?" Grell said. "Maybe we can buy Prince Mince off with this."

Mention of Prince Mejnul reminded us that we had work to do. Grell handed the shining bow back to Horm, who let it shrink to its original size before tucking it away in his pack.

He looked at the rest of us happily.

Then his face fell, as he realized what he'd done. "If that's all right?" he said, worried that we might think he'd kept it for himself.

"You look after it, Horm," I said. "We'll decide what to do with it later."

He nodded, relieved.

There was only one level below that chamber. The steps led around its wall and down to a floor of stone flags, rather than the wooden boards of the upper levels. The arched doorway was not hidden, as it was from the outside. Its heavy, wooden door was reinforced with iron bands. Two thick iron bars lay across it, between brackets set into the tower's wall. Grell lifted them off. I fitted Oller's silver key into the matching keyhole that appeared in the door. I turned it, and the door swung open. Daylight flooded in.

We all felt the better for seeing it.

"Well, there's our way out," I said, looking out at the distant, encircling mountains.

The Ring of Fire, with its white peaks and red.

We breathed in the fresh, cold air for a few moments. Then I shut the door again. I didn't lock it. We might be running for our lives when we came back this way.

We had a task to complete before we could head home.

*There is something below.*

First, I needed to find the way to it.

I cast Reveals, and another ⊤⊬⊢ rune glowed into life on the flagstone at the center of the floor.

A silver keyhole appeared in it when I held Oller's key towards it. I turned it, felt a click, and the flagstone melted away.

Below us, steps led down into a tunnel, its ice walls glowing with a dim, blue-white light.

Once again, I cast Reveal Hidden Life and Show Traps.

No life was revealed. No traps were shown.

I glanced around at the others.

Qrysta drew her swords, and said, "Keep going forwards?"

I nodded and led the way down into the tunnel.

We stepped off the stairs onto gravel, and then snow and frost. We were in a tube of ice, heading down. Our breath rose in clouds around us. The tunnel sloped, gently. I had no need to cast Glows to light our way. The walls and ceiling shone with their own pale, blue-white light. Before long we came to a small cavern, which swelled out to either side of us around pillars of ice. Beyond it, the tunnel ahead closed in again. We went on down, our Muffled footsteps leaving impressions on the ice floor. I cast ahead continually for Traps and for Life. Nothing was revealed. No one said anything. Whatever lay ahead was what we had come all this way for.

Cavern after cavern.

Tunnel after tunnel.

No branches, no choices.

Only one way on.

Down, through the blue-white ice that shone around us.

After a while, Little Guy trotted past me, ears pricked, tail wagging. He was clearly on the scent of something and enjoying it. I was happy to let him take the lead. I knew that his clever nose would sense anything ahead of us long before I did.

As I followed him, I kept looking for guidance. Or, rather, closing my eyes, and listening for it. The Voice that I had first heard in the vault below the village did not speak to me. I wondered whether, perhaps, I was too late. Had he died? Was he gone? *He promised*, I thought. *He is my only hope.*

*Hope or husk.*

I did not want my story to end in oblivion. I had so much yet to do. Esmeralda, for one thing. I could not help her, or her realm, if I had faded into the dark. I felt, still, as I had felt throughout this long journey, as if I was hanging by a thread. Moon Nights, aboard *The Red Rose*. Hiring Nyrik and Horm, in The Ship Aground. With Urngra, to the village. The ball of white light in the woods behind Farnz's cottage. The Voice in the vault. The long way around, back to Eastbay. Conclave. *We've been told*. Horm aching to kill me outside Velaryn's apothecary shop, thinking that I'd killed Urngra. The voyage to Normark. Captain Rozlyn's mutiny, Master Bjarnevalt, Evall's family. Across the snowline with Gundur and the herd. Over the stockade to avoid the Ice Wights. Desmond, his wolves, Isvellir. Shaman Sylmond. Ogretzk. *We've been told.*

Why wasn't I seeing it? Told what? For the hundredth time, I went over Dean Eilwen's words. As before, some of them seemed obvious, while others made no sense to me.

*Run and hide. Hide and run.* Been there, done that. *Don't assume. Assume the form.* What? How can I do one without the other? What do you want me to do—assume, or not assume?! Again, as I went over Eilwen's eighteen lines, I found them maddeningly frustrating.

I also knew that it was my fault that I was frustrated. I couldn't see what I was looking at.

*We've been told.*

Told, damn it to all hells, *what?!*

Once again, no answer came. Once again, I told myself to stop banging my head against it. *The answers will reveal themselves in their own sweet time. Or they won't. In which case, you're doomed. Meanwhile, give your mind a rest, keep your eyes and ears open, and gather information. Okay, so you don't know the answers, and you're meant to be the puzzle king. Just remember: You only don't know the answers yet.*

*Yes, possibly you never will. In which case, you lose.*

*It happens.*

*Forget the ending. First things first. Get the cure. Live longer than the rest of this moon month. Then worry about what's next.*

Esmeralda. Prince Mince. A hundred dragons, raining down fire and fury. A hundred thousand chalkers, knights, and archers. Midsummer Day. I can only deal with that little problem *if* I get to come to it. If I don't, well … I failed. So, let's not fail. Find the Voice. He's down here, unless he's dead and gone. Help him if I can, even though he says I won't be able to, because he has promised to help me, and that would be the least I could do for him in return.

And I need his help.

*Help or husk.*

Everything else can wait.

Keep going forwards.

We trooped down the blue-white ice tunnels, and caves, and chambers, down and down, lower and lower. Ceilings reared above us, crystal stalactites hanging down, stalagmites growing up towards them. Ceilings closed down again, and we were in tunnels that were not much larger than we were. The walls gleamed blue-white. No one spoke. We listened, trying to hear into the silence beyond our Muffled footsteps. We all had our weapons in our hands, ready for combat.

The lower we went, the more eager Little Guy became. It seemed that he was on the trail of something. Jess whistled softly, to call him back to her, but I told her we should let him have his head and see what was interesting him. He scuttled here and there, tail wagging, sniffing, checking every part of every new space we came into. He was halfway across yet another small cavern, and I was following him, my mind working on Eilwen's baffling lines, when I heard Nyrik, behind me, yelp, "*Gaah!* What the ff—??!"

I turned around to see him standing there holding his nose, as if he'd walked into something.

It was something that Horm bounced off a moment later.

Grell, and Jess, and Qrysta saw what had happened, and came up beside them, wondering. They felt the air in front of them.

I said, "What's up?"

They tried to push their hands out towards me.

They couldn't.

Qrysta said, "Some sort of barrier."

That baffled me. "Where?"

"Right here."

She knocked on something that I couldn't see.

I went back to them. I felt around in the air and found nothing.

They tried again.

Qrysta shrugged. I got the message. *I'm the mage, over to me.*

Nothing that I cast at the thin air between us revealed anything. No barrier showed.

Yet they couldn't come any further.

It was no problem for me to walk up to them, and around them, then behind them, and back on down. Whatever it was, though, was still stopping them. I turned back and reached my hand out for Grell's. He took it. I drew him towards me. His hand stopped, mine still gripped in it. I pulled. His wouldn't come with me.

I had a feeling that I knew what this was. I tried, anyway, to Cleanse or Nullify the barrier. I couldn't, any more than I'd been able to bring down the shield around the tower. That confirmed my suspicion. It was as the Voice had told me. No human could pass through it. Only a mage who had been Gifted could reach him. Or, of course, a scruffy little mutt, who was more "pack" than I was. *Weres* are part-timers, compared with dogs or wolves.

Little Guy was standing beside me, wagging his tail, eager to go on down.

I knelt down, and ruffled his ears. I said, "Stay with Jess, okay?"

She whistled him in and he trotted to her side.

I'd have liked the company, but there was no need to risk his life as well as mine. "Looks like I'm on my own from here."

Grell said, "Shit, Daxxie ..."

Which was pretty much how I felt. "Listen," I said. "I'd never have made it here without you guys. I owe you. Bigtime. And I'm going to do whatever it takes to get back here. We have work to do. Right, Horm?"

"Right," Horm agreed. We still had Urngra's death to avenge. Not to mention the little matter of Prince Mejnul.

"But, just in case," I said, removing the Link of Impartment from my wrist, "you're going to need comms with Oller."

I passed it to Qrysta, who nodded.

She understood.

If I didn't return, the team would carry on without me.

Another thought occurred to me. "Talking of Ols ...." I brought out his silver key and handed it to her. "He'll want this back." I then reached inside my jerkin for the pouch of heartstones and Marnie's Infinite Notebook. "Look after these for me, all right? If I don't make it back, well, you don't want to lose these too."

Qrysta took them. "You've got it, Daxx."

"Thanks, Qrys."

She looked as anxious as I felt.

I looked at all of them in turn. None of us knew what to say. All I did know was that they'd wait there forever for me to return.

434

I couldn't allow that. I said, "If I'm not back before the full moon, I won't be coming back. You all know that, right?"

They knew that. They knew that I would have failed. I'd be gone. A husk. And they would return to Mayport without me, in time for Midsummer's Day, to do what they could.

Qrysta said, "You'll be back."

I looked at her, wondering if I'd ever see her again. A lump came to my throat. I was going to miss her so, so much.

"I'll do my best," I said. I turned and walked on down, and into the tunnel ahead. It soon curved around a corner.

I didn't look back.

The walls of the tunnel glowed with the same eerie blue-white, which reflected off my breath as I exhaled. The air around me felt both colder and stuffier. It was a relief to emerge into a small chamber, and a relief to see that it was empty. I knew that I had to deal with what lay ahead, but I was hardly looking forward to it. I knew that it would be a trial. I had no way of knowing whether I was up to the challenge.

I'd never felt so alone in my life.

The chamber narrowed into yet another tunnel, which led on down yet again—until it began to slope upwards. That felt like a sign that I was close to my goal. Once again, I closed my eyes and cast Reveal Hidden Life. At last, something bloomed ahead of and slightly above me: a shapeless, dark lump, outlined in slashes of fuzzy red.

I waited.

I watched.

It gave off the telltale sign of life, that unstable red aura around it—but it did not move.

I closed my eyes and opened my mind. *"I'm here,"* I thought into the empty air.

No answer came.

No answer had come in all the days and nights since I had last heard from the Voice that I had first encountered in the vault.

Well, I thought, if this is him, at least he's alive. Even if he's too weak to get through to me.

If I'm too late, I'm finished too.

So, let's see what we shall see.

I took a deep breath and walked on up the tunnel.

After a couple of bends, I saw an opening ahead of me. Another chamber, I thought.

I refreshed the Muffle on myself and crept towards the tunnel's mouth, making no sound.

I hugged the wall, keeping my back against it, and looked into the chamber.

It was long, and arched, and there was no other exit.

Journey's end.

I listened.

I heard nothing.

And then, as my ears strained, from across the chamber came the sound of slow, deep breathing. The rumbling of something asleep.

Well, I thought. This is it.

I gathered myself, and walked out into the chamber, and across it, my footsteps making no sound, my ears straining towards the source of the breathing.

A small, dark lump on the floor.

I studied it, as I approached it, first with my eyes open, and then with them closed. I saw a small, dark shape. A fuzzy red outline. Slow, deep breathing.

I felt both apprehensive and, somehow, disappointed.

I didn't know what I should do next. Try to wake him up? What was he, anyway?

This little thing bore no resemblance to the huge form that had filled the vault beneath the village.

I was filled with a sense of pity.

I thought, *Is this all that is left of him?*

Some moments later, I heard a faint answer in my head. *Yes. This is all.*

It was the familiar Voice at last, but so weak, and so soft, as if it was no more than a whisper on the wind.

# 36

## Double Trouble

I felt a wave of relief on hearing his voice again. At last. After so long. He was still alive.

And then, other feelings poured in on me: anxiety, urgency. What could I do? What did he need?

I hurried along the chamber. Blue-white light gleamed through its ice walls, as it had done all the way down from the tower, but its far end was in shadow. Some kind of structure stood there. I popped up a Glow and saw what looked like half a tumbledown shack jutting out towards me. A few feet of roof stood out from the ice, propped up on ramshackle planks. Its floor was a low, wooden platform covered with straw.

Lying on it was an unmoving form. It did not move, I saw, because it could not. It lay on its side, a cord trussing its four paws together. Another cord looped over its snout, holding its jaws shut. Around its neck a wide metal collar gleamed silver.

Silver?

Silver dulled over time. That collar was not tarnished. Starsilver, then.

I stared down at the poor, bound creature. As I watched, its chest rose, imperceptibly, and fell.

I had never seen anything so pitiable. Its hair was lank and matted. It looked old, and worn out, and abandoned. It was smaller than

Desmond's wolves, thinner and weaker. Its ribs projected out of its shrunken stomach, as if it had long been starving.

I had come there to seek its help; but, looking down at it, I was overwhelmed with the wish to help it.

*You poor thing,* I felt.

After a while, the Voice in my head responded. "I have no memories of the babe I was. I grew to adulthood here, in this Form, with only a monster for company. I lived, I learned. I tried what I could. He grows more powerful. I grow weaker."

The resignation in his voice was heart breaking.

I said, "Is there nothing I can do?"

I heard a sigh in my head. "No, child. It is kind of you to wish to help me, but no one can. Remember me, as he subsumes what is left of me, and tell my tale to those who should hear it. I am beyond help. But think: When you are long dead and gone, I will still be here, bound and sealed, to remember you, the mortal who wished to help. I will be here until the binding fails at last. Only then will I know the release of death."

It felt infinitely sad.

I said, "I cannot imagine."

I heard his slow, shallow breaths, and at last his weak voice again. "You do not need to."

That was his destiny. I knew that I should be thankful it was not mine.

I looked down at the sorry bundle of bones and fur, his legs and snout tied up, his eyes closed. "Where is he? The one you are bound to. I can't see him."

"You did before."

"I did?"

"In the vault, when you found me and I first came to you. Cast your spell and close your eyes."

I raised Shift and cast Reveal Hidden Life and closed my eyes.

Above me stood a gigantic, four-legged form, outlined in fuzzy red, its long snout reaching down towards me, snuffling at me.

"He is within," the Voice continued, sounding weaker by the minute. "I contain him. It is not easy. We … vie, with each other. You might say that I cancel him out. Or balance him out. Either way: If I were not here, he would be loose upon the world, and the heavens."

I was out of my depth. This was magic I knew nothing about. As Marnie had told me, it was divine magic, beyond the scope of mortal knowledge. "Tell me about him."

"He is nightmare. He is night. He is the end of all things. As long as I live, bound to him, that end will not come. My mother and father scried this, when they saw to their despair what had become of their child. They, too, are divine. Their love was divine, but it made a monster. Who can explain? They could not. I cannot. It broke them. He is divine, as I am. You mortals cannot understand. You think that those who are divine cannot die, but there is an end for all things. My life is the price of his. I am the sacrifice that keeps him at bay, and this world living, and the sun and moon and stars shining down, to light your brief lives.

"This is my end, my ending. He is strong. I am weak. When the time comes he will break these bonds that bind us one to another. For as long as I live, I will prevent that. At last, I will fail. He knows that. I know that. He is implacable. In the end, the victory will be his. That is his destiny, as it is ours. The moon will fade, the sun will die, and universal darkness cover all."

He was right. We mortals could not understand.

An end will come, in time. That is all that we know. We do not know the how or why or when of it.

I heard another sigh, then the resigned voice again. "But you will be long gone, by the time the wheel has turned, and that which was made in the beginning is unmade in the end. After all the noise, and light, and struggle, there will be darkness, and silence, and the peace of nothingness. The final curtain will fall."

I was filled with a sense of cosmic time, and completion. It felt like a privilege, to be allowed to see the totality that surrounds us. Beginning, middle, end.

We weren't at the end yet, though.

He would be there, at the final stop on his long, unwanted journey. I wouldn't.

No mortal would. We have shorter time spans. We live and die in the middle.

Which was where I had work to do.

I didn't know how to point that out to him. It seemed tactless, and selfish—not to mention insensitive. *While you're lying there, forever, bound to a monster, meanwhile, what about me?*

439

I didn't need to.

It was as if he read my mind. "But there is something I can do for you," his frail voice continued. "Something that I promised. Something that will help your little life, which will bloom, and be gone, many centuries before my doom falls upon me. First, though, I should ask: Are you sure?"

I didn't understand. "Sure about what?"

"Sure that you can live without the Gift? That my disciple gave you? Are you sure that you never want to know what it is to hunt again? To run, in the Form, alive as you never are on two legs? Inhaling the world, living that richness, that truth, of who you truly are?"

I wasn't. But I knew that I had to reject it.

Knowing is feeble when compared with feeling. I yearned for it, the pure joy of the Form. My whole body was urging me to say no. I did not want to be cured. I had to be cured. This wasn't about me. It was about Esmeralda, and my friends, and the land that had become my home. I had a task to do. I longed to take the easy way out. Run away, into the Deepwoods. True to myself. Complete.

It was a simple choice. Love or duty.

I loved Esmeralda, and my friends, and my new homeland. My duty lay with them. I knew what I should do, what I should feel.

The problem was that I knew that, deep down, I loved myself more.

And in the Form, I was more myself than I could ever have imagined before I was Gifted.

Choices, choices.

Well, I thought: I've known the Gift for a short while. I have rejoiced in the glory of it. It was nice while it lasted. And at least I won't shrivel into a husk.

I wished that I didn't have to say it. I said it. "I'm sure."

"Then I will take back my Gift."

"Thank you," I said.

Then a thought struck me. "I did not know it was yours."

"I was the first. It is an old tale, and a long one. You will be shown it, while the Gift leaves you. You will understand, as you watch, and listen. And then, it will all be behind you. That chapter in your life will have ended. You will go your way. I will go mine. Now, close your eyes."

I did.

"What do you see?"

"Nothing."

"Good. Keep them closed. Keep seeing it. Walk towards me."

I did as he said. My shins bumped up against the low platform that he was lying on.

"Reach down."

I reached.

"There is a cord around my nose and mouth."

"I saw."

"Cut it."

I said, taking my knife from its sheath, "Is that possible? Isn't it magic?"

"The magic is in the Binding, child. The cords are merely cords."

I hesitated. What he'd just said confused me.

I said, "If they are not magic, why are cords needed? What are they for?"

There was a tinge of bitterness in his voice as he said, "To keep me in my place. To keep me, and him, immobile, and weak. Unable to move, canceling each other out. In this feeble shell. This is all that remains of us."

He sighed.

"I can see why she did it. It is better this way. My life drains his. I nullify the threat. It cannot have been easy for her, to know that she must do this to her own child. But he is a monster. He must be contained. He will not forgive her, nor his father. He will wait. He will outlast us all. And I will be the last of those that he has outlasted. You will see, when you return the Gift to me, in the vision that is about to come to you. Past, present, future: All will be revealed. You will understand, mage. And you will be as you were. Lesser, without the Gift, but free. Free to go. Ungifted. If that is indeed what you want."

"It is," I said.

I felt for his head and found the cord that bound his jaws together. I slid my niblun-forged blade under it, and it parted easily. I heard his mouth open.

His freed tongue smacked against his lips. He took a deep breath and sighed. "Thank you." He sounded exhausted.

"I'm glad that I could help."

"And I am glad that I can give you your reward. Hold out your hand."

I did.

His nose found my hand. I felt him snuffling at it.

"The Gift," he murmured, "is received as it is given."

"Thank you," I said.

And then I was screaming.

His jaws clamped onto my hand. His fangs wrenched at my flesh, chewing deeper and deeper. His snarls filled my ears, as he tore at my hand, mangling its bones. I was on my knees, unable to pull my hand away from his terrible teeth. I stood no chance. They were sunk into it, through it. All I could do was cry out at the pain. I felt him working on my hand. Any moment now, it would part from my arm. He would swallow it.

Why?

I had no idea.

All I knew was that there was nothing I could do to stop him.

He spat out my hand and threw me aside so that I fell on my back. He turned to the cord around his paws, which he parted with a single bite. He stood up, over me, growing by the second, larger, younger, stronger. When he filled the cavern to its roof, he placed one paw on me, to hold me down, threw back his head, and howled.

The echoes of his howl bounced back off the cavern's walls and died away.

He lowered his head towards me again. He growled, his snout against my ear. "At last. *At long, long last!*"

I felt only the agony in my mangled hand, which had been chewed to a pulp. It hung off the end of my arm like dead meat. I cradled it with my other arm. I had never known such pain. I could hardly see through the tears that filled my eyes, but his shape was changing, as he tore at the skin around his paws.

"I should have warned you," he said, between mouthfuls, as he peeled off his hide, "that it would hurt."

His voice was no longer sorrowful, but amused, as lay I there, gasping.

He straightened up, now standing on two legs, and kicked me onto my side. "And now," he continued, "it is over. For me, that is. Not for you." He knelt, and wrapped the warm, bleeding wolfskin around me, turning me over and binding cords around my wrists and ankles. I lay there, trussed and helpless, the pain in my chewed hand unbearable, only—it was now a *paw*, taped to three others? I was in the Form again? Another cord taped my jaws shut. Something hard slid over my head, and around my neck, where it shrank tight against my throat.

And began to burn. The starsilver collar.

I heard footsteps as he walked round to stand over me.

I looked up, and saw myself, Daxx, smiling back down at me.

"Centuries of waiting," he said, in my own voice. "Of planning. At last. I do not have the time, or even the inclination, to explain, fool. You have served your purpose. You will see, soon enough. And I will be gone."

I could not speak, but managed to protest, in thought, *you promised to help me.*

He chuckled. "Oh yes, indeed, I did," he agreed. "And you believed me."

He leaned down towards me.

"*I lied.* You walked into my trap, as you walked into the trap beneath the village. You believed what you wanted to believe. Mortals are easy to convince, when they want to be convinced. You wanted a cure, for my Gift. I promised one. You did not even think to question it. *There is no cure.*

"It has all been a lie. You will have all eternity to contemplate that, and to realize how stupid you have been. I have to say, I expected a mage to be sharper than you are. Lie after lie I fed you, spinning my yarn, teasing you along, hoping that you would not see through it. You did not even think to do so! You just assumed that I was telling the truth. Such a simpleton. You took the bait, and swallowed it whole. I lured you here to do the one thing I needed someone to do. And you did it. You cut the cord. My teeth did the rest. They are your teeth now. You won't be able to open your mouth to use them, just as I could not.

"And so, now you take my place. And I will take yours. It will be interesting to be mortal, for a while. I shall have to try not to be killed." He smiled. "Luckily I will have this pretty staff to protect me."

He was inspecting Shift. Even through the torment of my own pain I could hear her shock, her protests. I kept trying to reply to him, to object, to argue, but my thoughts no longer seemed to reach him.

"Powerful," he said, turning Shift over in his hands, clearly pleased. "Good. I will put her to good use. You, and my furry friend here, will have each other's company for the rest of time. He's a dull companion, I should warn you."

He turned, and walked away.

A wind blew in along the cavern. It grew stronger, and louder. Everything swirled in on me as I watched "myself" walk off down the long chamber, in my clothes, bearing my staff, her heartstone gleaming green above red.

While I lay there, on a bed of straw, my neck burning, my ankles and wrists bound, trapped inside a coat of fur. In which I was not the only one.

I turned my attention to the other. In response, all I got was a growl.

*There's no talking to him*, I thought.

So now what?

I closed my eyes.

A huge form, outlined in slashes of red, bloomed into view around me, its snout close to mine.

And there was me, at his feet, bound to him—small, helpless, his shadow towering above me, and a wind roaring in my ears.

I blacked out.

Out of the blackness the story emerged.

Two people were leaning over me, looking down, frowning, concerned. She was pale, and beautiful, her white hair matching her white robe. He was dark, and lean, dressed in deerskins, his face hard, a horn slung across his chest. They did not like what they were looking at.

Then I was looking through their eyes, down at the monster that had formed around their child.

Me.

I felt his amusement growing within me, as the Voice spoke.

*They did what they could, my poor mother and father. They did it before it was too late. Had I grown to where I will one day grow, these heavens and this earth would have long ago been extinguished. They bound me to their babe. Even though they knew that I will kill them, when the time comes, they could not kill their own child. It is forbidden among gods as it is among mortals.*

*But I am a demon. I do what I will, forbidden or not. I let him grow to manhood, within me, until I had the full power of his divine mind. Which is now mine, as your form is now mine. And you will stay here in my form, until I return for it, and assume it once more. There is an end to all things. I am that end. It is a thankless job, but someone has to do it.*

*And I would rather do it sooner than later.*

*So I made my plans, and set my trap, and worked my way past the constraints that she placed on me.*

*I created the Gift.*

444

*I timed it to my mother's rhythm. I gave it to my disciples. I invented the myth that they tell each other, about how the Pack began. That, too, is a lie. They passed it on, when in the Form, under the full moon, as I knew they would, because the blood in those that have been Gifted yearns for the blood of others, of the victims that it Gifts in turn.*

*And so the heavens wheel, and the years pass, and in time a mage who has been Gifted comes to our sanctuary. He would spring the trap that I had set for him. He would believe the lies that I used to lure him to me. He would be so needful, and so want to believe them, that he could not step back and see the truth. No human can pass the barrier behind which she sealed me. But those of the Pack are no longer human.*

*I lured Tolmeth towards me, to where he could practice the forbidden arts that I whispered into his mind. He knew nothing of me. I worked on him, without his knowledge. As he studied the secrets of Binding, I studied them too. There was much to be learned. I used him, as I used the Ice Worm. The results were less than ideal. Well, you saw the creatures they produced. But I learned what I needed to. Where there is a Binding, there can be an Unbinding.*

*And now, thanks to you, I am free.*

The blackness receded, and I opened my eyes.

I couldn't move. I could hardly breathe. My neck was on fire. My mind was racing.

I'd come all this way for a lie?

The realization stunned me. I saw that he'd been right: I hadn't questioned anything he'd told me, in his web of deceit. He'd lied to me in the vault below the village. He'd played the martyr, to get my sympathy, to allay my suspicions. *He was my last hope. Out of the kindness of his heart, he would help me and give me the cure.*

I felt such a fool. How could I have fallen for it?

As I saw how he'd deceived me, I had to admit that I'd done all I could to help him. He'd told me the recipe, for the cure. Marnie and Velaryn hadn't liked the sound of it. Marnie's words echoed in my mind. "I don't know as I'd trust anyone as told me to drink *this.*"

Why hadn't I listened to her? It wasn't a cure: It was bait, to lure me to him. I'd been so wrapped up in my race against time that I'd never thought to step back and think clearly.

I'd been suckered.

So, what to do about it?

I couldn't think.

*Well you'd better damn well start thinking,* I told myself. *That's the one thing you can do. You can't move. You can't look around for help. It's up to you now, and you alone. All you have to go on is what you already know. So work it out, if you don't want to stay here forever.*

What did I know?

What I'd been told.

Marnie's words came back to me, and I saw her as clearly, in my mind, as if she was talking directly to me.

Her old face was grim, her voice urgent: *We've been told.*

I recalled my baffled question, *Told what?*

*Everything. It's all there. All we need is the eyes to see it, and the wit to know what we're looking at.*

Marnie. My mentor. *Listen to her. She's never steered you wrong.*

If I don't see it now, I thought, I never will.

I have all the information I'm ever going to get.

So use it. Get to work.

I've been working on it for weeks—I can't make head or tail of it! Nothing's come to light.

The thought echoed in my mind.

*Come to light …*

Why had I used those exact words?

It felt significant that I had. I waited, for an insight.

And then I remembered what Avildor had told me. *When you wish to seek your own Light, cast Insight on yourself.*

And my reply: *Why would I want to seek myself? I know where I am.*

*Do you? At the moment, perhaps. That may not always be the case.*

I certainly did not know where I was as far as Eilwen's lines were concerned.

I closed my eyes and let my Insight guide me.

As I grew still, and trusted myself to it, a picture grew in my mind, gradually becoming clear.

I was back in Conclave, in Archmage Faldruti's house, the eight of us seated round his table.

I heard Dean Eilwen speak again:

*Run and hide*

*Hide and run*

*Been there,* I thought, *done that.* That's how I escaped the village and avoided the Wild Hunt. I ran, I hid.

*Don't assume.*

Yes, I thought: Look where assuming has got me! As he had said himself, I'd just *assumed* the Voice was telling the truth, and that he was what he presented himself as. Honest. A victim. My last hope. I'd heard what I wanted to hear, hadn't I? He'd been no more trustworthy than Captain Rozlyn, and we'd all *assumed* she was working for us.

So, what else have I *assumed?*

I let my mind think over what I'd learned, since Conclave. There had been a lot, from learning about Ogres to learning about dragons. What Oller had told me, via our Link of Impartment, about what he'd seen in Sarmen, had been as unexpected as traveling with Urngra had been. Mejnul's beasts were as different from Vagg's, or from the Wester Isle helldragon, as Urngra had been from what she looked like. She looked terrifying and savage. She'd been shrewd and insightful.

So, where to start?

How about at the beginning?

*Run and hide, hide and run.*

We already did that. Next?

*Whoa*, hold on a moment!

Look at the next line, idiot. *Don't assume.* You're *assuming* those lines mean the same thing. If they did, why would Eilwen say it twice? Every word had been an effort for her to get out. She wasn't going to waste a syllable. What's she telling you? Don't *assume* "hide and run" is "run and hide." Don't assume *anything.* Don't assume that appearances are all there is to it. Urngra, and the Voice, and Captain Rozlyn all turned out different than you'd *assumed.*

*Dead reborn.*

There's been some of that, on this journey. The mob of corpses outside the tower, for example. But is that all there is to that line? Not necessarily. *Don't assume* so. Maybe there's more. More in the line. More to come.

I got nothing on the next two lines.

*Turn the tide*

*Sound the horn*

What tide? And I didn't have a horn, so how could I sound it? Maybe I just didn't have one *yet.* Okay, if that's so, how are you going to get one?

By getting out of here.

So, let's do that.

It was as I considered the next lines that the lightbulb went on in my head.

*Wield the broom*
*Sweep the sky*

I'd never been able to make sense of any of that, but I told myself, *hold on*. Not so fast. Have you really tried? No. You just skim over it. You think, brooms sweep, so you're making that link, but you're not putting your mind to it.

*Wield* the broom.

"Wield?"

That's not a word you'd associate with a mundane task like sweeping. You'd say "Use the broom," something ordinary like that. *Weapons* are wielded, in battle: Qrysta's blades, Grell's maul, my staff—

And that was when I made the connection.

He'd stolen Shift, so I didn't have a staff, any more than I had a horn—but we *did* have a broomstick.

Take the twigs off it, the broom, and what is it?

A stick.

A stick of what?

A stick of rowan, just like Shift. Marnie had found it significant that Jess had chosen the same wood for her broomstick as I'd picked for my staff.

Why had that happened?

I remembered Jewelwright Neva's words: *I don't trust Mr. Coincidence.*

Not only did we have a stick, we had a heartstone: a tourmaline that was the twin of the one in Shift's eye—a tourmaline, moreover, which I'd seen merging with Shift's in the Thieves Guild trading room in Eastbay, as if it was learning everything that Shift had to teach her.

*Wield the broom.*

I would have a new staff to wield—perhaps not Shift herself, but one who knew everything she did.

For the first time since finding myself trussed and helpless I felt a surge of hope.

*It's all there. All we need is the eyes to see it, and the wit to know what we're looking at.*

Okay, I thought, that's all fine, but in order to craft my new staff, first I have to get out of here. So, how do I do that?

I cast around for ideas. None came.

# 37

## Skin in the Game

*Look, it's not impossible,* I told myself. *Even if he told you it was. He lied to you before, after all, again and again, right? Ignore what he said. He got out, didn't he?*

*Yes.*

*So, you can too.*

*Okay, so how did he do that?*

*I don't know.*

*Okay, so analyse.*

Where am I?

Behind a barrier. Bound and sealed. Just like he was.

So how did he get away?

I came along and freed him.

So, now I need someone to come along and free me.

My friends were nearby, but *no human can pass the barrier.*

*Those of the Pack are no longer human.*

Who did I know of the Pack?

Byrneth and Farnz, in the village. Graycote, in his Oak Grove.

They were all far away, overseas. And I didn't know how to reach them. Let alone persuade them to come all this way—for what? What

449

could I offer them? Nothing. I had no cure. That had been a lie. Would I in turn have to lie to them, to be rescued?

It was a pointless question. I could not *think into* them, the way that Marnie could think into me with her Awareness skill. And not even Marnie could work on anyone from so far away. There was a limit to the distance over which she could *think into* someone. Within range she could get through as clear as a bell, because she was an expert. I was a novice. I'd tried, with Oller, on our flight from Rushtoun, but hadn't had much success. I'd Influenced him, maybe, a little bit. But Oller was in Sarmen, even farther away than Byrneth and Farnz and Graycote. They were all too intelligent, anyway. They weren't open to my weak probings. The only creatures I'd been able to Manipulate had been the stone trolls outside Niblunhaem.

Trolls, I thought.

Big as houses, thick as bricks.

My Induction skill was so poor that I could only work on minds that simple.

There were no trolls anywhere near me, as far as I knew—stone trolls or ice trolls or otherwise. Pity. Trolls weren't human. They'd be able to pass the barrier, if I could Manipulate one down here. Except that the tunnels were too small for a troll to get down.

*Concentrate*, I told myself. Stop wasting time thinking about non-existent trolls. I needed to think about who was nearby, and available to me.

Qrysta, Grell, Jess. Nyrik and Horm.

I'd have no luck there. They were all far more intelligent than stone trolls. Way above my skill level. And even if I could get through to them, they wouldn't be able to pass through the barrier and come to help me.

So close, but so far.

It wasn't as if I needed much. All I needed was someone to cut the cord around my jaws.

Then, I could chew through the one that bound my paws …

The words played around in my mind, as I imagined freeing myself.

*Cord. Jaws. Chew. Paws.*

Epiphany! Pieces of the puzzle slid into place.

I knew what to do.

Okay, I thought. I'm going to need to give this everything I've got, if this is going to work.

When I'd Manipulated the stone trolls outside Niblunhaem, I'd had line of sight on them. I wasn't able to see my target from where I lay on my bed of straw, so I needed to pinpoint him. Then, I would be able to focus my Induction abilities on him.

Locating him was something that I now knew how to do, thanks to the Light Magic that Avildor had taught me. I was little more than a beginner at that skill line, but I had learned enough from him to be able to find those I knew well.

I closed my eyes, and Sought for my objective.

I soon found him: a small, orange ball of life and light, no more than a few hundred yards away, back up the tunnel. *Of course,* I thought, as I remembered what Avildor had told me. *Orange is the light of the faithful.*

I focused Induction on him and sensed him suddenly become alert.

I could almost see his ears pricking up, and his eyes searching around for me, his tail wagging.

I exerted Influence, and Domination, and finally Instruction.

And then, the little orange ball of light was scampering down the tunnel towards me.

The closer he came, the more his scent filled the chamber. I inhaled it through my wolf nostrils, as hope and relief flooded through me. My tail thumped on the straw that I was lying on. My companion growled somewhere inside my head. I ignored him. I'd deal with him later. First things first. My sharp ears heard Little Guy's paws scrabbling on the ice floor of the chamber as he ran up out of the tunnel. I opened my eyes to see him hurrying in my direction. He jumped up onto the platform and stood over me, panting, tongue hanging out, eyes bright, ears cocked, his bushy tail wagging.

Our scruffy little mutt, who was more "pack" than I was.

I'd never been happier to see anyone.

As always, he wanted to know what he was supposed to do.

I don't think I could ever have managed it using words. *Little Guy, bite through this cord, okay?* That would have meant nothing to him. *Sit, lie down, stay, fetch, charge:* He was fine with those, and knew exactly what was needed. But we weren't communicating with words—not that I'd have been able to speak anyway, with my wolf mouth, even if it hadn't been tied shut.

As it was, words weren't needed. I Instructed the idea to him and it got through soon enough. A human might have held back, and said,

"Wait—you want me to do *what?*" It was, after all, an unusual request. Little Guy just got on with the task. He bent down, got his teeth into the cord binding my nose and shook it and himself and my head around as he tore at it. It soon parted. He stood back, and looked down at me, pleased with himself, the cord in his mouth, for all the world as if he was bringing me his leash for me to take him for a walk. I couldn't say *good boy* until I got my human mouth back, but I beamed him a torrent of praise, and his tail whirred in response.

Then I did what I had seen my captor do.

I bit through the cords that held my paws, and tore at the wolf-hide pelt that held me in its Binding.

The pain was excruciating—but that was just tough. It had to be done. As I flayed myself alive, tearing back first one leg then another, hands and feet emerged where my paws had been. It was easier stripping the rest of me with my one good hand rather than with my teeth. The hand that the wolf had mangled was still useless, and still hurting like hell. At last I was upright, my chest and arms and shoulders freed and now my own again, the hide that had Bound me now peeling off me, all the way up to my neck—

Where it stopped.

I pulled, and twisted, as if failing to get out of a too-tight sweater, but the wolfskin would not come off any further.

I was unable to get it past the starsilver collar.

Below it, I was myself again. Above it, I still had the head of a wolf.

And inside that head, something very angry was snarling at me.

I felt at the collar for its fastening.

There was none. It was a single, smooth piece of metal, like my Link of Impartment. There was no join in it anywhere.

I couldn't get it off.

How had he managed to do it?

I hadn't seen. He'd been behind me.

Maybe he hadn't got the collar off. Maybe he'd just assumed my Form, and I'd assumed his.

I had to get rid of it. I didn't want to have the head of a wolf for the rest of my life. That would be inconvenient. And it was hard to think, with all the angry snarling echoing inside it. Besides, the damn thing around my neck burned.

But was locked in place.

It took me a moment to figure it out.

I started running up the tunnel, Little Guy cantering beside me, the wolf hide flowing behind me, my unwanted companion now howling with rage inside my—our—head.

My friends were all facing the other way when we rounded the corner and ran up towards them. They heard us coming, and whirled around. I was not surprised that their weapons were in their hands the moment they saw me. Horm, I saw, had the starsilver bow aimed at me—which was good thinking, considering what he saw charging up towards him. I must have looked like some wild, barbarian warrior, wearing a wolf's head over his own, its bloody pelt trailing behind him. They were all yelling at once.

"Stop right there!"

"Little Guy, come here!"

"What in all hells is that thing?"

"No closer! We'll shoot!"

Their voices came muffled and distorted through my wolf ears and the snarling of my companion.

I couldn't blame them. I'd been expecting that reaction. They must have been on edge, and confused. They'd seen "me" stroll up from the depths. Obviously, he'd told them to stay there. Obviously, they'd done so, thinking he'd been me. Obviously, they were waiting for him to come back down for them. Instead, this wolf-headed apparition had come charging up behind them.

I immediately dropped to my knees, hands outstretched, in surrender.

I clasped them, as if begging, as I inched towards them. I could see that Jess was worried about Little Guy, so close to this monster that had emerged from the depths. She kept calling him to her, but I made sure he stayed with me.

Then I stopped and got him to sit. Then lie down. Then roll over. I scratched his stomach.

His tail wagged appreciatively.

They'd been babbling all the while, shouting at me and at each other, but I didn't listen. I just waited for them to fall silent. When they did, I got Little Guy to sit.

Then I straightened up, still on my knees, and looked at them.

I pointed at Qrysta.

I pointed at the metal collar around my neck.

I mimed an unlocking gesture.

I waited, till she understood.

She reached inside her jerkin for Oller's silver key on its chain.

I nodded eagerly, then crept forward, very slowly, on my knees.

Little Guy came with me and we crossed the invisible barrier.

Qrysta was still hesitant.

Through the cacophony of howling in my head, I could just about hear her ask Grell, "What do you think?"

"I think we can kill it easily enough, if it tries anything," Grell replied. His Kinfolk maul was raised in his hands. He'd be able to brain me with it before I could move.

I looked at him and shook my head. Then I crossed my heart, and nodded, slowly. I held his eyes.

"It might know what's going on," Grell said.

I nodded again eagerly, several times.

"Okay," Qrysta said. She brought the key towards my throat. I felt it enter the starsilver collar and turn. I heard something click. Qrysta stood back, holding in each hand half a starsilver hoop, one of which had Oller's key sticking out of it.

I was so relieved that the burning had stopped that I was about to get to my feet, when I saw their weapons snap up on me again. That froze me, for a few moments—and in those moments, I could feel my head swelling, and growing, and the howling and snarling getting louder and louder, as if there were a whole pack of wolves in there with me, not just one.

I felt a rush of panic. I needed to put a stop to it right away. Staying on my knees, I hauled at the wolfskin and tore the rest of it off over my head.

I flung it aside, gasping.

"Daxx??"

"What in all hells?"

"How did you get back in?"

"What happened to you, what was that thing on your head?!"

"It was growing, did you see that? As soon as Qrysta took the collar off—"

"What happened to your hand?"

When I could speak, I said, "Thanks, Qrysta. That was … grim."

I reached up and felt my head. It was the size that it should be. I exhaled a long sigh of relief, and got to my feet.

The barrage of questions began again. I cut them off, saying, "I'll explain later. How long since he came out?"

"Who came out?"

The person you thought was me."

"That wasn't you?"

"No."

"Of course it was you, you think we don't know you?"

"He had your clothes, your staff—"

"Then who—"

"I don't have time to explain! How long ago?"

"Maybe an hour."

"We have to find him."

"How—"

"What—"

"*Later*, guys! We need to move. *Now.*" I started to run back up the tunnel.

Nyrik said, "Hold on, Daxxie."

I stopped, and turned back.

He was holding the wolf hide. "Marnie should take a look at this, don't you think?"

"You're right," I said.

"Just like the old days, eh?" he said, as handed it to me. "You was carrying one o' these when we first met, remember? Back in Jarn."

"If you'd looked like you did just now we'd have steered well clear," Horm said. "Bloody great wolf head on you …"

"Yur," Nyrik agreed.

I tied the skin round my shoulders and said, "Let's go."

Lumbering along beside me, Grell said, "He had Shift and everything."

"Yes. And I want her back."

"How are you going to do that?"

"We're going to kill him and take her."

Grell looked down at me, worried. "Jeez, Daxx, I've seen what that staff of yours can do …"

"I know. Don't worry, I've got this."

"Yeah? You'd better, or we're toast."

Qrysta said, "So, who is he?"

I said, "The son of a bitch who lured me here, lied to me, suckered me into taking his place, and stole my staff."

"He sounds dangerous."

"You have no idea."

"Care to enlighten us?"

I said, "Not now, it would take too long."

"And you want us to take him on," Qrysta said. "And you won't tell us what we're facing. And without Heals?"

I said, "We'll have Heals."

"You don't have a staff!"

"Don't worry," I said. "I've got you covered."

"You do? How, exactly?"

"You'll see." I didn't add, *if my idea works.* There was no point in telling them about it if it wasn't going to. I needed them positive.

We ran up the stone steps and emerged into the floor of the tower. Grell hauled the flagstone across and set it back over the tunnel's entrance, sealing it off. Outside the tower's open door, a line of footprints led away across the valley.

"Bastard told us to wait down there till he came back for us," Grell said. "Could've been days."

"In which time he'd have disappeared," I said. "He's got an hour on us."

We all knew that it wouldn't be hard to find our quarry, but I didn't want to risk him seeing us coming up behind him. Like Grell, I was only too aware of what Shift could do, both to protect him and attack us. We needed to hit him before he knew he was in danger and used her.

I told Jess what I wanted her to do. She nodded, unslung her broomstick from her back, and mounted it. Horm straddled it behind her, I Levitated them, and they took to the air, gaining height until they were out of sight to all of us but Nyrik. My look-alike had my human form and therefore, I assumed—or rather hoped, because I told myself not to *assume* anything—that he would also have my human vision, rather than the much sharper eyes of Woods Kin. Horm would be invisible to him, far overhead, but he'd be able see down and find our quarry. An hour's start, on foot, would soon be overtaken by Jess in full flight. The rest of us set off at a steady trot on his tracks.

It was not long before Jess landed beside us, alone.

"We found a good spot," she said. "In the field of boulders. Plenty of cover."

Nyrik mounted the broomstick behind her and they flew off at speed.

When she returned, she said, "He was getting close. It won't be long before they see him."

She jumped off her broomstick and unbound its twigs until it was just a stick, which she handed to me. As we ran on towards the encircling mountains, I retrieved the pouch of heartstones from my inner pocket, then searched both ends of the rowan staff until I found what I was looking for: a dark fleck. I teased it open, the way Marnie had shown me, and inserted the tourmaline. The wood sealed itself around the jewel, which began to glow, green above red.

Well, I thought, as my new staff came alive in my hands, she may not be Shift, but she will have all the knowledge and power that was shared between the two tourmaline heartstones when they first met—

*Ah,* a familiar, teasing voice came, as the warmth of her flowed along my arm and into my heart, *there you are!*

I stopped running, astonished, and stared at the rowan staff I was holding.

*Shift??*

*None other.*

*What? But I thought … How …?*

She laughed. *There's much you have yet to learn about stick and stone, Daxx. Now, let's see what we can do about that hand of yours …*

I raised her and cast Heals on myself. My mangled hand mended and stopped hurting. It was a blessed relief.

Her merry voice, asked *Better?*

*Better indeed. Thank you, my friend. It's good to see you again.*

*It's good to be back. Now, we have a job to do, right?*

We ran on. I felt a surge of hope. *Payback time. My hand, Urngra's life.*

Three small shapes appeared at last ahead of us, black shadows on the white snow of the floor of the Valley of the Moon, scattered boulders beyond them. One of them saw us coming, and waved. Nyrik. Another stood over the third, his bow drawn. Horm. The third was slumped on his knees, his back to us, unmoving, the staff that he had dropped lying beside him. An arrowhead jutted out of one shoulder. Starsilver. He looked up as we arrived. His face was twisted with pain. Sweat glistened on his brow.

His eyes grew round as he saw me. "How—?"

I raised an eyebrow. "Does it matter?"

He shook his head. "No. Nothing matters now. I am mortal. You will kill me."

"Not me," I said. "Him."

My body double looked at Horm, who drew his silver-bladed knife. "Why him?" he said.

"You killed my cousin," Horm said.

The other frowned. "I did?"

"The Wild Hunt found her," I said.

He stared at me, his eyes hard. "As I will find you, mage."

"Not in this world," I said, and nodded at Horm, who stepped behind him. He put his knee in his back, took a handful of his long, fair hair, and pulled back his head. He put the point of his knife to the side of his victim's neck, its blade facing forwards, and waited for my signal.

I looked down at the face that was staring directly up at me.

"Not in this world, as you say. But in the next one. Where I will see you soon." He let that sink in. "It has many realms, some of them much nicer than others. I will find you, wherever you are. You can depend on that. I may be mortal now, in your human form, but my essence is divine. Freed of this flesh and blood, it can go where it pleases. And do what it pleases. We will meet when this moon month is over and your time here has ended. I look forward to it."

He smiled. "There is no cure, mage, remember? Or should I say, *husk?*"

I felt a knot clench in my stomach.

He saw my reaction, and chuckled. "You will pay for this," he said. "For a long, long time."

I tried not to think about it. What could I do? Negotiate?

No. If I had to go, I thought, at least I could send him on ahead of me.

I glanced at Horm and nodded.

"This is for Urngra," Horm said. He slid his dagger through his victim's neck and slashed forwards, severing his windpipe.

He pushed the dead body away.

The snow where it fell reddened around it.

We stood in silence, looking down at the corpse.

Which, as we watched, began to move.

# 38

## One Down, One to Go

"Uh-oh," Qrysta said, drawing her blades.

Instinctively we all backed away, forming a circle around the body, which was writhing within itself under its cloak. Our archers had arrows trained on it, tight on their bowstrings. Grell's maul was in his hands. I had Shift raised and ready for action. Beside me, Little Guy growled, his eyes locked onto the changing form in front of us. It was face down, so we could not see what was happening—but, clearly, something was.

After a while, all movement stopped.

We stood there, looking at a corpse under a travel-stained cloak.

For a few moments, nothing happened.

Then, a pale light grew around it.

It bloomed and hovered above the place where our enemy had died, growing until it covered the remains of the body.

I recognized it. I had seen it before, in the village, in the woods behind Farnz's cottage. I had seen it earlier that day, above the corpse in the bed in the topmost chamber of the Tower of the Moon.

A ball of pure, pearl-white light.

Which, slowly, faded.

As it did, two figures within it were revealed.

A woman, her hair as white as her robe, ageless, beautiful. A stern-faced man, dressed in deerskin, a curved, silver, star-studded horn slung across his chest.

They were looking down at the body beneath them.

The man knelt and turned it over.

It was still dressed in my clothes, but it was no longer me.

The woman knelt beside him.

They gazed at the corpse's face.

A fine face it was, of a young man about my own age—but it was not mine. Blue, unseeing eyes stared back up at them, below a mane of brown hair.

The man and woman looked at each other.

She nodded.

He reached down and closed the dead man's eyes.

They stood. They turned to us.

"Thank you," the woman said, "for returning our son to us."

I wanted to reply, but was unable to speak.

"It is good to have seen him as he would have been, had he lived," his father said.

I wanted to respond, even if just with a nod, but was unable to move.

"We know why you sought him," his wife said. "We know how he deceived you. That was not him, but the other who had subsumed him. We want to believe that some part of our child remained. But how can a babe resist such influence? He fed on our son. Used his growing, his nature, his essence, his mind. It pained us beyond your imagination to think what he would become. What he would do, to us, to this world and the heavens above it." She paused. "But which, now, he will not."

She smiled, a sad smile of relief, and of closure. "He is free, now," she added. "Beyond harm. Beyond harming." She made a gesture in the air, and, as she spoke her robe grew brighter. "As are you," she said.

It took a moment for that to sink in. Then, as I felt a warm tingling in my blood, I also felt a surge of hope.

She nodded. "I wax, I wane. I die, I shine again. I have many avatars. This is but one of them. You saw another earlier, in my tower." A brilliant, white light had grown around her. It was so strong that it hurt my eyes, but I could not look away.

"The Gift is cursed," she said. The tingling in my blood faded as the light around her began to fade. "The curse is lifted."

When the light had gone, she said, "You need no longer fear me."

The man turned to Horm. "You shot well."

Horm, too, was unable to move, or to answer.

The Hunter looked at me. "Remember what happens next."

He held my eyes for a moment, then knelt down and picked up his son's body.

He stood beside his wife and the pearlescent ball of light grew around the three of them again, becoming brighter and more opaque, until they were hidden inside it.

It faded away, and they were gone.

We were left, standing in the snow-covered valley below its high, encircling peaks, a cold wind ruffling our clothes.

It was Grell who spoke first as we unfroze and lowered our weapons. "One down, one to go."

I was lost in thought.

*Remember what happens next.*

What on earth does that mean? How can you remember the future?

I looked up at Grell, distracted, and said, "One what?"

"Problem. That's yours solved. What about Esmeralda's?"

That brought me out of my reverie. "Good point."

"Well?"

"No idea," I said. "I've been … preoccupied."

He grunted. "No kidding."

Qrysta said, "Well, now get on the case."

"I will."

"A hundred thousand chalkers," she reminded us. "A hundred dragons. A couple of months. What could possibly go wrong?"

When we got back to Ogretzk, several days later, it seemed that its entire population was waiting for us outside its northern gate. Front and center was the chief. At our approach he stepped forwards and held out his enormous hand, an enormous smile on his even more enormous face.

"Welcome back! Welcome, welcome, *welcome*, my friends!" he cried, as jovial as a host at some old-fashioned celebration. "We are so happy to see you here again. What a triumph! *What* an occasion. Oh, we must celebrate, celebrate indeed! Come on in, do, we are agog to hear all about it. Who would have thought it? Hey?"

He was so lively, and so personable, that it took me a moment to realize that he wasn't speaking gibberish. Or, rather, Ogrish.

"Aha!" He chortled, prodding me in the shoulder with a large finger. "I see you have noticed our transformation! Out of the blue it came, sir! Entirely unexpected. One moment we were bellowing and snarling among ourselves, like brute beasts—the next, we were engaged in the most civilized of conversations. Such topics we have been discussing! Agriculture to zoology, and everything betwixt and between. It is as if we have found our minds, sir, as well as our tongues. And it is our considered opinion that it is no coincidence that this has happened to us in the wake of your appearance in our midst! I see the surprise written on your face! But, believe me, my dear sir, it is evident—*evident*, I say—that we owe this most happy state of affairs to you."

He was capering about in front of me like a gigantic puppy. He seized my hand, and led me, or rather hauled me, back to the city.

"Our wise men and women are in no doubt. We have been under a curse, my dear fellow. A curse, you are thinking? Indeed, indeed, *indeed*, and we shall explain all, at this evening's celebration that we intend to be, *ha ha*, a MOAF—a Mother of All Feasts! Our fishers have been out, on the Ice Lake; our hunters have hunted with great success, and .... Well, I would not want to spoil the surprises that we have been preparing for you and your gallant comrades. Suffice it to say, for the moment, that under our curse we could only gargle, and argue, and distill sproj, and snap and snarl among ourselves. And, as an interesting side effect, not walk and talk at the same time. But now look at me!"

He chuckled, skipping happily beside me. "The truth is as clear as day to us now. We were charged with the task of keeping others out. Anyone who sought the Valley of the Moon. And we ourselves were not to go near the place. She ordained it so. We were, as some had suspected, her gatekeepers." He grinned an alarming grin down at me. "But now, her gate no longer needs keeping, that is clear to her, to us, and to you. Thus, that tale is concluded. And ours," he said, with great glee, "can commence again!"

They wined us and dined us.

Or, rather, sproj'd us and stuffed us full to bursting at a banquet that was, indeed, the Mother of All Feasts. There was more than we could possibly eat and more than we should sensibly have drunk—but we only found that out the next morning, the hard way. The fishers had caught arctic char under the Ice Lake, which had been marinated in oils and spices, and was served to us raw, in thin, delicious slivers. With it came a salad of kelp and roots, a tangy mix of salt and sweetness, and giant loaves of dark, soft bread and bowls of yak butter. Joints of reindeer and fur-elk and musk ox followed, accompanied by platters piled high with green vegetables, peas and beans and cabbages, and crisp, roast potatoes.

Finally, there were winter fruits preserved in sproj, along with lemon and orange cakes as huge and light as balloons, topped with whipped yak cream, and, of course, ices of every imaginable flavor. Our hosts promised us a tour of their hothouses the next morning, to show us how they grew plants that could never have survived this far north if not for the thermal pools within them that bubbled up from deep underground—and, of course, help from the mysterious root folk. I asked about them, but it seemed that our hosts knew no more about them than the Ice Orcs did.

It was a long, joyous night. The Ogres, it seemed, had rediscovered the art of conversation along with language. There was no more roaring, or bellowing, or banging of tabletops. There was, instead, politeness, insightfulness, shrewdness, and a complete lack of insensitivity. I have never attended a more civilized gathering. Dozens of conversations took place all over the feast-hall, erudite discussions on every topic under the sun. The noise level grew as the night progressed, and the sproj flowed, but no speaker was ever interrupted. Points were made, and conceded, and embellished, and countered. Counterpoints were admired and applauded; backs were slapped in congratulation; witty remarks prompted laughter, and often even wittier ripostes.

Each discussion flowed forwards and progressed as its subject was explored and expanded upon. We listened, and learned, and spoke, and changed our minds, in tune with the development of the argument. I felt that I'd learned more about everything in that one evening than I'd done in my entire life up to that point.

Thanks to the sproj, though, I remember none of it. All I can say is that it felt as if everyone was right, about everything, and that we had all discovered profound truths that would stay with us forever.

They didn't.

I woke up the next morning, late, as if from a delicious dream. And then my head began to throb, horribly. I drained the water jug beside my bed. It tasted ghastly, as if there was more than just water in it, but I knew I needed to rehydrate, and there was no way that I could walk anywhere to empty it out and change it. I turned over and dropped back into oblivion.

The only one of us who was fit to travel the next day was Jess.

When I emerged, groggy and blinking, into the feast-hall, she was sitting with Qrysta, surrounded by groaning Ogres.

Qrysta could tell how I was feeling just by looking at me. "Me too," she said. And then, "Jess has an idea."

I winced and asked her to please stop shouting.

"I'm not shouting," she whispered, as I lowered myself onto the bench beside her. "And you need more of this."

She poured me a mug of water.

It tasted like the water that had been in the jug by my bed.

"It's an Ogrish version of Over," she said, reminding me of the Orcs' hangover cure, *Hangoverover,* or Over for short. "They told me that the more you drink today, the less awful you'll feel tomorrow."

I drank a mugful and held my shaking hand out for more. "So, what's this idea?" I asked Jess.

"Why don't I fly to the refuge, where we stayed after the Ice Pits, and ask them to send their sled for you?" she said. "Then I'll go on to Isvellir, and get another sled sent over to the refuge to pick you up. That way we'll be there in three days instead of a week."

I began to nod, but stopped abruptly. The motion hurt my brain. "Good thinking," I croaked.

"I'll be off, then," she said, getting to her feet and picking up her broomstick. "Stay here, Little Guy." Little Guy's head appeared from under the table, to see what was what. His mouth had a half-chewed bone in it. His tail wagged against my legs.

Jess gave us all a cheerful smile. "See you in Isvellir!" She hurried out.

"Good kid, that," Qrysta said.

"You're not joking," I said. "If it hadn't been for her, and Little Guy ...." I didn't like to think about it.

I'd compared both "Shifts," on the journey back from the Valley of the Moon. They were similar, but it was easy enough to tell them apart. The lines of grain in the rowan wood of each staff were as unique as fingerprints, as were their palettes of browns and reds and purples. But they'd both been *her,* when I'd held them individually—so, which one really *was* her? She couldn't be in two places at once, surely?

Only when I was holding one in each hand did I learn the answer. *I'll go with you, Daxx*, her voice resonated along my right arm. My right hand was holding the staff that had been stolen from me as I lay bound inside the wolf hide, at the end of the ice tunnel. *My sister will go with Jess, and teach her everything we know.*

I asked, *Sister? But … you made her.*

*As Esmeralda made Jess her sister in Coven.*

*That's … hardly the same.*

*Perhaps not to you. To us, it is hardly very different. You could think of us as craft-sisters, crafted one from another. As Jess is now a sister in her craft, inducted into Coven by Esmeralda, her Covensister. But what do you know of such things? Of Coven, and of stick and stone?*

I had to admit, *Very little, it seems.*

I felt her amusement up my arm. *The more we learn, the less we seem to know, right?*

*It does seem that way*, I agreed.

One evening, as we made camp, I showed Jess how to close the tourmaline eye in her former broomstick. She bound twigs around its other end, whispered a few secret Coven words over it, mounted it, and took to the skies.

So, it still worked fine. Good. She'd be able to scout ahead, and be our eyes in the sky.

Then I wondered: Could she, maybe, fly with her stick's heartstone eye open?

She tried.

She could.

I said, "Well, you said you wanted to learn my skills as well as Qrysta's. No time like the present."

Jess was a quick learner. Even so, she was still novice at both Healing or Destruction by the time we reached Ogretzk. She could zoom down and cast feeble green Shields on us, which wafted apart in seconds. She could fizz off a weak Lightning attack at a tree, which did no damage, but at least showed that she was getting the basics. What seemed significant to me, though, was that we had discovered something that I thought could come in useful, in the battle that lay ahead.

She could fly and cast at the same time.

After all, her hands gripped her staff as she flew on it. As they would do if she were standing on the ground to wield it.

If Marnie, and her Covensisters, fitted stones to their sticks, might they not be able to return fire with fire, while flying?

We'd have to see when we got back to Mayport.

The missing pieces of Shaman Sylmond's tale were filled in that afternoon by the Ogre chief, as he gave me a guided tour of Ogretzk, from its hothouses to its workshops to its unexpectedly magnificent library. It was there, seated at a table with him and his wise men and women, that I learned what I needed to take back to Isvellir and tell Sylmond. Threads, I felt, were twining themselves together, forming the yarn that would be our tale.

I began to get a sense, at last, that I might even be ahead of the game, rather than behind it. I couldn't explain why I felt that. Perhaps it was my once-Gifted instinct knowing that it was on the scent of the truth. I didn't worry at it, demanding immediate answers. I let it lead me, and let it know that I would follow, ears and eyes open, ready to receive its enlightenment. I had, after all, the information, did I not? All I needed to do was process it.

*It's all there, if we have the wit to see it.*

Did I?

Maybe. Just because I didn't see it yet, didn't mean that I wouldn't one day.

But there was the thing. *What* day?

One, I sincerely hoped, before Midsummer Day. Which was less than two months away.

Yes. Sooner rather than later would be good.

But I was still lost and confused, even though I felt that I was closing in on the answer. And I didn't know why I felt that. I just did. I clung to that feeling, trusting it, as I'd trusted my nose while in the Form.

Every night since I'd escaped my Binding, I'd cast Insight on my-self, knowing that I'd been *told everything,* and hoping to find *the wit to see it.* I went over Eilwen's cryptic lines again and again, probing for the secrets that I was certain they hid. I believed that I'd found some of them and had used them to make progress. Somehow, out of the fog of obscurity with which they surrounded me, I'd worked out how to escape my Binding, by Influencing Little Guy.

I'd *wielded the broom,* by making her into a new staff when Shift had been stolen from me, using her to cast Heals on my chewed hand. Step by step, I'd inched forwards. I still could not see the big picture.

It felt closer than ever, as if just out of reach. I knew there were more revelations concealed within those simple words. I also knew that I had to find them.

Nothing came to me, awake or in my dreams; but I kept trying, and working my Insight skill, not only on Eilwen's lines but on everything that we'd seen and learned so far. More often than not, I felt as if I were banging my head against a brick wall. I'd drift off to sleep, frustrated, and dream uneasy, unhelpful dreams, and wake as confused as ever.

*A hundred thousand chalkers. A hundred dragons. A couple of months. What could possibly go wrong?*

The Ogres were delighted that we were spending another day in Ogretzk. There was, it seemed, some Big Surprise that they had planned for us. Thanks to their tincture, which we made sure to keep drinking, the aftereffects of too much sproj gradually began to melt away. Even so, our heads were far from as clear as the noonday sky as we made our way down to the Ice Lake, where dozens of Ogres were slithering about—on, we saw, as we got close, skates.

"Our smiths and cobblers have been hard at work as you can see, dear lady!" the chief told Qrysta. "They noted the devices that your companion made for you and have followed his designs with great diligence." He handed her a pair of Ogre-sized skates to inspect. "Pray tell me, ma'am: What do you make of these?"

Qrysta inspected the huge things, turning them over in her hands. The chief, and the assembled crafters who were grouped around us, waited with bated breath.

Qrysta said, "I think they're excellent."

She showed them to Horm, who cast his expert eyes over them, and, eventually, said, "Mm, nice crafting."

"Capital!" the chief cried, clapping his hands, as the crafters beamed with pride. "And now, we have one small favor to ask of you."

My companions' faces fell. We were in no fit state for a rematch at Fnyarrrghh.

"Would you be so kind, dear lady," the chief asked, "as to teach us how to use them?"

Horm had disassembled our skates and turned them back into normal boots before we left Ogretzk, but the Ogre wrights had crafted a pair for Qrysta—which fitted her perfectly. "We measured your footprints, which you left in the snow," the master cobbler said, as he offered them to her.

"I'd love to," Qrysta said. "A bit of exercise will do me good."

And that was how we got to sit back and watch Qrysta leading a mob of enthusiastic but inept Ogres in their first skating lesson. Which, to start with, mainly consisted of falling down, but soon progressed to ungainly slithering, and doing the splits, and grabbing hold of each other, and falling down together. The learners apologized and shrieked and whooped with triumph when they finally managed a few steps. The spectators kept up a stream of encouragement, and merriment, and laughter. After an hour, Qrysta gave them a break. Her exhausted pupils slipped and shuffled back to land, where they slumped down onto the snow-covered bank to watch her demonstration.

First, she said, it was important to learn how to skate backwards. "You can't play hockey if you can't skate backwards," she said, hurtling in reverse past us, stick in hand.

"Hockey?" the chief asked, puzzled.

"Our version of Fnyarrrrghh," I explained.

"Ah."

Then Qrysta got a small stone and demonstrated puck control, and dribbling, and how to stop at full speed, and turn, and, finally, to shoot into the normal-sized goal she'd asked to have assembled.

I heard mutterings all around me.

"I'm not sure about this *puck* thing," the chief confided. "It rather takes the fun out of the game, don't you think? And those little goals …. How are we meant to hurl anyone into anything that small?"

I didn't tell him that they weren't meant to. "It's a little different from Fnyarrrrghh."

"Hm," he said, watching Qrysta at work.

He brightened, as a thought occurred to him. "Still, those sticks will come in useful," he said. "Much easier to trip the other chap up than to have to wrestle the blighter to the ice!"

"Much," I agreed, and he nodded happily.

Finally, after another hour of lessons, Qrysta ended with a demonstration. It was, she later told us, one of her teenage dance routines, as best as she could remember it. She flew across the Ice Lake with all the grace of a swallow, taking to the air in leaps and spins and twirls that had us all applauding and whooping. She ended by gliding to rest in a tableau, kneeling on one knee, head bowed towards us, arms curled out like the wings of a swan, holding the pose while her audience cheered her to the skies.

That night, we steered well clear of the sproj.

The next morning the city square outside the feast-hall was packed with Ogres who had come to see us off. The sled that had arrived from the refuge waited at its center, its wolves harnessed and ready to run. Little Guy was as happy to see his pack mates as they were to see him. Only Nostë had any interest in me. The rest of the team ignored me, but he looked at me, curious, as I went over to him, and held out my hand for him to sniff. When he recognized my scent, his tail wagged, and he looked up at me, his dark eyes shining. I scratched his ears, and told him he was the best. Little Guy joined us and bounced with joy at seeing his savior, who had brought him barely alive out of the Ice Pits.

We thanked our hosts and told them that we hoped one day to return to Ogretzk.

Grell took the Glove of Strength from his belt and presented it to the chief with a smile.

The crowd cheered as he held it aloft.

Three days later we were in Isvellir.

# 39

## Our Last Hope

**And** *that is all we know,* Sylmond had said to me, the last time we'd been sitting in the little grotto behind the star tapestry, deep within Isvellir. She, and her grandson, Kalmond, listened as I told them of what we had endured, and done, and learned, since we had left for the Valley of the Moon. Our tale, their tale, the tale of the Ogres.

When I finished speaking, she smiled. "And that is all there is to know," she said. "An end. A beginning. It was well done. I am glad you lived to return and tell us."

"As am I," I said.

A thought struck her.

"Come with me," she said, rising to her feet.

I stood, and Kalmond climbed down from his high stool between us. His grandmother led us out of the grotto and through the cavern of curiosities that was her sanctuary.

We walked back down the tunnel towards the main hall, but, to my surprise, turned away when we came to the fork that led to it. Sylmond took us the other way, towards the red glow in the distance, and the low, rumbling noises and whiffs of sulfur that were coming from it.

We emerged on a ledge above a molten lake. Below us, yellow and red and orange bubbles rose out of the roiling lava and spat hot globules into the air. It was, strangely, calm, and beautiful.

"I come here," Sylmond said, "when I need to think."

I could see why. I felt as if I could watch that ever-changing spectacle forever. It was like contemplating a fire in a hearth—but this was no domestic fireplace. This was a fire of molten rock, in the heart of a volcano.

We watched, in silence.

Isvellir, in all his majesty.

Eventually, I said, "I need to think."

Sylmond squeezed my hand. "I know. That is why I brought you here."

All I could think was, *What aren't I seeing?*

*It's all there, if we have the wit to see it.*

I brushed those unhelpful thoughts aside, and opened my mind, and let my Insight lead me where it wished.

A long while later, Kalmond squeezed my other hand.

The sensation brought me out of my reverie.

I looked down at him.

"Have you finished thinking?" he said.

I realized that I had not had a single thought in my head for … I did not know how long. My mind had been completely empty. I had simply been absorbing the wonder of Isvellir.

I said, "I think so."

He stared at me for a moment. Then his small, serious face broke into a smile as he got the joke.

"You think you've stopped thinking!" He giggled.

We turned away from the fire in the mountain and walked back down the dark gray tunnels towards the hall.

"You've opened your mind to him now," Sylmond said. "If he has anything for you, he'll tell you. He always does."

Desmond led the convoy out of Isvellir the next morning. His sled was filled with us, the other two that trailed it containing our goods and a dozen Ice Orc warriors, including Zeygmond, who had insisted on coming. It took several days to reach the mountains—and several nights, in which they were amazed to see how our silver key opened trees for us to shelter beneath. "Could do with one o' them!" Desmond said the first night, as we settled in under a tall pine. "Don't suppose as that's for sale?"

We did not see a single Ice Wight on the journey. That, Desmond told us, was not unusual. "Keep themselves to themselves, they do, until they make their move on you," he said. Even so, he liked the feel of the run. His wolves sensed no threat. We left them and the sleds and four guards at the foot of the mountains, and set off to climb them, up one of the secret ways that they knew to the south. Jess mounted up and flew on ahead with our gift for Master Bjarnevalt. Once we were over the summit, Desmond felt that we were safe from ambush.

A day later we passed the snowline. "Ice Wights won't come south of here," Desmond said. "Not unless it's a hard winter, and the land is frozen." We stepped off the snow and onto the rocky path that led down to Aldfell, and, eventually, Sondehafn. That afternoon rain hit, and hit hard, driven by a bitter wind out of the north. It soon turned to sleet and hail. We opened a tree, and settled in for the night, while the storm howled outside. The others knew, by then, to leave me to my Insight after we'd eaten. I was dozing off, not having, as far as I knew, made any progress, when Qrysta said, "Daxx …"

I opened my eyes, and saw what she had noticed.

My Link of Impartment was glowing, blue then white.

Oller.

We all gathered round to communicate with him.

We told him we were still in Normark, but heading home soon.

He was already back in Westwich.

That was the good news.

The rest of what he had to tell us was anything but.

Alaryd, the young Lord of Westwich, had led his army to Commandant Bastard's muster at Mayport, leaving his town undefended. He had left his steward in charge, with orders to welcome Prince Mejnul with all courtesy when the Sarmen fleet arrived, and to offer him his castle to use as his own. That was only to be expected, we decided. Mejnul would, presumably, prefer to gain undamaged cities, and a submissive, prosperous realm, rather than one ravaged by war. Jarnland would soon be absorbed into the Sarmenid Empire, if we couldn't drive its forces back into the sea. As to how we were going to do that, we had no idea.

The weather was still foul the next morning, but we had to keep moving. We made good progress despite the conditions and the loads we were carrying, it being easier going downhill than up. The wind died, eventually, and the rain ceased. The clouds had cleared by early afternoon, when we saw Jess approaching in the sky ahead.

She landed beside us.

"Gundur's coming with horses," she said, as she dismounted, "and fast, as he doesn't have a herd to drive. He'll be with you before you reach Aldfell, he says. It's got a nice tavern. They're sending a cart for the Ice Balm. Master Bjarnevalt couldn't believe his eyes when I gave him the pot of it! Nor his ears when I told him we're bringing six big jars more of it. He's giving us his fastest ship. I met the captain, who thinks we'll be in Mayport by the end of the month."

The month was May.

Midsummer Day would fall three weeks later.

Gundur appeared out of the mists the next morning with his string of horses and the cart from Aldfell. Our mounts were hardy hill ponies, well accustomed to these steep paths. A massive drayhorse towered above them. Grell, Gundur knew, needed something larger and stronger. The Ice Orcs loaded the jars onto the cart. They'd carried them over the pass and down without complaint, but were happy to be rid of them.

We said our farewells. They knew what lay ahead of us. The GOAF, Desmond had named it: the Grandmother of All Fights. He and Grell had discussed the odds. Grell reckoned that any Orc was worth two chalkers in combat. Desmond was both envious and worried. "If there were fifty thousand of us, we'd be alongside o' you in a heartbeat," he said. "Not a one of us would want to miss a scrap for the ages like that! But, even with the bumpers and clumpers, we'd barely be five hundred. The Ice Lands don't support large numbers." There were, Grell thought, perhaps a thousand Orcs of fighting age in Jarnland. Desmond shook his head at the prospect. "Don't know as we'll be meeting again, friend," he said to Grell, as they shook hands. "But if we do, you'll have a tale to tell that I'll be wanting to hear."

They turned and trudged back up the mountain path, soon disappearing into the clouds that were drifting down it.

We were in the lowlands that evening, where we spent one more night under a tree and told Gundur our tale.

473

"Maybe as we can take back the stockade from those creatures," he said, "and deal direct with the Orcs. That would be a fine thing. And no longer needing to send our cattle up to cruel deaths."

The next night we spent at the tavern in Aldfell, eating and drinking by a roaring log fire. Two days later we were in Sondehafn.

There was nothing Master Bjarnevalt would not do for us when he saw the six large earthenware jars of Ice Balm we had brought with us. He had never seen such a quantity all at once. He promised that he would supply the north with whatever was needed. I handed him the list that Chief Izmond had given me. He looked at it eagerly. "Of course, of course!" he said. "I'll arrange a caravan at once."

We left five of the jars with him, to sell for us on our behalf, as his partner. He assured us, again and again, that he would get the best price for it. Our share of the proceeds would be held by his agent in Mayport, for us to collect at our leisure. We kept the other jar for ourselves. I had a plan for it, even though I didn't give it much chance of success. His cutter, *The North Wind*, was loading up with cargo for Jarnland and beyond, and would be ready to sail on the next day's evening tide. We declined his offer of hospitality, with thanks, and headed back to Birgit's house.

Jess persuaded me to Levitate Evall and his brother and sisters, one by one, so she could take them up for a joyride on her broomstick. The darkling sky was filled with their shrieks and laughter, until an old woman shuffled up and told Jess, in no uncertain terms, to stop such foolery. "Yes, sister, I'm sorry, sister," Jess said. "As you should be," the old woman grunted. "Marnie will hear o' this. Gallivanting around with outsiders, and in broad daylight!" She shuffled away. Chastened, we went back inside.

We ate. We drank. We talked late into the night. We settled down to sleep, wrapped up in blankets around the warm hearth. Little Guy curled up with old Mulnd in his basket. The orange cat slid in between them. That night, a dream came.

I was on the ledge, deep within Isvellir, looking down into his beating, molten heart. I watched. I waited. In most dreams, scenes change, and the action and sense and logic shift all over the place. In this one, nothing happened. I was just there, contemplating what I was seeing. I felt that that was important, when I woke the next morning and thought about it. Was Isvellir trying to tell me something? Or was he, perhaps, soon going to?

We headed for the docks, under another gray, leaden sky, and boarded *The North Wind* as the last of her cargo was loaded and stowed. She cast off, Master Bjarnevalt in his peculiar, multi-colored hat waving us off from the quayside. Once out of the harbor her sails were sheeted out. She caught the wind and leaned over, her rigging humming and her bows slapping through the swells, to begin the long run south and west.

We were a week out from Mayport, our captain estimated, when Oller got through to tell us that the Sarmenid fleet had landed at Westwich.

The next day, the dragons arrived, Prince Mejnul at their head.

Lord Alaryd's steward was waiting for him, to offer him the keys to Westwich Castle.

Prince Mejnul proclaimed three days of festivities.

He, and his retinue, strolled into the town, the guards at its open gates rigid at attention and saluting.

Outside the city walls, the Imperial Divisions assembled, and made camp.

We heard the rumors as soon as we docked in Mayport. *A hundred thousand chalkers. A hundred dragons. Half the lords in the realm safe behind their city walls and their moats, their drawbridges raised and portcullises down, their soldiers with them. And our army a third the size of the enemy's, most of them raw recruits, and not a single dragon.*

This was not their fight. This was nobody's fight. Their new king was waiting, peacefully, in Westwich—a town that was celebrating, unlike every other town in the realm, their populations anxious and uncertain. The girl knew what she had to do. It was her duty, to her realm, to all her subjects. What reasonable person would not spare them? She was a good girl. Everyone loved her. Surely she would not put herself above her people.

Esmeralda had no intention of doing that. Just as she had no intention of capitulating meekly and submitting to Prince Mejnul.

"Look," she said, at our Council of War that afternoon. "I'm going to have to be married to him for gods know how long. He needs to know that I know how to deal with him. And that means being steps ahead of him. He's vain, and entitled, and arrogant. He's not thinking around corners, like I am. He thinks this is a power play. He doesn't know how right he is. So, we keep him in suspense. *Will she, won't she?*

Yes, she will. And no, she won't. He'll learn that, before I've finished with him. After all," she added, "I'll still be queen."

None of us knew what to say—except Marnie.

"No need to plan the marriage before the wedding, my girl."

"What does that mean?"

"It means you're not wed yet."

"Well, I will be soon enough. Commandant?"

Jack Blunt shifted in his chair.

"City lockups are all full to bursting with deserters, Your Majesty," he said. "We don't have near enough stocks. They have to take turn and turn about sitting in them. There's not an urchin in Mayport who doesn't have a sore arm from pelting them. And the guards don't catch half those as make a run for it."

Esmeralda asked, "So how many do we have left?"

"Thirty thousand, give or take. My officers and I have been drilling them, but …"

He stopped, and sighed. "Scouts told me the chalkers were exercising outside Westwich. Going through combat drills. Thought I might as well ride over myself and took a look." He shook his head. "Our men aren't a patch on them. Prince Barthuq, one o' their generals, saw us watching and sent for us."

"Nasty piece of work, the word in Sarmen is," Oller said. "The emperor's firstborn son, older than Mejnul. But from a lesser wife, not the empress. Thinks he should be crown prince. Well, they all do."

Commandant Bastard nodded. "The word in Sarmen's not wrong. All sneers and smirks he was when I greeted him, polite like. I don't appreciate being sneered at, so I had to take him down a peg or two. Told him to put his best up against his pick of my Orcs, who I've been training up. They made short work of the chalkers—using blunts, mind, no harm done. 'You've less than a thousand of the brutes,' he said. Well, you don't name an Orc *brute* within their hearing! The chieftains were enraged, drew their weapons—I had to shout them down, remind them we were invited guests. So, I said to Prince Smirk, by way of cooling the Orcs off, that I'd take on two of his best at the same time, if he liked, and with sharps. Well, that's two fewer we'll be facing. Drop in the ocean, though. Still, it wiped the smile off his face."

Silence fell in the conference chamber.

Esmeralda said, "Your considered opinion?"

Jack Blunt shook his grizzled old head. "We're a third of their size and a tenth of their training. And we've no dragons. We'll go down fighting, Your Majesty, but go down we will."

Esmeralda shook her head.

"It won't come to that," she said. "All I need is a show of pride, and a parlay, and some heralds and the right words. There won't be bloodshed, I promise you all that now. But I have to make it look like I'm playing hard to get. He'll understand, he's royal, sovereigns have their pride, and that of their realm. It's a dance. The seamstresses have made me a lovely wedding dress, and I'll be sure to be looking my best. I will tell His Radiance that I am overjoyed to accept his offer, while letting him know that of course I had to wait till the last minute, as I'm sure he'd understand, for the honor of my realm, which is now also his, *blah blah blah*. And I would be honored if the noble lords and ladies of his court would please join us at the castle for our wedding feast."

No one responded, because none of us liked what we were hearing.

I looked over at Marnie.

She didn't need to say it, or even think it.

*We need to talk.*

The Council of War broke up. Marnie and I made our way to her room. A fire was burning in the hearth. She eased her old bones into an armchair at a small table in front of it. On it was a flask and two clay cups.

I sat opposite her.

She looked up at me, and studied my face. "Well, lad? Getting anywhere?"

I knew what she meant. Had I deciphered Dean Eilwen's utterings?

I told her the progress that I'd made; that the meanings of some of the lines had become clear, and had guided me to good effect.

"Mm," she said. "Like I said, it's all there. What about the rest of them?"

I shook my head. "I still can't work them out. I mean *'divide the blood?'* How do you divide blood? All I can think of is we have to kill some demon and catch his blood into three goblets or something, and place them on different altars—some kind of dark ritual like that. But who, where we find him, what it has to do with everything else, I've no clue."

She snorted. "The clues are there in front of you. You've been staring at them since Conclave. At this rate, that head'll be off your shoulders before you get where you need to. What else are you doing with that clever mind o' yourn, I should like to know?!"

I said, "I have been busy."

"Busy wasting time. I've taken a look at you, lad. Your thoughts are all over the place. Strikes me it's time to sort them out, once and for all."

She reached for the flask.

"I have one idea," I said.

"Which is?"

I told her about the large jar of Ice Balm that we'd brought back, and how prized it was in Sarmen—and how valuable. Maybe that would be worth a queen's ransom?

Marnie shook her head. "Prick him in the pride, is that the best you can do?! He'd be insulted that we'd even *think* he could be bought off! That'd only make things worse for the girl. You're not thinking clearly, lad, and you need to start."

She tilted the flask over one of the cups.

Green sludge began to ooze out of it.

"I hoped as it wouldn't come to this," she said. "It's a perilous path to take. But hard times call for hard measures. I got Velaryn to run this up for me special. She didn't like to, but needs must." She filled each cup to the brim. "It'll be the death of me, this," she grumbled. "One dose too many, and that'll be my lot. Still," she passed me one cup, and raised hers, as if in a toast. "Here's hoping this one isn't the dose as does it. Drink up, lad."

I said, "What is it?"

"Never you mind. I'll tell you what it isn't. It isn't usually fatal."

That was hardly comforting. "What does it do?"

Marnie grunted. "What *doesn't* it? All sorts o' things, as you'll see. Things that we need to get sorted."

"Yes, but—why are we taking it?"

"Because two heads are better than one. Drink, and let's get the truth out of you. As long as one of us lives, and comes back so we can use it."

I hesitated.

"Now then, laddie," Marnie said, a hard smile on her face. "Death's not as bad as he's made out to be. And this way, you'll know the truth before he takes you, which is what you've been wanting all this while, isn't it? Driving you mad, it's been. Die where we're going, knowing the answers, or die in battle, still wondering. I know which way I'd rather go."

She swallowed the contents of her cup and wiped her mouth with the back of her sleeve.

"Yeugh!" she said. "Tastes worse every time. Come along, lad, down the hatch. I won't come out of there if I go in alone."

I drank. I had to force myself to keep swallowing.

It was, as Marnie had warned me, disgusting.

The first thing I saw, on opening my eyes, was Ken. And not Ken as I'd last seen him, in his guise as an elderly clerk, but Ken the Amalgam, in all his weirdness, tentacles and feelers and stalks and all.

"Oh dear," he said, "I'm not at all sure this is wise."

Marnie stumped up out of the murk and took my hand. "Come along, young 'un, can't waste time lollygagging with riffraff! You," she said to Ken, not seeming in the slightest bit perturbed by his appearance, "be off about your business, we've work to do."

"This *is* my business," Ken replied.

"Oh. It's you we need to talk to, is it?"

"No, no!" Ken replied quickly, "that's against the rules. And I don't know anything anyway, I've told him."

"So bugger off."

"I just, it would …"

"It would what?"

"Be bad if he died. Daxx."

Marnie snorted. "We came all this way to hear that pearl o' wisdom, did we?"

"No, but—you don't understand …"

"Well, that's why we're doing this, isn't it? To understand. And this conversation's getting us nowhere." She hauled me off past Ken, hobbling along the pathway as fast as her old legs could carry here. "Blasted interruptions," she muttered. "Can't think straight with them coming at you from all sides. What we need," she said, as a door appeared ahead of us, "is a little peace and quiet." An old sheepdog appeared outside the door. Her tail wagged as she caught sight of Marnie. "Not now, lass," Marnie said, "there's a good girl." The dog faded. "One o' mine," she said. "Bess. Lovely girl. Right," she said, opening the door. "No more distractions."

There was nothing behind the door. At least, nothing visible.

"Perfect!" Marnie closed the door behind us.

We were in utter, silent darkness. The air was empty, odorless. The awful aftertaste of the sludge that I'd drunk had vanished. I realized that I could no longer feel Marnie's hand, although I hadn't noticed when she let go.

*I haven't,* her quiet voice came, in my head. *I'm still holding it. Here there are no senses. No feeling. Just thoughts. You'll have my thoughts and I'll have yours; and if we let them, mayhaps they'll show us what we need to see.*

Gradually, out of the nothingness, images emerged.

*Here they come,* Marnie said.

Images, and sounds. Words, and voices. Memories, and dreams. Places, and people. We were with them all, and not with them. They were coming from within us, moving in and out of each other. The barn at the Wheatsheaf, scuttling rats against tiny dragons. The hell-dragon under Wester Isle, huge and roaring as we fought her. Prince Mejnul walking down the wing of his Nightshade, outside Eastbay Castle. Oller's report from the Grazings. Mejnul again, with his royal entourage and brother princes, at the testing ground, smiling when flames erupted as pots dropped and smashed.

Eilwen's words weaving in and out of the scenes as they changed, and flowing around us, her voice as clear as when she'd spoken at Conclave. Our minds were attuned, synchronized with each other, as we gave each line our full attention. Eilwen's wasn't the only voice we heard. Others spoke: Sylmond, Velaryn, Archmage Faldruti; Commandant Bastard; Mabel, Mejnul; Marnie herself, me myself, the Voice itself. Their words conjured up images, which we searched for meaning. Finally, one image grew into being before me, blooming larger and larger until it replaced all the others.

I was on the ledge deep within Isvellir, looking down into the volcano that was his heart.

Sylmond's voice came back to me.

*You've opened your mind to him now. If he has anything for you, he'll tell you. He always does.*

And there it was.

As clear as day, all at once.

I felt myself laughing.

Marnie was far from happy.

I felt her mind withdrawing from mine.

"I can't say as you're wrong," I heard her say, as she saw what I saw. "And I can't say as I like it."

"It's the answer, though, isn't it?"

She grunted, thinking it over.

"The question is," she said, "what's the question that comes *after* it?"

I said, "We'll just have to see, won't we?"

"I dare say we will," she agreed, if reluctantly. "Die here, die in battle, or … well, you saw what happened to the last one who did what you're thinking of doing."

I had indeed.

I said, "I'll just have to cross that bridge when I come to it."

"That you will. Right. Job done. The sooner we're out of here the better."

The darkness had cleared and our senses had returned. Marnie stopped at another door. "Pay no mind to what's next," she said, before opening it. "It's what would have happened, if you hadn't found our answer."

What was next was chaos. Instinctively I covered my head with my free arm as it assaulted us, but Marnie led me doggedly through it. Where before, in the peace of the chamber, all had been relevant, and filled with meaning, now all was nonsense. "Wrong answers," Marnie shouted, above the cacophony. "They'll keep you here forever, if you let them." Image after image vied for our attention. Voices yelled, people implored and cursed, scenes burst in on other scenes that had nothing to do with them. It was as if all the waste material in the detritus that lay below our minds was coming to life and screaming its importance.

Feelings flowed in and out: shame, embarrassment, fear, remorse, guilt—above all, confusion. Marnie's iron grip on my mind was as strong as her grip on my hand. Together they dragged me through the maelstrom. On and on it went, harder and faster and wilder, and more and more overwhelming. And then there was a door, and we were out, Marnie slamming it shut behind us.

She looked up at me.

I was shaking and could hardly focus.

"It helps if you've done it before," she said.

I didn't think I'd have made it without her.

She was studying me, with a curious look on her face.

481

"You've a deal of strange things in that mind of yours," she said. "I'll want to hear all about them if we still live Midsummer night. The which we must see if we can do."

She snapped back into action. "Right, I've got preparations to make. I'll be gone when you wake. Round up the others, and bring the Commandant. He'll need to see this answer of yours, or he won't know how to play his part. Head northwest out of the city into the woods after dark. I'll guide you when you're in them. We'll all be gathered by midnight, where no one can see us.

"And then we'll see what we see."

I couldn't think why my cheek was cold and my legs were warm.

I came to, head down on the table in Marnie's room, my feet out towards the remains of the fire. It was late afternoon, I could see, from the light coming in through the window.

I shook the cobwebs out of my mind and got to work. I used my Link of Impartment to get through to Oller. I told him to find the others and bring them to the training fields, where I knew Commandant Bastard would be drilling his forces. I grabbed my cloak, and Shift, and hurried off, stopping only to give orders for our horses to be saddled. Shift, who knew me inside out, could tell that I knew something she didn't.

*What? What is it, what's up?*

*You'll see.*

Jack Blunt did not like what he was looking at any more than his son did.

Soldiers going through the motions. Their hearts weren't in it. They wanted to be anywhere but there at their drills. They didn't want to die for their homeland. They wanted to live in it. It didn't matter to them who ruled it.

His eyebrows rose as he turned and saw us.

"Good evening, Commandant," I said.

He grunted. "And it may be one of the last I'll be seeing," he said, turning back to watch his troops.

He shook his head. "I've done what I can. Trained 'em as best as I know how. They're not up to the job. They know that, I know that. The enemy knows that. This isn't a fight we can win."

"I agree. So let's not have one."

He turned to me, frowning. "If there's one thing I want," he said, slowly, "it's a damned good fight! I've not felt the itching for one this bad in a long age. I want to put that smug pup in his place, and drive him and his back into the sea."

"Don't we all?" I agreed.

He drew back, and studied me.

"And we stand no chance of doing that, against these odds," he said. "So what in all hells are you taunting me with, young man?"

"Come with us and I'll show you."

"Don't look at me," Oller said, when Commandant Bastard turned his glare on him and the others. "He hasn't told us either."

Jack Blunt turned to his son and said, "Over to you, Jack, lad. Keep them at it."

Young Jack grunted, with a nod.

"Scares them more than I do," Commandant said, as he came with us to the stables. "Wish I had more like him."

Evening was falling as we rode out of the city's north gate. After a couple of hours we reached the glade in the woods where Marnie had guided me. We dismounted to wait for her. It was a beautiful, peaceful night. Stars gleamed above us beyond the encircling trees. The Hunter stood on the horizon, his seven-starred horn raised. Beside him, the waxing moon shone. Silently, I thanked them both, for all that they had shown me. At last Marnie landed out of the sky, followed by Jess— and, to my surprise, Esmeralda.

Marnie said, "Take your mounts back into the trees. Tether them, give them their nosebags and blindfold them. It'd be cruel to scare them, the which it will, if what we think's going to happen happens. And if it does: Well, I trust you all, as well as I trust anyone living, but, one person can keep a secret; ten can't. Not without help. And we can't have word getting about."

She raised her oak staff. The diamond heartstone that I had given her shone in the darkness, casting a sharp light on her fierce old face.

"I'm going to lay a Gag on the lot of you," she said, and none of us liked the way she said it. "Get near to speaking of this, whether you know you're doing it or not, it'll gag you, and gag you hard. Choke the words in your throat, it will! You'll have to pull your tongue out to speak again, and that's a struggle. Gag thrice, and it'll be locked in

483

your throat till I cleanse it off you. So, I want you all to look me in the eye, and swear you won't breathe a word of this to a living soul."

We all swore, and quickly. We knew better than to disobey Marnie.

She grunted dismissively. "Not that eye," she said, reaching for her eyepatch. "This one."

She turned back the eyepatch and we were staring into the huge, red eye that it concealed. It was just as bad as I'd remembered it.

Glaring at us, Marnie cast her Gag.

A cold ball of brown fog grew around each of us, and writhed, and hissed, and threatened, and faded.

"Mm," Marnie said, replacing her eyepatch. "That'll take care of that bitch Rumour."

"Gods and demons!" Nyrik muttered beside me. I looked down at him. He was shaking, as if he'd seen a ghost. The others weren't in much better shape. Even Commandant Bastard looked rattled—a sight I'd never thought I'd see.

"Now stand back," Marnie said. "We'll need space."

The others did as she said, moving away under the shelter of the trees as she and I walked to the center of the clearing.

From high overhead the almost-full moon shone down on us.

"She's watching," Marnie said.

I handed Shift to her, and she stepped back.

*Hide and run,* I thought.

*Two heads are better than one.*

*Time to use the other one.*

I unwrapped the wolf hide from my shoulders and laid it on the ground, skin side up.

I lay down on it.

As I wrapped myself in it, I remembered what the Voice in the vault had told me.

*Me or you.*

Another lie.

It was me *and* you.

The hide closed itself around me, and I assumed the Form.

When I was complete within it, I stood.

I stared down at my tiny companions.

I smelled their fear.

It was delicious.

I looked up, at the heavens.

I threw back my head, and howled, at the Hunter, and the moon beside him.

I leaped into the sky and ran towards them.

I had never felt such freedom, such power. I circled the moon and ran among the constellations. The Gift was mine. I was in my element. I should keep running, forever. There could be nothing better than this. I was invincible, immortal.

The joy of it was more than anything I had ever known. It was equaled by the sadness that grew within me, as I knew what I must do. How could I give it up? I had to. The sooner the better, then, or I might never find the willpower do it.

I ran down and landed in the forest glade. I lowered my head for the starsilver collar. Grell held one half, Qrysta the other. The shards were far too small to fit around my neck. It was as Marnie and I had feared. The child had been a babe when the hide had closed in and formed itself around him. They had bound him before he grew from a cub. This, then, was going to hurt.

Horm raised the Hunter's bow and drew. An arrow appeared on its string. He loosed. The starsilver arrowhead buried itself in my shoulder, and began to burn. It had been bad enough the first time, as I'd peeled the hide off myself with teeth and hands. Nyrik and Horm were skilled hunters. They had butchered their kills innumerable times. They knew what they were doing. They set to work with their niblun blades, and skinned the hide off me as fast as they could. Marnie kept me alive with her best Heals, and Jess added what little she knew. Even so, the pain was beyond bearing. At last, oblivion claimed me. It was not soon enough.

Something was choking me.

I came to my senses, gagging. I was lying on the forest floor, Grell supporting my back as Marnie eased one of her healing potions down my throat. I opened my eyes and looked up. The moon was shining beyond her.

"Drink up, lad," she said.

I drank.

I was in no fit state to ride. Commandant Bastard sat me in front of him on his charger, which took us as far as it could before it tired.

We changed mounts, and came to the road. The silhouette of Mayport rose on the southern horizon, not many miles off. My horse bore us the rest of the way. Grell carried me to a chamber in the castle, where Velaryn was waiting, with her salves and potions.

She and Marnie settled me in bed, and tended me.

I slept until the next Moon Night.

# 40

## Midsummer

Our scouts galloped into the city, their horses lathered and steaming. The gates were closed and barred behind them and the portcullis lowered. Eight of the ten of us that Marnie had Gagged waited on the flat roof of the gatehouse, behind its battlements, watching for what we knew was coming. We had the space to ourselves, by Royal Command.

The walls of Mayport below us were crowded with soldiers and anxious townsfolk, doing what we were doing: watching the western horizon. Towards midmorning plumes of dust rose into the air. They kept on rising until the sky in the west was dark. Soon the sounds of approaching footsteps could be heard, stamping on the road in double time. The first Vu-Sant division emerged out of the dust cloud, at the trot; then another, and another—seven in all. Each halted, with perfect precision, and turned to face the city walls, rigid at attention, their spearheads glittering above their black armor.

The knights followed, casual in their finery, their harnesses jingling, their emblazoned shields bright in the morning sunlight. Last came the archers, strolling at their leisure, followed by the supply wagons. The royal pavilion rose at the center of the Sarmenid host, an ornate marquee of bright silks and satins. Prince Mejnul's imperial banners soon unfurled and were streaming from its tent poles. The seven chalker divisions waited, unmoving, facing us. The knights dismounted and handed their horses to their squires. They looked at us, and talked among themselves, lordling to lordling, relaxed and confident.

Beside me, Nyrik pointed to the sky. "Up there," he said.

It took us a few moments to see what he'd spotted.

The dragons emerged out of the blue, their huge wings beating lazily, rank after rank of them in formation. They reached the city and circled above us, uttering their low, mournful cries, their pot-filled harnesses on their backs. At the head of his air fleet Prince Mejnul rode on the shoulders of the largest and darkest of them all, his Nightshade. I heard screams of fear from the streets below. The dragons wheeled away, to land behind their army, thump after thump echoing back to us from the distance.

It was the day before the Midsummer solstice.

We all had our parts to play. Esmeralda's was to spread reassurance among her people. "Don't worry," she told everyone. "I'm not going to let anything happen to any of you. We just have to observe the protocols. Must do this properly. His Radiance wouldn't want it any other way."

That was where the heralds took over. And, I have to say, excelled. Even Qrysta, who loathed heralds, was impressed. Ours were on home turf, and knew their stuff, down to the tiniest detail. Mejnul's imperial heralds were out of their comfort zone, in a foreign land. They approached the city gates with confidence and blew their brazen horns. They made a harsh, discordant sound—a sneer, a command to be obeyed without question.

The gates opened, and our heralds emerged in full finery, red and blue and purple and gold. They halted, and blew the Royal Fanfare on their elegant trumpets, the banners of Esmeralda's Royal Coat of Arms hanging from them. They sounded sweet, and welcoming. Then came the bowing, and the exchanging of courtesies. Our heralds, it seemed, always had one more refined formality to observe, one more point of order to make. They acceded to every request that the imperial heralds demanded and told them to assure His Radiance that all would be done to his satisfaction, according to the correct, long-established customs and formulae, which would of course be observed to the letter, out of courtesy, as was His Radiance's due. The imperial heralds gave up enquiring what those might be, exactly, understanding that our Deputation of Surrender would present itself at the imperial pavilion an hour before noon on Midsummer Day, to await His Radiance's pleasure.

There was more bowing and scraping. The parlay ended, with a reprise of the Royal Fanfare. The Sarmenid heralds took their report to Prince Mejnul, who was seated on a throne outside his pavilion, flanked by his brothers and courtiers. Our heralds marched back to the city in perfect order.

But the gates did not close behind them.

Instead, below us, a lone figure walked out towards the Sarmenid host. Esmeralda.

She was wearing a wedding gown of shimmering white, a veil over her head. A single attendant held the end of the long train that trailed behind her—Jess, Glamoured by Marnie to look like a young noblewoman rather than the child of fisherfolk. She was also, I knew, taking with her an Eavesdropping—a casting from Marnie's Awareness skill that she had laid on the girl. Those of us gathered around Marnie would be able to hear every word spoken to, and by, Esmeralda.

Prince Mejnul rose to his feet as Esmeralda approached.

She stopped, and bobbed a curtsey, and drew back her veil. Even from that distance we could see the golden light that bloomed around her.

"Now there's *real* radiance for you," Marnie muttered.

Prince Mejnul bowed, and we could hear the smile in his voice. "Milady," he said. "You are beautiful beyond words."

"You are kind to say so, My Lord," Esmeralda replied. "A bride hopes to look her best in her wedding gown."

"I cannot believe that any has ever looked lovelier. My hand and my heart, and my empire, are yours."

"I will accept them with due humility for the honor you do me, My Lord."

The courtiers around him applauded and congratulated their prince.

"Tomorrow," Esmeralda said, and the applause and congratulations died away.

"Why not today?" Prince Mejnul asked, sounding puzzled. "Why delay our happiness by an hour?"

"Alas, sir, I cannot, much as I might wish to," Esmeralda said, sounding pained. "For the honor of my realm, as I am sure you will understand. Which will be your realm, when we wed. Midsummer Day, as Your Radiance himself proclaimed. Our people are humble, but proud. You will wish to honor them with your magnanimity. They see your army, sir, and are apprehensive—as who would not be, in the face of such a mighty force? They will love you, sir, if you treat their customs with kindness. A little forbearance, and their hearts as well as their lives will be yours. They are good people, docile, hardworking, honest, and diligent. They will reward your condescension with devotion. I know them, sir, and love them. I know that you will come to know and love them, as I do."

Prince Mejnul hesitated. He couldn't think what to say.

He wasn't being defied, exactly. Far from it. He was being flattered. The portrait she painted of him was that of a generous, noble ruler. He rather liked it. He was used to being feared. He was used to seeing masks of adoration on the faces of his subjects, and to looking through them for the ugly truth. Esmeralda, by contrast, was all innocence and sincerity. He looked into her cornflower blue eyes and was lost.

"As My Lady commands," he said, and bowed.

Esmeralda curtseyed again, this time to the ground, lowering her head.

She held the pose, then looked up at him, and rose, and we could hear the smile in her voice. "As Your Lady *obeys*, My Prince," she said, as if she was sharing some delicious, private secret with him.

And everyone knew that everything was settled.

"Until the morning," Prince Mejnul said, his voice thick with sentiment.

"Until Midsummer morn!" Esmeralda agreed, and the message in hers was clear. *I cannot wait.*

Prince Mejnul gurgled.

Esmeralda turned and walked back towards Mayport, Jess behind her carrying her train.

Beside me, Marnie snorted. "Should've been a play-actor, that one!"

"Played him like a fish," Qrysta agreed.

All was relief and joy that night in Mayport. The taverns were packed with citizens toasting their new king and his bride—his future *empress!* There'd never been one of *those* in the realm before. She'd brought honor to the land, glory to all of them, gods bless the girl! *A toast to Her Majesty. Their Imperial Majesties. Their Radiances. Whatever they're called. Another toast, to all of them. To peace. To prosperity. Never mind those thousands of monsters outside the walls. They're not going to be bothering us. They're our army now. And the numbers of them! Did you see them at their combat drills all afternoon ...? Bloody terrifying! Blimey, I wouldn't want to be anyone who messes with us from now on, eh? With that lot to fight for us? Woof … I don't mind admitting, I was worried sick. Not sure I like what I've been hearing about our new ruler. A cruel people they say, the Sarmenids.*

*Don't you worry about that, friend. He may rule us, but our Esmeralda will be ruling him, you mark my words!*

*Royal and Loyal!*

*Loyal and Royal!*

The next day, an hour before noon, the city gates opened, and our heralds led out Esmeralda's Deputation of Surrender. It halted at the imperial pavilion, where Prince Mejnul waited, seated on his throne amid his court. Our heralds raised their trumpets and unleashed the Royal Fanfare at him, at top volume, as they parted to reveal our Deputation.

Which consisted of me, Commandant Bastard, and Nyrik and Horm, carrying between them an earthenware jar which was almost as large as they were.

And no Esmeralda.

Prince Mejnul's smile of anticipation faded.

He rose to his feet, staring in annoyance.

He shouted at our heralds to stop that noise.

They, being heralds, followed the ordained formalities to the letter, and played the Royal Fanfare to the end. Which, this being a Deputation, and thus mandating the Full Ceremonial version, involved two reprises, a bridge, and a coda.

As its last notes sounded, thirteen black-clad women landed behind us and dismounted from their broomsticks. They shambled into an uneven line as our heralds lowered their trumpets with a flourish and stood to attention. Mejnul, and his court, did not know where to look, or what was happening. I was not surprised to see Lord Rylen of Hartwell among them. Esmeralda had noticed him the previous day. "So now we know why he threw the bout, in the Royal Tournament," Qrysta had said. "Bought off and turned his coat."

We waited as the echoes of the Royal Fanfare died away.

Eventually, Prince Mejnul broke the silence. "Where is my bride?" he asked, his voice icy.

"Before we get to that," I said, "I have a gift for you."

Nyrik and Horm carried the pot towards him and set it down. "Two elves?" Mejnul said, unimpressed.

"Oy! Don't you call me a fucking elf!" Horm roared, reaching for his dagger.

Mejnul was too shocked to reply.

"I'll cut your fucking balls off, you preening twat!"

Mejnul's giant Vu-Sant bodyguard strode forwards, pulling his broadsword off his back. Mejnul and his courtiers were shouting, Horm was scowling, Nyrik drawing his bow. I raised Shift and Rooted them both, and cast Muffle over all of us, and waited till things calmed down. Mejnul's sorceress had been too slow to react, but saw that I had defused the situation, so lowered her staff.

"An unfortunate misunderstanding," I said, inclining my head towards Mejnul. "We offer you our apology for our friend's bluntness, knowing that you were unaware of your error. It was a blunder that no one in this realm would make, but you could hardly know that, could you? You being a foreigner. The gift is in the jar."

I Cleansed the Rooting from Horm and Nyrik and they opened its lid.

It was filled to the brim with Ice Balm.

I heard the gasps as his courtiers realized what it was.

"Ice Balm," I confirmed.

Even Mejnul was taken aback at the prize that we had laid before him.

"Worth a queen's ransom, I know," I said, before he could speak. "But it's not a ransom payment. It is, as I said, a gift, to your realm from ours, in celebration of this occasion. And there's more where that came from. A thousand times more."

Mejnul glared at me, puzzled. "Why are you telling me this?"

"So that the news spreads. And so that when they hear of it, your merchants will seek us out, in peace, to trade with us."

"That is irrelevant. This realm is now mine."

"I think you're forgetting something."

"What?"

"The battle?"

"What battle?! Are you not a Deputation of Surrender?"

"We are. And we are here to tell you that we have decided that we will, if reluctantly, deign to accept your surrender, rather than put your people to the sword."

Mejnul, and his brother princes, and his courtiers, could not believe what they were hearing. Astonished, he barked, "*My* surrender?"

"Yours, Mejnul."

Again, the assembly behind him stirred, and grumbled. Prince Eilmar, one of his brothers, snapped, "You will address our prince as Your Radiance!"

"No, we won't," I said, amiably. "Any more than you and your brothers soon will."

More stirrings, more grumblings, louder and louder.

Mejnul waved his hand for silence. "Where is your queen?!" he demanded.

"That is none of your business."

He stared at me. When what I said had sunk in, he said, "So. She defies me."

"Actually, no," I said. "We defied her."

Again, that was not what he expected. "You will explain."

"She was prepared to sacrifice herself for the good of her realm. We love her too much to allow her to do that."

"*Sacrifice* herself? Do you not understand the honor I have offered her?"

"It is no honor. You have offered her bondage. You have no honor. But we established that long ago, when you cheated at her Royal Tournament." That was news to Mejnul's courtiers. *Cheated? How?* "We have placed Her Majesty under house arrest," I continued, "for her own good. We could hardly let you get your hands on her, could we? No, we felt compelled to disobey her orders. We will accept whatever punishment she thinks we deserve when this is over."

I was lying. Marnie had Mabelized Esmeralda, who was one of the thirteen black-clad women standing behind us with their broomsticks. She had insisted on being there. She wanted to witness everything.

Mejnul said, his face like thunder, "You will take your punishment now, for your insolence!"

"Insolence," I repeated, as if considering the word. I shook my head. "The insolence is yours, Mejnul, in bringing your army into our land. You are the one who will be punished."

"Produce my bride," he demanded, "or prepare for battle."

I said, "That is the choice you offer?"

"It is. I do not wish to lay waste to a realm that will soon be mine."

"Actually, Mejnul, it won't. As you'll soon see. And we're not offering you a choice. You'll be dead within the hour."

He could not believe what he was hearing. "You think you can defeat me? Look at my army!"

"They will run."

"Vu-Sant never retreat!"

"There is always a first time."

"You're mad!"

"And you are annoying. But you'll be dead soon and we'll be rid of you. And none of your brothers will stay to avenge you. Not just because they all, quite understandably, loathe you, but because they will be fighting among themselves to be the new crown prince."

By then Mejnul was purple with fury and shouting at me. I ignored him and turned to his brother princes. "You're welcome to start here, as soon as you like, my lords," I said. "We promise not to interfere. We'll just sit back and watch the fun, as your chalkers hack each other to shreds. But perhaps you will think it wiser to be the first to get back to Sarmen, and claim the Sun Throne? Rather than waste your strength, not to mention valuable time, in this little out-of-the-way realm? We know that your father is old, and feeble, and won't have any say in the war of succession that is coming his way. Just as you all know that none of you will kill him, because that would mean your own death."

The princes, I could see, were eyeing each other warily.

"Which of you will it be?" I went on. "Barthuq? Vashtenar? Perhaps not, your mothers being inferior wives."

"Hold your tongue!" Barthuq snapped, his hand reaching for his scimitar—which, as no one was permitted to carry a weapon in the presence of his crown prince, he soon remembered he was not wearing.

Mejnul had been watching his brothers thoughtfully.

When they saw him looking at them, they waited, respectfully. They knew not to speak unless spoken to.

He addressed Barthuq. "If I asked you, brother, to kill yourself now to demonstrate your allegiance, what would you do?"

Barthuq dropped to one knee, lowered his head, and said, "I would beg Your Radiance to allow me the joy of playing my part in your victory over these barbarians first."

Mejnul nodded. Eventually he said, as if considering his decision, "It would be cruel of me to deny you that pleasure."

Barthuq waited, head down, motionless.

"You may rise," Mejnul said.

Barthuq rose, and backed away, bowing repeatedly.

Mejnul turned back to me. "And you may want to kill yourself, rather than suffer," he said. "My question-masters are skilled, and patient. They will keep you alive for months."

I shook my head. "No thanks."

He nodded, slowly, and said, "I hope you survive this battle, mage."

"I intend to."

"Good. After it is over, I will enjoy personally overseeing your punishment."

"No, you won't. You'll be dead."

He laughed. "I will not."

"You will. But you won't be buried here. Or anywhere. There will be nothing left of you to be buried. Do you want to know why?"

"I'm not interested in your ravings."

"Because I will have eaten you alive."

I smiled.

He glared.

Then sneered. "Is this some kind of stupid attempt to scare me?"

"No. It is something for you to think about, when you have turned those pretty pink skirts of yours brown, and you see me coming for you."

"Enough of this nonsense. This parlay is over."

"Good," I agreed. "I've worked up a nice appetite."

Prince Mejnul snorted and turned to leave.

I said, "Oh … Radiance?"

He turned back in surprise at hearing me, for the first time, use his title.

"I don't like that name for you," I said. "I have a better one."

He waited.

I let him wait, because I knew that he wanted to hear. "Lunch."

I looked past him and addressed his brothers. "Enjoy your civil war, gentlemen. And you, My soon-to-be-former Lord of Hartwell: You know the penalty for treason."

Lord Rylen glared, but I turned away before he could answer and walked back towards the city, ignoring the threats and insults that were being hurled at our backs.

"Won't be getting this, then, chum," Horm told Mejnul, as he and Nyrik lifted the jar of Ice Balm to carry back to Mayport. Our heralds raised their trumpets and sounded the Fanfare for an Unsatisfactory

Conclusion to a Deputation: several long, discordant snarls of contempt, as if they were blowing loud brass farts at the enemy. Marnie and her Covensisters mounted their broomsticks and flew on ahead of us.

The heralds fell in behind us.

Beside me, Commandant Bastard chuckled. "That's him told!"

We went in through the city gates, the heralds marching behind us, sounding the Call to Arms.

The gates were closed and barricaded and the portcullis lowered.

We climbed the stairs to the gatehouse roof, where the others were assembled.

Horm's jaw dropped when I showed him what I needed him to do with his starsilver bow.

"Got it?" I said, handing it to him.

He nodded.

I said, "Go on, then. You saw."

Horm copied what I'd done. He whistled. "Full o' surprises, this thing!"

"You saw the Hunter. When he came for his son."

"That I did. I didn't see what you saw, though. And I'm supposed to be the one with the sharp eyes."

"So here's what we're going to do, you and I."

Horm listened, disbelieving. "Blimey," he said. "You're serious?"

"Very."

"All right," he said, sounding doubtful. "You can rely on me."

"I know that," I said.

"It'll be a tale to tell my grandchildren, this," Horm said, bending down to take off his boots. "If I live to have any."

"They're airborne," Nyrik said, looking out at the sky above the Sarmenid army. "Gaining height for the run in."

The highest dragons were just starting to turn and head for our city.

I spread the wolf hide on the parapet and lay down in it. My companions stood back to give me space to grow.

*Assume the Form.*

The hide closed around me. I grew. As I towered above the battlements, I heard the gasps and shrieks of the crowd on the city walls and below in the streets.

I crouched down and Grell lifted Horm onto my back.

He straddled my shoulders and sat astride my neck. He dug his toes into my fur and gripped, hard, feet and toes and knees and hands.

*Hide and run.*

I, the Great Wolf, sprang into the air and galloped towards the fleet of dragons.

They were upwind of me, so didn't catch my scent as I raced through the sky towards them, Horm clinging to my neck. They didn't know what to make of me, as I charged them. They'd never seen anything like me before. But I soon caught the scent of their fear and howled my blood lust. Their neat formation broke apart in panic as they realized what was charging them. *Predator.*

Just as one ice wolf could herd dozens of yaks, so the Great Wolf scattered the Sarmenid cattle. I slashed and bit as I ran among them. Some dropped, wounded. Others flung their riders and cargoes off their backs. Crews fell, screaming. Pots smashed onto the ranks of Vu-Sant far below, the mixture they held bursting into flame. The chalkers scattered. I felt Horm's hands leave my fur as we spotted our target mounted on his Nightshade dragon, radiant in his robes of the sun. I heard the *thrum* of Horm's bowstring. A starsilver arrow bloomed in the beast's shoulder and it stalled, bellowing.

Mejnul and his crew were shouting in panic. I swooped onto his mount and seized it by the throat. I shook it savagely until its neck snapped. Mejnul was catapulted into the air, shrieking. I threw his dead Nightshade beast aside. *Let Darkness Fall.* As it dropped into the scattering army below I caught Mejnul in my jaws, gently, so as not to harm him.

*Remember what happens next.* After slaying the Great Wolf, the Hunter had raised his bow to his lips. It became his horn, which he blew as he approached the Moon and laid his prize at her feet. Above me, on my shoulders, Horm blew the horn that his starsilver bow had become when he raised it to his lips.

*Sound the horn.* The sky darkened. Black clouds rolled in from behind us, lightning flashing within them. We heard the thunder of hooves before the Wild Hunt came galloping out of the clouds, riders of all descriptions, human and other, on mounts of all kinds: sabre-cats, manticores, stags and bears and wolves as well as horses. *Unleash the storm.* Thunder boomed. Lightning flashed. A wall of water slammed into the enemy dragons, tossing them around like leaves. Their harnesses broke and spouts of flame burst among the Sarmen forces below as firepots exploded.

*Sweep the sky.*

*Fire and Flood.*

The ranks of the enemy broke and ran as the storm passed over them, its Wild Hunters driving all before them. The dragons fled for home, south and west over the ocean. The Wild Hunt overtook them. The black thunderstorm rolled on behind them to the horizon.

When it faded, not a single dragon was left in the sky.

It was a clear, calm sky again as I cantered above the length of the Sarmenid divisions, as if inspecting them. Some shot arrows at me, but nothing could pierce my hide. When they saw the body in my mouth they stopped, for fear of hitting their prince.

I landed, and loped along in front of them, letting them all get a good look at my prey.

I stopped and spat Prince Mejnul out.

He landed in a heap. He was wounded, but still alive.

He staggered to his feet and turned to look up at me, in horror.

I threw back my head and howled.

He tottered backwards, confused, terrified.

I took a few, slow paces towards him, my head lowered, my red eyes burning as they stared at him.

He dropped to his knees, his hands raised in supplication. He was jabbering, gasping for breath. I could not hear what he was saying, but I could guess.

I shook my huge head from side to side, slowly. I understood the next word he said.

*"No …!!!"*

It was his last. I seized him in my jaws again, threw him high in the air, caught him before he hit the ground, and chewed him to a pulp.

*Devour the sun.*

I swallowed.

I'd never eaten prince before. It tasted good.

I turned my red wolf eyes on the Sarmenid army.

They waited, not knowing what to do.

I prowled along in front of them until I saw Prince Barthuq, at the front of his division. When he saw me heading towards him he turned and ran into the mass of chalkers behind him.

One by one, I stalked his remaining brothers. They all got the message. It was the question that I'd given them at the parlay that morning. Which of them would be the next crown prince?

And they knew why I'd left them alive. So that they would fight not with us, but among themselves.

*Divide the Blood.*

I sat on my haunches, and stared down at them, growling ominously.

Their divisions began to form up. And not to face the city any longer, but each other.

I trotted back to Mayport, Horm chuckling above me. I was too big to fit through the gates, so jumped over them, landing on the gate-house roof.

My friends were there, in the background, unmoving as if frozen.

Another figure was standing at the center of the wide space, a pale light shining around him.

The Hunter.

I crouched down.

Horm slid off my neck. He walked over to the Hunter and returned him his horn.

The Hunter held it out in front of himself, at arm's length.

It grew back into his bow, shining with its seven inlaid stars.

I waited. I knew what was coming.

*And end it all.*

The Hunter, who had slain the Great Wolf once before, at the world's beginning, drew his starsilver bow and shot me through the heart.

# Epilogue

**When** he flayed me, it didn't hurt at all.

"It is not your destiny to be immortal," The Hunter explained, as he peeled the wolf hide off me. The gatehouse roof, and my companions, were gone. We were alone, but I did not know where.

"My arrow will stay within you, in shadow. When your time comes, whenever that may be—tomorrow in combat or in old age years from now—you will take it to your grave. It will ensure that you stay there. And I," he said, holding the still-bleeding wolfskin aloft, "will take this with me. I know you will miss it. It would tempt you, and you would succumb. It is stronger than you are."

I ached with longing at the thought of it. Of what I would never be again.

He was right. I would have to be content with being just me. And to live with the knowledge of what I once, gloriously, had been.

"Look for us in the heavens," he said.

I wanted to reply that I would, but no words came.

He rose, bow in one hand, wolf hide in the other, and walked up into the stars. The constellations settled into place around the moon.

She was at her full. The Midsummer Moon. The Rose Moon.

The Hunter took his place beside her. The seven stars of the horn that had for so long been raised to his lips now formed the bow at the end of his outstretched arm, its arrow-tip pointed at its target.

Not the Great Wolf, but the Lamb, at its grazing.

Just in case it got any ideas.

The star map of the night sky that had enveloped us faded.

My companions unfroze, in the noonday sunlight, and surrounded me, and all was noise and relief and celebration. I remember little of what anyone said. I do recall asking Commandant Bastard if he was annoyed that he didn't get the fight that he was aching for. He laughed, and said, "Mayhaps I'll hang my blades up for good now. Strikes me as how I've done all the fighting one lifetime needs." Grell reminded him that he still owed him a bout, and Commandant Bastard slapped him on the back, and thanked him. "Dunno what I'd do without my trade," he said. "Sit at home by the fire, pulling my old dog's ears? I'd rather be dancing with you, friend Grell!" Nyrik and Horm immediately wanted to know where and when, but Commandant Bastard chuckled, and said, "We've some watching to do first, lads," and turned towards the view below the battlements.

It was chaos. Chalker divisions fought each other, then broke off as their prince generals saw their brothers' divisions heading west at the double, for the fleet.

"Get there first, load up, burn the other ships and seize the throne," Commandant Bastard said. "That's what our fine princes are thinking. There's going to be mayhem in Westwich, with that lot fighting it out. We won't be seeing them in this realm again."

The Sarmenid knights saddled up and cantered after them, followed by the archers and engineers. The supply train trailed their ox-wagons in their wake.

As the Sarmenid forces scattered, a single figure remained.

"I've set squads on the roads and byways," Commandant Bastard told Esmeralda. "He won't be getting anywhere. With your permission?"

Queen Esmeralda, who Marnie had unMabelized, replied, "By all means."

Commandant Bastard bowed and left.

Lord Rylen would not be returning to Hartwell. We watched as horsemen closed in on him, from either side. Below us, Commandant Bastard strolled out from the city gates. Lord Rylen did not want to die at the end of a traitor's noose. He had his pride. It did him no good. He drew his sword, and raised his shield, and did his best, but the Commandant made short work of him.

I felt a tug on my sleeve.

Beside me, Nyrik and Horm had their bows in their hands.

Nyrik said, "If you'd be so kind, Daxxie?"

Their arrowheads had oil-soaked rags wrapped around them.

I pointed Shift at them and set them alight.

Nyrik said, "On three?"

"On three," Horm grunted agreement.

"Your Majesty?" Nyrik said.

Esmeralda laughed, and counted, "One … two … three!"

The two Woods Kin loosed their flaming arrows. They flew high in lazy arcs towards their target, trailing smoke. They lodged in the silks and satins of the imperial pavilion.

Within moments, it was ablaze.

All around us, on the city walls, the people of Mayport were cheering.

"One other thing," Marnie said, after we'd watched the pavilion collapse, to the biggest cheer of all.

We turned back to look at her.

She had lifted her eyepatch. Her fearsome red eye was staring at us.

She raised her oak staff. "Time to cleanse that Gag off you," she said. "You'll be wanting to tell your tales, and folk will be wanting to hear them."

We were Queen Esmeralda's guests of honor at the victory feast that night in the Great Hall of the Royal Castle, where folk were indeed agog to hear all that we could tell them, from *run and hide* to *end it all.*

*Don't assume* took some explaining. We'd *assumed* so many things, without examining the evidence—or lack of it. We'd *assumed* that all dragons were the same, because "that's what dragons were like," as far as we knew—even though we'd seen with our own eyes how very different they could be. We'd seen, but we'd ignored the evidence.

*We'd been told,* and *it was all there*—but we hadn't *had the wit to see.* Some were big, like the helldragon. Some were small, like Vagg's. Some fly. Some don't. The helldragon was gray, the color of an elephant, but with a hide of thick scales and tall spines. Vagg's little ones, scaled and spined, came in all colors of the rainbow. The helldragon had a head like a dinosaur, on a thick neck. The Sarmenid dragons looked like oversized moose, their bulbous heads on long, snaky necks above humped, leathery bodies. Vagg's looked like vicious chickens. They weren't different breeds of the same animal, as dogs are: They were entirely different species of the same class—just as crocodiles and snakes are reptiles, and lions and sheep are mammals. Some eat others; others eat plants.

Vagg's tiny ones had useless wings. The helldragon had huge, powerful ones. Both were carnivores and breathed fire. *Camels of the sky*, Foreman Ildrutj had called the beasts at the Grazings. They were there to fatten up for the long flight ahead—but not to feed on cattle, as we'd *assumed*. They *were* the cattle. They ignored the oxen under their noses and spent their time on the ground head down, grazing, tended by herders and their dogs, as placid and obedient as the Isvellir yaks when Nostë was at his work. We'd simply *assumed* they'd blast down the *fire and fury* that Prince Mejnul had promised from their mouths, because Vagg's little beasts and the helldragon had breathed fire, and "that's what dragons did." But no. They'd needed harnesses and pots filled with highly volatile mixture.

As for *hide and run*, everyone wanted to know what it was like. I did my best to explain, but my words felt inadequate. I didn't want to think back and remember what I had lost. "It hurt like hell, being skinned alive," I said, to deflect the issue. "I wouldn't want to go through *that* again."

After the feasting, Queen Esmeralda knighted the five of us. Jess, Marnie had told her, was too young—and anyway, Coven didn't hold with titles; all were sisters in Coven, and that was that. Jess didn't mind. There were no gentry where she came from, on Wester Isle.

Horm was beaming with pride. I reminded him of something he'd once said. *I've had "sir" sometimes. I mean, Sir Horm? Fuck off.* He glared at me. "I'm keeping this—*me*," he said. "I've bloody earned it!"

That he had indeed.

Qrysta wanted the same title as the rest of us, and Esmeralda said that she didn't see why not, but the Chief Herald demurred. *No precedent for knighting a woman, Your Majesty.* His queen could, of course, grant any title that she wished, he allowed—as long as that title existed. If it didn't, the Company of Heralds had no protocol by which to ratify it. There could be no Sir Qrysta.

"What's the alternative?" Qrysta asked.

She didn't like the Chief Herald's answer.

"*Dame* Qrysta?! I'd sound like an old woman on my last legs!"

"I'll jump you a rank, then," Esmeralda said. "I'll give you a Ladyship. What name do you want?"

The Chief Herald saw no problem with that.

"Lady Blades sounds good to me," Qrysta said, and we could only agree. She knelt, and Esmeralda dubbed her *Qrysta, Lady Blades*.

"Suits you, My Lady," I said, as we rose to our feet.

She replied, her eyes shining up at me, "Why, thank you kindly, Sir Knight."

She was smiling. I knew that I was smiling back. I held out my hand. "Would My Lady care to dance?"

She took it. "Your Lady would love to."

I led her through the applauding crowd to the dance floor.

www.ingramcontent.com/pod-product-compliance
Lightning Source LLC
Chambersburg PA
CBHW032300020726
47495CB00001B/182